About the Author

Tomás Francisco Diaz was born in Northern California. He grew up in a bi-cultural American and Venezuelan household. At thirteen years of age, Tomás suffered from a pituitary tumor, which was surgically removed after it began to affect his vision. He continues to experience after-effects of the surgery, which prompted him to start writing as a way to cope with the disability. Tomás is interested in fantasy, sci-fi, and nonfiction, and especially enjoys books on antiquities. He has a bachelor's degree in history and has studied warfare and weapons, resulting in knowledge that he uses throughout his work.

Runt

Tomás F. Diaz

Runt

Olympia Publishers
London

www.olympiapublishers.com
OLYMPIA PAPERBACK EDITION

A CIP catalogue record for this title is
available from the British Library.

ISBN: 978-1-80439-075-7

First Published in 2024

Olympia Publishers
Tallis House
2 Tallis Street
London
EC4Y 0AB

Printed in Great Britain

Dedication

To my friends and family who believed in me and supported me.

This formality is for you. You know who you are.

Acknowledgement

Thank you to my parents Donna and Julio Diaz, to my grandpa Jack Sturgill, who would be proud. To Imogen Ronde and Julia O'Rawe, thank you for the work you put into this book with me.

MAIDEN'S HAIR

CAPHRI HOLT

SNOW HORNS

CLOUD CALLERS

BRUME

FIVE SPOUTS

FIORD EATER

WOODLAND

THAW TIMBERS

GOLD TIDE

E. HORN

W. HORN

ROUNS

CHITTER

THE COLLECTOR

RICHLYNS

THE GASH

SMALL COLLECTOR

CER

GERTAN

AN

SWORD GRASS

WEDGE WAT

N

FRESH WATER BIGHT

THE DAGGER

Prologue

"When the Alpha Father[1] created us, we Silverbacks[2] were more wolf than man. We preferred to move about on all fours, rather than walk on our hind legs the way the Furless[3] do. We had no desire to settle; we wandered freely across the land. We had not yet been betrayed by the other Taurs[4]. Like all Taurs, we followed the codes that our Confederation had agreed upon. There was a law code for those of the land, and perhaps there was one for those of the air and the waters. For us, this law code was simple: we would not hunt other Taurs; although we were beasts, we would not be savages; we would respect the presence of other tribe members and tribes, and acknowledge the consequences of ignoring their presence; we would not hunt or kill animals for sport; and hunt only the lame and the old for food to ensure enough for all. The Taurs which grazed need not fear us, and those who were larger did not threaten those who were smaller. These four laws ensured that our kind flourished throughout the whole continent of Loog Turra, no matter where we lived.

"Of course, this blissful time of plenty eventually came to an end, as all good things do. We would learn that the Taurs were not the only conscious life on the continent or beyond. We learned of both the Dwarves and the Fay Wild[5]. These two could not be more different. The Fay were more like us, relaxed and applying themselves only when needed, although their humor was a bit too refined for any Taurs' taste. The Dwarves, on the other hand, worked and worked and worked and built and built and built, all so that they could sell and sell and sell, because there is nothing that they enjoy more than wealth. For us, the Fay were too aloof, and Dwarves were too structured, and so we each mostly kept to our own clans.

"The odd thing about the Fay is that they seem to be blessed with

1	Silverback god
2	Wolf-Taur
3	Humans
4	The Beast Tongue term for their peoples; of land, sky, or water
5	The Elves and elven lands known as the Maiden

immortality. They say their longevity means no need to rush through life, and this is also the reason for their small population in comparison to us and the Dwarves. The Dwarves claim to be mortal, and thus must be always busy in order to make every minute of their long lives productive; however, there are Dwarves alive today that were known by my grand-parents and that have not aged a day since. They are always striving for that next project or job and always taking full pleasure from sore muscles and sweaty brows."

I ignored the hand that shot up as I began to talk about the immortality of the Fay and the Dwarves. I could recognize that unusual burgundy fur anywhere; Terrabyss always had the same question and always received the same answer.

"Grimmis, why aren't we immortal?"

"We don't know," was the answer. "They were supposedly given this gift, or learned how to fabricate it." I, of course, had my suspicions. I noticed that the pup's hand was still up, actually now both of them were raised, and—knowing Terrabyss' determination—would stay up. He knew that he could drive me nuts like this, especially when he started to sway back and forth like he was some sort of tree. How was it that he lacked this determination with any other task he was assigned? I could tell that ignoring him was going to be pointless; especially once he started swaying back and forth, back and forth. I finally had to ask what his question was, and, as usual, when I answered him, Terrabyss was dissatisfied with the response. I closed my eyes, taking a deep breath for the argument that was to come, when fortunately, his sister, Numa, put a stop to his objections before he could voice them by putting her elbow into the runt's ribs. I smiled happily as his angry little glare switched from me to her, and con-tinued with my story before he could interrupt me again.

"So, we had friendly but strained relations with both the Fay and the Dwarves." I paused to take a small swig of the honey beer that we brewed. It didn't taste as good as the Dwarven ale or the Fay wine, but it did its job. I put down the drinking skin and started up again. "Then, one afternoon, we were lounging under the large redwoods of the Green Wall[6] . A tribe of Rodentia[7] passed by; they were traveling to the massive mountain range that supposedly divides the entire continent in half, the

6   Large conifer forest, famous for its sequoia trees
7   Rodent-Taur

Division Mountains[8] . We found this surprising for several reasons, not least of which was that they were talking about trading for something called weapons and armor. We had traded with the Dwarves and the Fay before, mostly pelts, although sometimes we would contract to bring in some lumber, but for the most part we left the wood-cutting to the Ozars[9] and the Daunkirks[10]. In exchange, we had always asked for one of two things; either Dwarven ale or Fay wine.

"When we saw the exquisite items the Rodentia were bringing to trade, we became even more curious. They had brought fine woven winter blankets made of hemp. They were all dyed a multitude of bright colors, and in a myriad of designs. They had also found some rare amber hidden beneath old trees. We wondered how much these weapons and armor could be worth that the Rodentia wished to trade such precious commodities. We valued blankets that would keep us warm in the winter, and the precious amber would fetch endless skins of ale or wine. We asked why they needed these weapons and armor. None of them would answer. So, we realized that we needed to apply a little pressure to these sneaky Rodentia."

At that exact moment, I finished cutting the sigils in the ground with my paws while I paced, a trick I had perfected over many tellings. The pups had not noticed as I narrated the tale, their attention on my words and not on my paws. It wasn't going to hurt them, just give them a good fright, and besides, it wasn't like I hadn't done it before. With a chorus of yelps, every pup suddenly jumped to their paws, twisting around to see what had yanked on their tails. By the time they turned back, I had on a wooden mask that my father had made for use when he recounted this tale. Their eyes grew wide, and some of the pups even yipped at the sight of the large, triangular, purple mask, such a foreign color, with huge saber cat teeth that looked like rows of small mountains. They had been painted snow white to gleam against the darker purple. Long elk antlers had been used to make the four canine teeth of the beast, and were also a gleaming white. The eyes were made of amber, and they reflected the firelight as it danced this way and that.

I shouted out the Rodentia response, "BECAUSE THE TITANS ARE COMING!"

---

8   Mountain chain running from north to south that divides the continent

9   Bear-Taur

10   Deer-Taur

The pups fell back onto their rumps with a thud, some had flattened their ears and others averted their eyes. There were also those few that stared at the mask, teeth bared and hackles raised. They had usually seen the performance before. Terrabyss always surprised me the most; the runt never seemed to react, even the first time he saw my trick. He always stayed standing, but would quickly sit down when the rest of the group did. He was obviously not dumb enough to try to be a leader, but still it was always so strange. Of course, the next thing was expected, and all I could do was sigh as the little burgundy-colored hand shot up. He had waited for everyone to be properly surprised and awed, but could not restrain himself from asking the next question.

"What are Titans—" was all he managed to get out; this time, it was his alpha brother, Tarphyss, that put a stop to his question by elbowing him in the ribs. This assault was the last straw for Terrabyss, and the almost nightly fireside brawl began. Scars from these fights showed character and established hierarchy in the pack. Their fur rose as they both showed their teeth and took wide stances.

Terrabyss had no patience and went straight for his brother's waist, trying to tackle him. The other pups began to howl as they cheered the combatants, and nearby adults and I watched for the outcome, intending to get involved only if one meant to lame or kill the other. Terrabyss collided with Tarphyss, but didn't have enough force to take him down. Tarphyss wrapped his right arm around the back of Terrabyss' head, grabbing his brother's right shoulder from behind. Then, before Terrabyss could pull back, his brother swept his right leg horizontally while pulling Terrabyss' right shoulder in the opposite direction of his paw. Terrabyss hit the ground hard on his back, and Tarphyss quickly pinned his shin into the runt's throat.

"Yield!" he snarled at the runt.

Terrabyss squirmed, twisting this way and that, rolling to his left and his right, but was unable to free himself from his brother's grapple. His hands went up, trying to grab at his brother, anything to gain the upper hand.

Tarphyss just smacked the feeble attempts away. "Submit!" he yelled again.

I watched as some of the adults became tense with how long the fight had been going on, and I realized that I was gnawing on my tongue. I forced myself to stop as a small dust cloud rose around the two pups.

It was getting harder to tell what was happening with all the dust, and hard to tell which pup was which. The pups hadn't yet been scarred like adult Maulers, you could recognize each and every one of us by our scars. Out of the corner of my eye, I saw Numa; she was recognizable by the long scar across her ribs on her left side. She had earned it by foolishly challenging the next Alpha[11] of our tribe, my son Haxzus. It wasn't usual, but since we had been focused on simply surviving since we had left the Green Wall, I had allowed Haxzus to take on more and more of my duties as Alpha. Normally, he would have had to challenge and defeat me for them, but the Council of Elders felt that there had already been too much loss. Numa had demanded that she be allowed to join the adult Hunters. Haxzus had told her no, that she was too young to join, and he made an example of her when she persisted. No one challenges the Alpha.

Numa quickly stomped on Terrabyss' stomach—which made the pup vomit—and she gave Tarphyss a solid punch in his back, just shy of the kidney. He toppled over onto his knees and joined Terrabyss as they both heaved. She grabbed them both by the scruff of their necks, dragging them to their paws, and pushed the groaning pups back over to the fire circle. The other pups all howled cheers for Numa, except a few that had wanted to see more of the fight. I took another sip from the drinking skin, and realized that my break was almost over. I had barely even enjoyed it. I cleared my throat as the group settled down, and picked up where I had left off in my tale.

"So, apparently… no, that wasn't right… these creatures… no." I glared at Terrabyss. I had lost my place and it was all his fault. "The Titans… ah, yes… the Titans were fearsome and savage beasts that could fly through the air, water, and earth. They had the ability to bend the elemental forces around us to their will, and could control these forces to create permanent change within the physical world. They walked on four legs, each foot tipped with claws the size of our skulls, they had snake-like heads, some triangular, some oval, others thin and narrow, but all were lined with teeth that could chew through a mountain and not even chip. Their tails could fell even the mightiest trees with ease, and the horns that adorned their bodies could pierce through all flesh. They stood as tall as these redwoods, and were easily as long. Their scales were strong, strong enough that our sharpest claws would have no effect and we would surely lose our teeth if

11   Leader of a Silverback tribe

we tried to bite them. These creatures were the Titans; what the Dwarves call Dragons.

"We felt insulted that we had never been warned about these Titans before, and it was humiliating that one of the Rodentia tribes knew of them before we did. The Rodentia would be able to threaten our tribes easily if they got hold of the very costly weapons and armor they were trading for. They could change the rules established by our Confederacy in the beginning. This was all so foreign to us—the weapons and armor, the Titans—and we decided that we would join the Rodentia on their way to the Dwarven trading post. They hesitated at first, but we assured them that we wouldn't hurt them, so they eventually accepted our company on their journey.

"As we traveled with them, they were so sour and gloomy that we had to bring a little levity to the situation. So, as we traveled, some of us began to break off, not many at first, just one or two, until we had all left the path and vanished into the woods. The next time the Rodentia checked to see if we were keeping up, they found no one. We began to growl from behind the trees and bushes, moving in on the flanks. They would fall for it, kicking up their heels in fright as we bounded through the tall sequoias. This would get the rest of the group in a panic, and they would bolt down the trail in fright, only to come to a skidding stop when we leapt out on the trail in front of them. We even managed to make one of the older ones faint, it almost brought us all to tears." In fact, recounting the story was almost bringing everyone to tears of laughter as well.

"When this got boring, we began to let them feel like they had escaped us a few times, only to trot into their camp at night, talking to one another, and acting shocked whenever we would find them. They should have known that they couldn't hide from a Silverback; no one has a sharper nose than us. We would act like we had just come across them for the first time, and convince them to recount the tale about the Titans that they had told us when we first met. This went on for four nights, and by the last night they were so frazzled and scared that they didn't even have a camp properly set up by the time we arrived." I took another long pause and the opportunity to sip at my drink. The older I became, the more I needed to wet my throat.

"It was early evening when we and the Rodentia made it to the Trade

Den. It was in a massive canyon that ran between the Ice Kraggs[12] in the north and the Division Mountains in the east. The canyon was easily twenty-five miles in length, five miles wide, and at least a mile deep. All along the walls were balconies covered in some sort of woven—probably hemp—canvas which provided some shade. It always amused us how much the Dwarves hated not having something above their heads.

"The Trade Den was full of foreign smells, sights and sounds. It was also crowded with all different Taurs, and often left no individual space for anyone. We found ourselves yelling at Ozars, Daunkirks, Rodentia, Ramsyns[13] , Airluts[14] , and even the occasional Gorgel[15] . The last three we had hardly any usual contact with, so it was interesting to see how they responded to us. Many of the Airluts ignored us, but we got in more than one stare-down with a Ramsyn and a few of us even came to blows with a Gorgel. Their skin is like rock, and punching one of them is like hitting stone itself.

"Every Taur there seemed interested in purchasing arms and armor. They all gave the same excuse that the Rodentia had, that they were defending themselves from these so-called Titans. The Dwarves were eager to corroborate the stories and it seemed as though they were doing all they could to amplify everyone's fears. My opinion was that it was good for their business, since almost all of them were now selling weapons and armor instead of their wonderful ale.

"We inspected some of these weapons and armor for ourselves. The metal armor doesn't even cover the whole body, how will that protect someone? The leather and cloth armors are, well, leather and cloth, we shred through fur and flesh all the time. The weapons were sharp, yes, but many of them were heavy and too long to fight in the dense forest that is our home. There were some lighter weapons, but they were no better than my teeth and claws."

"Teeth and Claws!" the pups shouted the Mauler creed.

"They tried to boast about the distance that was gained by using the spears or bows, yet once again it is easy to duck behind one of the numerous trees of the Green Wall. We noticed a group of three Ozars purchasing some

---

12   Frozen mountains that run east to west across the North of the continent

13   Sheep-Taur

14   Bird-Taur

15   Bat-Taur

heavy axes with large, half-moon heads, and wide-bladed, single-edged swords. When we asked them what these were for, the Ozar who was in charge of them said that if we had to know, it was for the coming Titans.

"Have any of us to this day ever seen a Titan?" I realized my mistake before I had even finished the question. My eyes shot over to Terrabyss, having forgotten that the pup doesn't deal with rhetorical questions well. I was expecting a hand to shoot up or for him to completely ignore formalities and shout the answer. What I saw allowed me to breathe easy; Terrabyss was pinned firmly by his three siblings. Numa squatted behind him, holding down his shoulders and keeping his muzzle shut, while Tarphyss held his right arm firmly, and his other brother, Skoff, held his left arm.

"None of us, to this day, not one has ever seen a Titan. Yet the Dwarves insisted that... that... " I was trying so hard not to chuckle, but both Terrabyss' sour expression and the story I had first heard fifty years ago were so comical. "They said that their 'god'—a MOUNTAIN—had told them of the danger they were in! That this 'mountain' had taught them how to make weapons and defend themselves with armor!"

I took the opportunity that Numa, Tarphyss, and Skoff were giving me to really hammer my point home without any of the usual interruptions. "We all know that a god doesn't live in a mountain; gods live in the night sky above. You can sometimes see glimpses of their world through the stars as they let in the light from the god's home. While we roam the lands, the great Alpha Father lives in the sky and watches over us from above. Even the Cens'[16] god sits in the heavens, as well as the Ozars' god, and the Minos'[17] god.

"After all these crazy tales and poor lies, we were sure that the other Confederation clans in the Green Wall—probably most importantly the Ozars and Daunkirks—were getting ready to rewrite the rules. The Rodentia were likely just getting weapons to defend against the blatant plans of aggression. Even if the Titans were real, these pathetic weapons and cumbersome armor would not help against the stories we heard of their power and might. No, if Titans came to attack the Silverbacks, we would defeat them with Teeth and Claws!"

Again, the pups shouted "Teeth and Claws" in response, even Terrabyss and his siblings were shouting with the rest. I managed to hush the youngsters

16   Horse-Taur (Centaur)
17   Bull-Taur (Minotaur)

after about the third time they finished the chant.

"So, we left the Trade Den, none of us feeling at ease as we were nervous at what the other clans were going to do. We gathered all the Silverback tribes, the Lobu, the Cana, the Eclupse, the Varggs, ourselves the Maulers, and even the Mutts[18] . The Lobu—whose silver-marked coats all Wolf-Taurs take their name from—were proud of us Maulers for not having purchased any of these accessories that would not benefit the packs, and also for warning the other tribes of what the Ozars and Daunkirks seemed to be planning. The Cana and the Eclupse tribes thought that we should purchase these new items, that our clan would benefit from keeping current with the world around them. The Eclupse tribe especially said that there may be some validity to the story of the Titans, that just because we had never seen one didn't mean it wasn't real. The Lobu argued that it was true that there were many oddities in this world, but until they actually threatened us, there was no reason to concern ourselves. To which we agreed, tomorrow always comes with its own problems that you can never be fully prepared for. This meant that it fell to the Varggs, who had been pretty silent during this whole argument, to cast the deciding vote on how we would act. The Mutts, of course, were lucky to even be there among their betters, so they would not have an opinion. At least not one worth noting.

"Almost as one, the whole council turned and stared at the Varggs. The Cana and Eclupse urged the Varggs to take the opportunity to progress with the other clans. The Maulers and the Lobu warned the Varggs to take caution and not to upset the delicate balance that had been put in place by our forefathers."

I held the silence for a while, keeping the pups in suspense. They were leaning in toward me without even realizing it, waiting for my next words. I opened my mouth, then paused and took a sip from my drinking skin, at which every pup groaned. As soon as I heard their groans, I began speaking again, making them chastise each other for causing the other to miss what was said.

"Calm, calm down," I hushed them before another scrap broke out, as I didn't have much mead left in my drinking skin. I began to repeat what I had said. "The Varggs wisely followed the alpha tribe, the Lobu, and the

18   Not a crossbreed, but a Canine-Taur that is not a Wolf-Taur. It is a derogatory term for the "sixth" tribe

now esteemed Maulers. The Cana and Eclupse tribes threw a fit, shouting that we had doomed them all, and that we were all fossils so infatuated with the past that we missed the great things laid out before us. They accused us of spitting in the face of opportunity and progress and etc.… etc.… etc. They carried on in the way all losers cry when they feel they have been cheated out of their winnings. They said we were on our own against an attack, and that they would go to the Trade Den and purchase some of the arms and armor and learn how to use and make them. Of course, the Lobu, the Varggs, and us Maulers forbade it, but they decided they would no longer be bound by our council and its orders. We Maulers have too much honor to allow this insult, even from former members of our clan, but the Lobu ordered us not to stop them and to allow them to leave. All of the tribes left would face any foe with our—" This time, the pups beat me to it as they shouted, "Teeth and Claws!"

I regretted having worked them into another chant. Some of their parents had now gathered around, and were waiting to put their pups to bed, most notably Bia, the mother of Tarphyss, Numa, Skoff, and Terrabyss. I resisted having another sip from my drinking skin and hushed the pups as quickly as possible. The story wasn't even close to done yet. They still got another three chants off before I could begin again.

"The Furless claim that they were made refugees by the Titans, who destroyed their homes. If we believe them, perhaps the Titans were punished by the gods for having caused such destruction, which would explain why we have never seen hide nor hair of one. The only evidence we saw of the destruction came from the other side of the Division Mountains. It was early in the morning, shortly after the sun had begun to rise. Some of us had awakened, and shortly woke all of the rest as we watched the faint blue morning sky turn red, and then become completely black. It was as though a second night had fallen, although there was not a star or moon to see by. We spent the day in darkness, fearful and watchful for what might come for us through the trees, even the bravest of us on edge. We all expected something, anything, to happen, perhaps for a Titan to materialize in front of us, all fangs and scales. Later that day, it was hard to tell when, as time means nothing in the darkness, we all heard a single, echoing boom. The boom caused the needles to fall from the redwoods, the dirt to quiver and the waters to quake. Even through all this, the Maulers would have stood strong against any Titan, but we couldn't have stood strong against what was to come three days later.

"The early morning dew was just starting to vanish and many of us hadn't even fully woken up, but those of us who had were stretching and getting ready for another typical morning. We had been celebrating fairly vigorously since the day the sky went black, celebrating that we were still alive. Some of us spoke about traveling across the Division Mountains in order to find out what had happened, as there had been no other signs. By now, most of us were sure that it was safe to go, but many of us had never traveled more than a few days away from our normal territories, and only then for the Trade Den or if the Confederacy was called."

I hesitated and drew a deep breath. This part of the story was always the hardest for me, but it had to be told.

"I led your families well. My mate, Clea, had just given birth to Haxzus and the rest of that litter. The sun's warm, orange rays were trying to stab through the trees and every now and then, we would find a nice warm spot to lounge in. The winter was coming to a close, and the snows were beginning to melt. We were alerted by crashing sounds and, breaking through the trees came some Silverbacks from the Vargg. They were wounded and bleeding, shouting about how the Ozars had come out of nowhere with their weapons and armor and had laid waste to their camp. Apparently, right before the Ozar attack, some Silverbacks from the Lobu tribe had arrived in their camp and, before they had died from their wounds, they had warned that the Daunkirks were also on the march.

"We had to make a decision fast. There was no way of telling how the Cana and the Eclupse were doing, or if they were in cahoots with the Daunkirks and Ozars. With both the Lobu and the Vargg taken down, there was probably little to no chance that we, the smallest tribe, the Maulers, would be able to put up much of a defense. I didn't really have any good ideas though, so I first ordered five warriors to go ahead with the Vargg, to retake their camp and to free all they could. I told them that we would meet up with them shortly, after everyone had been properly woken up and informed. As we were getting ready to move out, Clea approached me and told me that when she was younger, her pack had gone north one year to try to hunt along the Ice Kraggs. There, she had found a small canyon, and had followed the trail, sheer cold ice looming up on either side of her, and clouds of powdered snow blown by the wind hitting her face and head. She had walked for what seemed like most of the day, becoming frightened that she would never escape this canyon, for it was not wide enough for her to turn around. She could walk backward, but we are not made for that, so forward she went. Finally, she came through a narrow crack in the mountains, walking out into a small glade of the Green Wall that had been cut off from the rest by the Ice Kraggs. She didn't know why, but she knew she was being called to that place now. It was sheltered from the Banshee Tundra[19] by the trees, and difficult for anyone to find unless they knew where it was, making it the perfect place to take shelter.

"I knew better than to question her wisdom, and I also knew better than to engage both the Ozars and Daunkirks with the Maulers alone. So, I changed my order. I said that we were to follow Clea, and anyone who fell behind was lost. We did not have time to spare the weak if we wanted to survive. With that, we marched out, trudging through the snow. The weather seemed to turn against us as the clouds grew dark, sending a heavy snowstorm into the Green Wall for one last time that year. It became difficult to see one another, so I ordered that we all hold onto each other's tails and keep moving. Half-blind, cold, tired, and panicked, we arrived at the Ice Kraggs. I yelled out for Clea to take us through, but there was no response; the wind here was howling and had almost enough force to slam us into the icy mountain walls. I began to move up the line, trying to figure out why Clea had stopped. Perhaps the pass was sealed already, perhaps the Ozars and Daunkirks had known of it and had blocked it off, perhaps the snow had buried any landmarks that Clea had known. What I found at the front of the line was much worse than what I had assumed.

"There, in front, was Clea, frozen mid-step with her blanket wrapped around the pups that she had pressed against her chest. I reached out, only one pup made a sound, the alpha of the litter who had managed to bury himself under his siblings. I held my son Haxzus, as the tribe realized that we weren't moving, and so began to gather around. I knew that it wouldn't be long before we all froze, even with our blankets. I didn't know what to do, for the first time in my life I felt unprepared. We never know what tomorrow will bring; if happiness or sorrow will walk hand in hand with the rising sun, and it is so hard... so hard living in a world like this. I was scared. I am a Mauler. I am an Alpha. I was scared, and I didn't like it. Something inside of me seemed to burn to life. We had to

19   Northern tundra

survive no matter what.

I ordered a makeshift shelter assembled; the oldest and infirm would have to remain outside, as would the youngest. Only those who could ensure our succession would stay alive in the shelter. Haxzus was to stay with me, and if anyone wanted to challenge those orders, they were more than welcome to fight me. I killed four other Maulers that night, who either tried to take Haxzus away from me, or to force themselves or others into the shelter. I made sure to kill every single one; the Alpha is never challenged. The next morning, those of us who survived were greeted by an end to the storm, which gave us a chance to look for this passage, not knowing how far behind our enemies were.

"I had led us through the worst of it, and I wasn't about to give up now. We were going to survive. It was about noon when one of the lookouts, Ornyss… " – here I paused for a moment to allow the Ravis pack to howl their pride at the mention of their father, but quickly kept talking – "came up to us searching along the mountain; he had spotted an advance party of Daunkirks headed our way. We didn't have long; they were several hundred lue[20] away and closing fast. Usually, I would have no problem going into battle against the Daunkirks; they are shy and fragile Taurs, and one Mauler is easily worth five or more of them. Yet, from the sounds of it, the arms and armor had made them brave and resilient, something I wasn't looking forward to encountering. I ordered another four fighters to hold back with Ornyss and buy us some time if the Daunkirks broke the trees. I went back to where Clea still stood. I was preparing to leave Haxzus at her paws and take the remaining tribe into battle. I knew the Fist[21] could buy us some time, but not an infinite amount, and we were still no closer to finding the canyon pass she had talked about.

"The Alpha Father must have seen my predicament though, and would not have the last of his fine creation be taken as slaves or killed by other Taurs. As I went to set Haxzus down, having resigned myself to this fate, I noticed that Clea had been walking forward but her shoulders were slightly turned, and her head was looking at an exact spot in the Ice Kraggs. I was sure I was hallucinating, convinced that fear had finally gotten the better of me, but I felt compelled to go where she had been looking. At first, I saw nothing, just more-white mountain. In frustration, I hit the side of

20   Distance of the average single lunge

21   Unit of five fighters

the mountain, causing some of the snow in the area of my impact to give way. The fresh powder from the night before had covered it up. It was a tiny crevasse in the wall; indeed, the adults would have to walk sideways to make it through, but it was here and not a moment too soon. I hollered for the Maulers to gather 'round and follow me through the canyon pass to our temporary paradise. I could hear the Daunkirk's advance party having engaged the Fist I had sent back as a rear guard. I could still hear them fighting as I led the way, hurrying our tribe to safety.

"I know that one day we will return to the Green Wall, and when we do, our brethren will no longer curse our names for having escaped, but praise us for freeing or avenging them, if any are even still alive. For I still trust the words of my father, the shaman, that taught me, 'One day among the Silverbacks, there will be a mighty Mauler, he will be Alpha-Taur[22] . Under him, the Silverbacks will rule from the Division Mountains in the east to the Maiden's Hair[23] in the west. His reach will spread across the Green Wall, to the north against the Banshee Tundra all the way to the Endless Plains[24] to the south.' Among us, among you" – I pointed to the pups – "is that Alpha-Taur. I know I will see this savior in my lifetime, and I don't have much time left." I chuckled, directing my eyes to Haxzus as he wrestled with another Mauler not far from the central fire.

No, I don't have much time left, I thought.

"Teeth and Claws!" I howled, bringing the tale to its end, the pups howling back as we finished the saying together this time, "Is all I have and all I will ever need."

I watched the pups go, pushing myself up from my cross-legged position, and took a long drink from my drinking skin.

***

The fire popped and crackled as it began to die down, and Grimmis collapsed. He felt numb on his left side and crumpled to the ground. His vision blurred, yet he thought he saw a young Haxzus running over to him. He was so small; a pup again, hardly any scars to his name yet. Grimmis felt Haxzus' hands take his head, but couldn't hear what he said as the

22   Ruler of all Taurs
23   Sea around the Maiden Islands
24   Massive flatland south of the Warm Wood

pup held the Alpha in his little hands. Grimmis smiled, reaching up and tapping Haxzus on the snout. "Now lead us back to the Green Wall, my Alpha-Taur." He slumped; his breathing became irregular; he heard the howling of the pack in the stars and went to join them.

Terrabyss knelt on the hard ground, unsure what to do. He held Grimmis' head, he had seen him starting to collapse out of the corner of his eye, as he and Tarphyss had started shoving each other to decide in what order they would go home. He had forfeited his spot in line, not because he had any real love for old Grimmis, but because no one else had reacted to his collapse. Terrabyss respected the old Alpha, although he would never have told him that to his face, and now never would. Grimmis' son, Haxzus, had mostly rejected him and had taken no interest in the shaman's teachings. Skoff had taken up learning the shaman practice, he had the talent for it. Yet, Terrabyss hoped one day to be as great as this Alpha, to do what no one else would, to ensure the survival of the Maulers, no matter the odds. Grimmis' sheer grit and determination had inspired Terrabyss in many ways. It wasn't that his own mother wasn't a good role model, she was much like all the other Maulers, and enforced the standard rule of conformity. Maulers didn't like anything different. Terrabyss wanted to be something more though, something greater than being the alpha Hunter like his mother, or a warrior like his father, Ornyss, had been before he had died holding the rear. He had always wanted to be the Alpha-Taur, ever since he had first heard this story. So, when Grimmis had reached up, saying something in a whisper almost too low for Terrabyss to hear – "Now lead us back to the Green Wall, my Alpha-Taur" – Terrabyss knew his destiny. He was going to capture and dominate the Green Wall.

Terrabyss

The snow reached to the Mauler's waists as they crouched motionless under the large, red-barked trees of the grove they called home. In the shadows of these trees, the five stock-still figures were practically invisible to even the most trained eye. Many of the animals that lived here passed within a whisker's length, taking advantage of the waning winter and the slowly melting snow to stretch their legs and find food. Squirrels and birds argued in the soft green needles of the redwood's branches, while deer and hares gingerly moved through the snow, trying to find shoots of last fall's grass. They were hoping to find the new sprouting ferns and mosses of the coming spring, but it was still too soon for those to venture above the frost-bitten soil.

Still, no matter how close the chittering, nervous little creatures got, the five Watchers[25] stayed unmoving, ever-guarding the small canyon entrance into their precious grove. This canyon was the only known way back to the Green Wall, their ancestral home. No matter how badly these five and their tribe wanted to go back, they couldn't. The Ozars and Daunkirks had ensured that; but what they could do was make sure that anyone who entered this sanctuary never had a chance to report what they had discovered. It was vital to their tribe's survival that the canyon pass through the Ice Kraggs should never be discovered. They may have lost their land, but they had made this grove their home and they would not easily give it up. As the sun shifted throughout the day, so too did the Watchers, remaining ever-vigilant. Occasionally, one would drop down into the deep hole they called home while on duty—in order to get some sleep or food—before being awakened by the next one in turn, making their number more often four than five. At the fragile times of day, when the sun or moon vanished behind the tops of the giant trees and the forest and mountains sprang briefly to life, there were always five.

As darkness finally began to settle in, the Watchers left the shadows

25   All-male packs who work as sentries

of the giant sequoias and made a small camp. They built a fire that would serve as a beacon to anyone who happened to wander through the icy canyon. The five of them didn't stay around the campfire, but eyed it from about twenty or thirty lue away, so they could easily ambush whoever huffed over to the fire for warmth. They stayed closer together than they had in the daytime, so that they wouldn't freeze in the cold night. Their thick fur had a warm undercoat which did keep most of the chill out, but this far north the wind was more ice than air. Oryss, a large brute and the alpha of this Watcher pack, decided to break the night's silence first. He usually did, and he did so in his usual manner.

"Terrabyss, the fire is getting low. Go put another log on it." He was the oldest and most experienced of the five Watchers here, therefore, had seniority.

Oryss was a capable fighter, having won most of the scraps that had scarred his body. He had a few scars on his biceps, and some on his chest as well, but, in Terrabyss' opinion, none were all that impressive. Oryss' fur, like the majority of Maulers, was a shade of black, and he had amber eyes that glowed against the onyx fur. He was the average height of most Maulers, and proportionately muscular. Like all Maulers, he wore no armor because it interfered with his prized hump, the overdeveloped shoulder muscles that allowed the Silverbacks to shift from bipedal to quadrupedal movement. The more pronounced the hump, supposedly, the more ambitious the Mauler. The Maulers alone had the exaggerated hump; all Silverbacks bore one to some minor degree or another, but Maulers took pride in them, deliberately running on all fours to shape them. For Oryss, like most Maulers, his sharp teeth and long, sharpened claws were his weapons of choice. He hadn't made Terrabyss' short time as a Watcher easy, and each day Terrabyss was becoming more and more fed up with Oryss and his superior attitude.

Terrabyss had been in more scraps than all four of these Watchers combined, and had the scars to prove it. Unfortunately for him, few of his scars had victory stories attached to them; most were simple reminders of his place as a runt. He was the youngest and newest member of this Watcher pack's five-male team, having joined two years previously, immediately after completing his first Hunt[26]. The Watchers alternated with other Fists

26   Coming of age tradition

guarding the pass, rotating at each full moon. Not only was Terrabyss the youngest member of this Fist, but he was also a runt. He was a head shorter than Oryss, but tried to compensate for it by standing straighter, sacrificing his hump by doing so. His stature was what truly made him stand out. His body was much stockier than most Maulers, and he had taken full advantage of that fact. He was extremely muscular, and outweighed most by at least a Boulder[27]. Unlike the others, Terrabyss felt the need to train beyond the usual brawls and wrestling they all took part in. His fur appeared black until the sun shone on it, revealing its burgundy color. His eyes were not the typical Mauler shade of yellow, they were almost the color of rust, or over-polished copper, and were the reason for his nickname of Rust-Eyes, or sometimes Drunk-Eyes. However, most who used these terms weren't foolish enough to say them in Terrabyss' presence.

It was never good to stand out in the Silverback clan, least of all in the Mauler tribe, and Terrabyss' mother had often been heard making it clear that she didn't encourage his behavior, but somehow, he still persisted in his uniqueness. He had even used the pelt from his first kill to trade with the Ramsyn, who wandered down from the Ice Kraggs to trade with those living in the Grove and out on the Banshee Tundra. For the exquisite caribou fur, he had received a kanabo, which—as many of the Maulers put it—was 'a bat with spikes.' Terrabyss hadn't cared about their snickering or their jeers, and had learned the weapon's deadly uses. It gave him a longer reach than his claws alone, but was compact enough that the trees didn't hinder his swing. He had permanently shut more than one mouth that had tried to mock his originality, and most had learned to whisper behind his back. He could live with that. As long as none of them had the gall to mock him to his face, he didn't care what they said.

Oryss, though, was not most Maulers. He was the alpha of his litter, and he was the alpha of this Watcher Fist. Terrabyss ignored him for now, just staring off into the grove with his back against Oryss to exchange body heat.

"Hey! Rust-Eyes! You hear me? Go put another log on the fire." He elbowed Terrabyss in the ribs to make sure he had his attention.

Terrabyss pinched his eyes closed to try to keep himself calm. "Yes, Oryss, I heard you," he responded before Oryss decided to use another elbow. "I can see the smoke from here and I can smell the burning wood,

27   Measured by the weight of a particular, well-sized boulder kept by the shaman's den

as well as hear the crackling of the flames. I am pretty sure we don't need more wood." He tried to sound friendly, but he had long lost his patience for Oryss. Anyone else, and he would have snapped their muzzle for the 'Rust-Eyes' comment. His tone was even, yet he wasn't able to hide the aggression in his response.

"I gave you an order, pup." Oryss growled, his hackles rising. "I am the alpha here and you will do as you're told." He still hadn't turned to face Terrabyss, and the other three Watchers with their backs to the two of them kept silent. Balt and Narz were brothers, and both of them had two or three scars, mainly on their arms. They were agile warriors, and were good at fighting in a pair. Neither had been an alpha of anything, nor were they runts and they had shy and quiet personalities. They were almost indistinguishable, except for the fact that Balt wore two daggers, one on each thigh. These daggers had triangular blades with long handles, and were among the few weapons the Maulers adopted, as they could be used for skinning hides or as extensions of their claws.

Calmus was another story. He was lanky for a Mauler, and he appeared frail, having a small frame and lean limbs. Terrabyss suspected that his shoulders were twice as broad as Calmus'. He supposedly did have a good eye, and was apparently practiced with a sling. Terrabyss had never seen him use it though, and like most Maulers, Terrabyss thought being a slinger was a poor profession. It wasn't that Maulers didn't have slings and didn't know how to use them, but they were childrens' toys and not something to hold on to. Still, every unit of Watchers was supposed to have a slinger in case of flying enemies, like the vicious Corvel[28] that lived nearby, and Calmus was allegedly the best out of the five of them. As far as the others were concerned, the only reason Calmus was here was because he was a childhood friend of Oryss, and an unabashed brown-noser.

Balt nudged Terrabyss. "He is not going to ask a third time, just do it and get it over with."

With a hushed growl, Terrabyss stood up. He again considered challenging Oryss—he considered it almost every day—but he knew that Calmus would side with Oryss, and without good reason for the challenge, Balt and Narz would end up on Oryss' side as well. If Terrabyss was being honest, he wasn't sure if he could beat Oryss in a one-on-one match, much less one

28   Crow-Taurs of the Airlut clan

on four. Fighting with your siblings was one thing, fighting with an alpha without a good reason was suicide.

"Do we have any more wood?" Terrabyss asked, brushing the snow out of his fur and picking up his kanabo.

Oryss was very much enjoying himself. "Don't know. Just toss that big branch you're holding into the fire." He and Calmus had a good laugh, as Terrabyss and the brothers rolled their eyes.

Terrabyss stomped off toward the fire, hoping that there were some logs stacked up next to the ring. "Five nights. It's been five nights of that same bear-shit[29] joke," he grumbled under his breath as he approached the hot, flickering fire.

"We can't hear you!" shouted Calmus. "You will have to speak louder if you need us to help you. We all know fire is scary, but it isn't going to jump out at you." None of the others made a sound, Calmus had joined the party a bit late and was now the odd one out.

"Shut up, Belly-Greeter[30] !" Terrabyss whirled around toward the gathered Watchers, not bothering to add an extra log. He had enough of Calmus. If there was a Mauler that exemplified cowardice, it was Calmus.

None of the Watchers came to Calmus' support as he swallowed hard, unable to lock eyes with Terrabyss. He kept opening and closing his mouth, as if he wanted to say something but was unable to produce any sounds.

"The only fame to your name is that you aren't a runt," Terrabyss said with a vicious bark, and feinted a lunge at Calmus.

Calmus fell onto his back in the snow, showing his belly. Terrabyss was sure Calmus would have stayed like that too if it hadn't been for Oryss, who instructed him to sit up.

Terrabyss turned back to the fire and noticed a small stack of logs almost hidden under a snowbank. Putting down his kanabo, he brushed the loose powder off the wood stack, and tossed another log into the fire, watching for a minute to be sure it had ignited. The wind around the flames blew up in a powerful gust as something landed in front of the fire. The snow and dirt from the impact rolled over the orange and yellow flames like a wave. The fire spat and sputtered, trying to maintain itself; but quickly died out, leaving only a few stars and a half moon to light the grove.

Terrabyss instinctively jumped back, in case the 'whatever' that had

29   A common curse among the Silverbacks
30   Derogative title among Silverbacks

just landed was an enemy and was following up its descent with an attack. From behind him, he could hear the sound of other beings crashing down around the clustered Maulers, and he could hear the shouts of confusion as they tried to defend themselves from the surprise assault.

Having lost the firelight so suddenly, Terrabyss was almost blind. He closed his eyes as soon as the fire had lost the will to burn, and now relied on his hearing and smell. It would take only a short time for his eyes to adjust, but a lot could happen in that moment. His nose told him what he was fighting as he sniffed at the air. The assailants were from the Gorgel clan, but he wasn't familiar enough with the group to be able to distinguish a tribal scent. He heard the creature stepping closer, and he could hear the clicking sound his opponent made with its tongue to help it see, since Gorgels didn't have the best eyesight. This echolocation helped them navigate their dark tunnels and lairs within the Ice Kraggs. They were a Harpyn[31] Taur clan, and weak around their unprotected midsections, a fact that Grimmis had always failed to mention, unlike the Maulers, who had thick fur to protect their vital organs. Gorgels had leather wings that sometimes hung from their arms, similar to the Airlut clans, or sometimes the membrane-like wings grew from their shoulders. They had sharp pointed teeth, and equally sharp claws. They wore no armor, but carried spears and were about half the height of the average Mauler, depending on the tribe. They were not exceptionally strong creatures, and depended on surprise tactics as well as numbers to gain the upper hand in a confrontation or when hunting.

Terrabyss heard what he could only assume was a spear cutting through the air as it was thrust toward him. He stepped to the left to try to avoid the stab, only to discover that this particular Gorgel wasn't using a polearm, as the blade sliced into his right hip. *The pellet[32] was aiming for my groin!* Terrabyss leaped back several times to try to create some distance, and opened his eyes. He didn't have the clarity he had been hoping for, but it was better than being completely blind. The gray-skinned Gorgel rushed after him, holding a wickedly serrated axe above his shoulder to hack down at Terrabyss when he closed the gap. As he stepped out of the way of another attack, he felt a nearly crippling pain from his right hip, but managed to push through it. The blade had torn rather than cut at his

31   With a human torso

32   An extremely vulgar curse comparing the subject to herbivore waste

flesh, and the crude wound was making it difficult for him to stay light on his paws.

This time, the attacker swung back across at Terrabyss with a back hand. Terrabyss quickly leaned back at his hips, narrowly avoiding the blade as it swung just out of reach of his abdomen. The axe had only two logical attacks; a downward cut that was either diagonal or vertical, and a horizontal cut. Terrabyss quickly changed his tactic, stepping to the right of a downward cut so that he would be on the outside of the attacker's arm. Then, with a burst of speed, he grabbed the attacker's right arm before he could pivot to square off and defend against Terrabyss' assault. Terrabyss brought his head back and—with all the force he could muster—slammed it into the Gorgel's. They both staggered back; fortunately, it seemed that Terrabyss' head was the harder one, as he shook off the effects rapidly and sprinted for his weapon next to the fire.

Oryss had one Gorgel by the neck, and was trying to snap its spine. Calmus was off in the trees, hopefully putting his sling to good use. Balt and Narz were standing over a dead Gorgel, but Balt only had one dagger in his left hand and his right arm hung limp. Blood dripped from the tips of his claws, running from some wound in his back. Narz had a similar tear to Terrabyss, but it was in his neck rather than hip and it didn't look too deep.

Terrabyss reached for his weapon; just as his fingers gripped the handle of his kanabo, he felt a sharp pain in his ribs, as something hard struck them. It hit with such force that he fell to his side and rolled away, hoping to pull away from his assailant and put himself in a defensible position. Standing to face the attacker, he realized he was alone. He had apparently hit the Gorgel in the face so hard that it had shattered the creature's sensitive nose. Terrabyss was confused as to who had attacked him, he reached for his ribs and winced at how sore they were, but there was no blood.

"If Calmus hit me with a rock!" he swore, taking a quick look at what was going on. He had knocked one out by crushing its face, Oryss had three on him, Balt and Narz were still fighting the second of their two assailants, and he didn't see Calmus or another attacker anywhere.

"Is Calmus already dead?" he wondered aloud as he decided that Oryss needed his assistance. He wasn't sure why Calmus wasn't helping Oryss with rock after rock, and the only explanation he could think of was that the little coward was dead, or had run far, far away.

Oryss was ducking and weaving between axe swings and, considering that he was fighting three opponents at once, Terrabyss couldn't deny the skill that the alpha was showing. He couldn't go on the offensive, though; whenever he tried, he was punished for it by receiving another cut. Oryss lifted his left arm, catching a spear under it as it slid past his chest; at the same moment he kicked out with his right paw, striking a Gorgel on his wrists as he tried to cut at his hip. In the same motion, he punched out in front of him, trying to hit the third assailant's throat before it could step in for a swing. The third Gorgel read the attack though, and stepped back to avoid the Mauler's claws, stepping right into Terrabyss' two-handed swing. The blow caught the Gorgel on the back of the neck right below the skull. The head folded back over the weapon as the spikes tore through its flesh, separating the head from the body. Terrabyss moved toward the Gorgel that had attacked Oryss with its axe. He swung down at the enemy, intending to smash its skull in, but the Gorgel had seen Terrabyss' grand entrance and wanted nothing to do with his weapon. He quickly backstepped and avoided the heavy hit from the kanabo.

There was a loud howl from behind Terrabyss as the Gorgel that was fighting both Balt and Narz managed to slice across Narz's stomach, cutting deep past the fur and flesh. Narz dropped back to recover as Balt flanked the Gorgel. The Gorgel couldn't defend in time, trying to rotate and get its axe in between itself and Balt's dagger, but failed miserably as they both collapsed into the snow. Balt rolled over, leaving the dagger stuck in the Gorgel's skull as he tried to catch his breath. Narz was back up though, and saw Oryss struggling with his enemy and decided to give him a hand, moving over behind the spear-wielding Gorgel.

Oryss had broken the spear, but had lost a lot of blood and was feeling his endurance and strength sapping. He tried again to bat away the snapped spear pole and grab at the Gorgel's neck. This time, there wouldn't be two other Gorgels to save this one. This time, when Oryss got him by the neck, he was going to snap it with no interruptions. Well, that was if he could get his hands on it. Again, the stick poked into Oryss' shoulder; again, Oryss batted it away and tried to wrap his hands around the Gorgel's throat. The Gorgel didn't duck out of Oryss' grip. Someone had grabbed the Gorgel by the neck, except it wasn't Oryss. Narz lifted the enemy up over his head and grabbed it by its ankles. He folded the Gorgel in half; the creature's back, neck, ankles, and legs snapped as Narz broke him in two. The wound in his stomach ripped open again and Narz hunched over, trying to stop from bleeding out. Balt saw his brother collapse back to his knees, he could smell the gore from here and knew that the wound was fatal. He stood to rush over to his brother, but the spike of a war hammer punched through his chest and he slumped back to the ground, unable to even make a sound.

Oryss slid down to his knees, thinking that Terrabyss was eliminating the last threat. Terrabyss deftly batted the axe out of the way and with a quick twist of his hips and shoulders sent the kanabo back into the face of the shocked Gorgel, obliterating all facial features. Terrabyss heard the snow crunch as he spun around, he hadn't heard Balt go down, but he could tell that whoever was creeping up behind him had far lighter pawsteps than a Mauler. The first strike Terrabyss blocked with the kanabo, but this Gorgel had more strength than Terrabyss' quick block could counter. When the second swing came, Terrabyss was unable to bring his weapon back down to intercept the attack. He did the next best thing, and twisted his body so that the hammer hit his powerful back muscles instead of his already bruised ribs. The blow still sent him rolling muzzle over tail, like a stone across a pond's surface.

When Terrabyss pulled his head from the snow, he was wheezing for breath, his head was spinning, and little ice crystals had formed around his watery eyes. As he tried to push himself up, he discovered with a yelp of pain that his right shoulder was dislocated and he felt faint as he got to his knees. His lungs demanded more air but refused to work and he had to steady himself with his weapon. He could see Oryss was standing now, but was still bent over trying to catch his breath and to keep from passing out.

Where did this seventh one come from?

He opened his mouth to warn Oryss, but all he could do was gasp for air. *Alpha Father, damn him!* Terrabyss swore, he seemed able to do that. "Calmus, you cur! Was one, one Gorgel too hard for you?"

Then he saw something worse; another Gorgel came sneaking from between the trees, wielding a club. This second one hadn't noticed Terrabyss beneath the snow, and had moved to sneak up behind Oryss.

The Gorgel with the hammer screeched loudly, which instantly brought Oryss to attention. Oryss turned toward it, as it bounded toward him. Oryss grinned maniacally.

"Come on, come on," he taunted as the creature swung down with

35

the spiked part of the war hammer. Oryss caught the weapon by its hilt, and brought his hand back with a cruel smile, reaching for the Gorgel's belly with his claws. The stone club hit Oryss without him even knowing it was coming. The smoothed rock that served as the club's head cracked into Oryss' back, barely missing the lower spine. If Oryss hadn't already been so wounded, he may have pushed through the pain and been able to claw out the stomach of the one with the hammer. As it was, Oryss was fighting on fumes and went to his knees when the club bruised the lateral muscles on his left.

Oryss wasn't going to live through this if Terrabyss didn't do something, and although he didn't like Oryss, he liked two-on-one in his favor rather than in his opponents'. Terrabyss grabbed his injured arm by the wrist and pulled it straight out in front of him to force the joint into the socket. He felt, rather than heard, it go back into place, and he let out only a soft whimper as a shot of pain rang through his neck and arm when it popped back. With a grimace, he moved as quickly as possible to support the outflanked Oryss. Oryss twisted out of the way of the hammer, but the enemy behind him moved with him, bringing the club back down for Oryss' skull. The club managed to connect, but not as accurately as the Gorgel had hoped; landing solidly on Oryss' left shoulder blade. Oryss stayed barely conscious from the blow; trying to sidestep around the Gorgel with the hammer, so that he could put both opponents in front of him, even if it was just briefly—that was all he needed to turn the fight in his favor. Again, the opponent behind Oryss mirrored his motion, lining up another swing for Oryss' skull.

The Gorgel with the hammer was tiring, the weapon's heavy head was exhausting the creature with each swing, and each swing took longer and longer for the Gorgel to reset the weapon and turn back to the side-stepping Oryss. It knew its ally was still behind the Mauler, so eventually Oryss would have to stop avoiding it. A dark figure loomed behind Oryss and Terrabyss tackled the Gorgel before it could get its club to connect. When Oryss heard the thud of something impacting the Gorgel behind him, he rushed forward for the Gorgel with the hammer. The Gorgel had just about reset its footing and had propped the hammer up on its shoulder as Oryss collided with it, easily slamming it back onto the ground. As they collided, Oryss drove his elbow into the creature's sternum, causing it to shriek hoarsely. Before it could recover, Oryss grabbed it by its face and shoulders, spinning its head around until he had broken its neck.

Terrabyss, in the meantime, had managed to pin the Gorgel with the club to the snowy ground, and had his kanabo pressing down on the creature's neck. There were grooves in the snow where its limbs thrashed about in protest, but the flailing was becoming less violent and frequent. When the eyes bulged, the lips were blue, and the whipping about had stopped, Terrabyss finally stood, surveying the battlefield. Balt had a hole in his chest and wasn't breathing; Narz was slumped in the snow, his hands no longer trying to hold in his entrails; and Calmus was probably dead.

He had better be dead.

"Well, we won, and I think we killed all eight of them," Oryss said as he slumped down on the ground, picking up a handful of snow and using it to ice his neck. "I don't see Calmus, do you know what happened to him?" he asked, trying to look over at Terrabyss, but giving up when his neck cramped up and he was unable to turn his head.

Terrabyss shrugged in response, unable to stop his body from sliding down near Oryss, and holding his own ball of snow against his sore ribs. "I am pretty sure he is dead, and if he isn't, then he will be the next time I see him," he stated, matter-of-factly.

Dio

"Are you sure that this canyon is going to lead to the Mauler tribe?" Luna inquired of her father as they squeezed between the freezing walls of ice that made the mountain range known as the Ice Kraggs.

Luna had just put her juvenile years behind her, she had white fur, and stood slightly over six feet tall. She had dark blue eyes that contrasted starkly against her fur; they gleamed in her snowy white face. Her father, Dio, was light gray, almost smoke-colored, except for the white mittens that highlighted both his hands and paws. Dio had very pale blue eyes, which were dull compared with Luna's. He was about six foot five, even with his hump, which was under-developed as with most Eclupse. They were both lean and had very narrow frames, which helped them to step lightly and remain easily concealed, perfect for two Eclupse on the run.

Dio's ears swiveled to hear his daughter's question clearly before he responded. "I am sure your grandmother's story from when she was younger is accurate. She was hardly a pup when she heard where the Daunkirks encountered the Mauler rear guard, and she was right about her assumption about them finding some canyon that cut through the Ice Kraggs." He stopped to catch his breath for a moment. He wasn't old by any means; Luna had been from his only litter with his mate Luma; he bit his lip to stop from letting out a sob as he remembered her vividly.

A week of marching was exhausting though, and he rested long enough for Luna to catch up to him. He forced his muscles to work, the need for vengeance still outweighed the grief and anguish over the previous week's events, and provided him the fuel to march on. That drive and rage was becoming faint, but every time he lay down to sleep, he vividly remembered the face of that one, slightly more sober, Ozar, that had recognized Dio and his group and it rekindled the mania that smoldered within him.

He could still hear the Ozar shout out, "Wait a moment! I know who you, and you, and you are. I know who all of you are. You're not from the commune, you're that pack of rogue Eclupse! You're wanted!" His tone had only become more and more excited as he became more and more confident in his accusation.

The other Ozars got excited and ordered them to stop as well, but the Eclupse weren't going to let themselves be rounded up like cattle. They had all tried to run, but more Ozars had been celebrating with the others, and the Eclupse pack ran into their waiting axes.

Dio had tried to keep his family safe, trying to keep Luma, Luna, Altz, and himself all together. Altz was hot-headed though and immediately rushed at an Ozar who grabbed Luma by the tail and dragged her back into the melee. Dio yelled for him to stop, but Altz had let his emotions get the best of him and charged into the fight. He was neither armed nor armored, and that made it extremely difficult to take a chainmail-wearing Ozar enemy down. The Ozar axes also made short work of the unarmored Eclupse, and Dio didn't need to stay and watch to know that both his mate and son had just been butchered. Dio had managed to grab Luna before she bolted after her mother and brother, forcing her into the undergrowth of the ferns and snow, and urging her to keep her eyes forward and run.

The following night, they were not reunited with any survivors from the incident, and by the second night, Dio had come up with this plan. Still, his doubts were nagging at him and beginning to make convincing arguments again. Just yesterday, he had managed to silence these often-logical counter-arguments to his idea of finding the Maulers and persuading them to kill all the Ozars in the Green Wall. It had taken him and Luna three days of inching along the face of the Ice Kraggs, searching for the almost imperceptible canyon pass. Each day of their hunt for the pass, the doubting voices had become stronger and more persuasive. He had almost given up and marched off into the Green Wall, hoping to avoid ever being found by Ozars again, but then Luna had found the canyon and the voices were silenced. Now though, he could hear them again. *This may not even be the right canyon, probably just a dead end. You're leading your last pup into a pointless quest for vengeance. You and she are as good as dead.*

He thought they should just turn around before they found it impossible to turn back in this narrow pass, it was only becoming more cramped the further in they went. Luna's silence informed him that the same pesky voices were in her head, and Dio wanted to comfort her, but he couldn't. Hope was a long-forgotten notion.

As the sun rose in the almost noon sky, its warm rays found the two travelers as they snaked through the icy canyon. The heat and light did bring some comfort to the duo, but they were so tired from trying to stay one step ahead of the Ozars, who were probably also searching for them. Luna's knees were starting to get wobbly, and she was finding it hard to trudge through the deep snow.

"You think we could take a rest soon? The Ozars probably weren't able to find the canyon, much less fit through it. So, we could take this moment to close our eyes for a few minutes, couldn't we?" She looked up from catching her breath when she didn't hear her father respond to her.

Dio was deep in thought, trying to ignore the constant jabbering within his mind. He didn't hear Luna as he kept marching, winding around another narrow bend. He never even noticed that he had stepped out of the canyon. As he walked and argued with himself, he came to a sudden stop as a large, black-furred hand grabbed his neck, squeezing so hard he couldn't shout or even talk. Next thing he was aware of, he was lifted into the air and smashed into the snow on his back. Small lights flickered in and out of his vision, and he managed a groan through the chokehold. His vision was starting to turn black as he weakly smacked at the dark fur on his assailant's forearm.

Dio noticed a second figure joining the one who was choking him, and staring off at what he could only assume was Luna coming to the aid of her father.

"Silverback!" Dio shouted as loud as he could, using all his energy to get the word out loudly enough for the two assailants to hear him clearly.

Terrabyss looked down at Dio and then to Oryss, who had a chokehold on this gray-furred Wolf-Taur, and then toward the white-furred female running toward them. He had never seen a Silverback that looked like her before, and Terrabyss' tail wagged slightly in his distraction. He almost didn't hear Dio's word, but managed to catch it just in time. He turned back to Oryss, growling. "Get off him."

Oryss either didn't hear either of them, or was choosing to ignore both of them and maintained the chokehold. "They are invaders, now kill that bitch before she starts giving us problems." He met Terrabyss' intense stare. "Well, Rust-Eyes? I gave you an order!"

Terrabyss clenched his kanabo tightly, his hackles starting to rise. "They're Silverbacks, not invaders," came Terrabyss' even response, "so let him go."

Dio's eyes were starting to roll back in his head and his body was barely thrashing in protest any more. Luna was so exhausted and tired that she was stumbling through the snow to try and get to her father in time.

"I gave you an order, runt! Hop to it, Rust-Eyes!"

Terrabyss was done with Oryss, he was tired of being treated like a pup, and tired of not putting Oryss in his place for the constant insulting nicknames.

"You're worthless," was all the warning Terrabyss gave as he swung his weapon. His hips rolled with his shoulders, ignoring the pain from his barely-closed wounds as they tore open, and his arms and torso flexed as he planted his paws firmly. He struck Oryss in the chest. Oryss wasn't a novice to combat and had seen the attack in time to put up a defense; Terrabyss' swing had been meant for Oryss' face. Oryss had intended to catch the weapon, stomp on the unconscious Dio's chest, and then step forward and drive his claws into Terrabyss' throat. The power behind the swing, though, caught Oryss off guard. He leapt back from Terrabyss and the unconscious one; the female seemed intent on caring for the male on his back, and two-on-one was not in Oryss' favor. He raised his hands, rethinking his tactic. "All right, all right. I just wanted to see how serious—"

He didn't get to finish the sentence. Terrabyss was past fed up with Oryss. It was under his command that Balt, Narz, and Calmus were killed and, as far as Terrabyss was concerned, that was reason enough to challenge Oryss.

"You don't have any more supporters, your right to power is over." He swung his kanabo across at Oryss who couldn't avoid the hit completely, and went skipping across the snow like Terrabyss had done the night before.

Oryss came to a stop face-first in the snow with his legs arched over his back. Luna stopped mid-run to watch as the black-furred Mauler rolled like a ball through the snow. She was intimidated by the ease with which the burgundy Mauler had cracked the other one. At Terrabyss' paws, Dio gasped, taking in a huge lung-full of air, coughing and wheezing. He extended a hand to Terrabyss, expecting to be helped up, but Terrabyss merely stepped over him toward Oryss. Terrabyss knew that Oryss could take a lot of hits, and he was almost positive that his second hit hadn't connected fully with the brute's body. Oryss groaned as he let his legs fall back and did a push up to stand back up, brushing the snow out of his fur. He still had his back to Terrabyss.

"Now, runt, with attacks like that, I might start to think you meant to—"

Terrabyss had already closed the distance and brought the kanabo down in a chopping motion, bringing the weapon down over his head. This time, though, Oryss wasn't interrupted.

"—kill me." Oryss concluded as he twisted around out of the vertical attack and punched into Terrabyss' left side, hitting his ribs hard.

Terrabyss ignored the blow, flexing through the impact and turning to face Oryss. Again, Oryss used his speed to keep up his aggressive offense. He bit into Terrabyss' neck as he lunged at him, trying to tackle Terrabyss onto his back. Terrabyss was also not a novice to combat, and had developed an easy counter for this popular Mauler tactic. Oryss was quick though, and he did manage to get his teeth past Terrabyss' defenses. Oryss could taste blood and fur. Using his left-hand fingers, Terrabyss found the space between Oryss' ribs on the right side, and punched forward hard, burying his claws deep into his alpha's flesh. Oryss opened his mouth, letting out a rasping howl as Terrabyss broke more than one rib with the force of his hit. Terrabyss grabbed Oryss by the scruff of his neck and twisted him back, away from his throat. His paw kicked out, catching Oryss in his sternum, and he stepped down instead of pushing out. Oryss crumpled under the force as Terrabyss pinned him to the floor, squeezing down on Oryss' broken ribs.

"I sub—" was all Oryss managed to gasp before Terrabyss brought his kanabo down hard, turning Oryss' skull to mush.

"You are no longer alpha," Terrabyss said with a painful chuckle, putting some snow to the wound in his neck. He could hear Luna helping Dio to his paws after he had caught his breath, and turned around, intending to determine for himself if they were a threat that should be eliminated, hoping to intimidate the two of them.

Luna, though, had stumbled across Balt's daggers, which Oryss had planned to take back to the Gathering[33] , along with the heads of the eight Gorgels. She had procured these weapons for now, unsure if she was going to need to use them on whoever was the victor of the fight.

When Terrabyss turned around, he was met by Luna and a dagger a whisker's length from his snout. Her arms were a bit shaky, but Terrabyss wasn't sure if that was because she was not used to the weapons or if it was because she was exhausted. Both she and her father looked as though they hadn't had a proper rest or meal in close to a week. For all he knew,

33   Mauler communal grounds

she was just as good with that blade as Balt had been, he had no reason to assume otherwise. He decided that he would play it safe and not risk a two-on-one fight, since Dio was now at least conscious and standing.

"Terrabyss." He pointed to himself, speaking slowly and very clearly.

Luna raised her eyebrows, curious as to where the Mauler was going with this.

"No hurt you," he said again, in an equally patronizing and slow voice.

"I am not a pup, nor am I deaf or dumb," came Luna's sharp retort. "Now go join my father!" she demanded, keeping the blade dangerously close to Terrabyss' face and motioning for him to get in front of her and lead the way over to her father.

Dio gave Terrabyss a weak smile, obviously still not completely recovered from the rough handling he had received from Oryss.

"That's far enough," she ordered as Terrabyss got just out of kana-bo-range of Dio. "Now, you're a Mauler, right?"

Terrabyss wasn't sure what the point of that question was. Did she know any dark-furred Silverbacks that weren't Maulers? "Yes, I am. What does that make you?" He let his curiosity get ahead of him. His voice was deep and had a firm tone to it, he was no longer talking slowly.

"Eclupse," came Dio's reply before his daughter could continue her interrogation of Terrabyss. "I am Dio, and this is my daughter Luna." He held out his hand, fingers spread and palm out. "Do you know who the Eclupse are?" he asked when Terrabyss made no motion to return the gesture.

"Yes, I know who the Eclupse are," Terrabyss responded indignantly. It was his turn to feel insulted.

Luna leaned over to her father and in her best Dwarvish said, "I don't think this was such a good plan."

Terrabyss looked at her, then back at Dio. "I understand more than Beast Speech, and I speak more than Silverback. Your Dwarvish is terrible by the way, it is a more guttural language."

"Like you could do better!" Luna responded in a huff, her hackles rising a bit as she managed to steady the dagger again toward Terrabyss' snout.

"I know I can do better," he said in what he considered flawless Dwarvish. Any dwarf would have called it atrocious, but Luna and Dio were both impressed that a member of the exiled Mauler tribe would speak multiple languages. "None of this debate answers the question of why you are here though," Terrabyss directed the statement at the much more amicable Dio.

"Of course," responded Dio, putting a hand up in front of Luna to stop her from giving a more aggressive response, and also to encourage her to lower the dagger. He knew that Maulers were not known for their patience and had a grim sense of humor, even among Silverbacks. He also wanted to control the story that the Maulers heard about the two of them. "We wish to liberate our tribe from the control of the Ozars and their Honchos[34] . The Ozars are expanding their authority and establishing themselves in our lands—"

Terrabyss interrupted Dio by holding up his hand, "This grove is small, there is hardly enough space for just us. We can't support another tribe in this area." With that response, he turned to walk back to Oryss' body.

"We aren't asking for permission to migrate here," was Dio's response. He realized as he spoke the words they could be interpreted as hostile, and swallowed hard when Terrabyss looked back over his shoulder, hefting the gory kanabo intentionally. Dio quickly put out his hands in a submissive gesture. "Wait, wait, that didn't come out as I had intended. I am not saying that we are going to challenge you or the Maulers for your sliver of paradise." Dio raised his arms higher as Terrabyss turned back toward them, stepping with purpose.

Terrabyss pulled up short when Luna got between him and her father again, and rested her hands on the hilts of Balt's daggers. She had gathered her composure from earlier, and seemed much more comfortable with the weapons. Dio took the opportunity his daughter had given him to continue. "I am here to hire you and your tribe to help me take back the Green Wall." He studied Terrabyss closely, hoping to see some spark of interest in the Mauler from his proposal.

To Dio's relief, there was something. He wasn't sure if it was interest, but there was a response that wasn't being hit by that brutal weapon. Terrabyss lowered his kanabo, his focus past Luna coming to rest on Dio, and gave Dio a response he hadn't been expecting.

"The Ozars and Daunkirks own the Green Wall. There aren't enough Maulers to fight both of those clans."

34   Leader of an Ozar Campos

He didn't walk away from them though, and kept his gaze on Dio, so Dio continued to try and reason with him. "They aren't united any more; they believe they have crushed us and that none of us remember what it was like to live under the four laws. Luna and I are not the last of our tribe either. We were but one pack in our large tribe of Eclupse. The Cana and Varggs are not happy with their situation either, and I am positive that they would be quick to join in a revolt against the Ozars." Dio watched Terrabyss, who seemed to be thinking about the information that Dio had given him.

"What about the Lobu, would they help?" Earlier campfire stories were beginning to retell themselves in his mind.

Dio shook his head disappointedly. "The Lobu are loyal serfs to the Daunkirk aristocracy and were transported to the far south of their border, a buffer against the Warm Wood Taurs."

Terrabyss turned back toward Oryss' body, grabbing it by the ankle and dragging it to the large fire where they had burned the other Watchers earlier that day. He would have to get it relit, but there was plenty of wood left that he and Oryss had dried while they cremated their allies. Dio and Luna watched as he placed Oryss' body on a mat of dry wood, needles, and pinecones. After a few curses, Terrabyss got the sparks to take hold of some of the kindling and watched them slowly grow into a large bonfire.

As Terrabyss stepped away from the growing heat, Luna spoke up. She felt as though she and her father had given Terrabyss enough time to consider what they had said. "So, will you help us?" She growled the question as Terrabyss merely kept staring at the flames, making sure that the fire would not go out as it began to burn at Oryss' fur. She snarled, feeling like he was ignoring her.

"I will take you to our Alpha at the Gathering. I cannot speak for the whole tribe," Terrabyss responded to Luna's growls, turning to face them as Oryss' body started to burn. "Come on, then." He motioned for them to follow him into the trees.

Luna looked back at her father, hesitant at first to follow the Mauler. Dio for the most part was unnerved; Terrabyss was intimidating, although it would be strange for him to attack them at this point. His casual and almost heartless attitude was probably a calculated response to them, but the fact that he could play the role so perfectly didn't make it any less disturbing when he signaled for them to follow him into the dimly lit forest.

"I think you are in a better condition to lead," Dio told Luna as he brought up the rear, emulating Terrabyss by picking up some ice and holding it to his throat to help with the bruising.

As Luna's and Dio's adrenaline from the encounter wore off, they began to remember how badly they needed to rest and could use some sleep as their paws more than once refused to step forward. This resulted in numerous stumbles as they tried to keep up with Terrabyss.

"He is going to wonder if we know how to walk," Dio complained as he tripped for the third time in twice the number of steps.

Luna helped him to his paws. "He would be having trouble staying on his paws if he had gone through as much as we have in the past few days," she assured her father as she helped him navigate a particularly uneven part of the grove. "I am just curious as to how far we are going to need to walk to find this Gathering, it feels like we have been walking forever."

"Soon," came the gruff response, as Terrabyss appeared from out of nowhere to her right. "We're not all that far away," he stated as he walked by, weaving back through the trees ahead of them.

Luna was still trying to get her heart back to an even rhythm, and her father kept chuckling nervously, like he always did when he had been surprised by something. She growled and practically dragged her father after the Mauler.

"Insensitive piece of bear-shit," she murmured under her breath.

The grove that Terrabyss led them through was much like the Green Wall back home. It was more diverse than just redwoods, although the giant trees did make up the majority of both the grove and the Green Wall. The sequoias were what made the Green Wall famous; they soared high, standing higher than a single other tree, and wider than ten trunks put together. The other trees included many conifers, like cedars, firs, and spruces. The ground in the grove was no different to the Green Wall, uneven with rocks and fallen trees, and branches strewn throughout. Ferns and moss covered these fallen trees and stones as well, providing a thick blanket of undergrowth to the forest floor. Now though, in the depths of winter, this lush green level of the forest was hidden beneath snow drifts that piled anywhere from the travelers' knees to their waists.

As they got deeper into the grove, the sun struggled to break through the heavy canopy, causing the temperature to drop significantly and the snow almost double in depth. No animals scurried about this far in; the cold kept them hidden snuggly in their dens and homes. Both Dio and Luna were losing strength fast, and the cold of the inner grove was not helping them to stay alert.

Terrabyss appeared suddenly from around one of the large sequoias. "A few more lue and we will be there, so gather yourselves; the Alpha won't take long to speak with you. Honestly, he will be more than a little upset that I brought you two here." He didn't notice, or pretended not to, that his sudden appearing act was making the two strangers feel nervous and unsettled.

"Is there a title, or a name we should know when we address the Alpha?" asked Dio, moving his weight so he wasn't needing Luna's support any more. He tipped a bit to his left, but managed to stabilize himself. Between his exhaustion and the fight earlier, he was surprised he was still awake, much less standing. "Also, perhaps you could give us a little warning before you just stalk out from amongst the trees." Dio chuckled, trying to lighten the mood.

Terrabyss stopped a few steps from the two of them. "I guess that would be helpful," he said more to himself than to them. "Okay, first, my 'stalking' is what keeps me, us, alive in the grove. It keeps me in practice" – he grinned – "and it's fun. Second, I don't know what that stupid greeting is that you do with your hand." He spun around to face the two of them again. "In the Mauler world, when you greet someone, it is done like this." He held his arms slightly out and open, his palms facing upwards and his stomach and chest exposed. "This is a proper greeting, especially for the Alpha." He turned back around, getting one step in before Luna spoke up.

"What is his name? The Alpha has a name, right?" Luna asked, trying to remind Terrabyss of her father's earlier inquiry.

Dio swallowed nervously, Luna's tone was still annoyed, and she was not hiding the hostility she felt toward Terrabyss. He smiled at Terrabyss. "Please, excuse her. We have been through a few very long days."

Terrabyss shrugged. "She is right to assume the Alpha has a name. His name is Haxzus," he responded, and gave them no more time for questions, leading them out into a small clearing that was apparently the Gathering.

The clearing was no more than ten or so lue in diameter. Not all of the Maulers were gathered in it, some were scattered through the trees on the edges. Those that were in the open space were lounging about in the few warm rays of the sun that were not kept at bay by the heavy canopy around the clearing. Those that weren't in the clearing were mostly older, probably relatives of the others, and were watching the few pups that were running and playing in the trees. The first thing that caught Dio and Luna's attention was that there were no structures, not even temporary ones. There was an obvious, unused fire ring in the center of the clearing and a large boulder to the northern edge of it, where the Alpha would stand to address the tribe, but other than those there were no changes made to the natural environment. The clearing itself wasn't exactly circular, having some sides that expanded into the trees and other parts that had been overgrown by smaller ferns and shrubs. The two of them, and particularly Dio, were also disappointed to notice that there appeared to be only eleven, mostly female, Maulers gathered in the clearing itself. With the elders and the few pups that must have belonged to them, Dio guessed that there were only about twenty or so total in the Mauler population.

"This can't be all the Maulers that are left," he said under his breath to Terrabyss.

Terrabyss snorted. "This is definitely not all of the Maulers, but it is where the Alpha will hear matters pertaining to the tribe."

By now, everyone there was staring at them, and Terrabyss quickly turned to a large, all-black Mauler who had been lying with his stomach up toward the sun when they had entered the clearing. A younger, female Mauler, with more ash-colored than black fur was crouched next to him, whispering something to him, and he barked a command to her as he saw the three of them. She shuffled back as he rolled over and pushed himself up, so that he was sitting cross-legged and facing the three new arrivals. The Maulers gathered around him also followed his lead and became alert, giving full attention to Terrabyss and the newcomers.

This one that was obviously the Alpha had numerous scars along his shoulders, and a few on his neck and chest. His most defining feature was a scar that ran from his left ear to his shoulder, where he had been injured by a Mauler who hadn't liked a decision of his father's. He had bright, golden eyes that Dio felt pierced right through him, intimidating him as he returned the Alpha's gaze. There was some gray in the fur around his eyes and under his chin, showing he was quite a few years older than Dio.

Terrabyss came to attention when this Mauler's gaze rested on him, and he instantly gave the salute he had explained to Dio. Framing his stomach and chest with palms up, to which the Alpha tapped his stomach and then his chest while nodding; Terrabyss relaxed in response. Dio and Luna instantly copied the salute to the best of their ability, and it was enough that the Alpha seemed to find it acceptable, giving them the same return gesture as he had Terrabyss.

"Let's hear what you have to say," came the Alpha's voice; it was deep like Terrabyss' but had more patience in its tone, and he had learned to weigh his words to add importance to even the most mundane statement.

Dio stepped forward and introduced himself and his daughter, and then began to tell the same story he had told Terrabyss. This time, he made sure to add in more details and dramatic flourishes, as well as describe the killing of his mate and son. He also informed Haxzus of the same things he had told Terrabyss, about the Ozars' broken alliance with the Daunkirks, and how other Silverbacks were just waiting for a signal to rise up against those who oppressed them.

Haxzus

It was just past noon when the Scout arrived at the clearing where Haxzus spent most of his time being available to the Maulers and weighing in on choices and decisions when the tribe brought them to him. He was lounging in a patch of sunlight, and had decided to get some sun on his stomach, so had rolled onto his back when the Scout had approached. Normally, he would have sat up and listened to the information, but the cloudless winter sky was so rare and he enjoyed the way the warm rays embraced him.

"What is it?" He wanted to figure out if her information was important enough to have to forgo his comfort. The Scout hesitated for a moment, then quickly saluted Haxzus, framing her stomach and chest with her arms. He sighed, sitting up and tapping his stomach and chest, along with a slight nod. She was obviously new to the Scouts; her age was a clear indicator of that. All young females had two choices when they reached adulthood, three if they wanted a family, but if not, they could either be Scouts or part of his Guard. The Scouts kept the borders of the Mauler territory safe and relayed messages between the inner and outer groves and the Guards helped him maintain order here in the Gathering. It was no different for males other than the choice of profession, they could raise a family or become a Watcher or Hunter; Hunters maintained the food rations for the tribe and served under his mate, the alpha Hunter, Hanora.

"It is Terrabyss, sir, he will be here soon, and he has two Eclupse, I believe, with him," she informed her Alpha respectfully.

Haxzus sighed, rolling onto his back again. Here he had thought this was going to be important. He stopped for a moment, and rolled back onto his side to face her. "What about the rest of that Watcher pack?" It did occur to him that it was odd that Terrabyss was returning without the other four Watchers, not to mention that he was more than a half-moon early in returning from his post.

"They don't appear to be with him," she responded nervously, not wanting to ruin his pleasant mood.

"That's odd," he stated, more to himself than to her. "Why would Oryss let Terrabyss escort two Eclupse here? It would have been more like Oryss to have left the others at their post, and escorted these two Eclupse to the Gathering." *Although that would have left Terrabyss with the other three.* "Maybe he predicted I would have been upset if he had taken that plan of action."

The Scout was unsure if she should answer his questions, or try to help him come to a conclusion with his inner monologue. Haxzus was rubbing his eyes now, having shut them and laid back down in the sun. The Ravis pack was such a problem for him; their mother, Bia, had served as one of his father's Guards and they had developed quite a friendship after her mate had passed away, fighting as one of the rear guard while the Maulers had made their escape. To make matters worse, there were rumors that the litter Terrabyss belonged to had been sired by his father, Grimmis. On top of that, Grimmis had taught Skoff, the second Ravis male, to replace him as the former shaman. It was the first time in Mauler history that the Alpha of a tribe was not also the shaman. It had been the worst day of Haxzus' life when his father had told him that he lacked the connection needed to be a shaman. Eventually, Bia was given the coveted title of alpha Hunter, a title that had been Haxzus' mother's before she had passed away while leading the tribe to the sanctuary of this grove. How he despised Bia. When his father had passed away, she challenged his decision to place his mate, Hanora, as the alpha Hunter. Haxzus was convinced that Bia would have beaten Hanora in the fight if he hadn't ensured that she lost. No one challenged the Alpha, and his mate was equally off-limits.

Still, this had solved little, because by the vote of the elders, Numa, Terrabyss' sister, was placed as the alpha of the Scouts, known as the Scout Mother. This made her second only to Haxzus and Hanora, and he worried about the amount of power it allowed her to wield. The only consolation was that many Scouts didn't spend a lot of time at the Gathering, and Numa was no different. Haxzus had worked hard to ensure that Terrabyss had ended up in Oryss' Watcher pack, reasoning that if anyone could keep Terrabyss in line, it was Oryss. The more he thought about it, the more uncomfortable he became with the information the Scout had told him. He had hoped that the Ravis' popularity would have died out when Bia passed away, and especially after Terrabyss had killed his alpha brother in a challenge. Tarphyss had taken credit for landing the killing blow on

51

their proving Hunt, or some nonsense like that. Bia had never been the same after the loss of Tarphyss, and had died that same winter. Haxzus was sure with her death that his problems with the Ravis were over. Neither Terrabyss nor Numa had yet found a mate, and, without Bia, there was no one with authority to pressure them into having a pack of their own. Skoff was far too engrossed in his position as shaman, and lacked any ambitions beyond that. He had never shown any interest in having his own family and litter. As long as this was the last generation of the Ravis pack, they would be little threat to Haxzus' own legacy. This last thought did bring some calm to the Alpha's mind, and he stretched out in the sun again, wondering what the Eclupse wanted.

The Scout hadn't left and was still waiting for instructions, and he motioned for her to lean in close so that he could issue his commands. He was hoping that this Scout didn't share a close relationship with Numa. Before he could speak, three Silverbacks stepped into the Gathering.

"Soon?" he murmured to the Scout, as he noticed them walk out from the trees.

She stayed hunched over, not sure if she should stand or not. She was sure that she had insulted Haxzus by giving him poor intelligence, and she truly had no excuse for how they had arrived here so suddenly. "He—he must have pushed them," she stammered, trying to find a defense for her miscalculation.

Haxzus just snorted. "Go back to your post!" he barked at her as he pushed himself up to a sitting position.

She hurried back to the edge of the trees, leaving just his Guard of eight females, his mate Hanora, and his eldest son Ammer in the clearing. Haxzus watched the arrivals closely as several pups from friends of the family, and those who liked to boast about being in the Alpha's favor, broke away from their parents in the trees and ran up to the three, circling them and sniffing.

Luna was shocked to see that the pups were still moving on all fours, and also how many of the adults seemed to be able to switch from walking on two legs to running on all fours so gracefully. The Eclupse trained their pups at an early age to abandon walking on all fours, as it was seen as uncivilized.

The parents finally found a punishment worth threatening the pups with, in order to give the Alpha some privacy. The pups ran back to their parents within the trees, whimpering and whining about how the world wasn't fair and their parents were the worst; usual retorts. Haxzus returned Terrabyss' salute, and copied the gesture toward Dio and Luna, even though their salutes were awkward and clearly foreign to the Eclupse. Terrabyss sat down close to Haxzus, and Haxzus motioned for Dio and Luna to sit. Dio sat cross-legged opposite Haxzus, and began to recount his tale as a heroic rebel fighter who had been a true flea in the Ozars' fur. Now, he wanted to be more, with the death of his loved ones and with the luck of the Alpha Father, he had found the Maulers and felt it a sign that they were destined to retake their homeland.

Luna let her eyes wander as her father spewed his obviously somewhat rehearsed story. Even though everyone who was there was sitting cross-legged, she could tell that she and her father were at least the same height as the tallest Mauler here, and on average as much as half a head taller. However, her father was probably only as broad as the leanest Mauler she could see. She couldn't get past the fact that there were families living in this area, and she assumed that the Alpha and his mate must live here, perhaps even their pups. Yet, as far as she could tell, there was not one building in the whole area, in or outside the clearing. She eyed Haxzus' son who sat on the right of his father and had been introduced as Ammer; he was probably just about five or so years younger than Terrabyss who couldn't be much older than her. He had all-black fur like his father, but it was lighter around his eyes, mouth, ears, and digits, similar to her father's mittens, only gray instead of white. His eyes were the same bright gold of his father's which was lucky, they could have been like his mother's dull amber eyes, almost brown. It must be from her that he had his highlighted features, because she was a very light black, practically gray. Luna thought it was odd that they had only one pup, since most of the parents with young pups had at least two, but she saw more groups of three and four. Then she noticed that Hanora kept looking over at some other young juveniles sitting under the nearest trees; they could have been around Ammer's age and probably were other pups of hers. One was clearly a runt and came across as pampered and bratty. That was obvious by his expression alone, he seemed disgusted that someone else in the Gathering had earned his mother's attention, and was just staring at her. The female next to him seemed more like a servant than a sibling, and it took Luna a moment to assure herself of the family resemblance. She was offering the runt food, but instead of either taking it or refusing, he snapped at her and smacked at her hands, causing her to drop the meat on the slushy ground. She had charcoal gray fur, a perfect mix of her father's dark black and her mother's sleek, almost gray fur, and no other markings. Her eyes were interesting, one was her father's bright gold, and the other her mother's dull, deep amber.

After Dio had finished his story, Haxzus invited Terrabyss to walk with him and join him in a private conversation. Luna strained her ears to hear what was being said, and although she was sure they were speaking some form of Beast Speech, she could only catch random words and she was convinced there were times when no words were exchanged at all. She glanced over at her father to see if he was having the same difficulties, but by the expression on his face he was keeping a better track of the conversation than she was.

"None of them are armed," she whispered to her father, seeing only Terrabyss' kanabo which was slung across his back and covered with a leather wrap. None had objected to her carrying daggers either. "Where are their weapons?" she asked pointedly when her father said nothing in response.

Dio gave her a warning growl; Luna knew what that tone meant and went quiet as her father kept trying to decipher what the two Maulers were talking about. Dio was following the conversation better than she, but was having difficulty comprehending all that was being said. His parents had sometimes used these methods to communicate, but the loss of their culture and land had left holes in his education on all the old Silverback customs. He wasn't even sure his parents had known what they were saying when talking in the manner before him, the only Silverbacks he was sure truly knew how to talk this way were his grandparents. Haxzus and Terrabyss were communicating less through words—although there were some words present—and more through their facial expressions, pitched tones of growls, yelps, and barks, as well as tail and body movement patterns. It was these methods, specifically the facial expressions and tail patterns, that Dio was not educated in, and it was here that he struggled to keep pace with the conversation.

"Who are they?" asked Haxzus as he and Terrabyss huddled close to one another. His eight Guards went from sitting to crouching positions, but did not invade the Alpha's privacy.

Terrabyss saw the way the Guards shifted position, but kept his concentration on Haxzus; it wouldn't do to be rude to the Alpha right now, especially with the bad news about the rest of the Watchers.

"They are who they claim to be, at least they told me much the same. Perhaps not to the same degree, but you are Alpha. It is your right to know all the information." Terrabyss was worried that he might have overplayed it with the compliment. He knew Haxzus' feelings about his pack, and to be honest, Terrabyss' feelings toward the Alpha were not very different.

Luna watched intently as the conversation continued, not noticing the newest member to arrive at the Gathering. She jumped a bit, startled, when she heard the rattling of bones next to her left ear and let out a surprised snarl as she spun around. She stood almost a head taller than the short little Mauler that had been behind her, and if it wasn't for his mature features, she would have assumed it was some juvenile trying to play a prank on the outsiders. This Mauler was the leanest member of the tribe she had met yet, excluding the runt that lounged off to the side and he wasn't full grown, this male was. He was the only Mauler, or pretty much Silverback for that matter, that wore any clothing. He was wearing a bright poncho with different patches of red and blue, and the staff he carried had numerous small bones and teeth strung to the gnarled wood. His tail was braided with amber and bone beads, and he smelled strongly of soil and fungus.

Even though Luna had no idea of the significance of this member of the tribe, Dio did, and was able to stop his daughter from reacting any further than she had. Dio couldn't help but wrinkle his nose up a bit when the shaman got close to him and rattled the staff next to his right ear. Luna was glad that she wasn't the only one having a hard time coping with the Mauler culture. Both Dio and Luna gave sighs of relief as the shaman strode past them, walking right up to the Alpha and Terrabyss in their little huddle.

"Excuuuuuse me!" the shaman said, loudly and intentionally drawing out the first word, and doing so at the most inconvenient moment.

Haxzus' lips quivered a bit as he tried to hold back a snarl, not appreciating the interruption. Terrabyss didn't have the same aggressive reaction to the sight of the shaman and merely sighed, giving him the same salute he had given to Haxzus. Opening his arms, he framed his stomach and chest, to which the shaman responded by merely touching his stomach. Haxzus gave the most rigid salute he could to the shaman. The shaman turned and responded by touching his stomach, and then mirrored the salute back to the Alpha. Haxzus then touched his stomach and chest, and from what Dio and Luna could gather the greetings had been made. Again, Dio and Luna were left to sit in silence, as Haxzus informed the shaman, Skoff, of what the strays had told them.

Skoff was jet black, very similar to Haxzus' color, and had no other defining marks, other than the single scar on his left pectoral that ran horizontal to his sternum. It crossed the whole left side of that muscle, and was a good inch thick. Most of the time, this scar was hidden under one of his numerous colorful ponchos, items that he would trade for with the Ramsyn that lived in the Ice Kraggs. The ponchos were expensive and made from the fur of the mountain goats that the Ramsyn herded. The Ramsyn would often bring these goats into the grove to graze in the spring, which was when the Maulers would trade with them.

Haxzus turned to Terrabyss to ask him the question he had been leading up to before they had been interrupted. "Where is Oryss, and the other Watchers?"

Skoff, on the other hand, felt that his question was more important, and so before Terrabyss could answer the Alpha's question, he posed one of his own. "So that explains who they are; what do they want?" He gave Haxzus an innocent look. "I cannot control when the ancestors wish to use me as a vessel," was the excuse he gave, because clearly this would be of the utmost importance to the ancestors. It was the excuse he always gave, no matter the situation.

Haxzus had to admit that it was probably a more important question to the members of the tribe that were gathered here, so he ignored Terrabyss' attempts to answer and asked Dio directly. "What exactly do you want from us?"

Dio had heard Skoff talk, and had been expecting to hear an old man's crackling voice, but was surprised when he heard the resonating boom of the shaman's voice. Dio was sure that this was done through some magical spell, although he could not be absolutely certain. Luna, on the other hand, found this a shocking vocal effect. Although she had her suspicions like her father, this was the first time in her whole life that she had witnessed any sort of magic. The other tribes had lost their privilege of an arcane magic user amongst them when they were subdued by the Ozars and Daunkirks. Amongst the Silverbacks, there were supposedly none who had maintained the talent to manipulate the arcane arts. This was one of the new laws of the Ozars and Daunkirks, and very unfair since both still had their druids and madha[35] .

Dio took a deep breath. "We want to hire you to help us take back the Green Wall."

The Gathering went silent. Luna was positive that she could have heard a dragonfly flap its wings. Then, Haxzus began to chuckle, and soon Ammer and Hanora joined him. After that, everyone joined in the laughter, many of them had no idea what they were laughing about, but the Alpha had laughed and so must they. Everyone except Terrabyss, Luna noticed. He was standing there with a bored expression on his face, as though he wanted to be far away from here. Luna wondered if he preferred the relative solitude of the canyon to this small crowd.

Luna stood up. "I don't see what is so funny." The Gathering went quiet, and she continued. "The Ozars have burned their bridges with the Daunkirks; neither one will fight for the other. We have lived oppressed and as strays in our own home. None of us want to feel like that any more. I have never known freedom, but I want to experience it. I know that every tribe stuck in the Green Wall wants to experience it. Are you Maulers going to give it to us?" She stopped and looked around at all of them, mostly because her little speech had seemed to catch Terrabyss' attention and his expression was rather more awed than she was used to. As she looked around, her words seemed to touch most of the Maulers there. Many of them had grown up fantasizing about returning to the Green Wall. As the years had worn on, many had come to believe that returning to their ancestral home was nothing more than a fable. Perhaps this was a sign, a signal of good fortune, and a reason to finally take back what was rightfully theirs.

Again, the Gathering exploded into noise, but not laughter. This time there was debate about the logistics. Some wondered if the military would go first, leaving the young and elderly unprotected, or if it would be better for them all to move back to the Green Wall at once. While some cheered for the glory it would bring, others concerned themselves with how long it would take and when they could begin the march. A din of excitement seemed to hang in the air around the Gathering, some celebrating while

35   Magical healer

others pondered, but all seemed excited at the prospect. Dio was having trouble controlling his elation; he had hoped that the Maulers would respond positively to the idea of retaking the Green Wall, but this was better than he had dared to dream of.

Haxzus walked past Terrabyss and Skoff, approaching Dio with a determined expression and a purposeful gait. Skoff opened his mouth to protest as Haxzus pushed past, but the Alpha gave him a threatening growl and held up his hand to stop any objection. Luna put the palms of her hands on the pommels of the daggers, feeling as though she should step between Haxzus and her father. This was an Alpha and Haxzus didn't give the appearance of being lenient to a challenge; he might view her actions as a provocation. On the other hand, Dio was her father, and he was unarmed, and a lot slighter than the approaching Alpha. As Haxzus got nearer to Dio, he gave both her father and Luna a broad smile, and stopped just out of arm's reach of both of them.

"You believe that my tribe, my tribe of forty or fifty warriors can defeat all of the Ozars?" His tone was demeaning. "You say that we can free the Eclupse and I assume after that we should free the Cana. Is that your great plan, to free the two most COWARDLY TRIBES?" His tone lost all levity as he yelled the last part, spitting the last two words at Dio's face.

As soon as he yelled, Luna came to her father's side, fighting every muscle in her arms to keep her daggers on her thighs. She understood that this was an Alpha and she only wanted to pull her blades on him if she felt she absolutely had to.

Haxzus continued, "You didn't fight alongside us before, you left the clan! The Eclupse and the Cana thought we, the Maulers, the Lobu and the Varggs were the ones that would destroy our clan, by holding on to our traditions and our culture! My father made sure to remind me each and every day what your choices did to our kin! There is nothing in the world you could give me to convince me to use my tribe to help you fight your rebellion!"

Dio couldn't deny the accusations, and had been expecting many of them, although he felt that the 'cowardly' label was harsh, but not completely unexpected. His parents and their parents had always made it very clear how their decision was the only one that had enabled them to stay in their ancestral lands. The Lobu had been transported to the border between the Green Wall and the Warm Wood, the Varggs had been shipped to the far northwest of the Green Wall, along the Berg Maker[36], and the Maulers had been forced to flee the Green Wall altogether. Only the Eclupse and the Cana had been allowed to remain living in the part of the Green Wall that had always belonged to the Silverbacks, the peninsula that was divided by the two rivers Cenwyn, which ran east to west, and the Ryndell, which ran north to the south. The peninsula had been known as the Howler Grove, because the way the rivers cut the land made the territory look like a wolf that was howling. Although, he was not going to point out these facts to Haxzus.

"Perhaps we did make the wrong decision," Dio conceded, "and in many ways, I can see how it might appear that your brothers and sisters abandoned you. We have suffered for our foolishness." He really struggled to get that last part out, but swallowed hard and soldiered on. "I am asking for your help, as my daughter did. Let the Maulers be the tribe that pulls us back together. Let the Maulers be the tribe that punishes the Ozars for how they have treated Mauler kin."

Haxzus listened for Dio to finish, having lost some of his wild rage in the face of Dio's arguments and pleas. Perhaps this was why his response was surprising.

"No," he said firmly, turning back around to go back to where he had been sitting when the three of them arrived.

Dio's face wrinkled up and he tilted his head in confusion. Luna's expression was not much different, other than tilting her head in the opposite direction. Before either of them could speak though, Terrabyss called out from where he still stood. His voice lacked any energy, and that made it all the more insulting when he said, "You frightened, Haxzus?"

It became hard to breathe in the clearing. The air thickened with tension as Terrabyss smirked in response to the icy stare that was plastered on Haxzus' face. Luna didn't hear the Alpha growl, but his teeth were bared and his hackles were up. She wasn't sure if it was confidence or stupidity that kept Terrabyss so calm in the face of such obvious rage.

"We have survived here; we have lives here. Why should we uproot for an Eclupse? For all we know, they are spies sent by our enemies to

36   Ocean to the north

discover our sanctuary." He matched Terrabyss' stare, the two Maulers locking eyes. "We will not leave this paradise for them. I am the Alpha and I have given my command. Don't challenge your Alpha, runt." He gave Terrabyss a taunting grin as he flexed his arms and torso.

Terrabyss glared back, it was his turn to bare his teeth and raise his hackles. Before he could respond further, Dio retorted, "Survived here, maybe, but having lives here?" He snorted his contempt for the idea of Silverbacks enjoying themselves in these conditions. "You don't have any shelters or homes."

"We have our dens; and we prefer not to spend too much time with our heads buried under the dirt," Haxzus snapped back over his shoulder at Dio.

"Mauler dens?" Dio asked with an obvious chuckle. "My grandmother told me stories about what those were like. Shallow holes that you cram yourselves into so that you don't freeze at night." He looked around at the gathered Maulers. "There is no smoke house for your meats, no steam tent for your health, no council pit for your assemblies, and no fields for your games. You might as well call your dens graves for how depressing your lives have become." He sneered at Haxzus' back.

Luna had never seen her father actually bare his teeth and stand up straight, completely hiding his hump. He had Haxzus' attention and the Alpha turned away from Terrabyss and back to Dio. That dangerous gleam in Haxzus' eyes made Dio uneasy and he had to gather his composure when being stared down by the Alpha. He unconsciously took a few steps back toward Luna, at least she was armed.

Haxzus had been curious when they arrived, and on more than one occasion had been genuinely entertained, but with Dio's last statement he had lost his patience. He wasn't about to be challenged by some cur Eclupse and his bitch, and he definitely wasn't going to be challenged by the runt of the Ravis pack.

"All three of you think you can tell me how to be Alpha?" he snarled the words, foaming at the mouth as he flexed his powerful limbs and stalked toward the two Eclupse. "Well, challenge ACCEPTED!" he howled loudly.

Terrabyss had been watching everything unfold and was not sure what Dio's plan was. While he enjoyed frustrating Haxzus, he hadn't really planned on challenging the Alpha. Terrabyss wasn't stupid and Haxzus, although older, was not frail and was extremely experienced in combat. Most of his early life had been spent putting down challenge after challenge from rival packs who viewed his position as unearned and his father a poor leader. Terrabyss didn't know if Grimmis had been wrong to lead them as he did, but Terrabyss did know that his mother wouldn't challenge Haxzus herself. He and his siblings were sure that their mother could beat Haxzus, but she had remained a loyal Guard to him. She had seen some merit in the Ballio pack and had felt that Grimmis had done right by the Maulers. There were few Maulers that Terrabyss respected, one had been Grimmis; as a pup, he had wanted nothing more than to be the shaman's pupil. In his adolescence, he had come to respect his mother greatly; she had played favorites with her alpha son, but she never blamed Terrabyss for what happened to Tarphyss. She had said, "It was a challenge, and one that Tarphyss would not easily win. It was his own ego that killed him, not his brother." Terrabyss didn't care who had been his brother's killer, but he preferred to think it was him. He would hate to think that his brother's ego had stolen his victory, but he had never corrected his mother. Still, Terrabyss' obvious skill at defeating alphas didn't make him feel confident about challenging Haxzus.

When Haxzus howled his acceptance of the challenge, Terrabyss wasn't entirely sure how to respond. Haxzus had his back to him, but he doubted that he could surprise the Alpha. Dio was frantically stepping back behind Luna, who had drawn both knives and had stepped in front of her father. This was what really made Terrabyss snap to attention; that Luna was now the focus of Haxzus' ire was not a fact that he could ignore. Dio was whispering something in Luna's ear, and seemed to hunch up more and more with each of Haxzus' steps. Terrabyss was reminded of cornering a rabbit, how it would huddle into a ball as if to make swallowing it easier. If he didn't get involved, Haxzus was going to kill both of them. Terrabyss didn't care much about whether Dio died, but Luna, for some reason, that was unacceptable. Before he could close the gap for the Alpha's back, Luna moved, which almost made Terrabyss panic even more, but he managed to control himself when he saw her engage with the Alpha. She was good with those daggers, really good.

As Luna got close, she tucked one hand behind the other, keeping the two blades almost parallel with one another. Her right hand struck out first and, as Haxzus sidestepped to avoid the blade, the second lashed out in rapid succession. The daggers kept Haxzus on the back-step, trying to find some moment in which he could counterattack. After a good three, perhaps even four strikes had punctured Haxzus' defenses, Luna jumped back, putting a good three or so lue between her and her adversary. Although, Luna was exhausted; she had been up for at least a whole day, maybe longer, and she hadn't been able to have more than quick snacks the whole time they had been running. On some days, like today and yesterday, she hadn't eaten at all. She couldn't keep that blurring assault up for long, and although her opponent was injured, he was not out of the fight, not by a long shot.

Haxzus gave her a nod. "Impressive and agile. You would make an excellent Scout."

Terrabyss wanted to get involved, but it seemed as though Luna had jumped in to accept the challenge. Haxzus had said he accepted all three of their challenges, but that didn't mean that Terrabyss could just attack Haxzus at the same time as Luna. There were customs and rules that had to be followed, and usually challenges were one-on-one. Honestly, Terrabyss couldn't think of a rule that forbade him from getting involved, but if there was one, and he did, the rest of the tribe would be within their rights to rip them all to shreds. If they wished to maintain validity to their challenge, *I have to wait my turn, right?* He looked around for Dio to see how he was responding to all this, and to perhaps figure out why in the Alpha Father's name he had let his daughter be the first one to challenge the Alpha. As the other Maulers made a circle around Haxzus and Luna, Terrabyss realized that he couldn't see Dio anywhere. A loud cheer from those gathered brought his attention back to the fight.

Luna had realized that her attacks were not deep enough to cause Haxzus any concern and decided to try a new tactic. She led with her left again, stabbing for the Alpha's stomach. He would predictably step back to avoid it, and she would follow up with a lunge and catch him off balance. Either she could knock him to the ground in a worst-case scenario, or plant the blade in his torso in the best-case scenario. The problem was, that wasn't the worst possible outcome. Haxzus did step back to avoid the first stab as she had anticipated, but he wasn't as unprepared for what came next, and as she tucked her legs and lunged forward, he simply rolled toward her. As he did so, his hand shot up, grabbing her by the ankle. Luna felt her body jerk as she lost all forward momentum. She was being lifted up into the air and with a sudden chopping motion, Haxzus brought her spine-first into the ground.

All of the air was driven out of Luna's body as she collided with the icy forest floor. Haxzus had easily slammed her through the snow blanket that could have cushioned the impact and made sure she came to a jarring stop on the hard ground below. Specks of light blinked in and out of her vision as she tried to crawl away to compose herself at a safe distance. Haxzus yanked her by her paw again, pulling her back to him and her stunned body gave little resistance. Luna had collected some of her senses and was able to briefly register that the Alpha's leg was swinging back, and she managed to mitigate some of the blow by rolling with the momentum of the impact and tensing her core muscles. The growing snowbank that she made as she rolled created a natural barrier, bringing her to a stop. She took a shuddering breath; her ribs were sore, but they didn't feel broken, and she sighed in relief.

She wasn't winded this time and she could hear his pawsteps through the snow as he arrogantly approached her. Her body was shaky and she had to push herself to her knees. Before she could finish standing, Haxzus got within striking range and punched out toward her face. She pulled her dagger up just in time and he instinctively pulled his arm back to avoid impaling his fist on the point of the blade. Haxzus had forgotten about her second dagger and, in a flash, she swung across with her left and slashed the retreating punch with the weapon. Haxzus had thought she was more injured from his previous assaults, and this time he stepped back to reassess his approach. Luna tried to capitalize on his hesitation and change the momentum of the fight. Her left dagger slashed almost imperceptibly fast as Haxzus tried to sidestep the jab, but again misjudged the speed and she landed another nick on his right shoulder. Her right hand slashed out for his injured arm since he wouldn't be able to put up a strong defense with the deep wound.

Haxzus had been in more fights than he could count, and many of them had been to the death. He had learned to read combat and understand how an enemy would think. He knew she would try to exploit his injury and he was already in a side stance. He did what came naturally as she slashed, and kicked out for her exposed stomach, under her arm. Luna's eyes bulged as she felt his paw connect, she hadn't been expecting him to dodge and attack in the same motion. Her torso was already bruised from the focused assault and her abs had been softened from the constant abuse. She barely had time to flex, which probably saved her life as she sat back on her rump with a thud. She couldn't breathe, and heaved up all the bile and saliva between her stomach and her throat. Her eyes were blurry from tears, and everything was spinning around her. There were too many Haxzuses, too many to win against.

Terrabyss didn't know what to do. "Come on, Luna," he whispered to himself, "get up."

She wasn't trying to get to her paws, she was punch-drunk and wasn't snapping out of it anytime soon.

"Haxzus!" Terrabyss howled. "Turn around or I will cave in the back of your skull!"

Haxzus heard the shout behind him and smirked. He had hoped the Ravis runt would get involved so he could eliminate him and give yet another pointed example of why you don't challenge the Alpha.

When he spun around, he was confused. No one stood there, and Terrabyss was still tensely watching from amongst the spectators. None of those gathered seemed to have heard Terrabyss' howl and threat, all were watching captivated at the brawl taking place. Haxzus' face scrunched up and he tilted his head in confusion, dropping his guard for a brief moment to try and make sense of what he had heard and what he was seeing. He saw Terrabyss' face relax.

Why had he stopped panicking? He must have yelled, but why was no one else aware of that? Why had no one else even acknowledged it?

There was a sharp pain in Haxzus' left ribs, almost before he had registered that hit, a second, equally painful sensation shot through his right ribs. He didn't need to look down to know; Terrabyss' satisfied grin was all the information he needed. Dio withdrew the two blades from Haxzus' ribs, looking almost heroic as he stood over his beaten daughter.

Haxzus collapsed forward as the daggers left each lung with a sickening sound. Terrabyss was unsure why Haxzus had turned around and locked stares with him, but whatever the reason, it had worked out to their benefit. Skoff moved to step forward as Haxzus dropped to the ground, but Terrabyss put a firm hand on his brother's shoulder. "No, no, you stay."

"You will never get away with this. The tribe will never allow this," Skoff growled under his breath, but was concerned when no one immediately moved to attack Dio or Luna.

"You stay still, and they will stay still," came the even, calm, and dangerous tone of his brother as Terrabyss gave Skoff a powerful squeeze on shoulder.

Skoff winced, feeling the sharp pain as Terrabyss put pressure on the nerve. *He is right, with the Alpha dead, the tribe will look to me for guidance.*

Terrabyss surveyed the dazed crowd, looking for a specific Mauler. He roughly pushed Skoff against the trunk of a nearby redwood when he saw who he was looking for and, before the already stunned crowd could object, Terrabyss grabbed Ammer by the scruff of the neck and slammed him to his knees. Ammer could try to become an adult this year, and then he would have a valid claim to challenge Dio. All anyone could do in response was howl as with horrific speed and efficiency, Terrabyss smashed in Ammer's head with his kanabo.

Blood and gore shot out in all directions as the weapon slammed down on the stunned pup's head. Those closest to the execution were speckled with the carnage. Ammer's corpse collapsed next to his father's. Hanora held onto her two other pups as she collapsed to her knees, wailing in agony. It was her turn to be grabbed by the scruff of her neck as Terrabyss pulled her to her paws.

"Get your pups in line and bow to your new Alpha!" he demanded and let her go, turning to those gathered and holding his weapon aloft. "That goes for all of you! Bow to your new Alpha, Dio! Bow to the one who will take us back to the Green Wall," he ordered the spectators. He snarled as no one immediately responded. "Or do you challenge the Alpha?"

Terrabyss had no illusions about Dio's claims to the title of Alpha—he had none—but with both Haxzus and Ammer dead, there was no one left in the Ballio pack who had been groomed for such a position. Anyone who threw their support behind the Ballio pack now would do it to place a puppet Alpha in the position with one of Hanora's remaining two pups, or take the position for themselves and their pack. That's how things were done, but not many packs had the power of the Ravis, and few could compete with their influence. With Terrabyss' display of force, as well as Skoff's and Numa's status, the Ravis were the only true pack in a position to change the Alpha bloodline. Terrabyss watched everyone closely, he was well aware of all these facts and anyone who left now without bowing was blatantly refusing to accept that shift.

Dio was shocked by what had happened and had almost dropped Luna face-first back into the snow when Terrabyss flew into action. He hadn't been expecting the brutality, although that wasn't what really caught him off guard; it was the fact that Terrabyss was clearly stating that Dio was to be the new Alpha. That hadn't been part of his plan, he had simply meant to bring the Maulers back into the Green Wall, to make the Ozars suffer. He hadn't planned on leading that force. *Although, is it such a bad idea?* He knew how the Ozars thought, he knew how they fought, and best of all he knew their habits and customs. He was honestly the best choice for the job. He looked around, helping Luna to her paws as he tried to gauge the response of those gathered.

Silence was the response, and that wasn't a great reply to Terrabyss' instructions. It also didn't help to build confidence in Dio, and slowly his ideas of leading the Maulers into the Green Wall began to fade away. From behind those gathered there, a two-note howl filled the Gathering, and from the trees Numa and fourteen of her Scouts stepped into the clearing. The one that had reported to Haxzus was close behind Numa, and had obviously informed her commander of what was taking place. Many of the Alpha's Guards had finally shaken off their bewilderment, but only managed to let out a weak growl in reproach of what had happened, before quickly changing their tune at the sight of the Scouts.

Numa was built like Terrabyss, and was barely a half-head taller. She had a solid frame and powerful muscles that were easily visible with each movement. She had pitch black fur and dark orange eyes, and could easily be identified by a long, jagged scar that ran down her ribs. She had lost the confrontation, but she had put up a good fight and the fact she had only been a pup hadn't hurt her ego. It had been Haxzus' first real challenge, and he hadn't won a lot of honor by beating a pup. Numa used a mixture of blood and beeswax to keep the fur on her shoulders and hackles spiked and bristly, it made her look constantly angry and always as if she had just won a fight, and was an iconic identification marker for her. As she stepped out of the trees, Numa quickly took in the scene before her and then turned to face Dio, clearly and obviously saluting him. Terrabyss watched as the spectators slowly began dropping to their knees and framing their chests and stomachs with their arms; behind them, the Scouts followed Numa's lead and mimicked the onlookers. It was never a good idea to stand out in the tribe; best to follow the rapids than fight the current.

Terrabyss' stern glare came to rest on Hanora and her remaining pups, she had managed to stop sobbing and with some dignity she stifled her sniffles. She also managed to keep her pups from crying out as well as they acknowledged Dio's ascension to the position of Alpha.

That evening, all those who lived close enough to the Gathering crowded at the edge of the grove. Some of the young juveniles clawed their way up the branches of the nearby pine trees, the redwood branches growing too high and out of reach. All of the Maulers watched as a large pyre was made in the center of the Gathering and, as the sun set, Skoff approached the bier on which the bodies of Haxzus and Ammer lay. He began to whisper a chant to maintain his rhythm as he circled the pyre. His movements were dynamic and full of energy, he spun and dipped and spun again. His paws began to thump, matching the cadence of his chant, and he beat on his chest with the same rhythm. As his speed increased, so did the words, and on the stones that formed the barrier around the pyre, small sigils began to illuminate. As Skoff rounded the bier the fifth time, the sun set behind the trees in unison with his abrupt stop. He flung his arms outward and upward and the sigils, that had been slowly pulsing, brightly shone in the darkness. The bodies and kindling were swallowed by red, yellow, and orange flames; as the fire burst to life the flames rose, trying to outgrow the mighty trees around it.

Dio had to remind himself not to reveal his shock at seeing magic. Luna, on the other hand, did not have to adhere to such formalities and she stood open-mouthed, watching the fire roar to life with no flint or friction. Her eyes wide, she watched the flames surge up and up and up. She could feel the warmth as the fire swayed about to some unseen music and she was so entranced by the display that she missed most of Skoff's declaration of her father's ascension to the position of Alpha. If it hadn't been for the shouts of inquirers as to where Hanora and her pups were, Luna would have missed the ceremony completely.

"She must have slipped away when some of my Scouts were sent to outer packs, announcing Haxzus' loss in a challenge and naming Dio as the new Alpha," Numa said to Dio, Terrabyss, and Skoff who were standing in the center of the Gathering.

The majority of those gathered joined in the search for Hanora, and had spread out calling into the forest, thinking that she hadn't realized it was time for her mate and Ammer to join the Alpha Father in the night sky above.

"Is that such a problem?" Dio wasn't sure why Numa and Terrabyss seemed so upset by this information, and why Skoff had a hangdog expression. "What is going on?" Dio demanded.

Skoff took the opportunity to rub in his siblings' faces how poor this idea had been. "It probably means she has gone to the outer packs to gather them in opposition to your claim, which is pathetic, at best." He smirked confidently; he had shown them.

"So?" Dio responded. "Haxzus said he could only manage something like thirty or so warriors for an invasion." Dio still wasn't happy about that, but he had some ideas of how that limited force could be helpful.

"It was forty to fifty," Skoff corrected, repeating his smirk. Dio must simply not have understood the expression, he would give him another try.

Dio did fail to understand the smirk even with Skoff's second attempt. "Okay, those numbers I would assume are coming from her fighters," he motioned to Numa, "so, how many troops could she possibly get?"

Skoff was starting to lose his temper, he had given Dio two smirks, not one but two. Before he could form a snarky response, Terrabyss helped Dio understand.

"The forty to fifty would have come from the loyal outer packs. The outer packs have little interaction with the Gathering, and tend to go about their lives outside the everyday bureaucracy of the elders, of which the Alpha sits at the head" – Terrabyss ignored Skoff's offended expression – "the shaman is among this council of stupidity as well."

"Council of stupidity!" Skoff was beside himself with anger. "That 'council of stupidity' as you call it is the one that appointed Numa to her position. A position—"

"That I could have earned through challenge," Numa finished, making her opinion of the council obvious as well.

"You, you are on there as well!" It was a good thing that those gathered had strayed pretty far from the Gathering by now in search of Hanora, because Skoff was jumping up and down in frustration as he shouted at his siblings.

"It doesn't sound like much of a council of elders," interrupted Dio, at probably a bad time.

Skoff's head slowly turned back to face him. "You aren't born an elder. You got to grow into it." That was all the argument the shaman gave before stomping off, grumbling about being surrounded by pellets.

Dio looked awkwardly at Terrabyss and Numa as Skoff stomped off.

"So, you can explain the elder thing later, but I am still a bit confused. If she can get that many troops from the outer packs, then why wouldn't Haxzus include your, um… " he motioned to Numa.

"My Scouts," she said, helping him finish his thought. He nodded in response to her statement. "Simple, because I wouldn't have given him command of them. He was smart to assume that he wouldn't get their support, even if he had by some miracle beat me in a challenge."

"Pfff," Terrabyss snorted, "he would've beat you." He dodged instinctively as she went to punch his arm. "I am not saying that the Scouts would have not remained loyal, but I am being honest, and I just saw him fight. He would've beat you." He managed to dodge the second blow as well.

"Well, what can we do about it?" Dio's question stopped the playful taunts and hits that the two siblings were exchanging. "I don't want my start as Alpha to be fighting a civil war."

Numa stopped, and she and Terrabyss turned to face Dio. "Well, we could try to hunt her down," Numa suggested.

Terrabyss nodded his agreement. "If we find her before she manages to spread her own story amongst the outer packs, you could probably consider that group loyal. To finish my earlier point, before I was cut off by Skoff about his precious council, the outer tribes are fiercely independent but very loyal to the Alpha. Don't ask me how it works, we are a culture of contradictions."

"Well, I want someone to represent me, and I want someone who I can trust." *Someone that won't just side with her once they get out of my sight.* Dio looked toward Terrabyss and Numa. "I want you to take Luna with you, and then choose however many Scouts you think you will need. I am sure I don't need to emphasize choosing only those you trust."

"Doesn't sound like a bad plan." Terrabyss nodded. "What about you, though? Sure you're ready to deal with this all on your own? You are aware of how power is obtained and maintained, right?"

"I will be fine, I have Skoff so I won't be alone, and I am very well aware of how one obtains and maintains power." He gave Terrabyss a confident smile and, for a moment, Terrabyss didn't recognize Dio's character. He wasn't hesitant, nor nervous or humble. Terrabyss remembered again how Haxzus had stared at him confused, as though he had been expecting Terrabyss behind him.

"You know Skoff can be pretty stubborn about who he works with, and as you saw he can be very temperamental." Terrabyss didn't know why he felt the need to probe Dio, but something was there, just beyond the surface of this Ecluspe.

It was gone as Dio gave his response. "Oh, well, I am sure at some point we will find common ground."

Terrabyss nodded as Numa had already begun to walk away. He turned and jogged to catch up to her. "Why do you care if he is on his own? If he is dead when we come back, I am sure Skoff won't let some other pack take the title of Alpha until we could properly defend it. Besides, my Scouts will support me, we needn't fear being usurped." Her tone was icy as Terrabyss slowed to a walk next to her.

"I was just curious." They walked a bit in silence, but before Numa could call over two of her Scouts to join them, Terrabyss probed her mind. It wasn't a bad idea to know where she stood in all this, she obviously didn't care if Dio died, *but did she intend to depose him?* "What if he isn't dead when we get back?"

Numa had almost called out for Jabyn and Essall, two of her best Scouts. "Well, we are in a good position now, and patience is a virtue." She barked for the Scouts to join her and Terrabyss.

"It's probably the worst virtue amongst all of them," Terrabyss grumbled as he watched the two Scouts hustle over to their commander.

Jabyn and Essall were older than Numa, and had been Scouts for nearly ten years by the time of her appointment. Considering that most Scouts' tenure was typically five years—especially Banshee Tundra Scouts—the fact that these two had no crippling injuries and were still alive was amazing.

Jabyn was darker than Essall, having no white or gray features blended into her jet-black fur. She had bronze-colored eyes, and had a vicious set of claw marks down her back from a saber-tooth attack on her pack who had lived in the outer areas. The cat had killed the whole pack except her father who had been out hunting, and her, who had followed him. Her disobedience had saved her life. Her father had called her his delinquent miracle and had died two winters past, around the same time Bia had passed away. Jabyn and Numa had bonded over their parents' deaths, and had become close friends.

Essall was the exact opposite in family status; as far as she knew, her pack was still alive in the outer parts of the grove. She had three brothers and all of them had decided to start families instead of being Watchers or Hunters. She had decided that they could raise pups and teach them how to thrive, but she had been a pup once and it was an experience she would not wish on her greatest enemy. She was a lighter black, and had smokey gray highlights around her muzzle, eyes, and also peppering her stomach and chest. She had dull orange eyes that looked more brown than bronze. Both of the Scouts were taller and leaner than their commander, but didn't look nearly as powerful.

"We're going hunting, girls. Get your things and meet me at the Hollow[37], tell no one where you are going. I need to talk to Delthyn so she knows she is in charge while we are gone." Without a second thought, the two Scouts vanished to fulfill their instructions, and Numa turned to Terrabyss. "Go find—" she began.

"Nope. I ain't a Scout and you don't boss me around. Change that tone if you want something from me," Terrabyss said gruffly, obviously meaning it. The memory of Oryss ordering him around was still too fresh in his mind.

Numa gave him a curious look, tilting her head. "Fine. Would you go find Luna and take her to the Hollow? I will meet the two of you there, along with Jabyn and Essall."

"Are you going to see Ulvoue?" It wasn't that Terrabyss had anything against her spending time with the male; none of Maulers really cared unless one participant was part of a mated pair. Oath-breaking was unforgivable. As long as Numa was a Scout, having a family was not an option. He just didn't want anything to hurt her, even if it was herself. She had been the one good thing in his life, his mother was hard on all of them. It was because she needed to be twice the parent, since his father had died so bravely. For some reason, Terrabyss had always thought that meant double the disciplinarian. As he reflected on it, she was doing the best she could with four absolutely wild pups. Numa though, Numa had always beaten him up just like everyone else, but she didn't let anyone else beat him up in her sight, and she had always bandaged him up after making him submit.

"Never you mind." Numa giggled as she skipped more than ran off into the trees. For a brief instant, Terrabyss saw her as a pup, giggling and barking as she wound between the trees. He turned, letting the memories fade as he searched for Luna; there were still things he needed to do.

37   Skoff's abode

Unkyss

"I didn't think that there were any tribes that lived this far out in the grove. I actually had no idea the grove was more than two days' travel from the tundra," Terrabyss shouted to the rest of them from near the rear of the five Silverbacks, as they ducked under branches, hopped over boulders, and slid down icy inclines, trying to gain ground on their prey.

Terrabyss hadn't been sure if he liked the idea of Luna joining them, but he did like not being the slowest one in a group. He always had to conserve his energy when running; it was the only time he would admit that his kanabo hindered him. He also didn't run like this very often. It wasn't that Luna was actually slower than Terrabyss; she was faster than probably all of the Maulers, and far more graceful. When she wanted to, she could move with almost no sound and with her speed she could close huge gaps before her target could respond. Luna's struggle was with running on all fours like the Maulers, who seemed to do so effortlessly. All Silverbacks have padded paws and humanoid hands; they are covered in fur unlike the Mino, Gorgel, and Ramsyn clans, who have fleshy—but tough—torsos and arms. Like the Ozars, the Silverbacks have long claws on their fingers and toes, but unlike the feline Swifters[38] , are unable to retract their claws when they need to. The Silverbacks' legs tend to be a bit longer than their arms, which makes for a lunging gait when they move on all fours. It is a movement of confidence; they have to commit their entire body to each stride or fall flat. Luna was struggling to mimic this gait; she had long forgotten how to move like this. No Eclupse is ever seen on all fours; by the time the pups open their eyes, they'd better abandon the idea and are soon walking bipedally. The balance was awkward, and she couldn't stop mid-lunge, so if she misjudged the distance between her and a tree or a boulder, it led to a face-first collision with the often-unforgiving object.

Luna skidded and ducked to avoid yet another branch that whipped back at her as she tried to keep up with Terrabyss. "Alpha Father!" she

---

38   Cat-Taurs

swore at him for what hadn't been the first time that day, and especially not that trip.

"You said no special treatment," he huffed as he nimbly jumped from one stone to another to avoid a deep drift, before landing back onto the snowy trail they had been running on.

Luna had learned this lesson on day one, and she copied him as best she could. The first time she had seen him do that, she had thought he was just showing off until she lunged face-first into a deep patch of snow and almost buried herself. She had no idea that snow could get that deep, and she hadn't heard the end of it; in fact, she was sure she was never going to hear the end of it. It hadn't been a life-or-death situation; it had just surprised her, and she had panicked. Once she had composed herself, she realized that she could stand up and push through the drift until she hit firmer snow up ahead. Nevertheless, Jabyn hadn't failed to wake everyone this morning by crying out in loud, desperate whimpers, thrashing about on her stomach in some snow. Numa hadn't liked that and had lectured the veteran on false alarms, but Luna had also overheard Numa quietly congratulating Jabyn on her impressive and almost identical performance. A day ago, it would have made Luna mad, but this morning she had found it funny, and had flicked her hand up her neck and off her chin when Jabyn got pulled away.

Even her curse at Terrabyss had been halfhearted; he was a fountain of information when he apparently wanted to be. He had been teaching her all sorts of things, from Mauler customs to ways to survive blizzards, how to effectively conceal a trail, and how to determine the cardinal directions by using their senses. He had shown her how to use the slight incline of the terrain to determine if they were closer to the Ice Kraggs, the Banshee Tundra, or the Berg Maker. How to sense through the heat and melting patterns of the snow where the sun's path was as it traveled from the east to the west. Granted, sometimes that information was a bit rough and needed some refining, but, in many ways, Luna saw what her tribe had once been in this crude and energetic Mauler. The Maulers, and especially Terrabyss, wanted everything with a drive that she had never seen. Most Eclipse were no better than slaves under the new Ozar laws of commune, but the Maulers were truly free. Her father had resisted, not as aggressively as the Maulers probably would have, and Dio had been far from the leader of that little band of rebels. Now, she believed her father could become a heroic Silverback, if he could just become as confident as them. Most of all, the Maulers gave her hope, and that had been the best feeling of all.

"Can you still see your sister and the others?" she called as she jumped off a little embankment so that she could land several lue further down, but in front of, the rapidly panting Terrabyss.

Terrabyss was a little impressed, but then gave out a loud laugh as Luna collided headlong with a small fir. He came to a skidding stop, digging his claws into the icy path to stop himself from sliding, and waiting for her to pull herself back up and out of the needles. "I saw them just round a cluster of trees about fifteen lue northwest, but I can always track them down."

This was another thing Luna had come to respect about the Maulers; nothing seemed to escape their perception. It was as though they had a sixth sense, especially when it came to combat. Terrabyss had explained that he could "smell and hear when someone wanted to attack him." She wasn't sure how that worked, and she was trying to focus more of her senses through her nose and ears, instead of relying so heavily on her eyesight.

"Just so you are aware, I don't think we travel any faster on all fours." She rolled out from the lower branches of the small tree, covered in sap and needles.

"Well, we do. As long as we stay out of the trees and as long as we don't get caught in a snowbank." He dropped to his stomach, giving out a mournful howl. "I have been buried in an avalanche; I am going to die here!" He wailed and thrashed about.

Luna didn't want to smile, but that was a challenge she was sure to lose if she kept watching his comical display. She lunged past him. "Well, then, we best catch up before Numa wonders where we ran off to."

"More like where I ran off to, and where you were lying unconscious," Terrabyss teased as he chased after her. His kanabo was covered in a thick leather skin that he had slung across his chest, but it still jostled around on his back as he ran and made it difficult for him to catch up with Luna now that she had gotten in front of him. As he came around the cluster of trees, he barely managed to stop himself before he ran headfirst into his sister's rump, who had stopped on the other side of the trees. Luna was picking herself up off of Essall, who was growling with frustration as she wiped the dirt and snow out of her fur.

"What's going on?" he asked quietly, pulling his weapon off his back. Numa wouldn't stop suddenly without good reason.

"Quiet," came Numa's harsh whisper, directed at Essall and Terrabyss who were the only ones making noise at the moment. She peered out past some ferns to what looked like a small campsite that she pointed out to the other four. "Smell that?" she whispered. "That is the Sabor pack." She looked directly at her brother. "We don't have time to get in a fight. We are going to ask if they have heard anything from, or seen, Hanora and her two pups, and move on if they haven't."

Terrabyss took a quick sniff, he had no reason to doubt his sister, but there was a part of him that needed to be absolutely sure she wasn't pulling his leg. The Sabor were legendary, their name meant huge and supposedly they didn't disappoint. Terrabyss knew the name and knew he had met the Sabor when both had been young. The Sabor litter was several years younger, and Terrabyss hadn't mixed with the little tykes. He had been almost a juvenile at the time and had no interest in the pups. Still, he was excited to have his memory refreshed as they stepped out to the perimeter of the small camp. All five of them approached slowly, looking around for any signs of life, hoping to figure out where the Sabor pack was.

Luna slowly followed, taking a sniff. The smell was more rancid than anything else, and she was sure that scent couldn't have been what Numa and Terrabyss were talking about. She could hear Terrabyss and his sister arguing in hushed whispers about how if Hanora were here they may not have an option but to fight the Sabor pack. She could easily see how much the prospect of getting into combat with this outer pack was exciting Terrabyss, his tail was practically vibrating.

"This Sabor pack, they are Maulers too, and I understand that if Hanora got here first, she might have convinced them to join her. I just don't understand why we are being so cautious. Did her tracks lead here, and what is so dangerous about the Sabor?"

Jabyn whispered to Luna, telling her the legend of Unkyss Sabor, who had fought alongside the Ravis' father, Ornyss. His son, also Unkyss Sabor, had apparently been such a fine specimen that he had competed for Bia's affections.

"It's not that impressive," Terrabyss added nonchalantly, "besides, Mother didn't choose him, and our father fought in the rear guard as well."

Both Essall and Jabyn rolled their eyes, and Jabyn continued. "They are massive, taller than any Mauler. Maybe even taller than you. And strong, maybe even strong enough to make Terrabyss nervous." The three females laughed, and Terrabyss wasn't sure if he should feel challenged or not. He wasn't scared of either Jabyn or Essall, but before he could give some off-color remarks, Numa spoke up.

"Either way, I want this done efficiently and I am not taking any chances. Jabyn, I want you on the right flank. Essall take the left. Luna, you are probably the stealthiest out of the five of us, so I want you to sneak around the camp. I don't want anyone running out of here without us seeing, is that clear?" She looked around to the other four, her Scouts gave the traditional salute of exposing their bellies, but didn't wait for Numa to tap any part of her torso before they moved out. Luna tried her best to copy the gesture, and was becoming much more fluid with the salute. She hadn't realized she didn't need to wait for Numa to acknowledge her, and so there were a few awkward moments of her standing at attention before she realized she could dismiss herself.

"I suppose then that you and I are walking in together?" Terrabyss asked his sister, as he pulled the leather wrapping off his kanabo.

She gave him a serious look. "Yes, but only so I can make sure you don't do something extremely stupid." With that, she stepped past him and made her entrance into the clearing, with Terrabyss a mere half-step behind. "By the way, it would probably help me keep the respect of my Scouts if you would actually salute me," she commented to Terrabyss as they slipped through the underbrush, getting close to the boundaries of the camp.

Terrabyss almost stopped mid-scooch, tempted to just stand up and ruin her whole sneaky approach. "You are not an alpha of anything; not of a pack, not of the Hunters, and not of the Watch. You lead the Scouts, which makes you a beta at best. If I were a Scout, I would consider saluting you, but I am not, so I won't," was his indignant reply.

"You do realize that me being a beta still outranks a grunt of the Watch, right?" she asked in a most condescending tone.

"That's it!" Terrabyss barked, annoyed. "I am not your pup, and you best remember what I did to the last one in our pack who challenged me." He snarled and stood up from amongst the ferns, abandoning her plan for stealth.

Numa had known she was going to touch a nerve with that last comment, but she had hoped her brother would have kept some of his composure. She expected to hear the howl of the Sabor pack as they barreled down on him in support of Hanora. When that didn't happen, she expected the treacherous Hanora to make a break for it and flee the camp; her tracks had led the group here, after all. Numa was again a little disappointed, but also relieved when she didn't hear anyone trying to make a frantic getaway, or the howls of Essall or Jabyn to alert her of a runner. She did cringe as she heard Terrabyss' next statement.

"We are here looking for a bitch who goes by the name of Hanora, and her brood!" he shouted as he arrogantly walked out of the trees into the clearing, getting a good view of the camp.

It seemed almost abandoned; there were no meats, gourds, or roots hanging from the tree branches, and he couldn't smell anything buried in the snow around the clearing. There was a small open fire burning in a hole in about the center of the clearing; a little more to the south and it would have been right in the middle. Terrabyss could smell the wood burning in the pit and he could see three figures huddled close to the jumping flames. Two of the figures had their backs to him, while the third was obscured by the smoke from the wet wood that the fire was trying to consume.

"We are looking for the Ballio traitors," Terrabyss said calmly, stepping toward the fire. "They did not submit to the new Alpha, who won—"

The figure who was sitting alone and hidden in the smoke interrupted Terrabyss. "This note here says that the Ballio pack is no longer in charge." He tossed the Scout's message into the fire, which greedily consumed the dry bark tablet.

Numa stood, feeling that there was no point in remaining hidden since Terrabyss had made it clear that he wasn't alone. Maybe if I give my position away, the others won't need to, she thought.

"That message was not a lie," she called out to the figure and stepped up to the clearing with her brother.

"Wasn't what I was told," was the response. The voice was gravelly and Numa hadn't thought that there was a tone lower than that of her own brother's. Even some of the females in the tribe had deep authoritative voices, like Jabyn. The voice she heard now, that voice was deep, deeper than anything she had ever had the privilege of hearing, and it rumbled pleasantly through her mind as she tried to keep calm.

"Well, I can assure you that Hanora will say anything to excuse the crime she has committed against the tribe," Numa responded as she motioned for Terrabyss to go left while she went right around the fire they were slowly closing in on.

"Doesn't really matter to me," the Mauler who had been sitting by the fire said as he stood up. "Besides, didn't you hear? The Sabor pack no longer exists. They have become nothing but a Lone Wolf[39] ."

Numa listened as Terrabyss kept stepping forward. The statement 'a Lone Wolf' had made her stop. She recalled how the previous Scout Mother, Rymmall, had informed her that during her last years the Sabor had not sent any females in for the position. That, in and of itself, wasn't extremely odd; sometimes, Maulers decided they wanted to raise families rather than be Scouts, Watchers, Hunters, or Guards. Still, during Numa's tenure, she hadn't received any females from the Sabor pack either. Since the Scout numbers were growing at the time, she hadn't put much thought into the fact, but when this Mauler from the Sabor pack announced himself as the last survivor, things made a lot more sense to her.

"You have a name, Lone Wolf?" Terrabyss asked as he saw the Mauler stand up. *It isn't a myth, at least not with the evidence right before my eyes. The Sabor are truly giants.*

The Mauler in front of him stood head and shoulders taller than Terrabyss, and was easily taller than Luna by at least a head. Terrabyss didn't recognize him, his scent, or his voice from the previous year's Hunt, and he definitely would have remembered this colossus from his own Hunt if he had been there. There was no way he was older than Terrabyss, and honestly Terrabyss was sure that he was closer to how old Ammer had been. His coat was lush, and he had hardly any scars besides one that ran along his right arm from the shoulder to his elbow. He was a glossy black in color and his chest and stomach were salted with sprinkles of white. His eyes were a fiery yellow and seemed to almost shimmer with intensity.

"Name's Unkyss," was the reply as the muscular giant walked around the fire toward Terrabyss. Unkyss couldn't hide his excitement as he locked eyes with Terrabyss. He might have been much taller, but Terrabyss probably outweighed the tall Mauler.

"Unkyss?" Terrabyss asked, with a quizzical look. "Unkyss the Ambusher?" A single memory of when he had met the Sabor pack popped into his mind. The tribe had been gathered by order of Haxzus, for a meeting with the Ramsyn, the Maulers' first one. At this meeting, the Ramsyn and the Maulers developed an agreement and set up an annual trade between the

---

39   Exiled member of the Clan

two groups at the end of each spring. Terrabyss had been off, licking his own wounds from several unsuccessful fights with Tarphyss, and some of his friends and Numa had been building a little snow fort nearby. Out of nowhere, this black streak had bolted from his parents' supervision and collided with Numa at full force. It had sent them both sprawling and Numa had quickly recovered; although she had, at the time, sworn never-sleeping vengeance on the pup. She had threatened to shave him if she ever saw him again, and ever since that day when the tribe talked about it, they needed a way to distinguish between this Unkyss and the others in his pack. The Unkyss in front of Terrabyss had become known as Unkyss the Ambusher. Terrabyss' tail began to wag with somehow even more vigor.

"Hey, Numa, guess who it is?" he teased his sister.

Numa's eyes narrowed as she heard the name, and her ears shifted forward as her lips curled back, showing her teeth. Terrabyss smiled as he turned back to Unkyss. *Well, she definitely hasn't forgotten him.*

The massive Mauler was stretching his neck and shoulders as he looked down at Terrabyss' kanabo. "You plan on swatting some butterflies to take home as trophies?" he teased, pointing at the weapon as he rotated his hips in a circle to loosen them up.

It was Terrabyss' turn to show his teeth. "I am not here for butterflies, but I will collect your head as a trophy. I promise you that," he growled as he tapped his kanabo on the ground.

"Alpha Father! Terrabyss, stand down!" Numa ordered her brother. "Trust me, I would love to see you smear his hide all over this clearing, but we just need to know where Hanora and her pups are." She was stepping toward Unkyss as she spoke, no longer trying to flank him. She was pretty sure that he didn't intend to run. Terrabyss did stop, to Numa's relief, as Unkyss did a few squats. "Just tell us where they are, and we will leave you in peace."

"I know where Hanora and her runt are," he directed the last few words at Terrabyss. Obviously, some memories from his first encounter with them were starting to resurface in his mind as well.

"Why don't you come here and see how much of a runt I really am?" Terrabyss snarled, taking another step unconsciously before his sister ordered him to stop again.

Before Numa could continue her information gathering, Unkyss sprinted for Terrabyss. Her brother hardly registered the attack, it came so suddenly.

Unkyss' right fist hit Terrabyss in his left cheek; Terrabyss had to ram his kanabo into the ground to stop himself from crashing down from the impact. Unkyss' left hand shot out, claws aimed for Terrabyss' exposed throat. Fortunately, Terrabyss was more prepared for the second blow and put some distance between himself and Unkyss, managing to backstep away from the jab. Unkyss' attack on Terrabyss had been a diversion, he had used it to get some space between himself and Numa. Unkyss spun on his paws to Numa who had lunged forward, expecting to grab his hips and throw him to the ground. Unkyss had already outmaneuvered her and caught her by her throat; with a powerful shove, he forced her to collide with one of the large trees near the clearing's edge. Terrabyss rushed back in and had taken aim for the tall Mauler's hips, his shoulders and his own hips twisting as he swung the kanabo horizontally. It was a smart attack, a tall opponent like Unkyss would be forced back on his heels if he wanted to avoid the attack. He was too tall to easily duck or jump over the swing, and he had no weapon of his own with which to parry the blow. Unkyss was unfamiliar with this weapon, and spun about, intending to catch the kanabo like he would have done if Terrabyss had tried to kick him. The problem for Unkyss was this wasn't a paw or leg; it was a spiked, redwood bat and it was swung by a very powerful Mauler. By the time Unkyss realized his mistake, all he was able to do was drop his bicep to intercept the blow. Fortunately for Unkyss, he had enough muscle that the spikes didn't pierce anything vital, and he didn't resist the impact which minimized the damage. He slid to the right a couple of lue and his arm throbbed from the hit, as droplets of warm crimson blood dripped onto the white snow below. Unkyss was fortunately not left-handed and although he would find it difficult to beat these two without the full use of both arms, he didn't mind his odds.

Numa was getting to her paws, her back was sore and her skull was throbbing from the impact, but it would take a lot more than that to put her down. Unkyss saw her, out of the corner of his eye, getting up, as he tried to recover from Terrabyss' hit. At this moment, Jabyn, Essall, and Luna all charged into the clearing. Unkyss twisted out of Essall's tackle and managed to hop over Jabyn's sweep, but as Luna closed in on him, he knew he wasn't going to get to Numa in time and switched his tactic. His paw caught Luna in the shin, sending her face-first into the icy hard ground. She managed to twist her head, so she didn't hammer her muzzle into the solid forest floor; some of her practice while running paid off there. Unkyss snatched her up by her ankle and shoulder, throwing her into the charging Terrabyss. Terrabyss managed to drop his kanabo and catch Luna, but was unable to hold his balance and they both slammed backward, rolling a few more lue back. By now, both Numa and Essall had recovered and Essall tried to kick Unkyss in the face with her paw; quicker than Essall could register, he knocked her planted paw loose with his right hand, sending her up and back. If she hadn't been a trained fighter, she would have landed on her neck and probably snapped it. She let her body move with Unkyss' momentum and landed face-first into the snow. Still low to the ground, he spun with his left leg out, trying to sweep Numa. Numa was quicker though and jumped up to avoid the leg. Unkyss finished his rotation and, as he did, his left leg was now his pivoting paw, and his right leg angled upward, catching Numa in her stomach and sending her back into the trees again. Jabyn had recovered from her failed tackle and had turned back toward Unkyss; she tried to kick down on his calf and then bite into the back of his neck. He let her knock him to his knee, but his arms flipped back over his shoulders and grabbed Jabyn by her head, flinging her across the campsite.

"Do the five of you surrender yet?" he taunted, standing and turning to face the group, letting out a ferocious howl.

He was lucky that Luna had a bit of a limp from being kicked in the shin, and she stepped poorly as she launched her attack. Unkyss jumped forward, spinning to face Luna, impressed that she had recovered so quickly and almost got the drop on him. He remembered just in time that she had collided with Terrabyss, and slid to his left to avoid the chop of the kanabo to his right shoulder.

"You shouldn't brag until you are sure you have won!" Terrabyss barked as Unkyss slipped just out of the weapon's reach.

Unkyss twisted a quarter turn, so that he now had the five of them in front of him again, ignoring Terrabyss' advice and continuing his previous thought out loud. "Hanora told me that the Eclupse had taken over. She also said that it was you" – he pointed at Terrabyss – "who was the one who put them there." He continued to step back as Numa, Jabyn, and Essall had also recovered by now, and the five of them were trying to hem him in.

Caught up in the moment, Luna had her own wisecrack to add to the witty remarks. "Terrabyss didn't put my father in the position of Alpha, he put himself there."

Unkyss stopped backing up for a moment, recognizing the Silverback that had actually snuck up on him. It wasn't that he hadn't noticed that she was an Eclupse, he just hadn't known her relationship to the Eclupse who was now reported to be Alpha.

"Well, that changes everything." He relaxed his body and saluted Luna, framing his stomach and torso with his arms.

"She doesn't know what that means yet," commented Terrabyss as he hesitantly lowered his kanabo, glancing over at Numa for further insight.

Luna spun to face Terrabyss. "I know what it means!" she barked and, as if to prove her point, she turned to face Unkyss, responding to his salute by touching her stomach and chest, in that order. This only caused Unkyss to look confused, and caused Terrabyss to break out into howls of laughter. There were quieter and more polite giggles from Numa, Essall, and Jabyn, and Luna lowered her ears, embarrassed and confused.

"You aren't the Alpha of the tribe, nor are you the alpha Hunter, or shaman. When another Silverback salutes you, you should just salute them, or at the very least bow your head in recognition. If you tap your stomach and chest, you're signaling, in no uncertain terms, that you intend to be or are Alpha. Because of Skoff's position as shaman, he is given the honor of returning the salute by touching his stomach," explained Numa.

Terrabyss raised his eyebrows and was still catching his breath. "See, you don't know what it means yet."

She stuck her tongue out at him in response and turned to Unkyss. "You said that Hanora had told you about my father and me." She was trying to make sense of the whole confusing situation.

"She is not wrong about that, you said you knew where Hanora and her runt were," remarked Numa, trying to bring the conversation back to something constructive. "So, where are they?"

"Hanora arrived here yesterday, I believe it was in the evening, but it could have been late in the afternoon. Either way, she came here with two juveniles, one holding each hand. I say juveniles because they were like me, definitely of age to have competed in a Hunt, but hadn't been able to yet. One was a female with eyes of different color, and the other was a male who was a pompous little brat. She told me all about what happened and tried to convince me that it hadn't been fair. Your messenger had arrived the day before." He motioned to Numa. "The message was very clear how the fight went and, on many points, Hanora told the same story. She failed to mention what he had said when he accepted the challenge conditions; I was honestly surprised that all three of you didn't attack him at the same time."

Terrabyss was relieved to hear that he was not the only one with conflicted feelings about how that challenge should have been handled. "All right, well, will you invite us over to the fire?" he asked, starting to move toward the dying flames as his adrenaline started to drop and his body reminded him that it was too cold to not be moving around.

"Oh, no, I can't do that. That fire was made so that I could offer my apologies for how things ended for the Ballio pack."

Luna looked absolutely bewildered, as she looked from one face to another. Unkyss felt that he should explain, since he had contributed to her befuddled state.

"When we kill someone, intentionally and without challenge, especially someone we respect, we spend the night by the fire with them. We listen to their stories, and we offer our condolences for their misfortune and their arrival to this moment. I killed her and her runt. It's as you said, she committed treason and did not submit to the Alpha."

Terrabyss looked over at the fire. "There were three traitors we were looking for. I only see two next to the fire. Where is the third?" He turned back to face Unkyss as he asked the question.

"Alpha Father knows." He shrugged.

Luna hardly heard the rest of his words. She had silently moved up next to the fire. Sitting cross-legged in front of the fire, with their backs previously to them, were the corpses of Hanora and her youngest boy. Hanora's neck was snapped, and her head hung limply against her chest. The boy's eyes bulged out and his tongue hung out of his mouth, and it wasn't hard for Luna to recognize that he had been strangled to death. She turned back to the others, who were talking as though there were not two dead bodies less than five lue away. She wanted to scream at them to stop and to look at what that savage had done, but she couldn't find her voice. Things were so different than she had imagined.

I always pictured the Maulers as so free and unconcerned with hardship or struggle. Is it really in the Green Wall's best interests to bring this vicious tribe back within its borders? she wondered.

Jabyn and Essall noticed that Luna had stepped over to the fire, and had motioned to Numa. Numa saw them and looked over to Luna. She wasn't sure how to approach her; to her, this was natural, this was how life was. Numa was much more comfortable here with Terrabyss and Unkyss, discussing what had happened to the other juvenile and where she might have run to. She wasn't sure if she could explain it to Luna in a way that she would understand. These measures were drastic, but had to be taken to ensure the rest of the tribe's survival. *Does she want a civil war?*

Numa motioned to the two Scouts, and they approached her as she moved to join Luna. "Fetch some wood. We are going to make a proper pyre and get this death out of our sights." The other females were a little unsure of why Numa cared; the sooner that Luna got used to the way things worked the better, as far as they were concerned. They would not disobey their Scout Mother, and they moved out on her order, to search for dry wood for the pyre.

Terrabyss and Unkyss continued talking, both happy that the other's reputation had not disappointed.

"What happened to your pack?" Terrabyss asked, as Numa and her Scouts stepped away from the two males.

"Our parents left to meet up with the tribe last summer, and head to the trading camp at the base of the Ice Kraggs, where we meet the Ramsyn. Fall came and went with no sign of them. My brother, the alpha Unkyss, formerly Hald" – Unkyss sneered at the name – "said he was going to go to the Gathering to see what had happened. One can only guess what happened to him. That left me and my other brother; we were doing all right for ourselves until about a moon ago when a group of four Gorgel found us. Those blood hunters went quickly to work." He shook his head, kicking a snowbank. "Vikryn didn't stand a chance; he was staked and drained before sunup. I managed to kill at least one, I hope it was two. I think I only managed to injure the second one by pulling off his arm, but we can dream. For the last moon I have been looking for a new camp, and I found this one about a half-moon ago."

"Alpha Father!" Terrabyss breathed. "That sounds like an awful year, Unkyss."

Numa joined Luna by the haunting remains of Hanora and her youngest boy. "I take it you have never seen a power shift, or really even remember the stories of what's involved when one happens?" she commented as she stepped up next to the Eclupse.

Luna's ears shot up as she heard Numa's question, and she looked over her shoulder to the other female. "No, to both," she responded quietly, going back to looking at the two corpses.

"We gave their pack a chance to submit, she refused to accept the terms. The consequences rest on her shoulders, not ours." Numa tried to comfort Luna. "If we hadn't acted, we would be going to war with each other instead of the Ozars. If she had gathered enough support out here, she could have easily challenged your father, and to be honest I don't know how well we could protect you two. I could almost guarantee that the Guards would provide you little defense." She scoffed as she mentioned the last group. "They are passive as long as their position isn't threatened."

"I knew that nothing good was going to happen when we caught up to them," Luna said honestly, slightly comforted by Numa's attempt, no matter how poor that attempt was.

"If it helps, I wish they hadn't run. I don't get any enjoyment from this and despite how they may act, no one here wished for this outcome," Numa said, resting her head against Luna's. "It is never easy doing what has to be done."

Luna did feel better, and she took some comfort in seeing Jabyn and Essall starting to erect a pyre. "What about the other juvenile, did Unkyss tell you what happened to her?" she asked, almost dreading the answer but needing to know what their next move was and if the other juvenile had escaped.

Numa sighed reluctantly but knew there was little point in delaying the truth of what was going to need to happen next. "Yes, she went east and Unkyss assumes she is running for the Tundra, since there are no other packs in that direction that we know of. We will lay her mother and brother to rest here, and then pick up the trail in the morning after we have given them a chance to join the Alpha Father and his pack in the heavens." She hoped that the fact they were going to have a proper service for Hanora and her child would bring some relief to the burden that she could tell was weighing on Luna's conscience.

"The girl is not an adult; she will have no supporters to back her if she were to challenge my father. She isn't a threat to my father or to the stability of the Maulers." Luna was trying not to plead, but she knew how this looked and sounded, she had to find some way to lessen the guilt.

Numa gave Luna a gentle nussle and spoke softly but firmly. "The law is written and cannot be ignored. If the Alpha is challenged and the challenger fails, then they must flee or risk being purged from the tribe. If the challenger succeeds, the pack must submit; if it doesn't, then they must be expunged." Numa could hear how much Luna wanted to try to change the already predetermined outcome and she admired her compassion, but she knew where compassion got you in the wild.

Luna and Numa joined Jabyn and Essall as they used the fire pit to get a small pile of tinder lit, which they then transferred to the fuel stacked up below the pyres. Terrabyss and Unkyss carried the two bodies over to the \pyres, setting them atop the wooden frames. As the fire stack slowly smoked to life, the pyre began to be consumed by the hot red, orange, and yellow flames. Luna watched the smoke rise up to the sky above; as though to show its solidarity in the moment the sky remained clear so that the Silverbacks could watch twisting gray and black plumes snake their way up to the stars. Luna found herself standing next to Terrabyss. They watched in silence as the two Maulers joined their ancestors.

"When I and my father first met you, you killed that other Mauler who was trying to kill my father."

Terrabyss nodded. "You're talking about Oryss. Why did you think of him?" Terrabyss slightly turned his head to her so that he could hear her over the crackling fire.

She was not trying to attract attention to herself but had become curious about how Terrabyss had handled the cremation of Oryss, in comparison to how Unkyss treated Hanora and her runt, and compared to the treatment they were even showing her now. After Terrabyss had listened to her questions, he chuckled a bit as he answered. "I didn't respect Oryss." That was it, that was all he felt like he needed to say, and Luna knew that was probably the best answer she was going to get out of him. Another question occurred to her as Terrabyss turned to face the fire again.

Luna nudged Terrabyss with her elbow as she asked her next few questions in an attempt to regain his attention. "What was all that Lone Wolf talk? I understand that his pack was killed, but wouldn't he just be the survivor of his pack?"

Terrabyss turned back to her, as usual he had that confused look on his face when he didn't understand how she couldn't know about something. "Sometimes, I forget how much you Eclupse have forgotten," he began, unnecessarily.

"I am not looking for a history lesson," she grumbled at him as he began his long-winded explanation.

He grinned and nodded. "Fair enough. A Lone Wolf most often refers to a criminal who has been exiled from their pack, and the tribe will shun them as well. They are allowed to exist, away from the territories of their former family and friends and they are not allowed to interact with them in any way. If they do, the Lone Wolf can be attacked without warning, and often submission is unacceptable." He looked over at her slightly annoyed expression. "Look, your father is Alpha, you had better learn how our customs and rules work if you want to be a part of this tribe."

Luna growled at him. *He is right though, she thought. If I want to understand how this world I have been thrust into works, I need to learn about all of the Mauler culture, which in turn will teach me Silverback culture.* She stopped growling. "You're right, please continue."

Terrabyss looked a little stunned, he had obviously been expecting some argument or at the very least a debate to come out of their conversation. His tail wagged slightly as he continued. "So, the juvenile we are chasing is a Lone Wolf, no one should shelter or aid her. In Unkyss' case, however, it was a self-imposed exile; probably in his grief, he swore off his name and his attachments. When he learned that the former Alpha that he held alliance to had been replaced, he came to a crossroads. He would have to choose one or the other, to join the new Alpha or remain on his given course of neutrality. His former self-exile could have been forgiven by the new Alpha's ascension, as was customary, or he could remain a vagabond and an outlaw and survive isolated and alone."

"I understand all of that, but when he announced himself, he declared to us that he was a 'Lone Wolf.' According to what you have told me, he chose to remain in exile, and he didn't leave when we arrived so isn't he supposed to be… well, punished?" She shrugged, not wanting to say killed, but trying to wrap her head around the confusing customs of the Maulers.

"Well, that was your call. You are your father's representative on this hunt, you act with his authority. When he submitted to you and when you, poorly" – he had to remind her at least once – "returned the gesture, you essentially told us that his crimes were neutralized."

"So that is why when he found out I was the daughter of the new Alpha, he assumed that he could submit to me in his place. Okay, I understand that, but I do have one more question that this whole scenario creates.

What would have happened if I hadn't been here, or if there hadn't been a representative of my father here?"

Terrabyss gave her an obvious expression. "We would have killed him for declaring himself a Lone Wolf, or he could have tried to get away."

"Or, I could have killed all five of you and continued living my life free of interference," Unkyss called over, having caught the end of the conversation.

Terrabyss snorted his opinion on that response and the others—excluding Luna—echoed his sentiment.

Unkyss just shrugged. "You never know, never know."

The six of them gathered some way from the burning pyres, much to Luna's annoyance. Terrabyss had explained that it was to give the dead privacy to reunite with their ancestors. Luna did find that to be admirable, but it didn't make the chill night any warmer, although she quickly silenced her complaints and frustrations. It was well into the night, and every now and then a few stars would shine through the black clouds that were beginning to roll in. Luna was surprised at how quickly it had gotten dark since they had found the clearing.

It couldn't be much later than past noon, maybe mid-afternoon. I still have so much energy.

Most winter days in the Green Wall where the Eclupse had been living had sunlight for about seven hours. Here, the sun had only been out for about five hours, Luna estimated.

"Looks like bad weather," commented Numa.

All of the Maulers sniffed at the air. "It is definitely going to start hailing, you can smell the moisture in the air," commented Jabyn.

"There is going to be thunder, and lightning. Perhaps it will rain early this winter," Unkyss commented. "I can feel the static in my fur."

"My bet is on a blizzard, and an accompanying thunderstorm," predicted Essall, as she finally lowered her nose.

"Well, that isn't good, none of those options are good." Luna looked at all of them. "How will we shelter from something like that? Did any of you bring the proper items to build a shelter?" She looked at the sparse resources everyone had brought. Essall had two skins of alcohol, more for wounds than drinking, but some for drinking. Jabyn had a small bag of dried meat strapped to her back. Terrabyss had his weapon. Numa had two skins of milk, also for drinking, but only if they ran out of other food and couldn't find enough to hunt.

Jabyn and Essall looked at one another and Numa looked at her hands. "Yeah, we have what we need to make shelters."

Luna was caught off guard; she didn't see any rope, canvases, axes, or anything else that the other clans in the Green Wall used to build shelters.

That night, Terrabyss taught Luna how to dig a deep hole in the ground. Until now, they had just snuggled up next to each other in the open air. It had started chilly, but Luna had been surprised at how warm it would get within just a few minutes of sharing body heat. Now, they were going to sleep in holes. The Maulers called them Dens and with a blizzard on the horizon, they built what they called a Deep Den. Maulers were not the most imaginative when it came to naming their inventions. Luna looked into the hole as Terrabyss poked his head out.

"See, easy," he said as he pulled himself up out of the Deep Den.

"My father was right, these are more graves than homes," was Luna's response as she bent down and stuck her head in. She had noticed the occasional hole in the ground near the Gathering, but hadn't thought to ask about them. After meeting at the Hollow, where Skoff lived, Luna had assumed that all of the Maulers lived in similar dugout spaces beneath the sequoias' roots. Skoff had inherited the Hollow from Grimmis, as the shaman needed storage space for his many ingredients, ceremonial tools, and ponchos. It had been a major point of contention between himself and Haxzus, who felt entitled to the space as the Alpha.

"Well, it will keep you from freezing to death," was the pragmatic Mauler response as Terrabyss began to work on his own Deep Den. "I won't help you next time, you will need to dig your own." His voice faded as his head and shoulders were already beginning to vanish into the earth.

Luna was thankful for the hole; it did keep her very warm as the wind howled and snow whirled above. There were a handful of thunder cracks and more than a few flashes of blinding light that ripped through the dark clouds above, but to Luna's ears the noise was muffled by the cozy den. Two nearby trees were struck by the flashing, zig-zagging strokes of electricity. Both were sequoias and one was mighty and full of life, it merely split, but would survive and either grow back together or maybe become two separate trunks within one tree. The other redwood had seen many years and had long since lost more needles than it kept. It crashed to the forest floor, uprooted by the force of the lightning bolt. It fell to the ground, splitting in two as it collided with several large boulders that had taken up residence about a hundred lue to the right of the giant tree. Yet, deep in this den, snug in the warmth of her own body, Luna slept soundly, only rolling to her other side when the huge sequoia crashed to the ground.

Rellik

Mother lost her mind, we could have just stayed in the Gathering. Isn't this the way of power shifts within the Mauler tribe? Unkyss had asked Hanora to explain certain gaps in her story, something Rellik had thought was perfectly reasonable. Her mother, on the other hand, had thought it was insulting. *She obviously expected that tall Mauler to be on her side and help her retake the Ballio title.*

"Alpha was a dumb title, anyway," Rellik said out loud as she slipped into another huge snowbank. She didn't know what her mother had been thinking. *Stupid, smacking him.* Rellik grumbled as she pulled her hips and paws out of the deep snow. She had tried to grab Druce before he got himself killed, but if she was being honest with herself, she hadn't tried too hard. She had definitely thought about running, but something inside told her to stand her ground. That hadn't lasted long, and she had run as far and fast as she could to get away from the Maulers. Druce had tried to stop the massive Mauler, who called himself Unkyss, from trying to twist his mother's neck. Hanora had a better chance of achieving that, and instead of either submitting or standing his ground, Druce had become even more enraged and tried to bite Unkyss in the groin.

Her younger brother hadn't stood a chance. He was a runt, and he was the definition of the word. He was weak, small, and had a soft mind. That big Mauler had picked him up by the throat, after Druce had actually tripped trying to attack him. With one hand, he had choked the life out of her little brother. There had been nothing she could do, nothing Druce could do. She was definitely tougher than Druce, but it had been almost two days since their last meal. Rellik had caught the squirrel, but her mother had let Druce consume almost the whole animal before she allowed herself or Rellik to have any.

Rellik kicked a clump of snow, crying out as her paw hit an ice chunk hidden below the powder. "I just want to go home!" she howled at the top of her lungs, before pressing on.

She reached for a handful of snow and shoved it in her mouth. It wasn't food, but it was something to chew on while she scanned the horizon. All she could see was a desert of white snow that was shaped into small dunes by the deafening winds of the tundra. She had no idea where she was, and she had no idea where she was going to find food. Even her nose could only smell the cold. She rubbed her arms with either hand as she marched on. Her mind kept going back to that encounter with Unkyss.

I should have been angrier at him, right? After all, he killed my mother and brother. Perhaps I should be furious at that Terrabyss, he killed Ammer. Or should it be Dio? It was Dio who actually killed Father. No matter how she thought about it, the Maulers she was most angry with were her own pack.

Her father, Haxzus, had never even seemed to notice that she existed; his attention had always been on precious Ammer. He had taken Ammer with him everywhere, even on personal hunts when the siblings had been just pups. Haxzus had always said it was "because Ammer was going to be his successor, he had so much to teach the next Alpha," that was the reason he had no time for the rest of his pups. Ammer learned how to fight from the best Guards that Haxzus had protecting him, and the best Hunters that brought in the Gathering's rations.

Did both of them a lot of good, Rellik mused as she came to a tall snow dune and slammed her fist into the top of it. It reminded her of the way she had seen Terrabyss hammer in Ammer's skull. Her stomach grumbled. *If only we had been allowed to go on the Hunt this year, I would have a little experience in how to get food for myself.*

She still couldn't believe that she had caught that squirrel, and she doubted she had the energy to replicate the endeavor. The whole reason that they hadn't gone on this year's Hunt was because Haxzus had said that Ammer wasn't ready to spend multiple nights away from the Gathering. Also, her mother had insisted that her baby Druce was not ready for such exhausting activities.

Rellik had heard her father complain many times about Bia and the Ravis pack; how they were practically the only obstacle to stable leadership. The way she saw it though, Bia had prepared her litter for the realities of the world far better than her own mother and father had done.

Terrabyss is a runt, yet he was vital in the demise of my pack, she mused as she crested another snowy dune. "Alpha Father! There is nothing out here but snow, snow, and guess what, more snow!" She growled as she stepped off the dune to continue, slipped, and ended up falling on her butt and riding the small hill for a few lue until she reached the bottom.

Rellik was tough. She had turned her parents' almost constant neglect of her to her benefit. She had taken many of those opportunities to sneak off and play with the pups from other packs, who made their homes at the edge of the Gathering. She had learned all of her fighting from wrestling with the other pups. This did have its drawbacks. Firstly, that she had never been properly trained by an adult how to fight or hunt, and had learned all of her techniques by herself, and had no idea if they were really effective or not. In contrast, her brother couldn't even remember the names of all his teachers. Secondly, after her fights were over, she was the only one to bandage up her wounds, Alpha Father knew her mother and father were far too busy.

That night, Rellik found herself digging into one of the snow dunes to try to make a shelter so that she didn't freeze to death. The weather had become violent, and the dark clouds had completely hidden the stars and moon, which brought some distraction to Rellik's predicament. She lay on her back as the clouds began to cluster and blot out the heavenly canopy above. She shivered, trying to dig into the snow, but much of it was so loose that it kept collapsing in on itself. The night was spent forming and reforming a small crevasse that she had been able to carve out of the side of the dune. Every time the wind blew away the edges of her makeshift shelter, she would have to dig further into the dune. She got little sleep, and by the time the sun had beat back the clouds she woke up in a panic, having become buried by the dune and the fresh snow fall. The morning sun had caused some of the topmost layer of the snow to melt slightly, and the wind had ensured that it had then hardened to solid ice. Rellik panicked, trying to push her way out of the cold coffin in which nature had sealed her, but was having little success. She had never been in the tundra before and although she had lived in the grove, she had still never needed to dig a Den, and especially not a Deep Den. As the day moved on and she still found herself trapped, she stopped panicking, figuring that she would soon suffocate like her brother, and accepting her fate. It was fitting that the Ballio pack was wiped out, they hadn't done a good job at preserving their bloodline and it would seem that this punishment made a suitable ending.

Rellik could just barely make out the sound of muffled pawsteps and she could hear singing. She couldn't hear the words, but the tune was friendly enough, and stars, she was going to die in here so she might as well gamble and see if the voice was friend or foe. Perhaps it would be just indifferent, she could work with that as well.

"Help!" she called out from her icy tomb. "Help me, please! My parents never taught me how to fend for myself." She said the second half of the statement under her breath.

The singing stopped, and it sounded as though the muffled crunch of the pawsteps through snow were coming closer. "'Ello, could it be? Is someone stuck under the snow?" The resounding voice was barely audible to Rellik's muffled senses as she pressed her head to what she thought was up.

The accent was thick, and sounded nothing like a Mauler, but then again, she was buried under Alpha Father knew how much snow. She shrugged again, she was going to die in here and she would prefer to die out there. "Yes, I am trapped! I fell asleep and the drift I was using for shelter has fallen in on me!" She beat her fists on the walls of her grave, trying to make more noise, since her voice was hoarse and cracked from all her panicking earlier. She was also starting to feel lightheaded, and she wasn't sure if she was pounding on the walls because she was getting scared again or because she was excited.

"Now, that be a bad idea. Falling asleep under a drift, no, no, no, that's not good." There was a heavy thump, and Rellik wasn't sure if he was pressing himself against the snow floor to hear her or if he had just collapsed.

"Are you alive?" she called out when she didn't hear anything for a few moments after the thud.

"Now ain't that kind, asking how I am while you be stuck under all this snow. You are very polite, I bet we will have a good laugh about this when I get you out." There was another bang, closer to Rellik this time. "I recommend you keep talking," came a rumbling suggestion.

"Oh, oh, okay," Rellik said, a bit at a loss at what to say. "Well, thank you for the compliment, you sound rather nice yourself. *Uh,* I suppose I don't mind agreeing to be your friend. You are saving my life, after all." She wasn't sure what to keep saying. "So, you come out here often?" she blurted trying to think of a new topic.

"Oh, no, not often," came his infectious laugh, and Rellik found herself smiling despite the situation. "Lucky for you, though, I seem to come by often enough." Another thud, and Rellik saw cracks appear in the snow below her.

"Bear sh—" was all she managed to get out before the cracks gave way to a massive fissure, and Rellik's tail popped out like a single tiny tree trunk from the tundra's surface. All the snow that had been formed around her rump fell in and covered her face and neck, silencing her before she could finish the curse.

"Well now, that can't be comfortable?" It was still just as hard to hear with all this snow in her ears, and she still had no idea who she was talking to, but she was almost positive it wasn't a Silverback. She felt strong hands grab her legs and waist, pulling her up out of the snow. Her nose felt like it wasn't there, and she had to lick her lips several times to get them to warm up enough so that she could say something in gratitude.

Her eyes got wide as she saw the Ozar, her expression of shock needed no practice. The strange Ozar was very, very tall, he would have put the giant Unkyss to shame. He had smokey white fur that almost made him invisible against the backdrop of the tundra, and Rellik was sure that if he wanted to, he could vanish in this terrain. He had dark yellow eyes, which surprised Rellik; she hadn't ever heard that Ozars had any eye color besides dark and beady. His hands and paws were huge, which probably helped him move across this wasteland without falling through the soft snow like she had. His shoulders were broad, and he was extremely strong as was made apparent by how easily he lifted her out of that hole. The Ozar wore no clothes, like Silverbacks, but had a beaded satchel that was decorated with a mosaic of bright purple and green beads. He carried a bundle of two or three spears that he had put down on the dune, and he picked up a large net of fish that he began to open with the other hand. The Ozar's neck fur had been braided into short, tight braids, and he had black fur that highlighted his lips, eyes, and ears. Rellik wasn't sure if she should attack him, run from him, or thank him. He tossed one of the fish from his bag out at Rellik's paws. It was small, but it was food.

The Ozar watched her, he was honestly just as surprised as she was at what he had managed to pull out of the snow. He looked at her smokey black fur and her different-colored eyes, one bright yellow the other a dull brown. "Sorry about the fish. The Red Martyr don't get big till fall. They hatched early this year." He looked up at the sun, shading his eyes. "Judging by how much light is left, be maybe a month or little less before spring."

Rellik shaded her eyes as well and looked up at the sun. "How do you know that?" She couldn't help but be curious. She also didn't know what he meant by a 'month', but she didn't want to ask too many questions.

"Oh, sun stays out longer closer to summer. The sun's favorite season!" He chuckled loudly as he patted down the snow behind him and flopped down onto the makeshift bench. He reached back in the net and pulled another fish out. "They are best cold, makes it so you can really taste them." He gave her a big smile and began licking the skin off the meal.

Rellik was starving, and her stomach protested at her hesitation to eat the small fish. She knelt down and picked it up, sniffing it for a moment. *ALPHA FATHER!* her mind screamed as she got a good whiff.

"That's a strong smell!" she said reflexively as the Ozar saw her cringe at the first sniff.

The big Ozar just laughed. "That's how you know it's good!" He gave another hearty laugh.

Again, Rellik found it infectious and started chuckling softly. She wasn't able to ignore her stomach any more, and she mimicked how the Ozar licked the flesh off the fish. Silverbacks rarely ate fish, and she found the exotic taste repulsive but at the same time intriguing. She had never tasted something so bad, and it made the experience so good.

"So now, what is your name, little snow-Taur?" he asked in a very fatherly tone. With her head no longer barricaded or submerged in snow, Rellik found his accent interesting. It did make it hard to understand him sometimes, but it also made him sound that much safer, she didn't know how to explain it.

Rellik gave him a shy smile at the notion of being half-snow half-humanoid. "I am Rellik," she said finally, getting to the meat. The skin of the fish had tasted terrible, if she was going to be honest. The meat though, oh my she had never had anything so potent before. "This part is good," she said, digging into the meat of the meal.

"*Woah, woah,* slow down, you must be careful, or you will choke on them there bones. See how small they are?" He held the fish up right under her eyes.

She tilted her head back. "Okay, okay, but I can't see just because you put it that close." She began to slow down; it was hard, her stomach just kept demanding more and more, but she thought it was best to listen to the one who had experience with such meals. "Do you have a name?" she asked as she went back to her fish, picking the meat from its skeleton with her claws.

"Huh, me? I suppose I do." He remained silent for a few moments, and Rellik wasn't sure if he was going to inform her what his name was. "Burrum," he said suddenly, "it be a pleasure, Rellik." He wiped his hand in the snow and reached out.

Rellik wasn't quite sure how to respond, this greeting was nothing like the Silverback salute. She gingerly took his massive hand in hers. When he gave her an approving nod, she shook it up and down.

"Pleasure," she said with a slight grin, before going back to her fish.

"This ain't normal Silverback territory, odd that Rellik be out here." He turned to face her as he pondered.

She finished the fish, and as the meal vanished, so did her trust. *This is an Ozar; anything he wants to know isn't going to be for the benefit of the Maulers.*

"Does it matter to an Ozar why I am out here?" she replied hotly, trying not to lick her hands, when he looked back down to his meal.

"Ozar?" was his reply. "I am Hax[40] , not Ozar." He tossed the fish skeleton out into the snow. "Big, big difference."

Rellik was obviously confused. "No, there isn't. I am a Mauler but that doesn't make me not a Silverback," she responded impulsively.

*"Ahhh."*Burrum nodded, seeming to understand. "You think we think like you think," he concluded. "Ozar no think like you think they think. Mahuer[41] and Norrus[42] ." He clapped his hands together. "They think like you think Ozars think." He pointed to himself. "Hax be different. I care not that you be Silverback." He pulled another fish out for her. "I just care why you here."

She thought about asking for it, but her stomach was now complaining about how much food she had given it and she thought it might be better to just wait awhile. "Well, that's something an Ozar would say to make me drop my guard." She growled, showing her teeth a bit more than she had intended.

Again, that belly-shaking laugh echoed out through the tundra as

40   Ozar tribe, "Forgotten"
41   Ozar tribe, "Great"
42   Ozar tribe, "Second"

Burrum stopped licking his second fish clean of its skin. "Rellik needs to change her thoughts. Out here, I am Burrum, simply Burrum. I am not an Ozar. Out here, we have the luxury of choosing who our enemies are and who our friends are." He looked over to her. "And I choose for you to be a friend. Now you choose."

Rellik allowed herself to lick her hands and claws clean, her stomach was still protesting that it had eaten too much, and she wasn't sure that she wanted to keep talking. She swallowed hard to force down the saliva that was gathering in her mouth. "We can be friends for… " She shut her mouth tightly and looked around in a panic. Burrum raised his eyebrows, looking over his shoulder to see what she saw. She took the opportunity, and when he turned around, she vomited. It was so much worse coming back up, and the mixture of the skin and meat, along with the bile just made her more nauseated.

Burrum's head snapped back around as he heard her begin heaving, "Oh, bad idea to eat so much if been long time since you eat."

"That doesn't make sense," Rellik grumbled as she shoveled snow into her mouth to try to get the taste out.

Burrum chuckled. "Well, at least you kept some of it down. Maybe in little while you have more. While you wait, you can tell Burrum why Rellik here?"

Rellik did feel slightly better, now that she had gotten that up and out. She was still upset with her stomach for the mixed messages, but she figured there was no point in not telling Burrum what happened. If what he said was true, as she felt it to be, it wouldn't do any harm to talk to this Ozar; the ones she was supposed to hate were in the Green Wall, not the tundra. As her tale unfolded, she found herself snuggled up next to the big Hax, sobbing into his embrace about how she didn't understand why her parents didn't want her. She had tried to be good, and she didn't know if she was bad because she didn't feel sad that they were dead. By the end, she just sobbed into his chest.

"I just want to go home, but I don't think I ever can."

Burrum listened to the tale in silence. In his heart, he felt so sorry for this poor juvenile. He would nod, and every now and then he could be heard saying, "mhmm," "wow," and, "I am sorry." He didn't know what else to say, her life had not been easy, and from the sounds of it, it wasn't going to get any easier. He was relieved that he had been able to aid her.

Burrum felt that he was usually a pretty good judge of character, and one of the advantages of living out here in the tundra was he was isolated from others' opinions and free to make his own assessments. He found that those that were sincerely vulnerable were often also honest and worth helping. He hadn't always been right about others, but he had become wiser from the experience.

"Sometimes, it is best, if you don't know where to run, to just stop running," Burrum said in a soothing tone as he rocked her slightly.

Rellik couldn't help but give a sniffle as she looked up at Burrum, she felt so safe here and she didn't want this moment to ever end.

"I am sure trusting others always worked out well for you," she said sarcastically. "You never needed to run away." She sobbed more to herself than to him.

"You're right, for the most part trusting goes horribly. For example, these fish trusted me. It did not end well for them," he lamented with a smile. "You're wrong though, I have had to run, and I found that I only started enjoying life when I stopped." Burrum handed her some fish he had picked off his second meal with his claws. "Now slow, or Rellik will do that again." He pointed to the now-frozen puddle of puke.

She tried to look innocent, but followed his advice and picked at the pieces of fish. This time, her stomach protested much less violently to the amount that was being added. They exchanged a bit more information; she explained that the Eclupse had arrived just a few days ago. She told him about what they looked like and gave him their names, and also informed him how her father had been defeated in the challenge and that her mother swore that the Mauler, Terrabyss, had used some trick to get her father's attention. Burrum did dwell on that for a moment, asking Rellik to elaborate, but she just shrugged. Her mother had said that she had heard the Mauler's voice, but Rellik hadn't, and as far as she knew no one else who had witnessed the challenge had heard anything. She had been curious why her father turned around when he seemed to have beaten Luna, but she had figured it had been due to his ego. It was a better explanation than her mother's.

Burrum noticed that she kept yawning as she was trying to explain what her mother said Terrabyss had done. "Well, you can't take a nap in the open, even with the sun out," he said in his usual jovial tone.

In moments, he had helped her build a little shelter that wouldn't collapse and bury her. Rellik didn't stay awake for long, it could have been the fish, or maybe it was the cozy shelter. Either way, Rellik found herself in a restful sleep for the first time in just over seven days.

***

"I think I found her!" shouted Essall, who was off to the left flank of the troop as they marched slowly through the snowy dunes, following the last Ballio's trail. She looked over at the Silverback closest to her, which she was pretty sure was Jabyn. They were coming up on the end of the second day in the Banshee Tundra and they could see another storm rolling in from the Berg Maker to the north of them. The wind was screaming past them, and easily choked out Essall's announcement. The Scout tucked her ears in frustration, packing a small snowball and taking aim for whom she still assumed was Jabyn.

Jabyn could see Essall to her left, but she had no idea that the other Scout was trying to get her attention until a snowball flew past her shoulder. She looked toward Essall. "Coming!" she growled, walking over to Essall and having to duck as a second snowball was chucked at her face. "Alpha Father! I am coming. Don't you dare throw a third one at me," Jabyn warned as she joined her companion. They both looked down at Rellik, an awning of snow that had been packed to hard ice covered her from the sun that had just begun to set. She was curled up with her tail over her nose to keep it from freezing, but she need not worry about such things. The shelter was extremely well built.

"This was not built by an amateur," commented Essall as she looked over the shelter. "It is built to block the wind and the opening is to the south, out of the sun's path so the juvenile wouldn't have to deal with the snow reflecting the light into the shelter." She called attention to the detail and craftsmanship of the construction.

Jabyn nodded, having lived on the outskirts of the grove near the Banshee Tundra, she had seen these temporary structures before. Her father had said they were built by a tribe of Ozars known as the Hax, who live isolated lives with only their mate, if any.

"What are you thinking?" she heard Essall ask, as she noticed the scowl on Jabyn's face.

"This was made by an Ozar. The Ozar hid their tracks when they left." She pointed to where there were a couple of deeper stroke marks in the snow, from where someone had tried to rake the snow. "If we had been any later, we would have never known someone else had been here other than by the building. By morning, it would have seemed to us that she built it herself."

Essall shrugged. "So, a Hax helped her. They know some Maulers live here and they don't mingle with the other Ozars. They aren't a threat. So, do we just kill her and go back to Numa and tell her that it is done? It would definitely be easier that way, considering Luna's position on this whole thing," she suggested, hoping that her companion would agree. She knew better than to hold her breath.

Jabyn gave her a disappointed look, their orders had been to find Rellik, not kill her. "That is what you think we should do?" She shook her head. "No, Numa will want to execute her personally to ensure that she is dead, she wouldn't want there to be any mistakes." Essall nodded, having guessed that was going to be Jabyn's response. "The question is, do we take her to Numa or bring Numa to her?"

Essall furrowed her brow. "Just grab her by the back of her neck and I will snatch up her paws. I feel like you are making this more difficult than it has to be."

Jabyn gave a sidelong glance at Essall. "Okay, then what? We wander around aimlessly, shouting for Numa in this whiteout? I was lucky I saw you!" Essall had to keep her mouth shut at that one; Jabyn made a very good point. The storm had come out of nowhere, and the dark clouds would take most of the night to clear out, if they did. The last few rays of the setting sun were vanishing beyond the horizon, and soon it would be pitch black because no star or moon light was getting through the looming clouds.

"Okay, well, Numa said if we got split up, we were to head back to our marker at sundown," chimed Essall. "So, we can just take her there and wait for the others to show up."

"What if she fights us?" asked a concerned Jabyn, but she wasn't coming up with a better suggestion.

"Then we kill her and drag the corpse back for Numa to inspect and confirm," Essall responded matter-of-factly. "Now grab her neck, you have a stronger grip."

Rellik's pleasant sleep was rudely interrupted when she felt something grab the back of her neck. Her eyes shot open, and she suspected that it was the Ozar, thinking that he was finally showing his true colors.

How could I have let my guard down? Just because he seemed friendly! Now I am going to get killed all because I was a gullible fool.

She tried to struggle free as she felt someone dragging her out of a shelter. Another one grabbed her paws. Confused, Rellik kicked out.

"I trusted you! I thought you said we were friends!" Rellik shouted as her paw landed solidly with the second assailant's chest, shoving them back into the shelter. She tried to reach back to get her claws on whoever was behind her.

"We are definitely not friends, especially after you kicked me," came Essall's growl as she stood up, pushing the snow off her. She reached out again for Rellik's paws, which weren't kicking at the moment as she was trying to get at Jabyn, who was holding her by the scruff of her neck.

Rellik looked back at Essall as she came back at her, and tried to get another paw into her body to kick Essall back again. She instantly recognized the accent as Mauler, and she had been too slow anyway, because Essall wrapped up her legs by the ankles under her right arm. Essall clamped down her arm with all her might, and Rellik groaned in pain as it felt like her ankle was going to snap.

"Stop struggling and we won't hurt you. If you keep struggling, we are going to have to hurt you. If you try to hurt us, we will simply kill you. Our orders are to bring you back to Numa, and we will do that whether you are a corpse or not," the one behind Rellik told her. Again, Rellik noticed that the voice lacked the thick accent of the Ozar she had been talking with earlier.

Slowly, Rellik began to piece things together and recover from her surprise. The Eclupse who had challenged her father and the death of Ammer, her mother's foolish decision to try to lead a rebellion, and running out to the outskirts of the grove to try to recruit an army. The death of her mother and brother Druce because they had foolishly challenged that monster, Unkyss. Running out into the Banshee Tundra and her meeting with Burrum, and her feeling of just wanting to go home. *Perhaps this is it. Maybe this is as close to home as I will get. Burrum is right, though; I think I am done running, let's see what life has to offer,* she thought to herself.

"You won't get any trouble from me, I choose my friends and my enemies, and I choose to have you as my friends," she quoted Burrum, they had been wise words and she didn't mind if they were the words she died by.

Essall looked at Jabyn, who in turn looked to Essall.

"All right," replied Jabyn, nodding to Essall to release Rellik. "You know what happens if you run." She released Rellik's neck as Essall begrudgingly let go of Rellik's ankles.

There was a moment when Rellik thought about running, but instead she took a deep breath and waited for the other two to take her to where Numa was. The return took about half the night, and they were silent the whole way. Rellik thought for more than a few moments that she should hate the whole Ravis pack, *and the stray Eclupse.* That thought didn't last long, she couldn't deny that it had been her parents' decisions as much as anyone else's that had put her in this position. If she had just stood up to her mother and stood up for herself, she might not be in this situation at all. Still, it was hard to defy your parents, no matter how they treated you. The whiteout continued the whole way, and both Essall and Jabyn were on high alert for a good portion of the journey back. They soon realized that Rellik had no interest in running, and both respected the courage in her determination to see this through.

"I can't promise that you will live," Jabyn felt the need to clarify as they neared their destination. She could smell the marking and it was fresh, which meant that at least Numa was back already. Rellik simply nodded in response as they escorted her to where they had established a type of base camp the morning before. As they approached the small fire in the camp, they noticed that they were the last to arrive. Unkyss and Terrabyss were trying to explain a popular Mauler game to Luna. It was known as My Skull. Every Mauler knew how to play the game, and My Skull was a common recreation at most Mauler events. It was played by all age groups, but to keep it fair the age groups only play amongst themselves, not against one another. It was a one versus all game, and the Mauler would score points by running the skull to the border of the given game zone. The other players would try to tackle or strip the skull from the other player's hands, and this was the point that Terrabyss and Unkyss were arguing about when Rellik, Jabyn, and Essall arrived.

"When someone is tackled, the skull is no longer active, that is when you make a huddle around the skull and have a melee for possession of it!" Terrabyss was practically shouting, this argument seemed like it had been going on for some time.

"Bear-shit!" Unkyss yelled. "Okay, let's say that I am running with the skull, and you come charging up and yank the skull out of my hand. You are telling me everything stops, and you would just drop the skull and form up a huddle?" Unkyss was standing now; it was rare for any Silverback to communicate without frequent movement and facial expressions, especially when agitated. The extra body language always helped to punctuate certain points.

Terrabyss threw up his arms. "That is a strip, not a tackle. It is completely different; you better keep running if you strip someone cause they are likely going to turn around and run you down. It is a really bad tactic if you ask me, better to hit the skull holder and put them on their rump and scramble through the huddle than to try to outrun everyone," Terrabyss stated, providing a glimpse of how often he was able to outrun anyone.

"That is maddening, why do you inner-groves add extra rules?" Unkyss exclaimed, jumping back to his paws, having sat back down during Terrabyss' response.

Terrabyss was up on his paws as well now. "Because we aren't simpletons and our minds can handle more than a handful of rules, unlike you outer-groves."

As both of them got up, growling at one another, Luna saw past them to the three Maulers entering the camp. She instantly recognized Rellik as she saw the dissimilar eyes. To both Unkyss and Terrabyss' surprise, Luna was on her paws as well now, and for a moment they were both confused that she had something to feel so passionately about in this argument as to become involved.

She ignored the two of them—as she had previously anyway—and moved toward Jabyn and Essall, who were standing slightly behind Rellik now as they escorted her into camp. Numa also noticed the three of them, and had started moving toward them. It became apparent to Jabyn and Essall that Luna was going to make it to them first, her long strides were inching out Numa with each step. The Scouts were a bit surprised when they registered that Numa hadn't adjusted her gait and remained behind Luna. Jabyn stayed behind Rellik as the other two females approached them, but Essall's hackles went up and she stepped around Rellik to intercept Luna. Luna noticed the female move, and a week ago she would have probably just backed down, but she was learning what it meant to be Silverback. Her lips curled back, showing her teeth as her ears stood up and pointed slightly forward. Her tail was almost perfectly diagonal to her trunk, not hovering between her legs. Her vibrant blue eyes reflected the fire between her and Essall, causing streaks of red and orange to flash across the intense blue irises.

Essall found herself swallowing hard before she spoke up, as though she were about to confront an alpha. "There is nothing of interest to you here." Her voice cracked a bit as Luna closed the distance between them.

"Get out of my way, Essall!" Luna snarled viciously as she came face to face with the Scout.

Essall had found her nerve by now, and remained rooted where she stood, "No! This doesn't involve—" She wasn't able to finish the sentence as Luna's left hand flipped to her thigh. In one easy, fluid, and quick motion, she slammed the pommel of her dagger into Essall's sensitive muzzle. Essall was too late in registering the attack, and before she could dodge or defend, she felt the impact. She reeled back, her heels caught on the slight snowbank behind her, and she fell onto her back as a plume of powder puffed up around her yelping form.

Luna stepped past her, as she had done with Terrabyss and Unkyss, and moved straight toward Rellik. Jabyn was a little taken aback by what had just happened and went to step around Rellik as well. She had thought that Luna was just going to yell, or at the very least argue with Essall, not slam her pommel into Essall's face. The only thing that made her stop was that she caught Numa's eye, who by now was standing over Essall. That stare from her Scout Mother meant stand down, and she knew it. She didn't go back to behind Rellik, but instead remained to her right flank, so that if Luna attacked with her strong left, she might be able to prevent it.

Luna saw her, and instinctively knew what Jabyn was intending with that movement. It wasn't important, what was important was that no one else was killed.

Numa looked down at Essall. "You all right?" she asked with a slight wag to her tail, which Essall didn't fail to notice.

"My nose might be broken," she pouted, and gingerly touched it with a finger to check if it was all right. She winced, but didn't howl out, which probably meant that it was okay. It would be sore for a while, but it wasn't broken.

"She will become a Mauler yet," Numa said, reaching out a hand for Essall to help her up out of the snowbank. The fresh powder crunched under Essall's paws as she took Numa's hand and pulled herself up.

"We should probably execute her and get it over with, the longer we leave her alive the more attached to her Luna will get," Essall commented, looking over her shoulder at the Eclipse as she stalked right up to Rellik.

"We will let it play out," Numa responded in a soft but firm voice, with no room for debate.

Rellik's spine stiffened as she saw Luna punch Essall with her pommel. She became a little relieved when she noticed Jabyn circling around to get in front of her, but then became frightened again when Jabyn stopped on her right. She didn't have time to ask why, and again the thought of running came flashing across her mind. She forced herself to stay.

"You must be cold, come sit by the fire while we discuss what is to be done."

Luna's tone was gentle and soft, with no malice or anger, which caught Rellik off guard. She could no longer see that determination or savagery in Luna's eyes, just a look of sheer sympathy. She hated it, and hated to admit that it felt nice to be pitied. She nodded as Luna escorted her silently over to the fire, and as Luna helped Rellik sit down, she looked up at Terrabyss and Unkyss as if to say, "Touch her and I will skin you both." She then turned back to Rellik. "if you need something, ask them and they will provide you with it." Again, she locked eyes with both Terrabyss and Unkyss, who each gave her a slight tail wag and a nod.

Luna turned around and walked over to where Jabyn had gathered with Numa and Essall. They were only about ten or so lue away, but with the fire crackling and the wind that was still screaming across the tundra, Rellik couldn't make out what the other females were talking about.

"What is your plan?" asked a very curious Numa as Luna rejoined them. "You know she can't be spared."

"If she lives, it will come back to haunt you," added Jabyn. "I know you mean well, but the chaos that will erupt with her reunion with the tribe, I fear, will require more authority to control than your father has."

"Besides," Essall grumbled, still a bit upset at Luna and her tone didn't hide it as she continued, "the law is the law and if we don't kill her, your father will have to when we bring her back to the Gathering."

"Unkyss was a criminal and he submitted to me, why can't the same rule apply to her? If she submits, her crime is forgiven and we can just move on," responded Luna hotly. "And don't tell me that is just the way

106

it is, because that is more hypocrisy than I can take right now."

Essall's hackles started to go up again, but Numa responded, letting her Scout stew. "Even if she submits and we take her back with us, anyone who was loyal to the Ballio pack will use her as their call for revolt. Whether she condones it or not, they will rise up in her pack's name and if someone of that pack still exists, then there is validity."

Jabyn, who had become the last of her pack when her father died, spoke up. "My father and I often talked about my options if he was to pass away before I went on my Hunt. If he did travel back to the stars before I had become an adult, then I was to be adopted. He had already arranged it with Haxzus, and the families could choose who would take me into their pack. Fortunately, my father passed away after I had become an adult, but according to our laws, the Ballio name would vanish if someone were to adopt her."

Luna's tail began to swing back and forth excitedly. "That solves it. There we go, we will bring her back and put her up for adoption. She gets to live, and the Ballio pack name dies out. So, everyone gets what they want."

"Jabyn was a pup," Essall just couldn't let it go that easily and in many ways she was right. This was not the usual way that the adoption worked, and to the best of all their knowledge, it had never been done in the case of a purged pack.

"She is technically still a pup," Jabyn put in, "and the whole tribe is aware of that. No one would easily forget last year when we were all sure that Ammer, Rellik, and Druce were going to compete. The Hunt was delayed a whole day while Haxzus and Skoff argued over if they should go." All three of the Maulers nodded; it would be hard to forget, especially since the year before had been the fateful year that Tarphyss and Terrabyss had gotten into a challenge over who had brought down their kill.

"Well," Numa finally spoke up, "it is our Alpha's representative's call. She decides what we do. Take her back for adoption or execute her here and take back evidence?" She looked over at Luna as she finished, saluting her as she acknowledged her status in the tribe.

Without any hesitation, Luna responded, "We are taking her back for adoption." She saluted back to Numa before she turned around. First, she knew she would have to convince Rellik to submit to her, and she didn't know how much time the Maulers would allow for that. She spent less than an hour talking with Rellik before the outlaw stood up, facing Luna and, so that everyone could see, she submitted.

The Heart

They had put the Banshee Tundra, its never-ending snowy dunes, and the constant wailing wind far behind them. The grove was a welcome sanctuary from the exposed tundra, where the winter was fighting to hold onto its grasp of the continent. The days were getting longer, and the sun was warming the grove more and more; each afternoon, they could hear the *drip drip* of the melting snow as it plunged from the needles above into the snowy pool below. More and more animals were out and about each dawn, and the group depended less on their rations and more on their natural predatory skills, often returning to camp with each having caught one or two meals apiece.

Rellik tended to stay close to Luna, and if she couldn't be, she was next to Numa. Unkyss had tried to approach her, and although she had no ill feeling toward him, she became extremely shy and quiet whenever he got near. Jabyn was pretty indifferent to the fact that Rellik was traveling back with them, but Essall, on the other hand, had not kept quiet about it for most of the trip. Essall was superstitious, and she had already been hesitant to have Unkyss join their group as they would no longer be the Silverback sacred number of five. When Rellik joined, Essall went on and on about how the Silverbacks "are not Airluts, and have no need to flock together in large groups." For the most part, she was ignored, and when she couldn't be ignored, Numa sent her ahead to ensure the way home was clear. Terrabyss had also been reluctant about allowing Rellik to join, and he had many hushed conversations with Numa when Rellik wasn't near. Most were about the risk of Rellik damning the Ravis pack to face the same annihilation that the Ballios had faced in the prior days. He had been cool toward Rellik, and both he and Essall had managed to find rare common ground. But they both accepted that the decision had been made, and tensions had seemed to start easing away, especially once the party had left the harsh tundra behind.

Despite Luna's objections, Terrabyss enforced the Proving Requirements[43] that were usually reserved for pups. Rellik had to make her own shelter, fight for her share of the food, and she was the last to go to bed and the first, excluding Terrabyss, to get up. "She has lost any position she once held, she needs to fight for her survival until she has earned a place back in our tribe," was how he had put it and, to Rellik's credit, she had taken the treatment in stride. She had learned a lot in just the amount of time it had taken them to get back into the grove. She was quicker, more skilled, and, to Luna's surprise, she seemed happy.

Rellik was happy. She hadn't thought that she would ever get to return home. She had expected when she had been captured and taken into the camp that she was going to be executed, and every now and again the thought that she was still going to be executed before the next morning would arise. Since she had arrived in the grove, she had managed to completely shut that voice out. She wasn't foolish, and understood that there was a good chance that when she got back to the Gathering, she would be killed rather than adopted, but she had a sliver of hope with Luna.

They were still at least two days away from the Gathering, and it was starting to get dark as the group picked their ways through the trees. Essall had just returned to the main party, and over her shoulder were two good-sized snow hares that she had snatched for dinner. With their leftovers from other hunts, they would eat well again that night, even Rellik, after she had participated in a nightly sparring match with Luna. It had been decided that they were the closest in weight so it would be the fairest, and both had the most to learn about combat. Although Luna fought well with her daggers, there was much about the Mauler way of fighting that she had to learn. Rellik had even begun to put some meat on her bones and build up some muscle with having to fight for everything. Days of being on the run and having her brother eating almost all the food had, unsurprisingly, weakened her.

It was an unnaturally cold night even for winter, and it seemed as if the winds from the tundra had chased them into the grove. The trees were helping to block some of the wind, but freezing gusts broke through the barriers, sending chills up the spine. They gathered back-to-back to share their body heat until the fire overcame its struggles to stay alight in the wind. The trees were being stripped of their needles and the trunks were

43   Ways of determining hierarchy, usually in a litter

creaking and groaning in the unrelenting gale. Little was said around the fire as they ate; Rellik had been given a reprieve from having to follow the normal rules, much to Terrabyss' annoyance. He had such a good argument; he couldn't remember it now, but in the moment, it had been monumental—*No one had heard me because of this bear-shit wind!* That was the only reason that Luna had won the debate about how things were going to be done tonight. No one spoke, no one really could; the wind just shushed them tirelessly, it had no respect for any of them and their opinions.

After dinner, the bones were added to the fire and the Silverbacks went only about five or so lue away before they began to punch or kick at the hard icy ground, to loosen it before they dug their Deep Dens. Luna cursed as she slammed her paw down into a rock, hopping back on the other paw from the pain. Terrabyss popped his head out of his already-completed den at the commotion, and Numa and Essall soon joined him. It would have been a pretty comical sight for most onlookers, seeing one Silverback hopping mad, and three disembodied Mauler heads spinning around to find out what was going on. This evening's onlooker was in no mood for a show though, it was solely interested in dinner.

Rellik had been a quick learner and, to Luna's annoyance, was nearly halfway done with her den, only her tail and her haunches sticking out. Unkyss was similarly far along; and Luna stood, surveying the small camp for a more advantageous place to start work on her 'grave.' Her ear did it instinctively, moving to her left away from the fire and near where she had originally begun digging; she thought she heard some snow lightly crunch under some unseen pressure.

"Numa, we are still in Mauler territory, aren't we?" Luna shouted, hoping to be heard over the wind, her head turning to look where her ear had heard the sound. Her eyes locked on to two small specks that shifted from orange, to red, and then yellow as the fire flickered behind her.

"Yes!" came the shouted reply as a clump of dirt shot out from Numa's den. She was trying to make the entry a bit more spacious, so it would be easy for her to get in and out more quickly.

The deeper, somewhat disinterested voice of Terrabyss was barely heard coming from his den where he had already settled in for the night. "Do you need help? If I get up there and you start to chew me out about how you can do it, I am just going to stop even offering to help." He wisely waited for a response to his first question.

Rellik had been nearer to Luna and didn't have her head as submerged as the others. She had recognized the panic in Luna's voice over the howling wind, and she started scooting out of her den. Unfortunately, she had to go rump-first, because she had not yet dug deep enough to start the larger resting space, where the occupant could usually adjust their position and turn around. As she was almost out, she heard a thud as something or someone hit the forest floor hard. She tried to go faster, but it was difficult crawling backward quickly. As soon as her shoulders cleared the opening, she just shoved up with all her might, breaking through the dirt with her head so she could see what was happening. She instantly howled as she saw the huge, dirty-white saber-tooth tiger pinning Luna to the ground. Both its front paws had caught her shoulders, and his rear legs had slammed into her hips, easily sending her sprawling on her back in surprise. Its two long canines seemed to shimmer in the firelight as its head reared up, preparing to bite down into Luna's throat with those huge teeth. Luna couldn't scream, she was barely able to breathe. The predator's pounce and her crash to the ground had knocked the wind out of her, and now that the cat was standing on her chest, she couldn't get any air back in her lungs.

Terrabyss thumped his head on his den's roof as he heard Rellik's howl. He had already been crawling out when he had faintly heard Luna crash into the ground, but the howl had added all the urgency. He didn't bother to keep crawling out, instead pushing up from his knees, simply tearing the ground open as though he were some undead ghoul. Dirt and snow tumbled and blew off his fur as he grabbed his kanabo and ripped off its cover. Rellik slammed into the flank of the saber-tooth, and they both tumbled into the ferns away from Terrabyss. He growled in frustration as the fight moved out of his range, and climbed out of the dirt, howling gleefully in pursuit at the prospect of killing a saber-tooth.

Rellik and the saber-tooth rolled across the ferns, stopping when Rellik skidded into a small spruce. She groaned as she pushed herself up; she really hadn't expected the creature to be so strong and she certainly hadn't expected to almost bounce off it. The cat planted its right legs and stopped itself from rolling. It had no interest in fighting everyone it had smelt back at the camp, but it was starving, having just woken up, and it just needed to get its jaws around something and run away with it. It had almost succeeded the first time. It would just have to try again before that

112

one that had been in the dirt caught up to it.

Fortunately for Rellik, she was not too disoriented from her collision with the tree trunk, and she both heard and saw the saber-tooth tiger coming for her. She hopped up as the cat lunged, its claw nicked her right arm as she pushed up. She could hear Terrabyss slamming through the undergrowth. "Here, kitty-kitty!" He was howling at the top of his lungs.

Rellik didn't have time to get Terrabyss' attention before the cat swiped at her, forcing her to lean back out of the way. The saber-tooth was quick, and upset that its dinner was trying to escape. It lunged up toward Rellik's face, trying the same maneuver that it had performed so successfully against the first one. Rellik twisted to the cat's left flank, the last few days of constant fighting for her meals had provided some life-saving muscle memory. Now she was on the same side that she had hit the first time, the cat was in the air this time too and couldn't plant its paws. Rellik used all her strength, putting all of her weight into her elbow and she dug it into the saber-tooth's ribs, crashing into the beast again.

Luna got to her paws pretty quickly and followed after Numa, who followed Terrabyss. Unkyss was behind Luna, with Jabyn and Essall bringing up the rear. They eventually caught up to Terrabyss, and Luna noticed that he wasn't proceeding to help Rellik. Instead, he was standing about twenty or so lue away, watching the spectacle. Angry at his stubbornness to accept that Rellik was no longer a criminal, Luna moved to storm past him to where Rellik was fighting for her life. She felt his hand rest on her shoulder as she tried to push by.

"Let her earn her place back in our tribe," he said flatly, he wasn't being threatening and she could see that the others weren't pushing past him to join her. She had obviously been outvoted here, and she was pretty sure that either Terrabyss wouldn't let her go to help, or wouldn't come to her aid if the saber-tooth tiger proved too much for both of them.

"Fine, then I have a den to dig." Luna turned and walked back to where she had been working. She might not be able to help, but she wouldn't watch. Numa looked over at Jabyn, who nodded and joined Luna. Luna wasn't too excited about this, but the savage snarls of the saber-tooth were a pretty good argument that none of them should be alone in the grove.

Luna glared over at Jabyn as they got back to where she had been working. "You Maulers are barbaric; I don't understand why none of you will help her. She is going to get killed by that monster."

Jabyn replied in a patient and even tone, "You want us to trust her, let her prove her submission. Let her risk her life for the safety of the Alpha's bloodline."

Luna didn't have any good counter and decided to vent her frustration on her den, clawing large chunks of dirt out angrily as Jabyn added a few more small branches to the fire, trying to bring it back to life.

The saber-tooth turned to face Rellik, hopping to its paws after hitting the floor from her charge into its left flank. It roared its rage; the attack had been stressful for the beast and it was not at all happy that its dinner was being so belligerent. It stalked around to her wounded arm, not wanting to feel that elbow again and trying to keep its right side between her and its left. Rellik circled with it, unsure what to do at this moment.

Perhaps it's going to give up, she thought. It's probably best not to antagonize it and just stay on the defensive.

That wasn't the predator's plan, and it clawed at her leg, making her shuffle back, bounding in closer as she tried to backpedal. Rellik let her legs collapse as she narrowly avoided having her throat torn out by the lunge, and spun on her knees to face the cat; she knew better than to keep her back to it. The hunter had also spun around, and a bit faster than Rellik. Her body twisted to meet the cat's, and its heavy body slammed down on top of her. She scrambled to get her hand up under the cat's neck so it couldn't snap down at her, its huge canines scratched along her forearm. She lifted her legs up under the creature's stomach; she had originally planned to roll back with the saber-tooth against her paws so that they would simply change position. As soon as her paws were planted against the saber-tooth's gut, she realized that it was far too heavy, and it was more likely that her legs would give out and the cat would just crush her. She pushed with all her strength, using her back to plant her body and shifting all the energy she could down to her hips and out through her paws, launching the cat through the air and a sizable distance. Rellik howled as she kicked out, encouraged as her spectators joined their voices with hers.

Luna heard Rellik's howl and stopped working, she was almost done with the entrance and had only just begun to dig out the sleeping chamber. She shuffled backward as fast as possible and saw Jabyn just sitting by the fire. She looked over to where the other four were gathered. At first, she wasn't sure where the clapping sound was coming from. She looked at Jabyn at first, who was obviously not clapping. Her ears twisted back toward the four spectators as she narrowed down the sound. When she finally picked out that it was Terrabyss, he had already stopped applauding Rellik's ingenuity, and for some reason his encouragement made Luna want to see what was happening. Jabyn gave her a knowing look, and then jerked her head over to the group. Luna's tail wagged a little, embarrassed, and soon both had joined the rest of the onlookers.

The cat rolled back onto its feet, this time a bit more slowly. Jabyn nudged Luna and pointed to how the saber-tooth was moving. "It is guarding, it's desperately trying to keep its left side out of her reach. I am willing to bet when she kicked it, she hit a sore spot."

Luna followed Jabyn's gaze, the creature was stepping lightly with its front left paw, not wanting to strain the muscles on that side. "The left ribs are hurt!" she shouted to Rellik. "Focus on the left flank and this fight will be done in no time."

Caught up in the moment, Essall even shouted out some words of encouragement. "When it jumps for you, twist to its left, wait for it though! It will lose patience before you!" Everyone, except Rellik, who was otherwise focused, looked over at Essall. She gave them a side look and shrugged. "What? I don't want a saber-tooth to win."

Numa saw how Terrabyss was watching Luna as she cheered on Rellik. "She could have been right, you know, to spare her." She locked eyes with Terrabyss as he turned back to face her. "She sees the good in everyone; it's a special gift."

"It's naïve. We are only surviving. There is no good or bad," was Terrabyss' response, but his tone lacked its usual confidence.

"If everything goes the way we hope it will, we might not be only surviving for long. Then who will be the naïve one?" She smiled and wagged her tail at his expression, a mix between 'nah' and 'maybe?'

Rellik was concentrating on the cat, she had heard the advice of the others and had observed they were right about the cat defending its flank. She tried to do what Essall had suggested. Every time, the cat lashed out with its right and she wasn't timing her own movement to its left quickly enough. She was also worried the injury was only in the flank and not through the shoulder, then the cat may be quick enough to cut open her legs as she leapt to get to its left side.

Okay, you know how to hunt and fight, it just comes naturally for all Maulers. She reassured herself, With the others' advice, you can win this.

Just get to the left.

It was Unkyss' shout that really turned the tables. "Get to a snowbank! With the injury, the creature won't sidestep easily. In the deep snow, it will definitely be slower than you!" His booming deep voice resonated in Rellik's mind and she shuffled toward the snowbank that she had rolled through after her first collision with the saber-tooth. Unkyss had been right; as she scuttled around, the cat began to walk into the snowbank. She took another step and the cat responded, but had to yank its left leg free, lacking strength. With a burst of speed, Rellik changed her direction, quick-stepping to the cat's left side. The predator tried to whip its hind legs around so that it could twist about, out of the charging Mauler's way. But its paws were slow to respond to its brain's commands, and it was having trouble breaking free from the deep snow.

Rellik's mouth snapped down on the saber-tooth's neck and her claws raked down the left flank of the beast. She could taste the iron fluid, the crimson blood dripped from her lips and into the snow, instantly melting some as it connected. Now that the cat was injured, panicked, and off-balance, Rellik released her bite and shoved with all her might to get the cat to land on its back, or at the very least its side. She didn't want it to be able to use its weight or get stable purchase from which to attack. The saber-tooth tried to kick its paws and roll back up, but Rellik didn't pause.

"Don't let it get its paws back under it!" shouted Jabyn, holding tightly to Luna's hand as they watched in suspense.

"You just need to keep up a bit more pressure, you are going to win. Don't back down!" Luna shouted, following Jabyn's encouraging lead.

Unkyss and Terrabyss were standing next to each other. Each one had an arm on the other's shoulder, or rather, Unkyss had an arm on Terrabyss' shoulder, and Terrabyss had a hand up on Unkyss' arm. Unkyss gnawed on his bottom lip, tasting blood, and Terrabyss kept his other hand pressed against his mouth as if he were about to bite it off. Numa and Essall were wringing their hands as they watched Rellik push the predator onto its side. Both let out excited yelps, pumping their fists in the air when she managed to successfully shove it over.

Rellik was sore and was running on adrenaline, but she knew that the others were right, she had to keep the pressure up. This was life or death; she didn't have the luxury of submitting to this opponent. She lunged forward before the cat could roll back to its paws and her teeth again sunk

116

into the cat's neck, but this time found the delicate underside. The saber-tooth thrashed under the suffocating, vice-like grip of Rellik's jaws, and Rellik applied her claws to the creature's ribs again, sapping the fight from the creature as she maintained the clamp on the cat's windpipe. She could feel the saber-tooth's thrashes weakening. Eventually, there was a slight wheezing sound next to her ear and the cat stopped moving all together.

There was an outburst of noise from behind Rellik as she heard her fans shouting how impressed they were and how well she had done. Rellik's heart was pounding as the adrenaline raced through her body. She jumped up, grabbing the dead saber-tooth by its teeth and used all her strength to lift the creature up to show the others. She lifted it about halfway up before its weight caused her to teeter, and before she could stop herself, both of them had fallen back into the snow. The six others rushed over to Rellik and helped her up.

Luna was beside herself with joy. She began brushing the snow out of Rellik's coat. "We should just make this your Hunt," Luna said, caught up in the excitement of the moment.

All of the Maulers, including Rellik, got that awkward look on their faces, as if they were pondering if they should tell Luna the truth or not. "I suppose that there is some tradition that dictates that this can't be her Hunt," Luna said, slightly exasperated as she looked at each one of their faces.

All of the Maulers, except Rellik, drew lots every morning to see who would be the one that they jokingly called the "well, actually" Taur. Today, Essall had been the one to pull the single black tooth from the pouch of assorted white canines that was part of all Scout's gear. She had been excited that she had drawn it, but hadn't had a chance to flex her power because Luna had been fairly accurate in her comments today. When she finally had this opportunity, she did not let it go to waste.

In a loud and authoritative voice, she yelled, "A Hunt has to be recognized and is a competition amongst the numerous litters. Each team of juveniles that comes back with a quarry that matches the Hunt's parameters are recognized as adults by the alpha Hunter." Essall's wish to enjoy her authority was fulfilled this evening because Luna didn't let it go at that.

"I really don't see the problem if we count this as the Hunt. I represent my father, so can't I just recognize this hunt?" Luna responded sourly to the eager Essall.

Essall was more than happy to clarify, "If we recognize this Hunt, then Rellik Ballio would be a recognized name." Luna opened her mouth, thinking that she understood where this was going, but Essall just kept talking. "And if her name is recognized, then we have to kill her, because someone who wanted to depose your father could just rally behind her pack name." Again, Luna opened her mouth to clarify to Essall she had understood, and again Essall kept talking; she was on a roll. "Because whether Rellik supports the claim or not, the fact that there is the possibility of challenge legalizes the challenge."

Luna gave Essall an exhausted look, wondering if she was actually done this time, or if she meant to continue as soon as she tried to say something again.

Essall couldn't resist one more quick comment. "Not only that, but if she were to take Materimony[44], her mate could cast off their name and take hers. Then it wouldn't even have to be in this generation, but it could be her litter, or her litter's litter that defies whoever is in charge, all because we lacked the stomach to clean up all the loose ends in our original power shift."

"Okay! I understand!" Luna growled at Essall as they began to follow the rest back to camp.

Unkyss and Terrabyss were carrying the kill over, and Jabyn had her arm over Rellik's shoulder commenting on how those fang cuts on her forearm would scar nicely and boasting about her own. Numa watched Essall and Luna as they brought up the rear, joining them as they got back to the area that they had chosen to camp, noticing that the wind had died down in their distraction.

"Ever clean your own kill before?" Terrabyss inquired of Rellik as she joined him and Unkyss by the fire. She shook her head no; even while they had been traveling, she was usually not privy as to how the meals were made. She was often one of the last to build her den and so she hadn't seen how the others had gone about preparing the food. She wanted to look away as Terrabyss propped open the hind legs and Unkyss began to rip open the abdomen. "You have to be really careful when taking the guts out. You don't want to have the stomach or intestines rupture and contaminate your meal. It is often best to try to hang up your catch by the neck or front legs and allow the intestines to fall out naturally."

"Some of the insides are pretty tasty but don't keep well, so we will

44   Official union between two Taurs of the same clan

have to cook those up tonight and eat them for breakfast." Unkyss added to the conversation as Terrabyss lifted the creature by the front legs so that Unkyss could dispose of its insides.

Terrabyss nodded his agreement. "Especially when you have the opportunity to cook the testes, it is a rare treat." Rellik's mouth was drooling at just the thought of the meal, she had never had some of these delicacies before, not even as the daughter of an Alpha.

"Come here," Unkyss encouraged, "you won't learn anything from back there." He motioned for her to get right up to the carcass. "Now, reach up into the opening and pull out all the parts that didn't want to fall out."

Rellik took a deep breath and stepped forward, most of the intestines and other guts had fallen out onto the snow in a steamy mess. The smell was difficult to stomach, but the excitement of trying this for the first time overcame her finer senses. Luna watched as well, she had seen them clean and gut smaller game, but this was the first time she had seen them prepare something this large. Numa joined her brother, Unkyss and Rellik, and cleared away the innards as Rellik let them drop into the sloppy mess below. Jabyn and Essall began adding small branches to the fire and stacking larger pieces next to it to be dried in its heat. It didn't take long for Numa and Rellik to separate the edible from the inedible organs. Terrabyss and Unkyss worked on stripping the hide from the saber-tooth while Jabyn, Essall, and Luna stripped the meat from the creature's skeleton. When the two males had finished skinning the creature, they spread out the hide and placed rocks on the edges of the pelt to keep it stretched. Then, they buried it under the snow, once they had been sure to clean all the fibers off the pelt that had kept it attached to the muscle. All seven of them worked on this, cleaning the bones together, while the meat and organs cooked on spits. The bones that they weren't going to use went into the fire, the ones that they would keep—primarily the skull and the teeth—would be taken back with them for the shaman to choose what he wanted. These, they cleaned by scraping the top layer from the skeleton with stones, which got rid of any flesh they hadn't managed to strip. Skoff might take the whole skull for a new mask, or might just want the teeth for ingredients. Any material he didn't need could be kept by Rellik as a trophy.

After the group finished up all the necessary steps to preserve what they could from the saber-tooth, they sat around the fire, tired and hungry. Since most of it had cooked by now, they dove into freshly cooked items that had been skewered over the fire. Terrabyss was quick to snatch the heart, to everyone's very audible complaints, but he snarled and ignored the comments, turning to Rellik. He extended the skewered heart to her. "You took it down; you deserve the best part." A hush fell over the group, and they quickly stopped complaining. Luna's tail was thumping as she looked at Terrabyss, which quickly turned attention from Terrabyss' offering to Luna's tail. She yowled nervously as she concentrated on bringing the appendage under control.

Rellik reached out slowly, expecting Terrabyss to pull it away, or throw the heart off into the woods to make her sniff it out. Her hand gripped the skewer, yet he made no move to torment her. She tensed her arm, thinking that she had figured him out. He was going to make her yank it out of his grip. She pulled back suddenly, hoping to catch Terrabyss off guard. He looked surprised as he felt how hard she tugged, he hadn't planned to make this difficult for her, and had been serious when he said she had earned it. With an 'oooff,' she landed on her tail in the snow behind her, and matched his confused expression with one of her own.

"Overdoing it, much?" He cocked his head sarcastically, trying not to laugh at her and maintain his sour expression.

"I thought, well, I mean... " Rellik stammered, not sure if Terrabyss was mad at her or not. "So, I can have it?" she finally managed.

"I meant what I said, you earned it." He turned and smacked Unkyss' hand as he reached for the stomach. "But that is mine."

As they finally settled down to get some sleep, Rellik found that for the first time in a long time, she felt like she was part of a pack. I could die happy, she thought, as she drifted off to sleep.

The next couple of days to get back to the Gathering were joyful ones. No longer on the hunt, the original five travelers allowed themselves to go at an easier pace than they had when they had set out, and in doing so were able to teach Luna more about the grove. She learned about the nettles and poison oak that grew amongst the ferns hidden out of sight. She learned about how Maulers choose their professions, and how everything is done for the benefit of the tribe. She learned more about their games and what they did for fun when not working. Another argument broke out over the rules of My Skull, when Unkyss stated that once the skull had switched hands, then the one with the skull could go to the nearest border point to score. Terrabyss was of the opinion that they would need to go to the furthest point.

"You always have to go to the other side of the boundaries!" he shouted, both of them were on their paws and within a whisker of the other's face.

Unkyss rolled his eyes. "Again, you inner-groves and your complications, it is almost as though no one is supposed to ever score in your version."

"If you are playing it right, that is exactly how it should go!" Terrabyss shouted back, both of them taking a growling step closer to one another.

Rellik elbowed Essall and leaned over, whispering something. Essall let out a burst of laughter as Rellik finished and Jabyn, Numa, and Luna gave them both curious looks. The two males paused for a moment and looked over at Essall as she was still chuckling. She just nodded to Rellik in agreement.

"What was that about?" inquired Unkyss, who was immediately supported by Terrabyss, asking much the same question.

"Hmm, what?" Rellik responded, feigning confusion. "What do you mean? About what?"

Essall and Rellik both snickered, but would not reveal more than that, acting bewildered when confronted. Long after both Terrabyss and Unkyss had fallen asleep, Numa gingerly crawled on her belly over to Essall.

"What was that about tonight?"

Essall slowly opened her eyes, her muzzle was hidden under her puffy tail. The night had been moderately mild, and they had decided to sleep huddled together under the stars. Essall thought that maybe they were getting ready to move and almost stood up to stretch, but Numa stopped her.

"No, we aren't moving out, I just wanted to know what Rellik told you."

Essall leaned over, snatching up a mouthful of snow and letting it melt slowly as she drank the refreshing water. "What now—?"

Numa cut her off, "When Terrabyss and Unkyss were arguing. Rellik told you something, you laughed. I want to know what she told you, and if you play stupid with me again, I will make sure you are brain dead by the end of this conversation."

Essall could tell when Numa was serious, and Numa was very serious. "Okay, don't clip your ears, relax." She started wagging her tail again and it swooshed in the snow. "It wasn't anything important, just when they were nose to nose, she said it looked like they were going to snuggle."

Numa looked at her disappointedly. "Really, that was it? That comment had you busting your gut?"

"Wouldn't say busting my gut," responded Essall, a little incredulously. "I guess you had to be there," she said with a shrug.

Numa shuffled back to her spot. "I was there. You're just a juvenile, and find another juvenile's humor funny." She teased as they went back to bed.

Essall mimicked her in an inaudible tone before laying back down. *Numa needs to relax.*

They arrived at the Gathering the following afternoon. Dio was lying on his side with his back to Skoff, who had not yet noticed as he stared at a set of charcoal sketchings on sheets of tree bark, depicting Dio's confrontation with Haxzus. There were many more families around than usual, apparently the Scout's message had caught the tribe's attention. Almost every outer-grove pack had come to the Gathering after receiving the information about the power shift.

"If I were to guess, I would think that there are over a hundred Maulers here," whispered Numa to Terrabyss. "I didn't know there were so many."

"Neither did I," he whispered back as they walked out through the trees into the Gathering. He was quick to notice all the different looks that they received, in particular the ones directed at Rellik. It wasn't that he thought she might be up to something, but because he knew that her presence could become extremely contentious. He noted the expressions of anger against her, particularly because much of the tribe viewed her as a Lone Wolf. It was not hard to see the faces of excitement as well, in those that recognized an opportunity in seeing the last living Ballio. Any pup that tried to venture out of the trees to greet or inspect the new arrivals was held back by their parents.

Rellik could feel the tension as well, and could feel every single eye as each of them was locked on her. As a nervous reaction, she shuffled toward Terrabyss. As soon as he felt her clinging to him, he pushed her away.

"Walk tall, you earned your place."

She gave him a weak nod, and did her best to do as instructed. It was hard at first; it is ingrained in most Maulers to never call attention to oneself and to not stand out. Her natural instinct was to try to melt away and, although she wanted to follow Terrabyss' advice, she found herself gravitating toward Unkyss. That wasn't very helpful for either of them, because Unkyss was not accustomed to so many Maulers and the crowd unsettled him. It worsened when the eyes that followed Rellik fell on him, and he heard the and ahhh's of the crowd as they noticed his height.

Dio had been listening to Skoff for well over half of the afternoon; a while ago, he had rolled over in an attempt to piss off the shaman. Skoff hadn't noticed, and Dio lost all interest once his rudeness had failed to check Skoff. Skoff was going on about wanting to capture the moment of Haxzus' demise, and he didn't think it looked impressive that Dio had stabbed him from behind. Dio had stopped bothering to correct Skoff on where he had actually stabbed Haxzus.

"Technically, the back and flank are the same area of the body," Dio had responded to the shaman's last adjustment to the sketch. Skoff hadn't agreed with that reasoning, but he did think that the picture with the daggers in Haxzus' flanks was much more impressive than the one with the daggers in his upper back. At the same time, he felt it was important that the picture told the facts of the story, which meant daggers in the back. Dio didn't care; Skoff could have drawn him punching Haxzus' head off, or biting him in half. He only cared that it showed him defeating the former Alpha. Dio's tail thumped and he sat up when he saw the group come through the trees.

"There she is." He sighed with relief and stood up quickly, walking out to meet Luna.

Skoff rubbed his forehead, accidentally smearing some charcoal on it. "That doesn't answer the question. I really get the feeling that you think this is a waste of time."

Terrabyss howled in greeting as Dio approached, and quickly saluted the new Alpha. His sister and the others were quick to follow. Dio tapped his stomach and then chest as was customary, and his tail was wagging as he went up to his daughter and embraced her, before catching sight of Rellik and hesitating, looking at the group.

Skoff jumped when he heard Terrabyss' howl and spun around, confused as to what was happening. He growled as he saw that he had lost Dio's attention and bent over, picking up his sketches.

"They will all regret it when they want to remember how it happened and no one knows, all because there was no pictorial representation," Skoff grumbled under his breath as he stood up, wiping away his scowl and replacing it with his more traditional frown.

"Alpha Father! It is good to see you!" Dio exclaimed as he hugged his daughter. She nuzzled him respectfully, before he turned to the rest of them.

"I thought that I sent five of you away, but I now see seven. Of course, I am curious when the number I sent seems to just magically produce more, so you can imagine that I have some questions. Let's start with the simplest first." He turned to face Unkyss. "I would not be shocked if it turned out that you had some Cana blood in you," Dio began, "but whether you do or not is not my question. I am curious who you are, and who you pledge loyalty to?"

Unkyss' ears and tail lowered respectfully as he framed his stomach once again. "I am Unkyss, the last of the Sabor pack. I pledge myself and my pack to my Alpha's service." He knelt and exposed his neck. "You are my Alpha, do what you will with my blood."

He stayed like that until Dio approached him, touched his forehead to Unkyss', then stepped back. "I do not require your blood today, although I may need it, and all of your pack's blood one day."

With that, Unkyss stood, and the tribe let out a howl that echoed throughout the grove. Never had so many Maulers been gathered together since they had fled the Green Wall.

Dio turned next to Rellik. "And would someone care to explain why one of the traitors I told you to hunt down and eliminate is here in front of me?"

Essall gave Luna a little nudge. Luna glared back at her, but stepped forward. "She submitted to me, and as your representative, I accepted her submission. She is to go up for adoption, should the Alpha agree with my decision."

Dio looked from his daughter to Rellik, and then around to the gathered Maulers. Skoff shuffled up next to him and stared at Rellik, and then to the group that had been sent to hunt her.

"You thought that you could just bring back a Lone Wolf and we would want to adopt it?" he shouted, rattling his staff. "How dare you!" The staff came to a quivering stop in front of Luna. "This could end—"

Before he could finish the sentence, Terrabyss grabbed the staff, pushing it back into Skoff's chest. Skoff looked at him in shock, and Terrabyss himself was honestly surprised at how defensively he had responded.

Skoff liked to prattle on about his doomsday prophecies; after all, what self-respecting shaman wasn't proud of a good doomsday prophecy? The thing was, for as much as Skoff wanted to claim that the spirits told him the fortunes of the tribe, the shamans were actually using their best guess.

Sometimes, they were right and, sometimes, they were wrong; the future was never a sure thing.

"You're not the Alpha," Terrabyss growled. "Let the Alpha make the decision on her fate."

Everyone now looked at Dio, who had become just as nervous as Rellik had been when she first walked into the Gathering. He thought for a moment, not wanting to make a choice that would cause him to appear weak, but at the same time having some sympathy for Rellik.

"I will discuss with the Scout Mother and our Shaman; your elders will come to a decision, but until then she is to be treated as an orphaned pup. Care for her and treat her as one of your own, for she may become a member of one of your packs," Dio announced to all those listening.

Terrabyss had to admit that Skoff had done a pretty good job teaching Dio how to be a Mauler in the time that they had been gone. The three elders went away from those gathered, and everyone else began whispering their own speculations about what would be the fate of the orphan of the Ballio clan. Terrabyss, Luna, and Unkyss stuck around with Rellik, and soon the four of them ended up gathered near a group of pups that were playing My Skull. Both of the males were shouting about how this was the right or wrong way to play the sport. Eventually, the pups started arguing with them as well when a pup kicked the skull across the border line, and was given one point instead of two. Both Unkyss and Terrabyss agreed that the rule was completely made up.

Pack

Dio had been busy while the others were off hunting Hanora. He established two councils; the first remained the Council of Elders, with minor adjustments to the members and how they would be replaced. The only Maulers that would be eligible for such positions in the future would come from the eldest and most fit members of the tribe, and only when a former constituent had been removed from the position. Terrabyss hadn't been too concerned about these changes, as he was not a member of this council, nor did he intend to be one.

The council Terrabyss was in had been fittingly and predictably named the Invasion Council. Dio established this second council to consist of six members. It wasn't as auspicious a number as five, but it wasn't as bad as three or double digits, so most of the Maulers didn't complain except for Skoff and Essall, who were becoming attached at the hip with their doomsday prophecies and superstitions. The members of the Invasion Council were Dio, Numa, Terrabyss, Luna, Maxyss, and a familiar-looking Mauler by the name of Suskyss. She was impressive in both physique and intelligence. She had become almost inseparable from Dio, and when Skoff was busy with his predictions or other shamanistic duties, she had been teaching Dio about the customs and laws of Mauler society. Terrabyss wasn't sure how he knew her, and Numa said that she had never seen her in the Scouts. Terrabyss doubted that Skoff would have any useful insight, even if she happened to sleep right next to the Hollow, and so hadn't bothered to ask him.

It took Terrabyss two days of keeping everyone in order while taking a tally of how many fighting troops they had, his first official task as a council member. As it stood, they had just over seventy, or maybe a few less. It had been a difficult assignment.

"I think before we march out that we should have as many fighters as possible," Terrabyss suggested to the rest of the council as they sat around a small central fire in the Gathering.

"I have over seventy warriors, according to your count," was Dio's response. "I feel like that's plenty to lead an assault on the Green Wall."

Terrabyss was shaking his head even before Dio had finished his rebuttal. "It isn't a question of troop numbers; it is a matter of earning the Maulers' respect. Let them see you uphold our traditions, let them see you hold the biggest Hunt the Maulers have ever seen." He had Dio's interest with that suggestion. Terrabyss was starting to get good at these politics, or 'scheming' as he called it. "I am not sure who proposed that we move out without holding a Hunt." He looked directly at Suskyss; where had he seen her before? "If you hold a Hunt, not only will you swell your ranks, but also you will grow loyalty and admiration amongst the Maulers."

"It will take time, time you don't have," interrupted Suskyss. "Terrabyss' plan will take moons in the making; by the time we are ready to march, it will be winter all over again."

Terrabyss growled at her, he hated this back and forth. He wasn't entirely sure why he was even on this council; he would much rather be off doing his job. However, since his last Watcher Fist had been eliminated, no new spots had opened up on other Fists, and so he was stuck here. Also, Dio had asked for him to be there, and he wasn't going to turn down a request from the Alpha. Now Suskyss was challenging him, as far as he was concerned, but Dio silenced him.

"Terrabyss! You will have respect for your fellow speakers."

I would if they were contributing, instead of trying to poke holes in my ideas, he thought.

"How long would it take you to organize a Hunt of the size that Terrabyss is suggesting?" Dio asked, turning to face Maxyss.

Maxyss had been the beta Hunter under Hanora, and Dio had thought it best that there not be the custom of alpha Hunter any more. Since Dio had no mate, he didn't have anyone who could fill the spot appropriately. He also felt that the tribe would run more smoothly if only one Alpha oversaw it, but since he also couldn't go on every hunt, he had installed Maxyss as the new Prime Hunter. None of the Maulers could argue with this, because the tribe had been this way until just before they had been exiled to the Ice Kraggs. The position of alpha Hunter had been created by Grimmis for Clea. Maxyss was older, probably a true elder in terms of classifications for the title of the Elder Council, and had multiple gray patches in his once majestic black coat. He was still strong, and had a small hump in his back allowing him to stand tall, about a half-head taller than most Maulers. He had one milky-white eye that he had earned on his first Hunt, when he had been kicked by a moose his group was trying to bring down. Even with his face bleeding and his vision severely damaged, he had managed to get his claws in the creature's stomach as it tried to trample him. The shaman, Grimmis, had been able to heal his vision, and true to Silverback form, Maxyss wore the scar proudly. His other eye was the traditional yellow, but a little dulled with age. His right ear had never grown back right, after the stomping, and had remained a gnarled mess on the top of his head. "It is true that it would take at least a moon to find enough game for thirty pups." His voice was slow, and he spoke with purpose, and even in his old age his tone was firm and steady as he answered truthfully.

"We could just avoid the Hunt altogether," Luna added nervously. She knew that her suggestion would not be well-received and wasn't sure if she really even wanted to suggest it. As the debate had continued, she felt that it could be a simple solution to the whole problem. "We could use the Eclipse custom that we had to adopt when the Ozars took over our half of the Green Wall; it's known as the P&E Method."

All the Maulers in the Gathering had fallen silent at her suggestion, and Maxyss was obviously trying to hold back his outrage at such an insolent idea. Suskyss' expression was not so polite; she had obvious contempt on her face and her lips peeled back a bit as she growled. Terrabyss matched her gaze, barking at her when she wouldn't turn to face him instead of Luna.

"ENOUGH!" Dio snarled as he stood up. "No, we will not use the Paw and Ear Method here. We are among Maulers and have a chance to partake in real Silverback customs. I will not let a practice started in defeat become a custom within the Maulers. From the sounds of it, we will have to delay the Hunt."

"Delay the Hunt?" came Maxyss' shout. "Wouldn't we just have it when we got to the Green Wall?"

Dio was shaking his head no in response to Maxyss' question; it was Maxyss' turn to become upset. Before he could start a new branch of arguments, Numa spoke up. "We could go after the mammoths that the Corm[45] herd." Everyone who had been sitting around the fire looked over to her, waiting for her to elaborate, but that is all she said.

45   Mino tribe that live in the Banshee Tundra

"The mammoths are on the tundra, and the Corm shepherds are not going to just stand by and let us attack their herd," Suskyss finally said, after Numa didn't explain any further.

"I have never met the Corm, and don't know who they are or what clan they are from," Dio informed the Maulers.

Both he and Luna had a mystified cock to their heads.

Numa and her Scouts had the most interactions with them, so she informed the two Eclupse who the Corm were. "They are a tribe of the Mino clan. They are not as large as their brothers, in terms of height or even muscle, but they have very thick long coats that allow them to survive in the tundra easily, as well as long, slightly curved horns. They are a Beast Back[46] like us, and don't have furless torsos like the Ramsyn or Boofilou [47]to the southwest along the coast. We have never raided them outright in the past because we lacked any unified numbers, but now… " she trailed off, letting the council use their imagination.

"We could use the fighters to distract the Corm while the pups drove the herd and picked off what mammoths they could!" an excited Maxyss exclaimed. No alpha Hunter had led the Maulers on such a Hunt, and he was very much a supporter of this plan.

Terrabyss almost wanted to put a stop to this plan right now. *I wasn't able to hunt mammoths!* He wished that he had, instead of the caribou that had migrated through the grove in the spring. However, the idea of going into combat against the Corm was enough incentive to keep Terrabyss from derailing the proposal.

"We don't even know how many Corm tend the mammoths," was Suskyss' ever-negative outburst. "Is it worth our veterans' lives to throw them at the Corm, and let a bunch of untested pups fill the veterans' former positions?"

Terrabyss clenched his hands into fists before he realized that he didn't have his kanabo with him. Dio had asked him to leave it near the trees, along with Luna's daggers. Something about making sure that everyone felt heard, and again, Terrabyss wasn't about to argue with a direct request from the Alpha. He was sure he could beat Suskyss without it and he was tired of her constant objections with no new ideas of her own. He could tell that Numa was thinking along the same lines when both managed to

46   With animal torsos rather than human, in contrast to a Harpyn Taur

47   A tribe from the Mino clan that lives in the Endless Plains

glance at each other.

"I think our veterans can handle some shepherds," was Numa's measured response. "Besides, my Scouts have often kept an eye on the Corm when they come to the grove's edge in the spring. There are usually no more than ten to twenty shepherds, depending on the herd's size."

Terrabyss gave Suskyss a condescending look as he spoke up, "I am sure that our seventy fighters can handle even twenty of their most experienced shepherds," he stated confidently.

It was Suskyss' turn to get an arrogant tone in her voice. "The Corm are armed and armored, they do good trade with the Ramsyn."

"It would be good practice against the Ozars, who are also armed and armored." Even Luna had heard enough from Suskyss, and cut her off with an annoyed look.

"According to my Scouts, they only wear light armor, usually just cloth. When it comes to weapons, the Corm actually have very little trade with the Ramsyn." Before anyone could shoot Suskyss a triumphant look, Numa continued. "They do have a direct trade with the Dwarves, being on very good terms with the stout people." Suskyss sat up straight, giving the council a victorious grin as her tail thumped on the frozen ground. "Luna is right; we need practice against armored and armed opponents. If I have understood both her and you correctly" – she turned to face Dio – "the Ozars are well-trained with their axes and are comfortable in their chain armor. It is best we start with hills before trying to scale a mountain."

Dio had been listening to the whole exchange, weighing all the information given and, although he had come to trust Suskyss' advice, he knew that seventy Maulers weren't enough to overthrow the Ozars and free all the communes. Numa's point was also valid; before he threw the Maulers against the Ozars, he should see how they handled fighting against those that had both weapons and armor.

"All right, I think it is in the best interest of the tribe to engage in a large Hunt before we leave. Given time constraints, we will have the pups hunt mammoths, and have the main force test their skills against armed and armored opponents. I will only have sixty troops go; the other ten will remain here with me and the other adults to start preparing for our march back into the Green Wall." Dio's tone was not as official as he had hoped, and there was some obvious tension as it seemed that Suskyss still wished to offer some precautions. She held her tongue as Dio ended the meeting, not wishing this to drag on any longer. He still had to meet with the Elder Council to discuss Rellik's adoption into a pack. Terrabyss and Suskyss stood and saluted their Alpha before leaving. The two moved out of the Gathering, beyond the boundary that Dio had marked for the meeting. Suskyss didn't bother to linger, giving Terrabyss no chance to confront her about her constant negativity; leaving him to wander off to find Unkyss to wrestle with to work off some frustration.

Numa waited for Skoff to take his seat on the right-hand side of Dio around the fire. He was wearing one of his ponchos; this one was bright yellow and green in alternating colors. He had his walking stick—with the numerous bones, teeth, and other knick-knacks laced to it—that rattled as he walked. His tail was not braided today, which caught Numa off guard since that was such a common practice for him, as much as it was for her to spike her collar.

"You look ridiculous," she teased, and was surprised at Skoff's non-reaction to her comment.

She couldn't pry into why Skoff was not his usual gloomy and crotchety self, as Dio began speaking and it drew her attention away from the shaman.

"We are here to discuss one thing, and one thing only. As you are all aware, the former second pup of the Ballio pack was brought into the Gathering a few days ago. Although I know this is not customary among Silverbacks, I have decided not to have her executed, or banished as a Lone Wolf. I will agree to open up an adoption for her." He held up his hands to stop the murmuring that followed the announcement. "I have heard all of your opinions on the matter, and although I appreciate your views, I feel this is the best way to move forward. I am not erasing our old customs and traditions, but simply adding a small clause to them. I am unfamiliar with all your practices and so I will need you to explain to me how this process will work." He was silent for a moment. "Numa, since you were in charge of the group that was sent to hunt her down, could you please explain the procedure to me?"

Numa looked around, hoping that someone else would take her place, but since the Alpha had spoken directly to her, it was a stupid notion to think that someone else would respond. "It is pretty simple really, all those who wish to adopt the pup will speak for her. Usually, if multiple families speak up, then it is settled through challenge." She promptly sat down once she had finished explaining the process.

Dio nodded as she finished. "So, it is not so different than I had pictured. What happens if no one speaks for her?" He wasn't sure that he wanted to know, but he had to ask.

Numa again hoped that someone else would answer the Alpha, but the passing silence was too much for her and she just blurted out the response, "She is exiled as a Lone Wolf." She looked at Luna, noticing the upset expression on the Eclupse's face.

Dio nodded, slower this time, also seeming not to have expected that outcome. "Okay, well I know that some of you are worried that those who adopt her will simply cast off their pack name and take hers, so they can have a legitimate challenge to my position. I don't want any of you to think that the tribe's cohesion is less valuable to me than my personal desires, or my pack's needs." Luna couldn't help but flinch at that last part of his little speech. "Fortunately, I will not have to prove this to you, since one of our loyal council members has agreed to have Rellik join their pack."

All but Dio and Numa looked back and forth to one another, trying to figure out if it had been the Silverback next to, or across from them.

"We will have the bids as usual, but we will ensure that Rellik will go to a pack that will not cast off its name for hers. A pack that has worked hard to have their own name recognized, and would not willingly discard that name for the Ballio name."

Luna had put it together before the rest of those gathered. "So, she is going to become a Ravis?" Suddenly, the constant murmuring and shifting of glances stopped as all eyes turned to Numa and Skoff.

"*Huh*, what?" Skoff stammered, and he reflexively started growling at all their stunned stares. "What is wrong?" he snarled.

"Nothing," Numa said in an easy tone. "We are simply adopting Rellik into our pack." She glanced over at her stunned brother.

"Does Terrabyss know about this?" asked a bewildered Skoff, as he tried to process what his sister was saying. "We will be a target for anyone who wants to claim her!" He paused after he said the last part, understanding now.

"Exactly," Numa responded, her tail now thumping on the ground, "even if Terrabyss doesn't like the idea, he will love being able to put down any challenge that will surely come from our announcement of adoption."

Skoff had to admit, if you needed to get Terrabyss on your side, all you had to do was dangle a fight in front of him. Numa needed Skoff's support, and hopefully Terrabyss wouldn't challenge her.

"You realize that Terrabyss may not care who I support? You may be the alpha now, but we had one before you."

"I remember Tarphyss better than you," was Numa's savage response, "and I have the support of my Scouts. You should be more concerned about who would save you from his anger. Not whether or not he will challenge my decisions."

Skoff looked around the gathered council, he wished that he had not tried to question his sister. He suddenly felt very vulnerable and humiliated. He nodded his consent to Numa. "She will be a welcomed pack member." He forced his tail to wag a bit.

"All right," Dio said slowly, unsure if he should speak up. "Unless any of you have any argument, we will gather everyone so that we can find Rellik a proper pack to be a part of." The council was quick to stand except for Skoff. Numa approached her brother.

"You should probably get your things, so that her transfer to our pack can be official," she said soothingly, lowering her ears and tucking her tail in apology.

"Hmm?" Skoff asked, as though she had shaken him from a deep sleep. "Sorry, I missed what you said, could you repeat it?"

"If you are fishing for more of an apology than what I just gave you, you better be on your deathbed or have me in a submission," Numa responded, upset and thinking that her brother was trying to milk the sympathy she had just shown.

"What? No, no! You misunderstand. I am the shaman; you would have to do a lot more than that to undermine my position. I just had a rough day, that is all, super tired." He yawned and stretched. "But yes, I must get my things." He hopped to his paws and jogged off, quite spryly for someone so tired. Numa raised her eyebrows and tilted her head as he went. *I will never understand him.*

As was customary among the Maulers, Rellik's adoption was held at night, after Skoff had assembled the ceremonial fire pit. This was considered a sacred time for the tribe; as night fell, the heavens revealed the precious glimpses into the promised afterlife of the Taurs. When they slept, they were spiritually ascending into those heavens and taking part in the joys and challenges of the place. The whole tribe was there; over a hundred Maulers, including pups and elderly. The young were off playing, under the supervision of Maxyss and Numa, as well as some of their Scouts and Hunters. Several games of My Skull had broken out and the pups would be easily entertained and out of everyone's business until all of the challenges for Rellik had been decided. Numa had told Terrabyss that he was to be in the group of those putting in a bid and, if he didn't want his tail shaved, he would be there. Normally, Terrabyss was not impressed by others' threats, but something about Numa told him she would do it. Perhaps it was because she had actually done it to Skoff once, after he had temporarily turned her pink by failing an illusionary spell he had been practicing. Skoff had managed to convince their mother to let him stay with Grimmis for a moon, which had given Numa a chance to calm down and for his fur to grow back. She had the same look in her eye as on the day she threatened Skoff, so Terrabyss had stopped wrestling with Unkyss and had jogged over to the Gathering. Now that he was here, he was very bored and was debating if having his tail shaved would be so bad a punishment for skipping out on this. The tribe would shun him until it grew back in, but maybe he could convince Skoff to force it to regrow with his magic. Then, he wouldn't even need to worry about the humiliation he would need to endure until it grew back.

He was starting to turn to leave when howls around him erupted, and so he turned back, finding himself joining those gathered as they saluted their Alpha and the shaman.

"Well, now I am stuck here," he grumbled.

Dark clouds had gathered overhead and were blotting out the starry sky, as winter attempted to bring her fury one last time. There was a little over a moon of winter left, and she was getting desperate to keep her grip on the planet of Sarm and the continent of Loog Turra. The grove still had deep piles of snow in some areas, having had little rain to speed up a melt, and where the canopy easily held the sun's warm rays at bay. Chill winds blew in from the Banshee Tundra and from the Ice Kraggs, trapping the Gathering in a crossfire of freezing cold. The Maulers shook off the wind, their dense undercoats would not be shed for a couple more moons, until spring had actually staked its hold.

Terrabyss looked around to those gathered, he noticed that Suskyss was here and, for some reason, that bothered him. It might be that he was still worked up from their previous encounter, but he felt the aggression in her looks and heard the anger in her tone no matter how well she thought she hid it. He still couldn't place why her sleek black fur and yellow eyes reminded him of someone familiar. Terrabyss forced himself to look away and assess the rest of the packs gathered; he noticed with a bit of concern that, as far as he could tell, all of the packs here had been to some degree loyal to the Ballio bloodline. He had told Dio that this was going to happen, and he was curious to see how the Alpha was going to sneak his way out of this one.

Skoff was wearing ceremonial clothing; a bone-beaded chest piece with all of the long beads dyed black and the small, circular beads dyed yellow, typical for funerals and adoptions. It represented how sad a day it was when any pack had its members diminished, or was expunged all together. On his head, he wore the elaborately painted skull of a saber-tooth tiger. Half of the skull was gold, and the other half was a dark brown. If Terrabyss was to be honest, he didn't see much of a difference in the two shades. He remembered when Skoff had first made the mask; Terrabyss had talked him into repainting it six times, and honestly it looked the same as the first time he had seen it. The skull of the saber-tooth was another ill omen and fitting to wear on a sad night like this since the cats were the top killer of pups.

After the salute was finished, Skoff took a step in front of Dio, rattling his walking stick. "May we all honor and obey," he called out in his unnaturally thunderous voice that seemed to echo in everyone's mind at once.

"We will," everyone shouted back in a loud chorus as Skoff stepped aside for Dio, who now walked to the center of everyone's attention.

As the two passed each other, both saluted to one another. Skoff was sure to just tap his stomach in response, and then returned the salute. Dio tapped his stomach and chest, nodding at the same time, and then turned to the Mauler packs that had gathered.

As all attention went to Dio, Skoff stood off to the side and began a brief stomping dance. Terrabyss and the other Maulers knew what the shaman was doing—they had seen it every time the tribe had gathered to any degree—but both Dio and Luna were having a hard time not watching Skoff. Through this simple spell, Dio would be able to reach all ears with his words, so no one was too interested in watching the shaman beyond the introductions.

"Maulers, I know that you have been subject to many changes in the past moon. Before then, you had to make many changes from how you had lived in the Green Wall. For the past fifty years, you have survived

135

out here in this grove. You have not only proven to yourselves, but to the entire Green Wall, that you are both adaptive and resourceful. I want you all to know that I have not forgotten my promise to lead you back to the Green Wall. I have been in consultation with both the Elders and the Invasion Council, we have agreed that there should be no delay in our advance back to our homeland." The whole space erupted into howls and tails wagged enthusiastically, cheering for the Alpha. Dio waited a moment for the noise to die down before continuing. "To do this successfully, we must be unified, we have to be not just one tribe but one pack. To maintain this belief of being all one, I have decided that Rellik shall be spared her execution and shall not be branded a Lone Wolf." There was silence, the group was obviously done pretending that they were here for anything other than the opportunity to get their hands on the last living member of the Ballio pack. "As there is no objection to this... minor adjustment to our laws, we shall abide by my decision. So which pack is willing to accept Rellik, to treat her as one of their own?" He looked out at those packs who had come to participate in the adoption.

Several small outer packs who had felt that Haxzus was still the rightful Alpha—as he had actually been a Mauler—raised their hands. Some hands went down as others went up, weaker packs seeing stronger ones entering a bid and opting to not challenge them. They all wanted the same thing after all. Terrabyss couldn't help but wag his tail. Told you, Dio, he thought to himself.

"*Ahh,* and now the Ravis have entered a bid." Terrabyss looked around for a moment, Dio's statement catching him as much off guard as everyone else.

"Now Terrabyss, let's not play games. Once your hand goes up, you have to keep it up."

Terrabyss locked eyes with Dio. I hadn't even raised a finger, and even if I had, I could still back out.

It all made sense now; the conversations between Numa and Dio for the past few evenings. Her insistence that he be present for this adoption. One thing was for sure, their little scheme had just made this much more interesting. Terrabyss lifted his hand, holding his kanabo high and smiling as hand after hand dropped; no one was going to challenge the Ravis. Especially when it came to fighting Terrabyss, whether he had the weapon or not. He had proven that with Tarphyss. His gaze came to rest on the one hand that was still in the air.

Suskyss had been hoping this would happen. She was Oryss' sister, and some Watchers had reported back to her of their discovery of two separate pyres on which had burned the Watcher corpses. One that had been built about a half-day after the other. Since Oryss' pyre had not been built with much care, many had thought that someone from another Taur clan had done it to try to frame it as a Mauler-on-Mauler fight. Suskyss had heard many stories about her brother's job as a Watcher, and how he was not looking forward to having the runt from the Ravis pack in his Fist. How he was planning to put that runt in his place for all the stress the Ravis had put on the Ballios. The fight had definitely been Mauler on Mauler, but it had been that one Mauler that didn't respect the other, and she was going to change that. Suskyss was now the alpha of the Mallmee pack and she would regain their honor.

Terrabyss gave Suskyss a confused look; true they had not seen eye to eye earlier, but why did she really care where Rellik went? He wasn't even sure he knew her pack name, so it was plausible that she was loyal to Ballio, but she had been brown-nosing Dio so hard he was finding that hard to believe. Dio was also at a loss; he first looked to Skoff, then back to the two raised hands, and finally back to Skoff, who just shrugged in response.

"Well, as I said, we are becoming one, and there is nothing wrong with some friendly competition between those of differing opinions," Dio tried to reassure those gathered, or more reassure himself; he had no desire to lose either one of these Maulers.

"Oh, it won't be friendly," growled Suskyss in response. "I had hoped that being on the council would have allowed me to challenge you, Terrabyss. You murdered my brother Oryss! I worked hard to get close to you, figuring I could just upset you and earn a fair challenge. When I got a place on the council and learned you would be on it as well, I was ecstatic, but since that ball-less whelp over there won't let us settle council disputes the proper way, I needed to find a new way to get to you. Fortunately for me, you and your bitch sister brought the answer to me."

Those who had come to bid instantly made space for Suskyss and Terrabyss. Her eyes were burning with rage and her fur was on end. She was foaming slightly at the mouth from the excitement of finally getting her vengeance as she squared off with Terrabyss.

Dio wasn't sure what made him more upset; that she had called him a ball-less whelp or that Suskyss had befriended him just to get to Terrabyss. Terrabyss almost instantly saw the family resemblance as she mentioned Oryss, and had to chuckle for having not noticed it before.

"You are practically a clone of your brother, but I was always told by Oryss that he was the only one of his siblings who took up a profession. Were you a secret from him, or perhaps you chose to have a family?" He nodded. "No, I can tell you and he were close, by your expression, so you obviously have a litter. Go home to your pups. I won't fight a mother and a mate, and, just to clarify, it was a challenge and he lost." He turned away from Suskyss and looked to Dio, making it clear that he had no interest in this challenge.

Dio breathed a sigh of relief. *Good, my council members aren't going to fight, and we can move on with Rellik's adoption.* But Suskyss wasn't done.

"Oh, I don't need to be a professional to smear the Gathering with your blood, runt! Better tell your siblings they're going to need to burn another one tonight when I finish with you." Dio looked over in shock at Suskyss. She had to be crazy; he had seen Terrabyss fight Oryss, and both outweighed her.

Terrabyss stopped trying to ignore her and he turned, squaring up to her. "I don't want some pups or some mate to come crying to me because I beat your skull in like I did your brother's. If you go through with this, that is what is going to happen."

Dio noticed something very different and unsettling about Terrabyss' response. It was calm and collected, he wasn't driven by passion, anger or any other emotion, which made him all the more intimidating, at least to Dio.

"How did I never notice what a killer he was before?" Dio murmured to himself, but made no moves to stop the challenge. He honestly couldn't, no matter how much he wanted to and no matter the authority that came with his position, some things were just out of his control.

"Save your warnings!" spat Suskyss. "You don't scare me and I will just attack you anyway. No one gathered here is going to let you leave until this is settled." As if to hammer home her point, the circle let out a growl, showing their teeth.

"Not a lot of Maulers would go through this much trouble to plan their own funeral," Terrabyss said, still calm, but not dropping his eyes from Suskyss and waiting for her to make the first move.

Dio knew he could do nothing now other than legitimize the challenge. As he opened his mouth to speak, Suskyss lost patience. She rushed forward, trying to take Terrabyss off guard as he still hadn't lowered his hand or his kanabo. Howls of excitement erupted from those gathered as Terrabyss dropped his weapon in a rapid downward arc across his chest, intending to catch Suskyss face-first as she charged. She read the attack, and quickly sidestepped, putting her on the outside of the weapon now. With sudden speed and power, Terrabyss raised the kanabo up with a single hand, reversing his previous trajectory. Suskyss was not prepared for that and she barely caught sight of the weapon as it swung back toward her shoulder. She just managed to get under the kanabo, but before she could recover from her dodge, Terrabyss' left fist caught her square in the chest. She skidded back, coughing, as she tried to gather her wits.

No words were exchanged and Terrabyss didn't immediately follow up his attack. He needed to get both hands on his weapon if he wanted to control it; that little display had almost dislocated his right shoulder again. The bravado had an effect, and Suskyss was hesitant to run back in, especially now that he seemed to be taking the fight seriously. She motioned for those gathered to make some space, needing more room to work around Terrabyss' deadly kanabo. The two of them lunged at one another again, crashing headlong, but neither one gave up any ground. Suskyss managed to catch Terrabyss' side swing, her hands heavily calloused from constant heavy work. She was obviously skilled and practiced at moving on all fours and her arm muscles were over-developed. Suskyss' hand was bleeding slightly from the sharp spikes on the kanabo, but she didn't seem fazed.

Terrabyss growled, caught off guard by her strength as she succeeded where her brother had failed. He tried to yank the weapon free of her grasp, Suskyss easily read his intention and released the kanabo with a shove, sending him spinning like a top. She followed immediately; with blurring speed she appeared on Terrabyss' left flank and her teeth bit into his shoulder as he struggled to regain his balance. A sudden shock of pain ran up his flank and Terrabyss howled in agony and surprise as Suskyss raked her claws along his left side. Terrabyss twisted his neck to try to bite her face, since she was too close for his weapon to be effective. His jaw snapped around nothing as she had already moved; she knew that Terrabyss was probably far too muscular for her bite to get in deep. She was looking for a weak spot to strike. She decided to focus more on wearing him down, slamming a paw into the back of his calf and raking her claws down his leg. Another growl escaped Terrabyss, and he fell forward, catching himself with his weapon before hitting the ground face-first. Suskyss wasn't done, she sprinted forward and jumped up, using all of her body weight to slam into Terrabyss' back to ram him into the frozen floor. Terrabyss let go of his kanabo, not wanting to risk having his shoulder dislocated again, but managed to plant both hands to stop Suskyss from body slamming him into the dirt. Suskyss felt him stop her, so she slipped her arm under his neck and yanked back, lifting Terrabyss back to his knees. She kept pulling back, trying to snap his spine as he clawed frantically, trying to get either his weapon or her arm in a position to free himself.

Suskyss felt Terrabyss get a grip on her wrist and needed to gain control of the flow of combat once again. She quickly found it; flexing her arm, she pulled her wrist and Terrabyss' head back away from his hand, and, in the same motion, planted her knee directly into the small of his back with all the force she could muster. "Everyone will remember this evening, the evening the runt of the Ravis pack was sent to the stars by a Mallmee!" Suskyss snarled in his ear, pushing her knee forward and pulling his neck back.

"...dun... snp... sy... " was all Terrabyss managed to get out as she applied more pressure to his neck.

Why in Alpha Father's name had she not been a Scout, or a Guard at the very least? She is so damn strong, and obviously battle-hardened. That last thought made Terrabyss very uncomfortable. How dangerous is she if she isn't scarred, but is this experienced in combat? He felt her grip his muzzle and begin twisting, trying another tactic than suffocation. Terrabyss slammed his elbow as hard as he could manage into her ribs, but it was like hitting a glacier. Her muscles and bones barely protested under the impact; without air, his attacks were losing all their power.

"Wha—?" Suskyss leaned in to ask.

Thank the Alpha Father that the Mallmee are too arrogant for their own good, Terrabyss thought, thrusting his head back as she started to lean in. All Suskyss could manage was that 'Wha' before he connected with her sensitive muzzle. She cried out in both pain and surprise as he managed to hit her square in the nose, and Terrabyss felt her arms slacken in response. Terrabyss shook his head as he managed to free his mouth and bit Suskyss' thumb clean off, spitting it into the snow in front of him. Suskyss howled in pain and let go of his neck, quickly shuffling back to avoid the elbow that he launched back at her ribs with new vigor.

Terrabyss snatched up his kanabo as Suskyss tried to make space between the two of them. "I said, I don't snap easy," Terrabyss clarified as he spun to face her, grasping the weapon higher on the grip so that he could attack faster. The blows would be less powerful, but he would have to match her speed if he wanted to win. "You're a good fighter, better than Oryss ever was," he taunted Suskyss. He wasn't lying, and he would have liked to have fought alongside her rather than against her. But neither one of them was going to submit.

Again, the two closed the gap almost in unison, but this time Terrabyss' speed caught Suskyss off guard. She hardly registered the blur as the weapon collided with her left ribs. She didn't have enough time to fully brace for the hit, and her flank took the brunt of the blow. She spun a quarter turn, but still hit the snow hard, struggling to catch her breath. Her ribs were definitely broken, and there was a loud crunch as the kanabo slammed into the back of her skull. Her head shattered like a rotten melon. There was a perfectly-timed crack of thunder—as though the Alpha Father was applauding—as Suskyss' headless body slumped into the gore that puddled around her knees.

Terrabyss turned toward the crowd that stared, transfixed.

"Well, is there another Mallmee?" he asked the crowd and pointed his kanabo at them, brains and blood dripping off the spikes. The crowd stayed silent, but parted around a smaller version of Oryss and Suskyss. She was not quite as dark-furred as they had been, and the fur on the top of her head was in small tight braids, like how Skoff did his tail.

Terrabyss looked directly at her. "I guess that makes you the new alpha of the Mallmee pack. Do you challenge the Ravis bid of adoption for Rellik?"

Gentra didn't hesitate to shake her head no, and she even threw in a submissive salute for good measure. Terrabyss then posed the same question to all those gathered. Dio looked on with mixed feelings; it had become obvious that Suskyss had not been the most loyal of advisors. He was struggling with the idea that many Maulers seemed completely loyal to him, but thought of him as nothing more than a, well, a whelp. He was also upset with Terrabyss, because Dio hadn't hidden the fact that he wanted neither of them dead and now Suskyss was far beyond recovery. All of these emotions actually stemmed from one thing; Dio didn't feel like he was in control. He felt like the Ravis pack was in control, and he had unwittingly allowed them to be. The Ravis he honestly feared the most was Numa; Terrabyss just didn't seem that ambitious and Skoff seemed perfectly content to be shaman. Numa's point about her pack having too good a name to discard for Ballio suddenly felt more like a threat than a fact.

The Raid

Dio remained at the Gathering with some of the warriors, to watch over the families of those who stayed behind and to keep up preparations for the march into the Green Wall. Food needed to be gathered from every pack's hanging stores, placed in communal storage, and new supplies gathered from the few animals that had come out of hibernation a little before the spring arrived. Dio wished them all well, and now the group of thirty pups was escorted by a group of sixty different fighters, made up of Scouts, Hunters, Watchers, and Guards. Leading the juveniles who would participate in the Hunt was the Prime Hunter, Maxyss. Terrabyss had been appointed as commander of the sixty warriors, much to their indignation and his surprise, but Dio had asked him to do it so no one was outwardly complaining. Dio trusted that Terrabyss would complete the raid, given his penchant for combat, and also keep his daughter safe, who was there to represent the Alpha and his wishes.

Dio hadn't officially chosen a second and because he had no mate, it was assumed that Luna was going to fill that position the same way Haxzus had for Grimmis. There was still a lot about Mauler culture that she had to learn, so she always accompanied Terrabyss, who had become somewhat of a tutor to her. They had developed a strong connection and had both come to appreciate each other's talents. Luna had a way of calming Terrabyss, and he had a way of bringing out her inner Silverback nature, helping her recapture what the other tribes had lost, repressed under the Ozars' domination. They walked with Skoff, who was somewhat begrudging even though it was his duty to perform such tasks.

In past years, it had been enough for the Alpha who went on every Hunt to officiate the new adults. This year, since the Alpha would not actually be joining the juveniles and had a representative in his stead, Dio had thought it prudent to send another Mauler with authoritative power. Now, after three days' march to where the grove and the tundra collided, Terrabyss, Maxyss, and Luna were tired of Skoff's constant griping and complaining. The first day's pace was too brisk. The following day was too slow, and this morning everyone was too quick to pack up camp, but Skoff had yelled at everyone about how slow they were to get up and get going. There was truly no pleasing him and everything was a chore, even when he was doing nothing.

Late in the afternoon on the third day, the group crept up almost silently to the edge of the grove. Luna and Skoff had remained twenty or so lue back into the grove. Not because of Luna's lack of stealth—as had been the case with Skoff—but because the shaman hadn't liked the idea of being alone this close to the Corm. Terrabyss was replaying the conversation over in his mind. He was going to make sure Skoff never heard the end of his cowardice.

Luna now stood next to Skoff as they waited for the others to return. The sun was setting earlier and earlier in the day as they got further and further north, and now even though it was still afternoon, the sky was painting an evening masterpiece of reds, yellows, oranges, and purples. Luna had been curious about something, but Terrabyss had never given her a completely straight answer. She wanted to know about the events of his Hunt and the importance of claiming a kill, and Skoff was just sitting on an icy rock and grumbling as he mashed a ball of snow together and popped it into his mouth to suck on.

"Skoff, do you mind if I ask you something?" she asked politely, not wanting the shaman to go into some tirade about how she was ruining the wonderful silence. She thought she had failed to avoid that as he slowly turned to face her, smacking his lips together as he slurped away at his ice ball. It was one of the few times Luna actually wished she didn't have such a curious nature. She was so relieved when he didn't start berating her that she almost forgot to ask her question. Fortunately, she remembered, because nothing would have made the shaman angrier than if she had interrupted the precious silence and then not had anything worth saying.

"I was curious why getting the kill is so important in a Hunt, and why it led to such a brutal quarrel between Terrabyss and your brother?"

Skoff stared at her and then spit out the ice ball. "Well, it is important to have the privilege of taking down the quarry, because it gives you first pick of what you would like to choose as a profession if you are going to go that route, or increases your family's prestige for Materimony."

Luna looked at him confused. "But those are already your options."

She obviously didn't understand what he meant by first pick.

"Yes, but not everyone wants to work in the middle of winter, or summer for that matter. Also, the more connected your pack is with an elder, or Alpha, or shaman, the more benefits for that pack. For example, the Ravis pack is involved now in two councils, and heavily represented in both, so there is a lot of weight to our name. Few would challenge such a prestigious and well-connected pack." Skoff's tail was wagging, obviously Luna had found a topic the shaman was more than willing to discuss.

"Okay, I think I understand it, but that doesn't answer my question about what happened between Terrabyss and his brother," Luna persisted. She had heard enough hints to understand that they had gotten into a challenge over who brought down the kill, but outside of that and the deadly outcome for Tarphyss, she knew very little.

Skoff's tail twitched nervously; he had hoped to distract her from the tale by giving in-depth and interesting insight into the workings of honor and prestige in their culture and society. It obviously had not, and he honestly wasn't sure if he was the best to tell this story. Not because he was a bad storyteller, but because he was too good. Skoff was worried that because of his magnificent and well-practiced ability of public speaking, he would mislead Luna into thinking that one of his siblings had been in the right and the other had been in the wrong. Tarphyss had simply bitten off more than he could chew, and Terrabyss made that fact very obvious.

"Well, where to begin? Depending on the source of the story, it may seem that Terrabyss was defending his kill, others may make it appear that Tarphyss was simply defending his claim from a greedy runt—"

"I have heard both of those impressions, but I feel like you might tell me the truth of the matter," Luna interjected, trying to keep Skoff from straying too far from her original question.

Skoff didn't like being interrupted, but he did like having his ego inflated and Luna's reference to his 'truth on the matter' sent his tail slightly thumping.

"Well, that was a wise decision on your part." He couldn't help himself, and he was being honest, she was obviously 'very intelligent.' He motioned for her to take a seat as he stood, psyching himself up as he always did before one of his stories.

"It was mid-spring and the snow had almost vanished from the grove. There were still some deep patches under the shady canopy that kept the sun from melting away the last evidence of the winter. The Scouts, who at the time reported to Scout Mother Rymmall, came to the Gathering and informed Haxzus that a large herd of caribou were heading up to the tundra for the summer grasses that appear for a few months. As is customary, Haxzus sent Scouts to the outer packs to gather all their pups and the inner grove packs sent their pups to participate in the Hunt. Our mother, Bia, was sure we were all ready for our Hunt and immediately notified the Alpha that we would be competing. Since our litter, like all, was less than five, the Barchus' runt was made to join us. All packs must be five, so pups are added from other litters, or adoptees. If one member of a pack doesn't get recognized as an adult, they try again the next year as a member of a different pack. The alpha Hunter selects whose pack they will join. Tarphyss was angry that we now had two runts, as most die in the Hunt or afterwards from their injuries, and he thought we would be at a disadvantage. Bia was never one to let Terrabyss' life be constrained by how others saw him, and though she adamantly denied it publicly, she privately encouraged him not to let his status as a runt limit his life or his future."

"Really? Terrabyss always makes her sound tough as nails," Luna interrupted before she could stop herself.

Skoff gave her a growl but otherwise ignored her outburst and continued; this wasn't a discussion on parenting but on the challenge between Tarphyss and Terrabyss.

"As I was saying, our mother signed us up without even checking to be sure we were ready." Luna thought to herself that Skoff was probably the only one who was upset that their mother hadn't asked them before signing them up. "Proof that Terrabyss does not exaggerate her overbearing persona." He was sure that would answer her annoying questions, and would be the last improvisation to the story he needed to perform. "The Scouts led our alpha Hunter, Hanora, and our beta Hunter, Maxyss, and all us pups to where the herd would cross through the grove to get out into the tundra." He suddenly crouched down low to the ground. "We squatted down in the snow, with the wind howling as it smacked us in the face to blow our scent clear of the migrating caribou. Our eyes were so dry that we feared they would shrivel right out of our skulls." Skoff shook violently, adding a little air magic to his performance to give visual representation to his explanation. "Three days came and went, some of our fur solidified in this unrelenting wind, which Numa can attest to this very day." Skoff motioned to an absent Numa, but didn't skip a beat despite her not being there. "In a panic of excitement, a Scout came rushing to where we waited in ambush and signaled to us that our prey, seemingly unaware, was approaching the trap. Immediately, pack after pack stood to their hands and paws, stretching out the lethargy and shaking off the cold. Each one watched in hushed silence for the first of the caribou to run by. We hid amongst the trees or in the snow banks that were still deep enough. Their forward scout trotted into where we lay in ambush, you could see the breath steaming from its nose as it looked and listened to be sure that it was safe for the rest of the herd to come. We were all nervous now; every moment that caribou snorted and danced back and forth, shaking its head and pawing at the floor felt like an eternity, and more than one of us was having to tell ourselves to hold still." Skoff paced back and forth, shaking his body as though he were uneasy about something nearby. "Finally, when we all thought we could wait no more, the creature gave no alarm, and began running forward. The silence that followed its departure was fleeting, and a rumbling began to rise up from the southwest." He turned on point to the direction he had indicated, his rapid tail wagging came to a standstill as his ears pricked forward.

"The rumbling grew in intensity." As did the volume of Skoff's voice. "Our hearts beat with the sound of the hooves hammering across the grove's floor. From within the trees, the largest and fittest of the Caribou barreled through the low branches. Most of the males had shed their antlers the previous fall and were starting to grow them back as the spring had taken hold. The females still had large multi-branch racks that made them a very dangerous target this time of year. We waited anxiously; we had thought we were being tortured having to wait so long for the animals to arrive. It was much more agony to have to wait for the majority of the herd to run past, then, with a mighty howl, we sprinted out from our hideouts on either side of the caribou and tried to panic them, so that we could pick off the younger ones in the center or the older and lame ones on the outskirts or rear of the herd. Each pack went into action, competing against the other packs but also trying to collaborate enough that the majority of us would succeed and survive. Our pack came charging down on the rear right flank, along with another pack. The runt in that pack, Nayla" – Skoff gave an 'obviously' expression before continuing – "got yanked into the herd. She was trampled to death in moments, but her arrival did throw a small group of the herd off course to the right. Tarphyss frantically ordered us to drop back with it; claiming that he had seen one of the males limping. It had probably injured itself while colliding with Nayla." Skoff emphasized his point as he began limping on his right—and sometimes left—leg, depending on which one was closer to Luna. "Terrabyss had caught sight of some other target, and when we were about to take down the male that Tarphyss had chased down, we couldn't see the runt anywhere. We concluded that what had happened to Nayla had happened to Terrabyss." Skoff leapt back to his paws, after having slowly sat down as he talked about not being able to locate his brother. "But our brother was not finished, and he had not been trampled. The story was revealed to us later, in a far less interesting manner, mind you, that our brother had run and run until his lungs were going to burst from his chest. He had spotted another older female; she had a full set of antlers but she wasn't putting her full weight on her front left hoof. Terrabyss used all the endurance he had left, now alone against such a powerful beast. His teeth snapped into her back left leg, intentionally trying to weaken the legs on the same side so that the animal would collapse onto the ground, or just give up altogether."

Skoff had been working his way over toward Luna as he described his brother chasing the caribou down, and when he snapped his jaws to emphasize Terrabyss' attack, they clamped within a whisker of her face. She tried not to flinch, but she couldn't stop herself from reflexively jumping back as he suddenly bit down. Skoff had her completely engrossed in his reenactment of the event.

"The beast kicked back and hit Terrabyss on the left side of his collar," Skoff popped himself in the same area and tumbled backward dramatically. "It was such a foolish creature." Skoff seemed to rise from the ground without using his arms to lever himself back up. "It would take far more than that to stop a Mauler. Terrabyss lunged back after the creature as it hobbled weakly, trying to find some last bit of energy to save its doomed life. Another snap." This time, Skoff clapped his arms and hands together. Again, Luna berated herself for not having expected it and having flinched away from the crack of the colliding limbs. "This time, he had found his mark, the tendon of the creature was snapped in two. The creature cried in desperation as it tried to support itself, but could only slide onto its side and struggle to try and find its balance once again. Terrabyss jumped atop the lame creature, to get to its throat and finish the job quickly, but the caribou was not done fighting and it swung those impressive antlers back at him, to wound or perhaps even blind its predator."

Skoff bounded up, coming down hard, and began biting and clawing at an invisible carcass that Luna had no trouble conjuring to mind. As Skoff swung his body back and forth, she could see the antlers raking across Terrabyss' face or chest, as he ducked or leaned out of the way of the dangerous weapons.

"Alone, Terrabyss fought the creature, never backing down from the desperate thrashing of the much larger beast. The caribou had shown themselves close to noon and it was now becoming evening. The blood on the snow blended with the red in the sky as the two fought on, both locked in a life-or-death struggle. With a mighty howl, Terrabyss planted his hands against the creature's antlers; he pushed back using everything that he had held in reserve. Terrabyss knew he had to finish this because he would not be able to keep warding off the sharp antlers. Slowly, the caribou's neck craned back, it was a small opening, and Terrabyss had to take it. He suddenly let go and dove forward, trying to bring his jaws down on the creature's barely exposed neck. He tasted the warm blood as it flooded his mouth, it was like drinking iron he said, and the caribou's life force gushed out as he tore away the creature's throat. He had won!" Skoff collapsed down on the ground, sitting with his head between his legs. He lifted his head slowly, turning to the imaginary place where he had battled the invisible caribou. "Now, Terrabyss needed to get it back, to show as proof of his success. Terrabyss" – and Skoff – "rose to his paws, he wrapped his strong grip around each antler and began to drag the creature back to where the temporary camp had been established, just a few hundred lue east of the ambush site."

Skoff kept marching in place while seeming to drag a heavy burden across the ground before he stopped and pretended to drop the load. "He finally appeared in camp late that night. It was assumed that everyone who had survived had already returned, and most of the new adults were lounging about with full stomachs from the large feast held after the Hunt. At first, Haxzus tried to deny Terrabyss the title of adult, saying that he 'had not turned in his kill within the designated time.' Terrabyss, was not so convinced, nor were several others. This previously unmentioned rule would change the way the Hunt would be conducted going forward.

This was a point that even Maxyss was willing to challenge Hanora over, which was a pretty good indication to Haxzus that he had overstepped. As agreement seemed about to be reached, there was another voice that contributed to the debate. Our brother, Tarphyss, the alpha of our litter, claimed that he had wounded that same creature when they had first set the caribou into chaos. He had supposed that the creature would be too difficult a target, with its large rack, and had opted to take down the male that was also injured. Had he known that the creature was so badly hurt, he would have gone after it. Haxzus again declared that Terrabyss' kill was unearned, because he could not qualify as an adult by finding a creature that another had brought almost to death and claim it as his own." With a violent motion, Skoff pretended to throw the invisible carcass that he had been dragging into what Luna could only assume would have been a fire. Her assumption was confirmed, when out of thin air, a large gout of flame shot upward and then vanished. Skoff let his tail lift up confidently as he watched her enchanted expression.

"Terrabyss shouted in a rage that this was not the case, and that Tarphyss was trying to rob him of his rightful rewards of not only becoming an adult, but also getting either first choice or a title of prestige."

Luna felt the question coming, she tried to swallow it down. It was no use. "What is a title of prestige?" Her ears drooped as she tucked her tail slightly in apology. "Sorry, please continue. I am just so fascinated; I cannot help but want to learn more and I can't control my questions when you are so skillful at explaining." She wasn't lying about how interested she was, she may have overdone her compliments, but Skoff loved the flattery.

Skoff's face twisted up as though he were going to chastise her, but smoothed over as he basked in her attention. "A title of prestige is… how to explain? It's the ability to make your own pack, for example. First among the trade families, first among the rationed families, things like that." He could see his last few examples had lost her again, he sighed very dramatically, obviously not enjoying the diversion. "The first pack allowed to trade with the Ramsyn. The first pack to choose from the food rations if their hunts were unsuccessful. Things of that nature." He cleared his throat again excitedly as Luna nodded her understanding and signaling that he could continue.

"Terrabyss threw the kill on the fire in a rage," he muttered to himself. "That's right!" he shouted, having remembered where he was in his story.

"If Tarphyss did anything other than use the sacrifice of Nayla to his own advantage, it was minimal.'" Skoff paused, mimicking Terrabyss exceptionally well, for dramatic effect. As Luna felt the urge to speak, Skoff immediately talked over her. "'To my kill.'" Skoff pointed back emphatically to where he had thrown the invisible caribou. "'I bit its hind-leg, I took the kick to my collar and still chased it down and snapped its tendons, not you, Tarphyss. The kill is mine, Haxzus!' Terrabyss howled at the top of his lungs, the challenge was issued and accepted."

Luna listened in fascination; runts weren't exclusive to the Maulers, the Eclupse also had runts even if they had fewer pups per litter. The common practice that she had grown up with was to care for each pup equally. The Ozars had done so well in killing them off that they had no desire to help them in their endeavors. Runts hadn't been bad luck, or a curse that had been placed on them by the Alpha Father, they were just typically smaller. She remembered Altz and her mother Luma as she lowered her head, and although still listening to Skoff, she had lost much of the energy she had originally shown.

"Are you telling her how Tarphyss learned that I wasn't the runt he thought I was?" Luna jumped as she heard Terrabyss' deep voice, he and Maxyss—who Luna now realized was there as well—strode back into camp, having finished scouting and figuring out how they were going to attack the Corm and their mammoths.

Skoff had become used to Luna's compliments that had followed her interruptions and he was not so quick with his retort.

"Well, I need to know how likely it is that this Hunt may have challenges, and how those challenges might be resolved without senseless murder," Luna huffed. Skoff needn't worry about his brother getting away without some humiliation for his brazen rudeness.

Terrabyss' ears drooped slightly as he looked over at Luna. "A challenge was made and accepted, at that point neither one of us was going to back down. We had grown far beyond that stage in our lives." That was as good a reason as she was probably going to get. "Besides," Terrabyss continued, "this Hunt will probably be relatively non-competitive. At least to one another," he said with a slight wag to his tail. "Also, since we are leaving as your father claims, there will be no bid or relative prestige to go along with being the ones to take down a kill. The position will not be so hotly contested between the juveniles."

By now, Maxyss had dragged Skoff away and the two of them had begun dividing the pups into teams of five, the Silverbacks' sacred number.

"Why did you kill him?" Luna asked Terrabyss, making sure to not let him look away. "He was part of your pack, your brother."

"I was a runt, and no one let me forget it, especially Tarphyss. He would have done everything in his power to make sure that I remained a pup. It was all he ever talked about, how he was going to make me an eternal pup. When he tried to claim my kill and Haxzus was willing to enforce it, I proved to them, to all of them, that I was not a runt, or a pup any longer, and no one could assume otherwise. We are a culture of opposites, and the contrasts are proof of the others' existence. The weak affirm the strong, so the alpha needs the runts for their existence to be validated. My brother always felt challenged by any of my successes." Luna stayed quiet, processing the information. Terrabyss took this as his cue to start a new topic. "So, good news is, there is plenty of game for the pups to hunt."

Luna was dragged from her reflection at the sudden jump in subject matter. "What? Okay, why start with good news though?" She tilted her head in a befuddled fashion, as she was now very lost with the whole conversation.

"Well, because there is some bad news as well. Culture of opposites," he reminded her gently as he waited for her to catch up.

"Do I ask what the bad news is? Or were you just going to tell me?" Luna wondered aloud.

"Well, now I am going to tell you because now you asked, but customarily, yes, you ask what the bad news is. It seems that because the mammoth had such a productive year, there are more shepherds to help protect the beasts. There are easily over twenty."

Terrabyss shrugged as he watched Maxyss gathering the juveniles together to divide them into their packs. This year, there was no guarantee that family units would remain together. It was an idea that Dio had put forward before the group had left, and as Terrabyss watched the lots being drawn, he felt that it was fair.

"We should join the rest of them, things are about to get interesting." He hefted his kanabo with a big smile, and didn't wait for Luna's response before he jogged over to where the pups were gathered.

"What does that mean for the fighters under your command? Does that change your plan of attack?" she called after him, sprinting to catch up. She easily got to him in two lue, having become much better at shifting to all fours, and her long limbs meant she could outrun most of the Maulers without any difficulty.

Terrabyss slowed as she caught up to him. He didn't even know why he tried to outrun her any more, especially on two legs. "We still outnumber them, so we will hit them hard and make them run."

"Terrabyss, stop!" she commanded as she heard the awful tactic.

Terrabyss was surprised at how his body instantly responded to the authority in her tone, and came to a complete stop. He looked over at the pups who were now almost done being split into packs and then looked back at Luna, who had marched to face him.

"You seriously think that is the best plan of attack?" she scolded, trying to discipline Terrabyss but also not make it too obvious to those gathered, she respected him too much for that.

Terrabyss had started bending an ear to her instructions, and even though her tone sometimes grated on him, he appreciated her respect for him. His silence was all the permission she needed to explain to him a better tactic.

"You should send in a group of thirty or so, have them agitate the camp, and then run to the east. The Corm will give chase, thinking that they can overcome almost equal numbers. When the shepherds take off after the first assault group, then the second group runs in, puts out the camp's fires. There will probably be a few Corm left in camp, let them raise the alarm. It will pull the ones following the first group back to the camp. Now, this is important, allow the Corm to get back to camp, but the first group is going to stalk them as they run back in a panic to save their camp. Then both groups have pinned the shepherds, and you can snap down on them like a maw." She gave Terrabyss a confident look, and he had to admit that it sounded like a good plan. All except that now he was going to have to go and cast lots—like Maxyss had for the juveniles—to divide his unit up. Still, her idea was worth that inconvenience and so he turned back toward the assault team.

"Where are you going?" she inquired as he turned his back to her and began walking the other direction.

"To cast lots among the attacking force" – he shook his bag of teeth, a small leather pouch that contained a mixture of normal and black-painted animal teeth – "so that we can be divided into two groups, per your suggestion." He called out over his shoulder. "Perhaps you should come with me to make sure that I explain it to them correctly!" he teased as she sprinted after him, easily catching up to his slower pace.

Soon, the commands had been given and the groups had been divided into their units. This was followed by some downtime while they waited for the Corm to turn in for the night. Both the adults and juveniles took the opportunity to sleep or relax before the night's events began. Terrabyss spent the evening going over the signals with his group, and appointing a second to lead the diversion group into the camp and then back when they either saw the Corm retreating, or heard the signal from the camp. Terrabyss needed someone who could control the group and who understood the tactic well enough to execute it with no complications. He had chosen a Mauler by the name of Attaboye, a retired Watcher; he was older, nearer to Maxyss' age, and his fur that was once smokey-black was now mostly smokey in color. His intense, bronze-colored eyes showed his intelligence as he kept his gaze on Terrabyss, giving the young commander his full attention.

Luna watched the attack group especially closely, whose two units were now paying close attention to Terrabyss as he went over his signals.

"Ears forward then backward is the signal to get into position. When you see the next Maulers' ears go flat, you know it is time to charge. Copy the signal so that the message makes it all the way to either flank, then rush in. Remember, no looting or unnecessary risks; we need this to go smoothly so think on your paws and don't get slowed down."

Luna was getting better at understanding the Mauler's body language and their way of speaking, which used not only facial expressions and hand movements, but also pacing. The last was the hardest for her to learn. All the nuances of half-steps, double lefts and rights, half and full turns, and steps between turns, oh and she had almost forgotten stepping forward and backward as opposed to side to side, while including all the above patterns resulted in completely different meaning. She felt that Numa's example of how it worked was still best, "If I make a serpentine walk while going side to side, we are going to the river; if I did it front to back, it represents going to the mountains. If I do both of these backward instead of forward, it means coming from instead of going to." That alone had taken Luna a few days to remember, *especially because if they turn fully around and do the same pattern, back it means forest, as well as something about trust.*

"Well, it looks like they are off to start the raid." Luna was pulled from her thoughts as she heard Skoff. She realized that the groups were already mostly gone from the small base camp the Silverbacks had chosen. It was nothing special, but it was well protected from the wind by a row of tightly growing sequoias that stood strong against the Banshee's endless wailings. This line curved around on both flanks, making a good size bowl for the troop to camp down in. The snow here was especially thick, because the tight clump of trees that made the shelter also held out the sun's rays, making the base surprisingly cold even without the wind. Skoff was walking with his staff, and he wore a wolf skull, at least it looked like one, that was painted bright yellow, and a surprisingly undecorated deep-black poncho.

"I thought black and yellow were colors of sorrow, the loss of a pack name and all?" Luna commented as Skoff joined her, the last few stragglers of the two groups had left a few moments prior. He looked at her, surprised that he was going to even have to say it. "Opposites," she nodded dryly. "I understand, never mind."

***

Attaboye watched the Corm night sentries as they nodded off every now and then, jerking awake and often startling the one next to them—who was now dozing off—back to consciousness. The Scouts hadn't exaggerated the size of these Mino, every single one was head and shoulders above the Maulers, and had to weigh twice as much as most of them, if not more. They were wearing clothing, but given how thick their long fur was, Attaboye was sure the cloth wasn't to help keep them warm. The clothing had a linothorax design, completely covering their chests and stomachs. They had stout hide shields that were almost the length of their body, and were designed for deflecting attacks, rather than blocking. Each Corm shepherd carried a small, half-height spear that was made from a single iron piece. It had a long, leaf-like tip that could both cut and stab, and a small, smooth ball at the opposite end, for clubbing and to serve as a counterweight when throwing the weapon. It also appeared that under the shield they held another one or two of the weapons. Looped around the arm that held the shield was a leather thong that probably served as a sling, and they had

155

a small skinning knife attached to the small of their backs. As the group of Maulers got closer, Attaboye signaled first by moving his ears forward and then backward, the signal was repeated down either flank. By the time each end received the signal, they were a few steps in front of the lead Mauler, in this case, Attaboye. Each end then mimicked the signal back, and when Attaboye received the signal from both his left and right, he knew that everyone was in the right position. He dropped down to all fours, his right hand patted the ground a single time, two times, three, four, and then on the fifth his ears went flat, and the first assault group rushed in. As each Mauler to his left and right followed, they also flattened their ears, sending the signal to the flanks. Even if the flanks heard or saw the others charge, they were instructed to wait until they received the signal. This had been intentional; in this way, the Maulers hit the camp in a wedge formation, with Attaboye spearheading the charge.

Tents and shelters collapsed on the sleeping shepherds, as torches were knocked over and provisions were trampled in the panic. Some of the Corm simply ripped from their tents, just holding their spears and snorting in rage, trying to find who had ambushed them. One Mauler was taken by surprise when a Corm roared to life before him and shredded his shelter to pieces in a fit of anger. The Mauler tried to lunge into the Corm that had just appeared, only to be caught by the throat and gutted by the spear. Others did better. The Mauler to the left of Attaboye collided with the surprised sentry, clawing and biting at the Corm's face and neck. Rolling away, the Mauler was covered in blood that wasn't her own and she charged forward, leaving a throatless sentry in the snow. Attaboye had been a good choice; his howl kept the troops in line as they lingered but for a moment to spread chaos through the shepherds' ranks.

The Corm didn't need much encouragement to rally together and give chase to the Maulers. Shouts went from tent to tent as fewer of the Corm were taken by surprise, and the Silverbacks were forced to break off from attacking the camp in order to run into the tundra to the east. Behind them, the Corm thundered in rage, bellowing curses; with a few skidding to a stop to lob a spear or hurl a stone at the retreating Maulers.

Terrabyss crept up to Attaboye's starting position. He controlled the bulk of the troop, having kept forty of the warriors and given Attaboye control of the other twenty. This had been decided because if Attaboye wasn't successful in pulling the Corm out of the camp, Terrabyss would still outnumber the shepherds. Also, because it would be easier for a smaller unit to outrun the Corm pursuers. His division crouched down and waited for the chaos in the camp to die down. Terrabyss' attack was going to be rather different than Attaboye's. As they got to the edge of the trees, he gave the same signal with his ears that Attaboye had, to create the same spear formation, with Terrabyss at the center. The troop watched as a few Corm that had stayed back appeared and began to repair the collapsed shelters and re-light the fires or re-position the torches. As soon as Terrabyss was convinced they were focused on rebuilding their campsite, he let out a long howl. For just a moment, the tundra was hushed into silence, holding its breath as the new, ominous sound drowned out the wind.

The Corm hustled to defend, several of them trumpeting into hollowed-out horns. Terrabyss wondered if the horns had been their ancestors'. The howl launched the other forty Maulers into the disorganized camp. The flanks hit first this time, as intended; this time, the center consisted of many of the combat veterans, and Terrabyss. When the center collided with the camp to support the less-experienced flanks, the Corm were hit by a wave of ferocity they had never experienced. To their credit, the Corm made a quick and strong defense, given the circumstances. A fire to the far left was put out. *Good, that means the left flank is moving forward with little problem.* To Terrabyss' right, the fires weren't diminishing; in fact, he would swear they were increasing. Either the Maulers were looting, or they were experiencing more resistance than initially supposed. Terrabyss rounded up four Maulers to move with him, he ordered the others to keep clearing the center and to check all the tents for any Corm stragglers who might come up behind them. The center was to keep moving until it collided with the returning shepherds and pinned the Corm between them and Attaboye's unit.

Terrabyss then split off with his four and they moved over to the right side, checking tents so that they wouldn't fall victim to a rear assault. They were probably only a dozen or so lue from where he had seen the largest fire dance back to life, when to his left—less than a lue from him—another large sentry fire roared back up. Terrabyss motioned for the rest of the Fist to follow him, and they immediately turned to where the fire was now playing with the shadows that tried to gather round it. They snuck up to the tents that surrounded the fire, peering around the edges of the shelters. The tents were conical, with four large bones that had been laced together at the top and spread out at the bottom to provide a base for the structure. The material that made up the tent itself was mammoth's hide, and it had been shaped to fit snugly over the supports. The Fist had to steel their nerves, somewhat intimidated by what they saw at the fire. Two Maulers had been burnt into husks, and had broken apart as they fell to the snowy ground. The other three looked like they had been killed before being added to the fire as fuel, but the new group couldn't be sure. They couldn't see who had overcome this Fist though, and they took a moment to have a quick sniff around, hoping to locate an enemy hidden somewhere nearby. All they could smell was the slain bodies and the burning flesh of their comrades. Terrabyss sent two under the back of the tent to his right, and the other two under the tent to his left. He would rush the third tent across from them by himself. They all nodded their understanding, and he took five deep breaths before he motioned for them to go. Nomi and Vockyss went into the tent on the right; they both gave out yelps of surprise as something grabbed them by their haunches, hurling Vockyss out through the opening. She landed with a thud in front of Terrabyss and he skidded to a halt; she seemed okay other than having gotten the wind knocked out of her, and he quickly helped her up. There was another thump beside the two of them as Nomi landed next to them, lifeless as blood gushed from under her ribs where she had been skewered by an iron spear.

Snard and Groth—who had been retired Watchers—had rejoined at the idea of being able to fight in battles to retake the Green Wall. They had already gone under the tent flap to the left before they heard the yelps from the right tent. The sentry in theirs was not as lucky as in the other tent to have been facing the rear of the shelter, and was instead peering through a slit at the front of the tent. Snard let out a howl and charged the Corm, followed closely by Groth. The sentry turned, surprised, and managed to get his large shield in the way of Snard, but before he could stab after successfully blocking him, Groth got the Corm by his wrist and tried to yank him out through the flap he had been peering out of. The fight was on, and from the tent in front of Terrabyss and the recovering Vockyss, a third shepherd appeared.

"Alpha Father!" Terrabyss swore as soon as he saw the third shepherd. This Corm had his fur painted with yellow swirling patterns that covered his stomach and both arms. They contrasted strongly with his dark brown, almost black coat. Both his horns were painted bright yellow as well, with equally bright red tips, and his hooved feet were bright red. A tendril of flame shot from the fire in the center of the tents and ignited Groth as he tried to drag the off-balance sentry out of the structure. Terrabyss suddenly realized where the flash-burned husks had come from.

"Shaman!" he shouted, slightly pushing Vockyss. "Take care of that one." He motioned to the Corm that was stepping out behind Nomi's body. "Snard, Groth's dead. The one in there with you is your problem. Shaman is mine." The group needed no other commands and immediately went into action.

Before the Corm who had executed Nomi had even completely stepped out of the tent, Vockyss collided with his chest and stomach, sending the huge Yak-Taur back into the shelter. Snard also wasted no time biting down on his Corm's ankle, yanking the shepherd off balance again and onto his back. Terrabyss left no time for the shaman to get into his rhythmic motions, instantly going for the stone mace that he carried in place of a spear.

Vockyss rolled with the momentum, coming out of her tackle on her paws with her hands out to each side to catch whatever attack the opponent launched at her. Even though the tents were very large as far as the Maulers were concerned, the shelter was not the most ideal arena for the two combatants. Surprisingly, it was even less so for the Corm than for Vockyss, despite having a home advantage. Vockyss' agile movements, accompanied by her physical prowess, proved to be a difficult match for the Corm in such confined space. Again, her claws hit his shield with such force that they popped through the hide barrier, she tried to claw downward but the Corm was not feeble by any means, and he jerked his shield back. He stabbed forward and tried to slash across when his stab missed, but when Vockyss sidestepped the thrust, he caught his spear in the thick hide of the tent and for an instant lost all his momentum. His armor managed to keep several of her vicious claw strikes at bay, but she did manage to dig some of her claws in along the back of his neck where the armor didn't reach. It wasn't enough to bring him down, and he elbowed out with his left arm, since he couldn't get his shield up in front of her flanking maneuver in time. She was forced to back off when the elbow connected with her throat, but not before she clawed down the back of the opponent's neck. She moved back, coughing a bit. She had managed to avoid the brunt of the attack, but it had still caused enough discomfort that she didn't feel confident pushing her advantage.

Snard was not so lucky as to pull the shepherd back into the tent, but he did manage to make the Corm fall hard on its back. In the process, he had gotten a kick to the top of the head with the other hoof, and that had thoroughly dazed him. Fortunately, there is validity to the saying 'the bigger they are, the harder they fall', and the Corm was not hopping to its hooves anytime soon either.

Terrabyss was not having an easy time of it. He wasn't giving the shaman enough time to start any of his arcane motions, but he was obviously not a rookie shepherd either and had learned how to stay out of a dangerous animal's reach. Terrabyss' kanabo was deflected off to the left of the shaman for the third time, and the Mauler was again forced to go on the defensive and try to avoid the force of the stone cudgel. Cudgel, shield, cudgel, cudgel, shield, then the pattern would switch. The shield was becoming the largest problem for Terrabyss. The cudgel he could deflect, but he couldn't risk a heavy swing against the shaman. If the Corm managed to deflect the attack with his shield, it would leave Terrabyss wide open to a strike from that stone cudgel, swung by an opponent twice his size. No one wanted to be on the other end of that. The cudgel slipped past Terrabyss' defense and caught his forearm with a solid whack. He had to let go with his left for a moment to get some feeling back in his fingers.

At least it wasn't another tendril of fire, he told himself as he tried to shake off the sensation, blocking the second attack with his kanabo. This time, he wasn't able to counter, so the shield caught him in the face, causing him to stagger back a little.

Snard stood up, shaking his head, and then instantly regretting that decision. Everything was a blur, not just his vision. It felt as though he were in a den and listening to his parents talk, after the pups had supposedly gone to sleep. His fingers and paws sent shocks of tingling sensations up his spine, and everything felt like it was wrapped in a layer of material. Even if he had something to grab onto, he doubted he would have been able to. His nose felt like mucus was dripping from it, and it probably was as he could only smell his own congestion. He closed and opened his eyes, hoping to at least clear his vision so that he could orient himself. Snard felt something grab him by the top of the head, and he hoped it was one of his allies, but it felt a little too violent, or perhaps he was still confused from the blow to his head. Instinct screamed to fight it, and Snard, a veteran and a survivor, struck out with his claws. He felt himself suddenly drop and he tried to roll to his side with the impact, slowly standing as the din of battle started to become a cacophony, and he could see more than random blotches of color. The Corm, who had thought he was going to be able to easily defeat this dazed opponent, hadn't expected to have the whole left side of his face clawed, or his eye sliced open. It bellowed in pain, instantly dropping both its shield and spear to try to cover its face with its hands. Snard saw two spears hit the ground and took a guess at which one he was grabbing, the real one or the head-injury-induced one. His hand closed around something solid, but he was still not sure if he was holding anything at all; either way, he thrust forward, catching the Corm right below his sternum and they both tumbled to the ground.

"I didn't die!" Snard yelled, holding his arms up in the air, having forgotten that they were still in the middle of a melee.

Vockyss ducked under the spear swing and lunged forward under the cut. She hit the shepherd in its hips, causing them to buckle and it to fall back. Although as it did so, it flipped the spear vertically and stabbed down at Vockyss. The metal bit into her thigh deeply as she rolled off to its left side, not intending to but landing on the wound. She tried to scramble to her paws before the Corm charged her and she managed to avoid the horns but was still headbutted into the side of the tent, bringing the whole structure down on top of the two of them. Vockyss wasn't sure if this was to her benefit or detriment as she tried to orient herself under the collapsed hide. To her left and muffled through the fabric, she could hear the panicked sounds of the shepherd as it was trying to find her or its way out. She limped as stealthily as she could over to the continued sounds. Vockyss snapped her jaws down hard on what she thought was a shoulder or armpit as it flailed about. The shepherd screamed in horror as the area she clamped down on was actually his groin, and she snapped down on its genitals. Instantly, it lost the will to live as she pulled back, tearing both flesh and material. Spitting the gore out, she savagely attacked the wounded opponent as it tried to stay conscious. It had no defenses left, having lost the spear when the shelter collapsed, and now the pain was too much. The Corm welcomed its demise.

Terrabyss was trying to find some angle of attack that would take him from the defensive to the offensive. Right now, all he could do was keep that cudgel at bay and take the beating from the shield, which connected without fail each time. He didn't know how Vockyss was doing, having

161

only just noticed that the tent she had been fighting in had collapsed. He heard the Corm that had been fighting Snard let out an agonizing cry, so Snard had obviously gained the upper hand. Terrabyss saw the shield punch forward again, and he decided to try a new tactic rather than take the blow to his face. He shoved forward, ramming into the shield with his shoulder and knocking the shaman back on his heels. Terrabyss followed this up, taking his kanabo in both hands and trying to chop down to catch the shield and arm under his strike, to stop the continued use of the defensive item. The druid fell back, having not expected the Mauler to respond by throwing himself into his attack, and was also caught off guard at how well such a seemingly suicidal attack had changed the flow of this fight. Trying to recover and seeing the Mauler gear up for a chopping attack, the druid raised its shield slightly, angling the front so that the kanabo would slide off the surface rather than connect straight on. Terrabyss was getting used to the shield, and angled his chop to the right. If the blow connected, he hoped to yank the shield the other way, and maybe even twist the shaman's wrist and hopefully break it. The Corm felt the impact, Terrabyss flexed his shoulders and using his core pulled the weapon through the swing back toward his toes. There was a painful snapping noise as the shield twisted in the other direction and the shaman unwisely held on to it. Its wrist wasn't able to rotate that way and gave surprisingly easily, and the shaman had no choice but to drop its best defensive tool.

The shaman was left with little other option than to resort to the extreme. Amongst practitioners of the arcane arts there are three requirements for magic. Movement, found through rhythmic dance or other highly active rituals. Sigils were often used by more experienced mages, who combined the two practices by using premade sigils on items like Skoff's staff, but many items could serve as conduits. Finally, the most desperate or disciplined magic users sacrificed their own blood to amplify the effect of the magic. This was considered a desperate measure because a mage could siphon their own life force if they didn't find a way to control the amount of blood that the arcane practice would drain from them. Even a minute prick of a finger could lead to a mage's death, because a simple spell had sucked the life from its host like a parasite. Granted, the fire they could start with such a sacrifice might never go out, but they would never get to enjoy the benefits of the outcome.

The shaman smirked. *I am dead anyway*, it thought as Terrabyss closed the gap. He let go of his weapon and grabbed the bone sticking out from his forearm. "You're dead!" he shouted in agony as he tried to yank the bone up his arm to get as much blood as he could on the sigil he had hurriedly drawn in the snow.

Terrabyss was faster and swung upwards, connecting with the Corm's other arm before he managed to take hold of the bone. The Corm screamed in pain as his other arm was mangled in the blow.

"No, no, no, you're dead," Terrabyss corrected him, as he brought the kanabo back down on the shaman's face, silencing him. As he panted hard, catching his breath, he looked over at the other two. Snard was lying on top of his kill, panting as hard as Terrabyss. Only a moment later, Vockyss popped her bloody face out from under the collapsed shelter. There was a chorus of excited howls off to the east.

"We have them in our trap," Terrabyss said to the other two as he heard the howls, adding his own to the growing wave of sound as it crashed over the tundra. The other two quickly joined him; even though they were exhausted, they could always find enough energy to celebrate.

The Hunt

Kellij, Dardyl, Foyss, Worg, and Rellik were teamed up together, and they originally chose Rellik to lead the pack. She quickly rejected the role, telling them that she didn't have the training or the knowledge to lead a group in a Hunt. She had spent most of her life as the ignored middle pup, and was not accustomed to her new-found notoriety as the youngest Ravis. After she rejected the title the fourth time, they nominated Kellij as pack alpha. Rellik knew Kellij, at least by reputation. Her father had spoken highly of the Returin pack, and had encouraged Ammer and Kellij to spar whenever the two packs saw one another. Kellij was a typical Mauler in looks; with pitch-black fur and intense yellow eyes. His many scars criss-crossed his body even at this young age, but none of them stood out like Numa's ribs or the scarred head of one of the juveniles in Unkyss' group. He did have a patch of light brown fur that framed his left eye, which is how Rellik recognized him when they were teamed up together. She knew the other three even less than Kellij; Dardyl and Worg were both from outer packs, and she had never heard her father mention either of them or their families. Both were typical Maulers as well; they each had several large scars but none were remarkable. Dardyl had unusually orange-colored eyes, but what set her apart the most was she had begun to mimic Numa by applying beeswax to her fur. Unlike Numa, Dardyl liked to make the fur between her ears and down the back of her neck stand erect. Rellik thought it looked foolish, but she wasn't about to say that to Dardyl's face. Worg's eyes differentiated him; he had very dark brown eyes, but flecks of green could be seen in them in certain light. Foyss was an inner grove Mauler, and Rellik should have known him well as they grew up around each other. Foyss was a runt, and his parents had obviously followed Hanora's example of how to raise runts. Rellik wasn't sure he was going to make it through this Hunt, and had mixed feelings about trying to help him. He had the Mauler frame, but lacked the muscle and had a pretty significant gut. His head and tail were smokey-black, similar to Rellik's whole coat, but his torso and limbs were jet black. His eyes were arresting, the yellow was so faded in them that they appeared white. Her group of five waited patiently in the cold wind for Terrabyss' howl as he led the second assault team into the Corm's camp.

Unkyss, Aasha, Cycyss, Klain, and Oulyss were further up the line that waited to run out and startle the mammoths into a stampede so that they could pick out the young, old, or lame. Unkyss had accepted the title of alpha of his Hunt pack because of his experience surviving on his own, which had made him an accomplished hunter already. Aasha was a litter alpha that drew the same lot as Unkyss. She was just under average height, with a powerful frame and equally strong arms and legs. Her fur was sleek and she had bright golden eyes. A few scars were visible on her, but none so much as the one that ran directly down the center of her skull, right between the eyes. After her, Cycyss drew the same lot and was placed in the same pack; she was not an alpha, but she was an experienced hunter. Cycyss' mother had passed away giving birth to her litter, and Cycyss had forced her father to let her go with him on hunts. Her father was not in a good position to refuse since they lived in the outer grove bordering this very tundra, and further north. Cycyss' brother and litter alpha, Zelyss, eventually had to challenge her to claim his spot as beta Hunter next to their father on hunts when the whole litter started hunting. He hadn't scarred her in the fight, but she nevertheless stood out with her all-white collar and polished-brass eyes. The next two that joined Unkyss' group were also alphas of their litters, but couldn't be more different in their demeanor or appearance. Oulyss had the classic Mauler features, and a very distinct scar at his missing right ear. It had supposedly been ripped off by a Gorgel that had tried to carry him away when he had been a pup. Klain, on the other hand, was odd-looking for an alpha, and Mauler. He was short, similar to Aasha, but his hunch was extremely emphasized so he was almost as short if not shorter than Terrabyss. His coat lacked any sheen or luster, and his eyes were dull yellow. He had been the only survivor in a litter of stillborns, a fact which made him proud and of which he was fond of reminding everyone.

The six packs of juveniles stared at the large, elephantine beasts that might be sleeping, but they couldn't be sure as the mammoths were huddled together in groups and seemed to be keeping each other warm. It would seem a logical explanation; given the tundra's constant freezing winds, the

Maulers doubted that even the thick coats of these mammoths could keep the cold out. The creatures had long, wooly, deep brown to reddish-colored hairy fur coats. Both the females and males had tusks, but the males tended to be larger, and some even overlapped each other. The tusks were longer than even Unkyss was tall, which made many of the juveniles nervous. All of them were large, even the calves were giants in comparison to the Maulers. They couldn't even guess at the adult's weights, which made their only possible targets the calves, which looked at least three times the weight of a Mauler.

"Excited?" Kellij asked, noticing that Rellik's tail was wagging and thumping against his leg.

Rellik grabbed her tail, embarrassed. "Yeah. Sorry about whacking you with my tail; sometimes, she has a mind of her own." Rellik gave him a nervous expression as her tail started hitting him at a gentler pace this time. Again, she grabbed it. "Sorry."

"I am sorry about what happened to your family," he whispered to her, obviously not sure if the others in their group felt the same way he did.

"Don't be," Rellik said harshly. She wasn't upset with him, but she didn't want any suspicion about where she stood on the power shift. "They aren't my family anyway, I am a Ravis," she stated firmly, locking eyes with him to make sure he understood how serious she was.

"You're right—" he began, but Rellik quickly shushed him as she stared up the line back to the camp where the shepherds were. A fire shot back up to light, and then a few moments later, a second fire just burst up into flames again.

"What is going on?" he whispered, more to himself than to Rellik. She just shrugged in response, hoping that the raid was going well.

Unkyss watched as another fire cast its light, his muscles were tense and he wanted to get this started, but he made himself stay motionless until he heard the signal howl from Terrabyss.

"We should go, once they are done relighting the fires, they will come to check on the herd and will discover us," Klain's hoarse whisper broke the silence that surrounded them.

"No, we stay here until we hear the howl. If there is no howl, then we will fall back to our base camp," Unkyss instructed harshly, his hackles rose instinctively when he heard Klain's voice.

"You're packless, and alpha of nothing. I survived, like you, but I am still the alpha of something," was Klain's challenging response.

Oulyss' hackles rose this time as he snarled at Klain, "Show our alpha some respect and keep your bear-shit opinions to yourself."

"Are you going to make me?" Klain snapped in response, as both he and Oulyss started growling at each other threateningly.

Unkyss whirled around and grabbed Klain's muzzle, slamming him into the ground hard and making Klain shut up. "Yes, I will," Unkyss barked as quietly as possible. "Now, when I let you go, if you open your mouth again, I will personally break your jaw. Got it?"

Klain nodded slowly, the pain demanding that he agree and the tone of Unkyss' threat ensured that Klain kept quiet. Unkyss spun on Oulyss. "I can discipline my pack, and I will when I deem it necessary."

Aasha and Cycyss' snickers instantly stopped as Unkyss looked over his shoulder at them. Oulyss simply nodded his head in agreement, and the group settled back down, waiting for the signal howl.

"Remember, as soon as we get the mammoths into a panic, Aasha and I will take the flanks. You three are quicker, I want you to run ahead, and we are going to chase the target to you." Unkyss looked directly at Klain, who had put up the most resistance to the plan and was obviously still upset that he wouldn't be steering the mammoth. All four of them nodded, even if Klain's nod was a little reluctant.

They could see their breath rise in plumes as they panted in excitement, and then they heard it. That single echoing howl that was Terrabyss' order to charge. There was a brief instant when everyone remained motionless. This singular moment, freezing in time so that everyone remembered where they were on this night. Unkyss shook himself free of that paralyzing instant and let out a matching savage howl, as he and his lead pack broke the trees and charged into the herd of mammoths. The lead pack's job was to ensure chaos and panic gripped the mammoths, and ensure they stampede. The stampede would separate the young, old, and lame from the herd and allow the juvenile packs to target these mammoths. This would allow all of the juveniles the best chance to take down a target and earn their title as adults. As Unkyss' Fist reached the nearest group of mammoths, they snapped and snarled, jumping close to the beasts' faces to scare them with their aggressive display. The alarmed mammoths bolted, trumpeting terrifyingly as they turned tail and ran. One of the mammoths turned and beat Cycyss with its trunk. The force from the blow sent her up into the air, slamming down into the tundra's hard-packed snow. There wasn't any time to check her condition, and the group knew that if they took down a mammoth, she would still be entitled to the label of adult. The second pack had caught up with Unkyss now, this group was led by a lean Mauler by the name of Brutyss—Aasha and Foyss' brother. Brutyss was not as stocky as his sister, he was fast and had amazing endurance; most of the pack he was with were panting rapidly to keep up to his pace, and he had already passed by the alpha of his pack by three or four lue. With the second group's support and the third group closing in, the mammoths were routed; some collided into each other while others bolted in whatever direction they were facing.

Rellik saw the chaos mounting and the group just two lue ahead of them was now on the run. "Okay, we have the easiest job," Kellij announced. "We get to pick off the stragglers, so I am expecting all of you to be adults by the end of this."

Foyss groaned as he slowly got to his paws and Rellik was sure they would leave the lackadaisical runt behind. The pack right in front of them accelerated, howling that they had joined the fray. Kellij lifted his head and let out a loud, equally fearsome howl and his group sprinted from behind the mighty redwoods and into the now-frenzied herd. In the dark, the behemoths had almost no vision, having to depend solely on their hearing and smell. The Maulers' howling and ducking around them made them feel overwhelmed and trapped. This was a dangerous position for the Maulers. It would separate the weaker mammoths from the stronger ones, but as many of the groups were learning, even a weak mammoth fighting for its life was a fearsome opponent. Those driving the creatures into a frenzy ran the risk of being pulled into the herd and trampled. They could get flung into the air by the creatures' mighty trunks or, most frighteningly, be gored or bludgeoned by one of those very heavy and surprisingly sharp tusks. At least one Mauler in each of the first four hunting parties was killed or injured in one of these ways.

By this time, the lead pack and its support could break off and try to find a target for themselves to bring down. Unkyss spotted a larger bull, and normally he would have stayed clear of such a dangerous target, but he noticed that it had a long and deep gash in its side. Most likely, it had earned this in a fight with a dominant male, and the running had caused the injury to tear back open. The blood trail was easy enough to follow and, if they kept the animal in a state of crisis, it should wear out through losing so much blood. Unkyss barked a command, and he and Aasha started to herd the creature to his three runners that sprinted off ahead of him. Well, two had sprinted off, he couldn't stop to see where Cycyss was. As he and Aasha pressed on, he hoped that the four of them were enough to overcome the target he chose. They had already begun to steer it, and he had no way of telling the others ahead of him to break away. If he and Aasha broke off, they ran the risk of leaving the other two to fight a very scared and dangerous mammoth.

Rellik and her group followed close behind Kellij. Dardyl was the largest of them, and was at the furthest point from Kellij, who was in the lead of their diagonal formation. Dardyl was supposed to be the one in the rear, but it seemed that Foyss, if he kept his current pace, would fill that position. Dardyl barked at him, trying to yell at him to move up. She couldn't slow down behind him, or else the front three would get to the mammoth long before Dardyl could come in to take down the target. That was her whole job, given her stamina and power, and she didn't want to perform badly at her one responsibility because some overweight runt couldn't keep up. The plan was that Kellij and Worg were the most familiar with cornering tactics, so they were going to isolate the target and keep its attention. Rellik and Foyss were to harass the creature's flanks, and then Dardyl was going to leap from behind to get on top of it to bite down on the spine. This should sever the nerves to the hind legs and they could then pile on it to end their Hunt. Rellik looked about for Foyss, in the same position as Unkyss, in that she couldn't stop mid-sprint to try and orient herself, and she wasn't sure how they would box in their target without him.

Maxyss sat at the end of the row. He watched as the last group after Rellik's took off; all the packs were chasing down the mammoth. He stood and brushed the snow from his rump and legs, giving his hips a good shake to get off anything that was clinging onto his tail. He looked over to where Terrabyss and the second group were attacking the Corm camp, and he could barely make out the shadows against the fires that still burned. Maxyss wasn't sure he was comfortable that several new fires had sprung up since Terrabyss' charge, and was worried that they were getting overwhelmed. Maybe Attaboye's first attack hadn't pulled enough of the Corm out of the camp, perhaps there were even more shepherds than they had counted. The herd was especially large this year, and it would be logical for them to send double the number of shepherds rather than the additional ten the Maulers had counted. Maxyss was very old, his mother had been pregnant with him when they had fled the Green Wall, and he felt that his efforts would be more of a hindrance than a help to the warriors at the camp. He turned and jogged into the forest to meet up with Luna and Skoff, who were waiting for the juveniles to bring in their kills and receive their titles of adult. Besides, at his age, relaxing by the fire and listening to Skoff's tales was always a welcome way to spend the night. Maxyss had been proud of each group; he had sat down with them while they had waited to move and had listened to their plans of attack and how they were going to employ their pack's strengths. He sometimes helped them figure some things out, and other times just sat back and listened. Maxyss was an adamant believer in the fact that no one learned anything by being told how to do it, but by doing it.

he thought to himself as he wound between the trees, meandering back to the fire.

***

Unkyss and Aasha had little difficulty steering the injured mammoth where they wanted it to go. Its wounds and the pain kept it panicked, but because the two never closed too tightly on it, the creature never felt cornered enough to stop and defend itself.

"I don't think the others are much further!" Unkyss shouted to Aasha, but wasn't even sure she could hear him over the howling gusts of wind. He brought his attention back to the beast in front of him. Out of the corner of his left eye, he saw Klain charging the uninjured flank of the creature. "Alpha Father! No! Klain, for Alpha Father's sake, don't!" he shouted to no effect, as the other Mauler lunged onto the side of the mammoth.

Cycyss cocked her head as she saw Klain streak over from her right and leap at the mammoth that Unkyss and Aasha was driving toward them. "I think Klain just attacked the beast, and it's definitely stopping," she informed Oulyss, pointing to where the mammoth had halted and turning its head to the left.

"Bear-shit!" was Oulyss' first response. His vision wasn't as sharp as

Cycyss', and she had already forced him to admit it several times since they had been watching from their assault position. He squinted his eyes, staring off into the tundra; he wasn't sure how Cycyss saw anything through the snow flurries that whipped up into his face.

She shook her head. "No, I am sure that Klain attacked it, and I am definitely sure that the mammoth has stopped running." She looked over at him and wagged her tail slightly. "You know what that means… " She let the rest of the sentence hang in the air.

"I only made that bet with you because I felt bad for you, having taken that hit," Oulyss growled back at her, shading his eyes to try and block the snow as it gusted into his face.

"Well, either way if I am right, which I am, Klain wasn't trampled and you owe me first pick of your meat tonight." Her tail was pounding away now in excitement. "Also, you do realize that I don't use my eyes to know what is happening, I use my nose." She cocked her head curiously at Oulyss.

Oulyss felt embarrassed as he slowly lowered his hands from around his eyes. "Of course." He tried to recover. "Well, we should go help them out since the whole plan has just gone up in smoke."

Oulyss transitioned to all fours and ran toward where his nose told him the rest of his hunting pack and the mammoth were. Cycyss giggled and sprinted after him, her right arm and paw still hurting slightly.

Unkyss dropped his head and charged to where the mammoth had come to a halt. It was whipping its head and lethal tusks back and forth between it and Klain. He quickly glanced over his right shoulder to see if Aasha had heard him, or seen that he had increased his speed. He was relieved to notice that she wasn't even a lue behind him. Unkyss barely heard her question as she shouted, "Why has the mammoth stopped?" He just dipped more to the left so that she had a clearer view as they were now getting close. Her "Oh" told him that had answered her question.

***

Rellik's lungs were starting to burn, she had wished that the young calf they had picked out wasn't going to be too hard to encircle, but the damn thing was proving pretty quick and had plowed over Worg the first time the three of them had managed to get around it. It must have heard

171

Dardyl coming because once it realized something was behind it, it had just slammed past Worg as he tried to snap at its face to scare it back. He still hadn't rejoined the group. Rellik had heard something snap when the calf had barreled over Worg, and she had smelt blood, but she hadn't seen any on the snow around him. Worg hadn't gotten up, and he hadn't moved since the injury. Again, Rellik came to a sliding stop as the creature was cut off by Kellij, who managed to get a bite in at its front right leg. The calf came to a halt, fanning its ears back and forth and trumpeting loudly as it tried to circle around to get all the Maulers in front of it. Rellik again wished that Worg was there as she, Kellij, and Dardyl circled with it to try to get behind it. They tried a new tactic on the frightened calf; Dardyl and Kellij were to take each flank, placing the quicker Rellik at its face. Their hope was that the creature would be distracted by her for long enough for one of them to get up on its back and bite into its neck above the shoulders. At first, the plan was working well; the creature was so panicked by Rellik's bites and lunges directly at its face that it gave little attention to Dardyl and Kellij. Dardyl had almost made it up onto the calf's back, and she dug her clawed toes into the underbelly of the young mammoth. The mammoth panicked from the sudden pain and shook Dardyl free, slamming its other side into Kellij and throwing him onto his back, slightly dazed. The not-so-little calf, still scared, reared up and smashed down on the stunned Kellij. He was barely able to scoot most of his body out of the way of the mammoth's path, but its legs thumped down onto Kellij's right ankle. His scream of agony reflected his intense pain.

The calf easily outweighed Kellij several times over, and when the injured Mauler shrieked in pain, the frightened calf also trumpeted in panic, and tried to make the screaming noise stop by trampling it. Both Dardyl and Rellik tried to distract the thing and to get it to back off the prone Kellij; Dardyl was finally able to get up on the creature's rump during its frenzy and snapped her teeth down on its back right where it connected with the tail. Rellik got around in the creature's face and kept biting and clawing at it to try to get it to back off. Most of the time, her claws and teeth were unable to puncture past the thick, wooly fur, but every now and again she would nick its trunk. Despite their best efforts, the damage was done; Kellij's body from the chest down had been stamped into paste. The calf had trouble keeping its balance as it stumbled back and away from Rellik's vicious attacks. Dardyl had managed to find the creature's spine and was using all the power in her jaws to clamp down. Rellik saw a moment of weakness in the calf, and her body seemed to move of its own accord. She ran forward as the creature sank back, having lost sensation in its hind legs. Rellik's powerful jaws latched onto the calf's throat, and she tugged back with all her might. The muscles in her neck tightened and she tensed her shoulders and chest. With her legs planted firmly, she used her core and upper body strength to pull her head back. The sound of flesh tearing only gave her more impetus as she heaved with everything she had left, falling back into the snow as a shower of crimson blood covered her.

"We got it!" she heard Dardyl shout with pride, and Rellik stuck her hand up out of the snow with a thumbs up.

***

Cycyss and Oulyss swiftly arrived at their prey, and Cycyss wasted no time in trying to bring down the huge, injured bull. She slammed into its injured left flank, tearing at the already open wound with her teeth and claws. Unkyss was picking himself out of the snow, having been bucked off while trying to open a new wound on the right flank. Aasha had gotten up just moments earlier from also being bucked off, and now Unkyss saw her flop into the snow again, having been smacked by the thing's rump when Cycyss hit the creature's other side. Oulyss got clubbed by the trunk this time as the mammoth spun around, and he could make out Klain kneeling in the snow, panting, obviously out of breath. Then Oulyss cartwheeled a few more lue and was buried in a drift, Klain no longer in his view.

"What are we going to do?" asked Cycyss as she nimbly landed on her paws, unable to keep her hold on the wounded mammoth. Unkyss tried to bite into the creature's hind leg while it was facing Cycyss, but he came up with just a mouthful of reddish fur.

"We need to get up on its back!" Unkyss instructed as he tried to quickly wipe the taste and fur off his tongue with a handful of snow.

"What?" Cycyss shouted, not able to understand Unkyss with the ice in his mouth.

"He said the spine!" hollered Aasha. "We need to get up on its back somehow!" she clarified, before having to roll out of the way of the creature's whipping tusks as it swung its head defensively.

Cycyss nodded and tried to figure out a way onto the mammoth's back; she thought about climbing up its face, but the trunk seemed too maneuverable, and she was worried the bull might be able to wrap her up in it. The tusks could be good stepping points, and she was naturally quick. Even with her injured paw she had outpaced Oulyss here. Still, she had no desire to injure herself further, so she began to look for another way up. Oulyss shook the snow off his head and he used his legs to scramble backward out from the hole that his fall had trapped him in. Oulyss' whole back hurt as he tried to crawl free. He took a deep breath of the bitter cold air and looked back at the mammoth that was now charging right for him. He should be alarmed; he heard the snow crunching and felt the ground quake as the beast thundered toward him, even with his head in the snowbank. Seeing the creature this close and feeling it thundering down would put fear into anyone. Oulyss tried to get his paws back under him to jump out of the way, but lost his balance. The lumbering beast was less than two lue away; he was still scrambling. Suddenly, a blur of fur knocked him out of the way and onto his back, out of the way of the charging mammoth. Cycyss had saved him, and earned a gash in her left leg from the tusk that had managed to graze her as she ran past.

Unkyss wasn't sure of Aasha's intentions as she snuck behind the creature while it tossed the four of them about. Even Klain had found his second wind and had charged back into the fray. For all his faults, Klain didn't easily give up—as long as he had time to catch his breath. Unkyss didn't bother to ask Aasha about her plan though, as she actually made it around behind the beast in the chaos of the skirmish. He wasn't sure if he should laugh or be impressed as Aasha ran between the massive creature's legs and clawed at its scrotum, distracting it from the Maulers in front of it.

"What did that accomplish?" Unkyss shouted as the mammoth let out a surprised and furious trumpeting sound, turning frantically and charging away. All he got in response from Aasha was a shrug as she jogged past him to catch up with the angry beast. Cycyss and Oulyss watched as the mammoth bolted, sighing as they prepared to take up the chase again.

"What happened to the mammoth?" Cycyss shouted to Unkyss as he ran past them in pursuit.

"Talk to Aasha about it!" was all the answer that Unkyss gave her as he tried to keep pace with the beast as it ran for the forest. The enraged creature broke through the trees, redwoods that had stood as sentries against the Banshee Tundra. These sequoias had been growing for several decades,

174

having just begun to beat those around them in a race for the most sunlight. Now they were snapped and uprooted as the mammoth tore through the barrier. Cycyss, Oulyss, Aasha and Unkyss were no more than ten lue from the beast as it spun, protecting its rear by the few trees which hadn't been torn asunder. Klain was jogging up and panting heavily—his second wind hadn't seemed to last too long—and he was again desperately trying to keep up with the rest of the pack. The group could tell that the mammoth was on its last legs as well; the creature's breathing was extremely labored and blood flowed freely from his wounded left side. Its threatening trumpets became softer and less frequent as it pawed at the ground in front of it, as though it were going to charge again.

"We can take it down, don't let it get out of those trees, they will help us more than it!" Unkyss barked. The others nodded and ran forward trying to prevent the mammoth from rushing them.

Klain had just caught the end of that sentence and was confused when the pack ran in. "Wait, what are we doing?" he asked, hardly able to even whisper given his exhaustion. "Alpha Father, curse you all!" he had intended to snarl the words, but was glad that no one was around to hear his pathetic whimper.

The mammoth swung its head to the right and caught Aasha with its tusk. She was too close to be skewered but she was heavily bludgeoned by the blow; she let out a muffled cry as she was thrown into several small trees. Aasha came to rest under some ferns, panting; she was still conscious but finding it difficult to will her body back into action. Unkyss slid under the mammoth's cross swing as it collided with Aasha, and tried to lunge up under the creature's throat. The mammoth's flexible trunk whipped back, catching Unkyss by an ankle and hurling him back out into the tundra. He landed with several hard bounces, each one winding him more until he was clawing at the snow on hands and knees, trying to suck in just enough air to not black out. Now, the mammoth seemed to be turning the tables as its head swung back in time to catch Oulyss by the hip and flung him almost five lue up in the air. As he somersaulted, he managed to find his equilibrium and twisted his lower body to connect first. His paws hit the ground and he tucked and rolled, trying to absorb some of the impact and avoid completely breaking both legs. Neither leg broke, but the shock from the landing jarred his left ankle, and it snapped painfully. Cycyss was the only one that escaped the animal's counter, yet came up short as she was on the opposite side of the animal's wound. Cycyss jumped at the flank and her body gave out; she instantly fell back into the snow having lost her grip before she even found it. The mammoth saw victory, it saw freedom. It turned toward the closest opponent, which was Cycyss, still trying to pull herself up from the snowbank. She heard the beast focus on her as it trumpeted violently and stomped forward to trample her under its immense weight. Cycyss tried frantically to scramble backward, her arms sinking into the deep snow drifts. Her paws pushed through the snow, trying to find solid ground, but the powder simply yielded to her force.

A loud thud, trees whining as their trunks were snapped and splintered, then silence. Cycyss managed to get her arms under her, now that she wasn't scrambling for her life, and sat up, looking to the left of her where the trees had screamed their protest. The mammoth was lying on its side. Several small trees that had splintered under its weight stabbed through its thick legs, but the killing blow was a long, narrow, lance-like tree that the mammoth had snapped in its first charge for the grove. It protruded from the bull's side, pointing straight upwards as though it had planted itself again. About the center of the long, makeshift lance was Klain, his right arm wrapped over the weapon and his left holding on tightly underneath. His paws dangled over the dead beast as he slowly and gingerly climbed down the tree, he got about halfway before his muscles gave up and he slid painfully the rest of the way. The pack slowly moved toward the mammoth and Klain, who now lay on top of it, trying to find the energy to pull the splinters out from his groin and limbs. Unkyss was the last to make it over to them, Oulyss was leaning heavily on a makeshift crutch from an uprooted larch that he had snapped the branches off. Klain was pulling out the last deep splinter from his forearm.

"Is no one going to cheer for me?" he asked as he plucked the last annoyance out of his hide. "I made the killing blow, after all." Klain's tail wagged smugly as he hopped off the carcass in front of the others. He was starting to get a little annoyed that no one was saying anything. His tail stopped wagging and his ears flattened slightly. "Are you all just—" His sentence came to an abrupt stop.

Unkyss grabbed him by the shoulder, spun him around, and punched him hard in the face, right between the eyes. "Follow your alpha's orders," he barked viciously, "we could have avoided all of this if you had just done what I told you!"

176

There was no response or even resistance from Klain; Unkyss raised an eyebrow and put his head a bit closer to listen for Klain's breathing or heartbeat. *Babump, babump.* "He's alive." Unkyss sighed, disappointed. "We will drag him back with our kill."

Oulyss spoke up, "I am not trying to put a damper on this victory, but how exactly are we going to drag that," pointing to the massive body, "back to camp?"

"That is not a bad question," Unkyss responded as he considered the dilemma. He let go of Klain, letting him slump at Oulyss' paws. "If he wakes up, put him back to sleep," he instructed. "The rest of you, help me get a tusk as proof. We will go back to camp and see if we can get any help in collecting this kill."

***

Luna sat with Maxyss, Attaboye, Skoff, and Terrabyss around the fire. Her ears perked up when she heard the howls starting to sound off. Maxyss' tail started wagging and Terrabyss gave the Prime Hunter a nervous glance.

Perhaps it wasn't a smart bet that not all the packs would succeed. The size of those mammoths ensured that one group was going to come up empty-handed, right?

That had been the third howl though, and it was in the specific pattern to signal the pups' success.

No, it was a smart bet, no Hunt has ever been a complete success, and this Hunt was against mammoths.

"That is half of them," Luna commented, not realizing she was adding to Terrabyss' concern, but even had she realized, she wouldn't have censored herself.

The two ambush units had strolled back into camp not long ago, they had lost a few fighters, but overall, the raid had gone well. They had cleaned out the shepherd's camp and only a handful of the Corm had escaped. They had several large sacks that were filled with the Corm's culinary specialty, moldy and with a muddy consistency, they called it cheese. The Mino tribes on the coast also produced the same food, but it lacked the smell and potency of the Corm's. Luna had never smelled something so horrible in her life, and she wasn't sure why the Maulers had seemed so excited over the putrid food. They also had multiple sets of large ivory tusks, as well as several bundles of sheared fur from the mammoths. Terrabyss and several other fighters were wrapped up in the heavy, mammoth fur blankets. The two assault groups had now built multiple small fires, not worried about getting attacked by reinforcements from the Corm. Luna was told that the Corm's main dwellings were along the northernmost half of the Division Mountains. It would take the survivors several days to get back there, and they doubted that the rest of the tribe would mount any response before the Maulers marched out of the grove. They might return to herd what mammoths they could before retreating to their homes, but they also might cut their losses. Shortly after the assault group's arrival, the first hunting party had come in. It consisted of Brutyss, Wolg, Phier, Zelyss, and Molken. They had a good-sized calf, and were carrying it on a long and sturdy tree trunk that they supported on their shoulders. It had been at this point that Terrabyss and Maxyss had thought to make this interesting and made their bet.

Luna had expected that she would need to inspect the kill and tap the pups on their heads or some such gesture to bring them into adulthood as she represented the Alpha. She had eagerly rushed toward the group as they had come in, before she realized that she had no idea what she was expected to do. Thankfully, Terrabyss and Attaboye ran over and helped the group bring their kill to the largest fire at the center of the camp. The pups had hurried away from her with the others' help, and she strolled back to her original seat. When she arrived, Maxyss commiserated with her confusion; it seemed that nothing escaped his attention. She learned from him that her duties would come once all the pups had returned and all of their kills had been placed. As a formality, she was to inspect the kills to make sure they hadn't found an old carcass, or killed something else and tried to make it appear like the target they were supposed to bring down. After that, the pups would line up behind their kills and she would declare in front of all gathered that they had earned the responsibilities and status of adults.

Rellik and Dardyl came in third, panting heavily and dragging their mammoth calf between them. They didn't know where Foyss was, and hadn't seen him since he fell behind Dardyl during the Hunt. Luna was surprised that their pack had lost so many pups, and that no one went to look for Foyss in case he needed help. She knew that this was a rite of passage, and sometimes the pups didn't pass and sometimes they died.

The Maulers would not allow her to intervene.

With Rellik and Dardyl's arrival, all three howls were accounted for, as well as all three kills. As the night went by, another and then another pack's howls broke the hum of those Silverbacks gathered, as the hunters told the rest about their Hunt. The other two packs soon arrived, bringing the kill tally to five, but none of them had seen Foyss and a few mentioned that they had seen Unkyss' group isolate a large adult. Both Rellik and Dardyl were interested in the news about Unkyss, as were most of the females that had been part of the juvenile hunting parties. Something about the tall dark male seemed handsomely attractive to most of the Mauler females. Luna thought their swooning over Unkyss was silly, she had traveled with him and still felt as though she didn't know him all that well, so they certainly couldn't. Perhaps it was a difference in their attitudes, but she had come to find some of the shorter Maulers far more attractive. Perhaps because they were a novelty, *or perhaps because I am honestly attracted to him,* she wasn't sure, but she found herself gravitating toward Terrabyss more and more each day. By sunup, there was still no sign of Unkyss and his pack, or Foyss. The others that had died in the Hunt had been collected to take back to the Gathering for a proper funeral. The camp still hadn't heard Unkyss' howl. Terrabyss claimed he heard a howl that sounded like Unkyss, but it had been more savage than triumphant. It also hadn't lasted long enough to convey the message of a completed Hunt, and many were unsure if it had really been a howl or just a trick of the wind.

This close to the tundra, the sun was having less of a challenge breaking through the trees and warming the outer part of the grove. Much of the snow stubbornly hung on, hidden below the fanning branches and needles of the conifers, bolstered by the icy wind that blew off the Berg Maker. The tips of the tall sequoias seemed to act like spear heads to keep the sun at bay, as the sky slowly went from a pink hue to red, orange, and then a ball of yellow that climbed the sky. It was well on its journey when a howl cut the morning clamor of birds as they sang and cursed at the squirrels that sprinted along the branches.

Luna sat up, hitting her head on the dirt roof of her little den. Slowly, the night's events replayed themselves in her groggy mind, and she tried to organize them into a coherent timeline. She twisted around, rubbing her head slightly as she got her face pointing toward the hole that made for the exit and entrance of her 'grave.' She started to crawl out, and her nose poked out of the hole first. She sniffed about to be sure she was not going to jump out into an ambush or some other horror. All the scents were familiar, so she poked her head out. She saw Maxyss and Terrabyss stand up from the fire they had been huddled around, and both dropped those stupid blankets they had been wrapped in. Both of them were facing northeast, and their ears were pointing in the same direction.

"Was that Unkyss?" Luna asked, a yawn escaping her before she could stop it as she finished the question.

Terrabyss' wagging tail was a pretty good response so she didn't bother repeating herself when no verbal answer came. All three of them now stared toward the northeast, other Maulers were crawling out of dens or shaking themselves awake next to ashy fire pits. From the clearing, the last pack of five stepped out, carrying the head of a full-grown Mammoth. Rellik let out a cheerful bark as she saw them, which was quickly followed by Dardyl and others. Maxyss' tail wasn't wagging and Terrabyss' had stopped as well. Luna was pretty sure she knew why. A head wasn't actually a complete kill.

Skoff shuffled over, cutting off the other three as he approached Unkyss and Aasha, who were at the front of the group carrying the head by its tusks. His stance was critical as he planted himself in their path. "This is not a kill, this is a... well, it's a head." Obviously, he hadn't gotten a good night's sleep either, Luna was pleased to realize.

Unkyss and Aasha stopped and there was a loud "umph" as Klain hadn't noticed what was going on and had tried to keep walking with the head, as he supported the back with Cycyss. He lacked enough force to move Unkyss, especially while carrying the trophy, and instead walked muzzle first into its gory base. "By the Alpha Father, I am done," Klain growled, moving to drop the mammoth head, but he felt Oulyss tap his back with his free right hand. Klain decided to not make his injured comrade take his place and stayed there.

"That fact is not lost on us," came Unkyss' deep voice in reply. "We do have the rest of the kill a way back, and we would have left the weakest link back with the body, but we felt that did little to protect our kill," Unkyss continued as Klain gave a smug look to Oulyss at the comment of 'weakest.' Oulyss simply responded by rolling his eyes; he was too tired to get into another scrap with this fool.

"Well, you had best pray to the Alpha Father that it is still there," was Skoff's retort. He motioned to a couple of the warriors that had woken up from the commotion to go with the group.

"We will need more than two," Unkyss clarified. "Also, we will need you to see to Oulyss' ankle, it is likely broken." Unkyss called for Oulyss to head into the camp, and looked back at Skoff to see if he gave the pack more troops to bring back the kill.

Skoff locked eyes with Unkyss, and Luna wasn't sure why the shaman took so long to respond. Finally, though, he motioned for another three. "There, a whole new pack for you to work with. Think that will be enough?" he growled slightly as Unkyss and the others dropped the head.

"I am going with them as well," added Terrabyss as he picked up his kanabo. He intentionally hefted the weapon as Skoff turned toward him to interject. "Is that a problem, shaman?" he asked smoothly and coldly. Skoff just turned up his nose in response, and walked past his brother as he went to join Unkyss and the others.

"I am not sure why you came, but I can assure you that I don't need your support," Unkyss whispered very quietly to Terrabyss, his ears laying back a little to show his annoyance. "I know he is your brother, but you don't need to back me up." They turned to follow Cycyss, who was guiding them back to the kill.

Terrabyss' tail started wagging and he laughed. "Are you joking? I am not here to lend you any support. I just want to see how big the mammoth was before the others start carving it up. At least, I imagine that is how we are going to get it back to camp, if its body is comparable to that head you brought in."

Unkyss nodded, relaxing, and his tail began to wag as well. "Trust me, it is. I may have been a little greedy with my choice."

Terrabyss and the others were impressed when they arrived at the body and saw the sheer size of it. All the fighters that had come along to help, including Terrabyss, tried to hide their jealousy that these pups had the privilege of hunting something this large, and they all failed pretty miserably. It took the group of ten all of the morning to clean and strip the carcass, and it was mid-afternoon by the time they had carried all of the useful pieces back to the camp. By the time the whole process was completed, it wasn't long until the sun would begin to set again. Skoff re-assembled his ritual attire, and the mammoth bodies—and mound of flesh that was the last group's—were put out on display for Luna to look over. While this was occurring, a search group led by Maxyss returned to the camp with Foyss' frozen corpse. He had become too tired and lost in the flurries of snow. He had collapsed just four lue away from the trees and had frozen there. His body was carefully placed with those who had died in the hunt or the raid.

Luna watched curiously as the blood from many of the kills was gathered and preserved in skins that were buried in the snow, to make it thicken in the cold. She did as Maxyss had explained, and after she had declared that the pups had succeeded, she discovered what the blood was for. Skoff used a sequoia twig with some needles tied into a cluster at the end to paint the juvenile's exposed teeth in the crimson fluid. The result was terrifying to behold; their black fur, and golden eyes, along with their now dripping red maws was chilling. A cacophony of howls broke the night's quiet, as just over twenty new juveniles joined the ranks of adults. Luna found herself swept up in the excitement as she joined the celebration.

Confusion

A very auspicious five days had elapsed since the Hunt participants had left, and Skoff was still talking excitedly about how favorable a sign that was. He wouldn't shut up about it, and Terrabyss was missing his brother's usual crotchety doomsday prophesying. As they approached the Gathering, Jabyn met them; she had a piece of bark to write on, with several seemingly disorganized tally marks up and down it. Jabyn's tail wagged slightly at the sight of the number of those that returned and the amount of plunder they brought with them. Luna had to turn away when they opened one of the cheese bags and Jabyn scooped a handful out, lapping at it excitedly.

"What is that?" Terrabyss asked, motioning to the item she was holding and making a tallying check with his other hand.

Jabyn paused, suddenly realizing that she was supposed to be doing something; she quickly sucked her fingers clean and licked the fur along her forearm and hand. After which, she turned toward them, holding the piece of bark out in front of her. "I need to know how much meat you have, and... " – she scanned the scribblings – "oh, and any other foods as well as any non-edible... " She paused for a moment again, double checking she had listed off what the group was supposed to claim. "Non-food products include things like" – she looked them over – "like that." She pointed to the large pile of furs being dragged out on a travois. "Well?" she demanded, as they were still processing her request.

"Why?" Attaboye finally responded, having come up behind the rest and still feeling the privilege of his former rank as Terrabyss' second.

Jabyn shrugged and they could see that she didn't really know why, but she gave the answer on which she had been coached. "Because the Alpha says it will be easier to pack up what we have if we know what we have." It was her body language rather than her reasoning that got them to comply. It had been well before noon when the group had arrived, but after this diversion it was now well past. Sorting their haul and edible plunder had taken until noon on its own. Then she had thrown in perishable, and that had taken even longer to sort out. The precious ivory was bundled up along with the strong bones, and the meat was kept frozen by burying it in the deepest snow banks. Once they finished, Terrabyss and Luna made their way to the center of the Gathering, where they had been told Dio waited.

"That must have been some Hunt," Dio commented as they joined him. He was looking over several large piles of meat, probably rations brought in from the outer grove. Luna wrinkled up her nose, noticing that more than a few pieces had mold growing on them. Many chunks also appeared to have been damaged by the cold temperatures they had been stored in.

"Are we taking this stuff with us?" she asked, nudging one of the frozen pieces. *Most likely caribou,* she thought.

Terrabyss looked over at her with a slight chuckle. "Throw it in the fire and you won't even notice." He saluted Dio, waiting for the Alpha to respond.

Dio gave the appropriate response, "We are going to need all the food rations we can get our hands on. We will dispose of anything too bad, but much of this just needs a good trim and then it will still be perfectly edible."

"How long is this invasion going to take?" Terrabyss asked after the Alpha had acknowledged him. "Won't we be able to use the rations that the Ozars have stored up as spoils?" He seemed a bit upset at the idea of this conflict taking any significant amount of time.

Dio turned to him and gave the Mauler his full attention. "Have you ever fought a war? This is not a challenge where the winner takes all, or where any rules are followed. They want to win, we want to win; and both sides believe that they should win. This is not an easy undertaking, and it will not be complete in one night or even one year. This may be a never-ending war, and I am prepared for that if necessary." Dio's ears were down, and his tail was out straight. With raised hackles, he growled out the last sentence.

Terrabyss had to admit that all at once, the Eclupse actually looked like an Alpha. He wasn't sure where this sudden ferocity had come from, and he found himself wondering again how Dio had magically seemed to transform his demeanor. "Of course, Alpha," Terrabyss responded, again saluting Dio.

Dio acknowledged the salute and went back to sorting the meats. "How did the Hunt go?" Again, his tone was soft and patient, and his body language had changed back to that of an Eclupse.

Before Terrabyss could respond, Luna decided to give the report. "It went very well with very little confrontation within the hunting groups and packs. Also, the assault group losses were minor, only two Fist fulls." Dio turned to face his daughter at the expression 'Fist fulls,' confused by the jargon. Terrabyss couldn't hide his pride at her use of the term, his tail wagging slightly. "A Fist full." Luna looked at her father, surprised he had not yet learned such basic slang. "It's ten, a finger represents each Silverback. So, a Fist is five—"

It had sounded like Luna was going to give her father the whole long explanation that Terrabyss had given her, but she was cut short by Dio, who had lost interest.

"I understand." His tone was not curt, but he hadn't bothered to keep eye contact with Luna and had turned around before he had even finished speaking.

"Wouldn't want that meat to run away on you," Luna said under her breath, but Terrabyss heard it. His tail thumped her as he couldn't conceal his agreement with her hushed critique. She ignored Dio when he turned around and asked what she had said. He was aware that he had missed something, but unable to figure out what, and Luna wasn't going to inform him. Dio began to push for an explanation, demanding that she enlighten him on what was so amusing.

She was saved as she and Terrabyss heard the rattling sound of Skoff approaching behind them. He had changed back into his more traditional outfit of a bright poncho, with his tail braided once again. Skoff was different, he had a bounce to his step, still excited about how incredibly well the Hunt had gone, and happy to inform anyone he passed about the good omen.

"*Ahhh,* I see that our wise Alpha is looking over some of the feast that we will have tonight to celebrate, and to aid those who died to find their way to the stars above." Terrabyss and Luna stepped aside as Skoff walked past them, his mood immediately changing as he saw the meat that Dio was looking at. "This can't be what you are expecting to use for the jubilee? Those pups took down mammoths, and our fighters proved that they could go toe to toe with armored and armed combatants!"

"As well as a shaman," added Terrabyss, letting the stone club he had been carrying on his back fall into the snow at Dio's paws. There were small sigils etched into the weapon, much like Skoff's staff, but carved less skillfully and not very deeply into the club. 'Amateur scribbles,' Skoff had called them, but Terrabyss doubted that Dio would know that.

Dio gave Terrabyss a look of exasperation, but still bent down and picked up the weapon. It was a little longer than Dio's forearm, and the handle was made from one of the mammoth bones which gripped a solid stone about the size of Dio's fist. Dio ran his finger along the handle before finally touching the cold stone.

"Are these significant?" He turned to Skoff, but Terrabyss thought that he caught a glimpse of recognition in the way Dio ran his hands along the sigils. Both Luna and Dio claimed to have never seen Silverback magic, and from their reactions to Skoff's little tricks, Terrabyss believed them.

What is it then about the Alpha that doesn't feel right? Terrabyss wondered to himself.

"Pffff," Skoff dragged out the response for emphasis. "This, this is simply… "

"Chicken scratch," Terrabyss and Luna interrupted in unison, much to Skoff's annoyance which was easily recognizable on his scowling face. Terrabyss gave him an unapologetic grin, and for a moment Luna wondered if the two of them were going to come to blows.

"All right, before things get any more tense, Skoff, come with me to a more private place and describe what is expected of the Alpha this evening. And explain the events taking place this evening, other than feasting. Can Terrabyss or Luna assist you with anything you need to do before then? I am sure they are both more than willing and capable." His voice was stern again, and he challenged either of them to say something in response.

Terrabyss was close to taking him up on that challenge, but Luna again reacted before Terrabyss' anger got the better of him. "We would be happy to; Terrabyss will be able to teach me more about Mauler culture this way."

Her hips thumped him hard when he didn't immediately respond. "Of course, Alpha," Terrabyss said, on her signal.

"Well, I guess what I need from them won't put them in direct or dangerous contact with the phantoms standing between us and the ancestors. They should be safe," Skoff said, not very confidently. Terrabyss cocked his head, far more than would normally show confusion. Skoff ignored the sarcasm and moved on. "I need them to make sure that the large fire ring is dug out, and the stones mark its borders clearly. We don't want the phantoms able to step past the barrier." He intentionally looked at his brother. "Following that, I need them to choose enough meat so that the whole tribe can gorge themselves to their heart's desire. If you both complete those tasks before I am done with the Alpha, then return to me and I will explain how to mark the boundaries for the games and where to gather the branches for the strength test."

Terrabyss only half-heard these instructions as soon as Skoff listed the first chore; he knew all about these things, every Mauler did. Skoff just wanted to feel important, he also loved captive audiences, and Luna was a very good audience; something quite foreign to Skoff. If they stayed standing there, Terrabyss was sure that Skoff would divulge how to site the boundaries and gather the branches, two things that Terrabyss didn't actually know. Some of the Shaman's tricks were kept secret and vigilantly guarded. Terrabyss found himself remembering how he had been caged for two days as a pup because he had tried to follow Grimmis and Skoff one time. He hadn't seen the tripline, just felt it. The cage had slammed down around him, and what teacher and pupil did for two days off in the woods had remained a mystery to him ever since. Terrabyss still hadn't fully forgiven Skoff for asking his mentor to leave Terrabyss in the cage, when the two of them had discovered him in the trap on their way back. Terrabyss didn't want Luna to get the secrets out of Skoff; if anyone was going to do that, it would be him. His ego bruised from the memory, he encouraged Luna to leave the Alpha and shaman, and turned about without waiting for a response. Luna's head tilt was sincere as she watched him go, she had turned back to Skoff hoping for an explanation, but he was already spouting information to Dio, so she turned again, hurrying after Terrabyss.

They spent most of the pit-building in silence. Luna asked Terrabyss what was wrong but received a *"humph" in response*. He was more stubborn than an ass sometimes, but she had an infinite amount of patience, the one bane to Terrabyss' obstinacy. Luna followed his lead as he went about, without explanation, stomping out the fires of those around the Gathering. Terrabyss was intimidating, but he lacked any charm, and Luna found herself smoothing over some ruffled feelings as she followed in his determined wake. Not that anyone would have said anything to Terrabyss. She didn't mind it, and she found it comical how bewildered the victims of Terrabyss' wrath were with her quick apology. After the fires were out, Terrabyss and Luna gathered the stones from those fires, and she helped him to inspect them thoroughly. "No blemishes," had been his elaborate instruction, and as she watched she had learned what that really meant. The stones must have no chips, cracks, or have been obviously fractured. The stones provided the ring that would trap the phantoms that existed between this world and the heavens. Phantoms were those who had died without being properly sent to the afterlife, the body left to rot, buried, or any after-death treatment other than cremation guaranteed that the spirit would become a phantom. Phantoms would try to possess those living, in order to have another chance at redemption if their new host were to be cremated. The host's original soul became consumed by the phantom, which is why those who were possessed had not only the ability to mimic their host's personality, but also had their memories and quirks. It was a shaman's job to exorcize these phantoms, and hopefully the host's soul hadn't been fully consumed. Often, the exorcism left the host broken and changed. They could never completely recover what the phantom had stolen from them, and lived as a half-empty vessel, an easy target for another or the same phantom to repossess.

They had finished lining the fire ring with a stone border, five stones wide and five high. Terrabyss used clay to help set the stones, and to ensure that there were no gaps in the ring. The Mauler was starting to open up, having recovered from his hurt pride. Luna was fun to work with, she didn't complain, nor did she try to find ways to circumvent the work. She was encouraging and she was quick to learn, often finding better or smoother ways to get the job done to the same level of efficiency. Building the fire ring was not an uncommon practice, and even though the Maulers filled their large fire pit up after each use, it was not hard to locate its boundaries or to dig the soil out. Luna learned that there were special rules to even this simple task; again, the phantoms were cunning and desperate. The pit had to be dug exactly a half-lue deep, which was measured by Terrabyss laying a long branch in the snow and lunging once, determining the distance and snapping the branch at that point. Luna wasn't sure how accurate that was, but Terrabyss assured her that Skoff would have done it in the same manner. The pit was impressive, and as Luna worked with Terrabyss, she was shocked at the size of the thing. She had seen this same pit in action the night her father had been recognized as Alpha, but she hadn't realized that it was five lue wide. Once they had finished digging out the huge ring, Terrabyss went around the whole thing, packing the wall down and making sure it was solid. If the barrier had a weakness, a phantom could exploit it and any spots that seemed tenuous were patched with clay and the stones that hadn't been usable in the ring.

"With the dirt surrounding them, these stones are more than adequate to stop the phantoms' dangerous reach," Terrabyss said with confidence as he finished stuffing another weak point with stone and clay.

"Did we get it all then?" Luna asked, looking around at the hole. She still held a woven basket of clay on her right arm, the other basket was empty under her left arm, having used all of her stones.

"If you are finished with your side, then yes, we are done," Terrabyss grunted, standing and straightening his back before reaching back down for his two baskets.

"Well, that wasn't so bad," Luna said with a shrug, handing Terrabyss her baskets before she squatted and hopped out of the pit. Terrabyss almost dropped his basket of stones as he tried to juggle the addition of her clay basket and the empty basket as she hopped up.

"Alpha Father!" he swore as a stone fell from his basket and connected with his shin. "ALPHA FATHER!" he screamed as the rock came to rest on his toe. All was lost now as he dropped all of the baskets and fell back.

Luna peered over the edge of the pit. "You okay?" She was clearly trying not to laugh, but her tail was wagging back and forth and kicking up some loose snow.

"I am fine," came the gravelly response as Terrabyss collected himself and the baskets. "Usually, when we are done with the pit, we just toss our baskets over and then jump out after." He explained more pointedly than necessary, still a bit annoyed.

"I didn't think you could be defeated by a basket!" Luna giggled, rolling out of the way of the baskets as they landed near her. "You could have just handed them to me instead of throwing them up here." She jumped, startled by the sudden tremor in the forest floor as Terrabyss landed next to her. She looked up at him with a playful shrug. "So, meat, right?"

By evening, the two of them had finished Skoff's tasks, and they had even had some time to themselves, finding each other's company more and more inviting. They now sat with their respective packs as they watched a game of My Skull. The boundaries had been laid out, and only the new adults were allowed to compete. They put on a great show for their peers, and displayed the might and power they had shown in taking down the mammoths. Cheers and howls came from both sides of the field as they watched the new adults display not only their strength and endurance, like Unkyss and Dardyl, but also their tactics and explosive speed, like Brutyss and Rellik. Everyone was on their paws and shouting when Oulyss caught Klain by his hips and lifted him, slamming him on his back and winding him. Oulyss nodded in appreciation to Skoff and yanked the skull out of Klain's hands, sprinting for the boundary line. Terrabyss rolled his eyes as Oulyss ran for the nearest line under Unkyss' encouragement, and sat down in frustration when Dio counted the point. The game was almost over before Klain found the courage to stand up again, and he stayed well away from Oulyss. Rellik and Unkyss had the most points by the time the game was called, the sun almost completely gone, its last few rays outlining the forest dimly. The waning of the daylight contributed to a solemn feeling in anticipation of the serious rite and custom to next take place.

It was time for the large fire pit to be lit, and for Skoff to commemorate those who had passed away and to usher them home past the phantoms to the stars above, that had begun to glimmer here and there through the canopy. It was fitting that the last light from the sun had turned the forest a morbid gray and black, robbed of its usual color. The birds and animals seemed to still their chatter in recognition of the moment. Skoff stood before the stone ring, his arms outstretched before beginning to circle the pit with his customary chant and rhythmic dance. His staff was wrapped in leather lacework that was dyed white and green. These were the celebratory colors of the Maulers. Even though death was present, the Hunt was a time of joy. It made for a dazzling pattern, almost hypnotic, as he spun the staff. Skoff wore a wooden mask carved in the pattern of a large wolf's skull, and he was wearing a gray fur poncho and trousers. These had large wolf bones attached to them, making Skoff look like a dancing skeleton as he circled the fire. Legend had it that the bones were carved to resemble the very bones of the Alpha Father, the first Silverback. Each tribe had been given some of the bones, and then they had made casts of their bones for the other tribes. The Maulers supposedly owned the original leg bones of the Alpha Father. Terrabyss wasn't sure he believed any of it and his howl was indifferent when Skoff finally finished and the stones around the hole began to glow and smoke, before they magically manifested a fire into the great pit.

Numa elbowed Terrabyss when the howl had finished, she had noticed his lack of enthusiasm. Rellik giggled a little, enjoying sitting with her new pack, but that only earned her an elbowing from Terrabyss much like the one he'd just received. It was now Terrabyss' turn to laugh, at which Numa elbowed him again.

"Shut up, both of you," she whispered harshly.

The fire changed from yellow, to orange, to red and all the shades in between. Terrabyss silently mouthed Numa's instruction, earning another giggle from Rellik. The bright flames suddenly became a glossy black. They still danced and gave off a fire's heat, but no light was shed from the ink-like darkness of the tongues of flame.

"That's new," Terrabyss mouthed, suddenly finding it hard to vocalize, or perhaps not able to hear himself. The smoke became thick, almost like the morning fogs that swept in from the Berg Maker. Terrabyss couldn't pull his eyes away from the gathering gray plume. He felt like he was hallucinating as he watched the smoke form into five small, Silverback figures that seemed to be laying on a pyramid. They were all motionless, and a chill crawled up Terrabyss' spine. He felt nervous and on edge. *What is going on? What trick has Skoff learned?* More smoke beings began to appear and all bowed down, and although they had no face or other features, Terrabyss knew that they were all worshiping something. Terrabyss' gaze followed the rising pyramid, until at the very top he saw one smoke figure that was sizably larger. The figure was not only taller but broader, and there was strength in the wisp's pose. Still, no sound was emitted, and no other motion was made by any of the figures.

Instantly, the fire leapt back to its vibrant yellow, orange and red. Terrabyss was blinded but fought his body's urge to put his hands up and shield his eyes, managing to look away and blink into the darkness. He wasn't sure if it was the fire that had burned itself into his eyes, or if some other trick was being played on him, but something stared back at him from the night and mirrored his motion. When he blinked, so did the burning red eyes from the trees. Terrabyss reached over, to get either Rellik or Numa's attention, keeping his eyes on the eyes that watched him.

"Do you know where he went?"

The question was dumbfounding and unintentionally he pulled his vision and focus away for a moment. When he realized he no longer had sight of those eyes and turned to locate them again, he saw nothing. Well, nothing out of the ordinary, there were the trees, the snow, the ferns, but no eyes.

"Terrabyss, did you see where he went?" He turned back to face Numa, and noticed that the whole Gathering seemed to be in confusion.

"What? Who? What's happening?" Terrabyss asked, his mind in a whirl.

"Skoff," replied Rellik, as Terrabyss realized that she was staring where he had been looking. Her expression told him that she hadn't seen anything, and was confused too. "We are looking for Skoff. Are you okay?" she asked. "You acted like something frightened you."

Terrabyss glared at her and growled, "I am fine. What happened to Skoff?"

Rellik knew that was all the answer she was going to get, and she lowered her ears. "Fine, I should have known better," she replied gruffly, "and we don't know what happened to him, the fire went out and he was gone."

The fire went out, Terrabyss repeated to himself, turning to look at the pit. There was nothing, no fire, not orange, not red, not yellow, and not black. *What is going on?*

"What in the name of the Alpha Father is going on?" Dio's voice snapped Terrabyss out of his thoughts as he saw the Eclupse approaching. Luna was right on his heels and like Dio—bear-shit, like all of them—she was visibly shaken.

Numa turned to face Dio. "What exactly are you asking me? Your question could have numerous answers." Her tone belied her calm expression, she was not used to others yelling at her, and her voice snapped several nearby Scouts to attention.

Terrabyss gave Dio a cautionary look, and the Alpha quickly realized the position he was in. Terrabyss noticed that his apology seemed less sincere than in the past. *Or maybe I thought Dio was more honest than he really is.* For some reason, the thought reminded him of Dio's assurances that he would be fine alone while they hunted down Hanora. Dio brought his aggression down several levels, enough to make the Scouts and Numa relax.

"Was this supposed to happen? Is this part of the feast? Skoff didn't—" Before he could finish, Numa answered his many questions with a simple shake of her head. "Okay, so how do we proceed from here?" Dio asked Numa, now looking around at the nervous faces and hearing the confused murmurs from those gathered.

She looked at him, and Dio wasn't sure if he had insulted her given her expression. "You're the Alpha, we haven't ever experienced this. Like I said when I shook my head, this wasn't part of the celebration." She turned to Terrabyss and Rellik. "You two, come with me, we need to find our brother." She didn't wait for a response and pushed past them to see if she could pick up a scent or find a trail.

Terrabyss watched his sisters jog off. "I would tell them it had been," he said to a very confused Dio. "I would tell them all it had been a planned part of the feast," Terrabyss clarified for the Alpha.

"Numa said that this wasn't part of the custom, though?" Dio responded, still unsure where Terrabyss was going with this trail of thought.

"Yeah, but nothing about your arrival has been part of our customs," Terrabyss reminded him. He saluted the Alpha, framing his stomach with his arms and followed after his sisters, barely waiting for Dio to acknowledge the salute.

Dio realized as he watched the Ravis pack leave, along with Jabyn and Essall, that Numa hadn't saluted him. He didn't like how much power Numa seemed to hold, and he was beginning to understand why Haxzus had been so opposed to her being in a position of authority. Terrabyss and Skoff were easy enough to predict and control, but Numa was something else, or perhaps he was becoming paranoid.

He gave Luna a smile. "Well, we should probably go do as Terrabyss suggested. I can't come up with a better plan anyway."

The rest of the evening was awkward for both of them. The Maulers, to their credit, seemed willing to accept the flimsy explanation for the cause of the shaman's sudden disappearance. A few wondered where Skoff had gone, and why the rest of the Ravis pack had also left. Dio explained that he had sent them to scout the way, because it wouldn't be long before they began their march home into the Green Wall. Dio was a little surprised that this repeated promise still earned the same excited howls and cheers, and the feast seemed to resume as though there had been no pause earlier. By the end of the festivities, a very tired and well-fed pack had found space under the trees or in their dens for a restful night. Dio stayed with Luna for a while after the celebrants had trickled away into the late night. They sat together in relative silence, listening to the small popping of a nearby fire, one of many that now dotted the Gathering. Dio was sipping at his mead skin, and two others lay empty between him and Luna, who was pleasantly inebriated.

"You and Terrabyss have grown close to one another," Dio commented, having trouble putting the cork back in the skin.

Luna shot up, swallowing hard to keep her mead down from the sudden motion. "Wh… " She gave in to a small burp. "What?" She managed to get the whole word out this time before the belch that followed.

"It is pretty obvious that you both are spending a lot of time together. You can't be shocked by this revelation?" He handed her the skin, but she pushed it away, instead putting a ball of snow in her mouth and sucking on it.

Luna knew her father was right; it wasn't a secret that she had latched onto the Mauler. "Well, he is a good teacher," she said, embarrassed. Her ears drooped a bit, but her tail had a rhythmic pat.

Dio's tail was matching her rhythm, he was so proud of Luna and how she had adapted to survive. He took a deep quaff from the skin, draining the last of it before tossing it down with the other two. "You have been through a-a lot and you, well you… " Dio couldn't finish, surprisingly the mead was not creating the problem, his emotions were. *You have done so much, and I wish I didn't need to ask you to do more.* He rehearsed the line again in his mind, trying to push down the quivering that had begun to break through his relaxed facade. "Numa and I had time to talk while you were on the Hunt." The thought of how unpredictable and threatening the Scout Mother could be made him hesitate for a moment. *Is this really the best thing to do? Will she do it? Can I make her do it?* "Yes, it has to be done."

Luna swallowed the last of the little ice ball as she said, "You are starting to scare me. Are you okay?" She furrowed her brow in concern, and nuzzled her father to try to comfort him.

"I am f… " He sniffled a bit. "I am fine." He managed to lift his ears and wag his tail a bit more vigorously to convince her. *There is no easy way to do this, and I don't have a lot of options, not good ones, at least.*

"Numa and I have decided that you should be mated with Terrabyss," Dio blurted out. "It is the best option for you and me, if we want to keep our position and lives," he began to try to explain.

Luna was silent, and she wasn't sure that she had heard her father right. After all, he had drunk a lot and so had she for that matter, so perhaps her own senses had been playing a trick on her.

"Seriously?" was all Luna could manage at first, a million thoughts racing through her mind. Luna wasn't sure if it was the conversation or the thinking that was sobering her up more. "You're drunk," she sounded like she was more trying to convince herself than her father of the obvious.

194

"I am serious, and I am drunk, but I am drunk because I am serious." The conversation was sobering Dio up, but that wasn't helping him to explain.

"Why Terrabyss, though? Why a… " Luna looked around for a moment. "A runt?" she asked nervously, almost expecting Terrabyss to jump out at her for having put his name and 'runt' in the same sentence.

Dio let out a chuckle. "Well, I think you just proved that whether he is a runt or not, no one, least of all he, sees himself that way. Terrabyss will be a good mate; he is near your age and he has some ambition. You may not have noticed, but Skoff has made it abundantly clear that we are not Maulers, that we don't know their customs. This is upsetting to the ancestors, both theirs and ours. Like you, I have also been spending hours learning from the shaman and anyone else who will teach me so that I don't get challenged and we don't get killed. Skoff was furious when you brought back Rellik, and I went way out of their customs by sparing her. The Maulers respect power." Dio lifted his hand as Luna opened her mouth to interject. "Their definition of power, not ours, but one that needs to be upheld for now. Numa informed me, and she is right, that a union of our packs would solidify our position, at least in the eyes of the Maulers living and those to come. The best way to achieve that is to have someone from our pack mate with someone from their pack."

"Then why don't you mate with Numa? She is single," Luna snapped back, still not too excited about this idea. She tried to change her tone before she had finished the remark, and she hated herself for having said something so awful.

Dio's fist stopped within whiskers of her snout. "You dare!" He could barely form the words and his arm shook from his restraint. "You would have me disrespect your mother, Luma, and bind myself to a new mate? You know that is unforgivable in the eyes of the Alpha Father. Haven't you heard the rumors about Haxzus? The main reason that we stand here today, able to challenge an Alpha from a different tribe is because that Alpha's father did the very same thing you are suggesting."

Luna could see how furious her father was, she was more upset at herself than frightened of her father for having proposed such a horrible thing. Silverbacks didn't re-mate at the loss of a loved one; it was disloyal and caused chaos when that mate was finally reunited with their former mate in the stars. No matter the sex, neither male nor female could re-mate after they had taken part in Materimony.

"I am very sorry; I was caught off-guard and confused. I didn't mean to encourage something so taboo. I think I had too much mead to think clearly. Please forgive me?" she humbly asked her father, hoping that this would help soothe his ire.

Her expression did a lot to take the steam out of Dio's rage, and her apology left him feeling embarrassed for having responded so extremely.

"Terrabyss is headstrong, battle-hungry, and aggressive. He loves a challenge; you won't have to tolerate him for long. He'll get impatient and get himself killed in the Ozar fight, leaving you 'happily' widowed like me." Dio had honestly intended to try and cheer Luna up, but Luma's death was still fresh on his mind, and he found himself choking up again.

Luna found herself more upset at the notion that Terrabyss might be killed than at the idea of being mated to him. Sometimes, her father was a mystery to her.

"When will we have our Materimony?" She wasn't sure if she wanted to keep talking about it, but she couldn't think of anything else.

"As soon as Numa manages to convince Terrabyss, which shouldn't be too difficult. It is obvious he is attracted to you." Dio noticed Luna's tail thump slightly as she looked away, more out of embarrassment than anger this time. Dio looked into the fire. "Do you realize what we have accomplished? We went from being part of a pack of outlaws to controlling the whole Mauler tribe. That is something that no Eclupse, no Silverback has ever done. I just want it to be stable when I give it to you and your pups. I want it to last until the end of time." Dio hugged her. "Now, we both need sleep."

Her father let go of her and stumbled a bit as he looked for a good place to lie down for the night. Luna wasn't sure how much longer she stayed up, her thoughts just kept racing and wouldn't allow her to even acknowledge that she could be tired. She thought about running, but where and why? Terrabyss wouldn't make a bad mate, and he was hardly a runt. Besides, it was a Mauler custom to view the runts as outcast or an ill omen, but wasn't that what everyone here wanted? For her and her father to be more like Maulers than Eclupse? All of it was so confusing. She knew it was the Eclupse custom to arrange Materimonies, especially in powerful families. It was also, obviously, a Mauler custom, and most likely customary amongst all Silverbacks. Originally, the alphas of two given packs would arrange which of their children would be mated with which. This ensured that the best and strongest would breed with only the best and strongest. This custom evolved into first with first, and last with last. This was to make sure that the alphas always stayed the alpha, and the runts were always runts. The middle pups had more freedom with whom they mated under this custom, but the smallest pups were often left with no mates because of the short life expectancy of runts.

Luna lay down next to the fire. *Besides, if I had mated with an Eclupse, I would be a prisoner in one of the communes, like the others.*

She tried to get some sleep, and eventually her thoughts had run their course and exhaustion found her.

***

"Remind me why we are doing this again," Terrabyss called after Numa, ripping off another piece of meat from the chunk he had hurriedly grabbed when they had sprinted into the night after their brother.

Rellik was only a few lue in front of him as they trudged through the snow. "Wouldn't you want us to look for you if you ran off?"

Terrabyss just snorted his response as the two tried to catch up to Numa, who had come to a halt with Jabyn and Essall next to her. When they reached her, Numa had already issued her orders to the Scouts, who split off to the northeast. Numa, Rellik, and Terrabyss went to the northwest. Terrabyss took a quick glance at the snow around his paws as Numa ushered them onward. The only tracks he could see were those of the five Maulers; he didn't see any prints left by Skoff. Numa howled at him to catch up, and he slung his weapon over his back and charged off after her on all fours.

Dawn wasn't far away when the three of them collapsed in a copse of firs and hemlocks. They were panting hard, and as their lungs burned for air, Terrabyss lay on his back, gasping.

"How—how far—far back did you—you lose the trail?" he asked between breaths, rolling over and looking at Numa, who wasn't lying down but was bent at the waist, clearly just as winded.

"There never was one," Numa admitted to the two of them once she caught her breath. "I have no idea where he went." She was desperately concerned for her brother, and both Terrabyss and Rellik couldn't stop thinking about the possibilities of possession.

What happened if a shaman was possessed? Could they even get possessed?

"I thought as much," Terrabyss said after another deep breath. "I didn't see any trail, and I know I am not the best tracker, but Skoff usually leaves clues as to where he is." He took another deep breath, having almost winded himself with that sentence. "Did you send Jabyn and Essall on an equally ill-informed chase?" He felt a very loose snowball hit his chest. It was the best response Numa could muster at the time.

"Are we getting a break?" Rellik finally asked, she hadn't wanted to interrupt the two of them and had wanted to be a little conscious of their feelings before she asked for a rest.

"What's wrong? You aren't tired, are you?" Terrabyss teased as he tried to jump up. To his credit, he did get to his paws, but it was not as graceful or energetic as he had envisioned.

While he struggled to get to his paws, Numa scooted over next to Rellik. "Yes, let's take a break. Hopefully, we will find him before the evening." She looked over to Terrabyss who was up and had a triumphant look on his face, his tail wagging with pride. "Come here and warm us with your ego," she instructed her brother as she and Rellik snuggled together to share body heat. They were too tired to dig out a den, and they wouldn't be here long; by sunup, Numa hoped to be on the move again. Both Rellik and Numa snuggled up close to Terrabyss when they felt him join the pile; they would at least get some time to rest.

Magic

Skoff woke up. He was lying face-first in the snow. Slowly—and with a lot of effort—Skoff sat up and looked around. His head was still ringing with a chorus of different sounds. Garbled but melodic tones swam about in his mind, twisting and warping his senses as they still spun from his last clear memory of watching the flames fill the pit. Then, everything seemed to go black and those noises chimed even louder for a moment. Skoff held his hands to his ears in an attempt to block out the barrage of sounds, but this did nothing to alleviate the noise. There was another noise that was starting to drown out the other melodies that danced about in his mind. A gentle, lapping sound, and a rustling, like wind through the trees.

No, that wasn't it. He tried to swing his head about to perceive his surroundings. The melodic and gibberish sounds assaulted him again, and he was forced to lie on his back again to try to relax. It was well into the morning, according to the sun's position, and Skoff slowly recognized the sound of the ebbing and flowing water as the Berg Maker, which formed small waves that broke near where he lay.

Alpha Father! How long was I in that trance? Skoff thought to himself as he slowly oriented himself. He was about three days' run from the Gathering, and to the northeast. The tundra stretched far around him, and even with the unobstructed view, he couldn't make out the grove. His nose was fortunately stronger than his eyes, and he could smell where the boundary marks to the Maulers' territory were.

Ever so gently and slowly, Skoff got to his paws, popping a compacted snowball into his mouth to suck on so that he could start hydrating himself. *Perhaps my tonic before the celebration was a bit too potent*, he thought as he took one agonizing step after the other. It helped to be somewhat intoxicated when doing the ritual dances and chants. The ancestors seemed more willing to communicate with the drunk, which was another reason to imbibe the tonics. The more he thought about it, the more positive he was that he had prepared the mixture properly.

Rabbit fur drinking skin, and the brain of a woodpecker mashed and added to the mead. Both the woodpecker and the rabbit were sacred to the Silverbacks. The rabbit was the only creature that had learned the way between this world and the Alpha Father's—a rabbit had no fear of the phantoms because it was too fast. Hence, Skoff wore a rabbit paw around his neck before every dance. His eyes went wide as he reached for his chest, but he relaxed and breathed a sigh of relief when he felt the rabbit's paw.

Good, I wasn't possessed, he assured himself. *Perhaps, it was one too many yellowcaps,* another ingredient very helpful in achieving the mindset for the ancestors' communication.

As he walked and sucked on the ice ball, his thoughts began to clear somewhat and that—once obnoxious—melodic tone started to become less garbled. It was a laugh, a sinister one. The memory sent a shiver down his spine as he heard the sound vividly again. *Why can't I make out the words?*

"Eh ilwl hosoce em." It still made as much sense to him now as it did when he first heard it.

The Banshee Tundra was mostly flat, especially this far from either mountain range, and as he walked toward the familiar scent of the Gathering, he began to make out the tips of the sequoia giants that acted as a barrier to the emptiness and howling winds of the tundra. Behind him, the icebergs towered above the water, being nudged by the ocean's currents. Some of them were the size of small mountains, while others looked hardly as big as the circumference of the Gathering. There was something ominous about the northern ocean; its waters were so dark that they were almost black, and with the pearlescent white ice protruding from the surface, it was like staring into an alien world. Skoff hated the open water, not that he had ever been in it, but he knew he liked the comfort of the firm ground beneath his paws.

It was getting toward the evening when Skoff finally reached the trees. His stomach was angry with him and constantly complaining about being expected to sustain him on the water that he kept sucking from the ice balls he made. He felt under his poncho to the little stitched pocket where he usually kept some venison, roasted nuts, or dried fruits. Yet again, today, he forgot that he had already dug into these emergency supplies when he had been wandering about in his earlier stupor. His stomach gave another disapproving tone.

"Oh, just shut up already, we are both starving," Skoff chastised his stomach as he began winding between the trees, working back to the Gathering. By nightfall, he had set up a good little camp for himself and he stared into the fire as his small wood mouse cooked over the open flames. He had found the critter while he was digging out his den near one of the old redwood giants; it wouldn't be a large meal, but it would be a meal. His stomach had almost demanded he eat it raw, but he wasn't a savage; he enjoyed cooked meat. Only Watchers and Scouts ate raw, and even then, only when they had to. As he stared into the flames, he became lost in thought. That laughter rang in his ears again and he sat up straight reflexively.

Had the voice introduced itself? Surely it gave me a name, phantoms are not bashful about announcing themselves, and ancestors have no reason to hide their names. If it was neither of those, then what was it? Surely all that is beyond mortal knowledge are phantoms and ancestors? There can't be more, can there?

This path of thought started to make him anxious, and Skoff consciously tried to think of something else. As usual, he couldn't think of anything as interesting as the question he had just posed to himself. He rubbed his eyes; he had obviously been staring at the fire for too long. In a panic, he realized that his dinner was completely burnt, and he snatched up the skewer before the meal fell into the ash.

"Well, that doesn't look like much of a dinner." The voice was raspy, with an annoying whistle that accompanied every inflection. Skoff stopped mid-blow from trying to cool off his meal. His stomach yelled at him to ignore whoever was talking to them and stuff his face, but his survival instincts were fortunately stronger. He looked up and peered about him, trying to locate the voice, and his hand reflexively reached for his staff. When he didn't feel the sigil-carved stick, he remembered that he hadn't had it this whole time. He must have left it back at the clearing, or he could have dropped it somewhere in his semi-conscious state. These realizations just made him more nervous. Skoff was a novice caster as far as mages were concerned, he was still young and hadn't the need or desire to really learn more about the arcane arts. Magic was not an honorable way to fight in the Mauler society, and the only reason he had any authority was because he was the only shaman in the tribe. Skoff began carving a small sigil in the ground beneath him. He had never mastered Grimmis' ability

201

to draw sigils with his paws.

"It's one of dem Maulers," a second, equally annoying voice piped up. This one's voice was not as raspy but also had that annoying whistle.

Skoff knew that he should recognize the accent, but he was unable to recall the information. He was clearly too tired and dulled from the last few days' events. Skoff knew that he wasn't back in Mauler territory yet, but he hadn't picked up any scent of another tribe as he had entered the grove. Other than the migratory Ramsyn and fly-by Gorgels, the grove had a rather sparse population. *Numa would know where I am,* he thought to himself, trying to locate the voices out beyond the trees, but still he saw nothing. The Furless of Izwin lived much further northeast, so he doubted this was them, also the accent was definitely of one of the beast tribes. It wasn't that Skoff didn't know how to fight, he just hadn't needed to depend on it for some time, and—in Skoff's opinion—he was a better caster than he was a fighter. *I can always use my blood to amplify my spells,* he tried to reassure himself. Using blood came with its own dangers, dangers that Skoff was well aware of. With how fatigued and hungry he already was, blood was going to have to be a very last resort.

"If you know I am a Mauler, then you know I have a pack with me. They are nearby, obviously your senses are not sharp enough," Skoff bluffed. He was almost done with the sigil, he just needed a few more moments to get a legible trace in the hard ground. *You won't stay hidden from me for much longer.* "And done," Skoff said, more to himself than anyone else. The spell wouldn't be too powerful since he had only used a sigil; he had not wanted to betray his plan by doing any dramatic movements. It was enough though, and the fire seemed to whip back and forth, becoming one singular column that shot up to the sky above.

Skoff kept his concentration on his cast as they cried out, alarmed by the display, and he heard three different voices. One of them hadn't been smart enough to keep its annoying voice silent when the fire rose up. The fire shot orange sparks in all directions, and a single small ember came to rest above each of the three heads. A bright and obvious trail of orange light shot forth from where Skoff stood, and at the same moment the embers came to rest a few whiskers from the top of their skulls, the orange lines of light connected to them.

"I see you now!" Skoff shouted victoriously as he watched the light beams twist up to the branches above him, one each to his left and right and another almost directly behind him.

The three unwelcome guests immediately began shooting arrows down to where Skoff had been standing, but as soon as the spell had taken hold, he had ducked behind a large trunk, a little to the right of the tree where the enemy behind him was perched.

"Cracked eggs!" the third opponent swore harshly, looking to its allies. "Why can't the two of you keep your flapping beaks shut? He didn't even know we were here! Now where did he go?"

All three of them began to look around, trying to locate the Mauler. The sudden increase in the fire's brightness left their usually extremely sharp eyesight hazy and none had seen Skoff's retreat. The Mauler peeked out from around the trunk. The three enemies were Corvel, a tribe of the Airlut clans. Corvel were similar to the Gorgels in their customs, and the understanding was that both of them worshiped the same twisted deities. They were both practitioners of bloodletting and torture. Unlike the Gorgel, —whose entire clan worshiped these terrifying gods—the Corvel were the only tribe of the Airlut population that practiced the beliefs. They had glossy black feathers that hung from their arms in a fang-like pattern, with a sharp point and wider base. They had rough-skinned hands, with sharp, curved talons that protruded from each of their three digits. Their heads were beaked, and they had beady black or yellowish eyes. They had a humanoid torso, but it was covered in the same rough skin as their hands, which was also evident on their legs from the knees down. Their feet were long and narrow, with another three digits that protruded out much further than the Maulers' claws on their paws. On each digit was another of those wicked curved talons that helped the Corvel perch on the branches. From their waists to their knees, they were covered in those same inky-black feathers, and they had no tail, but a fan of feathers to help them when they chose to fly. The Corvel were not tall, and they were not strong, and rumor had it they had hollow bones; Skoff was more than a little curious to find out if that was true. It wasn't too difficult to determine the sex of the Corvel since, similar to the Ramsyn, they had humanoid torsos. Skoff always found the Harpyn Taur to be ugly, and these Corvel were no exception. There were two females and one male; one of the females was clearly older than the other two, and Skoff thought that she might be their parent.

Well, at least they will die together, he thought to himself as he crept up on the trunk on which the older Corvel was perched. She was lecturing the other two, and didn't notice as Skoff began carving a rough sigil into the trunk.

The beaded chest armor that the Corvel were wearing would do little to protect them from magic, and they hadn't anticipated finding a shaman when they had spotted this lone Mauler. Still, their god would reward them greatly if they drained a victim of his size into their cauldron. The fact he could use magic made him dangerous in a different way, and his blood would be a rarity to Corvis Minor, the god of the rejected in the Airlut pantheon. The Corvel were armed with D-style bows and short, thin arrows. Those arrows—although not very physically damaging—were lethal, and Skoff could smell the poison with which the tips were lathered. Along with about a dozen arrows in a hip quiver, the Corvel each had a knife or hatchet tucked into the small of their back. The ones that didn't succumb to his spells would be defeated by his teeth and claws, he just had to avoid the poison. The Corvel were now leaning from side to side, trying to catch a glimpse of him with their unnaturally sharp eyes. Skoff had been lucky so far, and they hadn't seen him or heard his soft scratching above the popping fire or the nightly sounds of the grove. His luck would not hold, and in his excitement his tail betrayed him, wagging into view of the younger male Corvel.

"There, there!" it screeched at the top of its lungs, jumping up and down excitedly. The older female on the tree above Skoff looked down and spotted the Silverback. She pulled the bowstring back; it couldn't handle much tension and only allowed her to pull the arrow back to her chest, but that was enough. The fingers released, and the missile came whistling for Skoff.

Skoff couldn't afford to get hit by that poison, and he swung around the other side of the trunk and into the path of two other arrows.

Alpha Father! Why am I so bad at this?

The sigil next to the fire was still there; he ducked under the first of the two arrows, the second scraped across his thigh but didn't embed itself. He waved his arms in a large circle and spun, putting his endurance into his next cast. His hands connected with the sigil and the energy of his movement flowed into it. Again, the fire leapt up, but this time with purpose. Skoff envisioned the younger female Corvel, whose shot had almost struck him. The fire snaked suddenly, twisting for her and igniting her feathers and flesh as she dropped into the snow, dead from the burns before she hit the ground. There was a thump as an arrow lodged itself into Skoff's lower back. Thankfully, it missed his spine, but between the thigh wound and now this, he could already feel the poison's soporific effects. Skoff stumbled forward from the hit, he was going to have to amplify his magic if he hoped to walk out of this. First, though, he needed to slow the poison. Using a claw, he painfully cut into his left shoulder; he knew the risks of carving a permanent sigil on his body, but he had to stay conscious. He hoped he carved it exactly as he had learned it, smacking the sigil hard to get the blood really flowing.

If this works, I will have a permanent counter to poison, as long as it doesn't get damaged. If it doesn't, or gets damaged, I will turn into a bonfire.

"Not the worst odds," he mused out loud as he shuffled under a fern then ducked behind a boulder, as yet another arrow skipped off the stone.

There was a rush of heat as Skoff felt his blood burn away the toxins; the sigil had been accurate, but not very deep. Most of the poison was gone, but there were some lingering amounts causing minor effects. Mainly, Skoff's ears and nose felt full of dirt, and he could barely use them to locate the other two Corvel. Fortunately, his marker spell hadn't run out yet, and he could still see the tracing lines even if they were a bit blurry. He was about four trees away from the one tree trunk where he had almost finished the large sigil. *If I can get there and finish, I will have won.*

He saw one of the lines moving as the older Corvel hopped from branch to branch; Skoff wasn't very good at hiding his trail. The second line was following the other but on the opposite side, as they both attempted to sneak up on his flanks.

"He is there!" shouted the elderly Corvel as it noticed Skoff pressed up against one of the tree trunks. It shot an arrow toward him. Skoff ducked as the projectile came to a humming halt above his left ear. *That bitch was aiming for my face.* Skoff bolted, doubling back to the first tree; his ears warned him that the second Corvel had shot at him, and he instinctively zagged to the left and tripped over a root, slamming into the dirt.

"I got him," cawed the younger male. "You see that shot?" he exclaimed, turning to face the older female.

The older Corvel was surprised, her son was a terrible shot. It was a hard blow to lose her daughter—she had been the one to truly inherit her mother's talent—but she couldn't deny what she had seen.

"You're sure it hit?"

"Of course, why else would he have gone down that hard?" the male shot back angrily, as Skoff slowly regained consciousness.

The Mauler's whole face hurt, and he hoped that the blood in his mouth was from biting his cheek and not his tongue. Even a loose tooth, or a missing tooth, would be preferred to no tongue. Skoff caught the end of the male's shout and wondered if it was better to play dead, or to try to move; he was still about two tree trunks away from his goal.

***

"Did you see that?" asked Essall, as she and Jabyn were settling down to get some sleep. They had just finished their dinner and had decided that they would get up before dawn to continue their search for Skoff. Neither Scout had any intention of returning to the Gathering without him, alive or dead.

Jabyn stuck her head out from behind Essall, they were cuddled together by the embers of their cooking fire and she had already begun to drift off.

"What was it?" she replied, yawning widely as she shook her head, trying to rouse herself.

"A huge pillar of fire shot up," Essall told her companion, looking back in the direction it had come from. "We should probably check it out."

Jabyn didn't need to be told twice and stood. "You're right, we should go see." The two of them quickly ran through the ferns, sprinting as they weaved between the trees. They were closing in when a second pillar of fire shot up.

"There!" Jabyn shouted, and the two Scouts dropped their heads and ran with all speed toward the sudden flash.

***

Skoff took a deep breath, the two Corvel had stopped debating whether he had been hit or not and, from the sound of an arrow slotting into a bowstring, he guessed that the older female wasn't prepared to fully trust the younger Corvel's word. The shaman jumped to his hands and paws, bolting for the tree with his almost-complete sigil. There was a snap and a twang, and the boy shouted and cracked an arrow over his knee in

206

frustration at the sight of the running Mauler. An arrow sunk into Skoff's hip; it didn't have enough force to stop him or knock him off his paws, but it had been slathered in the sleep toxin. Skoff pushed forward, he had purged most of the poison out the first time, and he doubted that even a double dose of the stuff would put him down before he finished the sigil. The shaman had twice the Corvels' speed as they moved through the grove; in an open space where the Corvel could stretch their wings, it would be a different story. Here among the trees, he easily outpaced their hopping strides. Skoff looked around in confusion as he ran. It was odd, the world around him wasn't moving but he was sure that he was sprinting.

Why am I not at the sigil yet? The shaman lunged forward, trying to close the distance with a jump rather than a run, but still he made no progress forward. *Oh, this is not good.* Skoff tried to support himself by leaning against the tree trunk he had apparently not left. The shaman frantically scratched a rough and perhaps not even accurate wind sigil into the tree. He was bleeding enough that he didn't need to add any cuts, and he smeared the blood over the sigil and crumpled to the ground as a massive torrent of wind hammered into the tree, centered on the marking.

"Was that thunder?" asked Jabyn, as she and Essall snuck up to the edge of the small clearing where a fire ring sputtered, having had its fuel turned to pure ash in some flash burn. Essall shook her head no, and pointed to a rather large hemlock that had started to tilt. The two Scouts watched, hearing the wood protest as it started to splinter and snap under the force as a focused gale pushed at the trunk, trying to crash it into the earth.

The older Corvel hopped to one branch and came to a quick stop, gripping firmly to the branch under her feet to keep herself from jumping into the falling tree. "Don't!" she shouted to her son as he came up next to her, intending to follow after her.

The young Corvel's knees bent, and the male's eyes went wide as he realized why his mother was trying to stop him. He tried to tell his legs to stop, but they had received the all-clear earlier and had already given him lift off. His mother reached out and grabbed him by his leg, yanking him back. There was a loud pop as his leg was dislocated, but he at least hadn't lunged into an avalanche of branches and bark. The elder Corvel lifted the male back up and helped him to sit on the branch, shaking her head in disapproval. She noticed a movement in some ferns, a short way back from where the shaman now lay, obviously unconscious. She clapped her hand over her son's beak before he could complain or cry any more, motioning him to follow her gaze.

Essall pushed a large fern leaf out of her eyesight, seeing Skoff lying there.

"Skoff," she whispered harshly, trying to get his attention. She couldn't see what he had been fighting, but she could smell the Corvel. Unlike Skoff, she and Jabyn were familiar with the Airlut tribe and were more practiced in conflicts with the Corvel. Essall let the fern drop back and she told Jabyn what she had seen by her expressions and pacing, rather than speaking, not wanting to draw attention to where they were or what they were saying to one another. Jabyn nodded, understanding that there were at least two Corvel, using sleeping concoctions, and that Skoff seemed unconscious. Jabyn responded by flicking her ears and flicking her nose up twice, Essall opened her mouth and gave two obvious pants in response. The two were of one mind.

The Corvel mother had lost her daughter tonight and her son was injured; with the arrival of the other Maulers, she didn't have high hopes for victory. Even if she had her daughter, she would not have wanted to tempt this kind of confrontation without more numbers. She gave one last, longing look at the unconscious shaman, and motioned up with one of her three fingers to her son, whose beak she still held. The other Corvel inclined his head, yes; having also seen Essall, he had no intention of continuing this conflict whilst in so much pain.

Both the Scouts narrowed in on the tree on which the two Corvel were perched. Their bluish-black feathers blended well with the shadows, having kept them out of sight, but the Maulers hunted better without their eyes. As Jabyn and Essall approached the trunk, they heard the squawks, and the two Corvel fluttered out into the night's sky. Quickly dipping and weaving through the branches, they shot for the sky above the canopy. Silverbacks aren't excellent climbers, and the two Maulers opted to not pursue the Corvel as they broke out into the open sky above. Jabyn was the last to keep her eyes on the Corvel as they made their escape, and once she was sure they weren't trying to feign a retreat and then double back on the Maulers for a surprise attack, she turned back around.

"Is he alive?" she asked Essall, as the other Scout knelt next to Skoff.

Essall placed her hand on the shaman's chest and waited patiently, letting out a sigh of relief as his chest rose and fell in a steady rhythm. Jabyn's tail wagged, relieved as well. She knew that Essall had feelings for Skoff. Jabyn didn't really care for him, but she cared for Essall. Besides, as long as Essall was a Scout she would stay with Jabyn, and the fact that she hadn't retired yet always made Jabyn feel better.

"What shall we do with him, wake him or drag him back on a travois until he wakes up himself?"

Essall let go of Skoff's hand. "I guess we could just camp for the night like we had planned, and see if he wakes up in the morning. We can carry him back to where we made our camp."

Jabyn agreed with her and helped her carry the shaman back, holding him by his knees while Essall held his chest under his arms. Between the two of them, Skoff was not too heavy and they easily carried him back to their camp.

***

"You want me to do WHAT?" was Terrabyss' response—a bit too aggressive—at least in Rellik's opinion. She didn't understand what he was complaining about; Luna was gorgeous, she was tall, proportionate, smart, fun, he could do a lot worse. "Besides, I am a Watcher, it comes with the same restrictions as a Scout," he snarled at Numa as they marched back toward the Gathering.

Jabyn had found the three of them the night before, informing Numa that she and Essall had located her brother, and that Essall and he were on their way back to the Gathering. Numa, Terrabyss, and Rellik had been combing the west side of the grove for the past five days, and they were looking forward to getting back.

"I won't repeat myself," Numa hesitated for a moment. She was tired of this argument; she had honestly thought that Terrabyss would have been thrilled. He spent so much time with Luna that others probably thought they were mated already. Her frustration was expressed in the rest of the sentence. "Little brother, you will mate with her and bring even more power to the Ravis name. Your brother the shaman, myself the Scout Mother, and you, the mate to the heir of the Alpha title. No one will challenge our pack; we will make a dynasty where Grimmis failed. He knew which litter deserved his legacy, that was obvious with Skoff."

She spat the name Grimmis, having never had much respect for the old Alpha. Her mother had to reinforce his decisions and Numa knew it, but when her Scout had reported the news about Dio's arrival and Haxzus' challenge, she had known that she had to bring support to her brother. She had assumed it was Terrabyss who had challenged the Alpha. Bia had deserved better, the Ravis deserved better, and she was going to make sure that they got what they deserved.

"Do you have a problem with that?" she snapped as she came to a stop in front of Terrabyss, who had spun around to her at the 'little brother' part. Jabyn came up close behind her, hackles raised, which made Numa feel better. Although she still wasn't sure if that would be enough of a deterrent to Terrabyss' anger, she wished that Essall were here as well.

Terrabyss locked eyes with Jabyn before meeting his sister's gaze; he could tell how serious she was, and he did enjoy Luna's company. He had never thought that he would have a family or a litter; he didn't know if it was because it had never been expected of him as the runt, or if it was because he didn't want it. "I can't imagine that Skoff thinks that our ancestors are okay with me mating with an Eclupse," was his only argument for the time, but he didn't turn around yet and was still holding his kanabo at his side.

Still, Jabyn didn't back down, and again Numa was glad of her support. "Don't worry about what Skoff thinks. Now, can we keep going? I am tired, and I want to get back so that we can start preparing you for the Materimony. It is likely that Luna is already ready, and given how quickly she learns, I would be surprised if Skoff hasn't already taught her the proper customs." Terrabyss didn't budge and she could tell he was thinking it over. "Besides, you want an end to everyone looking at you like a runt?" she asked over his response, having to speak loudly, forgetting that Terrabyss didn't really understand rhetorical questions. "If you are the first to mate in our litter, you will be granted the title of Mahuer[48] !" she shouted over him. "Now you may respond," Numa finished in a much softer voice, as Terrabyss had obviously not considered this fact.

Terrabyss nodded, then he cocked his head in confusion. "What about my position as a Watcher though?"

Numa rolled her eyes and pushed past him; if he hadn't lifted his weapon by now, he wasn't going to. "You already lost that, since we are going back to the Green Wall, and if you hadn't already noticed, you are

48 "Great" as for the Ozars, but for Silverbacks it is the one in the litter who inherits the pack name

a commander now."

That response made Terrabyss sling his kanabo back over his back, he hadn't thought about that either. *Is that my profession now?* He was pulled from his thoughts as Jabyn walked by, with a smirk on her face. "What?" he barked at her, but she gave no response. "Keep walking," he growled as he moved to follow.

Numa looked back at Jabyn, giving her a single obvious pant; Jabyn gave the same gesture in response. She wasn't planning on attacking him, and the fact she elicited such an angry response had been enough enjoyment.

"You make it too easy for her," Rellik informed Terrabyss as she jogged up next to him, glad that the tension had seemed to dissipate. She had begun to understand the Scout; she was beginning to understand all of them in a way that as a sheltered pup she had never seen. She loved every minute of it. This was life, and her only regret was having missed so much of it by never mingling, not even amongst her siblings. *What's that supposed to mean?*

"What's that supposed to mean?" Terrabyss mirrored her thoughts.

"You are too predictable," Rellik told him. "I know your moves before you move, I know how to get under your skin. You need to learn to have some control, like Jabyn, like Numa. Your rashness makes it easy to outsmart you." Rellik laughed as the two of them marched behind Numa and Jabyn.

Terrabyss knew it wasn't bad advice; he was at his best when he was focused, and that was usually in a fight. He knew how to fight. Terrabyss wondered, *Can a good fighter be a good mate?* That was what was really frightening him, not if he could be a mate but be a good mate. There were reasons that the tribe didn't take mated Maulers as fighters, although it seemed that Dio was about to throw that tradition away too, since Terrabyss had every intention of going to war to help get back their home.

The Pact

The Gathering was in chaos; not only were the travois being loaded but rations were being divided up between the traveling packs. Arrangements were only a few days away from launching the Maulers on their journey back into the Green Wall. While these preparations were being made, there was an equally big event taking place within the Gathering, depending on who you asked. The new Alpha of the Maulers had agreed to allow the runt of the Ravis pack to have the pleasure of being Luna's mate. Although, as Luna had learned, this Materimony would be a bit novel, in that the Alpha's pack would take on the name of the mate's pack. Skoff explained to Luna that this was done so that she and her father would no longer hold the title of their Eclupse pack, but a Mauler pack name, Ravis.

Skoff's condition on arrival back at the Gathering had been one of limps, groans, and moans. The shaman had wanted a whole moon to recover from his very frightening and harrowing ordeal, but the Alpha had other plans. The two had argued for some time, away from the acute ears of the other Silverbacks. Skoff was not impressed that Dio wanted a speedier recovery due to the Materimony between his brother and the Alpha's daughter. The shaman's tune had quickly changed when Terrabyss, Numa, Rellik, and Jabyn arrived back at the Gathering. Essall had been willing to stand by Skoff when against the Alpha, but against her Scout Mother was a different story, and Skoff soon lost his strongest supporter and had miraculously healed by the following morning. He did have a slight limp in his right hip, where the arrow had done a little muscle damage, simply due to the amount of poison. The following days were filled with planning and even unpacking several travois to obtain the items needed for the Materimony, mainly food and drink. Skoff spent every hour they were awake coaching Luna through the customs of the Materimony and Rellik, Numa, and Aasha helped prepare Luna's appearance according to the proper traditions. Terrabyss was also put through rigorous rituals, with Unkyss, Brutyss (at Unkyss' suggestion), and Oulyss (at Brutyss' suggestion) helping him. Terrabyss had never been instructed on the Materimony by his mother, and took up any of Skoff's time not spent with Luna in learning his proper place in the ceremony.

Brutyss dumped a large skin of melted snow over Terrabyss' head. Brutyss was perfect for this job, having both been too nimble for Terrabyss to bite and also stealthy enough to surprise him, so that he couldn't get out of the way of the freezing water as it drenched him. That had been before they had realized this job was going to take more than one skin of water, and both Unkyss and Oulyss had since been forced to pin Terrabyss down so that he couldn't run away. Although, Brutyss still needed to fear his teeth.

"Stop biting, we are trying to help!" shouted Brutyss as the young adult narrowly pulled his hands away before a finger got bitten. Terrabyss growled in response, trying to shake the freezing water out of his thick coat.

"Oh, stop your whining, you don't have to hold him down. My body is so tired I think I am just cramped in this position now," Oulyss snarled as he yanked Terrabyss by his hips, keeping him from leaning into his bite and preventing him from getting Brutyss.

"Well, maybe if you warned me before you dropped freezing water on me," Terrabyss growled, almost lifting Oulyss up as he tried to stand.

Unkyss' strong arm grabbed Terrabyss' shoulder and pushed him back to a sitting position, with Oulyss' help. "If he warned you, you would move. You have already proven to us that you won't stay still," stated Unkyss as he firmly held Terrabyss, "and if you don't stay still, I am not going to be able to get all these knots out of your coat." He motioned for Brutyss to make another skin full of snow, he was going to need more water to wash out the dirt.

"I bet Luna doesn't have to go through all this," Terrabyss snarled, as Unkyss pulled yet another knot of fur free.

"No, no, she doesn't, because she keeps her coat combed. Alpha Father, when was the last time you put a comb through here?" Unkyss said, finding another tangle of fur and beginning to work it out. "I comb every evening," he informed Terrabyss, almost getting the new knot out.

"I do it every morning," added Oulyss as he let his grip slacken slightly now that Brutyss was gone to fetch more water.

"It has been a busy moon, or so," was Terrabyss' response as Unkyss ran the comb down his spine, "maybe if you trained as much as you pamper yourselves it wouldn't take two of you to hold me down." Neither of them felt any tugs. They would normally just use their claws, but Skoff had given Terrabyss an ivory comb just for the occasion. Half of its teeth now lay in the dirt next to Unkyss, and he had resorted to using his claws for the largest knots. Terrabyss cringed, that meant it was time to comb out his chest and stomach.

"You better be far gentler than you have been," Terrabyss warned Unkyss, snapping his teeth.

"You want a shot at this, Oulyss?" Unkyss asked, stopping for a moment and hoping for a yes from the other Mauler.

"Alpha Father, no, we drew lots!" Oulyss shouted and held on tight as another skin of freezing water was dumped over Terrabyss' head. It was a miracle that the three of them had finished by the time the sun had risen to its noon position. The days were becoming longer and longer. The grove, with its fan-like needles that decorated the branches, had been successful at keeping the sun at bay throughout the winter. Now, that season was coming to a close, and the springtime heat was starting to gain an upper hand. In the less-shaded parts of the grove, the snow was nearly gone, and what was left was mixed with dirt. Tall ferns that had previously been covered now sprouted from the snow, stretching out their leaves again in the gaps under the canopy to catch the light. Patches of green clovers could be spotted where the warmth of a Silverback's body had melted away the snow layer to reveal the fresh green mat.

The animals were aware of this change as well, the birds sang and the squirrels chattered frantically back and forth. Terrabyss felt as though the creatures were having a good laugh at his expense and he let out a howl of pain as Unkyss worked on yet another knot. None of them had expected it would take them all morning to groom Terrabyss' coat. The three Maulers worked with even more urgency now as they brushed a mixture of sap and blood onto his teeth, making sure that each tooth had been covered by an obvious layer of the sticky red mixture. While that dried, they used a small amount of sap to spike up and exaggerate Terrabyss' collar and tail. Skoff even helped with the last bit, having shown up ranting about how the Materimony couldn't be held late or it would be a bad omen, among other words of warning which mostly went ignored.

***

Numa tapped Luna's nose lightly with the end of her brush.

"Stop licking, or it won't dry."

Luna grumbled a little, but obligingly opened her mouth and tried not to taste more of the sap and blood mixture that was being brushed onto her teeth. It felt and tasted strange, and although she knew that it was a Mauler custom, she hadn't had the opportunity to experience it yet. Numa and Rellik had been helping her to prepare, and Skoff was constantly badgering her with last-minute questions, making sure that she understood every part of the ceremony of which she was about to be part. As noon came and went, he would frequently storm in, clearly frustrated and making comments about how nice her coat was and what a true blessing that was. Luna still wasn't sure exactly how she felt about it all, it was all taking place very fast, but she also understood that it was necessary for her and Dio's security. Numa and her father had drilled that point often enough.

The sun had barely set, and the night sky was showing off a dazzling array of stars as Terrabyss and Luna stood facing away from one another. She was truly gorgeous, and Terrabyss had to concentrate to not wag his tail when he had first seen her, that would simply be crude. Numa shot him a harsh whisper, "Your tail better stop moving or I will cut it off!" Rellik gave her a puzzled look, as she had noticed that Numa's tail wagged a bit when she moved to lecture Terrabyss. Obviously, Terrabyss wasn't the only one impressed, or perhaps Numa was more pleased with herself, it was hard to tell with her. Luna and Terrabyss did make a striking pair. They were nothing like the other, and when placed next to one another, it was even more obvious. Terrabyss was broad and muscular, even by Mauler standards. His groomed and shining fur was highlighted by the numerous small fires dotted about, revealing the burgundy tint to his dark coat. Luna's coat shone pure white, glistening and reflecting the firelight, and, like him, her back and collar were spiked with wax to emphasize those areas. Her body was strong, but with her height she was leaner, and her torso was longer, giving her a much more slender build. They each faced their respective packs; Numa, Skoff, and Rellik sat cross-legged in front of Terrabyss. Luna faced only the Alpha, Dio. Both packs were looking their best as well, but neither had their teeth bloodied like the two prospective mates. The tribe circled around, with the elders and the young who hadn't been old enough to go on the Hunt this year, there was a total of a hundred and thirty-seven Maulers. It was an impressive sight, and no

Mauler there had ever realized how large their numbers were.

Over the last moon, these packs had come to know one another much better and with Dio's encouragement—coached by Skoff—Dio had held daily games of My Skull and Tests of Strength, and winners had been awarded first choice of commander under whom they would serve. Dio had chosen as his field commanders Terrabyss, Numa, Maxyss, and Rymmall, who had come out of retirement, but had insisted that Numa maintain her position as Scout Mother. Small hunting excursions had been led with some of the new adults under Maxyss, to ensure that rations were filled when they were used for an event such as this, and the community had begun to feel as though they were a tribe again. The many hard years and tough seasons seemed to melt away with the snow as the tribe bore witness to the union of these two packs, promising to those gathered of the Mauler return to the other tribes, and of the other tribes' need for the Maulers' might.

There had been an argument between Dio and Skoff as to how to stage this ceremony. Dio had wanted some Eclupse customs to be incorporated into the Materimony, but Skoff had laughed at the notion. Skoff had again made it clear that Dio couldn't be an Eclupse if he wanted to lead the Maulers, so he had better make this a Mauler ceremony. Luna had bravely agreed, not wishing her father to include any of the Eclupse customs. These consisted of her claws and teeth being agonizingly cleaned and stained white with chalk and sap. Given the chaos that had ensued during the last Mauler ceremony, Dio was anxious about the shaman having control over the Materimony, but he had little choice when Luna had agreed to the Mauler customs.

Dio now listened in silence, as did the whole tribe, watching the two mates recite their oaths to one another. They had turned to face each other, and looked at the other's pack as they swore both before and to them.

"I will hunt and fight by your side. Your pack is my pack. I will share in your glory and your grief. I will share in their glory and their grief. Your allies are my comrades, and your enemies are my foes. I will keep this commitment to you and only you, in this life and into the next. No other mate will I want, nor will I take. From alpha to omega, before Alpha Father and Alpha." Terrabyss then looked only at Luna and gave her the gesture of submission, framing his chest and stomach with his arms.

Luna had to fight to keep her tail from wagging this time, she had been sternly coached by Skoff about etiquette and custom and she meant to impress. Luna did impress as she held her composure and recited the same words back to Terrabyss, having memorized each word, expression, and to tempo her oath as he had. After she intoned the oath, she too looked at Terrabyss and gestured in submission to him. They both acknowledged each other's promise and in one voice—as best as two individuals could without practicing with one another—they said, "with these words and this act, I make clear the mate I choose."

Howls erupted from the gathered tribe, and the sheer number of the Maulers present sent up an echo of howls such that had never been heard in the grove. For an instant, everything fell silent after the massed howl from the gathered Silverbacks had ceased. Even the insects among the ferns and trees fell deathly quiet, nervous of what was to follow such an ominous noise. The new mates nuzzled one another, and there were shouts of joy and claps on the back as well as words of greeting between the two packs and those gathered as they recognized the new Ravis-Mahuer pack. If Skoff, Numa, or Rellik were to mate from now on, they would need to take the name of their mate's pack or petition to be recognized as their own pack. The name Ravis now belonged to Terrabyss and Luna, as well as their descendants.

Under the light of the full moon, the Maulers enjoyed the night with drink and food. The last few kegs of Dwarven beer purchased from the Ramsyn had been pulled out, as well as the last of the mead casks. The meat had already been accounted for earlier, and had been slowly cooking over the fires all day. As skewers were consumed and skins were drained, the celebration grew. Those more inebriated and who had overindulged sat out as the games began. Silverbacks are not known for pacing their celebrations, especially ones of this magnitude.

A group of some new adults picked up the skull first, two of these nine happened to be Brutyss and Oulyss, so within a short amount of time Unkyss had also joined the game. When he joined, this brought Rellik, Dardyl, and Aasha in, who had all begun to take more than a passing interest in the tall Mauler. More Maulers began to participate, and Unkyss knew that his winning streak and taunts would provoke Terrabyss to join the game. Unkyss hadn't been wrong, and other young adults quickly flooded the field to his cries as Terrabyss turned the tide on Unkyss' lead. Essall and Jabyn got roped in, and now complained to Numa, but their nagging fell on deaf ears as she said she would only play if Luna did. Numa was sure that Luna would not get involved, but she found that she had misjudged her when the Eclupse ran over. With Luna's addition, Dio couldn't refuse the call; by this stage, if you were an able-bodied adult and weren't playing, it looked strange.

The boundary lines that Skoff had so carefully placed were soon pushed to include areas of the surrounding grove, no longer contained to the original clearing. Those running with the skull now not only had to contend with other players, but also the actual forest itself. Dodging around tree trunks, sliding under, or over fallen logs, slipping around or lunging above scattered boulders, and using their nimbleness and reflexes to keep themselves from tripping over the many roots or dips. More than one player was out because of injury or simply unconscious; they had knocked themselves out trying to navigate the gauntlet. The contestants weren't playing forgivingly even with the difficult conditions, a matter of pride had become interwoven into the game.

As the night wore on, it became less of a game and more of a crucible of strength, cunning, and endurance. Many had come to realize this and chose to opt out, not feeling the need to compete against such giants. The whole tribe now watched as this grueling match began to define the top packs within the Maulers' hierarchy.

As the game had begun so it was starting to grind to an end, only nine players remained on the field, and again the boundaries fell within Skoff's original outline. The nine of them huddled around the skull that had been placed in the middle of the field, after Numa had just scored another point. More than one of the players were favoring one paw more than the other. Dio's right eye was almost completely swollen, having been hit hard by Unkyss on a possession prior to Numa's point. Unkyss spit out a bit of blood to Dio's satisfaction, he had seemed to bite his cheek or tongue during their last collision. Most of Rellik's wounds came from numerous cuts caused by charging through the branches earlier; they had stopped bleeding, but her fur was heavily matted. Luna obviously had a stitch in her side; she was favoring her left flank and holding her right slightly, trying to massage out the pain. Both Numa and Terrabyss had bloody noses from having collided into each other several plays back, and they were pulling out small wads of moss and changing them with fresh ones so the bleeding would stop. Dardyl was having trouble lifting her left

218

arm; it wasn't broken, but the muscles had been badly bruised when she had been knocked into the air by a surprisingly strong sweep from Dio, as she had tried to snatch up the skull when Unkyss had hit him. Aasha was panting hard, holding her side like Luna and was foaming at the mouth a bit; there was a pink hue to the foam, Unkyss wasn't the only one who had bitten himself. The last player, Brutyss, was probably in the best physical condition of all. His amazing endurance was on display, and he was hardly panting, but his smaller frame had taken some hard hits throughout the game. Brutyss' sleek black fur had some blood and dirt mixed into it and he had a slightly swollen lip, but other than that the Mauler looked fine.

The play before Unkyss tackled Dio, the first spring rain had appeared, showering the grove with an early dousing. This had turned the snow into slush and had made the game even more intense. The points had long been forgotten, as the players now stood until they were either the last one standing or they simply couldn't move any longer. The scoring of a goal did allow for breaks like this for the players to get a quick rest, so it was still worth it just to try. Brutyss had hoped that his agility and balance would help him in this mud pit, but so far Numa had been able to take the most advantage of the situation. He had earned his fat lip from trying to lunge at her and getting a palm to the face, he wouldn't try that method of attack again. Both Dio and Luna had depended on their speed early in the event, but both their stamina were starting to wane. Lacking their usual nimbleness, they had taken some hard hits, and Dio particularly was looking the worse for wear.

Dio knew that he needed the larger Maulers to focus on each other if he hoped to come out on top. He had used many of his 'special talents' to help him in the game, but his resources were getting depleted, and without the willpower to maintain his focus on his body, Dio wasn't sure how he was going to come out victorious. Dio had been sure that he had used his trick right before the impact, but Unkyss hadn't missed that time. If Dio couldn't fool their senses any more, he was not going to stay conscious much longer. He had been able to also use his cunning, at least at first. Everyone was getting wise to his tricks now, and Dio was pretty sure if he reached for the skull, they wouldn't even blink. Dio tried anyway; to his frustration, he was right about his assumption. Dio thought about not picking it up, but he was pretty sure someone would tackle him just for his attempt. He thought he might as well make it worth the pain that was to come; besides, he might shock everyone by grabbing it. Numa responded first this time, still full of adrenaline from her last point. She lunged forward, catching Dio by his hips and lifting him up over her head before pitching him back into the slush around her paws. Numa looked around frantically for the skull as Dio gasped for air.

Rellik caught the skull instinctively, she had seen Numa move and had intended to follow when she had caught the sight of the skull soaring toward her. She wasn't sure if Dio had purposefully thrown it at her, or if he had been hit so hard by Numa that he had just fumbled it. Either way, it didn't matter because she was now holding onto the precious item. Rellik's advantage had been that she could read the others; she seemed to have an ability to predict how they thought, spoke, and even fought. Rellik was only slightly bigger than Brutyss and she was more visibly muscular then both Luna and Dio, but compared to the other five she was not confident in her ability to withstand a direct hit from them. Rellik registered Dardyl's move first and Aasha was close behind her, having been on either side of her when she caught the skull. She flipped backward and the two collided like stone on stone, both hitting the ground from the impact like fallen sequoias. Rellik tried to keep track of Terrabyss and Unkyss, those two being her biggest concern at the moment. She could take a hit from Luna, and having seen Numa desperately trying to locate the skull, she wasn't worried about her just now. Rellik landed, holding the skull tightly; she heard some movement behind her as her paws hit the snow. She spun about, hoping to avoid whoever was going to tackle her, but no one lunged by. Then Rellik realized she wasn't holding the skull. "I don't have it!"

Terrabyss heard her scream that she didn't have the skull, but he was already moving and the mud and slush were not conducive to his stopping as he collided with Rellik. Rellik heard a thump, thump, thump as she rolled backward, head over tail. As she came to a stop in a snowbank, she seriously considered if she wanted to get back up after that hit. Terrabyss came out of the impact rather well; Rellik was not a soft target, but she hadn't had much time to brace, which had worked in his favor. He dug his claws into the mud trying to find some purchase, also using his hand to dig in. Slightly winded, he tried to get his sights on who had the skull.

Brutyss had come up with a new tactic, let the sadists pound on each other and then snatch up the skull while they were not paying attention. Brutyss' nimble fingers and speed would keep him in this game, as long as he remained mostly unscathed. Each point is another chance to catch your breath, Brutyss reminded himself. He was closing on the boundary line, when in the downpour, right next to him, Luna appeared. He was a bit more muscular than her, but his endurance and speed had been his ace. Yet here she was, right next to Brutyss, her height adding distance to her long lunge. Brutyss couldn't believe how quietly she ran, even in this slush, and he had no idea she was there until she had already begun to close the gap. He debated going to all fours and sprinting for the goal, but at her speed if she hit him, it might put him out of this game if he didn't brace for it. He could perhaps turn and duck under her if she lunged, and then he could just make a dash for the line while she tried to recover from the error. It took him too long to decide and she hit his legs with her shoulder, sending both his body and balance spinning. Brutyss tried to keep his grip on the skull, but the need to brace himself before he landed face-first into the ground forced him to let go of it. There was a smacking sound as though someone had clapped, and Brutyss' hands slid out as he hit the muddy slush hard.

Luna scooped up the skull and tried to finish the last few lue to the goal line. Numa hadn't needed much time to figure out that the skull wasn't around Dio's gasping body, and had sprinted after Brutyss when he had snatched the skull from Rellik. Numa was sure she wasn't going to catch up with Brutyss, but then when Luna had shouldered him, Numa had charged onward, spurred by the delay of the collision and Luna's desperate search for where the skull was dropped or thrown. Numa's side was sending sharp pains of protest to her brain as she gasped for air, she was less than a handful of lue from Luna, and she ignored the pain as best she could. There was a thudding noise to Numa's left as Terrabyss—now on all fours—tore past her, heaving for air as he panted desperately. Numa came to a jogging stop, her side aching and her brother showing her that she was losing speed rather than gaining.

Luna also heard the sound of the approaching Terrabyss, few wouldn't. She looked over her shoulder and noticed with some frustration that the Mauler was closing the distance. Luna wasn't sure if what she thought of was against the rules or not, since she hadn't seen anyone running on all fours with the skull before, but Terrabyss was closing alarmingly fast. Now they were mated, she felt as though Terrabyss was even less likely to hold back. In mid-stride, having become very adept at switching between the two stances, she tossed the skull out and up in front of her. As her hand released the skull, she allowed the right to mirror the left and both hands connected with the slush gracefully. Luna lifted her head, and with a smooth snap, caught the skull in her teeth. Terrabyss caught only a mouthful of muddy slush as she sprinted away from him, her long gait again serving to easily outpace anyone who attempted to tackle her. Terrabyss slowly came to a jogging stop, gasping for air as he looked back at Numa, who just shrugged in response to his frustrated and slightly impressed expression.

"She is a quick learner!" Brutyss shouted from where he still lay on his stomach, not having seen what had happened, but he assumed that Luna had scored as it was her voice that was cheering happily.

Luna jogged past Terrabyss, who had now collapsed like his sister in the slush, trying to catch his breath. Both Dardyl and Aasha had regained consciousness during the last play, but neither moved to stand as Luna returned the skull to the center of the field. Dio hadn't even bothered to move when he saw Brutyss take off with the skull. Unkyss sat at the boundary line, pulling meat off a skewer and taking a long draft from a skin. Brutyss was mimicking Numa and Terrabyss and had sprawled out in the slush. He sat up slowly, but didn't bother beyond that.

Dio was on his back, but had managed to catch his breath again. "I think you win," he said to Luna as she set the skull down. The voices of the other players joined him in agreement, except for Unkyss, who was too busy trying to drain his drinking skin. All about them, the tribe howled their approval at the outcome, and some of the pups who had been entranced by the game started a small match of their own that was no less competitive. Injuries were taken care of, and snowpacks were applied to aching bones and swelling muscles. Terrabyss walked close to Luna as they left the field, reaching for her hand and grasping it in his.

"I know it's probably not what you wanted, but I will do my best. I will try to be a good mate to you," he said gruffly, not looking at her.

Luna's tail wagged. She had grown up running from the Ozars, she had never put much thought into what she wanted out of life, other than to survive. Isn't this just another way of surviving? Luna thought. If so, she might like it.

By now, the shower had passed and the storm clouds lifted to reveal a gorgeous canvas of stars above the trees. A central fire—as the one created a half-moon ago—had been built in the center of the Gathering,

222

and the whole tribe sat around it, some watching a little nervously. Many had accepted Dio's reasoning and hadn't bothered to think much beyond the previous incident. Terrabyss, Numa, Rellik, Dio, Essall, and Jabyn watched on edge as the shaman finished his five ceremonial rotations, and the rocks that circled the pit seemed to glow before shooting flames back into the center of the pit. A gout of red, yellow, and orange twisted and swayed and the invisible fuel still popped and smoked as though the fire was consuming wood, Skoff relaxing visibly as the magic worked.

Terrabyss hadn't told anyone what he had seen that night, and Luna was still confused about what had happened. She had been told by her father that something had scared the shaman, and he had run off in the night. Luna didn't know what had frightened Skoff so much, and she wasn't sure if her father was even telling her the truth. She had hoped that someone in her new pack would give her a bit more insight, or at least more honesty, and she patiently waited for that Mauler to present themselves.

Skoff had been nervous about re-opening the bridge between them and the heavens above. The shaman was sure that no one had been possessed, and although he couldn't explain what had happened, he believed that no phantom had managed to slip through the barrier. Skoff's hesitation was obvious to those who truly knew what had happened, in that they knew he had simply vanished. Skoff had told the Alpha and his siblings—excluding Rellik—what had happened and about the odd voice. He kept what the voice said to himself, telling the others that he had only heard constant laughter. The shaman knew the importance of solidifying the Materimony before the Alpha Father, and tried not to let his nerves interfere with what custom demanded. Skoff was relieved when he didn't experience the sounds or the madness that had previously driven him to run as the fire's light filled the Gathering. He watched the flames intently; however, caution is always necessary when creating openings between the mortal and spiritual worlds. The shaman repeated Grimmis' advice silently in his thoughts as he watched earnestly.

Terrabyss also watched the flames closely, he could feel Luna's head resting on top of his, and her hand in his. He was happy that she seemed happy, and he hoped that he could keep her feeling this satisfied. The game had obviously worn her out, and the food was rapidly sending them both into a contented drowsy state. Luna's breath was rhythmic, and it was a relaxing sound, almost managing to pull Terrabyss out of his anxiety at watching the flames.

"Terrabyss," a voice spoke to him. For a moment, Terrabyss looked about, it sounded far away, and he knew from the volume that it hadn't been anyone near him. The voice was enthralling, with a kindness to its honied tone. "Terrabyss," the voice seemed to coax him, and Terrabyss' attention was drawn to the fire. The way the flames danced was hypnotic and the sound of crackling fuel made a seductive melody in harmony with movement of the flames. The heat was becoming more intense, and Terrabyss felt sure that the snow all about the Gathering was going to melt away. He could smell hot stones, and then a smell like rotten eggs, which made him feel as though he wanted to vomit. Terrabyss could hear powerful gales of wind which drowned out all nearby sounds. His body felt both cold and hot at the same time, as though he was being stewed in the Berg Maker. He tried to keep calm, unsure of what was going on, and berating himself for not having talked to Skoff about what had happened to him at the last ceremonial fire. Terrabyss was sure that he was the only one having this experience, because no one else seemed to be feeling the heat from the fire or hearing the loud wind. He strained his ears, trying to pick up the sound of the voice that was calling out his name. A soft, almost faint whisper managed to force its way through the wind to his ears, "Lucurael."

Luna looked down in confusion as Terrabyss slipped into her lap. His body relaxed so suddenly and so completely that it startled her, and took all her strength to stop him from knocking her over. He seemed to collapse, his head resting on her thighs. Luna had been pleasantly napping, the fire's light had managed to bring her to a groggy consciousness, but Terrabyss' sudden need for sleep had woken her up quickly. She gazed at him, puzzled; she was sure it was the same for him, but she couldn't help but appreciate his unconventional looks. There was something about his uniqueness—he was different from every other Silverback she had ever met that made her attracted to him. Luna wasn't sure if she was ever going to get used to all the things he did—like passing out without warning—but they had had a busy and exciting day.

"Lu—Lucre-el," Terrabyss mumbled. Luna leaned down, trying to hear him clearly.

She laughed softly, stroking his head. "Well, I hope that isn't another female, for your sake," she teased as he dreamed.

Intermission

"Lu-cur-a-el," I enunciated again slowly. I was beyond frustrated. I had to remain patient or I ran the risk of repeating the previous debacle, and worse, the arid winds of He-Lah[49] were practically drowning out my amplified voice. The last Wendovi-Kanul I reached had gone completely mad. I remember watching the creature wander into the trees as the portal it had created began to close and shut me back out. I couldn't be blamed for that blunder; any intelligent being would have assumed that a creature creating a portal with that amount of magic would be able to comprehend a single word. This time, I wasn't depending on the power of the simple caster to keep the portal open. This time, I would use my own magic to maintain a connection to the material world. I needed a subject that I could establish a link with, one of my own creation. A Titan would have been ideal, but since being trapped in He-Lah I haven't been able to find one. The Wendovi-Kanuls[50] had less of my power coursing through them, thanks to my siblings' interference, but I hoped it was enough to influence one. I had assumed that they would need to be versed in the arcane arts, but since that didn't seem to be a good enough foundation to build a connection with a Wendovi-Kanul, I needed to find a strong spirit that manifested different qualities. Anger is a quality I could work with. It is so easy to twist anger into jealousy, rage, cruelty, and so much more, and this one has anger.

I could sense the growing resistance of He-Lah to my magic and knew my portal would not last much longer. But the name had been planted, now I needed to give it time to grow and for my influence to take hold. These mortal races have such soft minds, it should only be a matter of time before my name is the only word to escape his mouth.

There was a sudden gale of wind that enveloped my tenuous connection. I had allowed my mind to wander and my focus faltered. "No!" I was again

---

49   Prison plane of existence
50   Fiendish name for Silverbacks

trapped within our prison. I slammed my open palm into the smooth wall of my mercury tower. I am tired of being here. I want freedom. The constant fights and the pointless bickering of my siblings over who controlled what had never enticed me. They never seemed to grasp that as long as the Puradean[51] had us trapped here, none of us truly controlled anything.

I bit my lip and my sharp teeth drew blood as I stared at the now portal-less wall. It had taken me millennia, or perhaps simply years, to learn the proper sigils to open that weak connection. Time doesn't have much meaning here, there is no way to track it and, as an immortal, no way for it to ravage me.

"Even if I studied for eons, I doubt I would truly be able to establish a connection that could last longer than that."

Tired, I settled down into a large throne, magically carved from the same single, fluid column of quicksilver. I wrapped my vulture-like wings around me, and crossed one bear-like leg over the other. The oppressive heat was enough to make me sweat, and it frustrated me that as much as I attempted to insulate my tower, it still seemed to find its way through. I glanced over at the shelves that lined the wall, summoning a fresh clay tablet to me and starting to scratch on it with a talon, documenting this latest attempt at reaching my creation and yet another tiny step toward freedom. The plan was in motion, the seed planted. Now I needed the patience and wisdom to snatch up the next opportunity that presented itself.

"The first step is taken; the Wendovi-Kanul, my creations, will provide me with the keys to escape this hell."

---

51   Creator of all known planes of existence

Forver

Urguss swallowed hard to keep from drooling as he ran for the Tavern. It was one of two genuinely permanent structures of the Ozar settlement known as Campos Ursyss. He wove between the small yurts that lined the outskirts of the large clearing that comprised Ursyss. He ran without trying to be silent, his information was too important to concern himself with fines for being out and about during the dead of winter. Besides, Forver was Mister Moneybags, he would probably pay off any fines imposed on Urguss. *Probably any that my children's children will acquire, this news will make him so happy.*

Urguss could imagine the reward now, he would get so much money for delivering this information; he could buy a fancy yurt like those that dotted the area around Ursyss. Maybe he could afford some of those pillows with their soft, smooth coverings made of spider silk, that Forver discovered when opening trade relations with the Arkem[52] in the desert to the far, far south, the Ember Sands. Those silk spinners sure knew how to make an elegant product, and perhaps he would be able to afford some himself with the reward he was about to earn.

Fortunately, Urguss had arrived in Ursyss late that night, and most of those living in the settlement were sound asleep. To be accurate, it wasn't that you weren't allowed outside of your home during winter, you just had to maintain minimal contact and activity to preserve your food stores. This had evolved into the formation of the What Not To Do's, a list of appropriate behavior and activities for the winter months. One of the things that was on that list was running through the Campos at full speed. Urguss was tired and his legs burned from the constant activity; he had been running since that morning when another Ozar, Bravis, from the same militia unit, had walked into his yurt. Urguss had hardly been able to contain himself as Bravis told him what his little group of drunks had stumbled across just the night before. Urguss let Bravis stay in his yurt

---

52   Spider-Taur

to get some rest and agreed to take his message to Forver, their former employer.

Even though neither Urguss nor Bravis were currently Forver's employees, both kept hoping for re-employment. They both had brown fur—although Bravis' fur was nearly black—and light brown, almost golden, eyes. Urguss, like Bravis, was the height of most Norrus, close to seven feet tall and heavy like most Ozars; with only slightly more muscle than fat. They had been employed by Forver some years back. Forver had a misguided idea that he lacked honor and status among those that lived in Campos Ursyss, and perhaps he did. Those who lived away from Ursyss and the current Honcho, Bardell, still remembered all the very generous donations made by Forver's Yukon bloodline. Forver had wanted to regain—or achieve more—glory within Ursyss, and had agreed to hunt down the rebellious pack that had refused to settle down in a commune. Dio and his pack weren't really a threat, but the Honcho of Ursyss wanted all the Eclupse in his area to abide by the commune design. It upset his prestige among the other Honchos that the group hadn't agreed to settle and had lived as fugitives.

It was five years since Bravis and Urguss had been employed, and they had been surviving aimlessly since their discharge when Forver had failed to capture the outlaws. They had been living fairly pointless lives, settling down where they could and surviving until they needed to move on to new areas with more resources. Now they had a chance to have some purpose, some responsibility, some violence. Urguss came to a stop in front of the door to the Tavern, built by Forver's grandfather when he had established the Yukon Mead brand. The best mead, probably the best alcohol, throughout all of Loog Turra. This was the family's prime source of income and, as far as Urguss knew, an unlimited and easy way to earn money. He only wished that his family had figured out how to make mead. *I could have been the heir to the Kolgur Mead brand,* he chuckled. Maybe with the reward money, he would pay someone to figure out how to make the beverage, and he could duplicate it, sell it cheaper, and make an even greater fortune. He took a few deep breaths to calm down, so that he wouldn't make a fool of himself when he stepped inside.

The Tavern was the most welcoming structure in the whole of Ursyss, and was just south of the Honcho's yurt. It was not glamorous; it had simple rough log walls with a matching roof that slanted toward the back of the building to allow the snow and water to run off. There was a large stone hearth around the fire that warmed the entire building. Around it were long tables and benches that were positioned in a diagonal pattern to provide as much space as possible for customers. Shael looked up, surprised, as the door to the Tavern opened and a light-furred Norrus stepped inside the building. He had honey-colored eyes and the fur around his face was in short braids. He carried a simple, very damaged, triangular bit axe, with a haft that was leather-wrapped to keep it from fracturing more than it already had.

Urguss stopped and looked around, surprised at how comfortable the place looked. He hadn't been to Ursyss in the last five years. Back then, the building was Forver's business hut; it was where he had laid out the plans for their hunt and where he had hosted them while they had gathered for the big event. The place had smelt of alcohol, vomit, and urine—a foul mixture. Now it smelt like smoke, wood, and faintly of alcohol. The hole in the roof had been enlarged so that more smoke could escape; it was no longer needed to hide the fetid odor that had been associated with this place. Urguss looked curiously at the female Ozar behind the counter. She had dark fur like Bravis, but there were highlights of honied brown that accented her neck, head, and back. She was taller than Urguss, or at least standing straighter, and she reminded him of a very young Forver. Her bright brown eyes locked onto him. He gave her a flirtatious grin, and began to saunter over to the counter that ran close to the back wall behind which she stood.

Shael wanted to vomit when he grinned. She hadn't intended to come into the Tavern today, but she was so bored at home that she had decided to go and do some minor chores at her Tavern. She certainly wasn't expecting customers until the spring. Forver had given it to her on her Materimony day with Oscord; an Ozar from the Mahuer tribe, and part of one of the southern garrisons. Her father had been so happy that she had 'married up' and was ecstatic to have a Mahuer as a son-in-law. As she watched this Ozar approach, she could almost smell her father and all his schemes wafting from him as he stepped to the counter.

"Now, you would look so much more attractive if you smiled," Urguss grinned widely, as if to emphasize his point.

Shael wanted to grab the small stone mace she kept under the counter and shatter his precious teeth; she had spent years dealing with these types.

229

She was once a server working for her father and not much had changed now that she owned the place. Well, she was able to defend herself now without getting lectured. She gave him a gorgeous smile that practically brought him to completion. He hadn't seen a female in some time.

"Is this better?" Shael cooed, batting her eyelashes at Urguss, all the while getting a good grip on the handle of the mace.

"Ho, ho, now! See, don't that feel nice?" Urguss gave her a big laugh; he would have never seen it coming. She could have brained him six times over before he realized he was dead.

Stars, some of these males are just too stupid; it's a wonder they survive out in the Green Wall.

"Urguss," came a voice to the right of Shael as Forver stepped through the back door, obviously having heard the brute's brainless laughter.

Urguss stopped laughing and looked over at Forver. "Mother Bear, you haven't aged a day," he swore as he saw his employer for the first time in several years, almost forgetting the whole reason he had come.

Despite Urguss' comment, Forver was obviously aging. The light-brown highlights that surrounded his face and streaked down his neck had turned gray. He stared at Urguss with his intense dark brown eyes that were swallowed up by his heavy brow and wide cheeks whenever he was enraged.

"You look like wolf-shit[53] ." Forver laughed as he walked behind the counter. "Shael, darling, how 'bout you let me and my old friend have some privacy?" He looked to Urguss. "Recognize our little wench?" he boomed.

"She's, she's Shael! Well, Mother Bear, what a beauty!" he sputtered. Somehow, this revelation made the whole situation even more uncomfortable.

Shael wanted to tell her father to piss off, this was her Tavern now and he was done giving orders in this building. She would give anything to get away from this Ozar though, and she had no wish to linger around her father either. She didn't want to stay longer than she needed to, and figured if she was rude about her exit, that may drag out the interaction. She kept the fake smile across her face as she politely excused herself from the building.

"Of course, I would hate to burden you both with my curious questions."

Urguss, not understanding the true meaning behind her tone, took it as flirtatious. "Ah, perhaps she could stay, yeah. Sit on me lap." He gave

53   A common swear among the Ozar tribes

her that repulsive grin again, but Shael had walked him into the trap she had set.

Forver was known for his money, but he was known for one thing far more than that; his temper. "What did you say?" His growl was just short of an echoing roar, and probably the only reason he managed to keep it remotely quiet was because he had no interest in being fined by the Honcho.

Urguss was stupid, but he wasn't completely brainless and realized that he had gone a bit too far. Shael sighed as the door closed behind her, she had hoped to hear the two of them at each other's throat. She didn't care how long it took her to clean it up; besides, she would always have Jakob's help. She wrapped her arms around her to keep out the chill and hurried off to her yurt. She was thankful that Oscord had asked his sister Ilka to stay with Shael during her pregnancy and while he was away at the garrison all winter. Shael and Ilka got along wonderfully, and she would be perfect company with whom she could vent about this experience.

Forver was practically steaming at this point as he glared over at Urguss. "She is mated to a Mahuer from southern garrisons. A cousin of sorts to the current Honcho. I could string you up by your ears here in this building and box your organs till they all burst. I wouldn't blink twice, no one would. Stars, they could even find you and no one would ask me what happened. So, before you go putting your hands on things, you best find out if you can." He picked up one of the heavy wooden mugs that were behind the counter. "Now, you wanna drink?" he asked, seeming to have forgotten the whole ordeal.

"Su—sure," stammered Urguss, still a little shaken up from Forver's outburst. This wasn't how he wanted their meeting to begin, but at least it was starting.

Forver slammed the mug into Urguss' muzzle, causing him to fall back with a resounding crash. Urguss was pretty sure that his nose and maybe even his jaw had been broken from the sudden impact. "I still haven't heard you apologize," Forver snarled to the surprised Urguss. He slid over the counter with surprising agility, landing over Urguss and stepping down on the prone Ozar's skull, starting to crush it under his weight.

"Of course, I am sorry!" Urguss shouted. "I thought that went without saying. I am very sorry. I swear I won't disrespect you by trying to get between Shael and her mate."

"Well then, what are you doing down there?" was Forver's pleasant response, holding out a hand to help the other Ozar to his paws.

Urguss thought about refusing it for a second, only a second before he reached out and allowed Forver to help him to his paws. "Could I have that drink, please?" he asked meekly, not wanting to set Forver off again.

"Of course, of course." Forver walked back around the counter. "Now, what is so important that you rushed all the way here? You took some big risks; the disruption fines have doubled this last year. Bardell is getting old and he is trying to find new ways to feel powerful, if you ask me." Forver filled the wooden mug with which he had smashed Urguss' face, not bothering to clean off the fur or blood. He handed the mug to Urguss, the dirty lip of the mug first. "This better be good," he said pointedly.

Urguss was beyond caring about the fur and gore on the brim of the mug, it was his own flesh and fur anyway, and it wasn't like he hadn't tasted those two items before. The golden liquid slid across his lips; it was delicious and Forver had obviously gone to great expense to insulate the cellar because the drink was as warm as a summer's day.

"Mother Bear, that gets better each time I taste it." He took another big swallow before putting down the empty mug and giving Forver a sheepish grin.

"Answer my question first, then I will top you off." Forver took the mug from Urguss, but made no motion to refill it.

"Right, of course." Urguss kept looking to where Forver had put the mug under the counter. "So, you remember Bravis?" he began, but when Forver gave him an annoyed stare, he quickly continued. He hadn't thought about how he was going to tell him; this had suddenly become difficult. "Of course, you know Bravis." Forver gave him the same expression although now his lip was twitching. He was obviously running out of patience with Urguss, which probably ensured that he wouldn't get that drink. "Okay, okay, let me start again. So, Bravis and I used to be employed by you. You know, for hunting that group of Eclipse?" He didn't wait for Forver to respond or lose his temper. "Well, turns out Bravis and a group of them were drinking and decided to have a sniff about. When who do they stumble on?"

Forver had already poured the mug and was sliding it over to Urguss, he had a hunch where this was going, and he was as far from angry as he possibly could be.

"You caught them!" he cried with a cheer, jumping up in excitement

232

as Urguss paused to take a drink. "I can't believe this! This winter could scarcely get much better; not only do I learn that Shael is pregnant, but you and this—this... " He was having trouble remembering the other Ozar's name.

"Bravis," assisted Urguss, finally coming up for air from the mug. He didn't want to ruin Forver's good mood or the possibility of more refills, so he decided to let Forver continue his speculation and drain the last of the beverage, getting another refill before he elaborated on what had actually happened. By the end of his story, he certainly wasn't getting any more refills, and Forver's face had twisted up into an angry expression. He was either having an internal tantrum or a stroke. Urguss doubted he was lucky enough for the latter.

"What do you mean, they killed everyone but two that escaped to the Ice Kraggs?" Forver roared in fury. He found the stone club and used it to smash Urguss' wooden drinking mug. Urguss had fortunately let go of it before it was destroyed by the enraged Forver. "You idiots lost them! You brainless savages killed the Eclupse we wanted alive, and then proceeded to lose two of them!" he grabbed another mug and threw it into Urguss' already bruised and slightly swollen face.

Urguss tried to move but his reactions were dulled from three large mugs of mead. The mug connected with his forehead rather than his muzzle to his relief, but it was still not a pleasant feeling. "If it is any comfort, I had no part in the attack or loss of the Eclupse," Urguss said, trying to defend against and deflect Forver's rage. "Also, Bravis knows where the two survivors went."

Forver stopped as he was reaching for another mug to throw. "Exactly where are they?" He started to walk around the counter over to Urguss.

Urguss had no idea how to respond, Bravis had said they had run toward the Ice Kraggs, but he hadn't actually said he had located them or even tried to track them down. "Well, he doesn't have eyes on them, but how far could they go with the Ice Kraggs and Division Mountains hemming them in?"

Forver stalked over to Urguss, he couldn't believe the stupidity of this Ozar. "Don't you remember what happened when my father tried to ambush a bunch of Maulers? Remember what the Daunkirk scouts reported after they had caught up with the rear line?"

Urguss was getting nervous, and he was trying to figure out where

Forver was going with this line of questioning. His eyes lit up, as almost in unison they said, "The Maulers vanished into the Ice Kraggs."

Forver grabbed Urguss by a handful of his braids and slammed him neck first onto the edge of the counter, causing the drunk Ozar to choke as he collapsed off his stool and scrambled to get his legs back under him while his claws raked down the outside of the bar.

"So, how in the stars am I supposed to find these two Eclupse?" Forver cursed, yanking again on Urguss' braids, and making sure that he wasn't getting back up. Urguss couldn't answer, so Forver continued, "This means that they have probably already found their way to the Maulers. How does that help me?" he screamed, the stone mace thumped against Urguss' face, right on his forehead.

Urguss tried to find his legs, but the pain from the blow, the lack of oxygen, and the inebriation were making it difficult to form a proper defense. This wasn't what he had been expecting at all, this was not how this was supposed to go. He was supposed to be rewarded, not beaten like some kind of slave. Forver wasn't done; again, the stone mace cracked against Urguss' skull, this time hitting right above his eye and there was a snapping sound as his orbital bone was broken.

"I am sorry, it can be fixed. Please stop, you'll break my skull open!" Urguss finally managed to yell, getting his arms in front of him and pushing away from the bar enough to get some air in his lungs.

Forver's grip hadn't loosened from Urguss' braids though, and he was not at all happy that Urguss was fighting back. "Don't make this difficult on yourself! What do you know? I ain't gonna break your skull with this wimpy little weapon," he growled as he bludgeoned Urguss again. Urguss' legs went limp with that third blow, and he almost dragged Forver down to the floor with him as his body became dead weight.

"Stars, you were fragile," Forver spat as he let go of Urguss before he was dragged down. "A woman's mace, not even an axe killed you! Mother Bear, you would have been useless in a fight." He wiped his hand over his face and snout, grabbing a mug and filling it with some of the mead before drinking deeply. "He was right about one thing though, this is some damn good mead."

Forver looked around the room and then back down at the body. All the gore and filth that accompanied a violent death had now created a puddle under Urguss' corpse. It was starting to stink up the place, and he would never hear the end of it from Shael if he left the Tavern like this. He couldn't risk anything happening to his grandcubs. He would have to find Jakob, at least that would give him some time to think. He stood up, filling the mug one more time so it would last while he searched for that cripple, the freakish murderer of Klarah, Forver's beloved mate. As he searched for the mute, he passed by the raven pen near the Tavern. This gave him an idea, ravens were used to communicate between the different Ozar Campo and their Honchos. He knew an Ozar that he could contact, who could maybe provide some leads about where these Ecluspe had vanished. It was a long shot, most of the spies that he had hired to try and find the Maulers that his father had lost had wound up dead, or there had been no news from them in so long that he had stopped sending them payments. He wasn't sure there were any ravens still in the pen that had been taken from the Banshee Tundra; he may end up sending his message to one of the other Campo by accident. That would do him little good; if he wasn't outright humiliated for the mistake, he would most surely be fined, and worse, the other Campo might end up actually finding the Ecluspe, or maybe even the Maulers. Finding them was Forver's right, his glory. The glory of their capture belonged to the Yukon family and he was going to make sure of that. The legacy he left his grandcubs would be far more than a jinxed grandmother and a failed grandfather.

How can I ensure that the raven will get to the tundra? He could ask Groll, the Campos Ursyss druid, to make the raven go to Friggi[54] . Groll was a Norrus, but he was also the religious and medical advisor to the Honcho. He may very well betray Forver to the Honcho, or try to find out why Forver was seeking his assistance. The last thing Forver needed was to pay one of Bardell's fines. Still, Groll did love a good drink, and what he would do for a keg may fulfill Forver's needs. First, he needed to find Jakob and get him to work, then he could think about approaching Groll with his idea.

He found Jakob in a shabby shelter made from fallen branches and piled snow. The mute had built a yurt to the best of his ability, based on the design of the homes around him. Jakob's light brown paws poked out from the entrance to the shelter; he had built one of these temporary homes every winter, and every winter he seemed to forget that he had grown since he was a cub. Forver hesitated for a moment before waking Jakob up. *The*

54   Communal gathering place of the Hax

retard is extremely strong, even with his limitations. Forver looked down at the twisted paw that had never healed right from a childhood injury. "Stars, you are an unfortunate creature." Forver instantly felt sickened by even this small glimmer of compassion, and quickly resorted to kicking Jakob in his lame leg.

Jakob shot up, his dark brown fur broke through the top of his little shelter as he groaned and whimpered in pain. Looking from his paw to Forver and back to his paw, he tried to understand why his father hated him so much. What had he done, and why couldn't he complain about his father's malicious treatment? He had learned when he was younger to just accept the bad and look for the good. Not to wait around and accept the good while looking for the bad, that had never seemed to work. It had been amazing to him how much good there was around him, and how much no one ever noticed. He wasn't sure why no one ever saw it. Those blessings were everywhere and, despite the pain, he was experiencing one of those blessings right now. He had woken up to a new day of fresh challenges and accomplishments. He quickly put his complaints behind him and reached out to hug his father, perhaps this would be the day he got that blessing.

There was a familiar sharp pain on the side of his face, on his cheek. He shied away from Forver, given the blow it would seem that today was not that day. *Oh well, I can always try tomorrow.* Jakob hopped to his paws as though he hadn't even been slapped, and shook the snow and dirt out of his fur. He was the tallest of his siblings, and even taller than some Mahuers. He stood just over seven and a half feet tall and, unlike most Ozars, he was not hefty. The years of never-ending chores and manual labor had transformed him into a solid, muscular beast of an Ozar. Forver unconsciously stepped back, in case Jakob was upset about being slapped. He had to keep a tight leash on the simpleton. He told himself to stand his ground, and as usual, Jakob was more than eager to assist in any way possible.

"Get your cleaning things and meet me in the Tavern." As Forver spoke, he made motions to try to help the dunce understand what he wanted. Making a scrubbing motion, making it look like he was filling a bucket with snow, and then finally pointing to himself and Jakob, and then at the Tavern.

Jakob instinctively wanted to follow his father into the Tavern after he had been given his instructions, but he reminded himself of how upset

Forver became when he just followed him about. He went over in his mind the items his father had said he would need, his scrub brush and his bucket with some snow. He had heard his father fine, and as much as everyone in Ursyss treated him as though he was stupid, he wasn't. Everyone just responded to him better if he played the part they expected. *There isn't anything wrong with that, is there?* He pushed the question out of his mind, these annoying reflective questions had begun to plague him lately, and he was finding them harder and harder to dismiss. He tried to focus on figuring out what his father could want. It was obvious that he wanted Jakob to clean some part of the Tavern, but which part and what was the mess? That is what made the game fun. *Perhaps, it's a broken keg or maybe –* he shoveled the snow into his bucket faster *– maybe my sister has given birth in the building.* He ran for the Tavern, his mind racing about how he would play with the cubs. He would show them how to build snow yurts like his, and show them all the mushrooms and roots that grew around Ursyss, which ones they could eat and which ones he knew from experience made you sick. Perhaps he would show them which ones made the trees and the animals talk to you, he and Groll had enjoyed themselves when they found those. It was one of the few times he had been treated like an equal, and it had been a special moment for him.

It took him a few moments to gather himself and force those thoughts back down, it was getting upsetting that he couldn't hush those darker thoughts. When he stepped inside, he was first disappointed and then disgusted; it took all his willpower not to run out the door and puke in the snow. Forver was standing behind the counter with an untapped keg on it and a mug of mead that he set down forcefully as he looked over at Jakob.

"What were you waiting for, an invitation?" he growled at Jakob, pointing to the corpse and mess below the bar.

Jakob just forced a half grin to keep himself positive.

"Clean it all up, spotless!" Forver emphasized as he grabbed the keg and strode for the back door. "Oh, some snow and mud got tracked in, get that as well. Remember, no drinks for you," he said pointedly as he shut the door.

It had to be getting close to sunup, so it wouldn't be too odd for him to pop in on Groll. It wasn't like the druid was known for being a late sleeper; most mornings, he would strut about the place cawing like a bird at the rising sun, unless it was winter. Forver wasn't actually sure if he had ever heard Groll making his morning racket in the winter.

"Zero risk, zero reward," he reminded himself, and stepped into the druid's yurt, waiting at the threshold to be acknowledged by the owner.

Groll looked up in surprise, true to form he was up and had already started to assemble his kindling into a little pyre in the fire pit at the center of the yurt. Groll's yurt was more traditional, built using the labor-intensive material known as fleece. The Ozars made it from wool they purchased from the Ramsyn in the Ice Kraggs, instead of the Rodentia-produced canvas with which most of the yurts in Ursyss were now built. It had a flexible softwood lattice of willow from the Warm Wood, instead of the stiff and more permanent redwood-beam structures that defined new yurts. The floor was covered in many different pelts and mosses instead of woven rugs, and it lacked the lavish silk cushions to which Forver had become particularly attached. From the roof above, and attached to the lattice of the yurt's frame on the walls, were various plants, flowers, roots, mushrooms, and mosses that were either drying or intentionally put in the path of the fireplace to smoke.

The old druid was ancient as far as all of the Ozars were concerned, almost a hundred years old, and his eyes had a milky haze that hid their once-piercing, polished-amber color. His body was hunched over, and he stood under seven feet tall, having lost at least a half-foot over the last decade. Forver and other Ozars often wondered how Groll was still alive and how much longer he would stay that way. He had trained three personal apprentices, but after he outlived the third the Honcho had decided that they all would probably die before Groll, so it would be his successor's problem to solve. Besides, Groll hated teaching and he had insisted that he would survive them all, which at this rate seemed true. His fur was now grayer than its former lush deep brown color, he had once had beautiful blond patterns in his undercoat that had highlighted his neck and chest. Forver was positive he was missing at least half his teeth by now, and probably that gruel he was cooking was a necessary—if boring—diet.

As Forver waited to be recognized by the druid, Groll took some time to look over his guest. Forver seemed in a rush and was, as usual, impatient; that much was easy enough to see in his expression and body language. The druid decided to drag this moment out and seemed oblivious to Forver's arrival, hoping to use this opportunity to fluster his guest. He took a sip of his breakfast and panted obnoxiously, feigning burning his tongue while he watched Forver out of the corner of his eye. Nothing about Forver was special, even with his markings he hardly stood out within Ursyss. If it wasn't for his extreme wealth and equally extreme anger, he would have been nothing more than a flea in their history, an unimportant dot. Forver switched his weight from one paw to the other, trying to keep himself patient. *Groll has obviously seen me, and he can always taste test his oat-mush later.* He knew better than to speak out, especially when faced with someone as powerful in the arcane arts as Groll. Forver reached for the water bowl next to the door and quickly cleaned his hands, hoping that his observance of custom would speed this process along.

Groll lifted his spoon from the gruel, which had finally been brought to a boil by the little fire below the bronze pot. This time, it actually was slightly warm, but nowhere near as hot as he pretended it was once again. Forver began to wonder if the old Ozar was going to get it to a scalding point just so that he could keep this stupid gag up. He was glaring now, and gnawing at his lower lip to keep himself from shouting out in rage. Perhaps that was Groll's plan, to make him fly into a tantrum so that he would wake up the Honcho next door and get a large fine. This made him eat at his lip with even more energy, not caring that he could taste blood as he kept his eyes fixed on the druid. Groll did wait until his meal was scalding hot before he added some molasses to the mix; he then emptied the contents of his little bronze pot into a nice, polished clay bowl, one of the new imports from the Endless Plains. Groll might like to give the appearance that he had no use for the commodities, but he obviously had a secret affection for them.

"I don't suppose you would have wanted any?" He seemed suddenly concerned, but he had at least finally acknowledged Forver's presence.

Forver's left eye was twitching and he had bitten into his lip hard enough to draw blood more than once. "No, I am fine. I do want to—" he began.

"Hold on, let me get comfortable. I imagine this isn't going to be a short conversation." Groll's eyes moved to the keg. "Well now, would that perhaps be for me?" As though to defy his age he was squatting, his rump mere inches from the ground, and his old legs weren't even quivering from the strain.

Forver decided to turn the tables a bit and see how long he could make the old druid stay in that low squat position. It had only been a few minutes, but Forver's patience was not able to outlast the old Ozar's powerful legs. "Stars' sake, sit down. It could be for you, but I am not simply going to just throw my bargaining chip at you before I have even begun to barter."

"Ah, so you are here for a favor," Groll said with a wise nod as he plopped down on one of the saber-tooth pelts. He really rubbed his hips into it too, as though he was humiliating the creature by scrubbing his butt on its coat.

"You think I would just come here for a social call?" Forver meant for the question to be rhetorical and put Groll off whatever scent he was trying to sniff out.

Still, Groll was quick and had expected an obvious retort from such a flustered visitor. "I know that Shael is pregnant, it is customary for me to be at that special moment. Others have brought me gifts before, so that is not as odd as you might have been hoping. You just lack most common courtesies." As was fitting his status, when the druid spoke, everyone else listened, so Forver had to tolerate this lecture. He couldn't risk the curses that a master of the arcane arts could put on his heirs.

It was so hard, he wanted to interrupt the smug old relic as he croaked about manners and customs. When he had finally finished, Forver tried to begin the negotiation; he didn't want to let Groll have another chance to humble him.

"Let's just stop this wolf-shit and get to the root of things. I need a favor, and I need you to keep your overly chatty mouth shut about you doing me that favor. Before you ask what it is, don't, because you don't need to know," he barreled on, not wanting to let Groll talk again. He couldn't stop it though, Groll just started talking over him and he had to stop and listen to what the 'wise' druid had to say.

"If you want to ask a favor of me, I need to know what the favor is before I can agree to it," he arrogantly corrected Forver, taking a long slurp of his mashed oats.

Forver wanted to bash the bowl into the druid's face but, for once, his need for redemption outweighed his rage. "Fine, I will tell you what I need, but you aren't to tell anyone what I told you or that I needed a favor from you. You won't ask any questions and will just do as you are instructed. If you do this and follow the letter of my orders, you may have this whole untapped keg of my finest mead all to yourself." Forver eyed the druid to see if he could determine if this bribe would be enough to keep the druid's silence.

"Depends," came Groll's nonchalant response with a mouthful of porridge. When Forver didn't respond, he elaborated, "Depends on what the favor is."

"Can you just agree to my terms before I tell you what I need?" Forver growled. He wished that he had brought Ol'Grim with him, she would have made him talk with her cold iron heart and her nasty edge. *Why did he leave his girl behind?* He shook his head as the thought entered his mind. He didn't want to turn out like that psycho Zolk, best to keep those feelings for his axe buried deep.

"How could I possibly agree to the terms when I don't know what I am agreeing to?" was Groll's wet response as he shoveled more gruel into his mouth.

"You know the terms, the terms are… " Before Forver could spit the terms back at him, Groll stuck up the porridge-covered hand he had been using to eat with to shush Forver. After which, he licked the fingers and appendage clean before continuing, practically scrubbing his tongue with his large furry hand. Forver was sure that the druid might just cut off his tongue with one of his big claws, with how vigorously he was brushing it. Anytime Forver began to speak, Groll would repeat the original gesture.

Groll set down the bowl gently, these clay dishes were extremely fragile compared to the Ozar-crafted ones, which were mostly wood, sometimes animal skins. The bowl itself was pretty plain, with just a wavy line along the brim for its only decoration. What Groll loved about it was its color, he had never seen such a vibrant purple in his whole life. He often wondered how the coastal Selee[55] managed to find an object or creature that naturally produced this color. The Selee were a migratory Taur tribe that only came up to the Berg Maker to the northwest in the summers. There, they somehow harvested the rich purple dye and competed in sporting events to show off their virility. They looked kind of like fish in that they had flippers, but they didn't have scales. They had thick, surprisingly muscular bodies and whiskers. Some tribes were known to have fur, and others had long tusks like a mammoth. They could shuffle along beaches and snow dunes rapidly, using their powerful lower body to essentially lunge across the ground. The Selee were more at home in the water, given their body's design, surprisingly, they had no gills like fish and would come up for air,

55   Seal-Taur

similar to some other tribes within the aquan clans, and could hold their breath for countless minutes.

"All right, all right. You give me the keg, and you make sure Shael gives me a refill when I drain this one, and, well, you will have yourself a deal." Groll turned to face Forver as he finished giving him his terms.

Forver thought for a moment. *Shael would not be happy to freely give away any mead, no matter who it was for. I have given up control of the Tavern, as hard as that was, and my daughter has made that fact very clear. I have to do this though, not only will it remove the blemish on the Yukon name caused by my father's failure to capture the Maulers, but also remove the blemish from my failure to capture the Eclupse pack. I am doing this so that my cubs and their cubs will have lives where no one can smudge their prestige.*

"Okay, you have a deal," he replied, reaching out for Groll's forearm. They clasped forearms and touched foreheads, sealing the agreement.

Groll listened as Forver explained that he would meet the druid at the raven pen tonight, he needed Groll to use his magical talents to persuade the bird to fly to the Friggi in the Banshee Tundra. The druid looked at him quizzically. "You just want me to persuade a raven to fly somewhere, and you are giving me two whole kegs for that? Why not wait till the winter is over in a month and have me do it for free? It is part of my duties."

Forver hadn't given him the keg yet, and held it above his head, threatening to smash it across the floor of the old druid's yurt. "The agreement was no questions and no talking!" he growled, letting the keg balance dangerously in his hands, high above his head and far out of the druid's reach.

"Woah, let's not get carried away. Just set it down nicely, you have my word you will not hear another question out of me and not another Ozar will hear about this," Groll promised, placing both hands over his sternum as a gesture of sincerity.

"Not just another Ozar, nothing, not a Taur, not a Fay, not a Dwarf, not a Furless." Forver waited for Groll to nod before he continued.

Oh, there is more, the druid thought to himself as the list continued.

"Not an animal, any animal, not a plant, fungus, root, tree, or leaf. Do you understand me, Druid?" Forver emphasized again.

Groll nodded. "Yes, understood." He had to stop himself from laughing as he saw Forver's eye twitch from the exchange. Forver set down the keg and turned to leave via the oval flap cut into the south wall of the building.

"Remember, be there tonight, not tomorrow, not a few days from now—tonight!" Forver let the flap swing shut behind him as he heard Groll rustling over to the keg.

That druid better keep his muzzle shut, or we may need a new druid this spring after all.

He hurried home so that he could start writing the note with the same code he had established with his spies when he had first hired them. He hoped there was still one loyal Ozar in the Hax tribe; those nomadic Ozars were his last shot at reclaiming his family's honor.

Campos Ursyss

The growing community, and the last outpost of civilization until arriving at Izwin in the far north of the Tundra, was known as Campos Ursyss. The center of Ursyss consisted of just over a dozen centralized yurts, mainly belonging to the influential and powerful. The outskirts housed the majority of the population who called the growing community home. Their yurts were spread out throughout the Green Wall, but surrounded the two permanent structures of the town and the dozen blue-furred yurts. Ursyss, like the other Ozar Campo, was home to the tribes known as the Mahuer and the Norrus. The third tribe of Ozars lived out in the Banshee Tundra or were dispersed throughout Sarm, and were known as the Hax, or the Forgotten Tribe. The Ozars had never been a communal clan, and for much of their ancestors' lives had lived as the Hax had. They isolated themselves from one another, and only came together to establish family units, usually only remaining a family until the cubs were old enough to leave the household and then the family would simply dissolve. After the Mahuer and Norrus united to subdue the Silverbacks, the two tribes thought it wise to maintain their merger and, mimicking the Daunkirks' way of living, the Ozars were starting to do well for themselves. They had become one of the leading tribes in two trade goods, mead and honey. They still sold lumber as well as furs and amber, but those were minor businesses in comparison. Jobs in those industries were more suitable for the Cana, Eclupse, and Varggs in the communes controlled by the Ozars.

The Mahuer were physically the largest of the two clans, but were often smaller than the Hax in the tundra. They made up the bulk of the military, after the subjugation of the Silverbacks some well-known Norrus were recruited into this group as well, but the majority were Mahuer. With their military status in a world that respects physical might, the Mahuer gravitated toward the top positions. No Norrus had ever held the position of Honcho, or chieftain of the Campo. The Norrus, not having access to these positions, struggled to find a place in the new society. Most became local traders, commuting between the Campo and the local market where they restocked with outside wares. Others had started their own businesses as mercenaries and menial laborers, being forced to work jobs in logging, mining, or local distilleries and honey farms. The Norrus were called into action only once after their discharge from the military ranks, and that was to fight against the Daunkirks in a skirmish that had permanently severed all friendly relations between the two clans. Many Norrus—whose parents had lost honor with the escape of the Maulers—were given this chance to regain their honor. The two tribes had been closer than ever since the Norrus and Mahuers defeated the Daunkirks and took sole control of the northern road that led to Izwin, becoming the undisputed masters of the northern and eastern Green Wall. The Daunkirks managed to hold onto the coasts and the smaller western half, but were being forced to branch out into the Warm Wood. Many military ranks were reopened to Norrus, and even though they didn't hold their former numbers in the army, they added to it substantially, even though this was the last battle the Ozars were involved in for almost two decades.

Campos Ursyss had fallen into peaceful monotony over these passing quiet years, and even held host to some of the Hax that would wander in from the Banshee Tundra, looking to trade in Red Martyrs, seal blubber, or a new commodity known as oil. It had changed the summer nights in the Green Wall, being used to fuel Ursyss' light sources during the shorter, warmer nights. According to the wild stories that the Hax would tell when they came in the spring and fall, this oil came from a fish the size of a giant sequoia, and about as thick around. They would also share stories from the other tribes of the tundra as well, mainly the Corm, who told stories of a fearsome creature with thick white fur that walked on two legs. These creatures had tusks like boars and intelligence which made them extremely dangerous to travelers. The monsters laid ambushes for their victims and buried them in the snow to freeze for later consumption. So, Burrum did not stand out too noticeably when he arrived at Ursyss, in the early afternoon in the last month of winter.

Burrum had eaten all the small Red Martyrs he had caught as rations a day earlier, and again his stomach complained to him about sharing his precious food with a Mauler. Burrum had planned to use the poor catches as an excuse for having come to Ursyss. He still had half a skinful of

245

some oil, and he could always claim he was here to trade this. Oil was so precious they wouldn't question why he had brought such a small amount, but he would like to keep it for his return trip back out into the Banshee Tundra. In those howling winds, sometimes the only way to start a fire was with this precious resource.

Hopefully, Forver will make it worth my while, he thought to himself as he walked toward the Tavern. *The information I have is at least worth this skin, as far as I am concerned,* he thought, noticing how many new stalls had been added to Middle Market, which was attached to the Tavern. "The last stop shop of civilization," Burrum mused to himself as he reached for the door to the Tavern.

As the door opened, he got a whiff of that sweet mead that the Yukon family was famous for. Forver was one of the few Norrus who had done very well for himself, even though he was still convinced that his family was cursed.

After the Dwarves were attacked and beaten by the Titans, they had needed to spend some time regrouping and they had stopped manufacturing and trading their usual merchandise with the Beast Tribes. The Taurs in the Green Wall could trade with the Humans of Wolkien for their beer, but it was too light for the cold winters and lacked the kick of the Dwarven Ale. The Ozars had focused their skills on bee-keeping, and transferred that to production of mead. No one had done it as well as the Yukon. Almost every Taur clan came to Ursyss for its mead, and bought it by the barrels. The Ramsyn had learned smithing, the Daunkirks masonry, and the Ozars had learned to make mead. In many Taurs' opinions, the Ozars had acquired the most important skill of the three, and Forver had used the talent to build an empire that could even rival the Honcho's. With Forver's money, Ursyss had the largest selection of goods in any Campo market. There were over twenty stalls, and the building, including both the Tavern and the Market, had gone through numerous reconstructions since it was first erected by Obarn Yukon. He was Forver's grandfather, and it was Obarn who had crafted the coveted mead recipe of the Yukon. Forver's father, Kodah, had ambitions to be more than a master-brewer and had added on the Market, which had originally been designed as lodgings for the traveling merchants to set up shop and sell their goods. It was Kodah who had failed to capture the Maulers and was, according to Forver, the progenitor of the family's curse.

Forver believed that curse had manifested itself in Jakob. Jakob was the youngest of Klarah's triplets. No other Ozar in the history of their clan had ever had three cubs at once and it had been her death sentence. Forver never let Jakob forget that if he hadn't been in there, Klarah would still be alive. Jakob the Love Killer had been what his father called him, sometimes just Killer, other times Love Killer, or, if Forver happened to be feeling good, rarely, 'you'. All three cubs had been raised by one of Forver's relatives, since their father had been so distraught that he hadn't even bothered to find a wet nurse for them. Jakob had enjoyed living with Nallus, her husband had been killed in an avalanche when trying to mine some amber and she was not a wealthy Yukon. In fact, other than Forver, none of the other Yukons were even known. Nallus became ill when the cubs were still young, but they had been weaned so Forver had brought them back into his home. Shael and Inlan were immediately recognized and groomed to take over the lucrative businesses of the Tavern and Middle Market. Jakob worked as a servant for the family; he was energetic and full of joy, never complaining about his lot. Often Shael or Inlan, when they were young, would sneak Jakob into the yurt, but Forver had always been enraged when he found the Love Killer in his home and would beat Jakob until he left. Eventually, his siblings stopped trying to bring him inside, still Jakob didn't mind; he understood that his siblings didn't want to see him getting hit, so Jakob didn't mind living in his little snow shelters, or sleeping under the trees in the spring, summer, and fall. Both Shael and Inlan, in their naïve youth, had argued that Jakob should be given as much responsibility and favor as them and their arguments were valid, often leaving Forver enraged and speechless.

Jakob didn't know if his father had planned what next befell him, in order to have a reason not to give him the same responsibility as his siblings, or perhaps it had just been a case of being in the wrong place at the wrong time. It had only been a few years after Forver had taken in the cubs, and all three of them were in the Tavern on a particularly busy night. Jakob had a toy that he had made himself, known as a circler. He had wanted to buy one from one of the merchants in Middle Market, but since he didn't make an allowance like his siblings, Jakob was unable to purchase the toy. Ever resourceful, Jakob had gone each day for a week and inspected the toy. By the end of the week, he had made an identical one to the item the merchant was selling, and his circled for longer. The

247

toy was a cone shape with a small stem that protruded from the large base of the cone. The owner would place the pointed end of the cone on a flat surface and twist the stem; Jakob planned to paint red and green lines in a spiral, so it created an interesting pattern as it spun. A large, drunk Norrus had passed out with his head on the table, snoring loudly. The sound had attracted Jakob over, and he proceeded to show the drunk his toy. Jakob got the circler spinning in a particularly quick and powerful motion, and, proud of his accomplishment, he had grabbed the drunk's forearm to show him the circler.

The drunk claimed he was startled from a particularly frightening dream. The Ozar responded suddenly and extremely violently. Startled by the cub, he stomped hard with his paw, crushing the cub's left paw bones. Jakob screamed in horror and pain, which, according to the drunk, startled him more and he gripped Jakob by his neck and slammed him repeatedly into the table's surface. Forver had watched, unmoved, from the bar, and only became involved when Inlan had tried to intervene so that Jakob wouldn't be beaten to death. Jakob had never fully recovered from those injuries, he had become mute from the battering his face and muzzle had taken, mainly from having bitten off his tongue during the assault. Jakob's paw fared no better. Having never healed properly, the bones struggled to support him in that leg and he had an obvious limp. He would often completely lift it and support his whole weight on his right leg. Still, Jakob didn't seem to care. Forver said it was because he was 'broken,' but no matter what it was, he still worked diligently and hard, never showing any self-pity for his condition. Shael and Inlan had often admired his courage, and Shael, in particular, always wondered what was going on in his mind that kept him so cheerful. Inlan, on the other hand, began to separate himself from Jakob after that night, and Jakob missed the formerly close relationship with his brother. Inlan insisted he would not work alongside Jakob. Since Forver wanted Inlan to learn to take over Middle Market, Jakob worked at the Tavern. Jakob wasn't sure if his brother was trying to spare him any more paternal abuse, but it had put an end to their time together.

Jakob was happy working with Shael in the Tavern, he couldn't deny that. Especially during the last month of winter, preparing for the flood of customers through the spring and fall months. Here in the Tavern, Jakob was inside a lovely warm building, protected from the nipping cold. Unlike

Middle Market's stalls, the Tavern's logs were chinked. Jakob had to admit that the log walls were at least an improvement to the Market that Kodah had built. The original Market had consisted of four posts, with hides that served as the roof and walls. Kodah had eventually made the building more permanent, with real log walls and a thatched roof. Forver had done little to improve upon this design, but had extended the clearing from a square of forty feet to a rectangle whose sides were now ninety feet long, so that stalls could be set up outside if the space was needed. This late in the winter and through the fall, the entire Market building had a smell of mildew due to the damp thatched roof and the dirt floors, without a front wall or door to keep out the elements. As long as the Tavern was attached to the Market's south wall, and while this was the only and largest market before the tundra, there was little incentive to remove these flaws.

Shael used Inlan's interest in the Market to establish herself as the owner of the Tavern, and eventually Forver had given it over to her when she mated with Oscord. Shael had done much to distance the Tavern from her father, forbidding any of his friends or employees to drink for free, and forcing Forver to manage his schemes someplace other than her establishment. Some of Forver's old friends had complained about her new policy, but Shael was not a fragile Ozar and she didn't repeat herself. She had sunk most of her profits into the Tavern since it had become hers. She had hired architects from Caphri, the Daunkirk capital, to help put a solid stone foundation in the Tavern. It had cost her double the agreed amount when tensions between the Ozars and Daunkirks had started, and she had figured out on her own how to finish it when the architects had left at the start of the conflict. Shael had then hired Ozars to chink the logs, and put furs along the floor and hides along the wall to help trap heat in the building. She had hired the best Harris[56] tribe artist from the Warm Wood to the south to paint beautiful scenes and images of sacred and important events and Taurs on the hides. Behind the bar, and framed by the kegs of Yukon Mead, was Shael's prized painting. The Harris had given her a painting of a field of flowers from his homeland, to the south of even the Warm Wood, in the Endless Plains. The Harris told her that these yellow-petaled flowers stood taller than him, even if you included his long ears, and Shael loved the way their dark black center contrasted with their bright yellow petals. The Harris had explained that each of these flowers

56   Hare-Taur

produced as many as two thousand seeds, and were a staple for his tribe.

Jakob put another log on the fire, masterfully putting all his weight on one leg and squatting down, a log in each hand and tossing both into the open stone stove, another addition the Daunkirks had help Shael build, along with the stone chimney, the only one in Ursyss. Jakob stood and turned to Shael, his eyes were cheerful, but the sounds Jakob emitted as he tried to speak would easily cause a stranger to fail to see the kindness in his intention. He motioned to Shael's stomach, and then wiped his forehead like he was tired. Shael smiled as Jakob tried to grunt and growl his question.

"No, I am not tired, but thank you for asking. We will need more wood if I am going to finish cleaning these mugs. Can you go fetch us a bit more?"

Jakob grunted twice, nodding his head and picking up the splitting wedge and maul to break up the big rounds. He was startled when the door opened and an Ozar about a half foot taller than him walked through the open door. Shael wrinkled her nose up in surprise as well.

"It's okay, Jakob, it is always good to have early customers. You keep going to fetch some wood, we are going to need even more now with our patron here."

Jakob studied the odd-colored Hax; he was sure it was a Hax because Jakob had never seen him in Ursyss and because of his height. The Hax's fur was not the usual pearly-white, but a smokey-white shade, more white than black, but with definite black undertones. The Hax stood over eight feet tall, with broad shoulders and narrow hips, making him triangle-shaped. He was wearing a satchel beaded in a green and purple mosaic with a motif of ice fishing. The green beads represented the ice, and a purple figure sat huddled over a gap in the green beads. The customer slowly and calmly put down a small bundle of fishing spears against the edge of the wall, his kind and bright eyes never leaving Jakob. His ears turned to listen to what the female Ozar behind the counter said, and he moved politely to the side, holding the door for Jakob to exit the building.

Burrum had to admire the injured Ozar's perseverance, he knew that no Ozar like him would survive in the tundra as the Hax did, and he was reminded again that the true value of society was that they support one another. Again, he thought of how the Hax might benefit from such a mentality. Burrum studied the crippled Ozar; he could have been near Burrum's height if he hadn't suffered such a terrible injury. Burrum recognized both the

Ozars as Norrus, typically dark brown in color. Both of them were leaner than him, probably weighing somewhere in the mid to high three-hundred-pound range. That didn't mean that he thought either of them was weak, even with the one Ozar's injury, his arms, chest, back, and core spoke of one familiar with swinging an axe and hauling a burden, and he didn't seem to allow his limitation to hinder him.

As the door closed behind him, Burrum turned to the other Ozar, who was obviously a female given that she was clearly with child. Even though she hid her stomach below the counter of the bar, Burrum thought of his own mate, Siya, and her own current pregnancy.

Soon, I will be home and holding you both, he reminded himself as he strode up to the bar.

As he got closer, he realized how much darker the female Ozar's fur was in comparison to the male who had exited the Tavern. She also had found another use for the precious oil, as her fur from her shoulders up was slicked back and appeared smooth, almost like ice. Under the counter, Shael's hand gripped her stone mace, she suspected that this odd Hax was somehow connected to her father; it was far too early in the year for them to be coming into Ursyss. He didn't seem like the greasy Norrus who had come in about two weeks earlier. She still didn't want to risk it, and really preferred to end this conversation before it began, taking a firm hold of her mace. Shael's arm didn't move as he sat down, as she pictured how he had held open the door for Jakob—no one, not even Oscord, had ever done that for him. It was a courtesy that Jakob wasn't extended for being a walking jinx.

Surely someone who does that has no connection to Forver, she thought.

"Excuse me, I am Burrum." He didn't wait for her response, and honestly Shael was used to that. "Could I get a mug of that famous Yukon Mead?" he asked with a smile, lifting his skin of oil. "I have payment," he clarified. True, Burrum needed that oil, but he didn't need all of it to get back home. Besides, he would get compensated from Forver, and perhaps never even need to exchange any of the precious resource.

Shael found herself releasing the mace at the pleasant tone to his deep voice. "I am sorry," she admitted, "but we have a strict rule of only coin for mead, and the Market is not going to be open for close to another month."

"Ah, that makes sense. I suppose I am early; I don't always remember how the campo handle the winters. It is practically always winter in the

Banshee Tundra." He laughed, putting his oil back into his satchel.

It is for the best. If I had used some, I would have ended up needing that exact amount going home, he thought to himself.

Despite her earlier wariness, Shael found herself giving a slight grin at the joke. She poured him a mug anyway. "Well, since you walked all the way here from the Banshee," Shael explained, handing him the mug she had imported from the Halflings[57] who were living along the foothills of the Division Mountains, in a settlement known as Whesscire.

Burrum looked at the clay mug for a moment, and then back to Shael. "Is it sturdy?" he asked, looking over the brim of the mug to see how thin the walls were.

Shael let out a lighthearted laugh, having been caught truly off guard by the comment. "They are a little frailer, but only if you were to handle them like a cub. The advantage is that the mead doesn't soak into the clay like it did with our wood mugs, and so doesn't become tainted with the taste of old mead."

Burrum picked up the dark, orange-colored mug and, ever so gently, as though he were holding a cup made from powdered snow, he brought the mead to his lips. He didn't come up for air, and until he had drained the mead, his muzzle didn't leave the mug.

"Mother Bear!" he shouted as he finished. "That was fresh indeed." He almost smashed the clay mug onto the hard redwood counter, and only just managed to stop himself from destroying it on the bar. "I am beginning to see a problem with these mugs," he mused as he slid the empty tankard away.

Shael smiled a sincere smile as she took the cup away. "Well, it has helped bring in a little more revenue." She pointed above her head to a sign below the sunflower painting, it read *"Break anything and you bought it two times over."*

"Fair enough," Burrum said after reading the sign. "I don't suppose my good conduct has granted me another free drink?" He gave her a friendly smile, but he doubted it would work.

"Well, not for free." Shael was curious about this Hax, she didn't understand why he had shown up, and she didn't believe for a second it was to sell that meager amount of oil. He was nothing like her father's other associates, and he had been so polite to both Jakob and her. "I will

57   Dwarf-kin, small humanoids that live above ground

charge you an answer to my question for a drink. Do you agree to the terms?" She held out her hand, waiting to see if he would take her forearm and shake in agreement.

"I see no harm in that, I feel I am making away with the better bargain," Burrum responded as he reached out and clasped her forearm and they shook.

She refilled the mug. "Why come to Ursyss so early? Don't tell me it is to sell that small amount of oil. I have seen how much oil traders bring in and how much those same traders keep on themselves for personal use. Your skin is for personal use and nothing more." She finished pouring the beverage and handed it back to Burrum, waiting for his answer.

"Well, you are observant," Burrum responded, trying to gain a little time to come up with a good reply. He wasn't sure how much this female knew, she clearly worked here but that didn't mean that Forver told her anything.

If I tell her something that Forver doesn't want her to know, I won't be going home. Forver is dangerous, and he may try to not only punish me, but her as well.

The door behind them opened as Jakob stepped in, carrying a bundle of wood under his right arm. Jakob looked at his sister and at the stranger; even he could sense the tension that had seemed to suddenly spring up in the building. Jakob put down the wood, starting to walk over to the two; Shael noticed her brother and figured that this Hax was waiting for privacy, since he had shut his mouth as soon as Jakob walked in.

She took Burrum's mug, which he had almost finished with anyway. "One more." She gave the confused Burrum a bright smile and went to fill the mug, but the keg appeared tapped. "Oh, wolf-shit," Shael swore. "Jakob, could you please get another keg out of the cellar?" she asked, starting to fill Burrum's mug at a different keg.

Jakob smiled and nodded, shuffling back outside to go down to the cellar. Shael turned back to Burrum, handing him another free drink.

"I expect an honest answer," she said, in the most threatening tone Burrum had ever heard.

Burrum was thankful that he had left his empty bag of fish by the door with his harpoons as he responded. "I had an early catch of some Red Martyrs. Figured your Honcho would like the first season's catch as Ursyss came out of winter."

It wasn't a terrible lie, and Burrum was good at making you believe what he said. Shael knew a little about the aquatic life in and around the Green Wall, but she wasn't sure how much of what she knew was what Taurs had told her, and what was actually true. She was always under the impression that the Red Martyrs were best in the late summer and early fall, when they were returning to their spawning grounds to lay eggs. Although the young juveniles did leave in the spring, it was still winter. Maybe it was different in the tundra, they were closer to the ocean there. Burrum smelt like a fisherman, and it was true that a lot of Philyp's, the fishmonger, exotic specimens were from the Hax.

"Well, I guess you will be off to see our fishmonger soon, but he doesn't live in Ursyss during the winter. He only comes here with his catches in the spring, his yurt is several days north of us back toward the Berg Maker."

"Well, that mead was delicious and will definitely keep me warm as I make my way there." Burrum stood and wobbled a bit as the door opened and Jakob came in, carrying a keg on his right shoulder. Burrum was amazed again—perhaps a bit more so, given his state of mind—at how easily Jakob had adapted to his injury.

"You're s-simpee maazen," Burrum stammered a bit, closing his mouth and shaking his head a little. "It drunk I am appears." Again, he closed his mouth, becoming a bit embarrassed. "Thanks," Burrum finally managed with a slight bow, turning and weaving his way a bit to the left, stumbling a bit to the right but reaching the door and fumbling with the knob until he shuffled out.

Shael watched the door close, and then noticed the harpoons and bag, she started to shuffle around the counter to fetch them, hoping to get the Hax's attention from the door. The door was opened in a jarring swing as Burrum gave a smile.

"Me things," he said, slightly less slurred, apparently the cold had sobered him up a bit. Burrum quickly pulled his items back out through the door, getting one of his harpoons caught more than once but with Shael's help, he was finally standing out in the open air again. The sun was getting low as the day turned to late afternoon, and he still needed to talk to Forver.

Let's get this over with so I can go home. At least, his thoughts weren't slurred, he assured himself as he went toward the stalls that made up Middle Market.

Burrum

"I still feel like we should give Middle Market a proper roof. It smells like an undried Silverback in here," grumbled Inlan as he and his father inspected the merchant stalls. They needed to see what parts of the roof needed to be repaired, what—if any—animals needed to be chased out, and how long it would take to clean out all the debris that had gathered over the winter. Inlan was built more like his mother than his sister Shael; he was leaner and the shortest member of the family. He had begun wearing clothes, but more as armor than for any other purpose, as though he needed it inside the Campos. Today, he wore a bright blue and dull orange checkered gambeson that had cost him a fortune due to the orange dye, along with some plain black trousers. Inlan did have to regularly cut some of his undercoat out in the winter so that his clothing didn't overheat him, but in late fall and early spring, when his heavy winter coat was falling out anyway, his clothing kept him quite comfortable. Because of this constant care and maintenance, Forver had started to wonder if perhaps Jakob would be a better heir. Since Jakob's accident, he didn't have the ability to inherit such a social position. Inlan delicately picked his paws around a small pile of rabbit pellets.

"Mother Bear!" he swore, trying to keep himself from retching as his heel pressed into the soft, still warm pile.

Forver rolled his eyes. *This was the seventh stall, for Mother Bear's sake, this boy had better toughen up.*

"Paying to put tiles on the roof for a building that we don't use year-round will cost us too much money. It is cheaper to have Jakob just clean out the stalls and to hire some Norrus to patch up the roof. Now, get to that back wall and check to see if it needs any repairs; if the wood has rotted, you will be able—"

"To stick your claw in it, I know," interrupted Inlan as he shuffled for the back wall, trying to wipe the filth from his paw. As he got to the back wall, he stuck one of his well-groomed claws into the wood. Inlan hoped it wasn't rotted, he was already going to have to spend hours cleaning out the other claws from the wood that had failed the test in the previous stalls.

Out of the corner of his eye, something sprung forward toward him. Inlan cried out—it was not uncommon to have a direwolf, a wolverine, a badger, or one time an actual bear hiding out in these stalls, and Inlan was not prepared for combat, now or ever. He spun about with a shriek, his arms flailing in what he hoped were both defensive and offensive maneuvers, and he stumbled back. He lost his balance in a large pile of old leaves and grasses that had once served as the roof, and sat back directly into the afore-mentioned pile of shit. A snow hare sprung past him, making a break for the front of the building.

If it is dumb enough to run right for me, I'll kill it, Forver thought, not wanting to expend too much energy; his frustration with his protégé growing as Inlan complained about his filthy pants and gambeson. Forver saw the hare make a quick turn, having noticed that it was running right for another of the frightening invaders of its home. Inlan's whining brought Forver's rage up and fortunately the hare was there to take the place of his son. Forver quickly stepped to the side, demonstrating that he retained all his skill and reflexes in his old age, and slammed his paw down on the hare's back legs as it tried to leap away from the new assailant. Unfortunately for the hare, the blow wasn't enough to kill it; fortunately for Forver, it made him happier to watch the creature suffer than to end its misery. He thought about letting it try to crawl away in the snow; if it was still around after the inspection, then he may take it home for a meal. Although its screaming was almost haunting, he was sure that Honcho Bardell would fine him if this hare woke Ursyss. Forver stepped forward again, scooping the frantic creature into his hands and squeezing its head until there was a crunching sound. The noise stopped, and Forver hurled the corpse out into the trees.

"That is an interesting way to keep predators away," commented a voice from behind. It was deep, with a pleasant ring to it, almost soothing.

Forver turned around, he had an idea of who it was but he hadn't wanted to hope that his scheme had borne fruit. Inlan came storming out, almost right into the side of the Hax standing in front of the stall; startled, he stepped back, his classic thrashing guard and attack on full display again.

"Boy, go home and clean yourself up, leave me and the Hax to talk," was Forver's order as Burrum looked at Inlan in surprise; he would have never guessed that this was Forver's boy. Inlan looked back at the large

Hax and pushed past him, marching off and grumbling under his breath, something rude about rabbits.

Burrum turned to face Forver after Inlan had gone. "Stars, does that mean that in the Tavern—?"

Forver nodded. "Yes, that is Shael, and she is pregnant with the cub of a Mahuer." He added the last part proudly, and somehow threateningly at the same time.

"So, the cripple?" Burrum began to ask but saw the look on Forver's face, and read it clear as any text. "The cripple is her helper," Burrum finished awkwardly, not really knowing how to end the thought.

"Yes, he is a servant," responded Forver emphatically. "Step inside my stall," he said with only a hint of mirth, "and mind the rabbit pellets."

Burrum did as instructed, following the Norrus into the stall and away from prying eyes and ears. "Well, Palgus[58] , since the winter isn't over and you are here in Campos Ursyss, I can only hope that the raven I sent arrived at your, I guess, home?" Burrum knew that Forver intended both the insulting title and the idea that he didn't have a home to be derogatory, and decided it was better not to rise to his taunts. "You wouldn't have happened to think that I would have wanted that expensive bird back? Of course, you didn't, since I don't see it with you."

"Yes, I got your message." Burrum didn't care how angry Forver got with this interruption, he wanted to go home. He was tired of being Forver's Palgus. "I would also prefer that you call me by my name, Burrum."

Forver actually looked amused by Burrum's last statement. "I think Palgus is a better name than some Hax gibberish, like Bur Rum, pa bum pa bum." He smacked his lips together as he hummed the random sounds. "I can see my banter is not entertaining to you. So, what have you got for me?" Forver asked, rubbing his hands together like a cub about to receive a gift.

Burrum ignored the mockery and chose to just continue the conversation. *The sooner it is over, the sooner I can go home.* "I do think that this Dio, that the message mentioned, is in the grove on the other side of the Ice Kraggs. I do not know how they got through those frozen mountains and I am unaware of any way to enter that grove other than by the northern border. I also believe that this is where the Maulers have been hiding for the last few decades, as my father, your brother, believed before me."

58   Lackey

Burrum knew he shouldn't be poking fun at Forver but he couldn't resist that last jab.

Forver's hips had been wiggling in excitement, but froze when Burrum spoke with conviction about where the Maulers were hiding. True, his father had always assumed this too, but he had never had any proof. To be fair, he wasn't sure what proof his Palgus had, but he believed him more than he had believed his father. Forver opened his mouth and then closed it, taking a moment to wet his lips before trying again.

"Do not play with my emotions, Palgus," he said in a hushed tone, as though he feared the air itself would betray this conversation. "We—we need to—the—no my—yes, my troops ready," he struggled to get his thoughts out in his eagerness. "I will finish what my father could not and march on the Maulers!" Forver exclaimed excitedly, his voice getting louder and louder.

"I wouldn't do that," Burrum commented. He had tried to stop himself from helping Forver, but the words had just come out.

Forver looked at Burrum curiously. "And why exactly wouldn't you do that?" Forver asked, all the joy and excitement gone like a puff of smoke, replaced by his usual smoldering attitude.

Burrum thought about saying nothing, but he had piqued Forver's interest, and he was like a Silverback with a bone when his interest was piqued. Burrum could try to lie, but he was having trouble coming up with one on the spot as he had done with Shael; he decided that the truth was probably the most tactical decision.

"I believe that Dio has somehow dethroned the previous Alpha, and become the new Alpha of the Maulers."

"That is a big assumption without any proof," commented Forver. "Your father made wild accusations like that, and as you know, no one believed him."

You didn't believe him, Burrum thought before responding. Burrum hated using such a wonderful chance encounter and corrupting it with this espionage. He had liked Rellik.

"I happened to meet a member of the former Alpha's pack, a female. She was being hunted by those loyal to the new Alpha, and from her condition I would assume she had little support."

"Interesting," was all Forver said in response. He thought for a moment before speaking again, "Well, I suppose that is some evidence, even if it is the word of a Mauler. Still, how big a threat can a tribe of Maulers be under the leadership of a cowardly outlaw like Dio?"

"I don't think you understand the danger that this Dio now imposes. If he has managed to unify the Maulers under him, that alone would be impressive. Grimmis, the Alpha when your father pursued them, was the last Mauler to really hold absolute power over the whole tribe." He ignored Forver's surprised expression; it was as though his uncle forgot who Burrum's father had been, and what he had known about the Green Wall and the Yukon family. "I believe it would be in your best interest to consult with Bardell and lead a unified front on Dio and the Maulers. If Dio manages to elude you, he has the charisma to spark revolts throughout all the Eclipse communes, and maybe beyond that," Burrum concluded. He knew his suggestion would likely anger Forver, but he also knew that his uncle clearly underestimated the Maulers, just as his grandfather had done.

"Shut up, Palgus, you don't know the shame my father had to carry after that fight! Your father couldn't live with it either and denounced the family to live a life in the wilds like some savage! I don't know what he told you or that sow of a mother of yours, but he was not a Yukon and you are not a Yukon!" Forver snarled his last comment, his breath coming in quick, furious pants as he fumed; he was tired of being corrected by a lackey.

Burrum was beyond angry now, and was tired of his uncle calling him a nobody, a lackey. "I am your nephew, not your servant. I am a Yukon!" Burrum shouted, obviously hurt by Forver's insults.

Forver did feel a little intimidated as Burrum seemed to corner him in the stall, his large body was not marred by age and he was holding those deadly, sharp harpoons.

"Oh, come on." Forver did his best to rein in his anger as that seemed necessary for his survival in that moment. "I didn't mean what I said," he lied. "Of course, you are a Yukon, far more than your father ever was," Forver said, trying to keep his voice calm and soothing as he saw Burrum relax a little.

Burrum was trying to collect himself; he had no wish to hurt Forver and he knew that—like his uncle—he had a quick temper. He had sworn to Siya that he would work on this flaw, and he meant to.

"I wish you wouldn't be so disrespectful about my father and mother," Burrum told Forver, managing to keep his voice at a normal volume this time around.

"Oh, come on, Palgus. You know as well as I do that your father deserves scorn after he ran off and humped a dirty Hax." Forver hadn't meant to be insulting again, but it had just rolled off the tongue so effortlessly and he wasn't wrong. It was time that Burrum toughened up and accepted the truth about his disgraceful father and hussy of a mother. Forver was already on the course, so he might as well cross the finish line. "Your father couldn't keep his lusts under control and then he goes and dies on you, tsk. When you have cubs, you are responsible for them." Forver stood proud as he continued his rant, choosing to ignore the expression on his nephew's face. "If I remember correctly, your mother became ill, no surprise with the condition the Hax live in, and then she left you to be raised by grandma and grandpa Hax. I can't imagine how awful that was, it is no wonder you always wanted to live here in Campos Ursyss."

Burrum's shoulders and chest rose and fell in heavy breaths of rage. "You didn't want me, you left me to be raised by them!" Burrum growled, his powerful, sharp teeth being slowly revealed as he pulled his lips back. "When my parents died, my grandparents wrote to you; you denied me."

"I had three of my own!" shouted Forver in response. He didn't like owning up to being Jakob's father but, in this situation, it helped his argument. "I didn't have the resources to raise another cub on my own." Forver threw up his hands in exasperation. "Where is this coming from? You're just upset because your parents would rather die than raise a mixed-breed freak like yourself."

Burrum's face twitched with fury, he knew his uncle had never wanted him, but he had always buried those thoughts, hoping that one day he would be accepted as part of the family. The fact that neither Shael or Inlan had recognized him had hurt, and his uncle was right; when Burrum was younger, all he had wanted was to come and live in Campos Ursyss. Siya had changed that, she had given him the one thing he truly wanted from anyone; love. Burrum's grandparents weren't bad Ozars, but they were Hax, and Hax raised cubs very differently than he envisioned the families of Ursyss did. As soon as Burrum had been weaned from his wet nurse, his grandfather had taken him far, far away from the place he called home. At some point in the night, his grandfather had left the young cub to figure it out from there, and Burrum had. He had never felt accepted by either Hax or Norrus, but he was accepted by Siya and that had changed everything. Burrum was not going to be like those who had hurt him so deeply, he gathered his emotions and snorted loudly.

"I found peace with who I am, both tribes. I felt as though I still owed you some familial respect and so I came all this way to bring you answers, but I realize now that I have long since paid my dues to you. I am having a cub, the druid said it was a girl. We have named her Hunnora. We were thinking about bringing her to Campos Ursyss when she is born, and we still might. If you're dead." Burrum turned to leave both Ursyss and his uncle behind.

"Like father, like son!" Forver spat. "You fell in love with one of those wild females in the tundra as well." Forver shook his head as though he were truly disappointed. "I had hoped you would be smarter than your father, but apparently you are just as stupid, or maybe it is the Hax females. I am sure those wild whores don't give you much choice in the matter."

Burrum had been able to suppress his rage at the comments about his father, his mother, and his grandparents, but Forver's words against Siya were too much for him. Burrum spun on his uncle, and there was an echoing smack as his backhand connected with Forver's muzzle.

"Keep your foul mouth shut, you bigot, because if you open it again, I will tear it off your face!" Burrum snarled, his tone was both forthright and terrifying. Burrum had made sure to hit Forver with his knuckles first to really make sure it hurt. Being a mix between Norrus and Hax, Burrum had the power of a Mahuer in his arms, and Forver was obviously thinking the same thing as he tried to reorient himself from the blow. Thinking that his threat and force had been enough to get his point across, Burrum turned to leave as Forver shook his head back and forth, trying to clear the spots from his vision.

"Don't you dare turn your back on me after a hit like that, Palgus!" Forver managed to spit out, having made his tongue and jaw work again. "That sow is going to be a widow, just like your mother!" Forver had got a bit carried away with himself, thinking that he could recover before he finished his insult, which turned out to not be the case.

Burrum was on Forver before the Norrus had time to finish his comment. Burrum slammed his head with all the force he could into Forver's face, sending his uncle crashing into the wall behind him and bringing a large section of the barrier down around Forver's body.

"What's the matter? Suddenly realized that you may have picked a fight you can't win!" taunted Burrum as Forver stumbled as he tried to stand up.

"If you weren't constantly hitting me in the face, it wouldn't take me so long to respond." Forver growled, spitting some blood out of his mouth as he used a broken beam to support himself. Forver's hands felt a strong hemp rope that had been used to lash the old beams together, on the end of the piece of wood he was using to stand back up.

Now you will learn your place, Palgus, he thought as he slipped the rope off the beam, keeping his back to Burrum but listening for the Hax to follow up the first blow. Forver noted, with equal joy and disappointment, that his nephew didn't seem to want to continue their little debate as he heard no follow up movements. Burrum hadn't left, but he hadn't continued his assault either, which worked well for Forver.

"Come on, boy, that can't be your best hit? If it is, you have a big problem because I am still standing. I mean, it does prove that you lack the strength to fight off that female's advances. Did she headbutt you into submission?" Forver laughed as he finished the question, baiting his nephew. He actually didn't think anything was funny, Burrum hit hard, and he didn't want to take another blow like that to the head or he could end up like Jakob.

Burrum forgot about his harpoons behind him in his rage and charged forward, roaring and having lost all self-control. Despite Forver's anger, he was, for once, in a moderate amount of self-possession. Burrum had the upper hand in both strength and speed, but he lacked Forver's cunning and experience. Burrum had been goaded into the attack and Forver read his assault well before Burrum launched it. Moving to the same side as the claw that shot forth from Burrum's right hand, Forver was now positioned behind the impulsive Hax. In one fluid motion, he slipped the strong rope under Burrum's neck and, catching the opposite end in his other hand, Forver yanked back. Burrum instantly reached up with his powerful arms to pull the rope free from under his chin as it dug into his throat, starting to close his airway.

Forver felt Burrum struggling and tsked disappointedly. He planted his paw into the back of Burrum's knee, knocking the large Hax down to his knees. Forver then planted his knee in Burrum's spine, and pulled back on the cord with all his strength. He could feel his arm muscles protesting the sudden force exerted on them, but Forver gritted his teeth and forced his arms to keep working.

"Come on, Palgus, stop fighting, don't you want to follow in your father's footsteps?"

"I am not your lackey," Burrum responded in a raspy voice as he felt his throat starting to collapse under the pressure of the rope. Burrum tried to jerk his shoulders from side to side, trying to shake off the paw that was planted against his spine, but his body was losing strength without air and his power was being sapped. His vision was beginning to shrink, and he was worried he wouldn't break free. Burrum had to keep fighting, he had Siya and would soon also have Hunnora.

Forver was beginning to lose what little patience he had managed to maintain at Burrum's simple stubbornness to yield and die.

"Damn, you're strong," he grumbled, kicking the leg he had planted into Burrum's back, hoping to maybe break a bone, either the spine or a rib.

Burrum took blow after blow, trying to dig his toes under him so he could stand. He was taller than Forver, and if Forver lost his balance, he could still turn this around. Burrum's lungs burned for air as he saw spots and his sight blurred. He felt Forver miss with his paw and slip while trying to kick him.

Forver fell forward as his blow glanced along Burrum's hip, having missed the lower spine. Burrum threw both elbows and his head back. *One of those three barrages should hit him,* he thought to himself as he felt his elbows connect with fur and then flesh as they drove into Forver's ribs. Forver gasped for air as Burrum's elbows worked as bellows to blow out all the air in Forver's lungs. Instantly, the rope around Burrum's neck slackened, and he was able to twist free of the noose. As Burrum spun about, he made sure to give his uncle one good backhand for a second time, to ensure that Forver stayed dazed. His right hand, which followed the left's slap, caught Forver around the neck. His left hand swung back as he started to choke Forver. Burrum's open hand slapped his uncle again, before letting his left hand take up position next to the right around Forver's neck.

"You're just jealous that no one ever really loved you, trust me, not even Klarah cared about you. Father was her confidant before he decided to abandon you foolish Yukons. He told mother all about it, how Klarah hated every minute of being mated with you and your brainless scheming. My mother made sure to tell me what my father had told her about how rotten you were. I never wanted to believe it, but the proof is irrefutable now."

It was Forver's turn to be scared, as well as hurt. He was sure that

Burrum was lying about what his brother had told that whore of a mother of his. Forver was sure that hussy had told Burrum nothing but lies. It still hurt, whether he believed it or not. Burrum squeezed tighter as Forver tried to punch at him. When that did nothing, Forver tried to rake his claws along Burrum's forearms to get him to let go. He couldn't get his claws past Burrum's coarse fur and tough hide. Forver felt like his eyes were going to explode, as the grip just tightened slowly around his windpipe. Burrum watched as his uncle started to foam at the mouth, and saw the whites of Forver's eyes as his pupils started to roll back. He felt a tinge of guilt but forced it back down. *He had his chance*, he thought to himself as he lifted Forver off the ground by the throat. Forver kicked out now that his paws weren't planted, again, his claws couldn't penetrate the thick skin of his nephew. Without air, his muscles started to feel like sand. Burrum looked past Forver's shoulder; their commotion hadn't disturbed anyone nearby and apparently Inlan was still grooming himself. Keeping hold of the choke, Burrum walked the two of them deeper into the stall. He wanted to make sure no prying eyes happened to see him kill a well-known figure in the community. Burrum's rage was ebbing, and he thought again that he didn't want to do this, but then logic helped seal Forver's fate.

"If I let you go, you will just hunt me and my family down because I bruised your stupid pride." His uncle weakly hit his elbow. "No, you brought this on yourself, you bitter old male!" Burrum shouted in his uncle's face as he slowly lost consciousness.

***

Jakob had finished his chores some time ago, and Shael wanted to go home for the rest of the day, since she had cleaned most of the mugs. The Tavern was well on its way to being prepared for the rush of customers it would have over the next few months until summer. During that season, they would have mostly local clientele, but in Fall they would be bustling with more business again. For as much as Jakob liked helping his sister and being around an Ozar who didn't despise him, he had come to enjoy the solitude that the winter brought. It gave him a chance to work on all his little projects. He hadn't completed any of them yet, but it was only a matter of time before he learned to paint like the Harris that Shael had hired, or be able to place stone and mortar as well as any Daunkirk. Perhaps this would be the winter that he finished his own recipe for mead. Jakob had thought about adding a bit of cinnamon to the brew; Wolkien traded for the commodity with the Taurs in the Verdegren[59] . The spice was very expensive, and he had only just been able to purchase some last summer. Given the expense, he was nervous about adding it to the brew. Jakob wouldn't have many opportunities to work out the amount to be added, given the supply he had.

That settles it, he thought, *I am going to finish learning to paint this winter.* It didn't matter that this was the project he had spent the least amount of time on, this was his winter.

Jakob wasn't allowed a yurt of his own, this had been made clear to him at a young age, so in the winter he had a little snow shelter that he had dug out about a dozen yards or so away from the northernmost face of Middle Market. Jakob's home was tucked away at the edge of the trees in the clearing in which Campos Ursyss was located. It was a good home in the winter and, when it got warmer, he was able to stick his head out past the barrier of trees and look up at the spring, summer—and sometimes—fall stars, depending on the weather. The downside to the winter was the temperature, the cold made his leg stiff which kept him less active and feeling low in energy. Pain was a sedative, and made it difficult for him to enjoy all life had to offer.

Remember, you have more life than you can already enjoy right here, he wisely reminded himself as he limped past the stalls of Middle Market. As Jakob approached the center of Middle Market, he heard a noise. It wasn't much of a commotion, more a single Ozar talking in a labored and obviously conflicted voice. Jakob was sure that he had heard the voice before, and the state the stalls were in was what had made him initially think of a commotion. The thatched roof had collapsed in on several of the stalls, and it seemed like several walls and supporting poles had been jostled loose. As he got nearer and nearer the center stalls, he realized why he recognized the tone of the voice.

That is the Hax stranger's voice. Jakob could only assume that he was talking to Inlan or his father, Forver. Slowly, Jakob crept up to the stall where all the noise was coming from and was confused at what he saw. From his position, he could only see the Hax, and he was talking to someone in front of him, but Jakob still didn't know who it was.

59   Jungle to the far south of the continent

The stall itself was a mess, the floor smelt of freshly smeared rabbit pellets, and the heavy mildew stink of the thatch almost made Jakob's eyes water. He put his hand in front of his nostrils to try and block some of the horrid smell. Besides the poop that had been smeared across the muddy ground, there were multiple Ozar tracks. Out near the opening of the stall, he did notice a few rabbit prints, and he didn't fail to notice the blood spots from where the hare had spent its last tortuous moments. The beams along the back of the stall that served as a wall of sorts to divide the left and right stalls had been splintered apart as it appeared something or someone large had fallen on top of it. Jakob's eyes had adjusted to the gloom of the stall, and he could make out what was happening more clearly. He had been right to assume the Hax was talking to someone; he took in a sharp breath of air when he saw what had been hidden in the shadows. The Hax had his father by the throat and was choking the life out of him. Jakob saw the harpoons next to the wall, in easy reach. He snatched one up and lifted it to hurl, but quickly thought better of it when he realized that he could skewer Forver if he missed, or perhaps even if he hit. He went with the second plan that came to mind.

Burrum groaned and his hands let go of Forver's throat. He felt his ribs crack from the blow, as splinters fragmented around his right flank. A bewildered look passed over his face as he felt his legs give. Burrum was trying to piece together what had happened.

Who hit me?

Jakob's strong hands grabbed the Hax underneath his muzzle. With a powerful pull from his shoulders and arms, Burrum's neck snapped backward, and he could now register who had been behind him. If he hadn't been dead.

Forver gasped for air as the stranglehold on his throat was released, and he fell on his rump back into the already destroyed wall. His starved lungs sucked down the life-giving air and his vision slowly cleared. Forver tried to speak, but his throat was too injured, and he could only gargle and spit up the saliva as it pooled in his mouth, the muscles in his neck in too much pain to cooperate at the moment. He spit out another large wad of built-up slobber and forced himself to breathe through his nose, the pain in his throat now outweighed the need to flood his lungs with air.

Jakob gave Forver a big smile and started explaining in a garble of sounds what he had seen and done. He tossed Burrum's body aside and reached down, trying to pick Forver up.

"Stop!" Forver wheezed as loud as he could, which sent him into a painful coughing fit. To his credit, Jakob did stop and Forver immediately collapsed, pitifully, back into the broken beams. He pointed to the snow and made a scooping motion, and then pointed to his neck. Forver prayed to Mother Bear that his son was as smart as Shael claimed and not as dumb as he supposed.

Jakob looked at where his father was motioning to the snow and then to Forver's neck. He clapped his hands excitedly, and again made noises that Forver wished he could ignore. The coughing had only aggravated the pressure in his skull and Jakob's sounds weren't helping. Jakob did step out to get some fresh snow, Forver noted with relief. Jakob first rubbed his hands in a clean patch, getting all the dirt and blood off them. Forver's relief dwindled at the sight of that, but it was renewed when Jakob moved to a different patch and began packing a wad of the snow into a firm ice ball.

Now don't throw it at me, you dummy, Forver thought as Jakob just stared at him while he packed the snow. A few seconds later, Jakob walked up and bent down, offering the cold ice ball to his father.

"Good b—" Forver was very thankful that his throat hurt so badly as he was thrown into another coughing fit. He had almost acknowledged Jakob; it was bad enough he had complimented Love Killer and he hoped Jakob hadn't heard. Forver's hopes were crushed when Jakob picked him up and hugged him tightly. In a rage, he mustered as much strength as he could and kneed Jakob in the stomach. It didn't hurt Jakob; even uninjured, Forver could do little to hurt Jakob without a weapon. Jakob did get the message and, although his stomach hardly registered the blow, his heart was bruised. Jakob's ears flattened slightly; he knew he would get over it as he had done in the past. He had just really hoped this time, given the circumstances, that things might have been a bit different.

"Stop crying," Forver managed to whisper through his sore throat. The ice was doing its job nicely as he gently rolled the ice ball along the bottom of his neck and up under his jaw. Forver pointed to the body of Burrum; he would have kept scolding Jakob, but his throat had barely let him get out those two words. "Get rid," Forver waited a few moments, so he didn't go into another coughing fit. "Of it," Forver eventually finished.

Jakob was a bit confused and looked down. He was pretty sure what his father wanted, but he wasn't positive, and he wanted to be positive.

Jakob pointed at the body and tried to say "dispose" but all that came out was a loud grunt.

"Yes, get rid of it," Forver could barely finish the sentence, but he wanted to make his point and he kicked Burrum's lifeless body. Barely keeping a cough back as he exerted himself.

Jakob was now completely confused; he understood the instruction but the body language that had followed was one that was unfamiliar. Jakob, again, was pretty sure he knew what Forver wanted and, given his father's frustration he gambled that he had solved the riddle. Jakob gave Forver a big smile and kicked the body hard, thinking that Forver wanted him to make sure Burrum was dead.

"No, you idiot!" Forver shouted, smacking Jakob on the arm and starting to cough again, unable to hold this fit back.

Jakob became worried as Forver's coughing persisted longer than the previous attacks, and reached out, thumping his father on the back the way that Shael would on choking drunks. A side wall of one of the stalls splintered apart as Forver went headfirst into it. Jakob winced as Forver crashed through the beams and went face-first into the mud in the other stall. A positive was that it had been one of the stalls that had little debris or feces so, other than the mud, Forver was still relatively clean. Forver pushed himself to his paws.

"You stupid wolf-shit curse," he wheezed between coughs. Forver spotted the coarse rope he had tried to strangle Burrum with and snatched it up. Jakob's concerned look switched to one of pure terror. It wasn't exactly like the whip the sadist had used on him when Jakob was younger, but it looked similar enough that it sent fear through the Ozar's body. Jakob bolted for a corner of the stall, immediately huddling up into a ball and beginning to whimper in fright. He tried to explain he had only tried to help making popping and groaning-like sounds with his mouth.

"Good, I am glad you remember some of your discipline," Forver rasped. He would have Groll give him some tea or perhaps just heal his throat if it was beyond herbal cures. "Now take." He pointed at the body to save his voice from saying the rest. "Then bury it." He again motioned away from Middle Market, flinging his arm in a gesture to say far away. "Bury it deep." He pointed down several times, hoping that the dummy understood what he was saying. Forver then raised his hand and shook his fist menacingly, waving the rope back and forth near Jakob's balled up form.

Jakob nodded, watching the dreaded whip with anxious breaths and nervous gasps. Forver rolled his eyes as Jakob didn't move and just nodded.

"Well, go!" Forver demanded, giving Jakob a good smack on the side with the rope. *That got the gimp moving!*

Jakob bolted for the body, easily heaving it up on his shoulders and shuffling for the trees as fast as possible. Forver balled up another snowpack and slowly massaged the new ice ball into his sore throat.

Now I need to tell Inlan that he is in charge of the repairs and opening up the Market. He had better not try any renovations. Forver moved to where he knew Inlan's yurt was pitched. *After that, I will need to gather up all those still loyal to the Yukon name, maybe hire some mercenaries, and march out of here quietly so Bardell is none the wiser.* Forver paused for a moment, realizing something. *Where are we going to march to?* If Burrum was right, then Dio will bring the Maulers back to the Green Wall, probably through the same pass the Maulers used to escape. The first place Dio would go would most likely be Kyron, the nearest commune that held a group of Eclupse, and had a moderately sized garrison. Forver's hips shook unconsciously in his excitement. The Yukon will have their revenge.

Call to Arms

"I am confused, why didn't we meet in the Tavern?" asked Zolk as he stretched his arms up to the roof of the yurt, his hands easily brushing the top. He was the tallest of the four Ozars that had gathered in Forver's home. The fire played off his black fur, and it seemed to reflect in the light gray that was sprinkled throughout, as though the Ozar had been salted. Zolk had an intense stare and bright amber eyes that seemed to glow when he was holding his prized axe, Headhunter. She spoke with him and, as Zolk would put it, "she understood him, and he her."

Zolk was the eldest of the four Ozars gathered in the yurt, having served under Kodah when he was younger. He had started his military career as an Axe Bearer; a title no longer used since the Mahuer consolidation of power. The Axe Bearers followed their assigned warrior around the battlefield and supplied them with their needed axe. Whether it was their two-handed axe, their battle axe, or one of their throwing hatchets. Now, warriors were expected to carry their own packs which included their weapon, so most fighters had adapted to using only the single-handed battle axe, but there were exceptions.

"It is because Forver is short," snickered Urrah. She was only a few years younger than Zolk and had been one of the first females to take up the axe as a fighter. There had been other Ozars who had put forward a case for female warriors before, but Urrah had been the proof of the notion. She had been an instrumental tactician in the victories over the Daunkirks in the northern territories and she had been recognized by multiple Honchos. Urrah's family had always owed much of their success to the donations of the Yukon family, who had been a patron to her and her family, the Moorgons. When she retired from the service, the Honchos had begged her to stay and train their colonels, saying that she could name her price. Urrah sat to the left of Zolk and on Forver's right, since she was the lead commander of the group. In her youth, Urrah had been strong, broad-shouldered, and had very little fat on her. She had been a fearsome and fearless leader, outmaneuvering enemies and overpowering those she couldn't outthink. In her retirement, she had lost much of her athletic physique, becoming more rounded and a bit plump in the cheeks. Her honey-colored eyes still showed their keenness, and Forver trusted no one else with the logistics and training of the army he needed to quickly assemble.

Zolk looked across to Forver, he seemed to be expecting their leader to give him permission to spring on Urrah for her rude comment. Forver didn't respond, so Zolk took the responsibility upon himself. "You should speak to your patron with more respect, or have the years off dulled your appreciation? Perhaps, we would have more room if you could have managed to keep your nose out of the sweet cakes and mead, you f—"

"You don't need to explain the insult, and if you do, then it isn't insulting," Ferda informed Zolk from where she sat at Forver's left, warming her paws in front of the fire and lounging back, her head resting on one of the large wooden columns that supported the crown of the yurt where the smoke exited. The beam was sturdy enough to support her weight and she leaned against it, a bit drowsy. She was the youngest of the three commanders that Forver employed. Ferda had massive amounts of respect for Urrah, who she knew had benefited greatly from Yukon assistance, and so had joined Forver's militia when he had gone on the hunt for Dio's rebel pack. Although they had never found the pack of outlaws, Ferda had made quite a name for herself among the militia, so much so that Forver had hired her to manage his security for Middle Market. Forver paid well, but she had recently become a mother and wished to improve her living status for Yoll, her cub. Ferda's mate, Erbun, was a den dad and had been a soldier in the Mahuer garrisons to the north. Erbun had been injured while on duty during a Vargg rebellion in the commune of Dolga. His left arm was almost severed by a Vargg that had got hold of the chopping axes for the logging groups. The druid in the garrison was killed and, without immediate magical assistance, the arm had to be taken off at the elbow. Since Erbun couldn't hold a shield any more, he was sent home where he now took care of Yoll, and had begun honey farming. Ferda was light brown in color, and in the summer, her fur seemed almost blonde. Her dark brown eyes looked black in contrast.

Zolk sat, mouth agape, looking between Forver and the two females that had insulted their, well, his, Mahzar[60] .

60   Title, Great Ozar

"Sir!" Zolk said loudly, trying to draw Forver's attention to the insubordination on display around him.

"Shut up, Zolk, so I can finish organizing the numbers," Forver said, sliding two blue beads across their column from left to right. Forver then looked over to Ferda. "If I move some money around, I could see to getting you what you need," he whispered to her in a low voice.

Zolk tried to listen in while remaining inconspicuous. He was already angry that he had been forced from his usual spot on Forver's left so that this private conversation with Ferda could take place. He didn't catch much of what was said, but managed to act nonchalantly enough to everyone besides Urrah. Urrah ignored both the conversation and Zolk, she was pretty sure she knew what Ferda and Forver were arranging, and it was about time Ferda was paid a little more for keeping his security tight. Since her employment, the security team was on time and attentive, which had nearly put an end to the frequent brawls that would break out between vendors and customers. Urrah didn't really care about the payment or the glory. She was doing this because she had been going crazy alone in her yurt for the past year, since her mate, Kevkel, had passed away. She was ready to find some action again. Urrah was pretty sure she knew why Zolk was here as well. It wasn't hard to understand that psychopath's mentality; he liked to kill things and he liked to get paid to do it. To be fair, Zolk was good at killing, no matter the threat to him. She had seen him cut down new recruits and seasoned veterans all with the same ease. He had zero problems with murdering someone or something, but lacked any self-control, making him useless at anything outside of battle.

Forver and Ferda clasped forearms and shook in agreement, obviously having come to terms on the question of her payment or reward for joining this campaign. "Now that we are done with that, we can discuss the reason I have pulled you out of your homes and brought you to the seclusion of my yurt. First." Forver looked at Zolk. Forver's face told Zolk and the other two that he was only going to humor them this once, and he expected no more dumb questions from any of them. "We don't meet in the Tavern because Shael is now its owner, and has decided that it is not a good place to have clandestine conversations." Zolk kept all of his smart remarks to himself. He had a lot of them, but none were worth crossing his Mahzar. When Forver realized that Zolk was done, he continued, "Next, I need to know how many warriors each of you can bring to Yellow Rest on the

East Road by the end of the week."

The other three Ozars looked from Forver to each other, there was no response other than the popping of the little fire in the center of the moderately sized yurt. Forver's wealth was not evident by the size of his home, but in the luxuries held within. The yurt was about thirty feet in diameter, with six-foot high walls and a seven-foot ceiling at the highest point. The walls were made of a polished redwood lattice that was moderately easy to collapse and reassemble. This yurt hadn't been taken down since the day it was put up. All the wood fittings except the lattice were elegantly carved with depictions of rivers, mountains, and trees on every visible surface. The felt wall coverings had been dyed in a deep red, orange, and yellow gradient near the crown, unlike the typical blue. The yurt was decorated with well-crafted wooden furniture, from small tables to short dressers. Since it was customary for the Ozars to move about in a squatted position in their homes and there were no chairs, all the furniture was at ground level. There was a small lap table for each of the guests propped up behind them, which Ferda had moved out of the way so that she could lounge comfortably. On the main table, to the right of the entrance, was a large basin made of imported clay from Whesscire, and filled with fresh water for the guests to wash their hands in, after they had brushed themselves off before entering. To the left of the entrance was a small cupboard that held a freshly tapped keg of mead and four large mugs that had been put out for the guests to take as they took their seats. On the shelves below the keg were several more cups that weren't needed, as well as some small plates. On the left side of the wall was a large, half-moon-shaped table, which had several hide maps and bark tablets strewn about its surface. Opposite this table, Forver's armor and Ol'Grim, his axe, were mounted. Next to the weapon and armor were several large chests that were locked, and a 'bookshelf,' as Forver described it, with nothing but candles on the shelves. There was a large wardrobe on this side near Forver's bed, it was made from cedar and brought a fresh smell to the yurt. In the center of the yurt, providing the most light, was the fireplace. Most yurts had their central pits lined with stones, but Forver had paid good money to have the Daunkirks install a brick stove in the center of his home.

The lavish furnishings and fittings paled in comparison to the fortune Forver had spent on his true love. Directly opposite the door was a large sleeping area, with a square woolen rug on which Forver slept. On top of this bed were numerous pillows, some long, some short, others round, but all of them were covered in smooth silky cases. These items were Forver's pride and joy, and he had spent a fortune in obtaining the hoard. They came in all colors: bright blue, green, purple, and many more. It was as though a rainbow had erupted. He had obtained these frivolous items from the Spilkot[61] , a group of Arkem who lived along the Charred Cliffs[62] that edged the Ember Sands[63] , meeting the Division Mountains in the south as the Ice Kraggs did in the north. Forver had learned about this group of Taurs when a group of Evems[64] , the Spilkot's more hostile kin in the north, had tried to assassinate him. It was assumed that they were sent by the Daunkirks, and one of the assassins had admitted this to Ferda after she had a few hours to torture him. It was through Ferda's patience and cruelty that Forver found out about the Spilkot city of Ebonhuw, which the Ozars learned was a huge and advanced society. The Evems had been cast out for being too warlike and because they worshiped Ploter, their god of poison and disease. This information had been extremely difficult to pry out of the Evem, besides trying to discover who had sent them.

It wasn't that Forver lacked the stomach for torture, but like Zolk, he didn't have the patience for it. Forver got too carried away, allowing his anger to govern the pace of the torment and killing the victim sooner than intended, or before they had revealed anything of use. When the assassins had attacked, it had been early morning, in the fall. All the travelers and denizens of the Green Wall and the Banshee Tundra were doing their end-of-the-year shopping before the winter set in and Ursyss was filled to the brim. Extra yurts had been hurriedly assembled for the massive influx of travelers, and the Tavern was full of sounds of laughter, shouting, crying, and singing. Shael was engaged to Oscord, the Yukon and the Slen family had agreed to the Materimony, and Forver wanted to make sure that Shael understood the position before she inherited the Tavern completely. The Evems, at the time, were an unknown Taur tribe in the Green Wall. The assassins had attacked Forver on his way home from the Tavern. Shael had just kicked him out, and she wasn't happy when her father had burst

61   Desert Spider-Taur tribe
62   Cliffs between the high desert and ocean at the bottom of the
       Division Mountains
63   Massive high desert to the south
64   Green Wall Spider-Taur tribe

back into the building, dragging the semi-conscious Evem with him.

"Get out of my way, I am going to cook it!" Forver had shouted as he dragged the odd-looking Taur across the rough wooden floor toward the open fire pit in the Tavern.

Shael had cleared the counter and the Ozar in front of her before Forver had managed to drag the grotesque thing halfway to the fire. The Taur was not Dotaur[65] , or Quataur[66]. Similar to spiders, the Evem had a large bulbous abdomen and narrow thorax, with eight, thin, multi-jointed legs. Attached to the thorax was a humanoid torso with chest, arms, and head. The Evem's whole body, including the humanoid half, was covered in a glossy shell that was as dark as onyx. It had eight eyes, two were located on the front of the creature's face and six, three on each side, were located horizontally under the creature's brow, and were hardly noticeable. These six had no iris and appeared just as black as the chitin hide. The other two seemed far too large for its face. They were centered, but also had no iris and were pink in color. The mouth was a horror-show, with a lower jaw that could split in the middle and gums lined with multiple curved, poisonous fangs. All of these deadly traits—their stealth, their strong hides, and their toxic bite—had not been enough to eliminate the fury that was Forver. At the time the Ozar went nowhere without Ol'Grim, even in Campos Ursyss. Be it the Tavern, the Honcho's yurt, or just to take a shit, he had his axe. The old girl had done her work that night, taking one Evem's life before its many legs touched the snow completely, and severing a whole arm of another before it fled back into the thick forest. His captive had taken the shoulder of the weapon straight between the eyes, robbing it of consciousness.

"Get that out of here!" Shael had demanded, brandishing a sturdy iron frying pan, her most deadly weapon. "If you want to cook that thing, you can do it at your yurt!" she lifted the pan threateningly as she closed in on Forver.

Ferda overheard the exchange, it wasn't easy to ignore, and decided to prove her worth to Forver. She quaffed the last of her mead and stood, swaying between the two of them before they came to blows. "It's no," she paused for a moment, swallowing a hiccup. "No good for you to...

---

65   Bipedal

66   Quadrupedal

" Ferda thought for a moment, either struggling with the word or having lost her trail of thought. "Fight," she suddenly said loudly, lifting an arm in triumph. "Let's take… " – this time, she didn't win against the hiccup – "take it outside." Ferda didn't wait for the two of them to respond, and stumbled slightly as she went for the door. Forver's eyes had narrowed as he glared at Shael, but she met her father's glare with one of equally furious intensity, still holding the pan aloft.

Forver, wisely, turned around, dragging the Evem out of the Tavern, giving its head a few good thumps on several tables on his way out. When Forver had stepped outside, Ferda was splashing her face with a handful of cold water to sober herself up. Between the dragging, head trauma, and now the sudden change in temperatures, the Evem woke up. By the time Ferda was done, it would wish it had stayed unconscious.

The Evem immediately began to struggle, instantly realizing the danger it was in. Forver was dragging the assassin by one of its eight legs, and the Evem decided to reveal one last trick of its sneaky clan. It ripped itself from its own leg, there was a gout of almost clear, viscous liquid that shot out when the assassin tore himself free, but the wound seemed to seal itself as the Evem tried to run for the nearest tree up which to climb. Both Ferda and Forver were shocked by this sudden display of desperation, neither had suspected that the assassin would have such an ability. The Evem almost escaped, but Ferda had sobered enough from the cold and the water and took up the chase, after a brief hesitation. It seemed that momentary hesitation was going to be enough time for the assassin to escape. Forver watched, impressed at the speed and ferocity with which the Ozar closed the gap between herself and the assassin. The Evem lunged for the tree, hoping to reach the trunk before its pursuer could capture it. In that same moment, Ferda also lunged forward and grabbed the creature by its large abdomen. The Evem had stretched its arms and front legs for the tree, but its three-and-a-half-foot frame could not find purchase as Ferda heaved back, bringing the Evem over her head and throwing it behind her into the ground, twisting and quickly closing the gap between herself and the stunned assassin as the Evem writhed on his back.

As Forver had approached to help pin the creature, the Evem had tried to bite the Ozar with its nasty, poisonous fangs. This earned it a rock to the face as Forver punched at the biting maw. If Ferda hadn't stopped him, Forver would have beaten the creature's face until it had been nothing but pulp.

"Stop!" Ferda had shouted at Forver, after the first blow knocked out several fangs. "It needs to be able to talk if we are going to learn anything." She grabbed the Evem by the shoulder, sliding it toward her in the mud and dew that was beginning to form as the dawn slowly fought away the night. Ferda planted a heavy paw on the creature's abdomen to hold it in place; the morning fog was beginning to set in, and she didn't want to lose the assassin again in the growing mist.

"What do we need to learn?" responded Forver, angry that she had taken away his punching bag. "It's an assassin, there were three, they all failed, and now it will join its friends in the stars."

"You don't know who sent him, you don't know why they were targeting you, and you don't know if he knows anything interesting." Ferda made good points, and Forver was forced to admit the logic in her trail of thought. Ferda stomped on the creature as it tried to free itself from under her weight, starting to pull at her fur with its arms. She was impressed with how strong it was, several of those tugs had taken handfuls of fur out, hence the stomp.

"All right, fine! You think you can learn something important, be my guest!" Forver dropped the stone he was holding, and moved the axe on his belt out of easy reach of the would-be assassin.

Ferda saw the gesture and gave another stomp to make sure the Evem wouldn't try to fight when she shifted her weight off him to pick him up. It had taken some time, and the loss of many of its limbs, but Ferda had learned many interesting things. She hadn't gotten anywhere with the eight small legs the creature propelled itself with, but when she got to the arms, the assassin had sung a different tune. Ferda still hadn't managed to extract any real intelligence on who had sent the assassins, other than confirming it was a Daunkirk. It seemed torture made the Evem say yes to almost any name, so it was faulty information at best. Forver was losing both respect and patience for Ferda and her methods, as by dawn they hadn't learned anything new. Forver's guesses as to the intentions of the assassins and who sent them seemed to be more and more accurate as time went on. So, Ferda chose a different tactic, knowing Forver's passion for luxurious things. By the time Campos Ursyss had come to life, Ferda had a decent map of how to find Ebonhuw, a city of constant warmth with walls that shone like copper, and whose citizens walked on paths of gold in the day and silver at night. As the cubs started gathering to see what was happening, she had figured that they had learned what they wanted, and the assassin was close to death by now. Apparently, the arms didn't have the same ability to stop blood loss when removed, also the torso bled crimson, like Ozars. Forver and Ferda left the body strung up by its fat abdomen and allowed the children to beat on it, as they did with Silverback and Daunkirk effigies during the Triumph Festivals.

It took six separate expeditions to find the city of Ebonhuw, and some of those ventures brought in some rare items. There was cheese from the Mino, who now lived on the peninsula along the western coast. The fragile clay mugs, bowls, vases, and other items came from the city of Whesscire, along the base of the Division Mountains that bordered both the Warm Wood and the Endless Plains. Yet none of these articles became popular enough within Campos Ursyss to completely refund Forver for his expeditions. The sixth expedition made large profits, since the city of Ebonhuw had never brewed mead and it became a highly sought-after product. Stories about the city itself and the places the explorers traveled between had become legendary. Supposedly, the Ember Sands becomes so hot during the day that if someone left the shade, they would puff into a small cloud of smoke, leaving no trace, not even a flake of ash. During the night, it becomes freezing, so much so that the expedition needed to sleep next to a roaring fire just so they did not die of cold. Shockingly, there was no snow, even though the temperature dropped to freezing conditions. Probably most fascinating were the tales of how those traveling through the region would see illusions of loved ones, water sources, strange beasts, and other fanciful things. Many believed these illusions so vividly that they would not leave them behind, or would run from the group, becoming lost in the endless waste that was the place. There were small trees that had sharp needles poking out from every inch of them, and the needles were strong enough to pierce even an Ozar's hide. There were also bushes that moved from one place to another, as the wind would roll them across the sands. When they began to speak of mountains that had their peaks smoothly sheared off, and giant worms that moved through the sand like a fish in water, the Ozars back home knew that the heat had probably made the explorers mad.

This journey alone was proof of the value of the many, many cushions that Forver had piled about his yurt. A pillow the size of an Ozar's fist and dyed a vibrant color would cost most Ozars the majority of their assets, and Forver had small hills of the items. Even more than the Honcho, and this probably was more intentional than Forver let on.

Ferda listened to Zolk and Urrah as they gave Forver the number of troops that they thought they could feasibly gather from the community without the Honcho knowing. A light snow had started to fall and the fire sizzled once or twice as a few flakes found their way to the hot tongues of flame. Forver's expression became more and more disquieted as he heard the small numbers. His stare came to rest on Ferda, and she had no wish to express how few she was honestly thinking she could recruit. She didn't have the seniority of Zolk or the gravitas of Urrah.

"I could probably get somewhere from ten…" Forver's face scrunched up, and Ferda thought he was going to make his eyes either implode or explode; she wasn't sure which would happen first. "To fifteen," she finished, hoping that the high end of the estimate would calm him down a bit. It didn't.

"Only ten!" scoffed Zolk. "I thought you oversaw those would-be guards at Middle Market? Aren't there around twenty of them?"

"Seriously?" responded Ferda. "Some of those guards served under you. Do you have so little respect for your troops?"

"I don't need to have respect for them, they need respect for me. Sometimes, I wonder how you maintain command with no balls." Zolk snickered. He was too good at touching a nerve and it seemed to bring him ecstasy.

Ferda was almost to her paws before Zolk had finished the sentence and Urrah wasn't sure if Forver was going to be able to stop this before it got physical. "Will the two of you measure your dicks somewhere else?" Forver's voice was on the verge of screaming and Urrah could see the tension in his face as he tried to restrain himself. "Ferda can't pull troops from the guard, you half-wit." Forver looked directly at Zolk, who had gotten as far as his knees in trying to get to a squatting position, to form some defense before an angry Ferda attacked. Forver's attention shifted to Ferda, who had stopped but hadn't sat. "Sit back down. If you stay standing, I will have you flogged for insubordination, and I will let him carry out the whipping."

Ferda knew he wasn't bluffing, and for all her anger at this moment she didn't want to give Zolk the satisfaction of being her martinet. After that spat had been settled, Forver leaned back, taking a deep breath.

"Now, let me make sure I understood the three of you correctly. Urrah can give me twenty troops, Zolk said that he could find as many as twenty-five. Leaving Ferda... " He paused for a moment, picking up one of his precious cushions. "THAT IS SIXTY!" Forver screamed into the pillow; even with it muffling the sound, the three of them could hear what he said clearly.

Zolk almost congratulated him on his ability to add, and for a brief moment Ferda saw what Zolk was about to blurt out, praying that the brown-noser would be so stupid. But Zolk shut his mouth before he said anything, and before Forver pulled the silk-covered pillow away from his face.

"By the stars, the three of you are the most famous Norrus in all of Ursyss and you can only get me sixty warriors!"

"It wouldn't be that way if more females were encouraged to join the troops," Urrah chimed in.

"Oh, hush," responded Forver. "I am in no mood for this debate right now. Besides, not all females are like you. They lack the savagery needed to be a warrior." Zolk nodded in agreement. He didn't bother to hide his position on the matter; a position he would have held whether he was Forver's yes man or not. Both Ferda and Urrah shot dirty looks at Zolk and Forver; to his credit, Forver wasn't looking for a fight and decided to ignore their expressions. Zolk, on the other hand, stared smugly at the other two, obviously baiting them.

Forver stood, as this, not yet physical, confrontation brewed. By the time he returned with a map from one of the many strewn across the half-table in the left of the room, the air was so thick with tension it could be cut with an axe.

"I swear, the first one to strike the other gets whipped by the other two," Forver warned, snarling as he saw the two females baring their teeth at a smug-looking Zolk. This worked in Zolk's favor, and both Urrah and Ferda knew that the Honcho would side with Forver if he told Bardell that they threw the first blow. Both females had failed to make great impressions on the Honcho; Urrah had refused him and Ferda had chosen to oversee the guards of Middle Market, rather than serve as a garrison Herder for Kyron.

Forver passed the map around to the three of them. "I have marked where a spy of mine from the Hax informed me that Dio has taken refuge.

Not only that" – the foul expression on Forver's face was replaced by one of excitement – "I know where the Maulers are." He looked over at Zolk, who looked at the map, puzzled.

"Is this charcoal?" the elder of the three commanders asked, peering at the hide drawing that showed not only the Green Wall but parts of the Banshee Tundra, the Warm Wood, all of the Endless Plains, and finally ending in the south at Ebonhuw.

"Does that matter?" Forver asked, frustrated. It was as though you could see the steam rising from the top of his head as the fire shifted for a moment and the smoke altered its course.

"No," replied Zolk a little nervously, realizing that he had upset Forver. "I just sometimes forget how wealthy you are. I wouldn't mark a map like this with something so permanent."

"Are you suggesting that I didn't know that charcoal was permanent?" Forver growled, snatching the map from Ferda before she could have a proper look.

"No, no, no, my Mahzar. I am so sorry, please forgive me," Zolk groveled as he begged for Forver's mercy.

"Enough!" Forver responded, trying to still sound upset, but he was obviously pleased by Zolk's prostration.

Urrah, who had seen the map well enough and was getting tired, spoke up, wanting to keep this meeting from turning into a worship of Forver. "From what I saw, you circled a section of the Ice Kraggs, about midway. You think that the Maulers and Dio are surviving in the Ice Kraggs? We have good relations with the Ramsyn, why wouldn't they have mentioned that the Silverbacks were living in their mountains?"

"Because they aren't," was Forver's quick retort. "My informant told me that there is a grove of sequoias there, and they believe that the Maulers and Dio are there."

"Wouldn't that be the same location your brother… ?" Ferda paused to think of his name, but was quickly interrupted.

"So, what if it was? He had no evidence then!" Forver practically shouted in Ferda's face. "My informant met with the daughter of the former Alpha of the Maulers. Dio has led a coup, and has somehow become those savages' Alpha," Forver finished, having backed off from Ferda a bit. He felt that he made his point. *No more stupid questions.*

"Are we going to march to this grove?" was the next stupid question, from Zolk.

"We can't. There is no way to feasibly gather enough supplies to even field an army as small as our estimates were without the Honcho's help. Bardell is not going to allow us to even consider marching out of Ursyss without waiting until the end of winter, which is still another three weeks away at least, given our hours of daylight," Urrah responded to Zolk's curiosity, which saved Forver from lecturing him.

But Forver wasn't going to let Zolk get away completely unscathed. "We are not going to march on the grove. I often forget how dumb you are," tsked Forver. He then looked at Urrah. "And we aren't saying wolf-shit to the Honcho, got it?" Urrah responded by nodding her head, having guessed Forver's reply. "Good," replied Forver as he continued. "Dio is going to bring the Maulers to us. As I was saying, my informant told me that he had a conversation with the daughter of the former Alpha. Dio had boasted about being able to lead them back into the Green Wall, and he will most likely go straight for Kyron." Forver looked to the three commanders, who honestly couldn't argue with that logic if his information was accurate. Kyron was the first commune that Dio would come to, if it was true that they were coming from near the Ice Kraggs where Forver had circled. The fact that the commune was populated by Eclupse also supported Forver's theory. Granted, Kyron was garrisoned with twenty-five Mahuer warriors, but if Dio was bringing the whole Mauler tribe down on Kyron, twenty-five troops would do little to stop the assault.

"Do you know when they are planning on marching into the Green Wall?" asked Ferda, with a very serious look on her face, obviously recognizing the dire situation for what it was.

Forver growled at first for his reply, but Ferda kept her stare on him. She was Ferda the Fearless; it would take more than a growl to make her back down. "My informant didn't know for sure," Forver finally replied.

That seems like a big detail to have overlooked. If this informant had such blatant proof, then how does Forver not know when Dio and the Maulers are coming? Ferda thought, but kept the opinion to herself. It was becoming obvious to her why Forver had not put up much resistance to her demand for a raise as the commander of the guards of Middle Market.

"I agree with the assumption that they will attack before winter's end," Urrah spoke. "It would be the logical time to launch an attack, and given Dio's relationship to the former outlaw band and their familiarity with our customs, I would be surprised if he didn't pull such a maneuver. However, how are you going to explain to the colonel of the Kyron garrison that you have shown up with some sixty-odd troops? If they don't let us bunk inside the commune, we will be forced to make shelters and provide rations for the troops until the moment the Maulers attack. That is a tall order, given that it is near the end of winter and few of us have any sizable stores left, much less enough to feed an army of sixty."

"She is right," came Zolk's voice. Everyone looked at Zolk as he agreed with Urrah. Honestly, it had been more blurted out than said deliberately, as though the thought had been unwittingly pulled from his mouth.

"Well, it is a good thing I am such a good tactician and have thought of all these problems ahead of time," Forver said sarcastically. The three commanders knew that the sneering tone was meant for them, but it had the opposite effect, making Forver appear as though he was probably not a good tactician. "I have already gathered the food that was left from last season out of the cellar of the Tavern. Shael may not serve it, but our battle-hardened warriors won't mind it, if they even need it. More than likely this will not even be a problem, as I have been instrumental in helping Dhon get her position."

Both Urrah and Ferda's ears perked up as they heard the name. Dhon was a Mahuer, and was the only female colonel. She had received her position after Urrah had turned down an unknown leadership role in the military. When Urrah had refused, everyone assumed that the position was going to be filled by one of Bardell's cousins or brothers.

"That is right, I convinced Bardell that Dhon was the best substitute for Urrah. His cushion numbers have doubled," Forver explained to them with a slight growl, "so, I am pretty sure that Dhon will be appreciative of the sacrifice I made on her behalf."

"You backed a Mahuer," Zolk commented, stunned at the revelation. "That is absurd, and… " His brain caught up with his tongue, and Zolk didn't finish the thought. "It's just not traditional," Zolk reasoned, hoping his slight slip would go unnoticed; it didn't, but it did go unheeded for now.

"It doesn't matter what I did, as long as it gets me the victory that my father foolishly squandered!" Forver had to hold back his voice from being too thunderous, the last thing he wanted was for the Honcho to discover that he was hosting guests in the winter. Zolk had never questioned him before and this new habit was not endearing. "We keep our mouths shut, and after we defeat the Maulers, capture Dio, and save Kyron from being leveled to the ground, the Yukon name will soar higher than the stars themselves, and my commanders will rise with me." Forver tried to ignore the constant doubts of his commanders and get them to focus on what the rewards of their success would be.

"What about weapons and armor?" Forver turned a crazed stare toward Ferda, and this time Ferda had to remind herself to stand her ground. This response was a bit more than a growl, but she pressed on. "Even if we get you these troops, not all the recruits will be as fortunate as us to have their own weapons, shields, and armor." Ferda swallowed hard as Forver kept that savage expression on his face.

"Well, I had planned for more warriors," Forver said to the three of them, seeming to ignore Ferda's question even though he hadn't stopped glaring at her. "Who knows, maybe this will give you a bit of incentive to find more fighters who will keep their mouths shut and who aren't Mahuers."

That last part is new, Urrah noticed, but didn't vocalize the thought, merely holding on to it. Forver motioned for them to follow him over to his bed, where he pulled back the woolen mat and pillows to reveal several smooth boards. They ran almost the full length and width of the sleeping area, and had barely been covered by the wool. Forver lifted the board closest to him up, and the three commanders could see a huge collection of hatchets and small bucklers hidden underneath.

"Mother Bear!" all three commanders swore in almost perfect unison.

"I didn't completely distrust Kaal, but I needed more proof than my brother's suspicions before I could march out of here. His suspicions were enough for me to begin purchasing hatchets and shields in moderate quantities. Looks like I was right to hoard such items," Forver concluded, lowering the plank back down and flipping the woolen mat back over. "The hatchets are a perfect weight, I had them designed after the same ones that Shael and Inlan used to throw, and you know how much money I spent on making sure those were balanced. The bucklers are not as large as I would have liked for the money I spent, but they will defend the warriors from the claws and teeth of the Maulers. I doubt the savages are using any weapons, but even if they are, the bucklers can easily block any stabbing or slashing blow. They may struggle against a bludgeoning attack, but I doubt the Maulers have many bludgeoning weapons." Forver had a good laugh at the notion and was quickly echoed by Zolk. Urrah chuckled softly, having a cheerful temperament. Ferda was more concerned about leaving and shrugged slightly. "The blades are sturdy iron, and they are about a foot in length and a half foot from toe to heel, with strong, black oak hafts," Forver continued, once he saw that his joke had little weight other than with Zolk.

"That many weapons and shields of such quality must have cost you most if not all of your wealth," commented Ferda, having a good eye for weapons and craftsmanship.

"It did, so make sure that it wasn't a waste, or you can forget any further patronage being extended to Yoll, or any of you for that matter," Forver warned sternly. "All right, that is all we needed to discuss. Get my troops and bring them to Yellow Rest by the end of the week. I will meet you there; I am going to have Jakob transport the items. The Honcho won't pay him any attention. You are all dismissed," he ordered as the other three Ozars crouched, shuffling for the door.

Urrah had almost made it to the fine redwood frame and matching door, both carved with a wondrous scene of the night's sky and the beautiful stars.

"Oh, I almost forgot. I suppose that now you realize how much money I have already spent, it should go without saying that I don't have the funds to pay for any fines imposed by the Honcho for not following one of those stupid rules. If you, and especially if any of those you recruit manage to get caught and fined, it will be expected that you or they pay it. I will deny all attempts to tie me into your problems. I hope that is very clear."

"Yes, sir," all three Ozars responded as they left the yurt into the late night air. The light snow had continued and had layered a thin sheet across all of Campos Ursyss. Once outside, the three split up, each going separate ways intentionally. Ferda watched Zolk leave. She had forgotten how unsettling that maniac could be, and in the back of her mind she worried that Zolk intended to creep up on her as she returned home to Yoll and Erbun. Urrah seemed to lack the same hesitation, leaving Forver's yurt in almost matching step with Zolk, despite her having equally, if not more, heated arguments with the psycho. Ferda's hand came to rest on Havil, her axe, and with a deep breath she marched off to the east side of Campos Ursyss.

Forver heard the snow crunching as Ferda finally walked away from his yurt. He stared into the fire and hardly noticed the silence that he found himself wrapped in. This was his last shot, the Yukons' last shot at cementing themselves as the most powerful family in Ursyss, Honcho or not. If Forver could redeem his father's error, other than Jakob, no one could find one blemish to the Yukon name. The disgrace of Jakob could be solved at a later date, when Shael was distracted with her cub, and he was such an easy problem to solve that Forver had almost come to ignore it. Who knows, perhaps the Love Killer died while disposing of the body in the woods. It has begun to snow; it is possible the curse got lost in the woods and died. Forver shook himself free from his thoughts as he remembered needing to transport the axes and shields to Yellow Rest. *I best go make sure Jakob isn't dead, I am going to need that ill omen.* He hadn't considered what he was going to tell Shael to convince her not to pry too deeply into why Forver needed Jakob's assistance, and began working on his explanation as he slid the axe cover over the bit of Ol'Grim. Forver hated this axe cover law; in his day, cubs had played with their fathers' axes and the stupid ones got cut. All these precautions and laws were absolutely unnatural—nature selected who lived and who died. Forver wasn't going to cover his axe up in his home, that was for sure. He was positive that Shael's cub would be smart enough to not cut himself on the axe.

What if my axe had been covered when the Evems attacked? he complained to himself as he trudged toward the Tavern, seeing smoke rising from the chimney and assuming that his daughter was still working. *Maybe I will get lucky and just find the Love Killer, and Shael will be off resting as an expecting mother should be.*

Forver opened the door. *Stars!* he cursed to himself as he saw Shael sanding a few knicks and splinters out of one of the tables. She looked up with her dark eyes, which narrowed almost instantly at the sight of her father.

"What do you want?" Shael asked flatly, not bothering to look at Forver when he responded. She decided that her focus was better placed in getting the splinters out of the table in front of her.

"I am surprised you are still here. I would have thought the little one demanded that you give yourself a break by now," Forver commented, ignoring her question and trying to start the conversation with some pleasantries.

"That is why you are here?" Shael kept her back to Forver. "You want to know why I am not resting?"

"No!" Forver proclaimed. He didn't like when his daughter did this to him. She knew he was trying to avoid answering her question and that he wasn't just trying to be polite. "I want to know where Jakob is," he said sternly, as she didn't reply to his original statement.

Shael picked up the plane and moved from the table she had just finished to the one next to it. "He is doing something for me," she responded evenly, and before her father could respond she continued, "What did you and the Hax talk about?" She finally turned to face him when asking him about the stranger that had been in the Tavern the previous day.

Forver didn't miss a breath. "I had no idea that the Hax were in town so early in the season. It is still winter, after all," he responded with a slight grin. Shael knew her father well, but he was like trying to read the surface of a smooth river stone. "I am going to need Jakob, where is he so that I can get him to do some things for me? It may take him more than a single day since he is not the fastest of workers. I hope you don't mind."

Shael slammed the plane down on the table, glaring at her father. "He isn't my slave. I don't own him. Jakob can work for you if he wants."

She is obviously having one of her mood swings, it's normal when females have a cub in them. "Okay, well I need to know where he is so I can get him." He noticed his daughter's face twitch with rage. "Ask him if he wants to help me," Forver quickly corrected.

"I sent him to his shelter so he could get some sleep!" Shael almost shouted, keeping her hands in tight fists, which usually helped her stay focused and calm down.

"You just said that you had him doing things for you," Forver responded. It was his turn to be frustrated.

"Sleeping is doing something," was Shael's snarky response. She turned and picked back up her plane, working on smoothing out the tabletop.

Forver moved for the door. "Your mother would have taught you better manners," he grumbled as he reached the door. He then recalled that he hadn't seen Inlan since he sent him home yesterday. "Have you seen your brother?" he turned back to face Shael, who kept her back to him.

"I just told you where my brother is," was the response she gave her father.

Forver wrinkled up his nose, confused at first as to what she was trying to say.

"No, not Jakob, your real brother. Have you seen Inlan?" Forver growled, starting to lose patience with Shael's poor sense of humor.

Forver wasn't the only one losing patience with the other, and Shael just wanted him to leave. "No, I don't know where Inlan is. I assumed he was working with you, inspecting the stalls for when Middle Market opens."

"I sent him home after he refused to keep working because he got some mud on him. I guess he still isn't done grooming himself," Forver responded, more to himself than Shael, but she still heard him.

"That would be my guess, you know he isn't a fan of dirt, and if you sent Inlan home, I am surprised you thought that he would come back," Shael said honestly, turning back to her work. "If I see him, do you want me to tell him to find you?" she asked as she heard the door shut behind Forver as her answer.

Forver didn't have time for her attitude, he had to get Jakob and get a sled packed up with weapons and shields and get Love Killer to start hauling the items. The sooner it was over with, the better, and late at night when the other denizens of Ursyss were more likely to be in a deep sleep. Forver moved through the fresh snow that was still sprinkling down, marching for the northern edge of the clearing where Jakob's shelter was.

Chosen Few

Urrah began recruiting yesterday, she had gone around to Ozars who lived near her and knew her to try to gather troops for the defense of Kyron. Urrah lived in the southern half of Campos Ursyss, where many of the older Ozar generation chose to pitch their yurts. This part of Ursyss had been where the Norrus and Mahuer had made their first alliance, and from there, Campos Ursyss had grown. Urrah had to time her recruitment as well, not wanting to go late in the evening or too early in the mornng. All the Ozars who lived in the southern section tended to be a bit more traditional in their thinking; the Mahuer tribe especially would not hesitate to tattle on Urrah for being out. Being recognizable and well-respected in Campos Ursyss didn't make you rich in Ozar society, and Urrah could not afford to pay a fine with the meager coins she had managed to stash away. She winced as a branch snapped under her paw. She was having trouble seeing the path in front of her past her ample belly. Urrah growled at her gut, warning it that it was not long for this world if it kept hindering her ability to perform her duties. She was comfortable with her belly, she was older now and no longer a fighter, so she hadn't seen the need to live her life so rigidly and she absolutely loved how she got the gut. Honey-made biscuits, fruit, tea, and honestly anything that tasted good, and the mead; when Kevkel passed, she had developed a scandalous love of both golden nectars. There was a second snap as she salivated, thinking about the food and drink. Urrah looked down at her stomach and whispered harshly, "Stars, you and I are over."

It was another few snaps and cracks before Urrah stood in front of the Baore family yurt. Like the other recruits, Urrah was quite a bit older than Arn, but Arn's mother had been a good commander of a platoon which had served under Urrah. She hoped to recruit both Arn and Penma, his mate. Most Ozars knew how to swing an axe, and she was hoping to get more than her promised twenty warriors recruited. Urrah ran her hands through her fur to brush off any snow, dirt, leaves, or other things that might dirty the home she was about to enter. This meeting was going to go one of two ways; either they would die tonight or agree to join her. She didn't want to kill the Baore family, but Forver didn't want news of what they were planning to reach the Honcho's ears. Urrah had sworn an oath to gain the Yukon's patronage and, no matter how she felt about Forver, she intended to fulfil that oath.

May my own axe slay me, she reminded herself of the punishment that awaited her if she broke her word. Urrah planned on dying of old age in her bed, especially after she had walked out of so many battles alive and not suffered the gruesome end that she had many times dealt out to others. To die by one's own weapon's thirst showed weakness of will, a weakness that Urrah didn't have. It was hard to predict when all the blood an axe drank would bring it to life, but once it cut you, you knew it was not only alive but now desired your blood. No enemies could sate an axe's hunger at that point, not until the weapon had drunk up all of your family's blood.

Urrah shook her head to force the thoughts to leave. She pulled her axe up in front of her face and gave Lopper a long stare. She knew that Zolk talked to his axe, so Headhunter had to be alive, and he was playing a very dangerous game by not disposing of it. Urrah was tempted to ask Lopper if it had achieved sentience yet. Forver had commissioned all three of his commanders' weapons, armor, and shields. Lopper was a thing of beauty, as was the shield slung over her back. It was made of hard redwood planks, bound by a sturdy bronze ring and boss to protect the hand. Her ring mail shirt was well-kept and polished, but since it no longer fit her, she didn't have the chance to admire it as much in recent years. The axe was made of some of the rare alloy known as steel, and had a slightly downward curve to the toe and a long bit with a pointed heel and a sloping beard. It reminded her of a scythe but with a sharp outer rather than inner edge. The handle was made from black oak that the Ozar had purchased at great expense from the Dwarves, who had brought it from the eastern half of the continent. Urrah took a deep breath and looked about to make sure no one had noticed her and when she was satisfied she hadn't been noticed, she pushed the unpolished wooden door open. *You can't keep putting this off,* she told herself.

Urrah stepped into a typical yurt, much like her own. The lattice was made of more malleable wood than the polished redwood of Forver's yurt, most likely fir. The cover of the yurt was weathered blue fleece; it was not dyed any fanciful colors, and there was a simple, stone fire pit in the center. Urrah turned to the right where the carved wooden wash basin was, together with the carved crown of the yurt, they would be among the most prized possessions of the family. She dipped her hands into the clean water to wash them, then sat down cross-legged, waiting to be welcomed by a member of the Baore family.

Penma and Arn's daughter, Doren, had moved out a few summers back and the couple had decided she would be their last cub. They had done enough, which was essentially the unwritten motto of the Ozars. Since she had left their yurt, the two had entered a quasi-retirement; Penma still collected honey from her bees and Arn kept his snares baited and ready.

"Urrah, it is nice to see you," said a confused Arn as he looked up from a wood carving he was working on. Penma glanced up as Arn greeted Urrah, she was dipping a long hemp wick in and out of a large vat of wax that she had harvested from her beehives the summer before. While most inhabitants of Campos Ursyss preferred to use torches, fires, and of course the new lanterns with the oil from the Hax trade, many still purchased her candles to add a touch of color to their yurts. They enjoyed the colorful dyes she added to the wax and the intricate patterns she applied to her candles, so she earned a good income for them to live on. Penma quickly tied the fresh candle she had just dipped to a small rack next to her and stood up. She made her way over to the mead, which was kept on the left side of the entrance. Penma pulled three mugs out from the shelf below the keg and pulled the plug out to fill the three containers. She had always been stout, and was one of the shortest Ozars, excluding Forver, that Urrah knew. Penma did have the lighter, more Mahuer-like coloring, making her size even more surprising. Her brown fur was almost so light that she might be considered to be blonde, but she still had the same dark and intense eyes of most Norrus. Arn was the more traditional Norrus in looks, with mostly dark fur and a lighter, brown-furred muzzle. His torso and underarms were slightly lighter, but still dark by most standards. He still wore his facial fur in small tight braids, even though he hadn't been in the military for some time now. Urrah knew that his height was comparable to Zolk's and his power was practically equal to that of Ferda.

Urrah got to a crouching position once she was acknowledged, and gave a pleasant greeting to Arn and Penma. "We weren't expecting company, given the season," Penma stated in a cheerful voice to make sure that

Urrah didn't think that she was chastising her for the visit. Penma held out a foaming mug of beautiful amber-colored mead. Urrah did hesitate for a second, remembering the threats she had leveled against her girth as she had made her way to the Baore yurt. *It isn't like you are going to lose the weight tonight*, she thought to herself and reached out, taking the brew. Urrah then gingerly made her way over to the center fire where Arn had laid out a nice wool rug for her and placed a small pine wood table next to the mat for Urrah to rest her mug. By the time Penma and Urrah had taken a seat, Arn had positioned each one of their side tables so it would be comfortable for the others and himself to rest his drink and now they all sat facing each other through the dancing flames.

"Stars, this is some good mead," Urrah began to say as she took a long drink from the mug. "You can really taste the honey in this one—"

"I doubt you are here to compliment our mead, since it is the same as the mead at the Tavern," Arn spoke up, not letting Urrah finish her sentence. Penma looked toward her mate accusingly, but Arn scoffed as he saw Penma's expression. "She is here to invite us to something violent, either participating or being the subject of it is still unknown." Arn looked back at Urrah. "Tell me I am wrong," he challenged.

Urrah slowly put down her mug, having taken the opportunity during Arn's assessment to have a good taste of the fermented honey. She let her tongue lick along her chops, making sure that there was no droplet hidden away. Urrah did notice that Penma was staring at Lopper at her side; it was customary for the guest to leave their weapon at the threshold but, for obvious reasons, Urrah hadn't been able to do that. Urrah gave Penma a reassuring smile, the last thing she wanted right now was for Penma to make a dash for some weapon stashed about in the yurt. Even if they didn't have a battle axe, they probably had a chopping axe or maul, at the very least a dagger or knife was somewhere in the abode.

"Well, it would seem that both of you are still observant, which is good. I wonder what other skills you have managed to keep honed in your retirement?" Urrah got very serious as she finished the question, placing the mug down on the table next to her. She didn't wait for either one to respond, their answers weren't important. "Forver has a very interesting plan, and it could be very lucrative. He needs those who are willing to invest in such an adventure to pack up provisions immediately and as stealthily as possible make their way to Yellow Rest."

Arn and Penma exchanged glances. Penma responded this time. "I suppose before you leave here, you need to know our answer." Urrah simply nodded. As they had talked, it hadn't slipped either of their notice that Urrah's hand had come to rest on the eye of her axe. "Perhaps it is more accurate to say that before you leave here, we will have given you our answer one way or another," Penma said as she reassessed the situation.

"I would prefer a positive response to all this," Urrah said between gritted teeth. "However, if I don't get one, and soon, I will be forced to make up your minds for you. I still need to go to Doen's today." Her voice was calm and lacked any emotion, hiding her true feelings, feelings she couldn't afford to have. She had nothing against Arn and Penma, if she were to be honest, she thought they were good Ozars. They fit the requirements, former soldiers who had no strong loyalties to the Honcho and no young cubs to take care of. The last rule was of her own design and she was sure that she could get Forver's numbers without having to break it. Urrah hadn't pulled her shield to the front, and it remained slung over her back. In close quarters like this, a shield would be of little use, but on her back it could protect her from being outflanked and she had secured it there for that reason.

Arn had locked his eyes with Urrah and they were both measuring each other. In their minds, the fight was playing out over and over, and, in Arn's mind, he saw few outcomes where he or Penma lived, and even fewer where they both lived. Penma, on the other hand, was not studying Urrah or weighing out the different end results. Penma had known well before her mate started his analysis of the situation what the outcome would be. She held Urrah in very high regard and there was little this legend could ask of her that she wouldn't do, even working for Forver.

"Of course, we will join in this expedition," she said.

Arn looked over at Penma, his mouth slightly open as though he were going to argue, but he wisely kept the words in his head. Urrah also was somewhat taken aback by the quick confirmation. No one really liked working for Forver, least of all when it could get them in very big trouble with the Honcho. Their punishment would be much more severe than a fine, they could be executed or exiled for marching out of Ursyss in the winter.

"You are aware that if you agree to this, I will be stopping in from time to time to be sure that you packed up and went to Yellow Rest and you are aware of what will happen if you haven't left?" Urrah stated, wanting everything to be very clear.

Arn gave Penma a sidelong look, but Penma ignored it. "Yes, we are aware of that, but we will share in Forver's glory," Penma responded emphatically, giving no room for rebuttal from either Urrah or Arn.

Urrah could read Arn, even with the flames writhing about before his face like a living veil. His furrowed brow and unblinking stare spoke volumes to Urrah. *This is a stupid idea. We are two on one; we could take her. Forver's a half-brained badger in an Ozar's body, why are we doing anything that mad Ozar wants?*

Urrah's eyes shifted to study Penma's expression. It was like trying to read the surface of a pond or the face of the sun; impossible. Penma was constantly smiling and had a cute, 'wide-eyed wonder' expression, as though she were still a cub. Urrah was again curious as to what the thrill-seeking Penma saw in the boring wood-chipping Arn.

"Well, if you are both in agreement," Urrah finally said, reaching behind her and pulling out a hand-sized bark tablet that she had kept in a pouch on her waist, "these are the directions, and will give you all the information about where we are going and what we are doing. Once you have memorized these facts, you are to destroy the tablet. Leave absolutely nothing that could help others learn our whereabouts." Urrah looked back and forth between Penma and Arn to make sure that the two of them were listening and processing her instructions. Penma and Arn seemed to be giving her their full attention, and Penma took the tablet as Urrah reached out, putting it in her hand.

"Just pack yourself enough food for about a week's travel, Forver has arranged for your arms and rations beyond the first week."

As Urrah concluded her business, there was little reason for her to stay longer and as she had stated earlier, she was still in need of going to the Doen yurt for recruitment. Urrah was sure that Cuskus had buried his mate the winter before Urrah had buried Kevkel and he, like she, had been mostly reclusive for the past two years. Urrah intended to put a stop to this, and she closed the door behind her as she left the Baores' yurt. The snow crunched underpaw as she stomped down the trail, the evening had given way to night and the encroaching darkness seemed to make the cold even more frigid as she approached her next destination.

***

Zolk lived on the western side of Campos Ursyss and was well-known among the community, especially by the Norrus families. There were few families that benefited from any patronage on the western half of Ursyss, least of all from the Yukon family. Zolk had come from here, and had become something of a local hero among the western block. Zolk allowed many of the benefits that were extended to him by Forver to trickle down to others on this side of Ursyss. Many of those who lived here were lumberjacks, amber miners, or simple trappers and hunters. Zolk lived like a king in this community, his wealth undiminished even by his generosity. He made sure that at every festival, he provided a personal feast for the community, and occasionally paid to rebuild and repair homes, fences, and other items. Despite this magnanimity, many Norrus feared him and were nervous around Zolk, for good reason. Fewer troops under his command returned from combat and training, and those who did had few positive things to say about their commander. This reputation didn't seem to stop the flow of recruits that Zolk could muster, mainly from the younger generations who desperately wanted to change their status and knew that one of the best ways was through joining the military.

Zolk had little fear of being reported to the Honcho by anyone who lived in the western block. He brazenly marched through the community, wearing his polished ring mail shirt with a brightly painted round shield of black and yellow checkers draped over his back. Over his shoulder was the black oak-handled haft of his axe, Headhunter. Its steel blade was uncovered, against the law, which Bardell had established to help control cub mortalities with family-owned axes. Zolk didn't have any cubs, he had enough trouble holding on to a mate. Many of them had mysteriously passed away. The only relationship that had lasted longer than a few weeks for Zolk was between him and his one true love, Headhunter. The blade itself was one-third the size of the weapon, and it had an equally long heel and toe, giving it a half-moon shape. The butt had a small chopping maul addition, for getting through tough bone or armor. The oak handle was wrapped in leather at the grip which stopped at the throat, leaving the rest of the polished wood haft exposed.

Zolk approached the Wozon family's yurt. His knees were aching from the hike from his yurt to the homes on the furthest west half of the clearing. *Stars, winter was created just to torture us*, Zolk thought as he neared the threshold of the yurt. His joints only hurt this badly in the winter, and he didn't understand why such a worthless season was needed. *This will probably be my last campaign,* he thought to himself. His body was hurting too much to keep up with the long marches or the grueling battles. Zolk had begun to prefer to kill quickly and quietly; it was easier than outright fighting and still sated Headhunter's need for blood, just far less than a battlefield of bodies. He had no fear of Headhunter cutting him; in fact, when she did, he found it arousing, but her appetite had been getting a bit out of control lately and he wasn't sure how much longer he could keep up with her.

"All right girl, you behave. We are trying to recruit some veterans because I don't want to show up to Forver with nothing but rookies." He paused for a moment while she answered. "I don't care what Habba and Urvek said to upset you... " Zolk stopped talking suddenly, as though he had been interrupted. "Hamba and Urkev, are you sure? Those don't even sound like real names," he responded to no one in particular, besides maybe Headhunter. If Zolk were being honest with himself, he was thankful that Headhunter had been so offended by Hamba being female. Urrah was an exception, but all other females were worthless fighters. Ferda was not an exception, and Zolk was baffled as to why she had such a prominent position in Forver's inner circle. Headhunter's easy dispatchment of Hamba had only solidified his opinion on her frail sex. This time had to be different, this time he was here to get Orald, the son of Orald, a true Ozar. No one passed on their first names any more, it had become such a shame.

"Do you understand? You keep calm or I will put the sheath on you. I swear I will," he said a bit louder, emphasizing the threat to Headhunter. "Okay, good, I am glad we have an agreement."

With that statement, Zolk walked up to the door and opened it. He didn't bother to brush himself off, he was cleaner than the inside of this Ozar's home anyway.

"Hello, Orald," Zolk announced, stepping into the yurt and squatting down, walking to the fire and snagging a fur from nearby and draping it out so that he could sit. Zolk didn't have time to wait to be acknowledged, he had to make up for last night's debacle of getting no veterans. Zolk looked to a cub that was sitting on the other side of the fire. "Fetch me a drink, girl, where are your manners?"

Gandrie looked over to her father, who nodded his approval, before jumping up and fetching two mugs for her father and this stranger.

"It is a surprise to see you here," she heard her dad say to the guest. Gandrie walked back slowly, being very careful not to spill any of the liquid from either container. She handed Zolk his first as was customary, and then gave Orald his.

"Go crawl into bed with Mother, so Daddy and this Ozar can talk."

Gandrie nodded at her father's instruction and quickly shuffled off behind a woven branch screen that served to give some privacy to the bed behind Orald.

"Who is she?" asked Zolk, not lifting his muzzle from the mug as he guzzled it greedily, even though he had kegs of the mead at his yurt and from the looks of it this was the last one the Wozons had. He still would have liked one more cup.

"My daughter," replied Orald in an even voice. "What are you doing here, Zolk?" asked Orald, not taking his eyes off the elder Ozar. "Also, I would prefer you put your axe next to the threshold."

Zolk, likewise, kept his gaze fixed on Orald and ignored the comment about Headhunter. Orald hadn't changed much over the years, perhaps a few gray hairs but not much. He had dark brown fur, Zolk always thought it looked like mud, but he did have very, very black arms and legs. Like Zolk, he had bright amber-colored eyes, and both reflected the fire between them.

"I am here because I have use of your chopping skills," Zolk said with a big smile, that to anyone who didn't know him would seem friendly. "Everyone knows that when it comes to felling a tree, there is no one better than Orald Wozon."

Most of the communes had been pacified, and the Honchos had developed and enforced a law making the Silverback denizens of the communes the lumberjacks for the in-demand wood of the Green Wall. This had put many loggers out of work within the Campos and, in their desperation, many had been great targets for Zolk to recruit. Since Orald's one-time service under Zolk's command, Orald had been willing to take his chances with the spotty work of logging.

"You need me to bring down a tree for you?" Orald was surprised by the notion. Zolk might have spouted about what a tragedy it was that the Silverbacks were putting lumberjacks out of work, but he had always hired from the commune if he needed something cleared. Zolk trusted 'military supervised work,' as he liked to call it.

297

Zolk's face twisted up as though he were going to start cackling. "No," he stammered trying to contain himself. "No, why would I hire you for that? I use military supervised work!" Zolk said emphatically. "I am surprised you forgot that Orald." He tsked.

Orald kept his responses to himself, and he had several, but none were likely to get Zolk out of his yurt anytime soon. Instead, he focused back onto an earlier request. "Please, if you intend to stay long, place your axe at the threshold."

"Don't worry, I don't intend to stay long," replied Zolk. "How is Berbra? I heard you tell your daughter to go lay down with her. Is she not feeling well?" Zolk tried and failed to sound sympathetic.

"That is why you stopped by? That is why you risked a fine from Bardell?" Orald was beginning to lose his temper, but the expression of pure hate that washed over Zolk's eyes and face brought his tirade to a quick end.

"Let's refrain from talking about such an unpleasant Ozar as Bardell," Zolk spit the name as he finished the sentence. His voice was stern and was full of violence. "Now, I am here to talk about hiring you again, for a campaign in which honor and good pay will be gained. I want you to join. Having a veteran like you among the novices I pick up will help keep them in line." Zolk's tone had changed again, back to the pleasant, conversational ring as he gave Orald a slight smile, which matched the kindness of his voice. Zolk could see that Orald wasn't excited about the idea and that he would have to do better if he didn't want to kill the Wozon family; which he didn't, they were such good lumberjacks.

"Orald, you are famous for your ability to bring down even the mightiest of trees, even the mighty sequoia falls to you before the sun can set in a day. Imagine what that kind of power would do in the service of troops."

"You tempted me with that exact same logic the first time I joined you," Orald responded before Zolk could keep repeating himself. He ignored the expression on Zolk's enraged face as it twisted with fury. "Maybe you can convince me, but first I need you to put your weapon back by the door." Orald had no interest in agreeing to this insanity, but he had a pretty good idea of where this was going if he outrightly refused, and he needed Zolk far away from his axe if he were to stand a chance.

Zolk took the hint, just not the one that Orald had hoped. "Of course, I am not going to impress you with flattery." He chuckled. "No, you require a different touch now that you are older and wiser." Orald wasn't sure he liked where this was going. "I never guessed you would have another cub after Rolph, such a tragedy that was."

Orald's eyes narrowed as Zolk spoke. Rolph had been his and Berbra's first cub and had died of a fever when he had been very young. Zolk had shown up to the welcoming of the cub, drunk and yelling about how Orald had dishonored his father Orald by not naming the boy Orald. The reason the cub hadn't been named Orald was simply because there were already too many Oralds, but that had mattered little to the drunk. Fortunately, intoxicated and unarmed, Zolk hadn't been much of a fight for the father Orald and, from Zolk's own lips when he awoke 'he respected an Ozar who could knock him out.'

"A lot has changed in the past five years," Orald answered harshly, growling a bit.

Zolk held up his hands as if to hold back Orald's aggressive glare. "Hold on, friend, I am merely saying that with the income gained from this you could ensure that you lived in a far better yurt, and guarantee that your new cub won't die of a sniffle." Zolk's voice had a jovial tone, but his eyes were stern and held no spark of kindness.

Orald was made painfully aware by Zolk's posture that the older Ozar had his armor, shield, and weapon at easy access. Orald wasn't intimidated by anything other than the axe. His own splitting maul and chopping axe were directly behind him against the screen, and if Zolk didn't have his weapon, then his armor and shield wouldn't save him. Orald had to swallow hard before he could get the next words out.

"You're right, but I am still not interested as long as you are holding onto that axe."

Zolk was starting to get upset and he could hear Headhunter's opinion on Orald's attitude loud and clear. He grinned, but this time it looked more like a snarl. "I am here to talk, I just have to take precautions. You wouldn't go to work without your tools, would you?" Zolk asked Orald, trying to keep the frustration out of his voice.

"You're not part of the military! At best, you're a mercenary and at worst you're a killer. Those aren—"

"Shut up! You're nothing more than a beaver without teeth!" Zolk spoke loudly and aggressively. Orald fell silent at the tone and Berbra woke up, if she hadn't done so before. Zolk was practically roaring in his rage. Then, unsettlingly, it was as though he had never raised his voice. "Forver has found the Maulers. We are going to intercept them at Kyron. I want you there, and I can guarantee that the rewards that Forver will divvy out will put you in a nice, warm, more central yurt. I need to know if you are going to accept or not? That's all, I just need an answer and then I march right back out that door." Zolk picked up Headhunter, using her to point to the door. Headhunter was screaming at him to kill this pellet for suggesting that he was nothing more than a common thug. Zolk was the furthest thing from a murderer, he was an artist and she demanded that he make this pile of wolf-shit acknowledge that fact. *No, not yet, just keep it in your sheath.* A smile flashed across his face as he thought of that.

"How 'bout I put the sheath on my axe, will that make you feel comfortable?" Zolk suggested to Orald.

Orald wasn't thrilled at that, but he figured it was at least a buffer, and hopefully by now Berbra had heard the argument and had already pulled off the sheathes from both his maul and axe. "Fine, you wrap it up and I will consider your offer and give you a well-thought answer." Orald watched Zolk closely to make sure he complied, as Zolk took out a leather cover that he bound around the bit of the axe.

After Orald was satisfied, he spoke up, "Give my family assurances, no matter my response." Orald knew this wasn't a custom or law that Zolk needed to abide by; murder wasn't encouraged in Campos Ursyss, but it wasn't pursued either, the family was in charge of the family.

Zolk sighed but nodded. "All right." The elder Norrus pointed to the door. "They gotta go outside."

"It is freezing outside," protested Orald, growling at the absurdity. "Gandrie is just a cub, you would expose her to the same fate as Rolph."

"You want assurances, that's how you get them," replied Zolk in a far too casual tone, watching with almost a manic smile as Orald turned about and poked his head behind the screen. They spoke in hushed whispers, but Zolk's hearing was excellent, and he could make out most of the conversation. Zolk made no attempt to intervene with the instructions that he heard Orald give Berbra and Gandrie. A few moments later, a very angry Berbra moved past Zolk for the door, followed by a very bundled up and confused-looking Gandrie. In all her three years, she had never been allowed outside at night and she was excited, trying to sneak past her mother while Berbra kept a close eye on her as they stepped outside.

"They aren't going to run to Bardell?" Again, Zolk spit the name, confirming what he knew from having eavesdropped.

"No, they are going to just huddle up next to the yurt, I assured them that this wouldn't take—" Orald had barely begun to answer before he was cut off.

"That long. I know," interrupted Zolk. "Now that they are outside, let's keep this short and simple. Here is what you need to do and some more in-depth information of where you need to go." Zolk tossed the bark scrap to Orald.

Orald gave Zolk a confused look. "I didn't agree to anything, I said that if you put down that axe and released my family from my decision that I would consider what you had told me." Orald could see that Zolk didn't find this amusing. "I follow the command of the Honcho, not you and Forver. I served under you once, but my recruitment was not a lifelong commitment and neither you nor that Yukon have the authority to force me to join your club!" Orald was getting more and more aggressive as he continued speaking.

Zolk chuckled, which didn't make Orald feel any more comfortable. Berbra had told him that she had unsheathed both his maul and axe and they were right behind the screen. Orald didn't want to kill Zolk—he wasn't a killer, which he had learned under this brute's command—but he would defend his family. That came naturally to him.

"Okay. I am surprised, I won't lie. I am very surprised. I was under the impression that my acquiescence to your requests, especially the last one, was a signal of agreement." Zolk's tone sounded more like a snake to Orald rather than an Ozar. Each word seemed coated in venom and almost hissed between pursed lips.

"Good," responded Orald with an equally clenched jaw. "Now leave and send my family back in, or I will make such a commotion that the Honcho will have to investigate, and he will find one of two things. You, dead, or you standing over my dead body; either way, you lose." Orald was not as charismatic as some Ozars, least of all Zolk, but his threat held a weight that Zolk couldn't ignore.

"All right," Zolk answered with that same chuckle as before. "All right, I will leave, but I need your word this time that you and your mate and your daughter won't say anything to Bardell about my visit or about what I told you." Zolk had a serious expression and Orald only saw sincerity in the Ozar's eyes.

Orald slowly nodded. "All right, none of us will breathe a word of any of this to the Honcho."

"Okay then." Zolk clapped his hands together. He shuffled back to the door, placing the mug back on the shelf. "I will send them back in, we wouldn't want your girl getting sick." With that, Zolk turned to the door, he left it open as he stepped out and Orald watched as each second felt like an eternity while Zolk instructed his family that their little meeting had come to a conclusion. Orald heard Zolk offer them a good night as Berbra closed the door behind her. Gandrie shimmied her way out of the bundle of blankets and rushed over to her father to describe to him the sounds of the winter night, the temperature, the sights, as limited as they were and much more.

Zolk stood outside as the door shut, the firelight vanished leaving him in the darkness of the Green Wall. The clouds above were thin and scattered, allowing the moon and stars to cast their light among the needles and ferns. He moved to step away from the Wozon family yurt, but Headhunter was furious. Honestly, he was pretty upset as well.

I agree with you, he thought to himself. *He is a tricky pile of wolf-shit. Making us believe that he was going to join us and then threatening to kill us. Us, the ones who were trying to provide a nice home for his spoiled little princess, the both of them.* Zolk nodded as Headhunter pointed out the obvious inhospitality of the Wozon family and he agreed with her that Orald should be disciplined, but it wasn't his place. It was up to Orald to discipline Orald, his father Orald that is. Headhunter was right, there were ways to ensure that Orald did punish Orald. But Forver had also made it very clear that they weren't to leave anyone that could inform the Honcho of where they had gone.

I am just following orders, he told himself and Headhunter as she pointed out the hypocrisy between her actions last night and his tonight. Plus, *I can't leave the tablet in his hands.* What made Zolk the most upset was that she wasn't wrong.

***

"I don't understand why you told us to wait outside, we could have easily notified the Honcho of what was going on," growled Berbra to Orald as he held Gandrie and rocked her slowly. After she had played out the few moments she had been outside through charades and immersive, but inaccurate descriptions of the events, she was tired and perfectly happy to nuzzle up to her father and drift off to sleep.

"If you had informed the Honcho, the worst that would have happened to Forver would have been a lashing. More than likely, he would have been fined, since Bardell thinks having the same wealth as Forver would give him the same credibility among the Norrus. Then guess what happens, he sends that psycho back here to chop us up when we least expect it for having informed the Honcho about Forver's plans," Orald responded. Suddenly, he dropped Gandrie, and his hands fumbled around behind him trying to find his weapons, having forgotten they were behind the screen.

"He is right." Berbra heard in her left ear, and before she could respond, Headhunter's half-moon blade sliced through the back of her neck and cleanly out under her chin. Berbra's head rolled off her shoulders into the fire.

Gandrie couldn't find her voice as she just stared in horror as her mother's head snuffed out the fire. "Don't touch my daughter with that axe!" Orald tried to scream, but his voice broke off as a fist slammed into his face, knocking him back through the screen onto the bed.

Zolk reached down and grabbed Gandrie by the throat, squeezing. "Headhunter doesn't like killing cubs." Gandrie's eyes popped out of her skull as Zolk snapped her neck in his powerful grip. "I, on the other hand, have no problem with it." He dropped her limp body in a heap on the yurt floor. Orald crawled for one of his weapons. As his right hand reached for the maul, there was a sudden pain that shot through his arm as Zolk chopped off Orald's hand. A paw collided with Orald's face so he couldn't make much more than a yelp from the pain before the same paw stomped on his now exposed chest, driving the air from him.

"If you wanted your family exempt, you had to agree, that is just the way this goes." Zolk shrugged as he swung Headhunter down, holding Orald in place through the paw planted on his chest. The blade met some resistance as Zolk chopped down. *C'mon, don't fail me, girl, don't ruin the reputation.* He grunted and let his body drive the axe down, placing a knee on the handle to help it go through. *Damn he has a big neck,* Zolk bemoaned as he sawed the blade slightly, hoping that would help finish the job. The head suddenly rolled backward and Zolk saw the root that

Headhunter had hit. "Oh, thank the stars, girl, I thought you were having trouble with his spine." He lifted the axe lovingly and gave it a gory kiss as he wedged the door open with Orald's splitting maul. Scavengers would clean up the evidence for him, and he turned, marching back toward his yurt. After two nights of unsuccessful veteran recruitment attempts, he was resigned to making do with newbies, but he would tackle that tomorrow. He was tired now, killing really took it out of him these days. Zolk was still going to have trouble coming up with the promised fifteen or even ten warriors if he had to keep killing them.

***

Ferda was on her way back to her yurt on the eastern side of Campos Ursyss. She had purchased the land from the Honcho with her earnings from Forver, but ever since her family had expanded she had new expenses that needed to be covered, expenses that she wouldn't need to worry about as long as she recruited enough troops for this expedition. The price she had managed to haggle was almost twice her current pay; Forver was obviously desperate for this scheme to succeed. Ferda also wanted it to succeed though, not to improve Forver's standing but to improve her own. She hoped one day to be independent from him and she hoped that after this campaign, the Honcho would recognize her worth and allow her to become the second female commune leader. Until then, she would keep mining Forver's coffers, which wasn't such a bad deal. Ferda pushed a branch out of the way, trying to work her way back toward the focal point of Ursyss since her yurt was on the inner side of the eastern block. This was the home of the Mahuers and some newer, wealthier Norrus families, excluding the Yukon. This side of Campos Ursyss was dotted with large yurts that were often dyed in colorful patterns. Ferda's own yurt was dyed in yellow and orange stripes, something her mate hadn't been thrilled about, but had learned to love.

The branches of the trees that provided natural fences and privacy for those living on this side of the Campos were groaning under the strain of the snow that covered them. The younger trees and branches often snapped under the burden and tumbled to the ground, dropping the snow that had built up on them down to the floor below. Ferda found the sounds of winter pleasant and enjoyed the beautiful white blanket that carpeted the Green Wall. She always felt the worst season was the one that was just a few weeks away. The spring always brought thunder and lightning storms that left the Green Wall on edge, and those booms and cracks echoed through the forest, terrifying all who heard. According to the Daunkirks, the closer one got to the western coast, the worse those spring storms were; a visible shiver went up her spine. *The Daunkirks can keep their frightening homes if those stories are true.* As Ferda arrived at her home, she looked over at the Tavern and Middle Market. She, like many of the younger Norrus and Mahuers, enjoyed living in the hustle and bustle of Middle Market. The stories, the goods, and the customs that converged in the only two permanent structures of Campos Ursyss was like flame to a moth for the youth of Ursyss. Secretly, she also wanted the place because it was the closest land any Ozar could own to the center of Ursyss, which put Ferda within jogging distance of Shael's amazing cooking over the spring, summer, and fall. To his credit, Erbun was trying to learn to cook, but no one could come close to Shael's delicious recipes.

Ferda opened the door to the yurt gingerly, not wanting to wake up Erbun or especially Yoll. Erbun had a blond coat year-round, although he had a handful of white hairs starting to grow in under his chin. He was massive and stood just under eight feet tall, and weighed easily twice as much as Ferda, who was not petite. Erbun's dark eyes were more typical in Norrus than Mahuer, which his son Yoll had inherited along with his father's size. Yoll had the more usual black fur, darker than Ferda's even during the winter, and although he was only a few years old, he already stood a good foot taller than most Norrus cubs. He was as tall as some of the tallest Mahuer cubs, pound for pound as powerful or more powerful than most cubs and he was Ferda and Erbun's pride and joy.

Erbun's head twisted around to see who was coming into the yurt as he heard Ferda open the door. He slowly pulled away from Yoll, who was curled up in a ball underneath a mammoth fur blanket that Ferda had purchased from the Ramsyn, who had traded for it from the Corm, the year she had been pregnant with Yoll. Ferda leaned over to wash her hands and get them both a mug from the keg opposite the hand basin. Erbun poked around in the fire to try and find some live coals among the ash, and soon both were huddled in front of a small fire enjoying their mead and using their bodies to shield Yoll from the light of the flickering flames.

"Did the Ummue and Tamess agree to march east to Yellow Rest?"

Erbun asked as Ferda rested under his arm, sipping on the sweet semi-warm mead.

"Yes," Ferda responded softly, glancing over her shoulder toward Yoll who was still sleeping soundly. "How long did he manage to stay awake?" she asked her mate as she watched her son dream.

Erbun snorted. "He was out after dinner. The boy is eating so much now, he puts himself into a coma every time he eats." They both chuckled at Erbun's response, but the slight groan and Yoll rolling over brought their voices back to hushed whispers.

"If you keep eating as much as him, you are going to be fatter than Bardell," giggled Ferda quietly as she gave Erbun's growing paunch a poke.

"It isn't my fault he likes my cooking," retorted Erbun as he smacked her hand away from a second poke.

"He will develop more discerning taste eventually," Ferda teased as she snuggled into his warm coat. Erbun was tempted to dump the rest of his mead on her head, but figured that her screams of shock would definitely wake up Yoll.

"I was a little worried with how late it was getting and the fact that you hadn't taken Havil, your armor, or your shield with you. Wouldn't it be more prudent to carry the weapon with you in case someone you approach feels like they could make a quick fortune on turning Forver in?" Erbun asked, staring at the beautiful weapon that hung above the mead barrel. Erbun was envious of a lot of Ferda's natural talent and sheer determination, but the thing Erbun was most jealous of was Havil, Ferda's axe. As a garrison soldier, the Honcho didn't feel the need to give him any customized weapons, armor, or shields. Those were provided to the warriors out of the Honcho's own armory, and were standard for all soldiers. This helped keep infighting between the Mahuers and Norrus less lethal, but also meant that garrison troops took little care of their equipment since they had little attachment to it. A problem that Erbun was still trying to argue with Bardell.

"Ever since Headhunter woke and how much influence it has on Zolk, I have become frightened of Havil," Ferda admitted honestly. To any other Ozar, she would have simply ignored the question or given them some random excuse, but she was safe here with Erbun.

"Zolk is the one who influences Headhunter, I guarantee it. Besides, that Ozar has never been right in the head," replied Erbun, hugging Ferda tightly. He enjoyed the honesty they shared. On the battlefield and among the other Ozars, she was Ferda the Fearless, but here she was just Ferda, the Ozar he loved. "You were young and out to prove something with that Evem, you are not a monster. That had nothing to do with Havil, you didn't even have the weapon on you at the time," reasoned Erbun.

"It isn't that I am worried that I was influenced by Havil. I am worried that when my father's soul finally does wake up and he realizes what I used him for, he will be disgusted with me." Ferda was sniffling a bit as her voice kept breaking and changing pitch through her gentle sobs. "The influence that Headhunter has on Zolk just proves how strong a connection Havil and I will have."

Erbun sat listening and waiting for the right moment to talk, he was never very good at this, always having a desire to fix a problem. "Your father was always proud of you, he boasted to my family that there was no warrior more talented than Ferda and he was right. You do what you must to survive and because of what you have done, you have ensured a good life for me and for Yoll."

Ferda couldn't really argue with her mate's statements. Her father had always pushed her to succeed, and both her mother and father had pushed her to join Urrah, her mother had even arranged for the two to meet. Her mother had died a year after she and Erbun had been mated and her father had died a few years after that. She originally hadn't named the axe that Forver had given her, but when her father had died, naming the axe after him had seemed a fitting way to keep his soul close to her, hoping that it would inhabit the axe. Like the other commanders' axes, Havil had a black oak haft that Ferda kept polished, and the throat of the haft was curved to give her a better chopping grip with the weapon. The top of the axe head was horizontal and there was no upward curve to the toe. The beard ran about halfway down the belly of the haft, and came to another flat heel. There was an armor spike on the butt of the axe head, and the cheek was a gray steel with a polished blade. The axe had never cut her when she had sharpened it, even one time when she had accidentally slid the long beard along her shin while sharpening the toe. Erbun had taken that as proof that the axe had been inhabited by her father's spirit. There was no explaining why the blade hadn't shaved a good few inches of flesh off her leg. She had started with the beard and she knew it had been sharp. At the time she had been excited with the prospect of having her father inhabiting the blade, but as she got older and reflected on her deeds she was becoming less and less proud of herself.

"With both the Ummue and Tamess, since you recruited both adults in both families, doesn't that put your count up to seven recruits? You still have five more days to gather up recruits! You will have fifteen troops in no time," Erbun said excitedly, knowing how stressed Ferda had been about mustering enough troops. Yoll groaned again and Erbun immediately whispered the last of the sentence.

Ferda pulled herself from her thoughts as she heard Erbun and smirked as he quieted at the sound of Yoll's quiet complaint. Erbun did notice for all her smirking that her response to him was just as hushed as his final words.

"I hadn't thought of that, that will hopefully make Forver less angry." She nuzzled his nose with hers as he scrunched up his face at her condescending smirk.

"Do you have any idea of when you will be back from Kyron?" Erbun asked in a suddenly serious tone. "Yoll's going to want to know," Erbun said with a shrug, trying to hide the concern in his expression and tone.

Ferda breathed a slight giggle. "No and I need you to do me a favor if I don't come back before the Honcho starts wondering where we went."

Erbun looked at his mate a bit confused. "Of course. I will do anything I can to help you."

"If winter is over and we haven't marched back into Campos Ursyss, tell the Honcho where we went." Ferda looked up at Erbun, she was not teasing and there was no mischief in her tone.

"Why would I do that? Won't that get you and Forver in trouble? If he were to find out that we had a hand in bringing Bardell in on this, he would not rest until we had suffered, or worse, let Zolk loose on us," Erbun responded, not understanding why Ferda would want to do something like that. "Besides, it would completely destroy your chances at ever getting a position as a commune colonel."

Ferda put a finger to Erbun's lips to get him to stop talking. "If we haven't come back by the end of winter, we are either besieged or dead, and in either case we will need reinforcements. Do you promise me that you will do this for me, Erbun?" She kept her eyes locked with his until he gave his response.

"Well, when you ask me like that, I don't see how I could possibly say no," Erbun finally responded as grudgingly as possible. "You promise me that you won't make me have to tell the Honcho where you are."

Ferda gave him a hug and nodded her response; they both knew she couldn't make that promise, but the nod at least told him she heard him. In the end, all Erbun wanted was for her to listen to his concerns as well.

Road to Kyron

Forver's mood hadn't remained cheerful for very long, given the traveling conditions as the troop marched for Kyron. The snow-laden branches dropped their burdens on the Ozars below, as they shed the weight or simply snapped under the pressure. A few Ozars were even injured by the falling limbs, none seriously, except for one Ozar who was buried whole by some of the cascading snow. Forver would have left the dummy to suffocate, but he needed all the troops he had if he planned to have an easy and swift victory over the Silverbacks. It had been several days since they left Yellow Rest and began the journey to Kyron. There were a total of fifty-six warriors, not including himself and his three commanders. The number hadn't been exactly what Forver had hoped for, but at least it was around what he had originally been quoted. He had hoped that his commanders had been underselling their ability to collect recruits, but it seemed they had been about accurate in that regard. Most of those who'd arrived had no armor or weapons of their own and were outfitted by Forver at Yellow Rest. It had taken Jakob three full days to move the cargo from Campos Ursyss to Yellow Rest and, as Forver had looked over his new armed and armored militia, he was glad he had forced Love Killer to finish out that last day. Every warrior had a small, solid iron buckler that was surprisingly light, and two hatchets. Well, except for the Ozars Forver really didn't like, he only had a hundred hatchets after all. The extra shields were buried again, and the troop planned on picking them back up when they returned to Campos Ursyss in victory.

Forver's cheerful mood had slowly waned throughout the difficult journey, each day brought an angrier Ozar out of his lavish traveling yurt. Every night, the same yurt greeted a more enraged and aching Ozar. Forver wasn't quiet about his growing frustrations with everyone around him, which wasn't helping morale. Of all the Ozars there, he was the only one with proper shelter, and Zolk had volunteered some of his rookies to be Forver's mules. Every other Ozar there was sparsely equipped, they had nothing more than single-person pitch tents, their rations, which included no water since they were surrounded by snow, and their hatchets and shields. Forver needed three of Zolk's rookies to carry his supplies, two of them carrying the small but luxurious travel yurt and its materials, while the third carried all of Forver's precious cushions. Forver had set out carrying his own rations and weapons, but that was a luxury he quickly abandoned by the middle of the week. A fourth mule was nabbed from the rookies and put to work so that Forver could travel unburdened.

Ferda had volunteered herself to guard the left flank, where many of her recruits had been placed. Unlike Zolk, she and Urrah had brought twenty-two and twenty-three troops respectively. Zolk had brought only eleven rookies, of which four were essentially pack animals. From Ferda's position, she was close enough to quickly put her troops in a defensive ring around Forver and the other commanders but far enough from Forver that she wasn't bothered by his quieter grumblings. The whole trip had been difficult, the end of winter was coming rapidly and by noon the troop was marching through slush. The nights were freezing and solidified that same slush into treacherous patches of ice, which became covered during the day by the melting snow from the canopy, hiding the ice from view and making the pace slow and cautious. Forver's insults and curses were no longer motivating the troops, if they ever had, and the mood was becoming dismal. Their pace had almost come to a halt this morning and Ferda wasn't sure if her presence alone was enough to make her recruits fall in line when Forver ordered everyone to move out before the sun had even risen. Urrah had warned Forver that if they had to spend another night in these conditions, the troops would run out of their personal rations, and even Zolk knew that he wouldn't be able to hold sway over his rookies if they were forced to eat the garbage that had been packed for them in case of emergency.

Ferda heard another branch begin to protest under the heavy snow that clung to it. There was a cracking sound, followed by a cascade of white. A moment later, the ever-predictable swearing soldier was heard as he was buried in the snowfall and bonked by the branch. The soldier had been wise enough to lift his small iron buckler, which at least stopped the branch from knocking him out in the snow. Urrah couldn't help but chuckle as she watched the branch bounce off the shield and the soldier shake himself, freeing his fur from the powdery snow. She was part of the rear guard, which comprised half her recruits, the most seasoned veterans of the troop and the ones least likely to abandon the campaign and turn back for Campos Ursyss. Although, Urrah wasn't sure how many more days that would remain true. The Ozars next to the now half-buried soldier began to help dig him out and they whispered in hushed, upset tones. Urrah noticed the rear guard had come to a halt as they also had taken the time to witness the spectacle. Urrah and her troop kept a close eye on the Ozars trying to get their friend out of the snow; more than one soldier had tried to desert using this tactic. Once the rest of the warriors started marching again, Urrah gave a low roar, signaling her troop to keep moving. There was a brief moment of hesitation, but the front line began to trudge slowly onward.

This scene repeated itself until nightfall when the group split up into their respective camps for the night. The camps were divided into three groups, the first group was composed of veterans from Ferda's recruits; in the second camp were Urrah's recruits and the rookies, to ensure that some experience was mixed into their ranks. The last and final camp consisted of the commanders and a handful of troops chosen to be their honor guard. The camps were laid out in a circular pattern, mirroring the Campo. The night watch lieutenants of each camp were located in the center, with the rest of the tents surrounding the central and customarily larger tent; although on this outing only the third camp mirrored this custom, as all of the party except Forver slept in pitch tents. In past times, all of the accommodations would have been yurts, but this had changed since the Ozars had become more sedentary and had developed laws to keep their community more rooted. The Honchos had wanted to ensure that war campaigns were seasonal and not continual, and had found that the best way to do this was to incorporate a new style of movable shelter that was not the yurt. The Rodentia had given them the answer to this problem and supplied them with pitch tents instead; far more portable and far less comfortable than the yurts. The Rodentia were a less martial clan; it wasn't that they couldn't fight, but they lacked the power of many of the other Taurs. Their lives were ones of stealth, or remaining within the safety of their tiered communities where they had not only vast numbers but also multiple escape routes, as well as built-in diversions to hinder any attacking force. One of their diversionary tactics was assembling the small pitch tents below their canopy homes and above their warrens. Guards in the tents could easily escape into the warrens, while the attackers would waste time by searching all of the empty tents to avoid being ambushed. But the tents were ideal for an army on the move; the hemp fabric made them easy to store, and the simple two-pole-and-rope assembly was much easier to carry than the whole lattice, crown, beams, and canvas of the yurts. There were some drawbacks; the tents were very small which allowed only one Ozar to use the shelter, and sometimes the tallest Mahuers still didn't fit completely inside the tent. Also, the thin, hemp walls of the shelter did little to hold back the freezing winds that blew in off the Ice Kraggs and from the Berg Maker, especially compared to the heavy canvas the Ozars would have in their yurts at home.

As the Ozars in the other two camps huddled around their fires for warmth before crawling into their freezing tents to try to get some sleep, much of the third camp was conducting an extremely audible argument.

"Two, two whole days behind schedule, we should have arrived at Kyron yesterday! Here we are having to pitch camp for a seventh Mother Bear night! At this rate, the Honcho will know what we have done, or the Maulers will beat us to Kyron!" Forver slammed his hands down on the small table in front of his crossed legs, looking directly at Urrah to his right.

Zolk smirked slightly as his Mahzar lectured the female. It soothed some of the resentment he was feeling toward Forver for not allowing him to sit at his left side. Zolk understood that Forver hadn't been happy with his mere eleven rookie recruits, but Headhunter hadn't been fed properly all winter and she clearly had needs. Zolk had thought that by now Forver would have gotten over it and forgiven him, but it would seem he hadn't since Zolk sat opposite his Mahzar, having to communicate through the fire.

He is not the same Forver, some curse has changed him. Zolk's smirk vanished as he heard Headhunter; she had become more and more adamant that Forver wasn't who he claimed to be, and that the Ozar before him was not the great Yukon he once knew. It was becoming more and more difficult to argue with her logic.

The warm yurt fell quiet after Forver finished yelling at Urrah. The warmth was trapped inside the fleece walls and the hide floor. The crown had a stiff hide flap that could be adjusted with long, thin poles that hung down from the opening. This way, the smoke could still be funneled out, but the wind couldn't find its way into the shelter. The lattice was Forver's preferred type of beautiful, polished redwood, and there were numerous comfortable cushions strewn through the yurt. Zolk and the others were making use of such commodities right now. The yurt was furnished with the bed, fire ring, and a small stand holding a finely carved wooden basin full of fresh water to the right of the entrance, as was the custom. Both Ferda and Urrah—who was taking the brunt of the tantrum—remained silent, knowing better than to point out that both of them, Urrah particularly, had warned him before leaving Yellow Rest that the march to Kyron would probably be arduous given the weather conditions.

Zolk, on the other hand, was quick to pucker up. "Who cares if the Honcho finds out? By the time he sends troops to apprehend us, you will have already subjugated the Maulers and that rebel Dio. I doubt that the Silverbacks will beat us there anyways; if it has taken us over a week to get to Kyron, it will take those savages double that amount of time."

Both Ferda and Urrah had doubts about the accuracy of Zolk's statements, especially the last one. They remembered the legends about the Maulers and how they still moved on all fours like animals. They doubted that fifty years in exile had done much to change the Maulers' habits. Again, they were wise enough to keep these memories and opinions to themselves.

Forver had shifted his condescending stare from Urrah to Zolk, peering at him through the fire, his beady little dark eyes reflecting the oranges, yellows, and reds. He intentionally mocked Zolk's tone and last statement, after which he chose to enlighten Zolk on why that was such a foolish notion. "You really have no idea how badly this will go if Dio and those savages make it to Kyron before us, do you?" Forver leaned close to the fire that divided the two of them; Zolk wasn't sure how Forver wasn't singeing his facial hair and found himself more impressed with that than with Forver's explanation. "Those howling savages will fall on Kyron like the winter snow and the garrison will be easily overpowered by both the Silverbacks outside of Kyron and those inside. The whole commune is populated with Ecluspe, which is the same tribe that Dio is from. Is it starting to sink in yet, you half-wit?" Forver was shouting again as he finished his sentence.

Ferda and Urrah watched nervously, they had seen the twisting expression that had been plastered on Zolk's face during Forver's rant. Both of them could see the emotions shifting as the older Ozar tried to maintain some composure. Ferda almost wanted Forver to keep going. She was convinced that his scolding would finally snap Zolk out of being the Ozar's palgus.

314

It might be entertaining to see the two of them rip each other apart. Urrah, ever the mediator, quickly tried to de-escalate the situation.

"We are all tired and disappointed in our slow progress to Kyron. I would assume that we are less than a day from the commune; if we can just motivate the troops to go one night with the stale rations, we can get them to beds, fresh food, and mead before the sun sets the next day. We are so close to our goal, we can't allow squabbles and depression to turn us from the objective on which we have set out. There have been no signs of smoke from the direction of Kyron as we could expect if the Maulers had beaten us there. If they had, the Eclupse in Kyron would have rioted and probably left the commune burning. Even if the Honcho finds out that we have left, he has no idea where we have gone, and it will be some time before he is able to learn of our whereabouts and how to proceed." Urrah looked to the other three Ozars gathered in the yurt as she concluded. There was no immediate response from any of them, especially from Zolk and Forver. Urrah's reasoning and rationale seemed to bring a measure of calm to the tension that had been building.

Forver slowly nodded as he looked from one of his commanders to the other. "All right then, we will strike camp in the morning and before sundown we should be in Kyron," Forver announced as he popped an olive into his mouth. He spat out the pit from the precious product, for which the Daunkirks traded opals with the Mino clan.

That wasn't exactly the time frame that Urrah had given Forver, but she kept her mouth shut, giving him a big grin in response. She then took a deep breath and spoke before Forver could start talking about some other nonsense. "I do feel the troops could use a boost in morale. Perhaps we could provide them with some of your private stock of mead?" she suggested gently, with cautious optimism.

When Forver didn't immediately respond, Zolk took it upon himself to enlighten Urrah as to his opinion of the idea. "That is idiotic. Stars! This mead is from the Mahzar's personal stock, this is the best the Yukon label has to offer, and we are going to freely give it to these troops who have done nothing but slow our progress and complain?"

Ferda was fed up with Zolk. "Besides carry our supplies and promise to leave their families and friends behind without an explanation? Oh, and become criminals to Ursyss, with their only chance of forgiveness being victory, lacking the reputation or money we have?"

Zolk looked offended. "What is this? Ferda the Fearless coming to the rescue of the common troop? Don't make me laugh, they don't need sympathy, they need to be reminded what it means to be a warrior, the hardships that entails."

"Hardships that you know nothing about! You live among the poor to flaunt your success in their face! There is no suffering within the walls of your yurt!" Ferda spat. Both of them were squatting now, having long since abandoned their sitting position. As their voices escalated, so too did their posture. At this point, Ferda would have agreed to shave her hindquarters if it would have pissed off Zolk, she was itching to find a reason to fight with the old Ozar.

Before Zolk could respond to Ferda's insult, Forver cut in. "Both of you, sit down and shut up!" Forver said sternly, waiting for the two of them to comply. Zolk immediately did as ordered, giving Ferda a smug look as she sat down after him. Ferda just wrinkled up her nose and furrowed her brow, disgusted with Zolk and making sure that he could see her opinion. "Urrah is right, the troops need something to lift their spirits. I could spare a keg, and if the troops were only allowed a single swill, the mead should be enough for all of them."

It was Forver's turn to earn Ferda's glare. "A swill." She scoffed before she realized what she was saying.

Urrah wiped her hand down her face as Ferda's tone was obviously dismissive of the idea. Zolk again shot a confident look to Ferda, he knew she had gone too far this time. All of them knew it.

Forver visibly had to regain his composure, he was not used to being mocked no matter how much he deserved it. Perhaps it was age, maybe he was just too tired to really care, or maybe, just maybe for once Forver realized how absolutely selfish he was being. No matter the reason, Zolk couldn't make sense of his Mahzar's response.

"You're." Forver cleared his throat. "You're right. We will let them enjoy an open bar for as long as it takes them to eat those stale rations. Keep your axes thirsty, I will not let you undo our success." He motioned to both Zolk and Ferda, who although they had sat back down had each undone the leather slip over their weapons' bit. "Besides" – Forver turned to Zolk – "I am sure that if anyone knows how well mead lifts one's spirits, it would be Urrah."

Urrah snapped her attention back to the conversation, she wasn't sure why Forver had felt the need to pull her name back into this debate. Unless he was trying to make a comment about her weight. Urrah had done well slimming down in the week before the march and during this passing week, she had become even leaner, surviving on rations and snow. She had lost enough weight before they left that she could fit into her ringmail shirt, barely. It was tight, but she had managed to squeeze back into it without too much difficulty. Now, the shirt fit almost perfectly, it was still a little snug around her stomach and hips, but it was a big difference from where she had been two weeks ago. Urrah decided that the good mood was not worth wasting by provoking Forver any further, deciding not to voice her feelings on his comment and choosing to view it as a compliment. Urrah gave Ferda a look to silence her, as the other female was opening her mouth in Urrah's defense and had shifted her glare to Forver.

"All right, you all get out of here and get some rest, we will be in Kyron tomorrow!" Forver pumped his fist in the air and the others responded with the same gesture, before shuffling out of the warm yurt into the freezing night outside.

Once outside, both Zolk and Ferda locked eyes. Ferda's face was twisted with rage and Zolk's wore his usual smug grin. Again, Ferda found herself uncomfortable leaving until she was sure that Zolk had walked away. She felt more and more uncomfortable around him, and after his goading in the yurt, she was struggling with not striking him down with Havil. After Zolk felt that Ferda was completely disquieted by his grin, he spun on his heels and walked to his pitch tent. The snow crunched under Ferda's weight as she subconsciously took a step to pursue Zolk.

It is just bait. Don't fall for bait, she reminded herself as she regained control of her steps and turned to go to her own tent. She checked over her shoulder more than once to make sure Zolk wasn't sneaking up behind her.

Zolk strode toward his tent, he had lowered his hand to Headhunter at his side when he heard the snow under Ferda's paw crunch but allowed himself to relax when he heard her wandering away from him. "*Shhh,* girl, she wouldn't taste good anyways and I promise that soon you will have more than enough to satisfy your thirst." Zolk hugged his axe tightly, earning him a little nick on his bicep from the extremely sharp blade. "Oh, calm down now. Don't be stealing snacks or you will ruin your appetite," he teased as he neared his tent. Zolk wiped the smile from his face as he came within sight of the two pitch tents that were on opposite sides of his own. Both of his chosen honor guards had fallen asleep.

Typical of Urrah's recruits. All of them are old and downright lazy. As he walked past both tents to go into his own, he reached out with both hands, gripping the front poles of the pitch tents and yanking them out from the hemp canvas they had been supporting. The two honor guards panicked as the tents fell on them and began to shout to raise the alarm.

"Shut up!" commanded Zolk as he went inside his own tent. "Tomorrow, there will be an open bar with Yukon mead as well as the rations that Forver packed for us. Now, pitch your tents, you are supposed to be the elites, and look at you! Any commander would be ashamed of your ability to pitch your shelter! If I wanted to, I could lash you for such disorganization, but I am tired and merciful. So, clean it up!" he shouted. "And keep quiet while you do so!" Zolk didn't like being the last one asleep.

The next morning, the sun fought another losing battle with the clouds and the Green Wall's canopy, leaving the forest covered in a cold shade. Urrah's suggestion had made a noticeable difference to the troop's morale. Not only were they up without any argument or delay this morning, but they were on the march within the hour and setting an exceptionally quick pace. The soldiers were paired up, excluding Forver and the rookies helping him, as well as the commanders. Each of the pairs carried a long pole between them. This pole had four smaller poles lashed to it which served as the supports for the pitch tents. Wrapped around these poles were the two hemp canvases of each soldier's tent. Slung over the opposite shoulder, the soldiers each carried their personal sack and shield, which was also strapped over this arm. Their hatchets were secured on their hips by a sinew cord that had a makeshift leather loop for the weapon. The axe was a tool as well as a weapon, and the hatchets lacked the lavish polished handles of the commanders' axes, or the bright steel heads. These axes were used as shovels, hammers, skinning knives, and, for chopping. The blades were extremely hard to break, and the bit could be smoothed to take out any knicks. The most fragile part of the weapon, the haft, was easy enough to replace, only requiring any wooden handle. Preferably hardwood, but one could use a softwood haft until they could find an oak, walnut, ash, or—more likely in the Green Wall—sequoia. Inside each sack were two bronze cooking utensils; a pot for boiling water or melting snow and a small pan for heating meats or roasting pine nuts. Depending on the season, the rations in these packs could consist of dried fruits, fresh vegetables, grains, and smoked meats. The satchel also contained a small sack that contained the soldiers' flint, sharpening stones, files for their claws and teeth, and tweezers to help keep their fur tidy. Finally, the last thing added to the satchel was the blanket and bedroll bundle that was tightly rolled up and mashed in with the other items.

Forver hadn't been able to bring his precious pack mules, literal ones, because Inlan needed the beasts to help him move materials to repair Middle Market. Usually, Forver had three mules with him that would carry his supplies. They carried his yurt and several different yurt covers, depending on the season and climate in which the troop was marching. Additional supplies included his kegs of mead, boxes of sweets, sacks of grain, bags of fruits, and crates of meat. Forver often said he wished his mate had given birth to mules rather than cubs, and only Ozars who didn't know him thought he was joking. When he traveled with Special, Precious, and Exceptional, he brought along a Moozer [67]slave he used for each beast. The sole task of these Rodentia was to ensure that the mules had all their needs cared for. The Moozers were probably one of the meekest of the Rodentia, standing just two or so feet tall and having tiny physiques which made them agile but easy to physically control. They were intuitive and very smart, so they could be trusted to keep the mules in good condition without needing to be constantly monitored, at the tiered slave community that was attached to Ursyss in the north. The Moozers didn't have a long life expectancy, and Forver was often seen at the market in summer buying new slaves who were then sent to the northern block and were communal workers. Most of these slaves came from rival Rodentia tribes, but there were a few Rodentia that felt the security of the Campo was better than freedom in the wild. Because of their short life spans, Forver had started naming them after the mule they each took care of. "It was best not to give them personal names, or you may get attached to them," he had always said, but he needed a way to tell the difference since they tended to have similar features. Often, they were some shades of dark brown to light blond, so he couldn't just yell blond or brown one.

Forver was honestly impressed at how well the four rookies were carrying his cargo. He had purposefully not packed heavily because he wasn't going to have his mules; he had brought only one yurt cover, as well as his smallest travel yurt, only half of his cushions, three kegs of mead,

67   Mouse-Taur

and a single crate of mixed rations. After the open bar that morning, the rookie carrying the mead was able to lighten the load of the one carrying the yurt by helping to carry some of the lattice for the walls.

By noon, the procession was no longer snaking its way through the massive redwood trees and other conifers, and appeared more like a slug meandering along. The tips of the massive trees seemed to keep the sun at bay, leaving the forest in twilight with their pointed tops. The groaning branches and occasional flop of the falling snow were the only sounds that could be heard other than the crunch of snow beneath the marching paws of the troop. Every now and then, a small bird or squirrel would peer out from the branches at the silent procession as it passed below them. One such bird, a small finch, became braver than the rest and skipped out onto a branch and ruffled up its reddish feathers. It had a bright orange chest and it craned its neck as it prepared to let out a chirp or a whistle. Suddenly, a puff of plumage appeared in its place. With a lifeless thud, it fell to the snow. Ferda shot a look over to her right where Zolk was. He was on the outside flank as well, obviously wanting to be far from Forver in case he started another tantrum. The Ozar smacked his usual grin on his face as Ferda met his gaze, and he securely tightened the leather thong that he had used for a sling back around his wrist.

"I was enjoying the silence," he shouted, as Ferda turned to ignore him.

"Stars, he is a monster," she murmured to herself as she trudged onward. Ferda wasn't wrong, but she didn't point out the obvious simply to condemn Zolk. She was disappointed in her initial response. She had almost laughed when she saw the explosion of feathers as the stone had caught the helpless creature by surprise. She didn't want to become a mindless killer, whose only pleasure was in inflicting pain on others, but she couldn't deny the joy she felt in those sadistic moments.

"You're not wrong," Arn commented as he overheard her whisper. Ferda looked at him, surprised; she hadn't realized she had spoken out loud. "The thing is, sometimes I wonder how much happier we would be if we gave as few shits as Zolk. I can at least rationalize my killing by saying I was ordered, and I had to obey. I don't know how you do it, but we all need to or else we will turn out like him."

Ferda was flabbergasted at Arn's brief epiphany. "I guess you're right, but I feel as though Zolk hurts others because he enjoys it. I feel as though that is what makes his actions wrong, and I am worried that is what makes my actions wrong."

Arn let out a long breath. "That is deep. Although I feel like your reflecting on these facts is also what separates you from him. Speaking for myself, and everyone who joined you, we don't see you as a monster but as a leader." Arn tried to give Ferda a reassuring smile before he was dragged away by Penma, who either hadn't heard the conversation or had chosen to remain aloof.

I am doing this so that Yoll never has to worry about being attacked by the savage Silverbacks. So that he can grow up in a secure and safe place, Ferda told herself, *my motives are pure, I am not the villain.*

The Ozars had simply done what was best for the Green Wall, their actions were no different than the Primjawl[68] in the Verdegren or the Mino along the coast of the plains. Sometimes, order was brought through the chaos of disorder; sometimes, the only way to bring peace was through force. The Taurs had learned this from the Humans, Dwarves, and Fay who had established great domains. *Under our leadership, the Eclupse, Varggs, and Cana have flourished. Their lives have only improved since the Ozars have taken the reins and modified the original four laws.*

She was unaware of the Lobu's condition under the Daunkirks' leadership, but she doubted that it was worse than how the savages had lived before, in scattered groups without homes, killing and taking whatever they wanted, with no regard for feeling or property. Ferda was pulled from her thoughts when she heard the bugle echoing through the trees; Kyron's sentries had spotted them and were announcing their arrival.

The garrison in Kyron rushed into action, donning their armor and gathering their weapons, unsure which Campo was sending troops or if these Ozars were here to raid them or for some other reason. It had been decades since two Campo had come to blows with one another, but Dhon, the colonel, was not going to take any chances. From the information she had been told, it was a sizable force that was moving toward them. The garrison troops consisted of merely twenty-five soldiers, but Dhon was not going to let that intimidate her. She quickly had her troops line up to the west from where the force of Ozars were arriving. She had a group of her soldiers round up the Eclupse and ensure that they were securely corralled. The front row lowered their shields to chest height so they could look over the tops and get an idea of who was advancing toward them.

68   Ape-Taurs

The line behind them held their shields slightly aloft, covering both their heads and the heads of the row in front of them. If a volley of arrows or spears were to signal the beginning of the assault, this line could lower the shields to provide a protective shell for themselves and the front line.

Ferda began to push up through the troops. She was excited; here at Kyron, her ideas about the better life the Ozars were providing would be validated. This would be proof that the soldiers following orders were not simply monsters on a leash. It would reinforce the idea that she wasn't the villain. As her eyes took in the sights, her steps became less determined, and she began to stop trying to force her way to the front.

This isn't right, this isn't a commune, she thought as she looked at the pens, the piles of feces, and the half-ruined shacks that housed the Eclipse. *How is this progress? How is this what we are fighting to preserve?*

Another Road to Kyron

The large procession of Maulers wound their way through the narrow icy canyon that had once guided them to the grove and would now take them back to the Green Wall. The Maulers had to move single-file in most places, and from above it appeared as though a black river was cutting its way through the Ice Kraggs. They had left the Gathering two days previously, and that morning had reached the entrance of the canyon and started their march through the frozen mountains. Dio and four chosen Scouts—Numa, Jabyn, Essall, and Rymmall—led the procession on its slow march. There were times when the whole group would grind to a stop, needing to lift fallen rocks, or cut out a wider path for the travois to pass. In the rear, several of the new adults watched to be sure that no one assaulted the party from behind, and to aid the elders and pups through the canyon. The rear group consisted of Aasha, Brutyss, Unkyss, Dardyl, and Rellik, who were trying to assist and hustle the older adults and herd the pups into the canyon. Skoff was near the rear, having to drag his travois with all his masks, unguents, paints, sigil items and other things that were necessary for him to be the shaman and communicate with the ancestors. Although he had refused any assistance, he did allow Oflyn to carry his antler stash, since the Mauler was his scrimshander. Terrabyss and Luna followed along behind him, taking the easy route through the snow by walking in the grooves left by Skoff's travois. The sun had no clouds to compete with today, and since the Maulers were out of the grove and not yet in the Green Wall, they were able to bask in its full glory. Terrabyss' fur gleamed burgundy in this light, highlighting his dark undercoat. Luna also seemed to shine, her fur appearing more silver than white, and her eyes became the softest blue in the bright sun. Terrabyss tried to flick some snow up at Luna with his paw to make her lose her balance; he fell forward, and she easily stopped before the snow even got near her. She cocked her head with a questioning look, they had been playing like pups for these past couple of days. The night brought more adult joys.

Terrabyss had woken up the day after their Materimony with seemingly no recollection of the word he had spoken in his sleep; at least that was what he told Luna when she asked. In all honesty, he had recalled some odd-sounding word, *Lucarael, Lucuril,* but the letters and cadence were strange to him. He didn't know how to pronounce some of the words that popped into his head as he tried to make sense of the oddity, so he kept much of his thoughts to himself. The more distant the memory became, the less he could recall the word and the more convinced he was that it had just been the mead.

Luna hadn't pried beyond her question the morning they had woken up together as mates. She wasn't sure if he was hiding anything from her, they hadn't known each other that intimately yet and she was still learning his quirks. She was certain that something else had been on his mind the past couple of days, but as each new day came the less weighed-down Terrabyss had appeared, so she didn't feel the need to investigate further. Skoff had predicted that it was a bad omen for the male to pass out on his mating night, and it was a portent of Terrabyss' death. Numa had told Luna not to bother herself with his doomsday prophecies; he was wrong most of the time and he had never successfully predicted someone's death. Those facts had reassured Luna that at least Terrabyss wasn't going to listen to fortunes, least of all from his brother. The past few days had done a lot to ease her mind as they now chased each other in the snow, ignoring those they bumped into and laughing playfully.

Rellik stood on the left side of the canyon alongside Aasha. The two of them had just rounded up a couple of pups that had learned to run during the winter and apparently needed to show everyone how fast they were. Aasha snarled angrily as one of the pups they had just guided into the canyon started to run back out. The pup slid to a stop, tucking his tail and lowering his ears before turning and whimpering back after the procession. Rellik hadn't noticed the pup; she was too busy staring jealously at Dardyl, as she and Unkyss were leaning against the edge of the canyon and playing Yield. It was not an official game like My Skull, but pups loved playing it, and apparently so did Dardyl and Unkyss. Each one took turns punching the other in the same arm as the opponent had used to punch them. The first one unable to lift their arm to hit the other back lost, or you won if the other declared 'yield'. Brutyss, who had just helped Oflyn with his travois that was piled with caribou antlers, came back out of the canyon to check that was the last one and retrieve the rest of the Fist.

"I don't know why Dio allowed Skoff to bring all those antlers, there are caribou in the Green Wall. Or why Oflyn is willing to carry the burden." Brutyss stopped talking as he followed Rellik's gaze. "For Alpha Father's sake, why? He doesn't have anything I don't."

"Other than that he is tall," responded Aasha as she joined the conversation, having made sure the pup was well down the canyon pass.

Rellik's tail wagged as she became aware of who everyone was talking about and why. She reached back and grabbed the appendage before it could embarrass her more. "You're attractive, Brutyss." Rellik wasn't lying, Brutyss was attractive. But he was short—not as short as Terrabyss, but close—and not very broad. His shoulders were barely wider than Luna's and she was an Eclipse. Although Brutyss did make up for these shortcomings with his speed and endurance, in which he was peerless.

"Don't lie to him," teased Aasha. "Maybe Oflyn will carve him a statue from one of those horns to help him find a mate."

"He carves exotic statues to help with fertility, not finding mates," corrected Brutyss. "Impressive, given that he is half blind."

Aasha just shook her head. "Rellik, you want to hear a funny story about old Oflyn's fertility statues and my brother?" she asked the other female with a grin. "I promise it will take your mind off of whatever it is those two are doing." She pointed across the way to Dardyl and Unkyss, who were now trying to push each other out of a small box they had drawn in the snow.

"Don't you dare," warned Brutyss as he knew exactly what story his sister was getting ready to tell. "If you do, I swear I will tell her how you got your most 'infamous' scar," Brutyss said sarcastically, running a claw down his own skull between his ears and eyes.

Rellik couldn't deny that she was interested, she almost hoped that Aasha would tell her the story, not intimidated by her brother's threat. In this way, Brutyss would hopefully tell her his story and she would have the best of both worlds. Apparently, Aasha knew her brother better than that and she could tell he was very serious. She clearly didn't want that story getting out. Rellik thought about using her new position as part of the Ravis pack and her connection to Numa to force Aasha to tell the story, since she knew that Aasha aspired to join the Scouts. Perhaps, if she was patient, she would find a moment when she and Aasha were alone, and she could get the other female to tell her. Then she could perhaps use that as leverage to get Brutyss to talk.

"Well, it looks like Oflyn was the last one, so we might as well follow him and head into the canyon," Aasha said, loudly enough to get Unkyss' and Dardyl's attention as well. After the five had made one last check to ensure they weren't leaving anyone behind, Aasha gave the signal for them to follow the tribe through the canyon.

"Do you hear that?" Brutyss asked the group as they followed Aasha into the canyon. Brutyss was slightly in front of Unkyss, who had an ice ball on his right bicep.

Unkyss looked at Brutyss, puzzled, his ears rotating, trying to pin down what Brutyss had heard. "No," he responded slowly. Suddenly, there was a thump as an arrow shaft came to a quivering stop in Unkyss' left trapezius muscle, just below the collar bone and above the lung. A half dozen other arrow shafts sunk into the snow around Unkyss' paws, only one having made it the full distance to the target.

Rellik had overheard some conversations between Numa and her Scouts, in particular Jabyn and Essall. Numa didn't want to warn Dio about the Corvel, she was of the opinion that they would take no aggressive action against such a large group of Maulers. Even if they had, the Maulers were leaving the grove and she doubted that the Corvel would pursue them into the Green Wall. Numa had probably assumed correctly that the Corvel wouldn't chase the Maulers into the Green Wall, but she should have known better than to assume that a Taur wouldn't take offense to another Taur being in their territory. Rellik turned as she heard Brutyss shout, "Alpha Father! Take cover!" Another hail of arrows began to fall from the sky above, difficult to see in the blinding bright sunlight.

"Corvel!" shouted Rellik; everyone there knew how this Airlut tribe fought. "Why do we live trapped between two murder-loving tribes?" Rellik breathed to herself as she found a small outcropping in the canyon wall and dove for it. Several arrows bounced off the icy wall of the canyon as she huddled for cover.

"Rellik!" Aasha shouted for the other Mauler's attention. Once she had it, she continued to relay her commands. "Go, sound the alarm. Bring reinforcements! We are outnumbered and will need some relief. Until then, we will remain behind cover and try to hold them off if they get closer." Aasha didn't wait for Rellik to respond, trusting that the Mauler would obey, and began shouting for Dardyl. "Brutyss can't drag Unkyss back on his own, help me get him back to some cover." Both Dardyl and Aasha waited for the next storm of arrows to stop, before sprinting toward the now-porcupine Unkyss.

Dardyl got to Brutyss and Unkyss first, having already begun moving before Aasha had given the order. She helped drag the giant of a Mauler behind a large boulder near the opening of the canyon. "After we get him safe, do we rush them?" she half-teased Brutyss.

Brutyss stared at her with wide eyes, "Are you nuts? You know how much poison is on those arrow tips?"

"Um purfuctly fin," Unkyss managed to slur. "Wek pusson!" Unkyss did his best to shout, but his muscles were not responding properly.

Brutyss helped Dardyl keep Unkyss behind cover as another volley bounced off the stone. "There is enough poison in one arrow to knock out any Mauler, and you were hit with at least—"

"Six," Dardyl hollered, yanking out the last barbed one that had been anchored in Unkyss' left shoulder, above the first one.

"Ima g-ant Mulur," Unkyss tried to reason with the two of them, but by now his lower jaw was hanging semi-limply and he struggled to keep his eyes open.

Brutyss looked over his shoulder to try to pinpoint his sister as he ignored Unkyss' attempts to argue. He saw Aasha poke her head out from behind an outcropping further in the canyon. She quickly moved her ears up and down four times, and shook her head from left to right, the same direction they had come from. Brutyss gave her a quick nod and leaned back behind the boulder with Dardyl and Unkyss. "There are four of them approaching us," he told them. "Aasha had a good view of the clearing and she signaled four were coming this way."

Another shower of arrows hit. "Okay, well, there are two of us so I would think we have... " Dardyl stopped talking as she slumped; it was as though the muscles in her back had turned to slush. As she fell forward into Unkyss' half-functioning embrace, two poisoned-tipped arrows stuck out from her mid-back.

"Okay," Brutyss said, more to himself than anyone else. "That's fine, there's still one of us." He ignored Unkyss' protest that there were still two of them. Mainly because he wasn't sure if the Mauler was actually protesting or just making sounds, but he was probably protesting. Brutyss finally clamped his hand around Unkyss' muzzle. "Please shut up," Brutyss mouthed as quietly as possible. He was straining his ears to catch some sound of the Corvel's approach, which was difficult with Unkyss yammering and the ping of the arrows bouncing off the stone. Brutyss looked back at his sister, their timing was off and she was still in cover. He listened closely, there was a slight crunch as a Corvel hopped near the boulder behind which it had seen three Maulers duck. They had released volley after volley and the Corvel was sure that all three of them were unconscious. Brutyss saw the beak first as the yellow bill led the Corvel's appearance around the corner of the boulder. He reacted with lightning fast speed and grabbed the Corvel by the side of the head. The Corvel was first surprised, then confused, then terrified, and finally its face was plastered on the boulder. Brutyss quickly pivoted around the stone for cover after smashing the creature's brains out over the side. The other three Corvel quickly shot arrows to try to catch the Mauler. Brutyss was back behind the stone before the tips bounced harmlessly to the snow. A stone whistled past his ears and cracked into the throat of one of the Corvel who had tried to retaliate against Brutyss. The enemy fell back, clutching at its collapsed windpipe as it suffocated. The other two Corvel quickly hopped back into the trees. As soon as the two survivors had cleared the area, shower after shower of arrows pinged and clinked off the Maulers' protective rock walls. A few arrows managed to get over the rock, but they only hit Unkyss a couple more times in his paws and legs. The sleeping giant was too spread out to keep him completely covered from the hail of flint and iron. Brutyss did his best to pile up some snow around Unkyss' legs to try to stop any more arrows from piercing his exposed limbs, and when he had another clear shot, he sprinted toward his sister to try and come up with a plan of attack.

There were several whistles as Aasha looked around the rocky outcrop, trying to find another smooth stone to pop into her sling that she kept wrapped around her forearm. She and Brutyss exchanged nervous grins.

"Well, it would seem they are tactical," mused Aasha, as this time the majority of the arrows bounced off the outcrop where both of them had taken cover.

"Is that a good thing?" asked Brutyss as an arrow bounced off the canyon wall above his head. "If they keep this up, they are going to hit both of us unless we pull further back into the canyon."

Aasha shook her head no. "We wait for Rellik to return with reinforcements.

I am not going to lose two Silverbacks to Corvel."

Brutyss took a moment to peer around the stone. "They aren't coming out of the trees again."

"They will run out of arrows eventually," Aasha replied calmly, as Brutyss ducked behind the rock cover again as another peppering of arrows were fired at the two of them. "Did the one you killed have any weapons other than the bow, was it armored?" Aasha asked her brother, trying to get some measure of their opponents.

Brutyss replayed the encounter back in his mind. "They are minimally armored, I am assuming a gambeson if that. I believe I saw a seax on its hip but other than that and the bow, I don't think it had any other weapons. Do you have a plan besides just keeping our heads down?" Brutyss waited for a moment, still there was no immediate response. He peered from behind their cover to see if he could make out any more details on the one he killed. "Are you looking for something specific?" he asked again, turning to face his sister when she still made no response.

"Bear-shit!" Brutyss cursed as he saw the slumped body of his sister leaning against the canyon wall, arrows sticking out of her neck and right bicep. Brutyss quickly balled her up as best he could in the corner and immediately piled snow around her legs, he didn't want there to be any chance that she could get stuck a few more times, as Unkyss had done. "Come on, Rellik, where in the name of the Alpha Father are you?"

***

"Explain to me what a commune is, and why we are stopping at Kyron?" Terrabyss asked as he and Luna leaned against the wall of the canyon, watching some younger pups run past them.

Luna stopped chewing on the bit of jerky they were sharing. "What do you want to know? Remember, I have never been to a commune, thankfully my father managed to keep us out of such places."

It was Terrabyss' turn to think about it for a moment. "Let's start there, why keep your pack from living in such a place?"

"Okay, well that is an easy answer," Luna began. "Communes are small prisons that the Ozars keep the Silverbacks in. There is a garrison that keeps an eye on the prisoners and makes sure they work for the Ozars year-round. Especially in the winter, when the Ozars practice what they call Hibernation, which is basically seclusion from others." Another handful of pups went charging by, a young gray one was giving chase to his darker-furred siblings. The pup running after them had almost orange-colored eyes and, for a moment, Luna saw a little light-furred Terrabyss. "Where are we in the procession?" Luna inquired absent-mindedly as she watched the little Maulers try to tackle and slip away from one another.

Terrabyss looked up, he had his pinky claw in his teeth and was trying to pull a piece of jerky from between his canines. "I think we are near the rear," he said with a muffled voice as he dug a bit deeper with the claw. He stopped when he noticed how Luna was staring at him. "What?" He shrugged and uncorked his drinking skin, taking a long draft of the warm ale. Luna just rolled her eyes and took the opportunity to pick her teeth clean as Terrabyss was looking further down the canyon. "Why don't more Silverbacks follow your pack's lead and choose not to live in such a miserable place?"

Luna was caught slightly off guard by the question, but managed to pull her claw out of her mouth before Terrabyss noticed. "Well, because it is outlawed," she responded bluntly.

"I don't remember any law about having to live as captives to those who conquered you, it just meant you had to move on, if I remember the four laws correctly," Terrabyss responded, watching as Oflyn dragged his travois past.

Luna had to keep herself from laughing, she knew Terrabyss wouldn't find her amusement entertaining. She often forgot how much the Maulers didn't know, how much had changed since they had fled to the grove. "The four laws are a long dead idea," she tried to make sure her tone wasn't condescending. "The Ozars make the laws now, and one of their laws is that if the Silverbacks want to remain a clan, they need to be subject to the laws of their conquerors."

Terrabyss was looking at her now and listening intently to her explanation of the Ozar laws. "I am going to have to remember that mentality when we conquer the Ozars." His tone was serious and there was no boasting in his voice. It was a cold and calculated voice, that lacked emotion and she had no doubt the words were never said in jest. Luna swallowed hard, he scared her a little when he spoke like that, but she managed to shrug a response. Terrabyss was intimidating and in the sunlight, he seemed to appear as though he were made of blood.

"All you need to understand is that the Ozars claim the communes are designed to harness our savage nature. I believe they are designed to enslave us, and break us of our free will," Luna finally managed to respond.

"That does sound like a dismal place," Terrabyss responded, offering Luna his drinking skin.

Luna gave a small laugh. "I told you it was. My father could explain them better, but if I remember his words correctly, they are places of eight, or maybe more, packs" – she paused as she tried to find the words – "who struggle to survive under the constant watch and power of the garrison. Dio always said that 'the Silverbacks are expected to do everything, except defend themselves and their homes. They grow the food and harvest it. They maintain the fields in the winter and prepare them in the spring. They do all the logging, and are in charge of maintaining their enclosures to satisfactory conditions.' It is absolutely infuriating that we need to maintain our own prisons." Luna was growling slightly as she finished informing Terrabyss of the things her father had told her. "They even cook meals for their jailors!" Luna was practically shouting at the last sentence; she took a deep breath and lowered her voice again. "The Silverbacks do all this, and their only compensation is living in rundown shacks and having only enough food to keep them alive and working. Those who live in the commune cannot leave to visit family or friends in another commune without special permission and escort from the garrison. You might guess how often that happens."

"Probably never." Terrabyss still didn't understand rhetorical questions. "This is probably a dumb question, but why not just rebel?" Terrabyss asked, pulling another piece of jerky out from his pack and tearing it in half, offering half to Luna who took it readily. "How many troops do the Ozars have stationed in their garrisons?"

"Depends on the size of the commune," Luna responded before biting into her piece of the meat. "Is this the mammoth?" It tasted more smokey, like it had taken longer to absorb the flavors and it was tougher than the previous piece she had eaten.

Terrabyss nodded. "The last one was caribou, but this is some of the mammoth the young adults took down. I think it is some of the trunk." He shrugged. "I don't honestly remember."

Luna swallowed, realizing that she hadn't actually answered Terrabyss' previous question. "There can be anywhere from ten to twenty-five soldiers, depending on the number of Silverbacks living there and the degree of pacification in the commune. The garrison can easily monitor and control the population of Silverbacks from a central keep." She recognized the confusion on Terrabyss' face. "A keep is something like a stronghold, a tall one. The Ozars clear out a circular area where they decide they will build the communes. In the center of this clearing, using the logs the Silverbacks cut down, the Ozars build a tall, tall lookout."

"All a lookout does is give warning; I feel like it wouldn't provide that much support from a mob of angry Silverbacks that easily outnumbered the garrison," Terrabyss responded with a snort as he heard Luna's explanation of the keep.

Luna gave him a pointed stare, raising her eyebrows. "Do you want to know what I know? Or do you want to make your own assumptions?" she asked in a condescending voice, not bothering to spare her mate's feelings.

Terrabyss' stare in response was equally level, but he couldn't deny how impressed he was that Luna was developing into a true Silverback and a Mauler. "All right, all right. Please continue," Terrabyss finally answered.

"The keep is not some platform stuck up in a tree like the Rodentia lookouts. It is made from redwood logs which are then stacked on top of each other to make a sturdy structure that even the strongest gales cannot move. Since it is made from sequoia, it would take a very concentrated fire to bring it down and it's almost impossible to dismantle. The Ozars are also an extremely martial race, they train day and night in both large and small groups. This makes them very disciplined and, like their keeps, almost impossible to topple. The Eclupse, especially, were not as warlike as the Ozars or you and the other Maulers, we are silent and quick. We are not suited for open battle, so when the Eclupse got hemmed in, they had little choice but to surrender. There were a few Eclupse, like my father, who used their speed to their advantage and escaped being captured, but that wasn't going to last forever." Luna sniffled slightly, forcing the water out of her eyes. "Hence why we are here." She tried to grin, but her lips quivered a bit.

Terrabyss wasn't sure how to comfort her, so he tried to see if she knew anything more that would maybe take her mind off her past. "Do the Ozars have casters in their garrison?" He also figured it wouldn't hurt to do a bit of reconnaissance.

Luna nodded. "Usually a moderately practiced Druid." This time, she reached for the drinking skin, as Terrabyss seemed to stare off behind her back toward where they had entered the canyon. "Is something wrong?"

"I think that is Rellik," Terrabyss responded. He lifted his head and took a couple of deep breaths through his nose. "That is definitely Rellik, and she smells panicked," he announced as he reached for his kanabo, pulling it from the leather covering.

Rellik was moving at full speed through the canyon, her tongue hanging out as she panted heavily, dashing across the canyon floor on all fours. She spotted Luna and Terrabyss, who were still leaning against the wall of the canyon, waiting for any others to pass them. Rellik took a deep breath and lifted her head, letting out an echoing howl to alert the others to her plight.

Luna followed Terrabyss' example when she heard Rellik's howl, and was glad she hadn't hesitated. Making sure her daggers were snuggly fastened to her thighs, she sprinted after Terrabyss, easily passing him as the two ran toward Rellik to see why she was so worked up. Terrabyss let out a howl in response to Rellik's. His was pitched less frantically and told Rellik of his coming support. Luna did her best to mimic his howl, still struggling with some of the nuances of the old Silverback forms of communication.

Rellik easily heard Terrabyss' response and was intelligent enough to discern what Luna's howl truly intended to convey, not what it actually meant. Rellik didn't wait for them to join her and—hoping they were enough reinforcement—turned and sprinted back to where she had left the others. Her hands and paws skidded below her as Rellik dug her claws into the snow and ice to find purchase so she could pivot back around to head back down the canyon. She skidded for a few feet, before managing to anchor her right paw and use it to spin her around.

We are coming! Just hold out a few moments longer, she thought to herself as she could already hear Luna closing the distance between the two of them and Rellik knew that Terrabyss wasn't far behind.

***

"Why is it that the three of you couldn't find cover big enough for your fat haunches?" Brutyss complained for about the fifth time as another hail of arrows came to a ricocheting halt. He quickly yanked an arrow out of his sister's thigh that had found its way through his little snow

333

barrier. Thankfully, the projectiles were being fired from too far away to achieve any significant penetration, but that didn't change how deadly an accumulation of the poison could be on their victims. Brutyss dreaded even thinking about the condition Unkyss and Dardyl were in. He was sure that the large Mauler was at least unconscious by now, because he had stopped trying to swear after the previous volley. Brutyss was starting to get desperate, he didn't know how many more Corvel were out there beside the two that had retreated to the trees. There had to be many more than two, because there were still more than two arrows being loosed at a time. Given the number of arrows that were strewn about, it was hard to get a clear count at how many were being fired per barrage. Brutyss waited for a moment as this time there was no immediate bombardment following the first. *That means one of two things; they are out of arrows or they are sending some archers in to clean up what they think are four unconscious Maulers.* With his back pressed against the stone, Brutyss listened intently to hear if any of the Corvel were approaching. He would pay attention if any moved for Unkyss or Dardyl, but they were further away and right now he wanted to ensure the safety of his sister and himself more than anything. Brutyss picked up his sister's sling and found a smooth stone still clutched in her hand. He had never been good with the sling, but it could be used as a flail if he tied the stone off in the leather thong, which he immediately did. *If you run, who knows what awful fate you leave your sister and allies in. For all you know, they eat their victims.* He had no idea how they worshiped their god, Corvis Minor.

The front Corvel hopped forward, his head swung left and then right as he surveyed the canyon's entrance. "Fly up and see if they are all asleep," the other Corvel archer instructed from behind.

"You go up there and get smacked by a rock like Scree," the first Corvel responded. This Corvel had been one of the two survivors of the first group. There was a clattering sound to their right, all six of the Corvel spun to look where the sound had come from. The leader of the party, who had suggested the first Corvel go up in the air, saw what had made the sound before the others did. Before he could warn them that it was a diversion, Brutyss shot out from behind the outcrop. It was like seeing a shooting star; for a moment it was there and then it was gone.

Brutyss didn't actually vanish, but the Corvel who had refused to fly would never have known the difference. His beak was shattered by the makeshift flail and he was most likely dead when he hit the snow. The leader of the Corvel now managed to squawk his warning.

"It's a diversion!" he shouted.

Brutyss was on top of him, his teeth sunk into the creature's neck and he ripped out its throat with his powerful jaws. The female Corvel immediately behind him let out a loud and foul-smelling fart, shitting itself in fright. The other three were a bit further away and were denied the sight of their leader's gruesome death. Three bowstrings twanged and three arrow shafts flew through the air. Brutyss lunged forward, slamming his hands into the terrified Corvel's fragile frame, crushing its lungs under his weight. Two of the arrows flew right overhead, and the third nicked the top of his head. He wasn't sure if a nick was enough to down him, and he knew he didn't have the luxury of considering the fact. He did a handspring somersault off the crushed frame of the female Corvel, landing on his paws and immediately letting his body tilt forward, planting his hands and sprinting for the remaining three Corvel.

"Holy Corvis!" one shouted.

"Bring him down!" another yelled.

"He is too fast!" the third one interjected as they fumbled with their arrows. Brutyss quickly turned to the right as an arrow thudded into the snow where he had just been. Another finally got his arrow notched and fired, trying to draw Brutyss away, he simply spun back to the left, letting the arrow drive harmlessly into the snow. The Corvel closest to Brutyss threw its bow down and, drawing its long knife from its sheath, tried bravely, but foolishly, to square its shoulders with the charging Mauler. Brutyss instantly pitched his body to the creature's left, bringing himself within one lue of the Corvel. The creature swung the knife-holding limb in front of itself, so it would have an easy stab for Brutyss' neck or flank. But Brutyss' agility was on full display, as even on the snow and icy ground he managed to twist back to the Corvel's right, ramming into the creature with his body and crushing the smaller Taur under his weight as they rolled through the snow. Brutyss' lungs burned as he twisted, coming to his paws. The Corvel had managed to bring the seax back, and its tip had dug into the Mauler's torso directly above his right hip. Fortunately for Brutyss, the Corvel hadn't coated its knife in the same sleeping poison. He could feel his limbs getting sluggish, some of the poison had seeped into his bloodstream from the arrow nick on his head. An arrow came to a quivering halt where Brutyss had reared up from his collision with the now broken and definitely dead Corvel, he had hit it hard enough to cause it to fold in half. The second arrow found its mark as it sunk into his upper thigh. Brutyss' leg gave out almost instantly as he tried to charge forward to the remaining two Corvel.

The Corvel with the broken beak regained consciousness and slowly sat up. Its senses were still obviously dazed because it was pretty sure it could make out another three Maulers rushing toward him. In the lead was the tallest and whitest-furred Mauler he had ever seen. "Ip, Ipper!" it tried to call out to one of the Corvel.

"Ipper got smashed," the elderly female Corvel said as she lowered her bow. "Is there something wrong?" she asked, watching with pride as Brutyss finally went down, collapsing face-first into the snow.

The strange, white-furred Mauler sprinted past, leaving the slightly stupefied Corvel spinning as it tried to keep his eyes on her. The second Mauler was also slightly thinner, but definitely had the black fur of a true Mauler, although she seemed rabid with how much she was foaming at the mouth. Then there was an explosion of pain in his back as the last thing he understood was being unable to support his upper body.

Terrabyss yanked his kanabo out from the now-shattered spine of the Corvel. Rellik, completely exhausted, lunged at the surprised Corvel that was a little way in front of the elder, female Corvel who had begun to approach Brutyss' body. The Corvel reached for its bow, but realizing Rellik was far too close, dropped it and grabbed for the knife. It was dead before it gripped the handle. Rellik slammed down on it, her teeth tearing at its flesh as black feathers scattered about.

The elder Corvel had realized her two allies had fallen victim to the reinforcements and despite her desperate drive for revenge, she tried to flee. She was never going to forgive that shaman for the death of her daughter, and she had made a lot of promises to gain permission to pursue her vendetta. She quickly began hopping, she could sense the thundering charge of Luna as she closed in on the elder Corvel. The Corvel dropped her bow and quiver, undoing her belt to let her seax fall, lightening herself so she could quickly take flight. Luna had become even more skilled with her knives, however. She came to a fluid stop and her left hand reached down to her thigh, easily slipping over the long handle. She exhaled and steadied herself, swinging her arm forward and the knife pitched tip over pommel, driving point-first right between the older Corvel's shoulders. The elderly opponent fell face-first, much like Brutyss, but she had one last trick. She whistled with her dying breath which was all the warning Luna had. It wasn't enough and she knew it, four arrows flew from tree branches. Luna's eyes closed as she tensed, knowing she couldn't avoid being struck. When she opened her eyes, she was still conscious, and there wasn't an arrow in her. Terrabyss stood before her, his left hand holding an arrow just inches away from her face, another arrow he caught in his jaws and the other two were embedded in his kanabo.

There were two loud snaps as the arrows in Terrabyss' teeth and fist broke. "You better run, or nock faster," Terrabyss called out with a savage growl, as he stepped toward the trees where the arrows had come from. The trees were fewer than four lue away; even on two legs the three Maulers would close that distance before the Corvel could get another clean shot. Those that survived had watched the one who had mustered them get killed, and were now dealing with three unscathed and very angry Maulers. There was a flutter as some black feathers fell from the branches, and the surviving Corvel thought better of their chances. They decided to return to their homes in the grove, safely away from the Maulers. Terrabyss scooped up the seax and tried to mimic Luna's skill with the weapon, hurling it at the only Corvel he could make out between the trees. "You're not getting away," he growled as the blade flipped much like Luna's had, toward the nearest fleeing Corvel.

Luna could appreciate the power behind the throw, the form was not bad either, but it lacked finesse and had zero accuracy. "That is a long throw, but you have terrible aim." The pommel of the weapon struck the Corvel's leg, probably leaving a good bruise and knocking it slightly off course, but not felling it.

Terrabyss smiled as the Corvel cried out. "You don't know anything about my skill. I hit him, didn't I?" Luna yelled over to Rellik to toss her one of the dead Corvel's seax. She caught the weapon, and Rellik and Terrabyss gave her questioning looks. "There is no way," Terrabyss stated.

Luna flipped the knife in the air once to get a quick feel, the Corvel was barely within sight, and she was using her hearing and smell to make sure she was actually seeing him and not just a random shadow in the trees. Her left arm swung back again as she took one, two, three steps forward, releasing the weapon on the third step. There was a mournful cry as something thudded into the forest floor.

"Close your mouth before a bee stings your tongue," Luna said smugly, turning back to the unconscious Brutyss. "We are going to need help getting these four back to the procession."

Rellik and Terrabyss were still staring off into the forest, neither of them had moved to confirm the kill. Luna knew she hit her target, and they knew it too, but at least without tangible proof they could convince themselves she had got lucky.

"She didn't even use her dagger," Rellik whispered in amazement to Terrabyss.

The male snorted. "Help us get the rest of your comrades back to the group." He wasn't going to admit how impressive the throw was, not to Rellik. He would compliment Luna in private later.

Rellik snickered as though she read his mind, but she left it at that and began to help getting Brutyss, Unkyss, Dardyl, and Aasha back to the rest of the tribe.

Monsters

Forver slowly picked his way down the ladder from the second story of the keep. He was bundled in a warm, wolf fur blanket to keep the cold out, and every breath of steam was a literal, chilling reminder of how cold the past couple of days had been. Tonight had to be the worst; somehow, the nipping wind was finding its way into the keep and freezing the occupants. There were too many pieces to these permanent structures, there was always a spot that wasn't chinked well or a gap at some opening. Forver hated the wind, be it cold or warm. The wind was always a fickle thing. The wind didn't care for your words, often carrying them away from the intended listener. The wind was the cause of the rain, hail, and snow blinding you in a storm. Worst of all, the wind couldn't be trusted, it could make you hear things that weren't there and wake you up from a perfectly good sleep.

The keep was three stories tall, with no inner walls, so each floor contained only one room. The kitchen, entry, and larder were all on the ground level. There were large stone pits in both the right and left back corners that were typically used for cooking, although Forver had a mind to use them for heating. Crates of provisions lined the walls: meats, roots, vegetables, fungi, and honeycombs. Hanging from the ceiling were a multitude of herbs, some drying, others ready for use, from nettles to flowers and everything in between. The floor was simply dirt, well-worn and packed down by the constant paw traffic, and assembled in a loose array at the center were several round tables intended for the garrison to sit to eat breakfast and supper.

The two floors above became narrower as the tower rose upward, the walls slightly leaning inwards. The second floor was the council floor, it held Dhon's moderately comfortable armchair. The chair was made of smoothed elm and had numerous large fish carved into the head post, with waterfalls cascading down the arms. Positioned directly in front of the chair were two large, rectangular tables with various maps, tableted notes, and a few extremely expensive bound books filled with the daily reports.

The walls on this floor were decorated with antler racks and tapestries with swirling patterns of vibrant blues, greens, and even yellows in some. The antlers were to impress, and the tapestries were to keep the chamber warm, which was pure wolf-shit according to Forver. This was the floor that he and his commanders were living on; the first night they stayed here, this had included their honor guards. Forver had since tried to pack more bodies into the second floor, in hopes that they would keep him warm from the wind. Although, when he had been rudely awakened by the groaning breeze, he realized that few of the many bodies he had packed in had remained, clearly uncomfortable with what had been to some the overwhelming heat. *Obviously, the keep was not built for comfort,* he told himself. After tonight, he would go back to his travel yurt, it was more easily warmed and could keep out a breeze more efficiently than this keep.

The third and final floor had twelve simple, fur, sleeping mats strewn about the room in no particular order. There were a dozen large rectangular chests for the soldiers to share and to store any belongings; personal belongings were a rare commodity in the garrison, usually reserved for the druid and colonel. Forver didn't understand how they stayed warm up there, there were fewer tapestries layering the walls and the bodies weren't packed together for heat. He didn't believe for one second that the bottom floor fires kept the top floor warm, not with this wind.

The very top of the keep was for the unfortunate soul who had to maintain a vigil. It did have a large iron brazier to help keep the sentry warm but other than that and the wood-shingled roof, the watch had no protection from the bitter cold. They could see the whole commune and beyond, losing the view just beyond the edge of the clearing. They could also survey the lumber site, about an hour or so walk away, depending on the trail conditions and the motivation of the traveler. Attached to the keep were two square buildings, one on the right side and the other on the rear. These two small buildings combined were the size of Forver's yurt back in Ursyss and it was beyond him why Dhon gave Carloe, the garrison druid, the larger of the two buildings at the rear. Forver hadn't yet seen inside either chamber, but he assumed it consisted of a bed mat, probably a horrid assortment of plants and ingredients in the druid's chambers, and maps, ledgers, perhaps a private keg in Dhon's quarters.

Forver wasn't very satisfied with Dhon's reception of him and his troops. First, she had complained that she had no order from the Honcho, any Honcho, especially Bardell, to expect Forver's arrival. After some convincing, Forver had managed to get her to stop quoting rules and protocol and had informed her and anyone else who would listen about the Maulers, who were probably on the march as they spoke. Dhon's second complaint was that Forver was now spreading panic among her troops. In his opinion, they needed to be panicked. The garrison should have doubled its patrols and extended the surveillance perimeter. Following this poor response, she then presumed to assume command over him, Forver, the Yukon who was solely responsible for her position today.

Once I am a hero for bringing the last independent Silverback tribe to heel, Dhon will feel so foolish for not giving me her quarters or presuming to put my troops on rations. I will make sure she feels foolish for her arrogant attitude, Forver thought to himself as he looked around at the numerous containers and all the stored food. Something in the shadows near one of the tables caught his eye. His paw missed the last rung of the ladder and he fell back, quickly rolling to a defensible position and leaving the warm blankets he had been bundled in on the floor. *Why, in Mother Bear's name, did I not bring Ol'Grim with me?* All Forver had been planning on doing was adding logs to the fires. *I have learned my lesson, he told himself.*

Zolk looked up, startled, from his seat at one of the tables as Forver tumbled backward into the room. He was a bit impressed with how well Forver recovered, squaring up as though he was getting ready to box.

"You okay, Mahzar?" Zolk asked as Forver got his paws under him. "That looked like it was a pretty rough fall."

It took Forver a second to register who was talking to him, even with the honorific that only Zolk used. The blood was pumping in his head as Forver tried to calm his heart rate by taking deep breaths. He was pretty sure he had pulled a muscle in his right thigh from his stunt, but he wasn't sure if he wanted to call attention to the fact by berating Zolk or keep the illusion of his performance. "Stars, Zolk, I could have killed you," he lied, trying to hide his limp as he moved to the wood pile between the two large fire pits.

"Of course," Zolk nodded respectfully. "Even if my girl was starving, I doubt she could match your sheer skill." Zolk hadn't meant for that last sentence to have such a sarcastic tone, he had honestly meant to compliment his Mahzar.

Forver paused for a moment when he heard Zolk's voice, he wasn't sure if the wind had just played another trick on him. Zolk was still riding a high from earlier and Forver could see the distracted look in his commander's eyes.

"Why." Forver cleared his throat. "Why didn't you add wood to the fires if you were down here? It is freezing up there," Forver scolded, but moved for the log pile and tossed a piece from the stack into the pit at his right. When he didn't hear Zolk respond, he pitched another log into the opposite pit and turned to see what was so distracting that his most loyal commander hadn't bothered responding. Forver wrinkled up his nose, finding himself actually repulsed by what he saw. Zolk was cooing softly to his weapon and lightly scratching the axe head under the beard with his index claw. Forver knew Zolk was a bit touched, but the extent had either never sunk in, or perhaps Zolk was getting worse. Forver clenched his fists, he could feel the anger welling up inside him from being ignored. Forver tried to keep his composure, he didn't have Ol'Grim and he wasn't sure how uncontrollable Zolk could get, especially coming down from a 'Kill Thrill' as he called them. Forver never thought he would be nervous around Zolk but he was, something about his commander and how he treated Forver had changed over the past few weeks. Zolk now stood menacingly between him and the ladder, and Ol'Grim was up above. Forever wondered why no one above them seemed to respond to the sound of him falling earlier. *Someone should have woken up by now.* Besides, it wasn't like he and Zolk were whispering. Urrah had been sent out to find Ferda and by the looks of it hadn't returned, so he wasn't going to get any support from her. For the first time in his life, Forver wished he had Urrah's talent to de-escalate a situation.

"I wasn't cold," Zolk finally responded nonchalantly, still standing between Forver and the ladder. He had a glazed look in his eyes and a manic grin on his face as he replied, making Forver more nervous. "Were we being too loud for you?" Zolk dangerously nuzzled the bit of Headhunter.

Mother Bear, Forver cursed to himself. Forver pulled his lips back, showing his teeth in a savage grimace. "No, I was cold. I wanted more wood on the fire!" Forver shouted at Zolk, not giving a damn if he woke the whole tower, or perhaps it was his intention. Above them some sounds could be heard as the yelling had finally woken some of the troops.

One of the rookies who had been near the ladder poked his head down.

"Is everything all right down there?" he asked, chopping his lips a bit as he was clearly still groggy.

To Forver's relief, it seemed to be enough commotion to snap Zolk back to the right state of mind as he slipped Headhunter, still uncovered, into the leather axe loop at his side.

"We are fine," Forver responded to the other soldier as he pushed past Zolk and started going up the ladder. "Are you coming to bed?" Forver asked Zolk, more out of habit then any actual concern as he got to the top of the ladder.

Zolk shrugged. "I could just stay down here and make sure that the fire doesn't burn down again."

Forver knew Zolk was joking, but he was still upset that he had felt nervous around Zolk. Zolk was his goon and he did what Forver said, Forver needed to remind him of that. Before Zolk had made it to the base of the ladder, Forver shut the hatch that provided access to the upper floors. "That is a good idea, you stay down there and make sure I don't get cold." Forver thought about following his words up with a threat, but something warned him to hold his tongue and for once he showed some wisdom and remained silent.

Zolk's brow furrowed as his eyes narrowed and his nose wrinkled up. Zolk heard the latch slide shut and knew Forver had not been teasing.

He has lost all respect for you, he has lost his balls and grown a nice bosom in their stead. Zolk slowly nodded as Headhunter spoke to him. She was right; Forver had changed, either by some foul magic or by some growth of conscience. Either way, Zolk didn't like this new Forver and he meant to find his old Mahzar. The fact that Forver had sent Urrah to retrieve Ferda and not sent him and a group of warriors to apprehend her and drag her back for her insubordination was proof of this. Eclupse died every day, why did she care if it was by Headhunter's doing or by something else? Sure, the target had been a bit younger, but surprisingly Headhunter hadn't complained about it, she only seemed to have an aversion to killing Ozar cubs.

"You are such a fickle mistress," Zolk teased her as he found his way back to the table he had been sitting at previously. He didn't make the rules, he just followed them as she ordered. He rested Headhunter—who was *already asleep—on the table and leaned back in the chair to get some rest.*

Chairs and cushions, Zolk thought, that's how I want to be rewarded

343

for this campaign.

***

Ferda finished patting the dirt over the third grave she had dug since they had arrived in Kyron. One for each day they had been there, and each had been one of Zolk's victims. It was late at night and particularly cold, but the work of digging and filling the grave had kept her warm. The activity along with her anger had kept the nipping cold at bay. She hadn't been able to stop Zolk from killing, not the first time, the second, and now the third time. A one-on-one fight with Zolk was suicide, and she hated having to admit that to herself.

Despite his age and my youth, peace has either dulled my memory of how talented he is with an axe or it has dulled my skills with one. "Perhaps it's a bit of both." She chuckled to herself. The laughter was empty; there was no mirth, only rage.

A familiar memory surfaced as Ferda stared off at the plume of gray and black smoke that began to funnel out the small smoke chutes on the first floor of the keep. In her mind, she relived the sound of the creature's raspy screams as she popped off leg after leg, it had hurt the Evem even though the creature could survive the injury. She could see the smile on her face as the Evem writhed back and forth, or tried to crawl its body and fat abdomen away from her with its hands, pulling up clumps of mud as it desperately tried to escape its captors. Ferda shook her head violently, trying to make the memories fall away or be shut out completely, although she knew she wouldn't be so lucky. As she tried to fling the memories from her mind, she heard the creature's whimpers as she had begun to work on the arms, 'those don't work.' He had cried over and over; she knew they functioned so she hadn't understood what he meant.

"Those don't work," she repeated, remembering how the Evem had bled out when she took off his hands, and how disappointed she had been.

"What doesn't work?" Ferda jumped to her paws, spinning around as she heard Urrah's voice. She hadn't even heard the elder female sneak up on her during her quiet reflection.

"N-Nothing," Ferda stammered, gathering her composure. "Why? How did you find me?" Ferda finally managed to ask.

"You know exactly why I found you," Urrah responded to the first

344

question, "the how is definitely more complicated. Forver was, and still is, pretty upset that you just marched out of Kyron, you must have heard him shouting for you to stop." Ferda leveled a stare at Urrah that told the older Ozar she had. "Well, with that in mind, you are lucky that he sent me and not Zolk," Urrah concluded sincerely, she had obviously seen the tension between them growing.

"I would welcome it," Ferda shot back, a bit more aggressively than she had originally intended.

"He will kill you," Urrah said flatly. "I hate to compliment him, and I find him to be an absolute ignoramus, but I cannot deny how well he wields that weapon."

"Maybe if someone had supported me, Zolk could have been stopped or at least challenged," Ferda responded, this time not bothering to soften her tone. "Maybe if I wasn't standing up to him alone, things would be different."

Urrah knew what Ferda was insinuating, and she couldn't deny that Ferda could be right. "Ozars, especially the youth and those who never matured beyond young adulthood, admire Zolk's brutality. They see his stars-may-care attitude as something to aspire toward and so Ozars like him will always have supporters. As long as his violence is aimed at those that have no connection to us, no one will care who he hurts, and many will praise him for it."

"So as long as he kills Eclupse or other Silverbacks, then he isn't bad?" Ferda was shocked at what Urrah was implying. "Those Eclupse weren't warriors, for stars' sake, Urrah, the last one was practically a cub!" Ferda felt the rage swelling inside her as she continued to speak. "No one did anything more than shrug when he killed any of his victims. We watched passively as he violated the dead, frolicking in their gore and parading their corpses around as though they were trophies."

"They were Eclupse, Ferda." It was Urrah's turn to raise her voice, which was very rare. "Even the Eclupse didn't care, how many of them tried to free their friends and families from his grip? None!" Urrah answered when Ferda gave no immediate response.

Ferda's shoulders rose and fell in heavy breaths as she clenched and opened her fists. She stared out at Kyron, the imposing and sturdy keep contrasted strikingly with the shacks that were the homes of the Eclupse. The Eclupse were kept in pens that were taller than even a Harris could jump, and the walls were covered in sharp thorns that could pierce the toughest of hides. Earthen walls surrounded the commune that stood about eight feet tall, and these earthworks were surrounded by a shallow moat which was filled by sharp wooden spikes whose tips had been heat treated. It was a strong design, and few armies would be able to assault Kyron with a force of any size because of the earthen walls and dangerous moat. An attack group would have to funnel their troops through one of the two openings, where there were gaps in the wall and moat on the east and west sides of Kyron. The enclosures around the shacks were positioned between the keep and the earth walls, with the four crop fields outside of the defenses surrounded by their own tall and thorny fences, which mirrored the ones inside Kyron. These fences were made of twelve-foot-tall poles between which the thorny vines had been laced, and the only clear patch was a small, four-foot high and wide door that the Eclupse had to crawl through to enter or exit the enclosed fields. The small door could be barred by a heavy wooden beam from the outside, and remained securely closed unless a garrison soldier was given specific orders to open the pen. The Eclupse were not even allowed to leave the pens to perform their bodily functions, forced to let it accumulate in distant corners of their cages. Those Eclupse who resisted, tried to rebel, disobeyed, or tried to escape were killed and skinned, their carcasses put out in the fields like scarecrows and their hides mounted on the outside of the keep. This constant reminder of the punishment for insubordination was an aid in keeping the commune in order.

Ferda heard the Evem's cries for mercy in her memory as she gazed at the horrible scene. "This, this is what we fight to maintain." She pointed to Kyron as it stretched out in front of them.

"It isn't perfect, but it is better than allowing them to run free and terrorize themselves and others. The Honchos have taken steps to improve their conditions as well, a great example is the Herders," Urrah tried to argue, perhaps she was also trying to reassure herself that it wasn't as bad as Ferda perceived. "The riots and bloody conflicts that were the defining factor of the frontier have been reduced to a distant memory because of these communes. Besides, think how much Erbun and others have suffered and bled to bring this much stability to the Green Wall."

Ferda nodded; her mate had been badly maimed in a rebellion, and it had been a Silverback, a Vargg, that injured him. Erbun had always

346

said, "Silverbacks needed a strong hand and an even stronger will to be dominated, and weak measures are never going to achieve peace." *Was this too strong a measure, have we taken it too far?* Slowly, the anger dissipated, it seemed with each fist Ferda made, less anger remained.

"How did you find me? I made sure to mask my scent, I even aggravated a skunk to spray me yesterday so that no one would be able to sniff me out. I used the snow to wash out my smell the first day, and I thought today the skunk's stench would keep me isolated for at least another day," Ferda asked Urrah, puzzled at what trick the wise female had used.

"Yes, the skunk's aroma is still potent, hence I am sitting over here and not downwind of you." She gave Ferda a smile. "You weren't hard to find, I simply found these graves yesterday and waited for Zolk to complain that he couldn't find where he had tossed his most recent trophy. After that, I made my way back here, almost positive you would do the work at night when there are no patrols." Ferda couldn't help but let out a slight chuckle, she hadn't even thought about burying the bodies in different locations. "Don't worry, Zolk and Forver aren't smart enough to figure out where you have gone," Urrah said, having interpreted the sound as a nervous one.

"You know you are practically soundless without that gut; I didn't even hear you creep up on me. I was lost in thought." Ferda felt like she should have some excuse for how oblivious she had been.

It was Urrah's turn to chuckle. "I am sure that the thought was particularly captivating. No one could sneak up on Ferda the Observant." Urrah paused for a moment. "That doesn't sound right," she teased as Ferda turned back toward her, a slight smile on her face and much calmer than she had been moments ago.

"Thank you for looking for me, it is nice to have someone to talk to who isn't insane or self-consumed." She motioned to the drinking skin on Urrah's hip. "Is that what I think it is?" Ferda inquired, licking her lips slightly.

Urrah gave a grin. "It sure is, the second most important thing any self-respecting Ozar carries is mead."

"The first is an axe," the two finished the Yukon motto in unison as Urrah tossed Ferda the skin.

"Are you going to tell him where I am, now that you found me?" Ferda asked as she caught the skin and popped out the cork, taking a long swig.

"I may have found you, but I have no idea where you are," Urrah answered with a wink, catching the skin as Ferda tossed it back. "I will go back to Kyron in the morning and tell him that you lost me on some switchbacks if you don't want to come back tonight. Although with how sulky Forver's been, I wouldn't keep testing his patience, he may send Zolk if he gets too upset."

Ferda nodded, understanding the risk she was taking by deserting Forver and the campaign. "Everything is so foreign to me and then with Zolk's attitude, I just needed some space," Ferda explained, slipping her ring mail shirt back over her shoulders and picking up Havil. "I think you are right; I should head back before Forver loses his mind." Ferda gave one last look at the newest grave that had been added.

Urrah respectfully waited a few moments before speaking. "Do you have any idea who it was? Did you actually see Zolk kill them?"

Ferda shook her head no, she didn't have the answer to the first question, and she hadn't witnessed this one's murder. "A pup," was the only verbal answer she could give, unconsciously she was removing the sheath from Havil's blade.

"*Woah, woah,* let's not get him out," Urrah said quickly, noticing the exposed metal of Havil's blade.

Ferda gave Urrah a puzzled look, not having realized what she was doing until Urrah motioned to her hip. "Oh, sorry," Ferda responded when she saw the gleam of Havil's edge, quickly covering it back up.

"The truth is that we all do things that we are ashamed of or at least should be ashamed of, but sometimes those things are necessary. Being a villain, a monster, is not a title that one usually chooses for themselves. There are exceptions, but those exceptions are true monsters, true villains. The Green Wall, before the order that we and the Daunkirks introduced, was sheer pandemonium and at the head of that chaos were the Silverbacks. Perhaps the communes were not the right response, but the fact is we cannot change that response, at least not without influence. Perhaps this victory here will be your opportunity to gain such authority and you can change Kyron and the other communes for the better. Either way, you can't achieve anything by staying out here, at least fight alongside me. After we have the fame and the prestige of this victory, we can find a way to improve these places." Urrah motioned out, back to Kyron, as she spoke.

"I know," responded Ferda, a bit more callously than she had hoped. Urrah was making good points and it had been Urrah who had fought to make a place for the female warrior class. She had done this by earning a name for herself, and had become so well-respected that she had almost single-handedly brought females into the military. Granted, there were still very few of them, the patriarchy was still deeply rooted and it had little space for new branches. It had been Urrah who had cleared that space. Ferda felt if there was anyone she should trust on this, it was Urrah; what did Ferda know about politics and what it took to bring change?

"If we are victorious, would you lend me your support if I were to speak up against the communes to the Honchos?"

Urrah had begun to walk back toward the commune, having thought the conversation was over. She turned back to face Ferda. "Of course!" she said sincerely. "I admire you, Ferda, and I support those I admire. A word of caution: be aware of who you defend. Those Eclupse would not hesitate to kill you, there are monsters everywhere and they come in all different shapes and sizes. We are much better off without the violent raids and cub sacrifices," Urrah concluded as Ferda joined her. The two Ozars meandered back through the trees toward the edge of the clearing that made up the borders of Kyron.

"You don't really believe that story about Ullym's cub, do you? The one about the Cana bringing forth a wolf the size of Middle Market, which snuck into his yurt and snatched up Kelv before vanishing into the trees." Ferda stopped trying to mimic Ullym's voice and became serious. "That Ozar is drunk all the time, and if he isn't spouting that story in the Tavern or at the corner of Middle Market, he is shouting about it from inside his yurt. It is a wonder Nill stays with him."

Urrah laughed. "No, I don't believe him. I knew him and Nill when they were young, old age and too much mead has made him spout nonsense. Nill is practically deaf as it is, so she probably just ignores his ramblings. You do know that Groll is their cub, the one they had after the supposed misfortune of Kelv?"

Ferda looked in shock at Urrah. "Are you serious? How come no one knows that or talks about it?"

Urrah smacked Ferda on the back with a powerful but friendly slap. "Druids are powerful; if Groll doesn't talk about it, then no one does. Besides, would you want to admit that you were related to Mister Comparison?"

Ferda was now laughing loudly, she had forgotten about the nickname that the whole of Ursyss had given to Ullym. Ullym had a nasty habit of wanting to compare his penis size with other males when he became extremely intoxicated. He had tried to get Erbun to compare lengths to see who was larger, a Norrus or a Mahuer. The look on her mate's face had been priceless, and she wished she had a talent for art so she could have a portrait of that single moment.

"I suppose not," was all the response Ferda could give as both of them started laughing again. Urrah had heard the story many times, few Ozars in Ursyss hadn't heard some version of it.

There was a long moment of silence as both recalled the other theory. Rumor had it that Ullym had sold his cub to the Gorgels or Corvel, since both would pay large sums of silver or amber for young flesh. Both had their doubts, but still the idea did plague Ferda's thoughts, it was as Urrah said. 'There are monsters everywhere.' The two of them broke the trees and stepped out into the open, the sentry rushed over to the northwestern half of the commune where the two figures were making their way to the western entrance. Urrah lifted a small whistle to her lips and blew a high-pitched, resounding note. The sentry's pace slowed as he heard the note, and he moved away from the large horn mounted on the top of the keep.

"Do you think that the Maulers have made it back into the Green Wall?" Ferda asked as Urrah lowered the small instrument from her lips.

"I don't know. Kyron's patrols haven't spotted anything. Forver has been adamant that the patrols need to extend their search area. He meets with Dhon every day and is often up before her and follows her around like some pet, constantly baying and barking." Urrah shrugged as they passed through the narrow west opening. The two of them could walk through adjacent to one another, although it was a bit tight.

On either side of them, the posted guards were gathered around a hide mat that served as the game board for the Ozar game known as Hoarding. The players each started with five polished stones, each about an inch in diameter. The players took turns stacking the stones on top of one another and when the tower fell, the player who had just placed the last stone was out. Then the remaining players would rebuild the tower until there was only one victor. There were often bets on who would be the winner, or the first one out, there were even bets for how many stones could be stacked before the tower toppled. Ferda and Urrah ignored the quick glances from the more inexperienced guards, whose turns were skipped for not paying attention. The two made their way to the keep entrance as they heard the rookie soldiers arguing with the veterans about the fairness of said rule.

The sun was beginning to rise over the Division Mountains to the east and started its daily conflict with the ever-dense canopy of the Green Wall. A few clouds aided the forest in the eternal battle, helping the trees cling to the cold and shadows. As Ferda and Urrah reached for the keep door, it swung open and Forver almost barreled over the two commanders in his haste to get to Dhon's room before she stepped out. There was a moment of hesitation as he saw Ferda, but his urgent need to find the Maulers was greater and he continued to Dhon's quarters without so much as a growl. Behind him, Zolk stared at the two of them, looking as though he hadn't slept all night. Ferda gave him one look and spun on her heels.

"I am going to check on my troops," she said flatly, and before Urrah or Zolk could comment, she hustled off to the small camp on the opposite side of the keep that housed the rest of the warriors that they had brought with them.

"What is her problem?" Zolk said with a snicker, moving for the ladder. As much as he wanted to antagonize Ferda, he was exhausted. He hadn't slept well with the smoke that had built up on the bottom floor. Even though there were smoke shafts for it to escape by, they were small and the smoke wasn't funneled out quickly enough. It gave the meat a wonderful taste but absolutely destroyed all the other rations, making everything taste like burning pine. Zolk's eyes were red, and he had a slight cough as he made his way up the ladder, not waiting for Urrah to give him an answer. Urrah just sighed and followed him, she was also tired and just wanted to get some sleep before the breakfast cacophony began.

Forver had wanted to stop when he saw Ferda, so many things went through his mind at the sight of her. He thought about yelling at Zolk to flog her, or to hold her down while he cut her with Havil, then strap it to her arm and let the axe feast. He even debated giving the axe to Yoll afterward and never telling the cub that the weapon had tasted his mother's blood and would soon desire the cub's. Forver had considered some less-extreme punishments after he had calmed down the evening before. He had thought that he would have her stomach shaved, or maybe drench her in honey, but that morning he had little time to enact any of these disciplines. Forver was wearing down Dhon and he knew it. He was already mad enough that the money he had added to the garrison's coffers hadn't earned him a bit more respect or authority. Forver couldn't believe how loyal the troops were to Dhon; she was a female and was young in comparison to many of the soldiers. In his opinion, if it wasn't for the fact that she was attached to the Yukon name, these troops probably would have sent her home crying, or worse. *She is an ungrateful little badger, and her attitude and treatment of me shows how ungrateful she is for all I have done for her.*

It wouldn't look good, however, if he used his troops to overthrow the colonel, and even if he did conquer the Maulers, the Honcho wouldn't be too happy about him seizing control of Kyron. *Keep your patience, patience will give you your reward,* he tried to remind himself as he made it to Dhon's building before she had left for the morning. Forver quickly pounded on the door, fearing that Dhon may have already slipped out.

Dhon lay in her bed, she hadn't bothered to get up when the sun started to rise. She knew that Forver would be a much more efficient alarm. She debated, once again, sending a messenger to Ursyss and informing Bardell of what was happening, but if Forver was right about the danger, she would need all the troops here. She had been relieved when she saw that Forver had been at the head of the army that had appeared two, three, now four days earlier. She had respect for the Yukon and appreciated the words of praise that Forver had used to recommend her. She honestly sympathized with the plight of the Yukon family, and the slight shame they had endured when Kodah had failed to capture the Maulers. Dhon had been excited to help Forver regain his honor, at first. But Forver's constant desire to control the situation and his sense of entitlement were becoming taxing, and Dhon was feeling less and less inclined to help him. She debated just giving in and doubling the patrols, but Forver didn't seem to understand that adding more troops to the patrol only made them more noticeable, and in a skirmish the tight conditions of the Green Wall would not be advantageous to the discipline and formations of the garrison. If she extended their search area and the Maulers managed to slip past the patrols, they would have no way of getting back to Kyron in time and the commune would have no forewarning besides the sentry at the top of the keep. The Maulers could descend on Kyron with no warning if she spread her resources too thin. Dhon appreciated the increase in troops and the extra money added to each of the garrison troops' pockets, but she wouldn't risk the whole commune on a poorly executed plan. Again, the thud, thud, thud of Forver's fist pounding on her door echoed through her room.

"For Mother Bear's sake, go away," she whispered to herself, but slowly stood from her mat and pulled Carver, her axe, off the wall. She wasn't going to take a chance with Forver's temper. "If you want more scouts, use your own troops!" Dhon shouted as she opened the door, glaring at the short Norrus as he huffed angrily.

"I have a new and better idea," Forver said with a gruff voice as he pushed into Dhon's chambers.

"Excuse me!" Dhon shouted angrily as Forver shoved his way past her and into the cramped room.

"You are excused!" Forver responded snidely as he kicked the door behind him closed. "Just let me speak in private with you and then I will leave."

Dhon thought about burying her axe in his skull, but she thought better of it when she remembered the army Forver brought and the lackeys he had with him. "Fine, say your piece and then leave. I don't want to miss breakfast because you have me held hostage."

"I would think you would show me a bit more gratitude, given the fact that you are the first ever female colonel." Forver was always quick to remind others of what his family had done for them. When Dhon just stared incredulously at him, Forver growled but decided to keep talking. "We are sitting on a perfect resource that can quickly find the Maulers, and will be accepted into their ranks without having to worry about being killed."

Dhon had already begun to shake her head. "If you are suggesting what I think you are, you can forget it."

Forver slammed his fist onto the small table in her quarters, he didn't know if he was more upset at the fact that Dhon hadn't even flinched or that he hadn't managed to break the table. *What in Mother Bear's name is that table made of?* he thought to himself. He was apparently angrier about not breaking the table. He channeled that rage into his next verbal tantrum.

"Don't, don't you tell me no! You don't even know what I am proposing, and what I am thinking. My plan will keep you and my troops here in Kyron to defend it from the Maulers attack! All of them! For star's sake, with my idea, you could keep all your patrols here!" Forver shouted, flexing his muscles and trying to stand straighter than was possible. It obviously bothered him that Dhon was taller.

Dhon wasn't impressed and she was positive she knew what he was about to suggest, but her curiosity was piqued when he mentioned being able to keep all her troops here. "Fine, you have until the breakfast call."

She gestured to the small table that Forver had been attempting to smash, offering him the chair. Forver wasn't sure how much he liked this private furniture, he understood the need for the chairs and tables in the Tavern, but to have that offered to your guests was almost insulting. Dhon didn't care if he sat or not and she leaned against the door, keeping a hold of her axe.

Forver eventually sat and out of sheer arrogance slammed Ol'Grim down on the table, making sure he didn't break the table with the weapon. If anything was going to break her invincible table, it was going to be him and him alone. He also wanted her to see that he was armed as well; he didn't care that she was half his age and all her limbs worked fluidly. He would tan her dark brown haunches from here to Ursyss with his experience in combat. He matched the glare from her light brown eyes with his intense dark stare, he did think she was larger than he remembered. Not that she had grown up, but out, and not that she got fat, but stalwart. She kept her arm and leg fur very trim, reminding him of Inlan's fashion.

I hope my boy is imitating a new soldier's trend rather than a female's vogue, he thought to himself. Forever pushed the thought from his mind, focusing back on the business at hand.

"I think we should set a group of Eclupse free toward the northern part of Kyron and have them sniff out the Maulers." Dhon didn't even feel the need to respond. She turned for the door and opened it, preparing to leave. She didn't have anything personal in her quarters and she didn't care if he wrecked the whole building. Carloe had enough druidic skills that he could just rebuild everything, since it was all made of wood. "Shut the door!" Forver roared, "I am not done! Let me finish! You said I had till the breakfast call, and it hasn't been called so… " Dhon could tell how much he was struggling with the next word. "Please allow me to finish."

The colonel smiled grimly. "Fine," Dhon responded, "but only because you seem to be learning manners in my presence and because I expect a damn good explanation of how we are going to ensure that the Eclupse go north" – she held a finger up – "go looking for the Maulers" – a second finger followed the first – "and will return to tell us their location." A third digit followed the trend.

"That part is simple, we will keep their families as leverage. If they don't come back with information, let's say… " – Forever looked at the colonel's gesture – "in three days' time, we will skin their loved ones. One each day that they are late. Simple," Forver said, wiping his hands together as though to clean them. "If they want their families to survive, they will do as they are told. Besides, we won't tell them anything important about us. The Maulers will be too stupid to see through the ruse."

Dhon had heard that before, she knew Kodah's story well, her father having served with him. A fact that Forver either didn't know or didn't ever care to mention, in her father's words Kodah had said "the Maulers are too savage to run." *Although if this worked, if the Maulers didn't somehow learn the truth and these Eclupse could convince them that they were allies.* The information was almost worth the risk; if she had actual logistics of what was coming, she could be well prepared. With that kind of information, even without Forver's troops, the garrison could hold out until reinforcements had been sent. Blind though, blind was no way to fight.

"All right. Speak to Travic, our Herder. He will know which families we have the most leverage with. I will instruct him to give you three Eclupse. I am not going to just throw a bunch of Eclupse away." Forver sat there silently. "I need to hear you say you will agree to these terms," Dhon said sternly.

"I would need five, at least," Forver responded, stubbornly glaring up at Dhon.

"And I said you would get three, I will not give you more. Now take it or leave it. I can smell that our Eclupse cooks are almost done with breakfast." Dhon moved her hand for the door handle to help add urgency to her point.

There was a long moment of silence, neither one of them moved. Forver could smell the food already as well, it smelt like roasted pine nuts with honey and what he thought was the smell of eggs. "Do you have eggs?" He almost forgot for a moment the whole purpose of why he was here.

Dhon wrinkled up her nose, confused. "Sometimes, the loggers find some up in the trees before they cut them down. Forver, I still need your answer."

"Yes, yes, I agree," Forver responded, somewhat distracted. "I assume you will send Travic my way."

Dhon nodded, opening the door. "I will speak to him over breakfast. The rule on the eggs is first come, first served, so you best hurry." With that, she marched off to the keep entrance, her stomach dragging her there as the breakfast call went out to gather the garrison and wake up the rest of the Eclupse for their day of work.

Spies

Unkyss sat up suddenly. His throat was parched, and his stomach felt empty. His head spun a bit as he sat up, and he almost puked from the sudden motion. He slowly opened and closed his eyes a few times; it felt like they hadn't been used in days and his vision was a little blurred. His whole body felt like it was made of pine needles, and his muscles and limbs were stiff. Unkyss almost rolled right off the little stretcher that he had been sleeping on, but he managed to get his hands down next to him in time and it was somehow enough to stop his momentum. The stretcher was made of narrow wooden poles only a lue or so long, and they supported a stretched-out hide that had been covered with a thick and soft mammoth blanket. There was a small fire at the stretcher's foot, it had obviously been burning brightly before but now it was nothing but dim embers that occasionally flashed to life with small pops. Unkyss was in a foriegn structure that he had never seen before; it looked like it was made of hide, but it didn't smell like it. There were long posts at the front and back of the structure, and there was a thick—probably sinew—cord running from one post to the other. The odd cover was draped over these posts and cord, which provided a basic frame for the structure. It was large too; inside, there were three other beds identical to his, but they were empty. Next to him was a wooden bowl full of milk, he greedily reached for it with his right hand, but his arm didn't respond.

"What in Alpha Father's name?" he tried to ask out loud, but ended up slurring his words. The right side of his jaw felt heavy, as though it were made of stone. *Bear-shit,* he thought as he tried to twist his torso so he could get his left arm to the bowl. Unkyss' whole right side felt like it was being poked by a thousand porcupine quills, he let out a soft whimper but gritted his teeth and forced his torso to twist. His whole back cramped, nearly leaving him stuck halfway to the milk. He gingerly lay on his side, and his arm came within reach of the bowl. His fingers snatched at the brim as he forced his abs to hold him up long enough to get a drink. In one guzzle, he finished the bowl, letting it clang to the ground next to him.

I'll pick it up later, he thought to himself, trying to lie back down.

For a moment, Unkyss stared up at the sinew cord as it ran from pole to pole, this shelter wasn't half bad. He guessed that with more poles, cord, and a larger canvas, you could house quite a few Maulers. His stomach suddenly cramped as the milk came to settle, his mouth began to salivate and he began panting at the same time, feeling as though he was burning up. It felt like his stomach was rolling around in his gut; the room spun a bit and he tried to keep focus on the light that crept from a crack that ran vertically that he assumed was the exit.

Fresh air; *fresh air and I will feel fine*, he thought to himself, trying to get to his paws. For a moment, his back seemed to forget about the cramp and he was able to force himself to sit up. Encouraged, he forced his hips to swing to the right, and went to plant his left paw. For a single moment, his stomach was so confused by the sudden and painful fall that it stopped its acrobatics.

Unkyss' head took out the pole at the front of the shelter, and the hempen material collapsed, the sinew cord yanking the other pole from its foundation and the back of the tent followed suit. He managed to push himself up to his knees, but now prone and reoriented, his stomach reminded him that it was ill and he threw up around his hands. The majority of the sick was bile, and it burned the whole way up, even now that it had been spewed forth it burned.

I was sure I drank some milk, Unkyss panted, trying to catch his breath. All he could smell at first was the stomach acid, but then a new smell began to mix with the caustic aroma. He swallowed, trying to keep himself from retching a second time. Unkyss sniffed about him, but he couldn't see anything because of the canvas that draped around him as though he had been swallowed into the earth. After he took one deep sniff, he began to cough; it was smoke that he was smelling. Suddenly, he could see again dimly as the shelter caught fire.

Unkyss sighed, he couldn't shout even if his jaw had worked properly, his throat was raw from the coughing, and he still only felt pinpricks of pain over and over, mainly in his right side.

Well, I am sure there are worse ways to die, he tried to reassure himself. At the moment, though, he was having trouble thinking of others. Isn't that how it always works out? He said to himself. *You hear all these horror stories about how Maulers die, and when you need to remember them most, they just abandon you.* Even his bad memories knew Unkyss was doomed.

***

Rellik smelt the smoke first. She, Aasha, Brutyss, Dardyl were all sharing another tent, similar to the one that Unkyss was managing to burn up. Like all the Maulers, she had been hesitant about staying in such a shelter. No one but Dio or Luna liked them. Terrabyss had flatly refused to sleep in one and had been hesitant to even enter it, until Luna had suggested how they could put it to use. Like all Maulers and the Silverbacks of old, Terrabyss was not so bashful about what he and Luna did and who witnessed it. Luna, on the other hand, had grown up in a different world, one of caution and boundaries despite their claimed freedom. In the end, Terrabyss didn't argue; he was sworn to Luna and if he wanted to keep that oath, it meant making some compromises.

Numa hadn't liked it, but she had reinforced Dio's argument that "if they were to sneak up on the garrison of Kyron, it wouldn't be wise to have just over a hundred Maulers camped out in the open." The Rodentia refuge was their best bet at maintaining the element of surprise. The forward guard had the pleasure of assaulting the Refuge, but the Rodentia alarm system had worked well and only the oldest and slowest had been captured by the attack. The rest had fled to some contingent shelter to regroup and probably simply rebuild; the Rodentia were not a particularly warlike kind, or known for seeking vengeance.

"Do you smell smoke?" Rellik asked Brutyss as she moved for the opening at the front of the tent, pushing back the flap to peer out.

Brutyss had been the first one back to consciousness and had suffered the least from the poison that had rendered him senseless. His hip muscles and pelvis had been a little stiff for the first half day since he had come to his senses. Now he seemed fine, as though he had not even been injured. Aasha and Dardyl had revived almost two days after Brutyss. To Brutyss' and Rellik's frustration, Skoff had refused to use his magic to aid their allies' conditions. Both were aware of the shaman's abilities to remove toxins from a body, and they were baffled as to why he refused to use his skills. Skoff's argument of "they are all young, and I don't see their deaths being caused by poison," in all honesty were weak excuses to both of them.

358

With Terrabyss and Numa out on patrols, they didn't feel like they had anyone of authority to bring their complaints to. When they had brought it up with Dio, his response was more logical, but no less frustrating. "No large fires. It would be a beacon to our location, and it would take a large fire for Skoff to channel the magic needed."

The Maulers had been camped in this area a day short of a quarter-moon. Winter was another half-moon away from ending, and the lengthening days and the sounds of the Green Wall were portents, warning the snow of its numbered days. It was only under the shade of the large redwoods and other conifers that the snow found sanctuary from the heat of the sun. In any openings of the canopy, all that could be seen of the drifts were patches and sprinklings of white, not deep enough to hide a pup. The whole forest echoed with droplets of water as the leaves shed their heavy burdens and icicles lost their winter girth. The mornings brought heavy dew and the sun created a fog with the evaporating water, making the forest slightly humid and warning of the summer heat.

Aasha and Dardyl were both still dealing with the side effects of having so much of the Corvel concoction in their blood, but in different ways. Dardyl's head moved laboriously to face the tent's opening, the muscles in her neck still suffering, and her left eye was unable to open completely. She had been blind for the first half-day she had been awake so she was hopeful that she would completely recover. Aasha was struggling a bit more; she was unable to talk but could relay basic information through hand signals, as long as a sporadic tremor didn't interfere. Her tail failed to reveal her moods and her face was—for the most part—expressionless. She remained on her bed in the back of the structure.

Brutyss hesitated to follow Rellik as he looked back at his sister, feeling guilty for the agony she was suffering through. Until he heard Rellik's shout of panic and extremely loud swearing. When he got outside, Rellik was kicking at a figure hunched up in a burning tent; the flames didn't seem to mind her beating at them and were just growing in intensity.

Brutyss quickly looked around, shouting at Rellik, "Stop! Get some snow! Suffocate the fire in snow and dirt!" Brutyss immediately sprinted to a small patch of snow near the front of the tent, not bothering to avoid the frozen leaves and twigs, they were too cold to burn anyway. It didn't take long as the two of them worked rapidly. Rellik began to just shovel dirt onto the flames from right next to them and Brutyss saw the sense in this tactic, instantly following her example. A few moments later, the two of them pulled a slightly charred and smoking hemp canvas off of Unkyss' body. He had reflexively huddled up as much as he could when Rellik had begun kicking him, and hadn't bothered to move as he looked up.

"Whikk eh kekt e?" he asked in a gargled voice, still trying to make his jaw move. Frustrated as the two Maulers just stared at him, he tried to lift his arms to signal what he was asking; again, his right arm remained motionless. Eventually, he just swung out at both of them, missing, but it was easier to just assume that they were both guilty of kicking him.

"What in Alpha Father's name is your problem?" Rellik shouted in a mix of tears and rage. Her tail wagged rapidly as she knelt next to Unkyss, nuzzling him. Unkyss learned at that moment that his tail was still working and Brutyss decided to leave them alone, stepping back into the tent.

Unkyss looked up, still unable to form words he looked around, and motioned with his left arm to their surroundings, attempting to cock his head but settling with half a shrug. Rellik nodded her head, giving a laugh through a slight sniffle, still so excited that he had woken up.

"Yes, we are in the Green Wall, we made it." Unkyss' tail matched hers as they put their foreheads to one another, both letting a few tears trickle out. They had made it home.

***

Terrabyss sniffed, looking off to the southeast of the encampment. "That's smoke," he said, glaring at Numa as she stuck an elbow in his ribs.

"Shush," she signaled with her finger, flicking her head back to the topic at hand.

Terrabyss gave another nod into the air, signaling he smelt something and then snorting as though he were sneezing to signal smoke. Dio and the other Eclupse present looked at him, both cocking their heads, confused as to what the young Mauler was doing. Numa glared daggers at her brother. She didn't care if the whole forest was on fire, they needed to pay attention.

This spy was full of useful information, even if half of what he was saying was a lie. Besides, the group Terrabyss was probably concerned about were adults now, and were probably fine. She visibly shook her head, flattening her ears to signal to Terrabyss that the discussion was over.

At that moment, Dio turned and looked at her. Numa instantly stopped shaking, trying to convince the two Eclupse that she was fascinated by the stars, as she left her head tilted toward the sky.

"Numa," Dio said in a slightly aggravated tone.

Numa turned to face him, raising her ears and eyebrows attentively. "Yes, Alpha?" she asked, trying to come to a greater level of attention, if that were even possible.

"What's wrong with Terrabyss? Are we missing something?" Dio asked crossly as Terrabyss hadn't felt the need to explain himself and was now just picking his teeth nonchalantly with a claw.

"Must be allergic to the… " Numa thought for a moment frantically, "the dirt, here in the Green Wall." To Numa's credit, her voice and tone—even with the slight pause—had made the lie seem logical and even though Dio knew that was bear-shit, she looked too sincere to question any further.

Dio turned back to Volg, an Eclupse that a group of Scouts led by Rymmall had found sniffing around. Dio was still a little upset that Rymmall had taken the Eclupse to Numa before him. He had just finished assuring Volg that he was deeply sorry for the rough treatment the Eclupse had suffered under both Rymmall's and Numa's heavy hands. Dio found the interruption too coincidental, but had little choice other than to continue his apology to Volg.

"I assure you, brother, you will be treated with the utmost kindness from now until you leave." Dio fixed both Numa and Terrabyss with stern glares. "And you will leave here, very alive and very well," the Alpha said pointedly at the two of them.

Numa nodded respectfully and saluted Dio, framing her stomach with her arms. Terrabyss copied the gesture, but the hesitation was obvious. In Terrabyss' mind, they had been in this Rodentia hole far too long and he didn't care what anyone said, this place was miserable. It had numerous hemp ropes that were strung between the trees. Between the ropes, wooden planks of varying sizes and widths created asinine bridges and lifting platforms. The majority of the Rodentia were excellent climbers, so it was beyond him what the pulleys were for. There were some more solid platforms that didn't move and were attached to the trees by braces wedged into the trunks. The forward group hadn't found much of value on the platforms. The stupid lifts didn't support more than one Mauler at a time, so in many ways it was a blessing that there was nothing of interest up there. The damn pulley and hoist would have probably broken under the weight of a looting Mauler. To add to their frustrations, the hemp tents were empty, completely, not even beds. All of the furniture—stretchers and firepits—now in the shelters was provided by the invading force. Below the tents was a maze of warrens that extended in all directions. The majority of the tunnels were too small for the Silverbacks to fit through and the few holes the pups could fit down had led to dead ends or had caved in. Fortunately, the tribe had been able to dig anyone out who had been trapped.

The Silverbacks were not novices to burrowing and making underground shelters, but their dens were much simpler then the Rodentia. The warrens were more of a maze than a simple tunnel. The advance party had managed to catch some older Harris and Moozers, as well as a Fillany[69]. The elderly Rodentia hadn't made any effort to keep their lives private and had been very forthcoming, which just meant that few of the Silverbacks trusted a word they heard. According to the elders, the Fillany were the tree-dwelling tribe of the clan, the Harris and Moozers were the ones that lived in the Warrens. They also claimed that their clan had the ability to smell gold and silver. Terrabyss doubted it, but no one had listened to his suggestion to execute the old Rodentia that were obviously useless. To add to his frustration, Dio had seemed to see some merit in these liars' words, and had been impressed with their abilities no matter how crazy the claim. The Harris earned their lives because they could chew through anything, even metal, although apparently at their age their spring-like legs had long worn out. *How are they going to be useful to the Maulers?* Especially since they were at least sixty years of age. *Besides, according to the Fillany, all of them can chew through almost anything.* Truug, the old red-furred Fillany, had told everyone that "a Rodentia was a Rodentia because of their teeth." It seemed true, too; all of them had those weird, buck teeth and needed to constantly chew on things to shave them down.

Personally, teeth like that sound like a nightmare, and what are cheek pouches anyway? Terrabyss thought to himself. *How stupid did some of these Rodentia think the Maulers were? Besides, what kind of claim to fame is that? Cheek pouches.*

Terrabyss was more impressed with the Fillany ability to bound from branch to branch with hardly a sound, that could actually be useful. He wasn't the only one with such biases toward the group. Many of the other

69   Squirrel-Taur

tribes viewed the Taur clan with distrust. Many of the Rodentia survived by stealing provisions, wealth, and anything else they wanted from other tribes and clans. Despite their shifty nature, many of the Rodentia were often employed as spies and thieves, to tip the balance between one tribe and another, or between opposing clans. That had been the normal order before the Ozars had taken over and dominated the eastern and northeastern half of the Green Wall. In the time of the Four Laws, the Rodentia had been used by the Ozars, Daunkirks, and Silverbacks to wound the other clans without actually coming to blows. After the Ozar and Daunkirk takeover, the Rodentia were hunted by both clans. Viewed as untrustworthy and as liabilities, they were imprisoned or forced into slavery. A few small tribes had fled to the Warm Wood where they lived out of the reach of the Ozars, and previously the Daunkirks. Ever since the newer conflict between the Ozars and Daunkirks, however, they had come back under the purview of the Daunkirk empire, putting their new small communities back at risk. Most had moved further south, or fled to the strongholds of their Darmin[70] allies, the dam-building Taurs who controlled the rivers and lakes that were especially numerous to the west. The Daunkirks developed a treaty with the Darmin, and they now accommodate the Rodentia that fled within their boundaries. The Rodentia that chose to stay within the Green Wall are forced to migrate from one safe place to another, living in what have been named 'Refuges.'

Terrabyss was positive that there were treasures hidden in the collapsed tunnels and caverns of the warren, and believed if the Rodentia didn't want to work to earn their keep and clear out the debris, they were useless. These elder Rodentia were consuming rations, and their sparse knowledge of Kyron and its defenses were especially useless, now that they had captured this obvious Eclupse spy. The Rodentia never mentioned having any relations, friendly or hostile with Kyron. This Eclupse could swear as much as he liked that he was here to discuss trade on behalf of Kyron with the Refuge. Terrabyss knew better, and he hoped that everyone else here didn't trust the Eclupse either. From the sounds of it, Dio was going to extend the same courtesies that he had offered to the Rodentia to this spy. If they kept throwing away their rations like this, they were going to need to start hunting further from the Refuge. That significantly increased the chances of a group of Maulers getting spotted by one of the Ozar patrols,

70   Beaver-Taur

which would mean that this whole tactic of subterfuge would have been a waste of time and effort.

It was hard to deny the advantageous area of the Refuge. The main camp was well hidden in a copse of trees and the Rodentia had clearly worked hard to make sure that it would be difficult to find. The Invasion Council was gathered in the moderately sized square that was defined by the surrounding tents. Here, the Fillany, Harris, and Moozer conducted business and had built an odd-looking space they called a compani, or common square. The compani had a small fire pit that was not in use, as all fires were to remain hidden by Dio's command. The edges of the compani were lined with large, fallen logs that had been rolled into the refuge. The sides of the logs had white chalk painted on them, and it was a bad omen to hold a meeting without first marking the logs. It was not a Silverback custom, but there was no sense taking the risk. At each corner of the compani was a pole, the two poles that followed the sun's path had multiple-colored cloths lashed to the top third. There was no particular order or color, but each family was represented by a cloth attached to the wooden columns. To the east were those cloths of the families that had joined the refuge, and to the west were the cloths of those who had left. The snow within the boundary of the logs had intentionally been removed, and the frozen needles, ferns, and clover could be seen as though on display through the slight frost that still clung to the forest floor.

Terrabyss looked around, forcing his mind to stop meandering as he realized that more than just Dio and Numa were staring at him. Obviously, everyone was expecting a response. *I need to get better at staying focused*, he berated himself as he tried to think of the least obvious way to ask for whoever to repeat the question or statement that he needed to respond to.

"Does what he said change your mind?" Dio finally asked again, having lost patience with Terrabyss' stalling efforts.

I am not sure what he said, but I doubt I agree with it, Terrabyss thought. "No!" If anyone had gasped at Terrabyss' obstinance, it was purely out of sarcasm. "What is to stop him from telling the Ozars exactly where we are? I still think we should kill him and I still think we should kill the Rodentia." It didn't hurt to bring that opinion up again, especially since they were on the subject of whom he thought should live or die.

"Please, I have a pack," begged Volg. "I am being honest; an Ozar, a Norrus. He has come with an army of over fifty fighters. The Ozar's name is Forver, and he seems to hold a grudge against the Maulers." Again, Volg's light gray-furred head swung back to Dio, his dark blue, almost sapphire eyes pleading with the Alpha to spare his life.

Dio was torn; in many ways, Terrabyss' assumptions were right. Both about this Eclupse, and as much as he didn't want to admit it, the Rodentia. Dio had hoped that the Rodentia would have had a bit more information. He had given his word, and he wasn't going to go back on that, and this Eclupse, well, it was an Eclupse. Volg had been through hardship after hardship, and Dio didn't want to deprive his pack of a father. Although, what was going to stop the Ozars from just marching up here when they sent this Eclupse back? *Nothing.* Dio couldn't deny it. Absolutely nothing. *Perhaps, if he could find some information out, perhaps enough to excuse sparing the Eclupse's life.*

"You say this, this Forver. He knows that we are coming?" Dio wasn't sure the point of the question, the answer had already been given on multiple occasions.

For a moment, Volg looked confused, his gaze shifting from Numa, to Skoff, to Maxyss, to Luna, and then the other members of the Invasion Council, unsure if Dio was playing a trick on him. "Yes," Volg repeated nervously.

Volg was a bit taller than Dio, making him the tallest Silverback the Maulers had ever seen, at least until Unkyss regained consciousness and they could have a fair comparison. Volg looked famished, he had some muscle, but his skin was pressed tightly to his frame. His gaunt form was not natural, and his bones were practically visible with just a thin layer of hide across their surface. As Volg kept scratching his neck and behind each ear, Terrabyss hoped that fleas were his only infestation. Volg's light gray fur was thin, and lacked the sheen that most winter coats had. He had long ears and a long muzzle, or the thinning fur around and on his head just emphasized its length. The worst part about Volg was the smell. It was like shit and water, mixed with a bit of mud and piss. Several of Volg's teeth were black and had rotted or were simply just missing. A fact that Volg was aware of, and it forced him to keep his head hung in a submissive gesture to all around; even if a Mauler pup were to pass, Volg kept his blue eyes on the Green Wall's floor. Terrabyss felt a bit of compassion for this Eclupse, he had never seen anyone so neglected in his life. Even the runts in his own tribe could aspire to be more than this. This feeling had done little to change his opinion on how a spy for this Forver should be dealt with. *Same as the Rodentia, dead.* Terrabyss wasn't opposed to trying to save the Eclupse's pack when they assaulted Kyron, he wasn't a monster. He would even be willing to tell the cubs and mate that Volg had died honorably and was awaiting them in the stars.

"I think we should send him back with a story, and try to round up the other two spies and make sure they return to Forver with the same information."

Terrabyss' ears twitched as he was instantly pulled from his reflections. He couldn't have heard Dio correctly. Terrabyss stepped forward. "When you say send him and the others back with a story, you mean a message, right? You mean to send them back as corpses, correct?" Terrabyss cocked his head, waiting for Dio to respond and the majority of the Invasion Council followed suit.

Volg looked to Dio with his earlier begging look, wide-eyed and head slightly tilted. Even Terrabyss felt a pang of guilt for the suggestion, for a moment, just a moment.

"No. I intend to send him back to Kyron and to his pack, alive," Dio emphasized. "I believe we can gain a great advantage in using him and the others to feed Forver with false information."

Terrabyss' tail dropped, not between his legs as though he had been beaten, but like he was disgusted. It didn't sway even slightly as he paced while he talked, not wanting Volg to be privy to the information discussed. It also helped to frustrate Dio, as he still didn't understand the movement and expressions completely. Luna was practically fluent, rarely missing a step or the proper manner. Dio focused intently on Terrabyss, not wanting to be made a fool in the council.

"I think that is a stupid idea!" Terrabyss began, and Dio was too far back in the translation to interrupt him. "He hasn't told us anything we didn't already know or weren't going to find out from our Scouts. Your sympathy for your former tribe is clouding your judgment, or perhaps it is that you have not truly committed to your new tribe. Is it that you are still more Eclupse than you are Mauler? This Forver who sent him wants you to do this, and you are foolishly playing right into his hand."

It took a moment for Dio to completely understand what Terrabyss had said, and the Mauler enjoyed watching his Alpha's different expressions as parts of the rebuttal were finally deciphered. To Dio's credit, he managed to maintain his composure, which was a slight disappointment to Terrabyss, but it hadn't been a total wash.

"He could not only mislead this Forver, but also give us valuable information. This is a war, not some challenge or raid, there will be defenses, choke points, and other fortifications we will need to overcome," Dio replied, using more words than movement, but his point was understandable.

"Then let him give us some of this valuable information," Maxyss shouted. "If he doesn't, then I agree with Terrabyss."

"I also agree," came Skoff's unnaturally booming voice; he had become a member of this council after Rellik's adoption, not because of any knowledge of war but simply because he didn't want to be left out of anything. His statement practically drowned out the wise council of Luna who stated that she left the tactics of war up to those who had practice in it. She honestly didn't know why she was on this council; the rest had their suspicions that Dio hoped to have a voice that would always side with his opinion. Luna, though, had a mind of her own and she intelligently stayed out of debates in which she had little interest or knowledge.

"I also agree!" Numa announced, and all others went quiet as the whole council hung on her words. "With my brother, and I would remind the Alpha that you are the leader of the Maulers, so long as you remain a Mauler in both word and deed. You cannot have one title without the other." She let her last sentence hold all the implications it needed and in her usual manner made no effort to elaborate on whether that was a threat or a warning.

Perhaps, it is intended as both, Dio thought as he weighed the emotions of his council. It was true that he was outvoted, but he was the Alpha and in the end it was his decision that mattered. As Numa had clarified, however, he had less real power than he was allowed to portray. A reality that he had submitted to, but one that he was finding less agreeable right now.

Dio turned to face Volg. "In case you did not understand what was being said, they intend to kill you unless you give us something useful. I am inclined to let them have their way," Dio lied. A skill he was surprisingly well trained in, Dio had made a practice of keeping things hidden and his practice was paying off. It also helped that Dio was able to transfer his real feelings of anger at the Ravis pack toward Volg, making his words hit all the harder against the frightened Eclupse's fragile psyche.

"What, what do you want? I swear I will and have told you all I know.

I just want to see my pups and my mate again. Give me the commands and I will fulfill them." Volg's words were sincere, and Dio knew the Eclupse wasn't lying. One of the benefits of being such a practiced manipulator of words, he was able to decipher when a subject's words belied the truth.

I only hope the rest of them believe it, he thought to himself.

"I believe him," Luna stated bluntly. Numa noticed with both a bit of admiration and jealousy, as Luna employed her earlier tactic and seemed to gain the group's attention even quicker then Numa had. "Volg, that is. I believe he is telling the truth. I may not be practiced in war, but I am practiced in survival, and Volg truly wants to survive. There is no denying that, given his tone."

"All right, let us test it then," responded Maxyss to Luna's statement as he turned to Volg. Very clearly and slowly, he spoke to the captured Eclupse, "How many warriors are in the... " He stalled for a moment, trying to remember the name of the complex the Eclupse had come from.

"Commune!" Terrabyss shouted, having lost patience with Maxyss' slow thoughts. "He is from Kyron, the commune."

Maxyss shot a glare at Terrabyss, who shrugged as the elder Prime Hunter finished his question. "How many warriors are in the Kymune-Commune?" he quickly corrected, casting another venomous look at Terrabyss, who was obviously trying to keep his tail from wagging, having easily heard the slip.

"I don't know... " Volg took a breath trying to respond quickly. "When Forver arrived, he brought a large group of soldiers with him. Before he came, we had a garrison of—" before he could finish Maxyss cut him off.

"What is a garrison?" Numa and Skoff nodded their agreement with this question, and found it surprising their brother didn't share their curiosity. Terrabyss was not just teaching Luna, but was also learning from her. Learning how the world had changed while they had been in the grove.

"A garrison is a standing guard. They are permanently in place, similar to the Watchers, only more numerous and in a much more defensible area," Terrabyss elaborated, as clearly Volg wasn't sure how to answer the question.

"Continue," Dio announced as he gave a nod of approval to Terrabyss and then cast an approving look to Luna, who was also beaming at her mate's display of knowledge.

"We, we had a garrison of twenty-five," Volg began again, having to remember where he had been cut off. Volg tried to match the submissive gesture that he had seen the Maulers display to Dio, and gave such an expression to Maxyss, hoping that the amount of information he had given had been satisfactory. It was an admirable attempt, but it didn't soften the glare that Maxyss fixed on him.

"Well, if that is all you know, then that was all you were good for," came Terrabyss' emotionless response. He reached for his kanabo, which was propped up on a stone next to where he had been standing.

Volg's eyes grew wide with horror, and Dio wasn't sure if this was an act or if Terrabyss actually meant to kill the captured Eclupse. Volg let out a painful yelp as Numa was behind him in a flash and had his wrists. She yanked back on his arms and planted her paw between his shoulders, giving her brother a clean target as Terrabyss aimed the weapon at Volg's exposed stomach.

"I swear," Volg cried out. "I swear I won't tell Forver where you are, or your troop numbers, not even… " Terrabyss was done listening to the pleas of a spy.

"This Forver will put your pack in danger, and then you will talk and talk and talk. Besides, you don't know our troop size," Terrabyss interrupted with an ominous grin and, bringing his arms back as he planted his paws, let his hips rotate back. His muscles were taut and ready to spring back into position. Dio thought he should intervene; this act was starting to seem too real.

Frantically, Volg racked his brain for information, pulling up weeds of useless facts. There didn't seem to be anything worth mentioning. He could smell the smoke of the small tent fire, that Terrabyss had complained about to Numa. *It is a better smell than the night soil that is piled up in the pens,* Volg thought to himself, as he resigned himself to his fate. Smoke, the thought lingered.

"Smoke, smoke!" Volg suddenly shouted, and Numa had to reapply her grip before Volg slipped free.

Dio took the opportunity to stop Terrabyss, he wasn't sure he would have been able to without this diversion. "Hold, Terrabyss, let him explain," Dio ensured that he added some authority to his voice. He wasn't sure how much longer this trick would work. Each time he used it, it seemed to be more and more difficult to soothe the Mauler's aggressive nature. This time, his charm seemed to be enough and Terrabyss slowly lowered his weapon to his side. Thankfully, it seemed Numa had fallen prey to his words as well, releasing her grip from Volg and allowing him to sit up straight. Although, both stayed within arm's reach of the terrified spy.

"Smoke," Volg began again. Dio cast him a warning glance, as if to tell Volg he didn't have time to start over. "The keep has smoke chutes for the fire's fumes to escape from the bottom floor slowly so that it helps warm the upper floors. These chutes are on the southern side of the keep, they send smoke up that side and make it difficult for the sentry to see out to the south of Kyron." Volg was talking as fast as he could. *Oh Alpha Father please let me see my family again*, he prayed as he blurted out the last bit.

Numa and Terrabyss exchanged looks, but Maxyss was the one to speak. "That is actually helpful."

Dio noted the disappointment in the Prime Hunter's voice, but it had been a long evening, he could have wanted to kill the spy just to get this interrogation over with.

Numa was not so convinced. "How can we be sure that these chutes even create enough smoke that it will provide our troops any cover?" She looked from Volg to Dio, and then back to Volg.

"We chop the wood!" Volg proclaimed, gaining courage with the council's hesitation. "I could inform the loggers to only stack fresh lumber outside the keep. The Ozars are too lazy to care as long as… if the wood… if they are kept warm at night." Volg was beginning to stammer again as he noticed Terrabyss' disinterest returning as Numa voiced her doubts.

"It is plausible," Dio announced, feeling his hold slipping and needing to refocus the council's attention. "With the end of winter, almost all the wood is probably soaked with water, the Ozars wouldn't have the time to wait for it to fully dry before putting it to use. We could assault the south side of Kyron while their sentinel is blinded by the plumes of *smoke*." Dio needed no trick this time, as it was a good tactic.

"If we are spotted though as we come to assault the rear, and this commune is as well-defended as Volg implies, the whole attack will be thwarted before it begins," Terrabyss added, having had a few moments to process the information.

"You could attack in two units," Luna offered. The council turned to face her; her tail thumped in a nervous rhythm and her ears drooped a bit in embarrassment. When she realized everyone was waiting for her to explain, she nervously cleared her throat. "If you assaulted the front of the commune while a smaller unit snuck around to the south, the sentry's focus would be on the first group that attacked. Most likely, they would never even think to look behind them. With the smoke covering the second group's advance, if the sentry did scan the horizon for another point of assault, they would likely not even notice the second unit," Luna finished, not bothering to look up from her lap. *Alpha Father, I hate being on councils.*

Numa nodded. "I could take a Fist against the rear, while the mass of our force hit the north of the commune."

"If what Dio says about the fortification of a commune are true, you will need something more like ten Fists to be a true threat to the rear," Maxyss huffed, finding the idea convenient. "Also why is this the first time we hear of, this, this smoke?" he asked, looking around at those gathered.

"None of us asked if the keep had any vulnerabilities," Luna pointed out.

"Besides, fear tends to bring clarity to one's thoughts," Terrabyss added, holding his weapon menacingly before Volg's face to help prove his point.

Luna didn't feel that this was the best time to educate Terrabyss on the gross inaccuracies of that statement and instead returned her focus to the subject at hand. "Perhaps, we should allow Volg to return with our message for Forver before we elaborate any more of our plan in front of the spy." Luna was obviously more cunning than she ever exhibited, as Terrabyss, Maxyss, and Numa all agreed without even considering their previous position.

"You will tell him what I am about to say, word for word. Do not stray from this explanation in any way, and it will ensure you see your pack again." Dio stared intently at Volg to be sure he understood the importance of the instructions he was about to receive. The captured Eclupse nodded keenly.

***

As Terrabyss escorted the double agent out of the forward camp, Volg couldn't help but feel nervous around the powerful Mauler. Terrabyss had never seen such a feeble and skinny Silverback in his life and Volg had never seen Maulers before. They were all impressive, muscular, fierce, and most importantly, free. Volg's initial response was pleasing to the Maulers, they worked hard to cultivate an aura of savage independence and they fought hard to maintain it. He had never before seen the black fur and yellow eyes that defined the Maulers, much less the Silverback culture that they had managed to preserve.

Terrabyss walked close enough that if Volg moved in a way that he didn't like, he could take out the Eclupse's legs before Volg could employ any cunning. The sheer presence of the armed and aggressive Mauler was enough to keep Volg in line like a newborn pup. The Eclupse spy wouldn't take a step before he ensured it was the right one. Despite Terrabyss' assurances that he wasn't going to kill Volg, and despite Terrabyss reminding Volg how lucky he was to be walking out of here alive, Volg did not change his timid behavior. The short walk to the edge of the refuge became a grueling ordeal.

By the time they hit the boundary of the refuge, Terrabyss was anxious to get rid of the Eclupse. He knew that if he killed him, Dio would be upset. *And more importantly, Luna would be disappointed.* Terrabyss almost lost his step behind Volg when that thought occurred to him. *Why in the Alpha Father's name does that bother me?* He wondered.

As the two arrived at the trees, Terrabyss placed his kanabo gingerly on Volg's shoulder. The Eclupse froze, thinking that he had let himself become too hopeful, apparently he wasn't walking out of here alive.

"You understand what you are going to tell this Forver?" Terrabyss asked, letting the arm that held his weapon relax so that a few spikes dug into the double agent's flesh. A light trail of crimson ran down Volg's gray coat.

Volg simply nodded in response, hoping that his quiet demeanor would help to convince the Mauler behind him.

"Good, then you're free," Terrabyss instructed, lifting his weapon off Volg's shoulder. The Eclupse didn't hesitate, and dashed into the trees before Terrabyss could change his mind.

Bad News Wolf

"If you touch him, I swear I will butcher you and add your skin to the keep. I swear this by the Mother Bear," Ferda warned Zolk as she noticed the psycho thumbing Headhunter's toe. She, Zolk, Urrah, and Forver were gathered in Forver's traveling yurt, located near the eastern side of the compound.

Volg had arrived that morning; the sentry had spotted him when he had exited the trees to the northwest of Kyron, as he had been instructed by Dio. To say that Volg was nervous would have been a gross understatement. Volg hadn't thought that he would have been more frightened of the Ozars than he was of the Maulers, given the novelty of the latter, but he had thought wrong. It was taking all his self-control not to burp, or worse, retch, all over the nice cushions on which the four Ozars sat. They had made a circle around him; the leader, Forver, was in front of a small fire that was being used to keep the yurt warm. To his left and right were the two female Ozars. The eldest of the two was on his left and the younger was opposite her. Behind him was the one Volg was most frightened of, as he had known Zolk's first three victims. Not well, since his enclosure worked in the fields and maintained the keep. The three Eclupse who had been killed had been from the logging enclosure, but he at least knew their names: Trel, Odan, and the juvenile Ryss.

Trel had been the first victim, she had been delivering the axes that the loggers used back to the commune's herder, Travic. Between the pens and the tool sheds, the savage Zolk had found her and torn her limb from limb. He had kept the torso for some time as a trophy. Odan, well, the whole commune had pretty much seen what had happened to him. It had been in the morning, when the whole of Kyron was starting its morning routines. According to the Ozar, Odan had spit on him, which was enough to warrant the reaction of stringing the unconscious Eclupse up and gutting him while he was alive. Odan hadn't lived long, but his screams had haunted all of the Eclupse for the rest of the day. Ryss had been Odan's

373

son, and had verbally assaulted Zolk, trying to goad him into a fight. It hadn't taken much goading, and Ryss hadn't taken many strikes of that steel axe before he was no longer moving. Zolk had managed to make the corpse twitch for several hours afterwards, but fortunately had the trophy snatched away by some half-decent Ozar, if there was such a thing. Volg was positive it was an Ozar, because no Eclupse in their right mind would have found a way out of their pen and voluntarily stuck around. It had been a huge wave of relief when he had been escorted past the pen that held his pack on his return, and he had seen his mate Hild and their two pups, the alpha Solgar and his brother Arvin. They hadn't noticed him, busy at their morning chores as he was shuffled by, but it had been good to see them alive all the same.

Volg had remained strung up in the Branch Pens—cages that hung down from the sequoia branches to the southeast of the clearing—until noon. He had finally been prodded here at Forver's request, while the commander was still eating the last of his lunch, to deliver his report.

Ferda didn't bother keeping Havil covered while she was in Zolk's presence, not any more. Zolk's savagery seemed to know no bounds; after she found her way back following her outrage at Zolk's previous cruel sadism and violence, his menace had only seemed to worsen. Even Forver had been forced to allow Dhon to put a watch on Zolk anytime he was out of Forver's immediate presence. Dhon had no love for the Eclupse, but she felt responsible for those under her protection and Zolk's acts of brutality had reached their zenith when the garrison couldn't find a handful of Eclupse. Later that night, some sounds had been heard coming from the punching bags that hung out near the northern earthworks in a training area. The garrison had discovered the missing Eclupse, who had been sown up inside the bags. Three had been beaten to death and another had suffocated, leaving only Velkurt alive. Dhon had warned Forver—in all of the commanders' presence—that if Zolk so much as flicked another Eclupse, she was sending them all back to Ursyss. It had been a strong enough threat to make Forver demand that Zolk comply, and it seemed as though Forver's orders were being followed.

Forver had spent the whole morning arguing with Dhon about how they should proceed now that the spy had returned. Dhon, logically, believed they should first interrogate the spy to see what he had learned. Forver felt that the spy's arrival from the northwest showed how deeply in the

Green Wall the Maulers had entrenched themselves and that all possible patrols should be sent to the northwest and as far as a day's march from Kyron. Fortunately for the patrols, Dhon was in charge of Kyron and she wouldn't give Forver anything until he had learned what the spy had to report. Now, the three commanders and their leader sat listening to what Volg had been instructed to tell them by Dio. Volg knelt behind the fire, facing Forver and uncomfortably close to Zolk. He was thankful that it seemed the younger female to his right was watching out for him. Forver was staring down at his paws as he spit another olive pit into his hand and tossed it into the fire. He missed, and it bounced off Volg's left cheek. He had flinched the first few times he had been hit by the pits, but by now he hardly noticed.

"So." Forver loudly sucked on his pointer finger to clean off whatever those disgusting fruits were soaked in. To Volg's sensitive nose, it was as though he had stuck his face in a skunk's ass, but the Ozar seemed to like them. *I suppose there is no accounting for taste*, he thought to himself. "So, you are telling me that they are camped here," Forver pointed to a spot on his map with his freshly cleaned digit.

Volg shrugged from behind the fire. "I am unable to see where you are indicating," he responded, trying to keep his voice meek. Volg had been here for almost an hour, and he hadn't eaten since the morning he had been captured by the Maulers. *Making it three days today,* he growled to himself.

Forver sighed impatiently. "Here, Ferda, look at where I am pointing and then show it to the simpleton," he instructed the female to Volg's right.

She also sighed, but Volg suspected it was directed more at the Ozar who was ordering her around than at him. Ferda picked up the map and carefully slid it past the fire, this parchment was a rare and expensive material. Once she was sure she had positioned it so that Volg could see, she tapped her finger on the same point that Forver had shown her. "Are they camped here?" she asked in a stern tone.

Volg looked at where she was pointing just to be sure it wasn't where the Maulers actually were. As he saw her motioning to just a random spot in the Green Wall, Volg suddenly found himself hoping that Terrabyss was serious about killing the other spies, because he was going to have to improvise. Volg studied the map, in hopes that it would add to the believability of his next statement.

"Would it be okay" – he asked Ferda, motioning with his own finger

– "if I were to touch it? I could show you exactly where I was. I have a mind for the directions." The last part was true, and he hoped that being honest at the end would hide the lie he started with.

Ferda looked back at Forver to await his reply, and when the Ozar nodded, she turned back to Volg. "Show me," she instructed, gingerly moving the map within his reach.

Volg tried to keep his hand from trembling too much, but he wanted it to tremble a bit. It wouldn't look natural if he seemed completely calm and composed. If he shook too much, the Ozars might realize that he didn't know what he was talking about and he was sure that would get him killed. *I am sure being killed by the Maulers would be preferable to being killed by the Ozars,* he thought to himself, *at least they seemed willing to make it fast.* He allowed his finger to rest on the banks of the River Ryndell, which was to the west of Kyron and ran vertically almost the whole length of the Green Wall until its confluence with the River Cynwyn far to the south.

"Smart." Volg almost jumped, not having noticed that the other female was leaning over his shoulder, looking at where the Eclupse was pointing. "With the river there, they are defended from the west and north by the Ryndell's bend, to the north where it connects with the Ice Kraggs. The only route we could take to them would be to march right where they will be expecting us. I would set up my camp there if I was going to launch an attack on Kyron. It is less than a day's march from us, and far from where we had expected them.

"The Ryndell is frozen," interjected Zolk. "What benefit would they gain from putting their backs to a slippery barricade? Do they think that we can't hold our balance?" Zolk laughed out loud but stopped quickly and awkwardly when he noticed that no one, especially Forver, found him amusing.

"The Ryndell was frozen where we crossed it, true, but that was a little over a week ago. The end of winter is right around the corner and the sun's warmth is a testament to that. The Ryndell has probably begun to thaw, and the ice would be too thin for us to cross as we did earlier," responded Urrah, as she again looked down at the map.

Zolk didn't bother to hide his scowl, and he left it on display even when Forver met his gaze.

"Since I have done as you asked, may I be returned to my pen and my pack?" Volg asked humbly, he knew he was probably way out of line, but he wanted to get away from these Ozars. He wanted to hold his pack against his fur, hear their voices, and smell their pungent scent.

"You can, or could, if I didn't think you were lying to me," Forver responded, looking up from where Ferda was now pointing at. She had respectfully and carefully placed the map back at Forver's paws, with a small stone marking where Volg had indicated. "Your numbers sound completely exaggerated, and I am curious if you even got a look at the Maulers or if you just wandered out to the Ryndell for a little vacation." Forver was staring at Volg; it wasn't that he actually believed any of his accusations, but he would feel foolish if he didn't make sure this Eclupse was telling him the truth, especially so if it caused him to repeat his father's mistake. He motioned to Urrah in the silence that followed his previous statements. "She has studied war, studied tactics, fortifications, troop movements, logistics, you name it she has learned it. If I was going to war against her, I would not think it odd that she had placed herself in such a good position. I am not fighting her; I am fighting a runaway cub who is pretending at being rebel with all of his playfield friends. I am fighting savages and barbarians. I am fighting half-wits and fools and you… you expect me to believe that they are smart enough to camp in such a good position?" Forver's voice was rising as he channeled his anger.

Ferda and Urrah exchanged knowing glances at one another. Zolk was silently cheering on Forver; this was the closest Forver had come to being the Mahzar that Zolk remembered in a long time.

Volg was nervous as the leading Ozar's tone became more and more aggressive. He had done exactly what Dio had told him. Volg had said the Mauler numbers were in the multiple hundreds, and that the Maulers were camped far from their actual location. He hadn't intended on choosing such a defensible position when he had pointed to the map. Dio hadn't told him where to tell Forver they weren't, just not to tell him where they were. Volg's mouth felt parched and his stomach dropped at the Ozar's words of doubt. *This means you are dead; you did good bartering with the Maulers for your life but unless you tell this Ozar the truth now, you are never going to see your pack again. Terrabyss was right, the threat of not seeing my pack again is going to make me talk.* As the thoughts filled his mind, Volg was a bit disgusted with himself, but the love he had for his sons and mate outweighed his guilt. *I only hope now I can convince the leader that this time I am actually telling the truth.* Volg swallowed, gathering what courage he had to betray the Maulers. Volg could feel his tail so far between his legs that it pressed on his stomach as he stood, and his ears seemed nonexistent with how firmly he was holding them down. He licked his dry lips, trying to form the words of treachery. *Perhaps, if you tell him that you were caught and forced to say these things, he will show mercy.* Volg stopped rationalizing. *No. For once you can be more than a slave. You have the chance to give your sons and mate freedom. The Maulers will win as long as this Ozar doesn't know where to look for them.*

Volg stared back at Forver and kept his lips sealed. He felt sick, and as though he was going to faint, but he stayed true to his word and did not reveal the true location of the invading Silverbacks. "I have been honest," Volg replied, expecting an axe to drive into his spine at any moment from the grumbling Ozar behind him. "Everything I said about their uncouth habits, their lack of discipline, and their arrogance was true." It seemed that half-truths were working, more convincing than all-out exaggerations. "They lack all forms of civilization which you Ozars have shown us, and their barbary will never hold sway over us. Not after we have learned what great advances you and your allies can bestow on us." Volg hoped he wasn't laying it on too thick, and by the sighs and expressions of those around him he was worried that he might have been.

Forver was smiling. "See, there are at least some of these animals that have learned humility." Flattery went a long way with those that harbor such arrogance. "Here is proof that these savages do have a brain, be it a small one. I suppose that even an Eclupse can get lucky in where they place their camp. Besides, with this information, I can convince Dhon to send scouts out that way, and then we can see if this Eclupse is honest or a liar that we can burn as a signal to the other spies to come back with truthful reports." Again, Forver locked eyes with Volg to see if the Eclupse would fidget or give something away, still Volg held silent and met the Ozar's stare. Not in a challenging way, for he kept his sapphire eyes toward the fire, but he did not try to move his vision from the leading Ozar, a sign that Forver took as honesty. "Put him in the Branch Pens until we confirm his story," Forver commanded Ferda. "The rest of you are dismissed. I need to go talk to Dhon," Forver ordered as his commanders shuffled out.

Ferda led Volg to the southeastern edge of the clearing. She couldn't keep herself from glancing over her shoulder to ensure that Zolk was not following. To her relief, he wasn't.

"You do understand that this Dio may be more intelligent than you give him credit for," Urrah warned, as she and Forver were the last to exit the yurt. "The reports that came into Ursyss about the little band he had been a part of described them as slippery and intuitive." Urrah almost reminded Forver of his previous debacle with capturing the group Dio had been a part of, but thought better of it. Besides, she had made her point. "If he is wrong, we may not get a second chance. Winter will be gone by the end of next week. I am sure the Honcho will be some time in learning our whereabouts, but we are now dealing with a time frame that we weren't two weeks ago."

"What are you getting at?" Forver grumbled as he walked rapidly to where Dhon's quarters were.

"I am saying that whether Dhon gives us troops or not, perhaps it would behoove us to just pack up and have this Eclupse lead us to the camp," Urrah finally explained. "If the Honcho learns of what you, what we did, he will send troops out here to arrest us and more than likely steal your victory. Time is a factor here, and this is the best lead we have had since we arrived in Kyron." Urrah had been doing so well until the last few sentences, she had kept Forver's attention and not earned his ire. All while causing him to reflect on her thoughts, so much so, that his pace almost slowed to a trot.

Forver's face scrunched up as Urrah mentioned the possibility of Bardell swooping in and nabbing the Yukon glory, his glory. "I know how much time we have!" he roared in Urrah's face as they stood in the path on the way to the colonel's lodging. Ozars and Eclupse alike that were within earshot stopped and looked over at the commotion. "You are the one that always speaks about patience!"

"Patience should be practiced as long as one has the time to practice it. You do realize that if the numbers are even half as large as the spy quoted, we will be hard pressed for victory, and if we do achieve victory, it will be at a massive expense. Perhaps it is time for a different tactic, maybe we should consider that Dio has outsmarted us, and we should either march on where we believe he is or abandon Kyron. Let Dio have the commune, we can convince Dhon and the rest of the garrison to return to Ursyss. The Honcho may fine you; but that will be of little consequence if you are the sole reason that the whole garrison of Kyron survives. The soldiers here will owe you their lives and Dhon will be even more indebted to you. I wouldn't be surprised if they speak out loud enough to earn you a reprieve from your actions, or perhaps even leadership of the reconquering force. Between the pockets you have enriched both here and in Ursyss, as well as the lives you have improved, Bardell would be a fool to pass any form judgment on you," Urrah pleaded with her commander; she had been a warrior for years and she smelt an ambush. Volg was probably lying, she had been stunned when she learned that Dhon had let Forver employ such a tactic. Urrah wasn't sure that love of family was enough to keep the Eclupse in line, and her worries weren't alleviated when Volg had arrived that morning. Urrah hoped that if Forver packed up the whole army and marched westward, a day closer to Ursyss, it would be that much easier to make him return to Campos Ursyss or to at least desert. She was beginning to feel that Ferda may have been onto something when she had left shortly after they had arrived. *Perhaps, I shouldn't have encouraged her to return,* Urrah thought to herself.

"Is this *your* army? Is it your honor that was tainted by those, those, those... " Forver was probably the most enraged Urrah had ever seen him. She imagined this was what he must have been like when he learned of Kodah's failure to capture the Maulers. "Maulers?" Urrah knew he was lost to his rage when there was not some derogatory slur or even spiteful tone to his voice when the word was finally uttered. "No! They are my troops! I will command them as I see fit! You, you will fall in line, or I will move Zolk to your position! No, actually, I will have Zolk lash you! No, no, I will let Zolk kill you!" Forver stomped off, meaning for the conversation to be over. He stopped and spun around suddenly. "I will command him to take you in Materimony!" he roared and then spun back toward Dhon's quarters, leaving Urrah to stare after him, shocked.

It was the first time in Urrah's life that she truly lost her cheerful smile. A vicious grimace came to replace it. "Try," she responded to herself, in a hushed but stubborn tone.

Forver stood in front of Dhon's door and swung Ol'Grim into it with all his might. The bit of the axe easily cut through the wood; the axe had two small wedge-like axe heads on either side of the haft. A long spike almost half the size of the haft protruded from the eye of the axe, hence Forver carried the axe horizontally along his lower back. Like his commanders' weapons, the haft was made of polished black oak and the grip had thin leather strips that had been painted red and woven around each other, creating a gnarled grip.

"Mother Bear! By each star in the night sky! What wolf-shit are you doing to my door?" Dhon's voice roared in almost equal fury to Forver's mood.

Forver froze and looked at the axe, he hadn't meant to do that. He didn't even know how the axe had gotten into his hand. Forver spun around, noticing the leather blade cover for his axe was lying on the ground at his heels.

"Noth—" was all he managed to get out before the door was kicked outward. The heavy wood slammed into Forver, almost knocking him on his back. He barely managed get his paws under him and anchor himself before using his shoulder to shove the door to his left. Dhon was standing in the doorway before the wood had stopped rattling in the dirt to her right. She wore the new garrison armor that had been issued to all officers, a chest plate over a sturdy and battle-tested gambeson. Around her neck, the collar of the gambeson was exaggerated to reach under her chin, and sown into the material was an additional set of small, rectangular plates for extra protection. She had no shield, but held a two-handed battle axe known as Carver. It was similar to Headhunter; in that it had a flat toe but a sharp beard. The handle was made of redwood with a smooth texture. Dhon had simply carved finger notches and cross hatches along the wooden haft to improve the grip, both toward the bottom of the handle and the shoulder, right below the long beard. There was no ornamentation other than the personal grip carving and the blade was a solid, polished piece of steel. Forver quickly planted his paws, ignoring the well-sized crowd of both garrison and militia, Mahuer and Norrus, that had gathered.

"Are you crazy? You could have smashed me beneath your door! How is that for hospitality?" Forver snorted.

"Oh, that it had!" Dhon roared. "But I know from experience that roaches are harder to kill than that!"

Forver forgot his earlier trepidations and waved his axe threateningly between him and Dhon. "Is this… " He spun about, getting an eye for everyone gathered. He knew Dhon had too much honor to rush him while he was boasting. "This how you want to retire? By my axe?" Forver yelled once he had finished his twirl.

Dhon rolled her eyes. "Beating you is not a bad way to leave my command." There were multiple snickers from those gathered. Even a few of the militia found themselves trying to cover up a slight chuckle. "Now either apologize for kissing my door with your axe or I will kiss you with mine."

Forver was not going to be insulted by this ungrateful, rotten, disrespectful, female Mahuer any longer. With surprising speed, he closed the distance between him and Dhon, and with surprising experience—given her youth—Dhon slammed the haft of her weapon into Forver's throat, knocking him on his back and leaving him coughing for air.

"Are you apologizing? I can't hear you past your wheezing," Dhon teased as she passed back and forth in front of Forver. "Get up, or have you already learned your lesson?" she yelled as Forver finally took his first deep breath in several seconds.

Again, Forver's speed was surprising as he leapt up to his paws, but again Dhon showed her prowess with her weapon as she slammed the butt into Forver's forehead as he tried to hop to his paws. The Norrus fell back, wailing about how she had almost hit his eye.

"I have yet to hear an apology. If you don't hurry, the whole commune is going to hear your apology and your groveling and begging as I beat the brown off you!" There was now no concealing the laughter, as many of those gathered hadn't seen this kind of entertainment in their lifetimes.

Zolk watched from near the back of the crowd, the old Zolk would have rushed in and shaved the fur from Dhon's body, putting her on display before the throng just for the verbal insults, much less the physical blows. He grimaced as Forver got to his paws, his legs were wobbling and he seemed to be having trouble orienting which way was forward. The cheek of Dhon's weapon smacked loudly against the side of Forver's face, sending him spinning through the air and landing on his back. His body slowly twitched and he muttered incoherently as his head rotated from side to side, staring up. Surprisingly, it was Urrah who came to Forver's rescue, not that he was conscious enough to realize it.

"Stop!" she shouted, pushing her way through the crowd that had gathered. Dhon hadn't been joking about the whole garrison seeing this. Zolk stepped back, he didn't want Urrah seeing that he had been nearby watching; besides, his supervisor was distracted, giving him a chance to sneak away. Zolk looked toward the southeast. Headhunter had a date after all, and he wasn't going to be the one that made her late. "He has had enough," Urrah said as she finally made it into the center of the circle that the onlookers had made. "I will apologize for him," Urrah announced, bowing before Dhon and exposing her neck by pulling the collar of her own personal gambeson down. It lacked the metal plates or the height of Dhon's, but the gesture was what mattered. "I am sorry for my rudeness; may you see fit to punish my savagery with your civility."

Dhon glared at Urrah, after a display like that and words spoken with such truth, she couldn't in all fairness strike Urrah down. Her glare passed over the bowing Norrus to the semi-awake Forver. "Fine, take him to Carloe, the druid can and will reverse any permanent physical damage he suffered." Dhon looked around at the faces gathered and recognized three of them. "Azbin, Frax, Gunthil, what in the stars are you still doing here? Aren't you supposed to be on patrol?" she asked, still a bit tense from the earlier confrontation. "Actually, I believe all of you have jobs to do!" Dhon shouted, growling at those who were lingering until it was just her, Urrah, and a mumbling Forver. Dhon placed Carver back in her quarters, then helped Urrah to lift Forver and carry the confused Ozar to the druid's room. There was a clap of thunder, and the sky began to darken as a heavy rain was released on the Green Wall. The first storm of spring, almost a week early.

Forver would be so angry that spring was already here, Urrah thought to herself as she placed Forver on Carloe's bed for the druid to treat.

After Carloe had told the two Ozars to leave, and had convinced Urrah that it was in Forver's best interest to be left in his care, Urrah stepped out into the downpour. The rain was so heavy that she couldn't see clearly more than twenty or so feet in front of her, and she wondered where Dhon had gone. Urrah had more than a few choice words to say to the colonel, but she would have difficulty sharing those feelings if she couldn't find her. Urrah decided to search for Ferda instead, she wanted someone to talk to. Her paws were sucked down into the mud with each step as the rain seemed to become even heavier. She could make out Forver's yurt and decided to wait out the worst of the storm in the shelter. Ferda probably wasn't back from the Branch Pens yet anyway.

As Ferda and Volg walked toward the Branch Pens, Ferda kept a watchful eye on the Ecluspe in case he tried to run or attack her. If she was honest with herself, he was so frail that she couldn't imagine him attacking her, although the running was a definite possibility. "If you run,

I will be forced to throw Havil in your back!" These had been the first words exchanged between the two of them, and so far both wished they had a better Taur to converse with.

Volg didn't have any illusions as to who Havil was, or how willing Ferda was to use the weapon, still he did notice a hint of remorse in her voice. Volg kept pace in front of her, he wasn't about to run. He knew that he couldn't outpace her given his condition, and he definitely couldn't beat her in a fight.

Volg finally broke his silence as they cut a trail through the melting snow. "Thank you for keeping that Zolk fellow from sending me to the stars." Ferda didn't respond and Volg interpreted the silence as a signal to continue. "You don't seem like the rest of the Ozars here, it is almost as though you care."

This did earn a response. "My compassion is solely for selfish reasons. I only want to improve your situation so that I can clear my conscience of any guilt," Ferda responded in a huff.

Volg chuckled. "A wise Taur doesn't snicker at kindness, no matter the motive. Also isn't good just good, no matter the rationale? Evil is always evil no matter the rationale, at least to those that label it evil."

"If you are naïve," Ferda responded, but less confrontationally than before. She had never considered being able to have a deep conversation with an Eclupse. Their pace slowed as they began to talk. "Evil will hide its true face behind good deeds. You need look no further than this commune."

Volg looked over his shoulder at her. "You think there is some good in this cursed place?"

"There was supposed to be!" Ferda responded defensively. "We were trying to help you put down roots, help you civilize, settle down. Teach you about what honestly has value to the world and what doesn't. Show you the savageness of your... " Ferda trailed off, not able to finish the last sentence.

"Of our what?" Volg replied aggressively, much more aggressively than he should have given his situation. "Of our culture, lifestyle, or perhaps the savageness of our joy, was it—" Ferda cut him off.

"Yes! Take your pick. You forced our hand; your clan wouldn't cooperate unless you were in charge. Your egos wouldn't allow you to be subjugated," Ferda growled, suddenly finding this conversation tedious.

"And who subjugated you?" Volg barked back, his hackles rising as he bared his teeth. "Who locked you up and told you that you couldn't leave? Who penned you in with your own filth, giving you scraps to eat, just enough to survive? Who took your culture from you because they said it was wrong? Who forces you to work, day and night for… this?" Volg outstretched his arms, although he didn't need the commune around him to make his point.

A voice in Ferda's mind told her he was right, but a different voice told her he had insulted her clan. *What about Erbun?* To Ferda's credit, she didn't kill Volg, although she did smack him with the cheek of her axe to get him to spin back around. "Keep marching!" she commanded the dazed Eclupse. The rest of the way to the Branch Pens was silent. Above, dark clouds started to gather. *Perfect, now I can command the weather with my moods,* Ferda grumbled.

She pushed Volg toward the circular metal platform on the forest floor that was chained to a stake. Volg gingerly stepped over the sharp spikes that poked upward from the edge of the platform. The spikes were just over a foot in height and tapered at the tips. Ferda lashed a leather strip around Volg's knees to hobble him. More than one Eclupse had been injured on the spikes by trying to jump over the brim while fettered. There was a low rumble of thunder in the distance as Ferda released the rope that held up the top of the pen. The top and barred walls slammed down roughly, fortunately for Volg it seemed that the spikes had found the openings in the metal bars and had sealed firmly. When a pen gave out, it was replaced by a new one. The problem was that a pen wasn't deemed worn out until the bottom dropped out, causing the helpless inmate to fall around thirty feet and break both of their legs or die. Sometimes both. Once Ferda was satisfied that the pen had sealed properly, by walking around it once, she began hoisting Volg back up into the branches above. Ferda ignored his concerns about the difference in her attention to detail between his earlier imprisonment and this one. *Once around was more than he deserved,* she told herself as she gave the rope another hard tug, making the top of the cage rattle as it collided with the branch.

There was a flash of lightning that cut across the black clouds, as the bolt punctured the gray veil, the rain poured forth, as though the thunderhead had been wounded. There was another boom of agony as the thunder responded to the blow.

"Pull him any harder and you will bring the pen right over the branch."

Ferda's ears rolled as far back behind her as they could, that slight chuckle to the tone, the almost excited edge. She had the forethought to wrap the rope she had used to lift the cage around its anchor before turning to face Zolk.

The older Ozar looked as though he had bustled over here, his breathing was heavy and he was swallowing excessively to try to stop from visibly panting. He was holding Headhunter and gently caressing the cheek of the weapon.

"What do you want, Zolk?" Ferda growled cautiously, her own hand quickly releasing Havil from his restraints and pulling the weapon from its loop.

"She doesn't think you are a good influence on our Mahzar," was Zolk's cryptic response. "Before you came along, Forver was a savage, he hung on to what made our clan great. Forver resisted all these new safety laws and allowances made for the weak and stupid. Then you showed up and he changed. Why do you suppose that is?"

"It is probably because I joined in a time of relative peace," Ferda responded casually. It belied the panic in her brain that screamed to just attack and get the upper hand before he assaulted her. If Zolk set the fight's tempo, she was going to be hard pressed to win; more than likely, she wouldn't. Zolk said nothing, putting his hand to his ear as though he had expected more. Ferda's temper bubbled. *Fine, I will oblige you.*

"How about because the rest of us grew? We changed over the years. You, you hang onto the past and let it feed your insanity. You cling to outdated ideas and fancy yourself an expert on what made the Ozars successful. It bothers you, doesn't it? That Forver sees the value in Urrah's and my council, and recognizes your advice as antiquated drivel."

Zolk's calm demeanor twisted into a visage of indignation. "You think Forver would miss you?" the elder threatened. "From what I saw, Forver isn't going to be around much longer anyways." *The old brute was too stubborn to let Urrah intervene,* was Headhunter's counsel and she was usually right. "Poor Ferda, no one here to protect you from me," Zolk smiled maniacally.

Ferda was so stunned by Zolk's comments that she almost hesitated, but Ferda was fearless and for one moment Zolk forgot that. Ferda matched his step, closing with him and the surprise on his face was evident. He and Ferda were muzzle to muzzle, not ten feet from where each of them had originally been standing. For a moment, Zolk thought he still had the upper hand until a knee struck his groin. His face scrunched up. Zolk was no stranger to pain, he was a veteran of countless battles, and his and Headhunter's relationship tended to be injury-inflicting. Ferda hadn't expected the psycho to drop on just one hit, but she wanted to distract him and on that account she succeeded. Ferda's head connected with Zolk's muzzle, but the veteran saw the predictable attack. Zolk moved his head back and tucked his sensitive nose so that she didn't dislocate his jaw or worse. The force was still enough to cause him to see spots. Now, Ferda moved in for her true attack, with Zolk on his heels and head down, she squatted down and jumped up, with Havil over her head.

"If he is dead, then he won't miss you!" she shouted, as gravity remembered that it had a job and yanked Ferda back down. Ferda swung down, chopping at Zolk's exposed neck and chest, using her weight to add to the impact.

Ferda let out a gasp, not able to understand what had just happened. Zolk's hand had shot up and his body had just suddenly whipped straight back into place. It was as though the old Ozar's bones were made of young spruce.

He caught my hands at the wrists, and kicked me straight back into, Ferda looked behind her, *yes into this fir. It could have been worse; I could have been kicked into a sequoia or a boulder.* She tried to reassure herself as she stood. *The cocky shit should have pressed his advantage,* she grumbled as she noticed Zolk was stretching.

At this moment, he was bending at the hips and touching his paws. "Staying limber is the trick," he said with a sigh of satisfaction. "You tried to sucker punch, well, sucker axe me. That is very rude. When you think about it, very dishonorable as well." He started doing jumping jacks. Ferda knew better than to be goaded, but he was really, really, really goading her. Ferda charged forward, this time saving her gloating for later, for after Havil had drawn blood. Once her axe tasted him, he would not let her lose; she had to believe her father was there and greater than whatever bogey possessed Headhunter.

"Should call you Ferda the Predictable," Zolk laughed as he kicked up a clod of snow and dirt toward Ferda.

She easily spun out of the way, and her tongue escaped the prison she had placed it in. "They should call you Zolk the Cheater!" she roared. Zolk had intended her to dodge, and Zolk seemed to know exactly how she would fight, moving to his left as she side-stepped to the right to avoid the debris. His head connected with hers, the blow took the strength out of her legs, and she willed herself to stay on her paws, wobbling back.

"Impressive, even on the retreat you managed to keep your axe in front of you and stand your ground." It sounded as though Zolk was honestly impressed with Ferda, or at the very least surprised.

Ferda blinked once, and then a second time. She was tempted to shake her head and try to clear her senses, but she knew that didn't really help and it would block her senses even more. Some were better than none, no matter how stunned they were. She focused her attention through her ears and her nose, and was trying to catch some sound that would clue her into Zolk's next move. To her left, her ears twitched, and she instantly hopped back, she threw out her arms as she landed, attempting to keep her balance on the slightly elevated terrain where some roots had pushed up through the ground. Zolk's swing came up empty as Headhunter chopped in a diagonal cut. He had thought Ferda would be foolish enough to simply try to duck.

She is smart enough to keep her distance while she is dazed, Headhunter chastised.

"We would have never known that unless I had tried," Zolk countered audibly. He rushed forward, hoping to still catch his opponent in a muddled condition. To his joy she was, and he tried to flank her left side as she hadn't brought her shield with her. Neither had he, but he wasn't the one being outmaneuvered. Zolk feigned another cut and made sure she heard where he stomped through the snow. Ferda's only option was to keep distance until her senses came back, her eyes already beginning to refocus. If he was cutting horizontally and she sidestepped to the left, she walked into the cut; if she went right, she was trying to outrun the cut. She could duck to avoid a slash, but if he was chopping down, that was a death sentence. She didn't know where to put her axe to block his, so her best choice was backward. She knew she was getting close to a tree because of the elevation in the terrain, still what was her other choice?

Well, I could... No, I know better. If he was chopping close to his body, I would still jump into the cut, but wasn't it better than backing up against a tree? She wisely, but also foolishly, chose the result that she felt had less unknowns, and hopped back instead of forward, right into Zolk's trap. As soon as Zolk noticed her body shift, he lunged forward, catching her with his right shoulder and ramming her into the sequoia that held the pens aloft. Ferda gasped for air, her grip released on Havil and she could barely see through the tears welling up. She was not weak, nor did she have a soft hide and pain was not foreign to her. But she couldn't fight her body's need for air or the sudden jolts of pain that shot through her nerves as her spine collided against the unforgiving tree. Zolk gave her two quick punches to make sure she was seeing stars, and backed up.

"I liked that lunging-jumping attack. What were you, five... " He looked at the distance between himself and Ferda, who was practically comatose after his last two blows. "Feet or so away? That looks closer than I felt it was, but I don't know if this old body can jump further than that without a running start." Ferda had barely moved, her head lolled from side to side once, but other than that she may already be dead. *Maybe if I took a running start, but if she doesn't regain a little bit of her senses before I attack her, then I am the only one who saw it.* Zolk noticed the rope. *Or am I?*

Volg tried to duck back before the Ozar saw his head pressed against the bars or his muzzle, the only part of his body that could stab between the prison's rods. He heard Zolk whistle a few times but decided he should still play dumb. Besides, it was deeply insulting to be called in such a manner.

"I will just drop you from your little perch!" Zolk shouted up. He noticed that Ferda's leg twitched slightly. Zolk eyed her closely to see if she was coming to.

"What do you want?" Volg shouted. He didn't snarl, but he didn't bother keeping his tone meek. Volg was pretty sure that after this beast killed the other Ozar, it was going to kill him.

Zolk looked up at the Eclupse, having pulled his focus from Ferda. By all accounts she was still unconscious, Zolk doubted that her pride would let her play dead. He kicked some snow at her just to be sure, looking back to the body to see if she reacted. She did not. Zolk looked back up.

"What do I want?" Zolk repeated, a bit at a loss.

You want him to see you submerge me in that stupid female's skull! Headhunter shouted admonishingly.

"Don't you take that tone with me, I was just caught up in making sure she stays stupefied, because if not we are going to look as dumb as she did when I kicked her." He emphasized his point by kicking another pile of snow on Ferda, a larger, more uncomfortable amount.

She isn't moving, for Mother Bear's sake, but the longer you keep this up the more likely she will wake up. Get this mangy Eclipse to pay attention to our glorious carnage. It was pretty obvious by her exasperated tone that Headhunter was not impressed with Zolk's caution.

Volg had kept watching during this odd exchange between the Ozar and his axe, at least he was pretty sure that the older Ozar was talking to his weapon. Volg didn't see anyone else about. He was sure that this Ozar was going to murder him after he was done with the female that lay crumpled at the base of the tree. Volg hated to admit how impressed he was that this old Ozar had completely obliterated his younger and clearly very experienced adversary. The same Ozar that had stood in that psycho's way when Zolk had wanted to put that same wicked-looking axe, to which he caressed and cooed, into Volg's back. Volg couldn't let them both die, but how in the Alpha Father's name was he supposed to stop this maniac? His prison tossed a bit as the rain pelted him; he had forgotten about the storm having been so engrossed in the battle. The pen groaned under his weight for a moment, and for an instant Volg thought the bottom half of the prison was going to slide out and they were both going to fall to the ground. An idea began to form in his mind.

Volg knew you didn't hold onto the pen if the bottom fell out. Xurzel and Igwulf, two Eclipse from when Volg had been a tiny cub, had learned that when their prison had broken apart. They had probably figured they would hold on and either jump away from the lower half, or wait for the Ozars to come and let them down. Either way, they hadn't cleared the spikes still attached to the bottom plate when they finally fell, and had met a probably very painful and agonizing death.

If I could make the bottom land on the savage's head, from this height it would have to knock him unconscious, perhaps even kill him. Zolk was standing near him again, trying to get his attention. Volg ducked back into the cage, trying to ball up and hoping that ignoring the shouting Ozar would help him think. *If it misses though, I will be dead. Probably by that lunatic's hands, or more accurately, axe. If I am lucky, I will die from the fall.* A ball of ice hit Volg, but he closed his eyes tightly, trying to concentrate. *What do I have to lose? Either way, I am not going to be that Ozar's next trophy. How do I get him under the cage? Or at least close enough that if it were to crash down, it hit him?*

"I swear on your precious Alpha Whelp that I will lower you and just start tormenting you until my opponent regains enough of her senses to make this fight entertaining again!"

Volg was positive that Zolk meant it, and that would guarantee that the Ozar would not be under the cage. Volg pressed his face into the bars toward Zolk, his eyes scanning, trying to find some way to coax the Ozar closer.

"I need you to bear witness to my glorious victory over this corruption in our ranks." Zolk didn't know why he needed to explain himself to the Eclipse. *It had sounded very august though.*

Volg hammered his head against the bars trying to think of a solution to his dilemma while loosening the base. He was committing to this one way or another, he was going to die but it would be on his terms either way.

"Did you not hear me over the cloudburst?" Zolk shouted, frustrated that the storm was stealing his thunder. The rain was practically a curtain, and he was having trouble making Volg out as the water pelted him in the face.

Volg watched in amazement as the Ozar took a step closer. *That is never going to work,* he told himself again, even though he just saw evidence to the contrary and he still hadn't come up with any better ideas. *All right, here goes.* "I couldn't hear you over the booms and… " he stopped for a moment. "And booms." He shrugged, not knowing what else to say.

It didn't even occur to Zolk why he could hear the Eclipse just fine but the prisoner couldn't hear him. Perhaps it was because Zolk thought he couldn't be outsmarted, or perhaps Zolk couldn't admit that his ego demanded an audience. Either way, Zolk moved closer, and began an exchange of clarification on whether the Eclipse could hear the Ozar or not. It wasn't until Volg thought the Ozar's voice was coming from beneath the pen that he stopped shouting his 'whats?' and 'huhs?'

"All right, now that you can hear me, I want you to… " Zolk began again with his earlier request for the Eclipse to watch his display of violence.

Volg ignored him and began jumping up and down violently. This, of course, caused Zolk to stop talking as he could hear the racket over the occasional crack of thunder and the battering of rain.

What is that imbecile doing? asked Headhunter as they both just stared at the display above.

"How would I know?" Zolk answered in an equally curious tone.

Ferda felt the water peppering her from under the tree, she had been kept out of the full fury of the shower by the stretching branches and fanning needles. A loud boom of thunder caused her eyes to flutter open and her leg kicked instinctively. She tried to collect her thoughts, but they were all jumbled and in a haze. A clump of snow seemed to drop on her. *Probably just from the branches,* she thought. Her whole body was wracked with pain, and she would have believed herself crippled if it hadn't been for her leg's previous reassuring kick. She thought she heard a familiar voice shouting, and then there was another larger snowy assault, still she complained neither physically nor verbally. There was a sudden flash of light as the lightning burned itself across the sky for a moment, her senses responded, and she flinched. Her memories were beginning to strain away all the muck they had become seeped in.

"Zolk," she groaned softly. She began to scan the area but all she could see was the downpour as the water clutched the Green Wall in its embrace.

Despite his and Headhunter's curiosity, Zolk managed to finish his instructions to the Eclupse and hefted his axe, seemingly walking away. In Zolk's mind, the Eclupse had told him he could hear him and with this rain, he would be lucky if the prisoner actually was able to witness this glorious moment. Headhunter was chomping at the bit to get her blade into Ferda, and Zolk was having trouble containing her passion.

"*Shhhh,* let me get a running start, it will look better that way." Zolk turned back around. "You ready?" he hollered to Volg as loud as he could. "Because here I go!" Zolk rushed forward, raising Headhunter behind his head as he counted each step.

Volg sat in the pen, banging his head against the unforgiving iron as he heard the Ozar finish his instructions. He hadn't paid any attention to the Ozar, so he had no idea what Zolk wanted him to do. His skull rang as he battered it against the metal to the rhythm of the alternating echoes of thunder and dazzling displays of lightning. *Maybe I could brain myself on the bars,* he mused cynically. The bottom of the pen groaned as it slipped slightly downward, jerking to a stop.

"No, no, no, don't stop!" Volg shouted as he had just heard Zolk announce the commencement of his performance. Volg reached up and gripped the top of the pen, he said a quick chant to the Alpha Father that he would succeed, and kicked his paws down with all his might, which was difficult given his confined space. Volg's gaunt form allowed him to curl his legs up to his chest and thrust them back down. There was a flash as another bolt criss-crossed behind Volg, he could make out the Ozar as he charged forward, he would be under him at the next step.

The nearby flare of the white cutting lines seemed to rekindle Ferda's senses and memories as everything suddenly fell back into place. "Where is Zolk?" she shouted into the raging storm, trying to stand, as just for a moment she could make out Zolk's fulminated form. His legs were bent and she recognized what he was about to do. Ferda's mind may have begun to function, but her body was stubbornly remaining inert. There was a loud squealing sound from above, as though metal was being grated against metal.

Zolk had no time to fathom what he was hearing; the sound already signaling that it was too late. Volg put all his weight into his paws, he was probably going to break something, hopefully not both legs, but he had to keep his balance when the bottom released so he didn't pitch forward or backward and impale himself. Volg was honestly hoping that he would be able to sense when the platform connected with the Ozar and spring from it. He had no idea if he could clear the platform, especially after it crashed into the Ozar.

Zolk's paws left the ground as he jumped up. The platform fell, and in less than a second the two objects hurtling toward one another collided. The Ozar's head crashed into the iron base as it dropped and Zolk crumpled into the ground below. As soon as Volg's paws felt the bottom collide with the Ozar's skull, he tried to jump clear to safety. His balance wasn't stable and was only made worse by the rain. His paws couldn't keep their traction on the slick metal surface. A conscious Ferda and an unconscious Zolk bore witness to the first flying Silverback as Volg came crashing down into the snow and dirt with an audible thud. Ferda stared on and no one moved for a moment.

"Help!" The voice startled Ferda as she looked over at the body of the Eclupse. Volg still didn't seem to be moving though. "Help!" the voice called out again, a bit stronger and a hand waved weakly as Volg managed to get an arm in the air.

Oh, thank Mother Bear! Ferda whispered, slowly forcing her body to move. It took a few minutes. Far more minutes than it should have, but she finally managed to crawl-stumble her way over to the Eclupse. "Are you hurt?" Ferda asked, as she managed to pull herself up next to Volg. She felt instantly foolish for having asked the question, given that she had such an obvious answer. She hoped her stupidity had been lost to the sounds of thunder and pelting rain.

Volg had heard the question, but had enough decency to not call attention to the fact and instead posed his own question. "Do you see my left leg? It is tingling and feels like it is on fire. As though a thousand fleas are marching along it with coals on their feet." Volg had to lay his head back down, he couldn't keep it elevated. He felt faint and his stomach told him it wanted to vomit.

Ferda carefully helped Volg roll to his back and off his left side. She was having trouble assessing the damage in the rain and only flashes of good light to inspect the injury. From what she could discern, he had fallen at an odd angle, he had probably been able to plant his right paw more firmly and hence he fell with his left side more exposed than his right. The Eclupse was lucky, he could have fallen straight back and injured his spine or cracked open his skull. Granted, he could have twisted toward his left but that would imply a level of intelligence that she wasn't willing to credit Volg with. Whether it had been skill or luck Ferda couldn't tell, but what she could see was that he had managed to avoid landing head or back first, which was a positive. The reason his leg seemed to be on fire and numb was because it was badly broken, probably in multiple places. He could thank his Alpha Whatever that none of the fractures had punctured through the skin. "You have broken your leg, severely. Honestly, it is astonishing that you are not screaming in anguish. It will start swelling soon and that will probably take your mind off the numbness and burning sensation."

"Because it will hurt a lot more!" Volg shouted. He wasn't trying to yell but he wasn't able to hold his composure any longer. Ferda had apparently given his body permission to writhe and cry in pain, and his body obviously didn't want to pass up the opportunity.

"Hush!" Ferda responded in an ironically louder tone. Embarrassed by her harsh response, she followed with, "But thank you for saving my life."

"I only did it because I knew once he was done with you, he would have come after me," Volg admitted through gritted teeth.

Ferda chuckled. "Selfish reasons, right?"

Volg's face scrunched up for a moment and then he gave her an honest laugh. "Yeah, for completely selfish reasons."

Skirmish

Azbin was the last member of the patrol who was still standing, probably the last member still alive. The Ozar stood against the three remaining Maulers; the others were definitely dead. The Ozars' axes had made sure of that detail. He was nearly two feet taller than the tallest among them and he was very insulted that all of them, all five of them, had been females. He was proud of the fact that he hadn't been numbered among the fallen, his other two companions had shamed themselves horribly by falling victim to these barbarians. They would hope they were dead when they woke up, if they had merely lost consciousness. His shield batted away the black-furred Mauler's attack as she swiped for his exposed face with her claws. She was young but powerful, and the largest of the five. He felt the breath of another one behind him, and crunched his head back into the unprepared jaws of the gray-faced one.

Dardyl fell back, her arms were exhausted. The armor these Ozars wore was a challenge to bite through, much less claw through, and this one had a bear-shit shield. Essall hit the dirt with a thump and rolled back to make sure that she wasn't caught in a follow up attack by the Ozar. She rubbed her jaw slightly, not sure if he had chipped or knocked any of her teeth loose. They were determined to take the last of these three Ozars down. They couldn't afford to let their location be discovered so there couldn't be any survivors. Cycyss' white collar was painted crimson as she lay face-first in the mud from the previous day's rain with her throat hacked open. Not three lue away, Rymmall was lying in a bloody puddle with huge wedge chops in both sides of her collarbone. The attacks had left her neck just barely attached to her spine before she fell back like a hewn tree. Jabyn was the only one seriously wounded out of the three left standing, with a deep gash in her right flank just above her hip, but fortunately below her ribs. She had managed to avoid most of the impact, but was struggling to be of much assistance against their single Ozar opponent.

Azbin squared off with the youngest of the Scouts, it was Dardyl's first mission with such a title and she wanted to wear it proudly. Rellik's fawning over Unkyss had earned her a special place in his poison-addled mind, and if he wanted that Ravis, he could have her. Dardyl still had trouble speaking because of her stiff neck muscles, but she could bite and move her head with little hindrance. Her vision was back to normal and, with a clean bill of health from Skoff, she had joined the Scouts, having been welcomed to their ranks amidst the previous night's powerful storm. Skoff had called it a sign of change and she was inclined to believe him.

Cycyss joined after we crossed through the canyon, and I have outlived her. I have even survived longer than the veteran in this fight. She tried to encourage herself, but instantly felt a pang of guilt as the thought came and went. She decided to focus her anger on the Ozar who was waving that wicked weapon of his about. She feinted forward and Azbin punched with his shield, hoping to stun her in the same way the eldest Ozar had stunned Rymmall. Dardyl had already set the fight's pace and she easily leaned back out of the way. The axe swung in behind the attacking shield, the heel and beard of the weapon were aimed at her knee, and he obviously meant to yank her leg out from under her. In an impressive display of agility and skill, Dardyl gripped the Ozar's large oval shield and planted it firmly into the ground, catching his wrist and causing him to almost drop his axe. She lunged over it, snapping at his face and raking her claws into the back of his head.

Azbin was no rookie like Gunthil and he wasn't about to let himself get his eyes clawed out or his throat ripped free. He let the shield go, it was getting in his way. The Maulers were too fast to be blocked and the chainmail shirt that the garrison wore was linked too tightly for the savages' claws to be much of a concern. Azbin used one arm to hold back the gnashing teeth, allowing Dardyl to snap down on the splint mail arm guard. He then lifted his axe to chop into the Mauler's side.

Dardyl caught the glint of the metal as it sped toward her and she quickly rolled away, snarling as the Ozar moved for his shield, flipping it back around to catch Essall in the gut with the boss at its center. After which, he pitched her over his shoulder, using the shield like a shovel to lift her up and over, her body collided with the mud with a sucking sound.

"Come on, is this the best you Maulers can do? If it is, you aren't going to win your little raid! You're like cubs with sticks and stones trying to fight a mountain!" Azbin roared in both laughter and disgust. He held his oval shield out before him, it was painted solid blue with numerous red fish across its surface. His axe, like most garrison troops' weapons, was simple and designed with a half-moon blade that was well-balanced, with an equally long toe and heel that curved back toward the haft. The beard was neither sharpened nor much more curved than the top, and the blade itself was thin, designed for chopping through flesh, not wood. Unlike Frax, Azbin had never felt the need to sink his own money into an axe if the Honcho was going to provide him with one. Now Frax's beautiful custom weapon was covered in mud and, as far as Azbin was concerned, lost. Azbin's chainmail shirt ran down past his waist and ended about mid-thigh. Both his arms and legs were covered in splint mail, which was laced to the gambeson and short trousers under the chain shirt. Like the rest of the Ozars, his paws and head remained unprotected, it being expected that they use their shields to guard these areas, hence the size of the shield. Azbin, like other Ozars, wore a thick leather belt around his hips which helped support the armor and distribute the weight evenly along his body. The Maulers had to break Frax's arm to get him to drop his shield, and Azbin chastised himself for having punched out like Frax had done.

If that Mauler was still half as quick as she was at the start of this fight, I would have ended up with a broken arm myself. With a shield crushing my throat. Azbin recalled how the one with six scars on her back, had held the large shield while her ally, that damn gray-faced one, had lunged forward, using her shoulder to barrel into Frax's elbow. Then, the one with the back scars who had held the shield lifted it and hammered down, once and then twice before Azbin had been able to dig his axe into her flank.

The brutish older one had tried to save the white-necked one from Frax's axe as she mauled poor Gunthil. That savage had felt the steel of Hacker's bit, and her neck only held on by her stubborn spine. Azbin pressed after the younger of the three remaining, the one with the scarred back was several feet away still trying to grit through the flank injury. The gray-faced one, he would have liked to let Biter have a go at her, given that she was still recovering from being flung by his shield. He was sure that this young, strong female would not allow him to simply let Biter have a nibble at the prone, gray-faced Mauler. He left Essall to try to get some air back in her lungs, swinging his axe's dangerous edge in controlled, accurate cuts.

Dardyl hustled back as the Ozar tried to close the distance between them. Her back met with the coarse bark of a large sequoia; she resisted the urge to skip to the side to keep retreating. *If I keep falling back, he will just spin around on Essall and Jabyn,* she told herself as she swallowed. The Ozar was less than a lue away. Azbin swiftly rotated his axe-wielding arm's shoulder forward, twisting his hips with the motion and anchoring his paws in the mud as he delivered what was surely a killing blow. The axe-blade sung as it cut through the air, the edge was aimed at Dardyl's collar bone, to mimic the same blow that had killed Rymmall. But Rymmall didn't have a sturdy redwood at her back. Dardyl used her better agility to outpace the swing and rolled around the trunk of the tree as Biter bit into the bark. The steel bit lodged snugly into the wood.

"Wolf-shit!" Azbin yelled as he tried to yank the weapon free.

"Rude," was Dardyl's response as she circled back around the tree. Thinking quickly, she planted one hand firmly over the shoulder of the axe, and with her other fist sent two quick jabs at the Ozar's throat.

Azbin quickly learned a flaw of the large shields. If your weapon was stuck, you couldn't bring the shield across your body to defend you without releasing your most valuable asset. The weapon. Azbin shrugged, pulling his neck down and moving his shoulder between him and the attack. Dardyl's blows missed their mark but didn't lack power. The first hit was moderately effective and connected with Azbin's right bicep, below the shoulder. The second blow was more successful as it connected powerfully with Azbin's right cheek.

Having finally closed the gap now that her target wasn't moving away from her, Jabyn clawed at Azbin's back, trying to get her own weapons under his collar and into the soft skin around his neck. The Ozar thrust his shield arm elbow behind him but didn't make an impact. Jabyn was too close to his back and her claws had finally drawn blood. Azbin let out a roar and Dardyl punched forward again, hoping that with Jabyn's distraction she could find her mark. Azbin felt the first hit; this time, it was his right cheek that took the first blow, she was getting closer. He swung his head forward at the onset of her second attack and felt Dardyl's wrist and hand bend unnaturally downward, there was a cracking sound as he broke her wrist. Her right hand instinctively dropped from the weapon's shoulder and Azbin let go of his axe for a second. His right elbow swung back and found Jabyn's injured side, sending her crumbling to the ground. As his elbow caused Jabyn to stumble back, his right hand shot forward, grabbing Dardyl's stunned face and slamming her back into the redwood, adding more red to the wood with the impact. His left hand let go of his shield and snatched up Biter, and he walloped Jabyn on the side of the skull with the butt of the weapon. With a loud clunk, then a thud, Jabyn hit the ground. Jabyn was well-trained and an extremely experienced Scout, but that meant next to nothing when getting concussed by a three-times-her-weight Ozar and his axe.

Essall screamed in horror and rage as Jabyn hit the ground and the mud splashed onto her dark coat. Azbin had lost sight of Dardyl and figured she had run off to lick her wounds, so he spun about at the sound of Essall's cry. His honey brown fur was braided around his muzzle and face. There were streaks of blood that marred his expression, from where Dardyl's claws had dug through his fur, and some droplets of crimson splashed into the dirt from under the chain shirt. His fierce brown eyes burned with rage as he let out a fearsome roar to match the primal sound that escaped Essall's lips. Essall ran forward, as did Azbin. Essall slid as she dug her claws into the slick mud, Azbin kept charging forward. Essall turned, spinning to her left toward Azbin's shield. He couldn't pass up the opportunity.

"You would think after the first time I tossed you with this, you wouldn't let me get a second chance."

Trust me, I am not, Essall thought, having seen a flaw in how the Ozars used these big, cumbersome defenses. Azbin was less than a step from her and he locked on to her for the last time before he ducked his head behind the wooden shield to keep his face protected from a counterattack.

Azbin would later explain that the impact was similar to having a rock the size of you hurled at you. Essall's paw kicked out and she yelped as her shin hit the charging Ozar's ankle; if her leg wasn't broken it would be a miracle. She had just slipped her leg under the shield and sent the charging boor face-first into a sequoia. There was a crunching sound as Azbin's muzzle broke in several places from the impact. The Ozar's body slid down the trunk of the tree until his knees folded under him, leaving him kissing the wood.

Essall was too panicked to ensure his death, the sound his face made when it hit the tree told her he was in worse shape than her allies and she wasn't losing another Scout. Especially not Jabyn.

"Jabyn! Come on, Jabyn, don't do this to me!" she demanded, trying to keep herself from sobbing.

Dardyl slowly came back to consciousness, she cried out as she tried to push herself up with her left hand and then almost passed out a second time when her fractured skull knocked against a tree at her back. Essall looked up, snarling, thinking that the Ozar had come back to life for a moment. She quickly lowered her hackles and hid her teeth as she saw Dardyl hit her head.

"Dardyl, Dardyl!" Essall called, trying to get the obviously woozy novice to focus. Dardyl opened her eyes and held up her hand to signal to Essall that she had heard her. "Can you walk?" Essall asked the slightly coherent novice. Dardyl nodded slowly, wincing when she tried to lift her head back up. Essall lifted Jabyn over her shoulders. "We need to get back to camp and see if Skoff can tend to your injuries. I will get permission to bring a Fist of Scouts back to collect the bodies, so we can send them off to the stars."

Dardyl was sure to use her right hand to get to her paws this time, she almost fell face-first into the snow the first time she bent down to pick up a clump of the cold substance for her aching head. It wouldn't be until the third attempt that she would manage to scoop up a handful. She worked hard to keep pace with Essall, but the other female moved with determination and Dardyl struggled to lift her legs with each step. Dardyl wasn't mad at Essall for the pace she was setting, Jabyn was in a terrible state. The blood had stopped dripping from her injured ear and the fur had matted along her neck and shoulder. Jabyn's side was still leaving a trail, the wound was reopened with each step that Essall was forced to take with Jabyn across her shoulders.

The Scouts had encountered the Ozars when the garrison patrol had strayed from their usual route. Neither Dardyl, Essall, or Jabyn had known why they had, and if Cycyss and Rymmall had known, then the knowledge had died with them. Skoff could possibly connect with them, but that information was not important at this moment. What was important was that for some reason the patrols had extended their search, and there was now a good chance the Mauler force would be discovered. No one really understood why Dio had not issued the order to attack yet, and many of the tribe were getting impatient with what seemed like cowardice. The Fist of Scouts had been only a short distance from the forward camp when they had crossed paths with the Ozars, seemingly by chance. The Maulers had acted first and Cycyss had quickly downed the smallest of the Ozars, but after that, things had snowballed out of control, especially when Rymmall, the group's alpha, was killed trying to defend Cycyss.

Jabyn remained unconscious as they marched back to camp. Dardyl felt responsible for Jabyn's injuries and the deaths of the other two. She would have blamed Cycyss as well, but it was poor character to accuse the dead. The three veterans hadn't wanted two rookies to join them, but the novices had been eager to go. Especially Dardyl; ever since Unkyss had started fawning over Rellik, she had felt nauseous at just the scent of them. It had been Jabyn who had vouched for them both, and what she had said made Dardyl proud. Jabyn had reminded Essall and Rymmall that Dardyl had been one of the last few standing in the game of My Skull at Terrabyss and Luna's Materimony. Now, that pride was long gone as she watched Jabyn's still form jostle about, even with Essall's care.

That was the last time Jabyn will support you, Dardyl thought to herself. By now, Dardyl was falling steadily behind Essall and was probably close to fifty lue behind her. It seemed to Dardyl that the more air she needed, the harder it was to breathe, and she hadn't bothered to pick up another clump of snow to relieve the swelling in her head. She was positive that if she bent over to scoop up another handful, she wouldn't get back up. Dardyl was beginning to feel dizzy and her muscles felt lethargic. She wove her way between two large trees, one a tall sequoia, the other was a fir who had lost the height race some time ago. Dardyl's paw caught on a large root from the redwood and she sprawled, nose-first into the mud. She put her right hand under her body and tried to push, her vision was going black, and she felt cold. She managed to flop the hand under her head to keep it out of the muddy ground, but that was the last conscious movement Dardyl made.

***

Azbin's eyes opened slowly, his whole skull hurt, and his face was grotesquely swollen. He looked a bit confused at the clearly Ozar teeth that had been sprinkled about his knees, trying to recall who they might belong to. Slowly, Azbin got to his paws, trying to remember why he had decided to canoodle with a tree. His whole body jerked with pain as he touched his lips, the sensation almost knocked him unconscious, but it did shock some memories back into place. He also realized that his bottom jaw was just hanging open. He told his mouth to stop this nonsense but there was no response.

"Mot—" he began to say but his eyes welled up and he found himself punching the tree to distract himself from how torturous that attempt to speak had been. Gingerly, he positioned his hand under his jaw but abandoned the idea of forcing it shut when the forest began to spin from the pain of just grazing his chin with a finger. Azbin figured he could deal with the discomfort of an open mouth; besides, he had to get a message to Dhon. The patrol had gone terribly off-course from their normal route in the storm that had been raging for the past twenty-four hours. There was hardly any snow left on the forest floor, besides what had taken shelter under the thickest branches. Now the floor of the Green Wall was a mud pit, at least until the sun could force its way through the clouds to bake the soil dry. The downpour had cleaned the Ozar's scent trails, and the shifting of the mud under the forceful groundwater had moved stone markers. Not to mention the gales of wind that had stripped the bark from the trees that carried the Ozar's claws marks. Their patrol had never intended on being this far northeast of Kyron. The thought occurred to Azbin that Forver would be very generous to anyone who brought him the information he now knew. Dhon might also recommend him to a different garrison if he proved to her that he was worth his weight in patrolling. He had spent his whole military career in a frontier garrison, and he wanted a job among one of the Cana garrisons. All he would have to do there would be to monitor the Silverbacks who caught Red Martyr along the River Cynwyn and farmed; the Cana communes were a lot less strict and didn't require nearly as much work on the part of the guards.

Azbin tried to roar in pain as he took his first jarring step, but that only made his pain worse, and he debated for a brief moment if impaling himself on his axe was a better way to handle his new injuries. *There is always Carloe,* he tried to encourage himself with the thought. The mere idea of the druid sent Azbin's thoughts back to the axe solution. Carloe wasn't an uneducated druid, just as far as druids went, he was very green. Supposedly, Groll could bring you back from the dead. Carloe, well, he could relieve minor wounds, but if the damage was too extreme, the patient still needed to spend time recovering and reminding their bodies how to perform even the most basic of functions. *Like eat, drink, maybe even speak,* Azbin grumbled to himself. *Why was it that the frontier always received the rookies and screw ups?* He wasn't a rookie, but he wasn't a screw up either. He had been transferred from an inner garrison when one of Bardell's cousins wanted Azbin's position. An Ozar by the name of Krell. Azbin found himself shipped out to this dump before the end of his first year of service.

Azbin noticed Biter lying in the mud, and he had to support himself on the tree trunk next to him to squat back down and pick up his weapon. He shouldered his shield, knowing how pissed Dhon would be if the Maulers attacked Kyron holding his shield. Frax's shield was broken from having smashed his windpipe and Gunthil fought with a two-handed axe like Dhon. It was beyond Azbin where Gunthil's and Frax's axes were, probably buried under the mud or tossed out into the trees and ferns. Gunthil's weapon was like his, simple and gifted by the grace of the Honcho Bardell. Frax's weapon, on the other hand, had been a work of art and Azbin knew he should return to Kyron with their weapons and armor as well, but he was in too much pain to actually care. Frax had been one of those rare soldiers that enjoyed the shitty responsibilities. He was always cheerful and far too positive for this profession. He had served in Kyron since its foundation and had planned to retire from the commune. Azbin felt a twinge of remorse; no one wanted to be a veteran of this awful place, but no one wore that title better than Frax. Gunthil, well, Gunthil was a novice and had gotten killed by a female Mauler and from the looks of it a pretty young one. *Like I said, the only Ozars out here are screw ups and rookies,* he repeated but made sure to keep it in his mind rather than try to vocalize it.

The evening fog was beginning to roll in, another sure sign that spring was here. Fortunately, Azbin wouldn't be assaulted by another spring shower as he made his way back to Kyron.

Each step brought new agony and a new curse from Azbin that he cast upon the Maulers. It was early afternoon when the Ozars and Maulers had collided in battle, but it wouldn't be until late in the night when Azbin would finally—in agony—arrive in the commune. His knees wobbling and vision spinning from exhaustion and pain, Azbin lifted his arms above his head trying to get the sentry's attention at the top of the keep, his whistle had long since vanished. It was futile as the sentry was apparently staring off to the south, trying to squint past the smoke. Azbin tried to yell out, but crumbled to his knees in sheer distress as he forgot for a moment about the condition of his mouth. He had managed to wander past the eastern opening and was now trembling, kneeling at the opposite side, on the western opening to the enclosure. The piles of shit and streams of piss from where the Eclupse dumped their filth was creating a suffocating aroma. Azbin had spent the last eight hours marching through fog and trying to keep his balance as the dew froze in the night breeze. *I am not going to pass out next to this excrement, he told himself. I barely avoided brain damage the first time; if I fall asleep next to this filth, I will wake up a dim-witted fool.* His stubbornness did little to fuel him, not after the day he'd had. He watched as the Star Flies[71] circled the night-soil, their butts flashing some strange language to one another.

I need to warn Dhon, at the very least get the sentry's attention, he told himself. *Honestly, haven't I done enough? I just need a few minutes, if I just rest for a few minutes, I will find the energy to continue to the keep.*

***

Dardyl could hear talking, but it sounded like she was in a den and the voices were coming from outside. Her whole body ached, and she wasn't sure if she was dead or alive. She recalled the Corvel attack, and wondered if the fight with the Ozars had been a dream brought on by the concoction that had been in her blood. As her consciousness became clearer, so did the voices.

"I don't care about the fire rule, I made the bear-shit fire rule! I wouldn't care if the Ozar's Mother Bear could see the fire from the heavens! I want one of the three of them awake and talking. I need to know what happened and why my Scouts were found outside of camp unconscious! One from exhaustion, one from blood loss, and the other it would seem from a head wound!"

Well, that means I wasn't having a bad dream. Dardyl tried to look around, but she couldn't shift her focus rapidly, at least not without the risk of slipping back to unconsciousness. It took her a moment to realize where she was, she had never seen this tent. The white hemp walls were painted with elaborate figures, simple and yet elegant drawings of animals from caribou to saber-tooths, and from the revered direwolf to the hated

---

71   Insects that only come out at night

grizzly. There was a stack of antlers in one corner and several makeshift stands that held paints and ripe-smelling poultices. There were different herbs hanging from cords above, which ranged from clovers to mistletoe. As she slowly rotated her head over to the other side, she noticed that Essall and Jabyn were both lying on what she assumed were similar stretchers to hers. Jabyn looked bandaged and Essall seemed to have an even breathing rhythm. She let out a sigh of relief when she saw that Jabyn, although clearly more labored, was also breathing.

"It will take a large fire to bring all three of them back to consciousness. Plus, I don't know the flows of magic yet in the Green Wall. I could say the wrong word, twist in the wrong fashion or hit myself in the wrong cadence and bring doom upon us all." A low, resonating tone hit Dardyl in familiar waves as she recognized Skoff's voice.

"That is not how magic works, both you and I know that." The first voice responded flatly. "Now get one of them awake with your magic so we can get some answers. There is a Fist out searching, but even if they discover where the Scouts were attacked and recover the bodies, we will still only be able to guess at what happened. I need facts. I need to know what happened from their own mouths." The first comment had caught Dardyl by surprise and had made her second guess who the first voice was. By the time the first speaker had finished talking, Dardyl knew it was Dio.

How do you know how magic works? she wondered curiously. A curiosity that Skoff didn't seem to share.

"All right, but if we all die, it will be on your head; if the world wilts away to nothing, be you warned," Skoff growled, taking a step into his tent. He turned back to Dio when the Alpha didn't join him. "Oh no, no, no, you want this done, you are going to help," the shaman said sternly to Dio, waiting for the Alpha to join him.

Dardyl's tail wagged weakly as she saw the two of them enter, she forced herself up onto an elbow but before she could speak, the room began to circle her and she became dazed again, slipping from consciousness.

"Grab her!" Dio shouted. To his surprise, his words were echoed by a deep voice at his side. Skoff and he met each other's gaze as neither one moved. Dardyl had some luck still with her, as her slumped form was too tired to fully pull her from the stretcher.

It took Dio and Skoff some time to get the fire pit dug and to place the stones carefully to barricade the fire circle. Skoff was not excited about this.

Ever since his little excursion to the shores of the Berg Maker, he had been doubly vigilant when channeling his magic through such a big conduit. The voice, had returned the night of Terrabyss and Luna's Materimony. His rabbit's foot was still around his neck after both instances, so he was sure that a phantom hadn't managed to get its claws into him. Both times, it had been nothing but jumbled words and terrifying sounds, but it had struck fear into Skoff's very core. Dio's rule about no fires when they had made it through the Ice Kraggs had been a blessing. *But who knows, perhaps the long hiatus has solved the problem?* Skoff wanted to cut out his tongue; if that is what positivity tasted like, he wanted no more of it.

They chose Dardyl because she had at least briefly become conscious, so they assumed that she would be the easiest to rouse since she only recently fainted again. Dardyl heard voices for the second time that night, but they were foreign to her. They chanted her name over and over, repeating themselves in a haunting chorus. She recognized a voice that gave shape, incorporeal but detailed. A long-dead memory fought its way past the barriers that a much younger Dardyl had managed to lock it behind. With a battering ram of force, it resurfaced to the forefront of her mind. This was her mother, not the mother she had remembered during her youth and young adulthood, but she knew the female Mauler was her blood mother. The memory unfurled, revealing the horrors that a pup had tried to forget. This female before her had died of some strange cough, shortly after giving birth to her only litter. Her father had isolated her and her siblings from their mother's illness, and had asked a neighbor if she would suckle the young. The neighbor was also a new mother, from the Barque pack. Her father had never again spoken her mother's name, but he had lovingly held onto her memory and nightly told the cubs of her beauty. Speaking her name made her illness too real, he preferred to remember her visage. The recollection continued to reveal itself as the illusions around her became the invocation. She could again see the day that Kiltra, the female who had suckled Dardyl and her siblings, pointed an accusing finger at her father. At Kiltra's paws were three dead pups.

"Your foul breed gave my lineage the same illness that left your mate a husk!" Kiltra was screaming at the top of her lungs.

Dardyl's blood father spit on the corpses and snarled his response, "I have told you a million times your pups fell ill of fever, we both know there was no cough from your den."

406

The insult was too much and both Kiltra and Hown, her mate, attacked Dardyl's father, the father who had sacrificed dying with his mate in order to be there for her and her siblings.

There was an old voice which echoed from behind Dardyl, it was then that Dardyl realized she was standing. They were in a land of darkness, of smoke clouds and trailing mists. *Am I in the stars?* she wondered as she gazed upon the elder, Phylyss. It had been because of this female that Dardyl had truly survived. Dardyl watched as Phylyss reminded her daughter Kiltra of the loss that all Maulers had endured, and demanded that "if they must satisfy their honor, they must also preserve the pack." It would be true that whoever they chose to spare would never truly know their pack's name, at least not until they joined them in the stars. Dardyl wondered if today she would know. But Phylyss would not accept a daughter who ignored her commands, so Dardyl had grown up a Barque. She had long buried the memory of her survival, purely out of her guilt at being the one that was chosen from her litter to live. She felt so much guilt, she could barely remember her siblings. She had been the alpha, that was all that had mattered. Kiltra and Hown weren't cruel to her; in fact, she had always felt as though she was one of the Barque. She was now their only pup, and they soon came to treat her like their own, also having long buried the memory of her orphaning.

"Why do you keep me locked away?" the specter asked in a wounded tone. "Do you care more for those who kidnapped you than those who truly loved you?"

Dardyl was confused, this was not Phylyss. *What in the Alpha Father's name is this? Where am I? This isn't the heavens, but if it isn't there, then where is it?* "Stop! This is an illusion," she responded weakly, feeling as though she was the only one lying.

***

"What is happening, Skoff?" Dio shouted nervously as he watched as the whole camp seemed to be wiped clean of all color. He looked around, he could see but all was dark, the day had given over to an unnatural night.

"I-I don't know!" Skoff stammered, equally nervous. Pulling the wolf bone mask off as he looked around at the sudden change. He hadn't even finished his second rotation around the fire. A sickly feeling crept up his throat, he could take a pretty good guess as to what was happening, a familiar chill running along his spine. *Told you this was not a good idea,* Skoff mumbled to himself.

The two of them watched in stunned amazement as a tendril of smoke slowly reached from the fire and lifted Dardyl vertically into the haze. She slowly spun upward, higher and higher into the wisps of smoke.

"Is it a phantom?" Dio asked, his tail pointing straight out and his ears lowering timidly as Dardyl's body became suspended above the flames.

It definitely wasn't a phantom that Grimmis had ever educated Skoff about, the dead were not known for playing with their victims. Much less performing supernatural phenomena like this, phantoms liked to be subtle in their approach. They didn't want to return to the endless nothing, neglected and forgotten, it was better to be stealthy and unobserved.

"No, I don't think so," was Skoff's expert opinion.

"Well, at least get her down, she is not responding to anything I try!" Dio shouted frantically. The camp was beginning to gather, having noticed the absence of color and the suspended body of Dardyl.

Skoff did catch that comment but didn't have time to mull it over beyond *What have you been trying?* "*Um,* okay... " There was a pulse of energy as Skoff started to explain what he would need. The shaman went silent, he couldn't move. *Bear-shit!* He couldn't speak. This was not good, this was bad, and Skoff had no idea what it was.

***

"Let me embrace you, my child, don't shun me a second time." Phylyss had shifted back, revealing Dardyl's true mother as she opened her arms. "There is so much of your life, of your ancestors you don't know." Dardyl didn't know why she was trying to resist; it could be some aberration, but she didn't think phantoms were so kind and gentle.

Still, something warned Dardyl that this was not a situation to let down her guard in. "Stop it!" Dardyl screamed. "You aren't real, this is some kind of a trick! You are a phantom trying to consume my soul!"

"Oh, child," the voice cooed as for a moment it lacked all Silverback or Mauler features, becoming formless. "Do you not see me? Is my form not pleasing to you?"

Dardyl looked about as the body seemed to vanish into vapor, she saw no phantoms lurking. A mist began to build from around her paws as familiar laughter, Kiltra and Hown's laughter, echoed around her. The mist slowly took shape, becoming an indistinguishable but humanoid form.

"Why can't I see the real you?" Dardyl asked cautiously, raising her arms and taking a defensive stance.

"Typical of my creation," came the response, "you were always so violent." The voice sounded far away, but it whispered in her ear. It had the melody of Kiltra but the resonance of Hown, yet it held the weight of Phylyss' age. "Wise though, wise enough to not trust any supernatural experience to be positive." The voice laughed. Dardyl wasn't sure if the laugh was just honestly contagious or if it was the familiarity in the tone, but she found her tail wagging.

She reached back, grabbing her tail. "You haven't answered my question. I don't like having to repeat myself."

"Puradean!" the voice swore with an unfamiliar word. "You really are brave; I am so proud. I hate repeating myself as well. Isn't it funny how we share that?"

Dardyl was becoming annoyed at this being's gall to claim that it had made her and that they were somehow similar. It was a lunatic if it thought it was going to convince her that it had done what she knew was the work of the Alpha Father.

"It is because you do not truly know me," the smokey form puffed; somehow, she saw sorrow in its expressionless face, or perhaps its words painted an image in her mind.

She felt heartache and sorrow beyond her fortitude. "Alpha Father," she whispered, barely able to contain her emotions. She wanted to cry and rage at the same time, she felt so much grief, so many losses.

"You cannot see what you do not know," the voice bemoaned. Its lament brought a quivering response from Dardyl.

"That—that doesn't make sense," she tried to say without sobbing. It took multiple tries, but she finally managed to posit the statement.

"Oh, not true," the voice soothed. Dardyl seemed to be relieved of the torture she felt and she took a deep breath. "Your knowledge is limited and therefore your sight is limited." The form became amorphous again and seemed to envelop her in a warm embrace. "Allow me to show you. Imagine what I know if I have waited patiently for this long for my creation to return to me. Imagine what I could teach you. Imagine what splendor

I can give you."

Dardyl peered out before her, she saw nothing. "There is nothing but emptiness and the gray that seems to be you," she growled, starting to feel like she was in danger, some inner voice screaming for her to fight.

"That cannot be," the beguiling voice dripped its honeyed words into her mind. It had not lost its compassion or grace despite her frustration, and a touch of guilt skipped across her heart. "I can see it clearly. I see a chance at redemption, a chance to redeem your pride."

Dardyl flailed her arms to make the smoke waft away. "What do you know of my pride?" she snarled as the image of Jabyn's labored breathing flashed before her eyes.

"I know that it aches, and I know that it was badly bruised at the hands of that Ozar brute." The silken words caressed her ears. "I know that you brought your friends into their doom. Your pride was wounded because he nuzzled another, and so you killed your friends. I can understand why, that Unkyss is handsome." The voice chuckled but sympathized in the same breath. "You think the shaman is going to help you earn Unkyss' love, isn't he the brother of Rellik? Do you think that Dio is going to allow you a second chance when he learns the truth? That it was because of the impulsive novices that the Ozars now know where his precious camp is. My dear, I think you give him far too much credit. I can offer you that second chance, you just need to reach out and grab it. It hangs there before you."

Dardyl found herself again staring into the void. There was nothing there, but she wanted there to be. The voice was right, it had been the novices' actions that had led to this blunder. Now Dardyl was the only one left alive to take responsibility for that decision. She wanted to make it right and she knew the voice was correct about how Dio would react. She would be lucky if she was allowed to stay a Scout after this. *More likely I will be labeled a Lone Wolf!* Her eyes began to water as the thought entered her mind.

"I don't see this opportunity." Her voice cracked as she felt a hammer blow of despair crush her. "It was my fault and I just want to make it right!" Dardyl's shoulders were trembling as she burst into tears. "I didn't mean to," she repeated over and over.

"*Sh, sh, sh,* my girl, you don't need to cry. You are right about not being able to see how to fix it and about whose fault it was, but that is why I am here." The smoke again embraced the kneeling, sobbing Mauler.

"I have the solutions; I can provide you with your desires." A tendril of smoke gently pulled her hands away from her eyes. "You have to let me give them to you, I can't give what isn't asked for." Dardyl stared back into a face of empty gray as it shimmered and she could see Kiltra, Hown, and Phylyss. The painful truth comfortably reburied deep in her psyche.

"That is just a taste," the voice cooed seductively. "You know, you know deep down how to accept my offer, just tell me you want me to solve your problems and I will. You will have your pride again."

"I... " Dardyl hesitated for just a moment, her inner voice tried to shout out a warning but seemed to be choked by smoke. "I want you to solve my problems. I want my pride back."

***

"Throw something at her! Use your spells to get her down! Find a tree and jump from it! I don't care how you do it, just get her down before her whole body goes up in flames!" Dio shouted as smoke had begun to rise and twist from under Dardyl's fur. By now, everyone in the main camp and even some Maulers from the middle and rear camps had begun to gather around. The whole tribe, excluding the Fist that had already left, were now within sight of the spectacle. They had been released from the silence and paralysis when the smoke had begun to appear.

Skoff felt as though more time had passed then they were aware of, but it was little more than a hunch. He looked about frantically. "I need my sigil stones. I have a flat, smooth gray stone that gets darker toward the center. It has a wind sigil that I can use to ground targets. I made it after... " Dio was already moving for the tent before Skoff had finished and hadn't heard what the sigil looked like. The Alpha came back out, holding the stone and running toward Skoff. The shaman didn't feel it was the right time to ask Dio how he had known which stone it was, given that he had several that faded to a black center. Sigils were not something that anyone could read, they revealed themselves to those who had the ability to read them. *There will be time for that after I get Dardyl down,* he told himself, turning back to her hovering form.

"Hurry up, Skoff," Dio commanded. "She is sm—" Skoff cut the Alpha off. If he needed someone to state the obvious, he would find a pup.

"Smoking. I know, now shut up and let me concentrate," was the booming command he gave Dio, turning his attention back toward Dardyl. Skoff's face transformed from one of determination into an expression of pure awe as he and all those gathered watched a large, wolf-like face begin to take shape in the smoke as it plumed from Dardyl's fur and collected above her head.

"Alpha Father," Skoff breathed in bewilderment.

An unsettling grin spread across the maw of the smoke wolf. "I am so thrilled to be among you," it howled into the night sky. "Where is the one that leads you?" it asked, shifting its gaze downward to all those gathered. All fingers pointed to Dio and the disembodied head followed their gestures.

Dio swallowed nervously, giving the Silverback salute that the Maulers had kept alive. "I am the Alpha," he stated nervously.

The eyes of the large smoke head narrowed as it inspected Dio. It didn't speak for what felt like an eternity to the spectators. Then it began to laugh, its laughter was maniacal and Skoff swore he heard a familiar rhythm to the sound.

"I do not have time for your games!" the voice suddenly shifted to one of pure rage. "Where is the one I saw in the fire, the one that was given my name?" Dio watched, but to his relief and the smoking wolf head's frustration, no one moved. Dio had been humiliated when this thing had laughed at him. He had never heard such a condescending sound and it caused his very subtle temper to flare for a moment as his hackles raised. He was smart enough to not falsely claim to be the Silverback that this thing or its messenger had tried to communicate with. He also wasn't about to verbally reveal his frustration to such an obviously powerful creature, or perhaps a mage who was using their conduit for some prank.

The supernatural is nothing more than phantoms, and there is no phantom like this according to Skoff. The thought brought Dio some comfort and worked better than his own assurances to help ease his fear. The fear still persisted, it was too deeply rooted and the logic too frail to truly silence it.

"Do you know the price that was paid so that I could have this brief moment? A price you will not easily pay again," the voice sneered, obviously upset. "Do you think that reaching through that which divides us is simple? It has taken me eons to make this one moment happen, and you fools cannot remember who I reached out to?" The smoking eyes fixed themselves on Skoff. "Surely you know, spirit talker?" Skoff gave a nervous and timid shrug. "Where is the one I marked?" The smoke head roared into the night as its form began to shift into something even more terrifying, its fury growing. A forked tongue flicked from between the canines and the ears seemed to elongate into spiraling horns that reached upward. "Where…?" Its snarling and gnashing were suddenly silenced as Dardyl stopped spinning in place. Slowly, the color began to creep back into the camp as the moon and stars began to cast what little illumination they could through the canopy and clouds. Dio watched in silence as the smoke was lifted into a gust of wind. The Alpha realized that even the breeze had been hushed during the ordeal. Skoff gasped and others soon joined, their cries brought Dio's focus back to above the fire where Dardyl's body began to flake. Her paw and some of her muzzle were the first to be picked up by the breeze, and then she fell in a heap of ash atop the fire.

***

"You said you would fix my problems, you said you had the answer!" Dardyl shouted into the emptiness as the smoke vanished. Her body felt warm, but she was shivering. "Why can't I wake up? I want to go home," she sobbed.

"I did!" an impatient voice echoed. It was vile and no longer tried to be soothing or comforting. "And look what good it did me!"

"But why am I still here, why didn't I return?" Dardyl asked, confused.

"You're dead, it is the answer to all you mortals' problems." The voice snickered treacherously. "Perhaps, I can still find some use for you."

Dardyl remembered nothing that followed, all there was, was emptiness. The ominous voice cackled her into a dreamless state of both death and life, trapped in He-Lah as the first captured soul.

The Howl

Arvin held the bucket with both hands and kept his elbows locked to try to steady the container and its gross contents. His fur was dark gray, much darker than the rest of his pack, but speckled with white. He had his mother's bright blue eyes and, according to her, she used to be as dark as him when she was a pup.

"Solgar, wait for me!" Arvin shouted in his tiny voice, he started jogging after his brother but quickly slowed as soon as some of the bucket's waste splashed out and hit his fingers, some almost hitting his paws. The morning fog of spring had come to settle over Kyron and waited for the sun to beat it back into a retreat. The dew was icy and made for a slick foundation, which wasn't helping matters as Arvin tried to step cautiously while still trying to catch up to his brother.

"Bear-shit!" Arvin swore as he felt the filth touch his fur.

"Mother's not going to like that you said that," Solgar's voice came from the mist in front of Arvin. The pup was so startled that he almost dropped the bucket, and more slop sprinkled out as he sucked in and hustled his paws out of the way of the droplets.

"You almost made me drop my bucket," Arvin scolded his brother as Solgar walked into view out of the fog with an empty bucket. "How are you done already? Did you actually take your waste to the pile? You know Mother and Father get upset if you try to dump it anywhere besides where it belongs," Arvin said smugly as he tried to nimbly step past his sibling.

Solgar had opened his eyes first, which according to him made him older than Arvin. Their mother denied this vehemently, but Solgar could be very persuasive. Solgar also looked more like their father, he had a striking white coat sprinkled with flecks of gray down his back and stomach. He was taller than Arvin, which only seemed to add credence to his early argument about age, and he had his father's dark blue, sapphire-like eyes.

"I am the oldest so, of course, I am done already," was Solgar's cocky response. "Also, I am going to tell Mother what you said, and she will give me your field mouse as punishment."

Arvin was a bit concerned; it was true that when Solgar had tried to take his breakfast a few weeks back—by telling their mother that Arvin had said it was okay—she hadn't fallen for the ruse. Although, given that Arvin had just cursed, she might see fit to punish him in such a way.

"What—what did you hear? Arvin asked nervously, but trying to act as though he hadn't said anything damning. Arvin was walking backward now as was Solgar, both of them keeping their eyes on one another as the gap widened.

"I heard what you said," Solgar said confidently.

"Yeah? If you did, you would know what I said instead of trying to trick me to say it again," Arvin responded with an upturned nose but not fully turning back around, causing him to do an odd shuffling sidestep.

"I heard you say bear-shit," Solgar called after his brother as he vanished into the fog and they lost sight of one another.

"Nah-uh! You just swore now!" Arvin shouted after his brother. He was tempted to just drop his bucket and run back to the small shack that served as their home. It consisted of one room with a small, dug out fire pit in a corner. The building was windowless, but that didn't stop it from being well ventilated and illuminated, as long as the sun or even moon and stars were out. There wasn't much material to prevent either the wind or the light from entering their home, which made it very cold in the winters. The family often had to stay huddled together, as long as they weren't away working, to keep warm. Recently, Dhon and Travic had seen fit to outfit the shacks with old hide blankets when the garrison had been restocked. They had a small table, essentially just a few planks of wood, that their father had managed to smuggle over from one of the lumber packs, Arvin thought it might have been Odan who helped him. Arvin missed the Kreal pack. His parents took turns hiding the table in the little mats that were stuffed with leaves and pine needles that the Ozars had given them to sleep on. Arvin and Solgar didn't mind sleeping on the mats so much, but their parents complained often, telling them they would understand when they were older. The two of them doubted that.

Arvin knew better than to just run after his brother, he would have to trust that his mother saw through Solgar's lies. *I know Solgar isn't lying, but Mother doesn't,* and with that logic he took a deep breath and almost retched, remembering how close he was to the waste dump. *Just a little further and you can go back home and eat breakfast,* he told himself as he tried to keep from salivating as he thought of the cooked meat. His mother might have even seasoned it with some of the herbs that she sometimes managed to smuggle from the keep. The cooks frequently did and it made the long winter more tolerable, especially when the adults snuck those skins that smelt sour into the pens, everyone had warm nights then. Hild—Arvin and Solgar's mother—worked in the kitchen as a cook, preparing meals for the Ozar garrison throughout the year. She had a talent for picking out spices and seasonings and mixing bitter and sweet, sour and savory. A talent that had earned her and her pack a slight reprieve from the garrison, especially Dhon.

There was a quick breeze and it ushered some of the fog onward, giving Arvin a clearer view of the piles of feces; he shuddered as he always did when he saw them. He walked quickly up, tossing the bucket and looking away as the contents flew from the container into the morning air. As he shifted his focus from where the waste was being flung, his sharp eyes caught sight of a glint from the first few rays of the sun that had come to defeat the fog. Arvin saw, face-first behind the waste piles, an Ozar sprawled out on the icy dirt. Obviously, the lookout hadn't noticed him hidden behind the filth, and Arvin could tell from the labored breathing that the Ozar was injured, perhaps fatally. He could even make out the disfigured muzzle of the Ozar, the damage was substantial enough that Arvin could plainly see it from this distance. The Ozar was definitely in pain, perhaps worse.

Arvin's first instinct was to get the sentry's attention so that the garrison could send someone to help the Ozar. A thought occurred to him, *But the Ozar cage us, beat us, and kill us.* He paused for a moment. *Wasn't this the just reward for such abuse?* Arvin studied the Ozar, he knew him. Not personally, and this one never oversaw the fields or kitchens. Still, he was an Ozar and he knew that Ozars were cruel. There was also a good chance that the Ozars might think that his pack or their pen had something to do with this particular Ozar's wounds. Arvin didn't have long to think, he still needed to eat his mouse. After breakfast, he and Solgar would be escorted out to the fields now that most of the snow had melted, and begin weeding and removing rocks from the ground to prepare the soil for planting. They would be doing that until sundown, no matter the weather, unless the fog got too dense for the Herder to observe them. Another thought suddenly

416

occurred to Arvin, *What if the garrison finds the Ozar outside my enclosure and blames us anyway?* Begrudgingly, his conscience gave him a little reminder. *I should probably get him help because it is the right thing to do,* he finally told himself. *What about your father?* Another voice in his mind chimed. *When is he going to come home? The Ozars took him away over a week ago.*

"Often the right choice is the choice you like the least." Arvin heard his father's wisdom, and nodded to himself. He had to be smart about who he told. He couldn't have his mother snatched away as well.

With his mind made up, Arvin ran back, still being cautious about the slick ice that coated the floor but now unburdened by the contents of the bucket. As he approached the thin canvas sheet that served as a door, he peered around at the other shacks to see if any buckets had been put out. Seeing none, he was pretty confident that no one else was going to dump their loads out back and he would probably be the only one aware of the Ozar. He sighed with the weight of his new responsibility, and he quickly rubbed his hands and paws in the closest snow drift before scurrying inside. He could smell the cooked meal. It was plain. His mother hadn't been in her usual borrowing mood since their father had been 'hired.'

"Did Solgar eat my mouse? Whatever he told you was a lie. In fact, he… " Arvin stopped mid-sentence as he noticed his brother's facial expression telling him to shut his mouth. Arvin quickly noted that Solgar had a mouth full of mouse, and was holding his and only his spit.

Hild cocked her head curiously at Arvin. "What were you going to say, Arvy?" she asked, holding his spit just out of reach.

Solgar snickered when he heard "Arvy," but quickly fell silent as Hild and also Arvin shot him glares, mainly because of his mother rather than his brother.

"He—he… " Arvin stuttered. *I can't believe I am about to do this, especially after he just laughed.* "He might deserve it, being that he is such a good brother." Arvin wagged his tail as convincingly as possible. Solgar almost choked, but managed an equally convincing wag.

Hild laughed, handing him his breakfast. "I would have thought after the last time he tried to steal your breakfast you would never want to freely give it to him."

"I wouldn't!" Arvin said firmly, sitting across from Solgar.

Hild looked at the two of them, confused, but turned around to grab her spit. Their father's meal was still cooking over the fire. Hild was convinced that Volg would be escorted into the pen at any moment, and it would be nice if there was a meal waiting for him.

Solgar smacked his brother on the head before he could dodge and while he was blowing on the still smoking meal. "You idiot, just a moment ago you burst in here saying that she should give it to me. But after what you just said, we obviously look like we were up to something," Solgar reminded his brother in a harsh whisper.

Arvin wanted to shout back that Solgar hadn't seen the Ozar, only he had, so 'they' weren't up to anything. Fortunately, he was still trying to blow on his breakfast so he could enjoy it, giving him a chance to realize what Solgar was referring to. He sighed dramatically, but saw his brother's logic.

"I mean, I wouldn't give it to him but if you had, I guess I would have understood," Arvin tried to explain to his mother.

"Okay, I may remember that," Hild responded, sitting cross-legged across from both of them.

"But don't actually give it" – *puff, puff* – "to him," Arvin responded with a mouth full of his still hot breakfast.

"Arvin, don't talk with your mouth full." His mother scolded, she only used his proper name when she was serious.

He quickly shut his mouth and nodded, which only caused Solgar to laugh with a mouthful of food and start coughing again. Hild swatted his back to force him to stop choking.

"Solgar, I am not always going to be around to save you from your gluttony." Both pups screwed up their faces in confusion. "You put so much food in your mouth you look like a Fillany with nuts in their cheeks," she explained. This earned a giggle from Arvin, which earned him another of his mother's glares and he quickly fell silent. "The two of you are going to kill each other with your eating habits." She sighed. Hild slowly ate her meal, picking the meat off delicately with her claws.

Solgar was the first to finish his mouse, it took him only four bites. A fact he would probably be boasting about for the rest of the day. As usual when Arvin saw his mother's refined way of eating, he began to lick at his meal, trying to savor what little he had left.

"Hurry up," Solgar groaned as he waited for Arvin to finish. "Travic is going to be here any minute and I don't like making the other pups wait while you eat your meal like a girl." His mother punched him firmly in the arm. "Ow!" Solgar yelped as he looked over at her. "Sorry," he said, rubbing his arm, embarrassed. "It wasn't that hard. It just surprised me," he grumbled.

"Well, next time, I will make sure to hit you harder," she teased.

"It hurt enough," Solgar responded frantically.

"Good, there is nothing wrong with taking your time eating and doing so properly. You might even stop yourself choking so much if you ate like Arvin." Hild's stern tone let both her sons know she was serious about the lesson.

"They haven't even shouted for us to 'get our mangy asses out here!' yet," Arvin did his best to sound like the Ozars.

"Arvin!" his mother scolded harshly, giving his muzzle a light tap. Punching an arm was one thing, but she wasn't about to actually hit her son's sensitive nose with any significant force. "Don't you talk like them," she instructed.

Arvin wiggled his nose slightly. "Sorry," he said bashfully. Arvin thought about the Ozar he saw. "Mama, what would you do if you saw an Ozar who was badly injured?"

Hild gave her cub a curious look, which was matched by Solgar's tilted head and uplifted eyebrows. "Why do you ask?" Hild asked, honestly curious.

"Just—just wanted to know," Arvin stammered nervously.

"That's easy, get a rock and smash his head in," announced Solgar.

Hild quickly looked over at him. "First, don't ever say something that cruel again, you never ever harm someone you find injured. There is absolutely no honor to that. Do you understand me, Solgar?" she asked, forcing him to look her in the eyes. He nodded. "Good," she continued. "Now, both of you listen to this second part. You find a way to help, Arvin, even your enemy deserves a chance at life. If they want to throw it away later by trying to harm you and you are threatened by them, then defend yourself, but do not go and kill just to kill. That is the lowest form of being, a senseless savage." Solgar and Arvin nodded and Hild was sure given the position of their ears and the looks on their faces that they had given her their undivided attention. "Did you see something you want to tell me, Arvy?" she asked, turning to face him.

Arvin wasn't sure how to respond. *Is it lying if I know something, but*

I don't want to tell her? Arvin was struck with a novel idea and stuffed his mouth with the last of his mouse, it was hot, and it was delicious. He gave his mother an innocent shrug pointing to his now full mouth. Hild shrugged back in response and crossed her arms, waiting for him to swallow. Arvin suddenly realized a flaw in his genius plan.

"Get your lazy mangy asses out here!" came the usual morning cry. Arvin swallowed.

"Lazy, that is what I forgot!" Arvin announced, hoping it would divert his mother's attention from her question, and it did. The sheer randomness of these two often floored her. "We need to go," Arvin hollered back to his brother as he leapt to his paws and bolted for the door, Solgar charging after him.

Hild watched them go, she would be called to the keep after the breakfast call to help clean since she wasn't scheduled to cook this week. Her specialty was fish anyway, and until the Red Martyr hauls came in, that wouldn't be served. She breathed a quick chant to the Alpha Father to keep her boys safe and finished up her meal before she was shuffled off to work as well. She missed Volg, he would have gone with the boys like the other males. The Ozars had snatched him up a week ago now, while the boys had been asleep. She was grateful they were deep sleepers and hadn't been woken up by their father's abduction. She knew this wasn't an unusual experience and honestly during the winter when the keep seemed to need the most maintenance, the Eclupse could be pressed into work at any moment. Volg had been gone for a long time and no other Eclupse or Ozar would talk about whether or not they had seen him. She hadn't been too concerned when it had been just a few days, but a whole week was rare and probably bad.

As the pups ran up to the gate of the enclosure, they were greeted by Travic, a Mahuer and probably the friendliest Ozar here. He was the Herder and was so named because it was his job to make sure that Eclupse got from one point to another, not so much safe but accounted for. Travic was young and had only joined Kyron in the last few years, he had been a ray of kindness in this place and many of the Eclupse found him tolerable. His unique relationship with the Eclupse allowed him to easily hold a modicum of respect from them, which made them more tolerant of his commands. This had allowed Dhon to garrison more soldiers since she only needed one Herder, which was rare for a frontier commune. This was one of the reasons that Kyron was one of the strongest border communes. It wasn't simply the number of garrison troops, but the amount of trained and drilled troops that the colonel could put into action that made Kyron so formidable. Herders had some combat training, but they didn't go through the same battlefield drills as the usual garrison troops, their training was focused on developing other talents better suited for overseeing the Silverbacks.

Travic's punishments were also not excessive. His lashes never numbered more than the promised amount and they 'drew only enough blood to make you learn your lesson.' This was at least how many of the Eclupse explained his punishments. The other garrison troops, especially those that had been here longer than the others, viewed the Herders, and Travic in particular, as an unnecessary and humiliating display of compassion for the Silverbacks. Dhon, on the other hand, understood the advantage of Travic's style and under her strict discipline the garrison had mostly learned to respect Travic and his position. Those who didn't were sent on the patrols; out far away from the garrison they could complain all they wanted. The Eclupse enjoyed working for Travic not only because of his moderation with punishment but because he encouraged a new practice in the Ozar community, called Lounging[72]. The Eclupse claimed—in hushed groups—that the Silverbacks had always practiced this custom, but all were thankful when the practice was finally introduced officially.

If Arvin should talk to anyone, it was Travic, he was sure of that fact. "Sir, Travic," Arvin said, walking up to the Ozar and standing at attention. A practice that Travic employed, which not all Herders did, was treating the Eclupse more like military grunts than slaves. He found that if he acted as their drill instructor and they as his troops, then they responded better than in a master and slave dynamic.

"Yes, cub?" Travic responded with a serious tone, saluting Arvin by tapping his sternum twice as the Ozar grunts were trained to do. It was a gesture that tended to fall from practice once you were out in the field or stationed at these frontier locations. Travic, however, felt that the custom should be reinforced. Salutes taught grunts deference to their superiors and respect for their peers' achievements. He felt these advantages reinforced his positive interactions with the Eclupse.

Travic towered over the cubs and was taller than any of the Eclupse, as were most of the Mahuer. He was not exceptionally tall, standing at nearly

72   Afternoon break or nap

seven and a half feet, and he weighed just under four hundred pounds. His fur was the color of pine nuts and was lighter toward his head and seemed to get darker close to his paws. He had an axe on one hip, typical troop design but, per his request, the blade had a wider wedge shape than usual. He found that the weight helped get through an opponent's tough shield. Travic made sure that his axe was always covered even around the Eclupse, another factor the Silverbacks respected him for. True power doesn't need to advertise. He also carried a shield, but it was not the large oval ones of the patrols or other troops. His was tear-drop shaped and smaller, it easily hung from his back like many of the round shields carried by the new arrivals several weeks back. His cheerful light-brown, almost gold-colored eyes were streaked with green that only showed in the sun. He wore a chest plate and gambeson similar to Dhon, plainer and looser in style and had no splint mail over his sleeves or shins, unlike the other troops. On his chest plate was a green shepherd's crook that contrasted brightly against the steel armor. Travic was proud of the symbol and he vigilantly maintained it. He spent the end of each week cleaning off the emblem and repainting the image with vivid and fresh paint on the polished surface.

The Herders had been introduced ten years ago by the Honchos of local Campo when the pup population had plummeted, especially among the frontier communes. It had been such a significant decrease that many of the Honchos feared that their workforce would soon go extinct. The response was the founding of the Herders, Ozars taught more about the Silverback culture and lifestyle so that they could perhaps relate with those they supervised. They weren't to be completely tolerant because that would be absurd, but perhaps just a bit more sympathetic. Even with these measures, the population of many frontier communes was dwindling quickly. Eventually, the Honchos undertook a whole overhaul of the frontier commands, and so Travic had replaced Reker, Kyron's former Herder. That had been five years previously, when it had been discovered that Reker was entering the pens and burying disobedient Eclupse in waste. The last Travic had heard, Reker had passed away in a drunken stupor somewhere north of Ursyss. As far as he was concerned, it was good riddance to a vivid smear that had been marked across the Herders' name. Even other garrison troops like Azbin and Frax who had served alongside Reker thought he had gone too far.

"Just kill the beasts," had been Azbin's words. Frax's were not much different. In the past five years, especially in Kyron, the pup population had boomed. In Kyron alone, the number of pups had more than quadrupled, from three to thirteen. Arvin and Solgar were among these pups, making Travic feel especially connected to them.

Travic squatted down, clipping a leather collar around Arvin's neck and attaching a thin chain to it. The Herder stayed at eye level with Arvin, he knew none of the Eclupse under his charge were going to run or attack him. His eyes grew wider and wider as Arvin leaned in and whispered what he had seen in Travic's ear.

***

Forver felt like ripping his teeth out as he stared at the map, the more he looked at the details the more his head started to spin. For the past day, his head hadn't stopped spinning. He had woken up in a panic in that wolf-shit druid's bed. The whole place had smelt like tonics and the sickeningly sweet smell of overripe fruit or rotten meat. Forver was sure that the disgusting concoction he was supposed to drink at morning and night wasn't helping. It smelt like onions and sweet potato, and he wanted to retch just thinking about it. Carloe had assured him it wasn't made with those ingredients; if he could be believed, he hadn't even known what a sweet potato was. The ingredients that Carloe had listed were so absurd that Forver was positive the druid was joking about what was in the potion. When he heard 'flea's stomach,' he was confident that Carloe was just having a laugh.

How could Dhon have sucker punched me like that? Who did she think she was dealing with? It had been a stupid door!

The star-staring druid had just scratched some sigils into the wood and smacked the pieces loudly, and they had simply fallen back into place. The door was perfectly fine, well, aside from a couple of odd-looking symbols cut into the wood.

Once I have dealt with those Maulers, I will make her shave her hindquarters as an apology. Actually, as he thought about it, that was too simple a punishment. "No, I will put Zolk on her, that will make her sorry," he said to the map. "And Urrah," he growled. Urrah was going to wish she had never put these doubts in his head. "How dare she patronize me, constantly asking if I need help up and down the ladder. I know you are planning something, Urrah," he muttered to himself.

The only commanders he could still fully trust to stand beside him in this fight were Zolk and Ferda, neither of whom were anywhere to be found.

Maybe I should just go out to the Branch Pens and get that Eclupse down, and march out to where he showed us like Urrah suggested. Forver slammed his fist down on the table; the impact sent pain all through his body as the force jostled his injured head and face.

"Mother Bear! Curse her for making me doubt myself!"

Spring was already here, which gave him weeks—if he was lucky—to subdue the Maulers who were just hiding in the woods like cowards. The constant downpours weren't going to make finding them easy, they would have had better luck in the melting snow. The Eclupse hanging from the cage was the only one of the spies that had returned. Forver was going to let Zolk have his fun with the Eclupse spies' mates and pups once his biggest problem was solved. All Forver had to do was find the Maulers. He stared again at the map, hoping for some inspiration, Urrah's words echoing in his head.

"STARS!" Forver screamed, he had never been so frustrated in his life.

Forver heard the doors to the keep slam open and a number of the Eclupse cooks shouting in confusion. He wondered if it was going to be Dhon, finally here to apologize for her brashness, or perhaps it was Urrah here to admit what a coward she was to suggest leaving Kyron. Forver watched the hatch in the floor leading down to the keep's first floor. It was flung open and the Herder, Travic, hustled up the rungs. He quickly shut the hatch behind him, stepping on it. Forver wasn't sure if that was a good sign or a bad one. Had Dhon sent her Herder to kill him, or to beg for his forgiveness? If it was the latter, she was going to find that sending a palgus wasn't going to cut it. If it was the former, this Herder was in for one hell intense fight. Forver's hand dropped to Ol'Grim on the table and his fingers tightened around the haft as he growled, "What do you want?"

Travic hesitated for a second, he wasn't intimidated he just didn't understand why he had been greeted with so much hostility. He honestly hadn't known what Forver had done to piss off the colonel, but he was sure the Norrus deserved it.

"I am not looking for a fight," Travic said in a gentle but steady tone, motioning to Ol'Grim as Forver held her aloft.

"Well, then say what you have to say and get out of here, or you will have found a fight!" Forver growled impatiently at the Herder, he didn't bother to lower his axe.

Travic wondered if Forver really wished to have his hide tanned twice in the same number of days but decided to deliver the message as ordered. "One of our patrol members is in the druid's quarters, being healed back to consciousness. He has claw marks in his shoulder and along his head, we think it was probably Maulers."

Forver nearly shoved him back to try to get the hatch to the ladder open. "Move! I must speak with this Ozar!" Forver said frantically, it was like trying to shove a rooted sequoia, Travic stood his ground. He knew that Azbin was coming to Forver, but didn't feel the need to inform the arrogant Norrus. Besides, it did boost his ego to have Forver pushing against him and not budge.

As soon as Travic had Arvin lead him behind the enclosure, he had ordered a random guard to put the pups back in their pens. Travic couldn't say he recognized the soldier, but he had been in a hurry. The Ozar he had instructed to handle the pups had seemed short for a Mahuer and had only his axe and no shield. He was walking around a bit dazed, but that wasn't too unusual for the night guard. This Ozar could sacrifice some sleep to get the cubs taken care of while Travic took the body to Carloe. Travic hadn't noticed the blood caked into the fur along the Ozar's head, specifically a Norrus head. He hadn't noticed the faces of the pups as a few recognized the monster. Travic was too rushed to pay attention and handed the leashes to the Ozar, gathering up Azbin and running off at a full sprint for the druid's quarters.

Once Carloe had assured Travic that Azbin would recover and that he would be conscious within an hour at most, the Herder had gone in search of Dhon. She always wore her armor now, and kept Carver on hand since her tussle with Forver. She wasn't so concerned about the militia that Forver had brought, more that no one had seen either Zolk or Ferda since she had fought with Forver. When Travic came knocking roughly on her door, she shouted her well-rehearsed warning. "If you want another beating, I will give it to you, or if you are here on behalf of that bigot, I will gladly send you to the druid half-conscious." Dhon's hands tightened on the carved grip of her axe, waiting for a response or for the door to be kicked in.

"Commander, it is Travic," he began, and before he had finished his explanation she had the door open and rushed him inside to finish his story.

After which, she had sent him straight here. "This may be our opportunity to be rid of this Norrus," she had told Travic and proceeded to instruct him to wait with Forver until Azbin was conscious. Then, she would bring Azbin with her and the four of them could have a private meeting. Forver had been allowed to have one of his generals at the meeting, but since he couldn't find Ferda or Zolk, he opted to proceed with the meeting alone. He still didn't trust Urrah.

It had taken practically the whole hour, but Azbin was finally coherent and Forver had chosen to pace the second floor of the keep during this time. At first, Travic found this amusing, but it soon lost its novelty and Travic found himself reading old garrison reports to distract himself. When Dhon and Azbin finally showed up, Azbin couldn't talk clearly due to the damage to his muzzle and Carloe's limited abilities. This problem wasn't helped by the fact that his mouth was bound shut by a strong leather cord, and Azbin found himself wishing the druid hadn't tied it so tight. But Carloe had insisted it needed to be tight if Azbin wanted the bones to set. The damn thing was so uncomfortable and there was a bow right on the top of his nose and always in his vision. As long as the keep remained silent and there was no ambient noise on the second floor, about half of what Azbin said could be understood.

The conversation was dragging on now, as Azbin had been forced to write down everything that had happened. Forever had lost all patience with trying to understand him. Azbin was already upset with Dhon for the lecture he had received about how he should have brought back the other weapons and armor. Especially since now the enemy could use them in the attack.

How bad could it be? he thought. *So what if two of them have axes? And like any of them could fit into Ozar armor. My face was smashed, she's lucky I made it back here at all.*

Despite Forver's earlier impatience, he at least seemed to appreciate the news, he was nothing but compliments and gratitude.

Dhon could learn from this Ozar, he knows how to show appreciation, Azbin thought.

Forver felt sympathy to some degree for Azbin, he had woken up in the same terrible place with the same horrid druid staring down over him. Forver thought Groll was eccentric, but Groll was downright conventional compared to Carloe. Like most druids, he didn't seem to bathe, or somehow encouraged lichen and mushrooms to grow in and from his fur. It gave a putrid green color to the druid's coat, a color that was enough to make most Ozars assume he was sick. He also wore some odd articles of clothing; today, for example, when Azbin had come to, the druid had been in a small—almost too small—loincloth, his scrotum barely covered. He was also wearing a woolen vest, dyed a variety of browns or perhaps extremely stained. Carloe, like most druids, was a Norrus; it seemed that this tribe had the most natural talent for the arcane arts although there had been a few Mahuer with the skill. As far as the Ozar knew, no Hax had ever shown any talent in magic, but they were an isolated tribe. It was pretty apparent that Carloe was a novice because his black fur was still somewhat visible and not yet hidden under the collage of green and brown that other druids cultivated. The druid obviously braided his own stomach and chest fur, and no one besides a druid would know if this was a common practice. It made Carloe easy to hear coming, since the beads added to the braids rattled as he moved along. Carloe always had a bag full of different items marked with a variety of sigils, and his prized instrument was a hand-sized bowl made of cedar. It had different sigils that Carloe could activate with a controlled amount of his own blood, depending on what he wanted or needed to cast. This item was for desperate measures but much safer than random slashes or carving sigils into your own flesh.

Forver wondered if Azbin had been startled back from the stars the same way he had. Forver had heard strange sounds, whistling, roaring, and cooing that had seemed to emanate from all about him. His vision had been blurred but he had been able to vaguely distinguish a large container, probably a skin that sounded as though it was full of liquid. Forver had thought, *I am going to drown if he tries to make me drink that whole thing.* But then suddenly he had sat straight up, alert and full of energy. The feeling had only lasted a few moments and Forver still wondered if he could get Carloe to give him some of the concoction he had been forced to smell that awoke him. He was sure if he went to Carloe's quarters he would be able to smell if Azbin's concoction had been the same, the aroma had filled the whole room long after the effects had worn off.

Azbin stared at Forver, Dhon, and Travic as he sat on the second floor, with the others surrounding him. He didn't understand why they couldn't have met in a more easily accessible area. His ears were still ringing from when Carloe had shouted, "Arise!" Following this, Carloe had smacked

Azbin in the side of the face repeatedly. A fact that Azbin was also still upset about, given his injuries and that he had already been conscious from the ointment that Carloe had put under his nose. The druid probably had just wanted him out of his quarters.

The secluded nut. Could've just asked me to leave, Azbin thought as he listened to Forver and Dhon argue. It was beyond his understanding why the colonel was waiting. Azbin had pointed out exactly where he had been attacked. *For Mother Bear's sake, they killed Frax, and, and Gundryl... Gungil... Gunthil, that was it. They had killed both Frax and Gunthil!*

"If they are marching this way, then we will simply cut them off!" Forver shouted at Dhon. He was pacing and stomping loudly with each step, Forver didn't care how much it made his head hurt.

"If they march around us, then what are we going to do? We have no idea the path they intend to take," Dhon argued sensibly. "Besides, if they are marching for us, we are better positioned if we stay here behind our fortifications." To her credit, Dhon was being very patient with Forver, who was having a real tantrum. "We also have no idea if the conflict between my patrol and theirs will force them to move. Azbin's survival with one against three may have made them reconsider the validity of this assault. They may even retreat back whence they came."

That is stupidly optimistic, Azbin thought. He was proof of their superiority on the battlefield when compared to these savages. Three Maulers hadn't been able to take him down. Granted, he hadn't been able to take them down either. A fact that he had been sure to leave out. Most of the injuries had been his own doing anyway, no sense in giving those females credit. The patrol had been only eight hours to the northwest of Kyron when they had been hit. He had described that in his report. A report that was right in front of them. Azbin had written down how the scouting group had seemed relaxed and surprised at the sight of them. That was proof that the Maulers hadn't been expecting them; the Maulers thought they were safe. Those savages would only have acted surprised if they had believed they were in a safe area or near their reinforcements. Yet here they were, debating what should be done. At least, Forver wanted to get out there and punish the barbarians.

"How in the stars are they going to get around us? Supposedly there are over a hundred of them, according to that spy. Your Ozars were hit in the northwest, what more evidence do you need for their location?" Forver was beside himself with rage. He had stopped pacing because of the pain to his skull, a pain that he vividly knew had been dealt by the very Ozar now standing in his way of redemption.

"I don't trust them, either of them," Dhon finally admitted. She turned to Azbin. "I don't doubt your wish to kill these Maulers, nor do I think you are trying to lead us into a trap. Your report clearly says that you got turned around in the storm. Given your severe injuries, you may have just assumed you came from the northwest because you entered on the western side of Kyron. Forver, your spy could have been captured and persuaded to give us false information. None of the other spies have returned, which either means they care less about their pack than gaining freedom or more likely they were all captured and killed except the one who was sent here to feed us lies. You are so focused on your revenge you don't see all the traps in between you and your goal." The colonel turned back to Forver. She didn't see Azbin's face twist with rage, even with the pain. But Forver did.

Travic also managed to see the roar growing on Azbin's healing face. Both he and Azbin made eye contact. Travic was second only to the colonel. The Honchos believed that the Herders needed greater authority than the average garrison soldier and so had bestowed on them a command. Nothing official like lieutenant or captain, but it was a fact that Herders held power in the Communes. Azbin should have lowered his eyes, and the fact that he didn't salute Travic when they made eye contact was, officially, enough for the Herder to have the patrol member lashed.

"Is there a problem?" Travic asked Azbin sternly.

"No," Azbin said, shaking his head from side to side sarcastically.

"Then lower your eyes, grunt, or I may get the idea you are challenging me," Travic answered snidely. He wished Azbin would blatantly disrespect him in front of Dhon; the veterans had not responded well to his replacement of Reker. They may not have condoned what he did, but his victims had only been Eclupse. It may have been easier if he and Dhon didn't see eye to eye on so many things and if the garrison felt like he was more on their side, but he honestly couldn't be. He had no love for the Eclupse, but there needed to be a measure of civility enforced within the commune, and Dhon provided that.

Azbin slowly lowered his eyes, and Travic figured that was good enough. No one in the frontier still saluted. Forver and Dhon had stopped arguing for a moment, Dhon looked between her soldiers. "You both okay?"

"Sir," nodded Travic, quickly saluting his commander, neither of them saw Azbin and Forver exchange disgusted looks.

Between Travic and Carloe, Azbin felt as though he was at the end of his patience. When Dhon had fetched him after he had been healed, if you could call it that, the druid had stepped outside of his room with them. Azbin had tried to ask if he were coming with them, surprised that Carloe was leaving his precious isolation. Carloe had faced him, blown a raspberry in his face and said, "I don't want to talk with bossy bear, I just need to replace what you and bossy bear used." Then the druid had skipped to the western exit, singing some song about mushrooms in the mud.

Mother Bear, I hate this place, Azbin thought, noticing Forver's gesture as Azbin rolled his eyes. Azbin wasn't stupid, he knew what it meant when someone rubbed their thumb and fingers together. He would love some money, especially if it earned him some friendship with the popular Forver, maybe some patronage from the Yukon. Azbin didn't care if the popularity was among Norrus, who was he to judge when it came to friends? It wasn't as though he was the best of one.

"The only reason you have this position is because of me!" Forver shouted, once he was sure that Azbin had seen his signal. He didn't even stutter or hesitate. It couldn't be denied that Forver had a talent when it came to maintaining his tirades. "The only reason you are a colonel is because you are attached to the Yukon name!"

Dhon tried to keep herself from laughing but failed, and Azbin heard a second raspberry blown that day. "You can't seriously believe that," she finally managed to say. "The reason I maintain my position is because for the past five years, Kyron has steadily increased in production of both wood and crops, enough for us, and excess to supply Ursyss. It is also because Kyron has not suffered a revolt since Travic and I were placed in these positions. A feat that perhaps one or two other communes, and certainly no frontier communes, can boast about. You know what I think is going to happen if one of us reports to the Honcho? I think Bardell will send his fury down on you, especially after he learns how much of our resources your little excursion has consumed. Not to mention when I inform him that we have over a handful of dead Eclupse because your man Zolk can't keep his axe sheathed. Forver, I wanted to help you, but your ego doesn't allow for anyone to aid you."

"What do you know of ego?" Forver replied, foaming at the mouth a bit. *I am too close, too star-falling close to let another wolf-shit Mahuer prevent me from establishing the Yukon legacy.* Ol'Grim still sat in front of him. *Obviously, Dhon has become confident since sucker punching me.* He had to be smart, he had to control his temper a bit. First, he had to make sure that no reinforcements could get to her. Forver was positive he could pay off Azbin, but Travic was another story.

"A lot," replied Dhon smoothly. "It would seem a lot more than you," she finished bluntly.

"It is funny you should say that. I believe that you know a lot about ego. I think that your ego is driving you to do something as stupid as keep your troops locked up here while the Maulers run about unchallenged! They murder your patrol, and you do what? Huddle up in fear?" With each sentence, Forver took a step closer to Dhon, his voice rising with each punctuation.

Azbin hadn't realized this was what Forver had meant to buy from him. Was he supposed to attack now? He quickly put the honey dipper back into the small barrel that he had been licking from. Carloe said no solid foods for at least a week. *Worst druid ever,* Azbin thought to himself as he brought his focus back to the dispute.

Travic also watched, unsure of what was going on. He was no longer leaning against the wall and was standing with a confused look on his face.

"You want to do this again, elder?" Dhon asked, thumping Carver's pommel into the boards at her paws.

"Do what?" Forver tried to say innocently. "I am not the one calling for my soldiers to come back me up because I don't know how to use words instead of fists." It was an odd insult for Forver to use, he was always the first to use his fists. Forver seemed to even have trouble saying it, his own tongue becoming confused on the first attempt.

Dhon almost laughed, but this time she wasn't as amused and found her mirth much easier to contain. "Oh, I don't need them to reinforce me. You are going to need them to help carry you out of here when Urrah comes to your rescue. You are a damsel in distress," she intentionally used the metaphor. Forver hated having his masculinity challenged, like most of the old guard. He threw tactics and self-control to the wind, yanking the sheath off Ol'Grim and running at Dhon with a savage roar.

***

431

Terrabyss could hardly believe where he was standing. He could hardly believe the events of the past day. First, Numa, Unkyss, Rellik, Brutyss, and himself had been sent to search for a battlefield where some Scouts were ambushed, then he had returned to the forward camp later that night to see Dio talking with that same Eclupse spy from a few days earlier. Skoff had just finished applying a splint to the Eclupse's obviously broken leg, and had simply walked past Terrabyss with a solemn expression. He had later heard Skoff explain to Numa that Dardyl had passed away from her wounds, and they had sent her to the Alpha Father just before the Fist had arrived back at the camp.

Numa had been furious when she had seen the condition of her Scouts. Especially when she had learned that both Rymmall and Cycyss had been killed. When she had learned about Dardyl's death, she had cursed the Ozars five times by five times. Now she was moving to the south with four Fists to lead an assault on the rear of the commune. Skoff hadn't told Terrabyss how the Eclupse had arrived in camp, and Dio's only response was that he was full of surprises. Perhaps the double agent had escaped this Forver, and if he had, then this was going to be a quick battle. Anyone who that Eclupse could escape from was not going to put up a tough fight. Dio still wanted to go about the assault tactically, hence Numa was going south accompanied by Luna, and the stupid commands he had issued to Terrabyss before they had lined up on the edge of the clearing. Before them was Kyron, before them was glory, before them was home. Terrabyss and his troops hid in the shadows, reminding him of the two years he had spent as a Watcher.

Jabyn and Essall had both regained consciousness and Essall now ran with Numa, but Jabyn's hip had been badly damaged by the axe blow. Skoff wasn't sure that even his skills in magic could completely heal the wound. "There is a chance she will recover," he had told Numa and Essall. Both females knew that when Skoff didn't foresee your doom, you were probably doomed. It would have been more comforting if he had said that Jabyn would never walk again. Jabyn could take comfort that she would live, but everyone knew that she wouldn't recover enough to maintain her position as a Scout. Dio had still honored her by leaving her in charge of the camp guard, a single Fist of mostly retired Watcher and Scout troops. Dio had taken a Fist with him and Skoff, a good several hundred lue back from the front line. From here, Skoff's magic was supposed to keep Dio in contact with the main force.

Terrabyss looked from right to left to make sure the Maulers were lining up adjacent to him. The morning mist had been defeated and the dew was now thawed by the sun's warmth. A light steam rose from the ferns as Terrabyss recalled the remarks about the smoking wolf head that had talked to the pack. No one would tell him what it had wanted and everyone seemed to believe that it had been the druid's magic from Kyron. As far as he was concerned, that was logical; how was he to know how druid magic worked? He didn't even understand how his brother's magic worked.

Terrabyss felt it was odd that after a half-moon of sitting in one place, Dio had suddenly decided to attack when the druid had goaded him, but he wasn't going to sneer at the opportunity. He had been itching for this moment since Dio had proposed taking them back to the Green Wall. He had distracted himself easily enough in the busy moon before their arrival, but the last half-moon of waiting had been more painful than any wound he had ever suffered. For a brief instant, Terrabyss remembered the odd dream that plagued him the night of his Materimony. He shook his head, freeing the memory from his mind. That was weird, he admitted to himself.

"Terrabyss," a voice whispered harshly, pulling him from the thought. He looked up and noticed Unkyss, Rellik, Brutyss, and Maxyss had gathered around for one last review of their orders. Terrabyss would be positioned at the spear point, usually his unit would hit first but because of Dio's plan he was to strike last. Unkyss and Rellik were to assault the west entrance, while Brutyss and Maxyss assaulted the east entrance. Once those units had hit, Terrabyss would attack the north wall. As soon as the invasion forces heard Terrabyss' distinct howl, the forward troops were supposed to retreat slowly, drawing the Ozars out of Kyron. The Maulers were sure that the Ozars wouldn't be able to differentiate between his howl and the cacophony of howls that the front lines would be vocalizing. In this way, Numa and her troops could scale the rear fortifications with either no or little resistance.

"It is each of your jobs to pull your troops back when you hear me," Terrabyss' captains nodded their understanding. Each one of them touched their foreheads to one another.

"See you at the end, or in the stars," they repeated to one another before they split to their designated sides.

Maxyss and Brutyss walked off to Terrabyss' left to prepare their troops for the assault. "You have lived through a lot of fights. Do you have any tips for me?" Brutyss asked the senior as they trotted toward their line.

Maxyss thought for a moment. "Kill them, and don't let them kill you." Then, he sprinted to the far flank where he was to lead the wing of this division

Helpful, Brutyss thought to himself as he stopped halfway down the line. After Maxyss had punched through the commune's defenses, Brutyss would follow with the rest of the troops for support.

"You know you are holding that wrong," Rellik said to Unkyss as they ran to their positions. Unkyss was stationed at the wing and Rellik was tasked with bringing in the reinforcements. "You don't hold that high up the handle. See, look at my hand," she instructed, forcing Unkyss to stop for a moment to look at his axe. "See where I am holding it, near the end of the handle, not right under the blade."

"Aren't you supposed to protect your fingers behind this curving part?" Unkyss moved his hand along the beard of the two-handed axe.

"If you hold it up there, what are you going to do with the rest of that handle?" Rellik motioned to the almost arm-length of wood below Unkyss' grip.

Unkyss shrugged. "I thought I might hit someone with it if they tried to creep up behind me. Are you sure this isn't right? If I hold it where you tell me, it feels extremely top heavy."

"Because it is two-handed; mine isn't, that is why I only use one hand," Rellik responded, a bit concerned. "Are you sure you have recovered enough from the Corvel attack?"

"I am fine," Unkyss growled, "and I am pretty sure I know how to use a weapon." With that, he secured the axe as much as possible on his back and jogged down to the end of the line.

Rellik sighed. At least I am supporting the arrogant fool. She liked her axe, it was beautiful and extremely well-crafted. It had a white oak handle from the Warm Wood, and the throat had a hide grip that was bound with leather cord which had been dyed green. The axe head itself was single-edged, but it had a slightly hooked spike protruding from the back. It had a sharp toe but a flattened heel, and the beard was razor sharp. Rellik gave her weapon a few quick swings. Yeah, she really liked it. Plus, the name wasn't bad. Hew, or Hewy according to her. Unkyss had taken the time to rename his axe as well. He had called it Dummy, because the name on it was Chopper.

"Anyone that needs the instructions on their weapon is stupid and shouldn't even own the weapon," had been his exact words. Her troop gave her a confused look as she realized she had laughed out loud at the thought.

"Eyes front," she growled, "we will be going any instant and you need to be ready, pups." She wasn't sure if the last part was necessary, but she had been caught up in the moment. No one seemed to object, at least not visibly or audibly. Maybe this will be my thing, Rellik the Responsible. That didn't sound good and she would need to work on it.

Terrabyss took five deep breaths for good luck as his captains got into position. He was a bit nervous; unlike with the Corm raid, he felt the weight of this conflict. If they won, they would be home again and free. If they lost, they may still be home but bound, a fate he doubted he could tolerate. He gritted his teeth, finding new determination in his stubbornness and threw back his head, letting out the loudest howl he could. The sound ripped through the early morning of Kyron like a bolt of lightning. The whole northern boundary of the commune began to echo the haunting howl, Mauler after Mauler adding to the chorus. Soon, the whole forest was trumpeting, the howl seemed to shake the very earth from where it was emitted. Silence followed. For one brief moment, the Green Wall was wreathed in a memory, an old memory, of a time when the Silverbacks had roamed her woods, singing to the sky over every victory and defeat. The animals, plants, and wind itself were captivated in a frightened moment of ominous silence. The Maulers rushed on Kyron.

The two flanks smashed into the two entrances. The sentry almost pitched himself over the railing at the top floor of the keep trying to get to the bugle, as the wave of black fur and yellow eyes broke the trees. Frantically, the Ozar pressed his lips to the instrument and blew as hard as he could, he had to call in all the patrols and alert the whole garrison. Their lives depended on his reaction and his ability to sound the alarm.

Forver saw the brief hesitation as Dhon looked over to Travic, who had the same confused expression on his face. Travic's expression changed from confusion to horror, as Dhon registered nothing beyond the howl and collapsed to the wooden floor. Her blood seeped through the planks and Ol'Grim was sticking out the side of her neck, having been wedged in by Forver's blow. The bit had become lodged in her spine and caused

Forver to lose his grip on the weapon when she fell.

"Kill those Maulers!" he screamed in rage, planting his paw on Dhon's shoulder and tugging his axe loose with a sickening squelch.

Attack!

Ferda shuffled into camp the morning before the assault. She had helped Volg back to the Mauler encampment, or as close as she felt that she could safely carry him, and now she meant to return to Ursyss. Forver could fight his wolf-shit war without her; she was tired of this place. Tired of the truths it held, tired of the questions it generated, and tired most of all of Zolk and Forver. Ferda stepped rapidly across Kyron in the gloom of the morning mist and rising sun. She went toward the eastern half of the commune, where all of the access troops were forced to stay in their pitch tents, hoping that Forver wasn't in his yurt. Ferda had been staying in a pitch tent since her little excursion during Zolk's brutalities and had enjoyed being among her troops and away from the keep. She bumped into another Ozar as he shuffled for the western half of the commune and she quickly lowered her head, trying to be inconspicuous. She was pretty sure Forver was looking for her again, since she hadn't been here much at all lately and had been gone again all night. A commotion was beginning near the Eclupse pen on the western side, but she had no interest in what was going on. She was glad when the other Norrus seemed to move away from her and rush for the commotion.

Probably on some errand for Forver, she thought curtly and turned back to her tent. She had pitched it in the middle of the troops, as was customary for the commanders so that they could be easily accessible to all their soldiers. It had been pretty well-established that the best way to achieve this was by being centralized. She looked around quickly to be sure no one was watching her, which was one of the disadvantages of this design. When she was satisfied that she wasn't being observed, Ferda dipped into the tent and began packing her things as rapidly as possible.

This won't take me long, and hopefully whatever commotion is going on by the pen will keep the garrison distracted.

"What are you doing?" Ferda heard Urrah's cheerful voice from behind her, she glanced over her shoulder and could see the Ozar's head poking through her tent flap. Urrah smiled. "Looks like you are trying to desert again." The motherly Ozar was carrying two plates with eggs, pine nuts, and some dried meat. She sat on the ground, pointedly handing Ferda one of the plates and started eating.

"Deserting implies that I am part of a military unit. I am not, we are mercenaries at best and hired thugs at worst," Ferda growled. She turned back to her packing, trying to ignore the food even though her stomach was screaming for it and her mouth watered at the sight of the eggs. "If you were smart, you would leave before the Honcho finds out you were here as well."

"I can't," Urrah replied flatly, "and you shouldn't. Now eat slowly and let's talk about it."

"Do you know what Zolk tried to do?" Ferda spun around, which was hard in the small tent. She managed to catch the front pole before it toppled over. "He tried to kill me, Urrah."

Urrah's face changed for a moment from a smile to a scowl. "Well, that is a problem that can be solved without you leaving."

"That isn't why I am leaving," Ferda said, turning back around and grabbing her shield.

"I tried to find you all day yesterday. Did you know that after our meeting, Forver got in a fight with Dhon? She almost killed him," Urrah said with a quivering voice. Ferda turned around, confused. She had never seen Urrah like this, not even when she lost Kevkel.

At first, Ferda had the impulse to say that she wished Dhon had just killed Forver, it would have done them all a favor. Wisely, she pushed that thought aside and instead responded, "I am sorry. I hadn't realized how much you cared about Forver." She personally didn't see it, and she would kill Forver before she let Urrah fall any deeper in his clutches. She sat down on her bed roll, finally taking the offered plate, and digging in, much to her stomach's approval. She realized that she hadn't eaten since yesterday afternoon, and was grateful to Urrah for thinking of her.

Urrah's face twisted back into a grin as she held back a giggle, giving a slight snort. "Stars no, Ferda! Mother Bear strike me down if I ever love him. I wanted someone to talk to because I didn't know what to do. I did end up trying to help him, although he is determined to shun my assistance. It hurts his pride, I guess. I don't know, I just wanted to talk to someone about what had happened between Dhon and Forver. I don't know who

I am madder at, Forver or Dhon," Urrah finally admitted. "Just wanted your opinion, I guess."

Ferda was shocked. "My opinion?" *I am half your age. What do I know compared to you?* Ferda thought to herself. "Well, did he deserve it? I guess I would have started with that question." Urrah lifted her eyebrows and smirked. "Well, if he deserved it, then why are you mad at Dhon?"

Urrah laughed. "Well, now I am not so confused over the matter. I had a day to pace the commune and a night to sleep on it. Now I am here to gloat that I saw Forver get his hide tanned by Dhon and you didn't. I think even Zolk was there for a bit." Urrah noticed the scowl on Ferda's face when she said the name, and remembered her earlier comment. "We can kill him together."

Ferda almost dropped the now-empty plate; she wasn't sure if this Urrah was an illusion. "Did you just… " she began, before Urrah answered her with a simple nod.

"I can tolerate a lot; I won't tolerate him lifting an axe to you. You are one of the good ones." She gave Ferda a motherly smile. Ferda couldn't help but feel her fur rise as she got goosebumps, and she would have blushed if it wasn't for her well-groomed face.

"I still think you shouldn't leave, but I won't stop you," Urrah finally said, as she could see that Ferda was fidgeting nervously.

"But I think I need to," Ferda responded softly. "Make sure Forver comes back alive at least so he can keep paying me," she said with a smile as she got to her paws, handing Urrah the plate and preparing to drop the tent.

Urrah smiled. "Well, that is a pretty good reason and I guess for that alone I can make sure he doesn't get himself killed."

As the two of them left the tent, Urrah couldn't resist any longer. "What did you do with his body?" she whispered into Ferda's ear.

Ferda turned to look at her, almost headbutting Urrah in her haste. "What, whose body?" she asked, honestly confused.

Urrah leaned back, a little surprised. "I thought by your silence when I made the offer, I thought you meant you had taken care of it when he attacked you."

"Why would you think that? You know how good he is with that axe. After our skirmish, I know I can't beat him one on one." Ferda wasn't ready to admit how she was saved to her hero.

"Because no one has seen Zolk since our little meeting with the Eclupse,"

Urrah responded, obviously perplexed. "If you didn't kill him, where do you think he is?"

"He could be dead," Ferda admitted. She began to recount the events of the night before. Making sure to tell only the amount of truth she wanted Urrah to hear. She and Volg hadn't checked the body, she had assumed he was dead; it had been a hard blow from the iron platform. But she had seen Ozars survive worse. "Hence the caution when I entered the commune, I didn't want Zolk to see me." She and Volg had watched as a fire sprung up in the Maulers' camp and the color vanished from the world. They were too far to hear what was said, but at one moment they lost the ability to move. After that, Ferda had told Volg he was close enough to get their attention, he could hobble the last forty or so feet to the camp. These facts she kept to herself.

Urrah looked a little surprised. "You helped a Silverback because his cage luckily smashed in Zolk's skull? You didn't just put him in a new pen?"

When Urrah put it like that, it made Ferda feel foolish that she had carried this Eclipse for a whole day over her shoulder like a cub, until she had left him to go the last measly forty feet. True, she should have just put him in a different pen, or taken him to the druid, but he had saved her life and it felt like the right thing to do to save his in return. Ferda continued to let Urrah believe that she had just let him go though.

A howl exploded to the north of Kyron. Ferda and Urrah exchanged curious glances. The bugle from atop the keep echoed through the commune and the forest nearby. "Maulers!" came the cry from either side of Kyron as the Ozars who guarded the entrances were suddenly flooded by a torrent of black fur, slashing claws and gnashing teeth.

Ferda stopped rolling up her tent. "Don't," was all she said to Urrah, but she knew that they weren't getting out of here unless they fought.

Urrah smiled. "Come on, Ferda the Fearless, maybe we can make them surrender," she said as she pulled Lopper from the leather loop and swung her shield over her shoulder in front of her, moving to support the eastern side.

Ferda threw her tent on the ground, frustrated. "One good act and you are damned to repeat them," she growled, charging after her ally. Her presence and cries were needed to rally her troops and soon Ferda was being circled by her recruits, excited to see her and more than happy to defend her.

The majority of Urrah's troops and Zolk's pitiful recruits were waiting on the bottom floor of the tower. The eggs had been a hit, and the 'first-come first-served' policy perhaps needed reconsidering. Behind them, to the north, there was a howl that broke the din of the Ozar chatter, the sound of the Eclupse preparing the food, and the shouting above them. A moment of hesitation fell over the ground floor. The Ozars had done a good job in keeping recent events a secret from the Eclupse, so as to avoid a riot. Now the Ozars—militia and garrison alike—thumbed their axes while staring at the Eclupse. The Eclupse were intuitive and observant, they had been curious, and rumors had passed about in the wind like flies. This sound brought clarity and evidence to the many theories that had been floated in hushed voices, and some of the Eclupse could barely hide their excitement as their tails started to wag. Some of them had never heard a howl in their lives, it had been banned in the communes since they had been started. Howls were used to start riots, in the Ozar's opinions, which was not entirely false. The Ozars could never understand the reverent sound of a pack calling to the heavens in joy, sadness, or anger.

The bugle above them sounded and it was echoed by a thud from the floor above the troops. Both Penma and Arn looked up as a warm, thick liquid dripped down onto Arn's face. Penma sniffed and looked at the red fluid.

"That is blood," she said matter of factly.

The discovery sped faster than fire down the line of troops, and the theories were dragged behind like most gossip. The whole keep heard Forver shout "Kill those Maulers!" and, despite the curiosity and confusion, the garrison fell into line. The Eclupse in the kitchen were escorted out rapidly to the nearest pen, and the troops broke off to support either side.

As Arn and Penma stepped out of the keep, they could see the two black spear points that thrust and punctured through the sides of the commune. Within seconds, the Mauler force was within a stone's throw of the keep and swarming the grounds. Arn pulled his iron buckler over his left fist just in time to punch a Mauler's teeth out as it lunged for him. Another Mauler tackled him, grabbing him by his hips and they both went rolling into the mud. Penma went to toss Arn his hatchets as he finished adjusting his shield, and now he was gone in the slick, shallow trench of muck. The Mauler to her left went for her arm, slashing with her claws. Penma swung the hatchet in front of her, she didn't have time to flip the blade side around. The Mauler howled in pain as she crunched its hand with the butt of the hatchet. Maxyss slammed into Penma's other side, bruising a few ribs as they both hit the ground. He quickly spun up and held her wheezing face into the mud. She swung at him with one of the axes, catching his thigh. Maxyss tried to push through the pain and keep her head down, but the second axe came within a whisker of his crotch, and he had to let go, leaping back. Penma pushed herself up, taking as deep a breath as her injured ribs would allow, and her head swiveled to the left and right. It was pure chaos and she couldn't make out where that Mauler had gone in the fray, or where Arn was.

The Maulers collided with the forward guards, easily smashing through the choke points. Rellik waited patiently for Unkyss' howl to send her troops in. Unkyss had to meet stern resistance before the reinforcements were committed. If he and Maxyss could take Kyron, that was all the better as far as Rellik was concerned.

I am not sure how Terrabyss would like that, she snickered to herself.

Unkyss charged forward, purposefully dodging some smaller, black-furred Ozars and making his way for a large, light brown, nearly blond Ozar. His tail pumped excitedly as he easily shifted from all fours to running with just his legs and pulled the axe free, snapping the weak knot on the strap and releasing the weapon from his back. "You're mine!" he howled happily, smacking the butt of the weapon into the Ozar's large oval shield. It was enough force to fracture the wood, sending a huge split through some of the planks and denting the metal brim.

"Bear-shit!" Unkyss snarled loudly, he had intended to cleave the shield and maybe the arm behind with the blade. The shield punched out and Unkyss experienced weightlessness for a moment, before falling back hard onto his tail. The massive Ozar stared through the new opening in his shield.

How did he generate that kind of power holding the axe so high? And who in Mother Bear's name says bear-shit? the Ozar wondered. Have I been doing something wrong?

"That was my fault," Unkyss said, springing to his paws. "Supposed to use the edge." He shrugged innocently as he and the Ozar squared off again.

Brutyss paced impatiently, waiting to hear Maxyss' *howl. It's a good thing if Maxyss takes the commune without me,* he kept trying to reassure himself. He heard Unkyss' howl and thought about how Rellik was now fawning over the giant. Brutyss' hackles rose, he wasn't waiting for Maxyss any more and he threw his head back, issuing his own howl and charging forward. *You are not getting all the glory for this victory, Unkyss,* he growled as his Fists slammed in behind Maxyss.

Terrabyss heard Brutyss howl and looked to his left, confused for a moment. *What's he up to?* He looked over to Rellik, who should have howled and been off to support Unkyss, but was now staring back at Terrabyss, confused. From the sounds of the fighting inside, the Ozars were in complete disarray. Alpha Father, curse Dio's caution! He thought to himself, nodding to Rellik and then perking his own ears up, his line all crouched in response, ready to charge.

They aren't going to have all the fun, the Ravis need to be represented in the victory! Numa has plenty of triumphs, I want this one! Terrabyss' ears went flat and he charged, the Maulers on either side of him flattened their ears and bolted after him, running with all speed toward the moat. If Volg's estimate about the distance was right, it was only a lue wide. They should easily be able to clear the sharp wooden stakes at the bottom.

***

Carloe turned back to Kyron when he heard the howl. He was on the western half of the complex, looking for fresh supplies to replace the ingredients he had used on Bossy Bear and BinBin? He couldn't remember the trooper's name. Carloe knew he was part of the garrison, but he felt as though the soldier avoided him, or perhaps he was rarely injured or in need of Carloe's talents. Carloe had just pulled another large strip of bark from one of the firs in the area that had been toppled in the storm.

"Grubs!" he shouted happily, and was now licking the bugs from his claws as the howl broke the usual chatter of the forest's wildlife. He could spend the time rummaging through his bag to get the small squirrel carving with the sigil on the bottom and attempt to find a critter to talk with to discover what was going on, but he was pretty sure that he already knew. He was definite that he had figured it out once he heard the bugle.

Carloe became excited, despite the unfolding situation. He had grown up in a family of druids and his grandfather had always told him a story of how he had a duel of wits with a powerful Silverback shaman. It was the story that poems were written from and that there should be records of. Everyone here thought that the Eclupse were sneaky and tricksters, but Carloe knew better. *Travic and those other Herders are amateurs, they don't know anything.* It is true that the Eclupse are quick and light on their paws but with the length of their limbs and their lean builds, that wasn't surprising. The Lobu were stealthy according to the Daunkirks, and they outweighed the Eclupse by a good fifty or so pounds. If you wanted to see stealth, you need look no further than the light and compact Varggs. They had small frames that held a surprising amount of power; it was rare even for an Alpha of the Varggs to reach six feet. What the Eclupse were really known for, at least in the right circles, was their magical abilities. They had a true talent for magic and it was an Eclupse that had provided his grandfather with such a glorious duel. Carloe had always wanted to test his own skills against that of the savage Silverbacks, especially after hearing the story. However, since about thirty years ago, the communes hadn't seen one Silverback with a talent for magic. The Ozars had rejoiced, but Carloe had lamented. The technique the druids had learned from the Daunkirk Madha had been too effective to allow Carloe to realize his dream. The Daunkirks had called it Clipping, and it was when a group of mages, or a very powerful mage, cut off a single mage's connection to the ley lines of magic that ran through the planet. There could be side effects, well, one really. Sometimes, the mage's brain was turned to mush, and it happened more often than Carloe wanted to admit. The desired outcome was that the mage would go on with a normal life, just without the ability to read or transcribe sigils. It had been close to forty years since the last known pup was born with any magical talent. It had been in Nelhel, a commune further west of Kyron. Carloe knew the clipping had been done by a single druid, Groll the Magic Stealer. Carloe didn't know who Groll had performed the Clipping on, and druids weren't taught the skill any more. It was seen as an unnecessary amount of information to memorize when a druid had so much else to remember as it was and so many other tasks to take care of. Carloe recalled listening to Groll tell the story to his father, Charbah. Groll was there to woo his sister, Kitren, known as Kit, and had told the story while he waited for her. Carloe reached into the bag at his paws where he kept the wooden bowl. Kit had died crafting the item, the folly of magic. It could literally pull you in too deep and consume you.

"The sky-eyed Eclupse," Groll had told his father, "the pup's eyes had been almost as light as its fur, blue but faint."

That was why Carloe was here at Kyron, he hoped that Groll's discovery of a magically connected pup was not a fluke. Once he found a pup, he had planned to hide its talent and secretly teach it the arcane arts. Then, one day when the pup was ready, they would duel. "It would be the ultimate display of magical superiority," Carloe chuckled slightly manically. *Could there be a chance that amongst those Maulers there is one that can use magic?* He was too far from Kyron to be able to really help. He looked at what sigils he had brought with him and the items they were carved on. *Oh, I did bring the Green Walker.* He pulled out a small wooden clog he had painted green and inscribed. He had traded several body augmentation potions for this. Mother Bear knew what that Rodentia was doing with a human shoe, and why it wanted to grow its ears; they were already huge and, well, the other appendage need not be mentioned.

"Foul creatures, Harris, always focused on one passion, it seems." Carloe tsked to himself. Carloe didn't actually need the clog for the spell, but he liked how it looked and technically anything was magical if the right amount of energy was put into the item. Some things attached to sigils better than others, but anything could work. "I could just step through one of these redwoods and arrive at my cabin, but the warriors are there and they probably would have little use for me," he said out loud, deciding on the best course of action. Carloe knew that shamans preferred large conduits over quick channels. They would be using fire, natural wind currents, a large stone formation, or be partially submerged in water. Kyron had been stripped of large boulders to allow for the building of the commune. The nearest large waterway was the Ryndell, about a day or so northwest of here. As far as Carloe could feel, there was no heavy breeze, those were more likely found in the mountains, along the plains, or by the shore.

That leaves fire, Carloe told himself with a shudder. Fire was not an element that druids especially liked to play with. Carloe had the bowl and he doubted that the shaman of a savage tribe like the Maulers had any true acumen for magical craft. *Now I must simply find him,* Carloe told himself as he looked back in his bag.

"Ah, there we go," he said out loud with a big smile as he took out a walnut from the Warm Wood, it was painted blue and had a bright silver sigil etched in it. He put it to one side. "After I find the shaman, you will take me to them." He patted the item gently as he went back to searching for his polished bronze dish that he used for scrying.

***

Skoff and Dio stood with a Fist of soldiers, among them was Oulyss and he watched over his shoulder at what the two were arguing about. He had wanted to be on the front line, but he and Aasha had started spending more time together and, even though she planned to join the Scouts once she completely recovered, they were having fun together. Oulyss wasn't sure what road he would choose. He wasn't sure what roads would even be available; for now he had chosen to be part of this group because Aasha was in the group. She had recovered from the Corvel attack, for the most part. She had an obvious limp and Skoff was constantly warning her that it would never heal. "The fire has told me." Or there was the time she burned her tongue and Skoff had shouted, "As your tongue does burn, so shall your wound for ever more!" It gave them comfort she was going to make a speedy recovery. The whole Fist was pretty sure that they were going to have a boring day, but by the tones of Dio and Skoff's voices, that seemed like it was about to change.

"What do you mean you won't do it?" Dio shouted in disbelief as Skoff stood resolute, arms crossed and tail pointing straight out. Skoff had one of his many ponchos on; this one appeared as though he had flung black paint at it and then used his tail to thump wild lines of yellow all over it. There had been more than a few delays due to his battle attire that morning. First bright pink, and then a dazzling red, which was followed by a vibrant orange, with streaks of soft but vivid blue. He had finally settled on this one and Dio—probably out of frustration more than anything— had allowed the shaman to wear the poncho with the bright yellow that gleamed against the black.

"You are the shaman, Skoff! Who else is going to make it so that we can communicate with the troops and coordinate them?" Skoff wasn't using his words, which was only irritating the Alpha more. His tail stayed pointing straight out and his ears weren't allowed to perk back up, they seemed to be stitched to the back of his skull at the moment. It didn't get much more 'NO' than that. "Skoff, I swear to the Alpha Father we went over the plan this morning before we marched. Why didn't you say anything then?"

"I was tired, and hustled out of camp I might add. I have a handful of sigils on me and nowhere near the precautionary items needed for a large fire. Alpha Father curse you, don't you remember what happened last night? Now you just want me to spit in the face of that portent and build another bear-shit fire?" Skoff replied, using words where he had to but forcing the Alpha to translate his expressions and gestures for the rest.

"Skoff, it wasn't a sign; it was most likely the druid from Kyron trying to intimidate us," Dio said in exasperation. "I have told everyone this!"

For the most part, everyone had seemed to accept that fact, except a few, and none refused to accept it as vehemently as Skoff. Everyone who had witnessed the events had told the members of the missing Fist the same story, as far as Dio knew, and he had worked hard to ensure that. But Skoff's willpower was making him more resilient each day to Dio's suggestions.

Dio pinched his muzzle below his eyes. "Skoff, just go to the fire pit that we made," he motioned to the Fist, but still somehow included himself. "All you need to do is open a channel so that all of the army can hear me."

"Oh, is that all?" Skoff sneered indignantly. "I am not summoning that thing again or making it possible for that thing to summon itself because I don't know how it got here. I know magic, Dio, and that was not any magic I am familiar with."

"Skoff, you know next to nothing about magic!" Dio growled, his voice seemed to carry and echo through the trees all around them.

Oulyss cocked his head and noticed that Aasha and the others had heard the sudden volume increase. It wasn't like Skoff's voice that seemed to reverberate off you. This voice, it pierced you and pulled you and your attention to the Alpha.

***

"That wasn't too hard," Carloe said out loud as the image of Dio and Skoff faded. He quickly shoved the bronze plate back into his bag. Carloe assumed at least one of those he saw was the shaman. They had soldiers around them which meant that they were guarded, and if he remembered correctly, the Alphas were always the shaman. Carloe reached for the magical walnut shell then stopped for a moment. He recalled the stories that he had heard from those militia brought by Bossy Bear, hadn't they said that the renegade Dio was supposedly at the head of this tribe? *That probably means that neither of them is the shaman. That Eclupse is probably*

Dio, which means that the shaman is probably dead, Carloe sighed to himself. The one Mauler with the poncho pricked at his mind, why had that Eclupse been pointing to what he had thought was a fire pit? Perhaps it is worth looking into, he thought to himself as he rolled the nut about in his hand, debating if he should crush it. The items weren't hard to make, but it was his last Earth Coffin token and he would have to wait for fall before he could get more walnuts.

***

"What in Mother Bear's name are you thinking?" Travic shouted in shock as he watched Dhon's body thud to the wooden floor. "You just murdered our colonel!" he roared, but was still unsure how to proceed.

"I executed a traitor," Forver responded through angry huffs. "Dhon would have had all of Kyron roll over in submission to these savages, or made you hide behind these earthworks until the army from Campos Ursyss arrived to steal your glory. Your fame." Forver pointed beyond the keep. "Out there is a chance for real renown. I am willing to lead you to those accolades you all deserve. This is a chance for you to earn the glory that your grandfathers and my father denied you." As Travic took an aggressive step toward Forver, the Norrus spun on him, holding his bloody axe.

"Makes sense to me," Azbin said, standing from the table at the same moment. He let his hand drop down to his hip where Biter rested. Azbin had no desire to become a true veteran of Kyron as Frax had been, and with Frax now dead he was the next senior member of Kyron. *Stars, I could just retire with that kind of prestige.* "I agree with Forver!" Azbin announced, tipping Forver a nod. *If nothing else, I walk out of here with money for helping Forver with his little coup.*

Forver and Travic exchanged glances for a moment. Forver had understood maybe a word or two of what Azbin had said, but when he saw the nod, he assumed it had been in support of him. He kept the weapon level with Travic.

"Choose your fate," Forver said, trying to keep his voice even and dramatic. He didn't succeed but still his point was made.

Travic looked from one to the other, stunned. First off, he had understood a good portion of what Azbin said, but even if he hadn't been able to, he knew what the nod meant. "You can't just kill someone, a colonel no less, commit mutiny, and expect that there will be no repercussions!" Travic growled at Forver, then turned to give his attention to Azbin. "Why even follow him? He holds no military rank and despite all the money he has used to convince us, he has no authority from Bardell to be here. Dhon and I knew the truth."

"He is going to pay me a lot more than she ever did. I will have a real chance of getting the position I deserve." Travic noticed Forver's expression as he semi-understood Azbin's mumbled claims. Forver's face clearly suggested that Azbin was making up this claim of wealth, or perhaps it was that the Norrus still didn't really understand what Azbin was saying. Travic had no intention of fighting the two of them. He had hoped that Urskoo on top of the keep would have made his way down by now. Travic decided he needed to buy a little more time until the sentry got his hide down here, or he successfully drove a wedge between Azbin and Forver.

"Won't it be interesting to explain to Bardell how Kyron was put under siege by an army of Maulers because the Herder didn't want to take command when his colonel fell? Worse, we may need to explain how Kyron was destroyed or taken by the savages because of the Herder's cowardice," Forver suggested with a curt tone. *There are other ways to make someone do what you want.* Forver was sure he could be just as persuasive without his money as with it, as long as he was holding Ol'Grim.

"Yes, quite the traitor you would look like if you were siding with the colonel," Azbin tried to mutter. They could all see that Forver's patience was wearing very thin, and he lacked the elegance he thought he had.

"A colonel who, guess what! Surprise! A colonel who didn't want to attack the savages either!" It was Azbin and Travic's turn to exchange glances, slightly confused as to what Forver was implying. Despite the look that Travic gave to Azbin, he thought he understood what the raging Norrus was saying. If the Honcho believed that Travic or Dhon had shown cowardice, and less likely but more seriously if Bardell believed that either one of them had been in cahoots with the Maulers, the Herders would be disbanded. The unit Travic took so much pride in would be relieved of service with a blotch on their honor that could never be erased or forgotten. In addition, what would happen to the prospects of female warriors? Forver looked between the two of them and their confused expressions.

"How many of you have to die before we start fighting Maulers?" Forver screamed, he was beside himself with fury. What happened next shouldn't have been so surprising to Azbin and Travic, it certainly wasn't to the rage ball that was Forver.

Travic meant to knock Azbin off his high stool with the information that Dhon had gleaned from Urrah, which was that Forver was impoverished. Urrah had told the colonel herself. This Norrus had sunk everything he had into this raid and this little coup had no monetary gain behind it. Fame, yes; fortune, no. Travic should have learned from what had happened to Dhon, but he was sure if he could just buy a few more moments with his argument that the two mutineers would be at each other's throats. The words never left his mouth, but his last breath did, when Ol'Grim sunk into his stomach behind the chest plate. The air left Travic's lungs as the axe was removed and replaced in his back. The gambeson wasn't designed to stop this weapon, with this much power and at this range. Finally, Travic's soul went to the stars when Ol'Grim socketed itself into the Mahuer's neck. Azbin watched, wide-eyed at the speed of this old Ozar, it would seem that rage was a powerful stimulant.

Forver spun on Azbin. "Now, are you going to work with me or do I need to add a third Ozar body to my kill count today? I would rather kill Maulers, but I really don't care any more," Forver said through puffs of air.

"No, sir!" Azbin tried to say while lifting the hatch to the lower level and sliding down the ladder. Forver yanked Ol'Grim free and slightly kicked both bodies as he passed, following Azbin down the ladder and out into the melee.

***

Numa led her group of fifteen Maulers down the western boundary of Kyron, staying hidden well within the trees. An additional Fist had cleared the way earlier, checking for any Ozar patrols that might intercept this unit. All of them had heard Terrabyss' howl and were moving at full speed, sprinting to come up around the back of the commune.

"Do... you... think... every... thing... is... going... accord... ing... to... plan?" Luna asked as she bounded off a rock, landed, hopped over a small fir that must have toppled in the storm, landed, charged through a fern, skidded slightly in a mud slick, swerved around a sequoia, jumped a growing spruce, landed, ducked under a low branch, and dodged some deer pellets.

"Every… thing… goes… accord… ing… to… plan… unless… you… know… it's… not… going… accord… ing… to… plan," Numa responded, performing her own acrobatic routine as she replied.

"With… Terra… byss… lead… ing… what… could… go… wrong?" shouted Essall sarcastically to the two lead Maulers. She was understandably still distraught about Jabyn's injuries. Numa just looked over her shoulder, giving Essall her silent response, which forced Essall to reply, "It… will… be… fine."

From their distance, the unit had to depend on their sharp hearing and powerful sense of smell to understand how the battle was progressing, given the din and stench of combat. The sounds of agony, the smell of blood, the cries for assistance, the reek of death, all these assaulted their senses. One of the five Scouts Numa had sent ahead appeared to the advancing party's right. She quickly doubled up where she stood and crouched down, as though she were trying to hide from an approaching troop. The whole unit came to a sudden stop, and everyone found a good amount of cover. A group of three Ozars who had heard the bugle came charging through the forest, none of them gave even a second glance to the shadows that seemed oddly larger for this time of day. As soon as the Ozars were out of the troop's range, the now sixteen ambush troops sprinted through the mud and slush toward the south of the clearing that surrounded Kyron. If the sounds of the battle were correct, they had already moved more than half-way to their designated area.

Defend!

Ferda and Urrah's arrival at the eastern entrance had stalled the troops under Brutyss' control, and now they were being funneled back through the gap in the earthworks. The two Ozar commanders kept their troops organized and reminded them that they had trained for this very situation. Soon, the Ozars had formed a shield wall and dug their paws in. They had divided Maxyss' troops from Brutyss' reinforcements, and there was nothing the two Mauler units could do at the moment to escape the envelopment. There was a roar, and the front line punched their shields into the charging Maulers, the force of the blow and support from the rear rows broke the flood like a boulder in a creek. The Ozars trampled over the prone Maulers, and the rear rows put axes in the creature's skulls or torsos. Urrah had taken rear command while Ferda led the forward division. They could both hear some shouts from the troops back at the keep, and thought they could make out Forver and another Mahuer exit the keep, barking orders. Urrah noticed the Mahuer who exited with Forver was trying in vain to get someone to focus on the northern embankment. Urrah's eyes tracked to the north, she suddenly understood the problem as she saw a dark-furred figure begin sliding down the earthworks into the commune.

"Ferda!" Urrah shouted. "I am taking half our rear to stop a breach in the north embankment." She didn't wait for Ferda to respond; from her perspective, the captain was pushing the Maulers back easily.

Urrah took a platoon with her and hustled to the northern fortifications, where now a dozen Maulers were on the inside of the earth wall. Terrabyss came to a skidding halt as he hopped the last couple of lue off the steeply angled dirt and grass wall. With his kanabo in hand, he had been expecting to be met by a fearsome Ozar. He didn't know how many of his troops had made it over the moat, and he wasn't about to look back to check.

That isn't important right now, I am sure they will be surging over the wall behind me at any moment.

He was distracted from his thoughts when he saw a group of eleven Ozars running toward him, axes out and shields in front of them. The majority of them were unarmored, but had small iron bucklers with hatchets. There was at least one that was armored with a sturdy round shield and had an interestingly designed axe. It reminded him of a wolf fang. The whole charging force was taller than him and for once Terrabyss wondered if they were broader than him. *Only one way to find out,* he thought, shouldering his weapon. He would have to make sure that no one got past him to his troops as they made it down the embankment.

Urrah saw the lone Mauler coming. *This one is definitely stupid,* she thought to herself as her unit closed in. Although more Maulers were coming over the northern wall. "Keep going!" she commanded the other Ozars. She was armed and armored, and it was time for her to let Lopper out of his sheath. The militia Norrus knew better than to disobey, especially in the panic that was unfolding, and they moved to give Terrabyss a wide berth. The Mauler obviously was disappointed about having lost the chance to fight the other Ozars and broke to his right to try to cut off a group of four.

"On your left!" Urrah's eyes widened as she saw the speed with which he collided with the four militia troops. Before they could square off with him, he had taken the legs out from two of them, caved in the chest of a third, and planted his paw into the buckler of the fourth, knocking him back. Urrah studied the weapon the Mauler was using as she tried to get to her soldiers. *That's new,* she thought, a bit concerned as she sprinted toward the four Ozars. Another two militia had also dropped back, trying to surround the brute.

Terrabyss was in his element; the battle seemed to fuel him and his senses, reflexes, and stamina were surging to their peak with adrenaline. The top spike of the kanabo found one of the Ozar's skulls, who had already had its leg almost ripped off by Terrabyss' first sweep with his weapon. The second one was already bleeding out, having actually lost his leg. The Ozar who had been knocked back planted his paws and stopped himself from actually rolling, looking on in panic as the Mauler brained one of his prone allies. His confidence was bolstered when two other militia troops flanked him and charged the blood-furred Mauler together. The Ozar took two steps, one for each blow the Mauler had delivered to the reinforcements. The Ozar that had been on his right got a face-full of kanabo, having underestimated the speed at which the Mauler could swing the weapon. The second Ozar was sure there was no way that the

Mauler could reposition his weapon to hit him, and roared in triumph. There was a thud as Terrabyss tightened his arm muscles and twisted his hips, forcing the weapon through the skull of the first Ozar and into the ribs of the second. The Ozar rolled away, ribs shattered and gasping for air.

"I will give you a… " Urrah tried to yell to distract the Mauler, she never got to offer him a chance to surrender. The kanabo hurled down on the collar bone of the last stunned opponent. The Ozar slumped to his knees as the weapon found the side of his face with the second blow. Urrah let out a savage roar, she was finally in range. Urrah's paws shuffled to a stop as the Mauler swung the gory weapon in an arcing blow toward her head. She quickly brought her shield up, and the sound of oaken shield colliding with sequoia kanabo echoed with a fearsome boom.

Urrah's whole arm burned from the impact. She was glad she hadn't tried to stop the blow straight on and had gotten her forearm behind the shield, not depending solely on the boss grip. If she hadn't, her wrist would most likely have shattered, if not completely smashed into her forearm. The block was jarring for Terrabyss as well; he wasn't used to anything blocking one of those blows.

Alpha Father knows the other Ozars were unable to block me.

The Maulers didn't put up defenses, they didn't usually block or try to catch opponents' attacks if the opponent had a weapon. Usually, it was fists on fists, no one was stupid enough to try to actually catch a dagger or his kanabo. If they were, they soon learned how dumb a response that was. Terrabyss had to step back to reposition his grip on his weapon as it was forced slightly loose from the collision with the shield. Urrah saw the dust that had built up on the shield—that she had thought no one could knock loose—scatter in the breeze. She moved to push the kanabo off her shield and strike. The weapon was already gone, and Terrabyss quickly dropped the kanabo down and caught the axe along its cheek, almost removing it from Urrah's hand. Terrabyss stumbled back as the boss from the shield punched into his right side.

"What bear-shit was that?" the question slipped out. Terrabyss had never been punched that hard by a shield before, and his body and brain weren't sure how to react. The Corm were powerful, but they didn't use heavy materials for their shields. The punch didn't hurt too badly, but it had knocked him off balance, so it was more challenging than anything else, far more so than with the Corm. Urrah wisely ignored the question and pressed the attack, she wasn't here for banter. Terrabyss stepped back hurriedly as the axe quickly followed the shield's punch. He recognized that the Corm had used the same tactic, but with the Ozar deploying a sturdier shield he was having difficulty in finding an opening. Urrah, also wisely, hid her attacks behind the shield. The Ozar rammed forward, keeping her body and axe behind the protective barrier. At the last moment, she pulled the shield aside and swung up with the axe, intending to catch the Mauler in his gut, flank, or hip.

Terrabyss had no idea what attack was coming from behind the shield, but his years of fighting and training honed his instincts so he saw the Ozar's right shoulder shift upward. He shifted to the left, letting his kanabo—which had come to rest on that side after his first parry—pull him through the motion. Urrah barely got her shield up in time, her axe grazed the Mauler's stomach as he moved, but not enough to even make him aware. The kanabo suddenly swung in diagonally at her face as the Mauler planted his paws and pulled the weapon across his chest with his back, shoulders, and chest muscles. The top half of Urrah's beautiful shield splintered, only the iron band holding the wooden planks remaining. Urrah's hand sang with pain, and she was sure that she had broken at least one of her fingers trying to maintain her grip on the shield as it was hit by the kanabo. This was nothing like Urrah had expected. The Ozars, up to now, had dealings only with Silverbacks that were cowed and, truthfully, malnourished. The Maulers were neither; they were fierce, powerful, and obviously very deadly. Her battles against the Daunkirks had required far different tactics. They preferred to use strong recurve bows with heavy iron arrowheads to spread chaos through the Ozar formations, before actually charging into the enemy. The Maulers seemed to be of the opposite mindset.

Do they send in powerful single opponents to spread confusion? she thought, a tactic that Urrah would honestly have never believed would work and by all rights shouldn't be working. But this Mauler alone had just slaughtered six of her militia. All were veterans of the Daunkirk skirmishes. Urrah had to create some space to try and find another plan of attack, this Mauler's body was too well-trained in reading even her most subtle movements. Urrah breathed a sigh of relief as apparently the same thought had crossed the Mauler's mind and he backed up for just a moment.

***

Ferda didn't bother to turn and let Urrah know she had heard her, a Mauler lunged forward while her axe was stuck in the skull of one of its allies and she couldn't bring her shield across her chest to block in time. She scrunched her head down and—as the Mauler's jaw snapped down at her head—shoved her skull forward. The teeth punctured her skin but her hard skull would take more than one bite to split. The Mauler, on the other hand, lost more than a few teeth and was quickly trampled under paw as the front line surged forward again.

Brutyss wasn't sure how to counter this well-organized attack; no matter how much force he threw at that shield wall, it just wouldn't break. He had to find a different way around it or through it. *If only I was the size of Terrabyss, I could just charge through that wall like they were dry leaves.* His tail started thumping excitedly against some of the troops around him. That is the solution! We are making our own problem. Brutyss' mind scrambled frantically to put his thought into a coherent tactic. He quickly instructed those around him to pass on the information to the front lines. It was honestly very simple. First, they needed to stop slamming into the shield wall at different points. "We need to pick a point and hit that point, if we can even punch a Fist through, it should be impossible for the wall to recover." This did create a problem; what if the signal was given to pull back? They were already funneled by the entrance to Kyron. If they were also forced to funnel back through a shield wall, his troops would be trapped inside the killing field. Brutyss hadn't heard Terrabyss' howl to retreat, and the defenses had obviously begun pushing back.

Maybe Dio made contact with him and gave him new instructions because of our initial success? he wondered to himself. Either way, he had to act now or he could lose all his troops. Brutyss commanded his soldiers to focus their aggression into the left flank and to follow his lead; the Ozars on this flank had become eager and were starting to pull ahead of the rest of the line. The small creek began to envelope the boulder that had once stood in its way, as the left flank almost instantly buckled under the concentrated assault, having ventured too far forward.

Ferda tried desperately to get her troops to fall back into line, even before they had been hit. She had just broken off the right flank to go and personally reorganize the line when Brutyss sent his spearhead of troops into the left. Once they were hit, she tried to urge the center forward, to support the wilting side. Soon the Maulers found other gaps on the right which had become timid in Ferda's absence. The line fell apart, some troops still moved to join the left side, others became bogged down, and soon Ferda and her troops found themselves isolated in a wave of teeth and claws. A set of claws raked down Ferda's back but were unable to find their way through her ring mail. She spun with her axe leading the way, hoping to catch whoever had tried to claw her. Brutyss watched as the Mauler next to him had his left arm severed before he could shuffle away. Brutyss ducked under an Ozar's buckler as the opponent tried to bash him, shoving his claws up under the Ozar's arm and ripping down the enemy's flank. He pushed the screaming Ozar at the enraged Ferda as she spun on him. His heel hit the hatchet of one of the fallen militias, and he fell back, cursing as he lost his balance for a moment. Ferda charged after him, but Brutyss was quick and agile. He picked up one of the iron bucklers, managing to put it between him and the descending bit of her axe. There was a loud gong as the steel head hit the small iron buckler. Brutyss shuffled back, still in a squatting position, having not been able to stand completely. Ferda was trying to maintain the grip on her weapon from the sudden and unexpected defense. Brutyss took the instant to try and find the hatchet he had almost fallen over as he half stood. His hand came to rest on the hatchet's cold and hard metal head. His fingers quickly traced their way to the haft and he grabbed it, trying to gain any advantage against this Ozar. Ferda was back on the offensive by now and Brutyss had barely managed to get his paws under him before he had to lunge to the right to avoid the savage chop from Havil. He was lucky, managing to land in a less corpse-strewn area and found himself rolling to his paws nimbly as Ferda followed in pursuit, picking her way over the bodies that he had avoided in his dodge. Brutyss quickly adjusted the hatchet and buckler, trying to mimic how Ferda held hers as she closed the gap between them. He winced as she buried her axe into the flank of a distracted Mauler that had become entangled with an Ozar between the two of them. Brutyss' hackles rose and he snarled, Ferda had to plant her paws quickly as he charged her. The sound of steel rang out again as Ferda's speed with her axe forced Brutyss to put the buckler between her and him. He felt his whole arm trembling from the impact of the blows and his digits were tingling. He had to drop the buckler and flex his fingers several times to make sure that his nerves were still working. Ferda hadn't been so stunned this time and now followed with a cross swing, bringing the blade across her chest horizontally. Without another shield and the attack now on the opposite side, Brutyss quickly changed his grip on the hatchet. He hoped that the wooden handle was sturdy enough for his plan, and he gripped the hatchet behind the toe and heel, along the beard between the haft and the bit, with the sharp edge protruding from between his thumb and pointer finger. The hardwood handle rested along his forearm now, and he used his impressive speed to intercept Ferda's attack. Havil hit the wooden handle, putting a good chip in the haft but not managing to cleave through it. Havil was designed to be a battle-axe, having long abandoned the wood chopping wedge-head for a more sleek and lighter head, designed to deliver deep wounds, and allowing the user to swing the weapon with greater ease for longer periods of time.

Brutyss hadn't been sure that his impulsive plan was going to work and for a moment he was expecting the steel to keep going and dig through both his flesh and bone. "It worked!" he said audibly, with a sigh of relief in Ferda's surprised face. Brutyss' next response was more instinct than skill and he punched forward with the hand holding the hatchet. Ferda was in the process of pulling her axe back to reset for another attack. She let out a sudden roar of anger as she felt the sharp bit of the hatchet in his fist slice across her shoulder.

Brutyss had his paws under him now and he ducked under Ferda's quick counter swing. She quickly reversed her swing, chopping back at Brutyss as he stood up from his previous dodge. Brutyss deftly swapped hands with the hatchet, taking the same grip in his left hand and blocking her back swing. Again, Havil struck the haft of the hatchet and Ferda was forced to pull her axe back only to receive another slash across her right shoulder this time. Ferda growled, taking a step back and putting her shield up before her defensively, trying to catch her breath a bit. She hadn't been able to get the heavy wooden shield up in front of her earlier because of the Mauler's attacking speed. *He is obviously not going to go down easy.*

Brutyss took the brief respite to find a second hatchet. He quickly adjusted his grip on the second weapon. Now I have one for each hand, he mused as he thumped the wooden hafts together, giving Ferda a confident grin. This was more his style. *A thousand quick cuts.*

***

Forver and Azbin stood in front of the keep, the scene unfolding around them was pure carnage and absolute panic. "We have to get these troops organized," Azbin tried to say to no one in particular.

"We need to organize the troops!" Forver yelled at Azbin. *Where the stars are Urrah, Ferda, and Zolk? I couldn't get rid of them two days ago and now I can't find any of them,* Forver bemoaned.

"There is a problem to the north," Azbin tried to say, pointing to where a singular Mauler was sliding down into the commune.

Forver tilted his head questioningly. "What?" He followed where Azbin was pointing. "One, one Mauler, is that what you are worried about? Have you seen the wolf-shitting east and west entrances?" Forver shouted, trying to gesture to both sides at once.

Azbin wasn't sure why he was even trying to help this little fireball of anger. *Maybe Dhon had been right.* He pointed above the single Mauler and tried to say "Above him!"

Azbin's frantic grunting sounds, despite being almost mute, caused Forver to look again at the northern wall. His attention went first to the lone Mauler, and then up. "Mother Bear!" Above the single Mauler, a group of at least twenty Maulers were beginning to descend into Kyron. "Do, do something!" Forver yelled at Azbin as he saw several handfuls of Maulers now jumping down the last few feet of the sloped embankment and making their way into Kyron. Forver let out a sigh of relief as he noticed two groups moving toward the north with a familiar Norrus in the lead.

There is that fat Ozar, he said to himself as he saw Urrah leading the defensive charge. "She has it under control," he said, more sarcastically than he should have.

Azbin began shaking his head as he heard Forver's comment. "It wouldn't appear that way," he tried to say, pointing again to the north as Forver turned away.

"Either take that stupid thing off or stop trying to talk!" Forver snarled. "Now, follow me to the west, we will push these brutes back yet!" Forver exclaimed, charging to the left and leaving Azbin to watch the one Mauler slaughter six Ozars. He had to look away. He hoped that Forver's confidence in Urrah's skill was not misplaced.

***

Rellik had made it to the western entrance around the same time that Terrabyss cleared the moat. Unkyss and his forces had almost reached the base of the keep, but the space between him and Rellik was beginning to get choked with Ozar reinforcements. The Ozars were beginning to recover from the shock of the initial assault.

"We need to break through to Unkyss, you runts!" she shouted, leading a howling charge into the Ozars who were trying to surround Unkyss' division. Rellik and her troops hit the Ozar lines hard and eager for combat. As soon as she hit the few garrison troops that had made a shield wall, similar to that which Brutyss was facing, she ordered her troops into a wedge and chopped through the defenses with astounding speed. Rellik felt like she was in her element, she could see everything around her, her ears heard whether Ozars or Maulers were buckling, and she could even make out the groan and whimper of bones and sinew as the battle raged on. Her speed through the shield wall seemed not to be quick enough as Unkyss' troops were still getting surrounded. Her supporting troops had put a dent into the Ozars that were trying to envelop him, but the enemy's organization and discipline allowed the majority of the Ozar troops to focus on tightening the noose on Unkyss, while the rest fended off Rellik's rear assault. The majority of her opponents were militia, unlike the eastern half of the commune which had managed to attract most of the garrison forces. There were a few garrison troops on this side, and their large defensive shields were creating the most difficult obstacles. With the militia supporting them, these garrison soldiers could cut down a handful of Maulers before they were even scratched. She noticed that Unkyss had snapped his axe haft and was using the handle as a club and the blade part almost as an extension—a sharp one—of his knuckles. He apparently hadn't adjusted his grip as she had suggested to him before the assault.

Rellik ducked under a two-handed crosscut from one of the garrison troops who wasn't using a shield. As she stood, she used the hook on the butt of her weapon to catch the shoulder of the two-handed axe before the Ozar could lift it back up above his head, putting her knee in his kidney and her other fist in his throat as he went down to one knee from the kidney blow. She let the weight of his body bury her claws deep in his esophagus before tearing them free. There was a ringing sound as Rellik felt her head lurch forward and she yelped loudly. Something sharp hit her back at her right shoulder, causing her to fall into the mud muzzle-first.

Unkyss used the axe blade to cut his opponents with each rapid and powerful punch. The beard of the weapon folded over his fingertips, and he had long abandoned the idea of using the elongated haft as a rear defense. Surprisingly, the haft had become his primary killing tool. He used his axe hand to punch repeatedly, in rapid succession, into the Ozar's little iron buckler over and over, putting him on his heels. Then, he brought the sturdy haft across the creature's ankles or paw, which usually put them on their back. Unkyss could then leap on top of them and maul them with the axe blade over and over until they stopped squirming. He was forced to change his tactic once the Ozars had recovered from the shock of the attack, and he no longer had the luxury of killing them while they were down. He needed to kill them while they were standing, which was proving to be a bit of a challenge for him. Unkyss could hear Maxyss' howls for aid echoing from the other side of the keep where he was trying to push back against the Ozar barricade.

Why hasn't Terrabyss howled for us to fall back? The Ozars have definitely mounted a defense, and we are becoming hard pressed! Unkyss scanned the battlefield around him, kicking his latest dazed victim into the corpse of the Ozar that he had just disposed of. As the Ozar fell back, Unkyss snatched up the buckler that the Ozar dropped and threw it like a discus into the back of another Ozar's head. The impact sent the Ozar sprawling, and the Ozar that was still trying to regain his balance from the kick fell onto the back of the Ozar that Unkyss had just dazed. There was a loud snap as one of the two Ozars broke their back, or maybe they both did. Unkyss raised his paw to stomp down on the Ozar's face who had fallen on top of the discus-stunned Ozar. The Ozar stupidly stuck its shield up. Unkyss used the metal object to smash down into the helpless Ozar's muzzle, shattering its skull. He heard what he thought was Rellik's voice and quickly scanned the battlefield, recognizing that her reinforcements had entered the fight.

"Rellik!" he shouted over the din of battle, hoping that she would hear his call. There was no response. Alpha Father, *where is she?* he thought, smashing his beat stick into the back of the other Ozar's skull as he groaned about his spine. It took a couple of hits, but the Ozar stopped complaining. *The black-furred ones aren't as fun,* Unkyss lamented for a brief moment before he was distracted. A terrifying howl emitted from Unkyss' throat; the vibration was enough to tremble the blood that was soaking the ground. That Ozar pellet with four hatchets was bringing her arm back from having lodged one of those weapons in Rellik's back and he could see Rellik falling forward from the blow.

Penma quickly tossed a second hatchet into her left hand, preparing to drive another blade into Rellik's back as she lay prone. Rellik blinked, she could have sworn that she had heard Unkyss howl. She gritted her teeth and winced as her body reminded her that she had been injured in her back. She wasn't sure how to get the axe out, but she was sure that lying in the mud wasn't the solution. Rellik pushed herself to her paws, her ears twisting behind her. She spun to her uninjured side, her brain told her that if they wanted to kill her, they were going to aim for her spine. The first blow had narrowly missed, lodging itself in her scapula a whisker's length from her spine. Ducking would have simply put her face in the way of the next attack. With this reaction she might get nicked, but she could survive a scratch. Her own axe was still in her right hand; the natural martial prowess of the Maulers and Rellik's own quick instincts instructed her to switch hands and throw. She did, and Unkyss stared in horror as the hatchet swung end over end toward Rellik. Then, in a mix of excitement and awe, he saw Rellik react by throwing her own axe. Rellik took the hatchet in her right hip, but the weapon didn't have enough of a target to lodge deep into her thigh. Penma saw the Mauler push to her paws and had to change the angle of her throw when the Mauler stood up so rapidly. Rellik's axe, however, came snuggly to rest in Penma's sternum and she fell back with a bewildered expression frozen on her face.

Unkyss didn't have time to shout a warning to Rellik as another Ozar started charging her left flank. Rellik was already losing her balance from the wound in her right leg where the hatchet blade had scraped deeply enough to draw blood. She heard the mud squish to her left and she frantically tried to spin to defend herself from the attack. She smiled as she saw Unkyss rush between the two of them. Honestly, it was Dummy's haft that pushed between them, the handle miraculously hit the assaulting Ozar hard in his hatchet hand, on the Ozar's fingers. The hatchet dropped as the Ozar roared in pain. Rellik lunged for the discarded weapon and snatched it up, managing to chop the bit into his right paw. The Ozar didn't know what to do, his hand, his paw, and then his face felt the blows in quick succession, as Unkyss' axe knuckles collided with the Ozar's cheek, sending him spinning with a broken neck.

"Did you see that? I love this weapon!" Unkyss barked loudly. Movement to his left and behind Rellik caught his attention. One of those damn black-furred Ozars had a hatchet and was looking directly at Rellik.

"Sorry," was all the warning Unkyss gave her. Her confused expression didn't last long as he pulled the hatchet from her back and threw the weapon with all his might. The knob smashed into the Ozar's eye socket and the Norrus fell back.

Rellik howled with pain, fortunately the hatchet had hit her poorly in the back. It had embedded itself under the skin rather than wedging between the muscle or bone. The Ozar who had thrown the weapon obviously didn't have a clear shot on her first attack. Fortunately, Unkyss had the forethought to realize that the weapon wasn't lodged and hadn't tried to tear it out. Rellik certainly didn't appreciate how gently he had removed the weapon. What made her most upset about the whole situation was that Unkyss hadn't even hit the Ozar with the bit. She saw the weapon's wooden handle, the bottom of it no less, hit the other Ozar.

"You are worse than Terrabyss," she barked as she watched the Ozar stumble backward.

"He didn't hit you with the hatchet though, did he?" Unkyss yelled to her as he sprinted off, intending to ensure the Ozar was dead. Rellik got to her paws and tried to pull her axe from Penma's corpse; it didn't budge and a horrible pain shot through her back. She leaned over and picked up one of the hatchets off Penma's body, strapping the buckler onto her left forearm. She would at least not die in this fight, although she wasn't sure how many more Ozars she could kill with her right shoulder like this. She charged after Unkyss; they were both going to survive this.

I haven't worked this hard for his attention to have him die on me! Rellik told herself.

***

Dio's Fist stood at attention, but all of them were watching or listening over their shoulders as he and the shaman argued. "Just dance around the bear-shit fire, you damn pellet!"

"Pellet! Pellet!" Skoff was beginning to squawk. "That is not how you talk to someone you want a favor from."

Many in the Fist were wishing that one of the two of them would lose

463

their voice, preferably both. To Oulyss and the others, it felt like they had been arguing since yesterday. Oulyss thought he noticed that Skoff's voice was becoming weak. He was the closest out of the Fist to them, and he noticed that Dio's voice was maintaining its amplified level while Skoff seemed to be losing this screaming match. He had always figured that Skoff's voice was magical and Dio's was natural, with a well-practiced talent for flair. Now he was beginning to have some doubts.

"Come now, your well-dressed friend is right. That is not how you should ask someone for assistance." The voice came from all directions. It was as though the seven Maulers were somehow submerged in the sound.

Oulyss didn't need to hear what came next to know that they had encountered another mage. Only masters of the arcane arts enjoyed announcing themselves in such a flamboyant manner. Oulyss heard the rumble behind him, and he spun around to see a massive root shoot from the earth, rising like a tree with no leaves or branches, whose tip was as strong as steel. It impaled Klain, who had been put in this Fist to avoid the liability he would have been in the main assault. Oulyss wasn't too distraught about losing Klain, or Klain the Cock as he had recently been nicknamed. He had mainly earned the title because he strutted around like a rooster, but Klain had come up with many even more insulting reasons that they should use the name in his paranoia and vanity. So they did, *or rather, had.* Oulyss shrugged as he tried to predict the next attack.

"Bear-shit," he swore as Oulyss realized that the root had simply vanished, no stem and no hole, just Klain's torn open body as it thumped to the ground.

"Bear-shit!" Dio and Skoff shouted, almost in unison with Oulyss as the root vanished. Everyone quickly looked around, hoping to catch some sign of the caster.

"Oh, no, no, I am not showing myself until all of you are gone, Alpha included." The ground vibrated faintly and Skoff jumped into Dio, trying to push him out of the way but the Eclupse simply caught the shaman.

"What are you doing?" Dio asked, a bit puzzled at Skoff's response.

Carloe chuckled from his hiding place. He had a cluster of glowing roots in one hand and was sitting comfortably in a hollowed-out space within the earth below the Green Wall. He was glad he had decided to use the walnut. The blood in the bowl was beginning to dry, and he wouldn't be able to keep up the root attack forever, so he was going to have to maybe spare a few of the Maulers. Carloe's other hand was rhythmically pounding on the bronze plate so that he could maintain a visual of the group above him.

The trembling stopped below their paws as suddenly another root shot through the surface, catching Snard in his stomach and leaving a gaping hole in the body, which also collapsed onto the forest floor as the root vanished.

"Run!" Skoff shouted. "He can't target us all at once!" the shaman declared, having recognized a few of the patterns of the spell. "This magic is limited to one spike at a time!"

By now, Carloe was sweating and breathing hard, his arm ached from hammering at the bronze plate and the blood had almost vanished, slowly streaming away as the bowl consumed the price. "Interesting," he panted, listening to Skoff's instructions. He yanked the root arm back up, as though he were lifting his hand to his shoulder. "Are you a shaman?" he breathed heavily as he felt the world resist his augmentation. Carloe closed his eyes and focused, he couldn't give his arm a rest, even if he wasn't seeing through the plate at the moment. If he stopped using the energy of his movement for one instance, the plate would go dark, and it would take him several minutes of preparation and a long nap to get enough stamina to do this again.

A third root speared upward, catching Ulvoue this time. He was skewered through his right hip and out his left flank, falling to the ground with a heavy thump.

Numa is not going to like hearing about that, Skoff thought.

"For Alpha Father's sake, do what your shaman tells you!" Dio ordered. That was all the rest of them needed; except Oulyss, he just needed to see Aasha start running.

Carloe's ears perked up, he could fortunately still hear what was happening even if he wasn't looking through the plate.

"I can help you or carry you!" Oulyss shouted to Aasha as he easily caught up to her. Her leg was still having trouble receiving her brain's signals.

She snarled at him, refusing his help.

Carloe took a deep breath. "I have one more in me." He looked to the bowl as he spoke. "Can you go once more?" He flexed his arm again as the roots turned to ash in his grip and the last of the blood in the bowl vanished. There was a rumbling and Aasha turned defiantly from Oulyss as an explosion of dirt showered them, another root erupting from the ground. Both Oulyss and Aasha came to a sudden stop as Attaboye—who was in front of them—was gutted by the root. Aasha swallowed her pride and allowed Oulyss to help her as they tried to make it to a safe area.

"Why didn't you run?" Skoff asked Dio as both of them watched the others flee.

"Because you are holding onto me," Dio responded, "also, you will probably need some help against this druid, wherever they are."

Skoff pushed himself from Dio. "Well, you should have run," Skoff said, brushing the dirt from his poncho.

Dio's knowledge of magic was limited, extremely limited. He had never been properly trained but he knew some basic spells through trial and error. He had never learned sigils like Skoff, he could understand them but couldn't create them. He had no idea how to maintain a cadence or rhythm in his casting, as both the shaman and probably this druid did. Dio had learned how to force his will onto others, how to make others see or hear things that were not there, or manipulate an individual's emotions. This was achieved through the simple elegance of his tone and he used the force of his voice to provide the spell with sustenance. He also had learned that blood could help amplify the arcane magic, but fortunately he had witnessed this lesson through another druid rather than having to learn it himself. With his lack of training, he would have surely been consumed by any spell into which he wove his lifeblood. With years of self-discipline, he had learned to add power to his simple charms, illusions, and sensory effects through biting his lip or scratching his palm, but those were tricks that Dio preferred not to resort to. He had always been a natural with the arcane arts and he had never needed much blood to coax the ley lines to aid him, but he had never put his wit against someone who obviously outclassed him.

"We will walk out of this," he told both himself and Skoff.

There was a loud pop and about two lue away, the earth seemed to vanish. Rising from the ground, an Ozar sat on a clay platform and pillar. Carloe looked for a moment at Dio, the eyes, the fur. *Is that the sky-eyed pup that Groll had told Father about?*

"I only want the shaman," Carloe announced. "You are welcome to go back to your soldiers and lead them over the walls," the druid offered politely to Dio.

"My troops have their orders; I can afford to aid my shaman."

Skoff wished that Dio would stop singling him out to this Ozar, but he was also impressed by the bravery that Dio was showing. It was stupid, but brave. The shaman could easily tell by the grandness of the entrance that the druid was leagues above him. *Perhaps Dio will be helpful, after all.*

"If that is what you want," Carloe said with a shrug. His clay pillar slowly formed stairs for him to march down. "Well then, Shaman, shall we begin?" Carloe shouted with joy, jumping up and slamming his paws into the ground. He had already scattered the thorns with their sigils at his paws. It was going to hurt, but it would keep that pesky Alpha busy.

Ten humanoid figures rose from the ground around Carloe's paws. The plants, needles, leaves, and seeds mixed within the growing figures. Before Skoff or Dio could figure out what the druid had done, the four-foot-tall thorn-covered plant humanoids all assaulted Dio, letting Carloe have his fun with Skoff. Dio doubted that his parlor tricks would work on these creatures, and he bared his teeth. He would have to do this the old-fashioned way, the Mauler way.

There are four known magics in the world: natural, spiritual, cosmic, and pacting. The shaman and druids are from the natural fields of magic, but this doesn't mean that mages can only use the field to which they are most connected. Mages can learn from all fields and can manipulate the ley lines to create a spell from any of the four areas. Both Skoff and Carloe knew how to manipulate the spiritual magics of the body's humors. Their ability to connect to this field of magic is hindered by how they perform their magic, since both practitioners depend on the physical aspects of magic, they can pull a great amount of power from the natural fields. If either practitioner had learned under the Madha of the Daunkirks or the Oracles of the elusive Fay, their magic could take on new forms; although, not many races have learned to merge multiple fields together, because of the time it takes to master the arcane arts. But a practiced and trained natural caster could perform a mixture of elements, allowing the caster to create a hybrid form of magic. Carloe had managed to perfect one of these hybrids; Gia or plant magic, a mixture between earth and water ley lines. He didn't even need his powerful bowl for something as mundane as creating ten Needle Arms. That was cub's play for him.

Skoff swallowed hard as he saw how easily the druid used a hybrid form of the natural arcane practice. This was definitely not going to be easy. Skoff had never learned to channel a hybrid mixture between his favorite elements, wind and fire. He had barely used wind techniques since he had fallen in love with fire, when Grimmis had finally taught him to open the ley line. Since then, he had devoted most of his practice to fire sigils and the warmth of the burning ley lines.

"Now that we are alone," Carloe cooed excitedly, "let us create a story that our cubs' cubs will speak of."

Skoff was pulled from his thoughts as he grabbed the small satchel next to him which had some basic sigil items. Carloe was also rummaging through his bag.

Okay I just need my staff, Skoff thought as he saw the perfect sigil on a piece of coal. Alpha Father, he swore as he realized that he had left his staff at the forward camp. *I am going to put sigils on my ponchos from now on,* he thought angrily.

A duel of wits required speed but also intelligence. Skoff could grab the charcoal lump and try making a smoke cloud. With his staff, he could have put the coal on the tip of the wood and traced the wind sigil near the bottom. That Ozar would stop rummaging quickly if Skoff had hit him with a piece of coal traveling the speed of a meteor. Although, if the druid was earth-based as Skoff suspected, the Ozar probably had a way to sense Skoff without the use of his eyes or nose.

"Ah, what about this one?" Carloe said, pulling out several sticks that were tied together by a hemp cord. He began flicking the item. The more his arm moved, the more the sticks transformed into a sturdy switch. As the druid flicked the switch, a droplet of sap seemed to fly from it, catching Skoff's paw and adhering it to the dirt around him.

That was amateurish, Skoff thought as he just carved a quick fire sigil into the sap and a small ember melted away the adhesive. He looked up as Carloe smacked him across the nose with the switch, this time the switch didn't leave a sticking line but a burning one. It was obviously covered in some arcane poison. Skoff hopped back and smacked his arm where the sigil was, returning blood to it and instantly the poison burned out of his system.

"Oh my, you are prepared," Carloe sang gleefully as he dug his hand around in his bag again.

Dio grabbed one Needle Arm by its wrists. He ignored the sharp spikes as they dug into his hands and pulled the thing apart. He then used the halves to beat back two others that rushed both his flanks. Trying to spin about to the ones that he could hear behind him, Dio hit the ground as a thorny foot kicked into his back, tripping him over a root. He let the blow give him some extra oomph, tumbling forward with the impact. He dropped the destroyed Needle Arm and quickly licked his bleeding palm. As long as Carloe was focused on Skoff, perhaps Dio could buy the shaman some time to figure out a counter. Dio fixed his focus on the druid as he tasted the iron in the crimson fluid.

Carloe thought of the perfect spell to hit the shaman with. "You like fire?" he hollered loudly to Skoff. "Well, I like water!" Skoff grabbed his one barrier spell that he now took with him everywhere along with his grounding stone, since the incident with the Corvel. It was a burnt piece of bark from a redwood into which he had carved a specific fire sigil. The flames could keep most attacks at bay, and it engulfed things that burned. It wasn't that Skoff had an aversion to water, it was what the water was going to do in the druid's hands that he was worried about. He fumbled the piece of bark.

"Alpha Father, don't let a druid kill me," he pleaded out loud. He yanked the bark from his satchel and looked up to the sun, waving the item back and forth. First in front of him then behind him. To the left and to the right. He paused for a moment having noticed something odd—the druid was frantically looking around.

"Help me, Skoff! The druid wasn't ready for my assault on his senses, but it will not last long. Especially if these little abominations manage to kill me!" the Alpha shouted to the shaman as Skoff received a small reprieve.

***

"Something is wrong," Numa said to the others as she put her nose to the air, taking several deep breaths. "I smell fear, and it smells like Mauler," she said matter of factly.

Luna had pointed out about fifty or so lue back that she hadn't had any information from her father, and none of the group had heard Terrabyss howl for retreat. They were less than a hundred lue from where they were supposed to wait for Terrabyss' signal. Numa's last Scout had just met up with them and explained that the rest of the way was clear.

"We are almost there," panted Essall, motioning with her head toward the southern end of the clearing that surrounded Kyron. "Once we are there, we can assess what is happening," she concluded, turning to continue to their destination.

"No, we need to go now," Numa said stubbornly, taking another long sniff.

"If we break the trees now, the sentry will see us. We are not far enough south. He will notice us charging if we leave from here," Essall countered, stopping only a few lue away.

"That is the risk we take," Numa commanded. "Line up!" she ordered and the unit fell quickly into place, except for Essall.

"We should stick to the plan," Essall said gruffly, her ears slightly flat and her tail straight out.

"Are you challenging me?" Numa asked, glaring at Essall. "Because if you are, I will gladly settle this before we leave. It won't take me long."

Essall knew she wasn't in a good position, plus she wanted revenge for Jabyn more than anything at this moment. "No, Mother," she responded with a quick salute.

"Good, now get in line!" Numa ordered.

This time, Essall fell in next to Numa, opposite Luna on the Scout Mother's right. Numa took five deep breaths for good luck and then her ears went flat. Twenty shadows burst from the trees southwest of Kyron.

Savage

Hild had been surprised when Solgar, Arvin, Rolg, Sernna, Essur, Indel, Nordyss—the third, if she remembered correctly, everyone called him Ordy—also his sister Nordyss the fourth, simply known as Fourdy, Fintorn, Vomi, Zarsyn, and the two youngest siblings Heb, and his sister Jennis were brought back into the pen by an Ozar she didn't know. Hild had never understood why Okmyss and Wilca gave their pups, Jennis and Heb, such Ozar names—perhaps they thought it would make the Ozars more tolerant of them. Perhaps they had intended to have their pups be more indoctrinated into the Ozar society and customs. Hild had never seen the Ozar that now held the pups' leashes; he was wearing different armor from Travic and the garrison troops, neither the tightly linked chain mail nor the single breast plate like the Herder and colonel wore. The rings in his mail were thick and large in circumference. They were attached to a thick leather jerkin, and he wore a thin, well-worn gambeson under that. His fur was black, and she couldn't think of any other Ozar in the garrison besides Carloe who had the distinctly colored fur. The Ozar's eyes were rather bloodshot, as though he hadn't slept well, but they were an intense amber color. It appeared as though he had been in a fight because at this distance, Hild could see and smell the blood caked into his fur that had matted around his skull. It was at that moment that Hild realized who this Ozar was, and she realized why the pups looked so terrified.

Most of the pups' parents were among the logging packs and lived in a different enclosure. Many of them had suffered terrible losses like Fintorn, whose mother had been killed by this brute when he first arrived. Hild's pups had told her that since Trel's death, Fintorn hadn't said a word. Others, like the girls Vomi and Zarsyn, Hild knew well as they lived in the other shacks in this pen. Their mother, Vozim, was working right now and Hild would go to replace her to clean up soon. Like Volg, the girls' father, Habyss, had been taken in the night and had not returned. Because of this, naturally, she and Vozim were having a rough time of it, but Vozim was putting up the bravest face of all of them. Wilca, on the other hand, was falling apart without Okmyss, and Hild almost hoped that he would come back before Volg just so Wilca's mind would be put at ease.

Zolk looked around the sparsely furnished shack; the roof had holes, the floor was uneven, and the walls' only purpose was to hold up the rickety roof. It was hard to get a good look at the Eclipse' living conditions from outside the enclosures. The druid had wound thick vines with foot-long barbed thorns around the bars that could prevent anything from climbing them. The top of the enclosure was no different; the wooden bars were laced with the same sharp deterrents. Some Silverbacks had tried to dig out; the living bars had to grow from somewhere though, making the enclosures deeply rooted. Short of killing the druid, these pens were never going to release their captives, not unless they had the key in and out. There was a possibility that the druid might not make the evening rounds and let the magical charge in the pens deplete, which would release the Silverbacks, but no druid had yet been that irresponsible. There were no chairs, cushions or even furs to sit on. A small fire still smoked toward the rear of the hovel, but it was nothing but orange embers and charred ash. A small pile of logs sat next to it, obviously for use later in the day or perhaps this evening.

Zolk yanked the pups by their leashes and Hild responded by leaping to her paws, concern for her own and the other pups driving her actions. She watched with bated breath as Zolk unclipped one after the other, but then stopped at Essur, holding the leash tight and close to the collar.

"What about your rule?" Zolk asked Headhunter quietly.

Essur tried to run after his friends but turned back to look at the Ozar, confused when he didn't move. Arvin recognized the terror in his mother's face as they ran toward each other and she quickly scooped the pups, all of them, into her arms.

"Fair enough," Zolk said aloud, "I mean, it is weird to distinguish between pups and cubs, but all right." There was a sickening, squelching sound and then a thud, all the pups but Arvin turned around. He understood from the look on his mother's face what had made that sound. It was the sound of Essur's skull being caved in and his limp body crumpling to the floor. The pups yelped in fright, some letting out cries of fear while others growled.

Indel, Essur's brother, had been one of the growlers, logically the loudest. Zolk moved like lightning, snatching Indel out of Hild's stretched embrace.

"Don't start a fight you can't finish," Zolk lectured the pup as he held Indel by the scruff of his neck and ran his blade along the pup's guts. The growling became whimpering and then stopped as another thump hit the shack's floor. Zolk ignored the cries of horror, not finding the same pleasure or reveling in their fear as he would have previously. He had to get some things off his chest, then maybe he would feel better.

The Ozar leaned back against the shack wall and the building whined under his weight. He was directly between both exits, Hild noted, and she wasn't sure if running was even an option. She doubted that this Ozar had left the gate open, and there was no getting past the bars.

Maybe he will get bored, maybe he is happy now, Hild lied to herself. She didn't know what to do, but she was sure that he would kill them all if they didn't just play along. She watched in bewilderment as Zolk looked over at Headhunter.

"You seem to be taking it pretty hard too, girl."

Hild wasn't sure, but she thought the Ozar was trying to console his weapon. *This could be our opportunity, perhaps if I could make him feel better, he will just leave.* She knew who she was dealing with by now; he hadn't been his usual sadistic and maniacal self when he had entered. She prayed to the Alpha Father that two dead pups had sated his hunger.

"What is wrong?" Hild asked nervously, trying to ensure that her voice was more empathetic than enraged. A very difficult achievement.

Zolk's eyebrows furrowed as he looked from his weapon to the Eclupse with the pups now huddled closely to her. She was darker than most Eclupse he had seen, although he thankfully hadn't seen too many. Her fur was gradients of gray, getting lighter toward her paws and hands and becoming darker the closer to her spine until it was essentially a smokey black line down her back. She had bright blue eyes and stood over six and a half feet tall; like all the Eclupse here, she was gaunt and her hide was held tightly to her bones.

Why not tell her why we are upset? Maybe she will understand, Zolk heard Headhunter's voice.

The Ozar sighed. "We both lost someone very important to us recently and we just don't know how to handle it," he admitted.

Since Ferda returned from her desertion, Forver has completely lost his spine. Watching him get beat by Dhon is undeniable evidence to that fact, but if I am honest with myself, Headhunter tried to warn me. All the dumb rules I had to follow, and Forver supported those wolf-shit rules. My great Mahzar, killed by peace. He almost spat the words from his last thought but he realized that the Eclupse was talking to him now.

"He has been gone for a long time and I don't know when he will be back. We aren't the only ones either; there are others of us who had the same experience. It is hard to lose someone," Hild finished when the Ozar suddenly spoke up again.

"Wait, what was that first part? I didn't realize you had been saying anything that might be interesting to me."

Hild wasn't sure if she wanted to respond, but she didn't want him to suddenly become angry and start snatching pups out of her arms again. "My mate was taken from me, and my pups... " Something inside Hild's mind told her to keep staring at the Ozar, and stopped her body from hugging her two boys tighter as she referred to them.

Zolk started putting it together now, among these pups were the offspring of that damned spy who had interrupted his fight with Ferda. "I understand now, so tell me a bit about your mate," he commanded her.

Hild was suddenly very grateful that she hadn't fought her instincts earlier. She still wasn't sure why, but she knew that this Ozar didn't want to know about Volg simply because he cared. There was another, more sinister reason in those gleaming eyes.

"I haven't seen him in a while, he could have changed so much." Hild didn't have a better response, and she knew that one was never going to be believable.

Zolk burst out in laughter, letting out several long rolling chuckles. Hild could smell the food cooking and heard the clamoring of voices as breakfast was called.

"Oh hush, it was funny. You just have no sense of humor," the Ozar said to no one in particular and, at first, Hild thought that perhaps her response had been enough. Suddenly, Zolk was standing, the wall complained again as his weight moved off it, and he took two large steps, bending down and snatching up another pup.

"No, please stop, not a third! Please!" Hild screamed, trying to reach up with one hand to grab the pup he took and keep the pups close in her embrace with the other.

"Relax!" Zolk said with a long, slow laugh. "I simply want to talk to him." Zolk held Ordy by the scruff of his neck, about half an arm's length from his face.

Start with something simple, Headhunter instructed.

Zolk rolled his eyes. "Now, what is your name?"

The Eclupse pup swallowed hard, looking first from the Ozar, then to the axe, and then to Hild.

"Don't look at her. Look at me and answer the question."

"Or… " there was a nervous pause.

"Dy," was the conclusion. The pup squeaked more like a mouse than a wolf.

"Is your name Or and your pack name Dy?" Zolk questioned, unsure how to process the response.

His name is Ordy, you half-wit, Headhunter berated.

"I am getting tired of your tone; you best watch how you speak to me! Besides, you just ate! Twice, I might add."

Ordy had no idea what to do. He had barely had breakfast in his pretty accurate opinion. "It is Nordyss like my father, mother, and sister, but everyone calls me Ordy!" the pup exclaimed in a panic, hoping that this would be useful information, and he didn't even need to try to sound terrified.

Now Zolk looked confused, which was arguably more terrifying than his conversations with no one. "Why?" was all he managed to get out.

Ordy opened his mouth to respond, he felt weightless for a moment and was confused before his body hit the floor hard. He let out a yelp of pain as his paws hit. He was more stunned than hurt. The next yelp was more of pain than surprise as Zolk smashed his paw down on the pup's torso, crushing him.

"Ordy!" one of the pups screamed in horror.

"No, Fourdy!" the words slipped from Hild's lips as the pup wiggled free. Zolk wasted no time in lifting the little whimpering pup into another raised grip, holding her by the scruff of her neck.

"Are you the other Nordyss?" he asked in a childish voice. "Yes, you are?" he confirmed as her little head bobbed up and down while she sniffled. "Good." He hammered the butt of Headhunter between her eyes. The gore splattered across him and the horrified audience.

"Stars, did you see the way she popped!" Zolk cried out, to what the

Eclupse hoped was his axe. "Glorious, simply glorious." He looked to the rest of the pups huddled in terror. "I did you a favor, no one needs four curs with the same name in their community." The muffled whimperings and silence were deafening but also wondrous. Zolk was starting to feel better and he basked in it, wiping his hand through his gory fur.

"Pop!" he chuckled loudly as he cleaned some of the mess out of him. "Now, where was I?" Zolk said aloud, tapping his bloody axe's shoulder on his own.

Hild was trying to frantically think of a way out; as the only adult in the enclosure at the moment, she felt responsible for all these pups. She couldn't imagine how Rolg and Sernna were feeling. Dessel and Koff had died shortly after their pups' births of an illness that spared the young— Sernna, Essur and Indel. Rolg's mother, Woydra, and his father, Modyn, had taken care of the three pups and made the two packs one, both were loggers and would be devastated at the loss of Essur and Indel. Nordyss and Nordy were also part of the lumber enclosure, and Hild hoped that they would forgive her for having lost their pups to this maniac. She hoped that she could keep Heb and Jennis safe for Wilca and hopefully her mate Okmyss, when he returned with Habyss and Volg. Hild had absolutely no idea who was taking care of Fintorn after Trel had passed away. The pup's father, Nio, had been crushed under a falling log, so she hoped that he had been adopted by one of the other families. All Hild could focus on was just getting the nine pups and herself out of here safely, but Alpha Father knew how she was going to accomplish that.

The shack's exits were facing to the east at the back and west at the front. Near the north wall, opposite of where Hild and the pups were, was a loose floorboard that held two small sacks of powdered spices. The Ozars had these delivered from one of their Campo, and over the years Hild as well as other cooks had taken pinch after pinch for their families. They exchanged these goods with the lumberjacks for pieces of scrap wood that their overseers allowed them to keep. One of the spice powders in particular was a chili spice from the Verdegren that the Ozars received through trade with the Mino, who acquired the items from the Primjawls that controlled the jungle. Just a puff of this powder had made Arvin sneeze for hours, and Hild had needed to stash the spices in a new space. Solgar had discovered their original hiding spot and wouldn't stop assaulting his brother with the ingredient.

I am sure the sack is loosely woven enough that if it hits this Ozar in the face, he will lose all his senses. Long enough for us to escape, but how am I going to get to that side of the shelter without him becoming suspicious? Hild had already reached the conclusion that the Ozar wouldn't imprison himself in here with them. He must have the item needed to exit the enclosure, although she had no idea what that would be. The garrison had kept these trinkets tucked away, perhaps in their braided faces, on the garrison armor, or maybe in their weapons. But Zolk had none of these items, so she was at a loss as to what it could possibly be.

"That's right, I remember what I was doing." Zolk turned that psychotic smile on Hild and the nine pups again.

"Sir," Hild quickly said. She didn't want to give this Ozar the pleasure of this respectful address, but it was a way to perhaps get to the other side of the building near the spices. "One of, or perhaps all of the young ones have become so frightened they have wet themselves. Perhaps it would be more comfortable for all of us if we were to move, say to… " Hild looked around, hoping that her ruse was working. It wasn't that she was lying, she just hoped this Ozar cared enough to allow them to move.

Before she could gesture, Zolk just shrugged. "It is good you baste in your fear." He laughed jovially.

Hild wasn't done trying as another idea sprang to mind. "Yes, we probably deserve that, but wouldn't it be more impressive if you managed to make us stink the whole shack?" She was trying to sound eager, squeezing all of the pups tightly to make them keep their confused questions and looks to themselves.

Zolk couldn't deny that sounded like an accomplishment worth bragging about. He ignored Headhunter's comments about how they were just going to kill all the Eclupse here anyway, so why did it matter where they killed them? But Zolk liked the idea. Sometimes, he wondered if Headhunter's heart was truly committed to this.

"Okay, why don't we go to that corner?" Zolk pointed with Headhunter, much to the weapon's frustration.

It was the right side of the shelter, but opposite the corner that Hild wanted to go to. "Why not where we sleep?" Hild blurted out, not sure how else to get them to where she wanted.

Zolk looked at her with a questioning expression on his face. It honestly didn't matter, he supposed he would make sure that they painted this house in their terror, both literally and metaphorically. The pups and her could sit anywhere for all he cared; he just wanted to make them scared, and he liked the idea of being able to boast about this triumph.

"All right, but you try to do anything tricky, and I will skin you in front of these pups," Zolk promised.

"No!" yelled Solgar as Hild tried to move them over to the corner. His hackles were up, and he was growling. His pride was wounded, his friends were being killed, and his mother had been insulted. He was done playing nice with this invader.

"Brave. Stupid, but brave," Zolk said solemnly, stepping toward Solgar. Suddenly, the pup realized his foolishness, turning to run back to his mother's protective embrace. Zolk snatched the pup up by his tail. Pain was etched across Solgar's face as he let out a loud yelp. Hild wanted to throw the pups aside along with her plans and rush to her boy's aid. The floorboard was right there though, she just needed to get a claw under it.

Can I leave my son to save the rest? she thought to herself, torn by the decision she was forced to make.

"That is some white fur, especially for living in the commune," Zolk said admiringly as he spun Solgar around a bit to get a good look at the almost perfectly snowy white coat. The pup's tail was the only colored part of him, a light stone gray. His eyes were like sapphires, and Zolk tried to remember where he had seen eyes like that. Somewhere, they had been peering down at him. *No matter, if it is important, I will remember,* he thought to himself.

"Does your mother bathe you daily?" he asked the pup as it whined in agony from being gripped by his sensitive tail.

The question solidified Hild's response; it was the hardest moment of her life and one that she would never forgive herself for. She remained motionless, except for her paws which worked frantically at the floorboard. Hild knew that if she ran for Solgar, it would tip the Ozar off as to who he could use for leverage to get the information about what Volg looked like from her. Once he had that, there was no reason for this monster to keep any of them alive and he would probably butcher them all, brutally. She felt Arvin tugging at her fur as he became frightened for his brother. She smacked him away, trying to give him a hint of the etiquette required in this situation.

Hild felt the floorboard give a bit as she heard Solgar's response. "I am just lucky," he tried to say with a brave face, but was still sniffling. The pup had managed to stop crying and Zolk didn't like that, so he decided to shake the Eclupse by its tail. That got the tears flowing again and put a grin back on Zolk's twisted face.

"Well, lucky little whelp. Tell... " Zolk began.

To Hild's frustration and dread, Arvin slipped from his mother's grip. He was not going to allow this brute to abuse his brother any more, not after the kindness he had shown to the injured Ozar.

"You stop it right now!" the dark gray pup yelled at Zolk, fists clenched and teeth bared. "You let my brother go, you... you lazy whelp!" the pup barked. "I... I helped save your friend and this... this is the thanks you show us!" The little Eclupse was doing his best to stay angry, it helped to keep him distracted from the panic welling up in him.

Hild had no idea what to do, did these other pups matter as much as her two boys? Her paws stopped working at the loose board as she swallowed hard, watching the terrible scene unfold and unsure how to respond.

Up until this point, Zolk had been happily batting at Solgar, or simply twisting him round by the tail to keep those cries and whimpers loud and constantly flowing. For a moment, all sounds of the tortured pup and Arvin's righteous tantrum were drowned out by a howl that echoed from the northern part of the enclosure. Almost immediately, the bugle atop the keep was sounded. Everyone in the shack froze, the Eclupse had never heard such a sound before. There were stories and rumors about how the howls of the Silverbacks had sounded, but nothing could have described the haunting vibrations that laid siege to the northern embankment. Zolk stopped for a moment, his eyes drifting back to the enclosure gate. He knew that he should probably go and help the defense. It was the moment that he and Headhunter had been dreaming of, after all. Unfortunately, it was a dream that at the moment no one could make a reality. Zolk had opened the gate with the bark sigil and then left it on the other side of the enclosure. He had wanted to ensure that none of these Eclupse were going to get away.

You imbecile, Headhunter roared savagely. Now look what you've done! The Maulers are here, and we are trapped in a pen with these things.

"Now just calm down," Zolk said out loud. "Besides, who cares about the Maulers? We have an opportunity to make that little cage-pooper pay, we are going to make him hurt." Zolk's eyes slowly scanned the room to build suspense as he began to shift his focus back to Solgar, before hesitating.

It wasn't that Arvin and his honest words had called Zolk's consciousness into being, it was that Zolk now saw why Hild had wanted to move to this side. She was trying to dig something out from the ground behind her.

"I warned you!" Zolk roared. With a powerful throw, he hurled Solgar into the wall behind him. There was a nauseating smack, and Arvin watched in outrage as his brother left a blood stain and smear down the wall of their home. There was a groaning sound from the building around them, obviously having not appreciated being struck by the pup, but then nothing. Zolk hesitated for a moment when he heard the shack's disapproval, but when there were no repercussions from the structure, he began to stomp toward Hild and the pups with new vigor.

The sounds outside the enclosure began to intensify as shouting turned to screaming and orders gave way to panic. Hild had turned away before Solgar had been splattered along the back wall, she hadn't wanted to see it. The home's protest to the murder shook her from her shock and she spun about, reaching for the chili powder as Zolk stomped forward. He batted away Arvin, who fortunately had seen the blow coming and had managed to jump back, only earning several scratches and bruises as he rolled across the floor of his house. He stood up with four long cuts along his chest, they hurt but the pup could ignore them.

Hild's eyes were watering, and her hands were shaking; she had to be able to see and force her hand to grab the right sack. If she grabbed the wrong one, she would simply throw a bag full of dried cloves at the angry Ozar. She felt his hand grab her leg, then her limb was released as Zolk growled in pain, the other seven pups surged for his hand, snapping at his fingers and wrist. Zolk yanked his arm back and Hild stretched for the sack, the small plume of powder that tickled her nose told her she had what she needed.

Zolk clutched Headhunter and with a fearsome roar he pulled the axe back, prepared to swing horizontally, meaning to cut the pups down as though he were reaping crops. His large body pitched back, and he lost his balance as a reddish-hued hempen sack flew into his open mouth. He blinked once, surprised, and didn't immediately spit it out. The cloud of red powder puffed, creating a haze around Zolk's face as the sack tore open on his teeth. Zolk wasn't sure what was besieging his nostrils or assaulting his eyes. He had no idea what odd substance had invaded his throat and stomach, but it wasn't long before he realized that these were attacks for which he had no defenses.

Hild watched as the Ozar staggered back, the pups' hackles were up and Arvin, now recovered, led the pups on the charge as they ran for the murderer's paws. Zolk's eyes burned, and his nose was dripping with mucus, the inside of his whole face felt like someone had stuck hot coals down his ears and rattled them about in his skull. His mouth was salivating but he couldn't swallow, his throat muscles were in spasm trying to break free of the awful ingredient. Zolk had never been one to expand his palette, he had found the introduction of new foods, ingredients, and delicacies to be frivolous. A good raw or slightly cooked chop of meat and maybe some berries or Red Martyrs roasted over a fire, that was Zolk's idea of a good meal. Not this, this was torture, this was pure and unbridled abuse. His stomach sent some acid warnings up his esophagus, making it very clear where it planned to unload this unwelcome substance. Zolk couldn't see and he couldn't smell, he could hear the charging pups but had no orientation to their attack or even where he stood so he swung wildly, wounding nothing but the air. His nerves still seemed to be working, as he felt the pups bite into his paws, more than one pulled away with a digit as a trophy of their first battle. Zolk kicked one off to only have two replace it, and he screamed in true and utter horror. It was the small wounds from those he once thought too weak to fight that were making the defeat all the worse. Zolk's axe finally hit something, and Headhunter's bit sank deep into the victim, but held firm and slipped from her master's grip.

Hild ducked under the weapon as Zolk spun about like a headless chicken, she heard the axe thump into the wood behind her and it anchored itself in probably the strongest part of the structure, the door frame. Hild was standing and held two pieces of wood from next to the fire. They were the heaviest ones she could comfortably hold. "Get out of here!" she shouted to the pups as Arvin pulled off the fourth now severed toe from Zolk's bloody paws. He gave a puppyish howl and the eight of them sprinted past her and out into the enclosure. Zolk spun about as he heard her and the pups moving past him. Hild brought both sturdy logs against either side of Zolk's head in a mighty clap, the Ozar's previous head wound was reinjured and Zolk spewed chili powder across the shack, before landing back-first as he was showered in bile and chili. Hild looked to the axe and grabbed it, turning to follow the pups out the door. Perhaps she could cut them a way out.

***

Terrabyss could see that the tide was turning and debated calling the retreat, but they were inside, he could see that Rellik was even within the walls and was sure that meant Brutyss was inside Kyron by now as well. To retreat now would be foolish, in his opinion. They could win, they just needed to get rid of some of these Ozars who were giving orders. Although that was proving easier said than done, as even with her mangled hand and destroyed shield, the Ozar in front of him was not going to just let him have this victory. She stepped forward and chopped her axe down toward Terrabyss' exposed left shoulder, having evaded his diagonal swing. Terrabyss could see that she was slowing down. He quickly stepped back and swung his weapon up to intercept the attack. Urrah hadn't thought that the Mauler could pull the heavy weapon up again quickly with only one hand, especially since he had just put what had seemed like all his momentum into that downward hit. Terrabyss hadn't, and his ruse paid off as the weapon caught Urrah in the elbow, shattering every bone the weapon could find as Urrah dropped Lopper with a shock of pain. Terrabyss was bleeding from several nicks to his forearms from her axe, but in the end her endurance had not been able to match the sheer savagery of the Mauler. She was glad, and ready to see Kevkel again. The kanabo split her skull with an audible crunch as Terrabyss forced the weapon to swing back down from his counter, planting his paws and using his core and body weight to pull the weapon, smashing down on the Ozar's skull on the right side of her face. Urrah's face folded down onto her chest as her skull was turned to mush from the blow, leaving no recognizable features.

The bugler from atop the tower let out another two quick trumpets, frantically waving his arm and pointing to the southwest. "They have reinforcements! They are moving to the southern embankment!"

Why had Numa not finished her circling of the commune? Terrabyss thought to himself. As he took a moment to catch his breath and truly survey the battle, he realized that the Ozars were mounting counter attacks on the wings. If they managed to push the reinforcements out of the two entry points, the Ozars could easily clean up the forces that were then trapped inside the fortifications. To the west, where Rellik and Unkyss should be, it seemed that the Maulers were dug in better. On the east, Terrabyss couldn't even see Maxyss, and most of Brutyss' division were being successfully pushed back. Terrabyss couldn't decide if the lookout should be eliminated or if he should help on the eastern wing.

An Ozar holding an iron buckler rushed the Mauler as he debated this dilemma, obviously upset that the female Ozar at Terrabyss' paws now had a head of mush rather than bone. Terrabyss caught the chop with his weapon across his chest, he stepped out, managing to step on this Ozar's paw with his own. Once this was achieved, he pushed his weapon back, lifting the Ozar's hatchet above its head and dislocating or hopefully breaking the opponent's ankle as the Ozar fell back. The Ozar tried to block the next blow with his buckler, but he only managed to embed the item in his sternum when it caught the full force of the Mauler's blow.

"That decides it!" Terrabyss yelled in the dying Ozar's face. "I need to get Brutyss some support!" If these Ozars weren't in a unit, they were easy enough. "Brutyss just needs to break up that wall on the eastern side," Terrabyss said casually, pulling his weapon off his opponent's—now concave—chest.

Several Maulers moved to sprint past Terrabyss and enter the fray; he motioned to the three and barked orders their way. "Get two more and get up the keep!" He pointed to where the sentry was. "See you at the end!"

"Or in the stars!" They nodded, giving their commander a salute and dashing for the tall wooden structure at the center.

Terrabyss still wasn't used to being saluted, and for a moment he debated bashing their skulls in for mocking him before he realized that they had been sincere. He turned to those behind him and put a fist in the air, barking at the closest group of Maulers. Once he had their attention, he smacked his chest, telling them to group to him and then motioned with an open hand to the western side of the embankment. The reinforcements understood, four began moving to him and the rest went to support Rellik and Unkyss.

Terrabyss chuckled slightly. *Things have really improved this last win*—there was a flash of light and Terrabyss' thoughts were interrupted as his fur stood on end. The bolt of lightning cut its way through the cloudless sky, to everyone's surprise, sending mud and dirt flying as a crater formed. Dust hid the place where Terrabyss had been standing and smoke wisped up from the hole that the bolt had punched into the ground.

483

***

Forver put his shield between himself and Maxyss' punch. The old Mauler was stuck between the Norrus and a massive, brown-furred Ozar, who, as far as Maxyss knew, had to be a Mahuer. Maxyss was in a dangerous situation and didn't have time to ponder the odd facial decoration that the Mahuer wore on his muzzle. He let out another howl, trying to alert any Maulers around him to his dilemma as he felt his hand connect with the shield and heard the axe behind him. Forver punched out, catching Maxyss off guard and making him stumble back. There was a sharp pain that shot up Maxyss' spine as the Mahuer's axe bit into his back. He felt his legs go numb for a moment and it seemed like half his body, the lower half, refused to work. The Prime Hunter collapsed forward on his hands, giving one last soft howl as Forver stole the glory from Azbin and planted Ol'Grim into the back of the Mauler's ribs, once and then twice for good measure. It was a good way for an old warrior to go to the stars.

***

Rellik and Unkyss had met back up and were now fighting alongside one another. Rellik still struggled to keep the shield in front of her, the buckler's weight felt awkward on her arm. Her right shoulder was extremely sore. Although, with her speed and her dexterity, she was able to use the buckler more reflexively, forcing axe blows to glance off the surface rather than landing with full force. Each blow she took was wearing her down a bit more, but the lightweight hatchet—which she had decided would be named Hewy Junior—was helping compensate for her fatigue. Unkyss, behind her, had Dummy and her axe Hew—he refused to call it Hewy. He had snapped off the haft of Hew—much to Rellik's frustration—as he had with Dummy, using the weapon's beard to cover his knuckles.

Another collision rang out as Rellik bounced the bit of an axe to the side and gave two quick chops with her hatchet into the attacking Ozar's bicep. The Norrus dropped his hatchet, only to receive hers in his sternum. The Ozar managed to stumble back and gasp for air before falling victim to the wound. Rellick's ears twisted to the east and she focused about four or five lue away, where a very fancy-armored, black-furred Norrus and a Mahuer were fighting. The first howl had slipped her attention as she moved to retrieve her hatchet. But the second, by either some blessing or curse, didn't pass by her unnoticed.

"Unkyss, they're killing Maxyss!" she cried, seeing Unkyss trying to keep his grip on his hatchets as they gonged into a buckler.

Unkyss felt the hatchet glance off his right bicep as Dummy forced the Ozar to lift his small shield. Hew sunk into the Ozar's exposed stomach, the Mauler ignored the cut in his arm and gutted the Ozar as he yanked the blade up into the opponent's heart.

"Do you know where he is?" he shouted back, slipping Dummy past a buckler and slicing the Norrus' forearm before the Ozar could pull his left arm out of the way.

"Four or five lue. To the east! The last howl was weak!" Rellik shouted, trying a tactic she had seen the Ozars use as she punched her new opponent in his face with the boss of the buckler. To Rellik's delight, the Ozar stumbled back, dazed, and she followed by putting her hatchet into his left collar bone twice, for good measure.

The bugle above them sounded twice as the lookout shouted information about the reinforcements. Unkyss looked up and Rellik would have followed if it wasn't for the fact that a familiar head rolled into view.

"Maxyss," she breathed in anger.

Unkyss hardly noticed her shoot away from him, her speed practically making her a blur. Rellik locked her sights on the two Ozars who seemed to be scanning the battlefield for specific individuals. Unkyss took a step to follow and then another to dodge a hatchet as he heard it whirling in from the right.

"Alpha Father! Really?" Unkyss raised his gory fists. "Really?"

Azbin saw the black-furred Mauler with different eye-colors first. The bright gold and dull amber contrast was hard to miss. Her hatchet slammed into the large oval shield of the garrison Mahuer, startling Forver as he hadn't even heard her approach. Azbin held his shield over Forver's exposed back and chopped Biter out from behind it, using the large object to keep his motions hidden. Rellik's whole body trembled as his axe connected with her buckler. She had tried to angle the shield so that the attack would just bounce harmlessly away but the swing had been so sudden she hadn't had time to position her arm correctly.

Forver spun around; excited to let Ol'Grim have another bite, he swung to Rellik's flank, preparing to chop his axe into her hip. Forver barely noticed Unkyss; if it hadn't been for the Mauler's savage howl, Forver may have never known the giant was approaching. The Norrus put his shield up as both Dummy and Hew dug into the wood façade, sending Forver sidestepping to try to maintain his balance.

Rellik had planted her paws again, squaring her hips and shoulders with Azbin as Unkyss and Forver locked weapons. Azbin tried to ignore her, his ego insisting that Unkyss was the more worthy opponent. Rellik's weapon and her reflexes were far faster than his, and if it hadn't been for his shield covering most of his body, she would have easily buried Hewy Junior into Azbin's flank. Azbin turned all his ire on the already-wounded female. The Ozar rushed forward, swinging down trying to catch Rellik, who was a little stunned after having been blocked by the shield, with a swift counterattack. Rellik abandoned using her buckler to block this Ozar's blows and leaned to the left, out of the way of his right-handed cut. Now standing on his left, she punched with the buckler as he moved by. The iron crunched into Azbin's healing muzzle and his eyes instantly watered as he let out an indignant growl. The Mahuer spun on the female Mauler, his axe leading the way and she was almost caught off guard by the speed. She jumped back just in time as the toe of the axe scraped along the front of her left thigh. That was the second time a female Mauler had broken his face which Azbin was not happy about.

Forver put the shield up again as the tall Mauler assaulted him. To Forver's frustration, this Mauler was taller than him by almost half a foot and his power would have made a younger Forver nervous. Forver intentionally tried to intercept the left swing of the giant Mauler, believing it to be his weaker hand and the side Forver held his round shield on. The Ozar managed to stop Unkyss' jab with the shield, intending to push and deflect the blow to his left to veer the Mauler off-balance. Unkyss punched through the block and easily kept his balance, earning Hew a scratch on the Ozar's neck and shoulder before his attack was fully stopped. Ol'Grim swung for Unkyss' waist, but the Mauler's right fist had already leapt into action and Forver's chop was stopped short when his bicep screamed in pain as the flesh and muscles were cut, Dummy sliding across the Ozar's arm before he could finish the swing. Forver stumbled back, barely able to stop the left fist from its second assault and holding a weak block to the right fist, again the blade dug into his arm, this time a few inches lower, right above the elbow. Forver's already injured arm could not lift Ol'Grim fast enough to intercept the second attack from the right.

"Azbin!" the panicked Ozar shouted, barely stopping a third punch with the left.

Azbin knew if Forver died, so did his dreams, and he ducked, keeping the shield above his head to stop Rellik from chopping him and punched the base of the oval brim at Rellik's hips. Rellik let out a yelp as her hatchet bounced from the treated wooden planks and the iron brim collided with her legs. Thinking the Ozar would pursue her while off-balance, Rellik purposefully lunged back despite the pain to give herself some room. She was instantly distracted as she collided with an Ozar behind her. Rellik just barely got her buckler in front of her throat before it was slashed out by the other Ozar's hatchet. The Ozar she had hit knocked her back with the blow and came charging after her. The Ozar was hit hard and lifted off his paws as he was tackled by Attawoolf, one of the sons of Attaboye, who had been a summer Watcher. Rellik jumped to her paws as the Ozar and Attawoolf rolled over each other. The Ozar came out on top and lifted his iron buckler, preparing to sink it into Attawoolf's throat. Rellik wasn't within striking range, unless—*Throw the weapon!* The thought suddenly arrived in her mind and without any hesitation she followed her instincts. With a resounding crunch, the blade wedged itself into the Ozar's skull and he collapsed atop Attawoolf. Rellik had no time to assist Attawoolf as he pushed the body off him, she turned back to find Unkyss.

Unkyss went for the third right punch, there was no block that was going to save this Ozar from his next hit. He felt a burst of pain in his right calf, as Azbin threw a nearby hatchet at Unkyss. The attack put a large gash in Unkyss' right leg, and the muscle was obviously badly damaged as his leg wouldn't respond completely to his instructions. Unkyss spun about and charged forward, abandoning the attack on the extremely injured and winded Ozar, much to Forver's relief. Azbin's second blow was with his axe, the half-moon blade chopped down with massive force for the Mauler's chest. Azbin was sure that this was over, the Mauler had no shield to block his attack and with the injured leg he hoped the Mauler would try to dodge. Unkyss' body reflexively lifted its arms in a cross to guard from the chop that was surely on its way.

Your funeral, Azbin thought to himself as he saw the guard. Unkyss smiled and stepped forward; suddenly, Azbin felt nervous. His confidence was shattered as the wooden shaft broke on the blades of the Mauler cross guard. Biter's head fell over Unkyss' shoulder harmlessly, he had obviously memorized where these hafts were weakest.

Azbin didn't see the final exchange between Unkyss and Forver. He was stumbling back, holding the broken haft of his weapon in shock. Forver tried to sneak up on, what he hoped, was a distracted Unkyss. He had abandoned his shield and now held Ol'Grim in his left hand. Forver saw the ears swivel first, then the body followed. Unkyss' shoulders, hips, and finally paws finished the rotation, coming face to face with a very nervous, tired, and wounded Forver.

"Mother—" was all Forver managed to say before he raised his arm to try and guard from the shattering punch of Unkyss' fist. It hit Forver square in the left shoulder, the nicely armored Ozar's chainmail protested from the hit, and the links snapped from the pressure as Forver thought he had lost his whole arm. Forver let the blow push him away, and honestly there was probably very little he could have done to stop himself from pitching back and rolling through the mud and muck. Azbin moved to pursue the giant Mauler and Forver, having gathered some of his courage back after Unkyss' block. Any pursuit was abruptly cut short as a hatchet sunk into his right glute. The Ozar stumbled for a moment and turned around, again seeing that female who had injured his face.

Perhaps I am not as good as I thought, Rellik thought to herself as she quickly looked down at her paws for another hatchet. *Note to self, always have a second one,* she mentally instructed as she scooped up a second hatchet. She had wanted the lower back; her intention had been to take his legs out. Though, as Azbin could attest, she had been a little bit wide of her mark.

Azbin didn't plan on letting her take a second swing and shouted to Forver, "The big one is all yours!" Unkyss felt a little honored. That brown-furred Ozar, who was easily a head or more taller than him, had called him big. Azbin gritted his teeth and awkwardly closed the distance between him and Rellik. The Ozar quickly ducked his head back behind the shield as there was a thud and a humming sound, as the hatchet the Mauler had thrown lodged itself into his shield.

Rellik nervously looked about again. *What did you just learn?* She screamed at herself in both frustration and panic. She readjusted her buckler; she was going to need it and all her strength to stop this Ozar's onslaught.

Her fingers still felt slightly numb from the other hits. Azbin yanked the hatchet out of his shield. He had originally planned to just brain the female with the oval ring but now he figured he could cut her down with the hatchet, Azbin charged in. It was jarring, and Rellik almost sat down from the blow. Her arm refused to lift itself a second time, still reeling from the first blow.

Unkyss knew he wasn't good at what he was about to do, but he had to do something. He threw Hew; the weapon was completely off balance because of the lack of handle, and Azbin ignored what felt like a stone hitting him on the back of his neck, as the butt and what was left of the haft bounced up and over his shoulder.

"I will deal with you soon enough!" he yelled, not looking back at Unkyss. *Let me just get some honor back*, he lifted the hatchet to hack into Rellik a second time. Her arm was still too numb to respond to another swing. Hew landed with a thump off Rellik's right thigh, almost perfectly in her right hand. Rellik's legs tensed as the signal went up her abdomen to her chest. Already her arms, shoulders, and back muscles had contracted. Her paws propelled her forward as the muscles uncorded themselves and she punched upward, digging the bit in under Azbin's ribs as he choked on his spit for a moment, too confused to swallow and fell back dead with Frax's precious axe-head in his lung.

"That... that better have been your intention!" Rellik yelled to Unkyss as she pushed herself off Azbin's collapsed corpse. Unkyss had his hands on his knees and was taking deep breaths; she couldn't really blame him, the battle was getting to them both. He just nodded to her, far too busy panting to talk. Three Maulers sprinted over to them from the north, just in time to be of no help to them at all.

"Terrabyss wants us to take the two of you to clear out the keep!" the three Maulers said to Unkyss and Rellik. Unkyss was too tired to even recognize them and Rellik was now mimicking Unkyss, trying to catch her breath.

"Bear-shit!" Unkyss responded, squinting to get a look at them.

Rellik waved them on. "Go, we will catch up," she responded.

The three exchanged glances but weren't going to argue with Rellik, and especially not with Unkyss. They charged into the keep, and were almost to the ladder leading up to the next floor as Rellik held her hand up, motioning for Unkyss to follow her before they were both too exhausted to move. Besides, they weren't going to let a strange number like three rush the keep. No matter how tired they were, they weren't going to leave any Silverback's fate to that risky number. Both of them heard the static and they could smell the electricity making their fur stand on end, then there was a cacophonous blast as the shock sent tremors through everything and everyone around the keep. Another bolt ripped to the top of the keep from its foundation, and three Mauler heads looked down to Rellik and Unkyss as a hole bored through the building, destroying floors and ladders. Ilkyss, a retired Scout; Bakcur, a Watcher and Attawoolf's alpha, and Devyss, a retired Hunter, were unsure how to get down or up from what was now left of the second floor with no ladders.

"Is the sentry dead?" Rellik yelled up to Bakcur, being the most familiar with him given he was the closest to her age group.

All three heads looked up and waited to see if someone moved or looked down, there was nothing.

"I think so," responded Bakcur with a curt tone.

***

On the eastern half of Kyron, Brutyss was frantically trying to keep his unit inside the commune. They had broken the shield wall but now the all-out melee was at its zenith. On both sides, the combatants threw themselves into the skirmish. The Ozars desperately trying to beat back the Maulers and the Maulers frantically trying to gain more ground inside Kyron. Despite Brutyss' earlier tactics, Ferda's shield was easily keeping the quick Mauler's attacks at bay, and the hafts of Brutyss' hatchets were becoming more and more notched with each passing moment. Both knew it was only a matter of swings before the weapon's wooden guard would break, leaving the young Brutyss exposed to Havil. Brutyss' attacks seemed to be making no headway against the sturdy wooden beams of Ferda's round shield. The eastern entrance was slick with blood and the embankments on either side of the entrance were sprayed with gore. Some troops lost their balance, others used the slick terrain to try to gain some advantage; the whole area had turned into a field of absolute carnage. The cries of the dying echoed about the combatants, and their cries for relief rebounded from ear to ear among the living.

Ferda's arm muscles burned, and she had multiple small cuts along her forearms, biceps, and shoulders where she had been punished for leaving her axe hand in front of her shield for too long. Her back had more than a dozen strikes that still leaked crimson off her fur from the agile Mauler who had managed to move around behind her on several occasions. Her lungs burned for more air, and she found herself jealous at the easy breathing pattern that Brutyss displayed. Brutyss quickly switched his grips on his weapons and locked the hatchet's beards over the top of Ferda's shield, yanking them down. Brutyss' strong legs and muscular core pushed his weight down and Ferda's weak arm was forced to comply. For an instant, the shield dropped. Ferda swung up with her weapon, managing to connect Havil's cheek with Brutyss' head, causing him to stumble back for a moment and preventing whatever following attack he had been planning. Ferda charged after Brutyss, bringing Havil's butt spike down to try to stab the Mauler's forearm with the sharp point and avoid the hardwood guards.

It was a smart move, and one that Ferda had already tried during this engagement with moderate success. Brutyss had a puncture wound in his left pectoral from having been unable to stop the weapon before it had dug in. He had managed to catch the haft of her weapon with his block, between the axe's belly and shoulder. Her second attempt at this attack cut along the top of his forearm, but not deep enough to slow his guard or assault. A few more of those cuts would have Brutyss thinking differently, Ferda was certain of that. Wisely, the Mauler decided to put some distance between him and the Ozar, to avoid a miscalculated block or worse, miss-intercepting the attack all together.

Ferda's shield lashed out, the boss directed for Brutyss' chest. Ferda hoped to tangle the hatchets up in her shield bash and then bring her weapon over the top and hopefully into the head of the Mauler, if not the back or shoulder. Any of those blows would bring this fight to a decisive finish, a conclusion she desperately needed given her lack of stamina.

Brutyss had let one hatchet slide down his forearm, he had liked how the beards and heels of the weapons had caught the Ozar's shield and he hoped his new idea would work. *I have been lucky so far,* he mused. Digging deep to find his reserves of endurance, Brutyss used a burst of energy to scoot just out of reach of the jabbing shield. In the same motion, he used his right hatchet, the one he had changed his grip on, and jerked it directly across his chest. His swing was accurate, and the hatchet's heel slipped over the brim of the shield. Ferda tried to stop her swing with Havil as it chopped down for what had seemed to be an off-balance and off-guard opponent. Her arm muscles contracted as she flexed, trying to hold Havil back, but it was a doomed attempt as the brim of her shield smashed into her wrist, sending both arms wide. She heard the blow before she felt the hatchet sink into her flank. Perhaps it was because she hadn't seen it enter, but she did feel it leave. Another violent sensation of pain as the wedged blade chopped through the ring mail and into her ribs. By the third hit, in her skull, she was probably dead, but Brutyss wanted to make sure.

He had also wanted all of the Ozars near him to know what he had done, shouting, "Here is your leader! Fall to the ground with her and perhaps you will not meet her fate!"

Needless to say, no one volunteered to collapse to the bloodied floor with Ferda, and the battle still went on. Rallied by Brutyss' victory, fewer Maulers let steel taste their blood and had the privilege of tasting the enemy's gore.

***

Numa was the first over the southern part of the moat, she landed with an "umph" and almost skidded into the steep, rising earth wall. Luna gracefully touched down next to her and instantly lunged up the side of the fortifications. Not to be outdone, Numa caught her balance and charged in pursuit of Luna.

"Curses to anyone who tampers with what should be left natural!" Numa barely heard Essall's comment as she couldn't help but give her opinion on the completely unnatural structure.

"What is waiting for us?" Numa shouted to Luna as the white Eclupse scrambled over the cusp of the embankment first. If Luna had all the time in the day to explain the chaos that was the ever-turning tide of battle, she could not have found the words. She had never seen battle, a truly savage battle. She had learned much from Terrabyss, Numa, and even Unkyss about fighting; all of them had been valuable teachers, but none of them had experienced this and nothing could have prepared her for what was on display before her.

"Luna, what is waiting for us?" Numa cried again, getting closer to the Eclupse as she surveyed the battlefield.

"It is pure chaos," Luna breathed as Numa finally joined her on the brim.

"Good, you can only bring order when there is disorder!" Numa hollered over the bugle which sounded their arrival. "Now, let us go put things in order!" was the last thing Numa said before she went sliding down the other side of the fortifications. Essall was on her Scout Mother's heels with a howl of excitement that finally managed to pull Luna off the edge she had perched on. Even with the long run that the four Fists had endured, only one had been killed on the leap over the moat, and soon nineteen Maulers came charging up the southern section of the commune. They met a group of fifteen Ozars, led by a garrison trooper who was trying to keep the militia in a tight shield wall so they could brace for the impact of the charging Maulers.

Numa, being at the lead, felt her fur stand on end and could smell the gathering static as she skidded to a stop in the mud.

"Stop! Stop!" she barked, hoping that everyone heard her command. Her heart sank as Essall slid by, frantically trying to dig her claws into the slick muck but finding no way to stop her momentum. There was a sudden flash as everyone was briefly blinded by a bolt of lightning whose clap robbed them of their hearing and ripped apart the ground just a lue away from where Numa had stopped, and right where she had seen Essall last.

Sparks

Skoff had just finished activating the sigil, he pounded his legs against the ground, keeping an even rhythm to maintain the incantation. Carloe was still distracted by the myriad voices that seemed to be everywhere but were nowhere. Although the druid had paid his price for the Needle Arms, so they kept pressing their assault on Dio. The Alpha planted his legs into one as it lunged for his prone form and launched it into a nearby redwood. Its body splintered into a shower of thorns, needles, and kindling as it smacked into the hard surface. Dio tried to scramble back to his paws as another abomination hooked into his ankle with its sharp, thorny fingers.

Skoff stopped pounding the ground with his paws and inhaled deeply, while starting a new, quicker rhythm on his chest with his fists. The fire around him suddenly began to retreat within Scoff's lungs as he turned toward the Alpha and the thorny creatures.

Probably should have warned him to go belly-first, Skoff thought, but there was no time for that now. There was no way he was holding in the flames for long and the next time his mouth opened they would escape.

Dio sighed in relief as the shaman turned toward him, cracking his heel into his assailant's bristly arm, earning another stab of pain but allowing him to break free. The other eight were almost on top of him now and he was struggling to stand when his fur felt the heat. Dio pitched to his side, covering his face with his hands and rolling on the moist Green Wall floor. The Alpha's attackers stood no chance, even if they had been standing in a downpour, burning to ash in the onslaught of flames. The water around the area quickly heated and evaporated, becoming steam and creating an unintentional escape route for the two Maulers. Their fur curled and puffed out in the humidity as they began panting instinctively.

"You could have warned me," Dio whispered harshly as he could smell Skoff less than a lue away, it was like mildew and the scent before a heavy rain had mixed together. "Alpha Father, you reek," Dio added as the two found each other in the haze.

"You don't smell like a field of clover either," Skoff snidely remarked. "Now come on, we need to get away from here before the Ozar realizes we aren't in this vapor cloud any more."

A million other questions were harassing Skoff's thoughts. How did *Dio assault the druid? He hadn't been holding any item carved with a sigil or performing any ritualistic motions, so how?* Now wasn't the time for that, now was the time to live. The two ran for a tight thicket of small spruces. The trees' lush needles and closely layered branches kept them hidden for a moment. They had put almost forty lue between them and the cloud of humidity that was beginning to dissipate. Again, Skoff's mind dogged him to ask Dio what he had done and how? He thought better of it, peeking around the girth of a spruce to see if the Ozar had recovered yet.

"Do you see him?" Dio asked in a hoarse whisper, trying to catch his breath and holding his hands over several large cuts in his arm and legs. His hands kept alternating for a few moments until he finally concluded that the cuts on his ankle were the deepest. He scraped what little snow he could find from under the spruce and packed it against the wound. Skoff brought a hand to one eye, the one nearest Dio, and covered it briefly as a response. It took Dio a few moments to understand what the shaman was telling him but nodded when he realized that Skoff had lost sight of the Ozar.

"Won't the trees tell him where we are?" the Alpha asked the shaman as they tried to remain hidden from the druid. Skoff's answer was a shrug of uncertainty.

Carloe looked to the east and west, then to the north and south. His gaze went above and then below, as he spun around trying to pinpoint the barrage of laughter, questions, insults, compliments, and statements. Everything went deadly quiet for a moment, and then there was the sound of distant birds, a breeze of wind, and a puff of cloud. The druid looked down at his curled and twisted fur, looking as though it had been blasted by a wind funnel. He ran a hand down his forehead, eyes, and down his short muzzle. *When did it get so hot? The shaman!* His mind raced back to take control of his confused senses as his eyes scanned the area. All he could smell was heat, all he could hear were the confused whispers of the birds and the squirrels as they questioned each other about the scene playing out before them. Carloe had no idea what trick that shaman had pulled but he was excited. *I'd best not underestimate him again.* The druid pulled his precious, carved bowl from his bag and placed it on the ground before him, looking at the different options. His gaze fell on the large canine head that had been so delicately chiseled into the beautifully polished face. It had been a long time since he had brought Planter out for a good hunt. Carloe quickly shifted behind a large cedar and rooted the bowl into the dirt. The druid squatted down over the conduit. He took out the only true weapon he carried on him; a small, wide-bladed skinner that had been a gift from his father when Carloe had come of age. The Ozar debated for a moment how long he would need Planter's assistance. *Probably not more than five droplets. Although, if the shaman pulls another surprise like that out of his bag, I may need Planter for a bit longer.* Carloe gave himself a good prick with the knife, *I think most likely more than five.*

After a few more moments passed, Dio took a sigh of relief. "I think we may have lost him."

Skoff wasn't so sure, his mind was arguing with itself. On one hand, he wanted to agree with the Alpha and use the opportunity to interrogate him on what in Alpha Father's name that spell had been? Also, while they were on the subject, what ley line was that? Spirit? Spirit was the only one that made sense. One last thing, how? How do you cast without a sigil? Because that is not possible. At least, it isn't supposed to be. The other side of his mind, the more rational side, was of a mind to try to find some way to put down the druid when he came back. Skoff could try to create a hybrid form of magic with his knowledge of fire and wind, but as he recalled earlier, he hadn't used wind much since he found his love of fire. He could always mix fire into wind but that could potentially just make his fire bigger, he wasn't sure of all the rules to forming a hybrid. Of course, if he mixed wind with fire, wouldn't that be the exact same effect? This is insane, Skoff thought to himself.

The first drop of blood hit the etching of the canine head. What am I supposed to do? Skoff mused.

The second drop of blood hit the hound engraving. *It can't be as simple as wreathing one hand in the wind,* Skoff picked up the stone with the wind sigil engraved.

The third drop of blood hit the whittling. *I would probably need to amplify it,* Skoff concluded, giving his finger a slight cut.

The fourth drop of blood hit the shape of the dog's head. *I guess if I am to follow this path of logic, I would need a fire sigil in the opposite hand, fortunately the one on my shoulder is still there.* He slowly reopened the original cut, making sure to not dig too deep, he was hoping he wouldn't need much of either element for his trial run.

The fifth drop of blood hit the tooled design of Planter's features. *With the fire sigil naturally amplified, I just need to focus and...* a small ember flashed to life and hovered in the shaman's palm.

The sixth drop of blood hit the mold. And now I just, Skoff shrugged and brought his left and right hand together. The larger wind flue caught the ember and, instantly, the ember died.

The seventh drop of blood hit the delicately hewn pattern. Dio stared at Skoff, unsure of what the shaman was attempting, having no schooling in the arcane practice whatsoever.

Did I do it wrong? Skoff thought for a moment.

The eighth drop of blood hit the blocked-out visage. *How else would you do it?* Skoff stared back at Dio for a moment, cocking his head to match the Alpha's expression.

The ninth drop of blood hit the sculpt of Carloe's trusted companion. Skoff's fingers began to tingle. *Well, wait a moment, this feels right.*

The tenth and final drop hit the growing crimson puddle. Dio stepped back, his fur was starting to stand on end and not because the humidity was returning. His coat was becoming stiff and the fibers seemed to be pulled upward by invisible strings. A surge of power pulsed through Skoff and all of his muscles locked painfully as his nerves seemed to overload.

Maybe this didn't feel so right, Skoff tried to say, but his jaw was held shut by his cramping sinews.

Carloe jumped up and began whistling and running back and forth, as though he were the very creature he wished to summon. On the first lap past the bowl, it began to rattle in place, another lap brought a more visible response. On the fifth lap, the bowl had a long body and legs, with a panting face and a long, branch-like tail. The creature's hide was bark, but firm like the sequoias around them, with bristled teeth and nettle-like fur.

Skoff's body convulsed slightly at first and then more violently. Dio was panicking, trying to get him to tell him what was wrong. It was pointless, the shaman could neither speak nor move and he felt as though his heart was going to explode. His head throbbed and he was sure he could smell his blood boiling.

"Well, there is a good girl!" Carloe exclaimed, running over to the twelve-foot monstrosity. As he neared the droopy-eared hound, her nettle-like fur vanished, so as not to agitate her friend's sensitive flesh.

"We have someone to hunt and here is the good news. We don't have to bring them back alive." The Growth Hound's tail shook violently with excitement at the druid's tone. Planter gave Carloe a splintery lick, that, had she wanted, would have shaved his fur and flesh right from his chest and face, but the Growth Hound had no such desire.

"Okay. Okay. Okay!" Carloe finally shouted to try to get Planter to calm down. "Now, let me get on your back and we can sniff these Maulers out." A strong gust of wind was created by the Growth Hound's tail as it shook happily, but she bowed her head and front legs so the Ozar could take his seat between her shoulders. Once Carloe was comfortably in position, he tapped Planter on the neck and she shoved her face to the ground, sniffing for the scent Carloe had sent to her with his touch.

Skoff still hadn't responded, he hadn't moved, and Dio wasn't sure if he was even breathing. The Alpha's ears swiveled around behind him as his paws sensed the floor below him trembling ever so slightly. Weakly rooted trees were being pushed aside and boulders were kicked out of the beast's path, ferns were trampled under paw. Dio took a glimpse around their clutch of spruces and saw the huge hound sniffing its way ever nearer.

Carloe was getting a little concerned, he repeated his concentration verse again in his head. Each telling was the length of a single droplet and he had gone through the script three times already.

"Skoff," Dio whispered nervously. The shaman remained the same, standing like one of the many spruces around him, only he didn't sway in the light breeze. *Maybe whatever Skoff was trying had been successful, and perhaps he just needed some time.* "Would have been nice if you told me that," Dio muttered as loudly as he dared, the monstrous plant creature was getting closer. "You owe me," Dio said, hesitating one last time before walking out from the cover of the trees.

Planter's head shot up and Carloe growled, disappointed. "Where is the shaman?" the druid demanded of Dio.

"I think you passed him," Dio lied. *So far, this isn't so bad, and I am sure Skoff will be joining me any minute.*

Carloe rolled his eyes, Planter wouldn't have passed anyone the Ozar told her to seek out. "Enough games!" the druid shouted. "Eat him, girl!" Planter lunged forward, to Dio's dismay. It easily cleared the distance

498

between them and the Alpha had little time to react. The Ecluspe slipped between the Growth Hound's front legs and narrowly avoided having his head snapped off. Dio slid to a stop under the creature's stomach, similar to the animal the creature was designed from, here the body was protected by a thinner layer of bark and far less nettle growth. Before Dio could reach up and drive his claws into the summon's stomach, the beast jumped up, intending to smash the puny Silverback below.

"Bear-shit!" Dio managed to breathe, quickly rolling to his left to avoid being crushed into the earth. Dio jumped to his paws, twisting as Planter turned, the hound's huge, powerful head whacked Dio in the flank, sending him cartwheeling across the ferns and into a sturdy redwood. Slowly, the Alpha re-gained his equilibrium as Carloe laughed with delight. Dio could barely suck in air and his ribs were definitely bruised and probably broken. The arm he had used to protect his face in the collision was wrenched out of place and broken. *Come on, Skoff, whatever you are planning, now is the time to reveal it.* Dio stumbled as he tried to put his right leg under him. *I guess I rolled my ankle,* that was the best-case scenario. Dio forced his good leg under him, knowing he could get one good lunge out of it, and he was going to need it as Carloe was lining Planter up with him again.

Skoff's fur was now standing on end and he could smell the growing static. An intense blue light cut this way and that up his left leg as a yellow one shot down his right arm. Small currents of electricity surged between each strand of fur. His muscles finally released him from their rigid constraints, but his nerves met with sudden spasms as sharp, needle-like pains rolled up and down his body. The two glowing lines ran toward his torso and his heart surged; at this rate, it was going to explode. The shaman's body felt too alive for a moment, everything was painful. The forest floor beneath his paws was torture, the breeze like a thousand lashings, and the spring morning a suffocating heat. Skoff had to find a way to release this energy or his whole body was going to overload, not just his heart. The shaman closed his eyes for a moment, trying to bring his focus in on the druid. He saw a multitude of Taurs and places at first. Kyron, the keep, the earth walls, Terrabyss, a multitude of Ozars, Essall, Dio, and finally, the druid. Forcing his arms to move, Skoff brought his hands up to above his head, clapping with all his force and releasing a loud howl. At first, the blue and yellow energies tried to resist, but the shaman's will was too much, and with an echoing boom the greenish bolt crackled into the sky above.

Dio didn't move at first as he watched the electricity twist and cut its way back into the clear sky above. Even Carloe and Planter stopped for a moment, hearing the sound and seeing the dazzling light. The sky stayed bright with a few, puffy white clouds meandering above them. Dio felt it before he saw, smelt, or heard it. The druid's fur began to stand on end as well, but he ignored it, thinking that the shaman had failed with whatever spell he was attempting.

"Let's get this over with!" Carloe cried energetically, not wanting to waste any more time with this magicless Eclupse. Planter charged forward, closing the distance between the two of them in the blink of an eye.

Dio's body screamed at him to move as his fur felt heavy but alive with the static at the same time. He followed his instincts and lunged with all his might for a patch of ferns; further to his left and out of the way of Carloe and the huge Growth Hound. The druid didn't have time to ponder the Alpha's odd response, there was a loud snap as a yellow bolt cut down into Kyron, once, twice, a third, and a fourth time. Planter's head was seared off as a blue bolt hammered down where Dio had been standing. Before Carloe could cry out in surprise, another blue spear of lightning impaled itself in the druid and the creature's back. Some way off in the woods, a beautiful wooden bowl with elaborate sigils split apart. Skoff fell to his knees, his eyesight flashing in and out before he fell forward, tired and drained.

***

Hild looked back to the shack, still nothing stirred inside. She turned back to the large vine and chopped with the brute's axe into the magical plant. The sound behind her drowned out the sound of the steel bit trying to even scratch the arcane creation for the umpteenth time. The dirt that shot out from the crater that the bolt created scattered across the north end of Kyron and then a second bolt bored its way through the keep. Another flash toward the south brought her attention to a rear defense against another group of Maulers that had appeared over the southern embankment. The fourth flash within Kyron stabbed into the eastern entrance, sending dirt and debris over the battling troops. The fifth and sixth bolts impacted further out, into the northeast of the Green Wall and then, miraculously, the vines around the compound began to wither and wilt. The thorns fell

500

from them, becoming dust as the wooden bars both above and along the sides toppled, no longer held together by the plant life.

"Come here, quickly!" Hild shouted to the pups as they gathered around her and she charged through the dying cell walls, breaking open an exit to freedom and away from the collapsing structure. Fintorn didn't move, the shock of the day's events had left him paralyzed and his fear held him rooted. He huddled with his arms around his knees, crying and tail tucked under his bottom. Hild almost didn't notice him as she glanced over her shoulder to make sure all the pups had followed.

I am not leaving another pup to die here, she told herself, charging back into the pen. Tossing the weapon aside, she scooped up Fintorn as a heavy wooden bar from above crashed down to the left of her. She turned back for the exit, another wall beam came down and crunched across the hole she had made, sealing them back in. The dust was becoming suffocating and Hild was having trouble making out where the next dangerous piece of the pen was going to collapse.

"Mama," she heard, looking to her right and spotting Arvin's little head peering through a gap in the rubble. Without hesitation, she sprinted for her boy. A loud crash sounded behind her as the shack was demolished under another wooden beam. She quickly pushed Fintorn through and, with Arvin's help, they had the pup on the other side of the gap in no time. She hastily followed, thankful for her gaunt physique as she squeezed her narrow chest and hips through the space. The wood above her shifted and she felt a sudden pressure on the back of her left thigh, the beam pressing down on her legs. Arvin and the other pups began to pull on her arms, trying to free her. All eight pups gave it all they had and, with a sudden pop, Hild was free and colliding with the eight exhausted pups.

"We need to keep moving," she panted, helping them back to their paws. Hild winced as she stood, but still the Eclipse ignored the pain. Her ankle could heal later. "We are going to climb the west wall and then slide down the other side. Do not try to jump over the moat, even with the momentum from sliding down. We will gingerly work our way down the moat wall and weave our way through the stakes and out the other side. Then we will climb to freedom. Understand?" she asked, looking from face to tiny face as they nodded. The serious expressions almost made her chuckle, and she may have despite their feelings if the mood had not been so desperate. "Follow me," she commanded, leading them toward the western wall.

"I hope that savage Ozar is dead," she heard Arvin say to Fintorn, who was jogging quietly beside him. She wanted to tell Arvin not to talk like that, but at this moment she hoped he was too.

***

Numa and Luna didn't have time to see if Essall was okay, the front line of Ozars had been only moderately stunned by the bolt of lightning and the long fissure it had created that divided the two forces was not much of a barrier. Snarling with rage, Numa barked for her troops to "spare no one." Leading them headlong into the clumsy shield wall, the captain had managed to cobble together again after the lightning strike. Unlike Brutyss, she had a bit more experience on the field and instantly the troop followed her lead, filing in behind her. All were experienced Scouts, excluding Luna, and she was a quick study. Numa directed the spear point into a militia Ozar who she had noticed step back when she barked her command. He would fold easy, and the rest of the shield wall would break. She lunged, slamming into the frightened Ozar with no mercy and rolling out of the attack with his throat in her jaws. The rest of the force followed quickly, throwing this rear guard into disarray.

Luna did well for her first true battle. She managed to keep her wits about her in the chaos, deflecting a hatchet as it was thrown at her and sending her own dagger sinking into the attacker's throat. The sound of a second hatchet flying toward her right side caught her attention and since her hand was now free from throwing the dagger, she rapidly moved her shoulder out of the hatchet's trajectory and caught the weapon by the knob, almost missing it. Hurling it back at the foolish Ozar, she forgot to turn the blade back around before she released the weapon and the butt collided with its forehead, knocking the Ozar out cold. Two more came at her, one from the front and another from her rear. She was starting to get into the rhythm and all her evening training with Numa and morning drills with Terrabyss were paying off. The one in front was the garrison trooper and he used his large, oval shield to keep her dagger point at bay. Despite her speed, she found that she was too preoccupied with the other Ozar behind her to slip the dagger past the oval guard.

Numa had her own problems, having become pinned in by a group of four Ozars trying to keep their shields in front of her blurring and brutal attacks. Luna let out a whimper as the garrison soldier's cruel weapon found her left shoulder. The axe was older in fashion, most likely an inherited weapon that had been passed down. Instead of the head being fitted over the wood with an eye, the axe head was socketed into the handle, making it harder to replace. The weapon was designed for war and had a spiked point instead of a curved blade. The spike expanded close to the haft, at which point the metal was sharpened to make a cutting blade. This was known as a dagger axe, and it was rare to find one on the battlefield.

Luna had managed to block the second attack with her dagger, she held it with the point angled back toward her body and smacked the attack away with the handle of her weapon. A quick jab shot the tip of her knife back at the garrison trooper's face, but there was a hollow thud as the tip connected with his shield. Luna was already moving as the second swing from behind came in, but her dagger had become wedged between the planks of the opponent's oval shield for a moment too long and the hatchet bit into the bicep of her left arm as she tried to twist away from the attack, but was halted by the inconvenience of her dagger.

The Ozars had regained their cohesion and they began blocking Maulers from supporting one another. They used their iron bucklers admirably, deflecting most, if not all attacks, and letting their hatchets respond by drawing blood more often than not. A lone Ozar was a dangerous opponent, in a coordinated unit they were ruthlessly efficient. Luna had to get some support to Numa so that the Scout Mother could re-organize her troops. She caught a slight break catching her rear attacker's buckler wrist with her blade before he could get his shield in front of the attack. She had to snap the tip of her dagger to free the weapon, but it was worth it as she caught the militia Ozar by his wrist, causing him to hesitate with his attack. Luna still had to dodge both axes at once but with the militia Ozar's injury, she managed to catch the hatchet with her free hand, planting a hard kick in the garrison Ozar's large shield at the same time. This scooted him back a bit, forcing him to reposition himself. The buckler punched out for Luna's face as she held the hatchet firmly, it struck but Luna had wanted it to. She slipped her left arm around the shield, driving the blade into the Ozar's elbow and out through his tricep. The militia Ozar's arm went limp as Luna yanked the blade free, still holding tightly to his weapon. He wasn't trying to free his arm any more and just begged for his life.

She wasn't interested in his pleas and drove the broken tip into his throat and up into his skull.

Spinning, she expected to be taking the full fury of the garrison trooper, but instead found Essall squared off with the Ozar. The Scout looked like she had risen from the earth, her fur was covered in dirt and mud, and much of her back and shoulders were burnt and smoking from taking almost a direct hit from the lightning. Her claws were deep under each of the Ozar's bottom ribs, and she was obviously tickling the garrison soldier's lungs. She finally released him with a grin and he collapsed, dead, joining Luna's kill.

"Numa," Luna said, a little shakily, unsure if she was seeing a phantom.

"I am alive, and you are welcome!" Essall shouted at her, turning to where the Scout Mother had one Ozar in a standing arm bar and was using him for now to keep the other three back. Luna stood stunned for a moment, but Numa's howl of joy at the sight of Essall brought her back into the fight as she joined the other Scout to give Numa some relief.

Numa kicked the Ozar she was holding in the hips, making him fall face-first. She then grabbed the same arm she had been working and planted her paw in his back before he could get back up. She wasn't worried about the other three now, Essall was on her way to reinforce the Scout Mother. She yanked the Ozar's arm up and heard the pleasant sound as it dislocated, before smashing her paw down into the back of his head. She had been right to assume that Essall was not going to let her get attacked by the other three. The one on the left of Essall had been the closest to Numa so the Scout had already flanked out, having all the assailants in an almost perfect line. The Ozar nearest to Numa raised his axe to chop into her exposed throat but she didn't even flinch at his approach. Two paws, in honor of Jabyn, connected with the Ozar and, had he survived, his feelings on how hard he was hit would have mirrored Azbin's. One, two, and then three Ozars fell over one another as their comrade was launched into them. Essall's adrenaline was at its peak and she barely noticed the impact as she landed from kicking the Ozar. Rolling back to her paws, she charged after hearing Numa's paw cave in the back of the other Ozar's skull, and soon it was three on three as Luna charged the rear Ozar. As the militia turned to face their new attackers, Numa reminded her Scouts of their orders and not one of the rear guards remained standing by the time her Fists were done.

Guilt

Terrabyss slowly stood up, about fifteen or so lue from the moderately sized crater to his left. The left side of his body was burnt, and much of the fur on that side had been singed short or was gone altogether. He took a cautionary sniff and wrinkled up his muzzle at the smell of half-cooked him. His eyes were still flashing specks in his vision and his ears were ringing as though a tree had fallen on his head, his left ear especially was only relaying a high-pitched humming sound. There were small fires around him and the northern half, almost the whole enclosure, was still slightly reeling from the shock. Terrabyss smelt the half-dazed Ozar that thought it had an easy target on its hands. Unfortunately for it, the Ozar hadn't realized the battle was over. Terrabyss didn't bother to enlighten him on how the keep, both entrances, and the north and south walls had all been breached, and that the Eclipse were no longer in their pens. Terrabyss did take some solace in the realization that the bolts had seemed to strike indiscriminately between Ozar and Mauler. He lifted his kanabo with his right arm, thankfully that limb wasn't charred and was still in its socket. He didn't want to risk injuring the left more, so he choked up on the weapon and planted his paws as the Ozar chopped randomly at him. Terrabyss was glad he had noticed the signs of the gathering energy, or he would have been ash. His instincts must have pulled him free and now he would let his instincts cave in this Ozar's skull as he batted away the axe and hammered the points of his kanabo into the opponent's head. There was a slight groan from the Ozar that was matched by Terrabyss' frustrated growl and another bash to the head. This time, the Ozar's response was silence.

A howl of triumph erupted from the southern part of the commune as Numa's Scouts brought down the last of the rear troops. From the eastern half of the commune—where the debris had settled from the fourth bolt—Brutyss and what was left of his forces had dug themselves out of the dirt. With a slight chuckle, Brutyss mustered as much energy as he could, adding his voice to Numa's. From the keep, both Rellik and Unkyss chorused the victory howl and their surviving troops joined them on the western half of the commune. No Ozar was left standing; if any had fled into the Green Wall, they were few and Terrabyss would guess no more than a handful at best. To their credit, the garrison and militia had fought until the bitter end and had proved their courage in the casualties that the Maulers suffered. Those facts didn't change the certainty that the Maulers had won.

***

"Skoff!" Dio shouted as loudly as he could, still lying on his side from where he had landed. Smoke rose from the burning remains of the Growth Hound, and Carloe had long since blown away in the breeze. Dio had caught a glimpse of the charred Ozar skeleton before it had crumbled to ash. "I am pretty sure you hit him!" Dio yelled when Skoff gave no response to his first statement. Dio tried to laugh, but winced, letting out more of a whimper than a chuckle when his ribs reminded him of their condition.

"I could use some assistance, and I am hoping you don't need any!" the Alpha was shouting into the sky at this point. He found himself whimpering a lot more when he saw the puffed out, static fur of Skoff's face as it looked down at him. "Fix your fur," Dio wheezed, trying to stop himself from laughing, "you look ridiculous."

Skoff scowled, rubbing his hands through his fur but just making it stand more at attention. "I can't. I have been trying," he responded, frustrated. Skoff reached down to help Dio up but sent a surge of shocking energy through his fingers into Dio's arm.

"What in Alpha Father's name was that for, you pellet?" Dio snarled, having not expected the sudden shock to his bruised body.

Skoff glared at him. "I don't have control over the residual static. I am hoping I had enough control over the actual bolts, and we have a tribe to get back to. Now, do you want my help up or not?"

"Funny you mention going back," Dio said in an innocent voice. "I seem to have hurt my paw so unless you can perform some healing assistance, I don't know if I am going anywhere." Dio pointed down to the swollen joint. "I didn't know you could do that," Dio admitted, "you hit that druid and his ugly pet good," motioning to the left of him and the still smoldering outline of the beast.

"I didn't know I could either," Skoff said, honestly, "and I am lucky I didn't end up like that druid… " The shaman looked around for a moment. "Wherever he is." Dio blew into his fist, opening his hand as he did so and Skoff understood the gesture. "Good," was the only response he gave before collapsing next to Dio. "I am sure someone will come looking for us if we won, and if we lost, I don't want to go back."

Dio nodded his agreement as both lay back and looked up at the sky. They heard the Mauler's howls not too much later and again debated going, but again found the forest floor much more comfortable than moving. Skoff's mind, still amped from the battle, had lost all recollection of Dio's earlier skill against the druid. The two of them lay there laughing about the absurdity of using plant magic, even though it probably could have killed them both. Slowly, the sun shifted through the sky above them and it was just past noon when Terrabyss, Numa, Luna, Unkyss, and Essall found them.

The Alpha and the shaman were made aware of their approach by the sound of Terrabyss' voice, obviously arguing with a much more covert member of the team. More than likely, his sister, Numa.

"So what if there is a druid? I will smash him like I smashed everyone else. I am not scared of arcane spectacles." There was a moment of quiet. "Well, then you can sneak up, I will just march through the trees until the druid is dumb enough to run into me," was Terrabyss' reply as he rounded one of the redwoods and almost stepped on Skoff.

"Watch where you are going!" Skoff cried as Terrabyss' paw came within a whisker of his brother's hand.

"I found them!" Terrabyss shouted over his shoulder to the rest of the search party. He turned back to Skoff, noticing the sticking-out fur and all the ferns adhering to the static left in his brother's coat. "You," Terrabyss sneered threateningly.

"Me what?" Skoff asked, suddenly revealing that he wasn't injured and shuffling back from Terrabyss. Hoping to get to his paws a safe distance from his brother.

"You brought that storm down!" Terrabyss shouted, full of rage. "Look, look at my arm! At my leg! Alpha Father, look at my side!" He thrust out his left arm, showing Skoff all the singed fur and burnt skin that had cracked and blistered in the heat from the lightning bolt.

"He had to; if he didn't, we would both be dead, and you would have a druid marching back to Kyron with that," Dio said, pointing over to where the massive Growth Hound had been burning, now just looking like a pile of burnt sticks.

Terrabyss looked to where the Alpha was signaling, he saw nothing but a large patch of charred ferns and mosses, perhaps some wafting ash.

"It doesn't matter, we are alive, and the day is ours!" Numa spoke before Terrabyss spoke his mind, stepping between her brothers.

"Besides, you have nothing to complain about," Essall growled to Terrabyss, "you still have hackles."

"That is awful," Skoff breathed to Essall. Terrabyss shot him a look. "Well, yes, what happened to you is… " He was obviously struggling for a word.

"A travesty?" Luna asked, hoping that Skoff had been trying to sooth Terrabyss' anger rather than stoke it.

"Sure." Skoff shrugged.

"Why are you still out here?" Luna asked rapidly, before Terrabyss could comment on Skoff's response or turn the argument on her for butting in.

"Skoff is pretty exhausted from his last spell, and I have twisted my ankle," Dio explained. "Neither of us has the ability to heal me, so we decided to let you have your fun."

"Skoff seems to have energy," Terrabyss commented, trying to take the conversation away from discussing the battle. He wanted to have that conversation with Dio, alone. "I bet you wish you were a shaman with your own spells now," Terrabyss added flippantly to the Alpha.

Suddenly, Skoff remembered. "He does!" the shaman blurted out. The stare Dio fixed on Skoff almost made the shaman's blood freeze and the rest of the group turned to Skoff in surprise. "Well, I mean, he did. The druid that is," Skoff tried to explain, hoping they didn't see through his ruse.

"You get hit in the head?" Terrabyss asked with a laugh as he bent down to look at Dio's leg. The rest of them began to laugh, and even Dio and Skoff started chuckling. Numa's laugh was for show, and it was a good show. Her mind was beginning to fit the pieces together. The odd atmosphere she felt exuding from Dio, her brother's remarks about Dio's magical understanding and, most importantly, the fact that she had made decisions but had no recollection of why, and it had always been in the Alpha's presence.

"Well, we can make a travois and drag you back," Terrabyss concluded. "We are too far from Kyron to carry you without risking hurting you more.

The travois will be uncomfortable, but it will jostle you around less than if we carried you over one of our shoulders."

"How did the fight go?" Dio asked as Terrabyss stood.

"We won," was the Mauler's response as he, Numa, and Essall spread out to find good pieces of wood for the poles.

"How will you lash it together?" Luna called after them. Terrabyss simply lifted his kanabo above his head, tapping the leather wrap around the handle.

Dio turned to his daughter. "I am led to believe we won by the way everyone is talking, but by the way they are acting I am having my suspicions."

"Let's just get you back to the commune," Luna responded with a half grin. Dio knew his daughter well enough to know when she wasn't telling him something.

"What happened?" Dio asked, laughing nervously now.

"When you are back at Kyron," Luna said, this time much more firmly. "Be happy we won and leave it at that."

Dio wasn't, but he had no energy to pry it out of her now. His body still ached and the tension was not helping. It took a while for them to make a travois and return to the commune—Terrabyss dragging the travois behind him—pulling Dio through the eastern entrance. Despite the intense fighting and sore limbs, the Silverbacks had worked to stamp at least a temporary presence on Kyron. The keep had kindling piled around it, and broken weapons and shields were being divided from ones in excellent, moderate, and poor condition. Most of the armor didn't fit, and most Maulers didn't want the armor that did fit. The armor in the best state was being preserved and piled near the tool shed that held the splitting axes and mauls.

Luna looked about for Rellik, impressed with how quickly things were getting done. Before the search party had left, Rellik had been placed in charge by Luna who had explained to her what items should be kept and what should be destroyed. Luna hadn't told Rellik to prepare to burn the keep and she wasn't sure that was a good idea, but she couldn't find her right now to tell her otherwise. The logs from the pens were being stacked by Maulers and Eclupse who were in condition to lift the heavy lumber and the beams that were in good condition were being moved to the western and eastern openings. It had been Brutyss' suggestion to block off the entrances by slotting the wood into holes that the new occupants were digging out of the side of the earthworks' entrances. There was a massive stack of Ozar dead to the south of Kyron and a large single pyre was being built next to the dead with the more damaged wooden beams. Toward the west, where the sun would set, was another set of large pyres, five in total, and at their bases were numerous dead Silverbacks. Dio couldn't believe how many he saw.

"Wha—what ha—what happened?" the Alpha finally managed to stammer.

Terrabyss took a deep breath, he instinctively wanted to blame Brutyss for charging in behind Maxyss, or Skoff for the bolts of lightning. He wanted to blame Dio; wasn't it the Alpha who said that he was going to communicate with them and survey the battle? He even debated blaming Numa for coming out of the forest at the southwest instead of the southern tip of the clearing.

The battle had been loud. No one could hear commands. I had to do what I thought was tactical. Besides, you left me blind and deaf. The excuses flooded his thoughts. "I didn't call the retreat." His mind screamed at him that his response hadn't been one of the options, but he knew the truth.

Somehow, the Alpha managed to glare at his commander even from his squat position in the travois. "You were given clear orders!" Dio shouted. The other Maulers within earshot tried to ignore the justified condemnation. "Once you felt pressure from the defenses, you were to pull back and allow the enemy to think they had won! The Ozars needed to see the huge number of troops retreating, or else they wouldn't have followed with a false sense of victory!"

"I know," Terrabyss growled. He honestly wasn't frustrated at Dio but at himself. The Alpha's comments cut deep into his pride and he found himself becoming defensive.

"Do you, Terrabyss?" Dio barked. "How many did we lose? How many?" he pressed when Terrabyss' initial response was silence.

"Forty-one," was the staggering reply. Terrabyss' muscles were tight, and he had to keep himself from shouting the rest of what he thought in Dio's face. *Their weapons and armor were more than any of us could have prepared for*—another lie he tried to tell himself. He should have pulled the Ozars into the woods where their defenses would have accounted for less. Where they couldn't organize and employ their discipline. He had become lost in the thrill of the combat and forgotten that he had responsibilities to others. He had been the commander and the death toll rested on his shoulders alone, a lesson he would never forget.

"How… " Dio swallowed, trying to keep his heart in his chest, it was pounding. "How are we going to continue the campaign? We will be lucky to fortify this position and keep it until the winter when we can march again." Dio's words were softer, not because he had regained his composure but because he felt lightheaded.

"I will make it up to you," Terrabyss promised.

"How?" Dio found a bit of a second wind when he heard the response.

"I just will. Know that." Dio found it hard to argue with the tone in Terrabyss' voice and the stern expression on his face.

"See that you do," Dio responded coldly. "Now, take me to the keep so I can rest."

Terrabyss looked back over his shoulder. "You could sleep in the leader's quarters or the druid's, or one of the many pitch tents that the Maulers and Eclupse haven't claimed."

Dio looked out over Kyron again as Terrabyss drew his attention to the keep. His anger subsided a bit, he was still unsure of how they would survive but the hugs, wagging tails, and nuzzling faces of the once-penned Eclupse brought a slight wag and painful motion to his tail.

"There is a large circular tent if you want to rest in there, fortunately all of these" – Terrabyss motioned to the small pitch tents – "were already set up when we arrived, or we wouldn't even know what all the material was for." Dio nodded, which was better than what Terrabyss had expected with the terrible joke.

"Take me to the yurt," Dio said weakly. Terrabyss gave the Alpha a confused look, cocking his head. "The circular tent," Dio explained. A gray pup with a small log went running up to the keep. "Are they going to burn the keep?" Dio finally asked, after noticing the young Eclupse dashing away after placing the wood in a small moat dug out around the structure.

"I think so," Terrabyss responded. "They started that after we left to find you," he added, his tail wagging slightly at the sight of the happy pup as he pulled Dio toward the yurt.

"Do you know why?" Dio asked as he felt the travois lurch forward and grimaced slightly.

"My guess? It is a symbol of this place. One they are not fond of," Terrabyss wisely said as they made their way to Dio's temporary abode.

"Were any of the losses extremely significant?" Dio asked; he hated the question, but he had to know the actual damage that had been done other than numbers.

Terrabyss slowly responded as they arrived in front of the yurt, "Fortunately, none other than Maxyss."

Dio nodded. A war councilor, Prime Hunter, and elder. "He will be greatly missed," Dio finally said. Terrabyss pushed open the thin wooden door and carried Dio into the yurt, helping the Alpha get situated on all the cushions which were strewn about the bed opposite the entrance.

"Fetch Skoff, please, I want some basic aid until he has regained enough energy to heal my paw."

Terrabyss stopped by the door and leaned down, taking a lap from the bowl of water next to the door. "Yes, Alpha," he responded, closing the odd barrier that shut his Alpha in the strange round tent.

The burgundy, red-eyed Mauler passed by Volg and Hild, who held Arvin tightly, and Arvin, who held Fintorn. The pack stopped and howled respectfully; many of the Ecluspe had been doing this to any Mauler that passed them. The Maulers had been caught off guard at first, thinking that the Ecluspe had meant to avenge their overseers, but Luna had quickly explained the law in the communes about howling and the Ecluspe assured their rescuers that they meant it as a sign of respect.

We can teach them the salute later, Terrabyss thought to himself. The other surviving pups had been reunited with their parents or welcomed temporarily into another pack. Many grieved and others celebrated together, but all came to an abrupt stop as Terrabyss passed; they all recognized the weapon-wielding Mauler as the first one over the northern wall and the leader that had been at the forefront of his troops. They all turned to thank their liberator. Shouts were raised to the passing Mauler and howls broke out around the camp.

"Terrabyss the Breaker of Kyron! Terrabyss the Bane of Ozars! Terrabyss the Blood Bather!" were just some of the accolades that echoed about.

Numa smiled as she saw her brother begin to strut slightly to the praise. Unkyss and Rellik stood tall, and Brutyss cheered from the eastern entrance. All his troops were quick to join in his glory and add their praise. Luna's tail wagged nervously as Terrabyss motioned for her to join him, and then her tail thumped heavily as he nuzzled her when she finally made her way over. Both their tails whipped back and forth as they were showered with raucous howls.

Dio sat in his yurt, his hackles on edge. *How dare those Eclipse and Maulers praise that runt?* It hadn't been Terrabyss' plan that had given the Eclupse their freedom, or the Maulers this victory. That prideful Mauler had almost gotten them all killed and lost everything. Dio would not allow his anger to sour the mood, for now they would celebrate and after everyone had their fill of the triumph, they would remember the casualties. Then, Dio could punish that uppity Mauler, he could really humiliate him. *Patience is a virtue,* he growled to himself as he waited for the shaman to arrive, by now a familiar mantra. Dio had to consciously change his expression so it wasn't sour when the door to the yurt opened.

The shaman hadn't changed his poncho and was holding a massive crate of different poultices, unguents, and other random concoctions. Skoff's tail smacked the lattice work of the yurt in his excitement. "I found all the druid's stuff!"

The scowl almost returned to Dio's face as he got a whiff of the smells that were wafting from the crate. "I told Terrabyss to fetch you after you had rested a bit to heal me," Dio said, scooting back ever so slightly from the odd items. Dio swallowed hard, beginning to guess why the shaman had brought all these things in here.

"Terrabyss hasn't talked to me," Skoff responded, which only made Dio more positive that he knew where this conversation was going. He forgot how upset he had been a moment ago. "I just figured that there was something in here that could help your injured paw. So when one of the Eclupse asked if I knew arcane magic, and I told them" – Skoff gave one of his typical flourishes – "yes, they took me straight to the druid's home. Dio, Dio, you wouldn't believe all the items in there. I never thought I would be jealous of a druid, much less an Ozar, but the organization, the labeling, the amounts! It is simply amazing!"

"Skoff. Skoff!" Dio shouted to try to break the shaman free of his trance. "I am sure that I can handle a bit of pain until you recover enough to just use some magic. I doubt that there is anything in… in there that will be useful." Skoff just raised his eyebrows, an expression that Dio was fluent in. "Of course, if you think that there is, I am willing to allow you to recuperate at your own pace." Dio knew he lacked enough energy to even attempt to persuade Skoff otherwise, magically or not.

***

Terrabyss raised his hands to get some modicum of silence. "Has anyone seen Skoff?" Terrabyss yelled over the last few howls. It had been nice, all the praise and recognition, but he didn't want to keep the Alpha waiting. His question was met with blank stares from the Eclupse and shrugs from many of the Maulers. "Figures," Terrabyss mumbled under his breath.

It was just getting toward evening when all the Eclupse and Maulers gathered under the open sky. The Maulers, per Dio's instructions, had built a very traditional Gathering directly in front of the keep, facing the northern embankment. He had wanted some changes made to how things had been done at the grove, so they had rolled boulders in from the nearby trees and had laid the largest one near the base of the keep, at the head of the new Gathering. Smaller stones were placed next to the larger one for Skoff and Luna. Patches were then cleared for the seating of the councils, and a single black canine tooth was placed in each of the empty seats for Maxyss, Rymmall, and—much to Terrabyss' frustration—Suskyss. The rest of the Gathering was left as natural as possible, according to Mauler tradition.

The Eclupse and the Maulers had begun to get acquainted with one another. A few fights had needed to be broken up when tempers flared because Maulers felt as though the Eclupse were ignoring them when they didn't respond to the Mauler's expressions, gestures, or pacing. Luna had found herself becoming an interpreter of sorts through much of the afternoon, explaining to both sides why the other seemed so foreign. She was a good mediator and the fights had never escalated beyond some growls and snarls; it didn't hurt that she was the Alpha's daughter and the mate of Terrabyss.

Dio had been spared these unpleasantries; once Skoff had cornered him in the yurt, he had tried several different poultices on the leg. One had felt as though it had frozen his paw before it began to burn. Another, which was wrapped in a long fern leaf, had caused Dio's leg, painfully, to spasm over and over as though the nerves were being poked. The third had been the one Dio had told Skoff was right. Honestly, the Alpha wasn't sure, but he couldn't take another random attempt to heal his ankle. Skoff had wrapped a hemp cloth that had a thick, almost ichor-like substance coating the inside, similar to the fern but clearer, around the injured ankle. When Skoff had wrapped the paw in the material, Dio's whole paw and ankle went numb. *It doesn't hurt any more at least.* Although Dio's head hurt slightly now, he dared not mention it to the shaman. Skoff had been so excited about all the different things he found in the druid's quarters that even after he had helped the Alpha, he stuck around. Pulling item after item out of the crate and explaining to Dio what he thought they were. It had been educational but also mind-numbingly dull.

Dio limped onto the large boulder that had been rolled in for him at the head of the Gathering. It took him a few more minutes than he would have liked, and he was sure he looked like a fool trying to scurry up the massive stone. They couldn't have found a smaller one? He growled to himself as he managed to get his claws into some pores in the boulder and pulled himself to the top of the pedestal. Dio's gaze traveled around those gathered, despite the losses he was proud of what he had achieved as everyone's eyes were fixed on him. His eyes trailed to his left where Skoff sat, opposite Luna on the Alpha's right. The shaman's tail wagged as he gave Dio a nod.

Of everyone who knows about my ability, why is it that I dread the fact that Skoff knows above all else?

The Alpha quickly shifted his gaze out to the group of Silverbacks before him. "You waited a long time for this!" Dio began in a booming voice so that all could hear. "Both of you waited a long time for this! The Eclupse, my former tribe! We beg your forgiveness for our delay! Maulers!" A loud chorus of howls broke out, interrupting the Alpha and startling some of the Eclupse, but not all as Arvin and his friends tried to join in the chorus. Dio raised his hands as Terrabyss had done earlier and the howls slowly stopped, especially when Hild clamped Arvin's mouth shut. Dio's eyes were closed, his head lifted to the sky. "Maulers, you have waited a long time for this as well! But I promised you I would bring you home!"

There was a moment of awkward silence as Dio announced this, and for a moment Dio's eye twitched. Numa, ever observant, tilted her head back and let out a loud, dominating, single howl. If Dio hadn't known better, he would have thought she had just missed her cue. But he knew better, or so he thought. *Was it her that set this up? Did she encourage everyone to wait for her so that she could drag it out? Maybe it was an idea hatched up with them as they had searched for him and Skoff? Why then had Skoff been in on it? He was with me this whole time.* Dio's thoughts were smothered by the howls that followed Numa. The Alpha kept his composure and nodded to Numa. "I have been made aware that the Ozar's stores have been cleaned from this… this sign of oppression behind me! I say we burn it!" There was no awkward silence after that statement as a cacophony of howls erupted.

Terrabyss stood, fetching the torch that had been set aside for this and Luna struck the flint to get the kindling and sap-covered wood shavings to light. Dio looked to Terrabyss and remembered the struggle it had been to get up and down this rock, although he really didn't want to give Terrabyss the honor. Not after his debacle. "Is there any among you who would like to have the honor of burning this symbol to the ground?" Dio looked out to those gathered.

A small, dark-gray paw shot up from in front of Hild, from Arvin who was sitting in her lap. *A pup that size is going to need Terrabyss' help,* Dio told himself. Everyone was looking at him and no one else had volunteered to take the pup's position. *Bear-shit!* "Okay, it seems we have a young, strong volunteer, perhaps his father or mother would like to join him?" Both Hild and Volg lacked their son's courage and stayed silent. Just bear-shit! "Well, come up here!" Howls rose, cheering the pup on as Arvin sprinted up to the Alpha's stone. "Terrabyss, can you assist him?" Dio said in a friendly voice, despite his thoughts.

Terrabyss looked over to Arvin. "Of course, Alpha," the Mauler responded bluntly as he turned to face Arvin.

The pup swallowed hard. "You're the one who broke through to save us." Arvin's tone was full of awe. Dio had to keep himself from snickering at the notion.

Terrabyss gave him an awkward smile, he wasn't sure how to relate to pups, much less Eclupse pups. "Yes… " There was a long pause. "Yes, but you will be the one who burns their stain from this land."

Arvin liked that. *Arvin the Purger,* he snatched the torch and almost fell forward from the weight. Terrabyss instinctively reached out and caught the pup by his shoulders, so he didn't go face-first into the ground. It took a little longer than it should have, and everyone tried to keep from snickering as Arvin almost spun around at one point and put the torch within a whisker of the Mauler's chest. To Terrabyss' credit, he didn't yell but he was perhaps a bit too gruff in spinning the pup back to face the keep. If Arvin had noticed that he upset Terrabyss, the fear washed away as he watched in awe with those gathered as the flames snaked up the keep and, for a moment, only the highest point left caught fire. The beacon showed for all who cared to see that Kyron was free. Then, the whole building ignited as Skoff casually adjusted his poncho.

The next couple of hours were full of chatter, laughter, shouts, praise, and thanks as the Silverbacks feasted in the temporary Gathering. Dio had been right about the Ozar's provisions being cleaned out of the keep and mead, meat, pine nuts, honey, and grubs were passed around. The Eclupse who worked in the kitchen had been more than willing to lend their ability to the meal, and more than one Mauler mate or pup was commenting that another should spend some time with the Eclupse to learn such an invaluable skill.

Several Eclupse were learning the rules to Test of Strength and Rolg cheered his father on. Modyn managed to break a bundle of eight fresh sticks. Unkyss nodded slightly in respect and then snapped a bundle of twelve with ease. This brought laughs from all watching, including Modyn and Rolg; Maulers weren't great at showing restraint. A lesson that some of the other Eclupse pups were learning too, as Arvin led them in a game of My Skull. To Arvin and his friends' credit, they didn't shed a tear when they were hit, and pulled themselves right back up out of the mud and kept playing. The Mauler pups played fair and didn't change the rules on the Eclupse or gang up on them. There was no honor in winning when you cheated, something all Maulers knew well.

"Are you sure we should be doing this?" Luna asked Terrabyss as the two of them made their way to the western embankment and the sentries stationed there.

"It isn't fair that Bakcur and Devyss as well as Delthyn and Zelyss don't get to participate in the celebration. The least we can do is take them some mead and some of these honied grubs. Have you tried these?" Terrabyss snatched his fourth grub from the wooden tray he was carrying.

"Yes. I told you it was better than that cheese," Luna responded as she could see Bakcur and Devyss on the western entrance of the embankment. "But this Ozar mead is a bit stronger than I think you Maulers are used to; shouldn't we be worried if our sentries become drunk?" Luna reminded Terrabyss again of her earlier concern.

"*Pfff,* don't get ahead of yourself. We have strong tolerances. Also, what are they even guarding us from? A few injured and humiliated Ozars? I am sure Dio is being a bit too cautious." *Besides, I owe them some reward for following me,* was Terrabyss' thought as they closed the last few steps between them and the watch. "We brought you some treats," he said to the two of them as he held out the honeyed grubs and Luna moved to give them the skin of mead on her left shoulder.

"Thanks!" Devyss responded with a wag of her tail as she snatched the mead before Bakcur could grab it. The male Mauler was staring awkwardly at the grubs Terrabyss held out.

"Take some, they are actually pretty good," Terrabyss instructed, putting the tray right under Bakcur's nose. He finally took one, then two, then ten.

"You're right!" he said with a mouthful, pushing Devyss back with his paw as she tried to snatch one.

A few minutes later, the mated pair was moving for the eastern side of the embankment with a mead skin for Delthyn and Zelyss, and—if Terrabyss kept his greedy hands to himself—another fifteen or so grubs for the two of them.

Rellik and Numa were talking with an Eclupse by the name of Byell, who with Dhon's permission had been taught by Travic to do simple smithing. She repaired the axe heads that the commune used to fell trees, and had once or twice fixed a chainmail link in the garrison's armor. Rellik was holding one of Luna's daggers in her wounded right hand, and holding a militia trooper's hatchet in her uninjured left. Numa was shrugging and Byell was nodding excitedly at what Rellik was describing. Brutyss and Oulyss were laughing across from one another, obviously trading stories about their positions in the battle. Aasha was with her brother, but laughing along with Essall, Jabyn, and a handful of Eclupse. Essall had just begun explaining the moment the lightning bolt smashed right behind her. Skoff, to his absolute joy, found a captive audience in the Eclupse. Everywhere he told the old stories, both adults and pups would gather round and listen, completely entranced, to stories that most Mauler pups were tired of hearing. Dio had to personally get Skoff's attention so that the evening could conclude. The shaman was needed to usher the dead to the stars and despite all of Skoff's earlier trepidations about large conduits, he knew he couldn't deny the fallen their right. Not even the enemy.

The Ozar bodies were stacked up on or against the single large pyre that had been erected in the south of the commune. Everyone watched reverently as the pyre caught fire and the flames consumed their enemies' bodies, sending them to the stars above as their souls rose with the smoke. Few, if any tears were shed for these, but the Maulers were not savages and would give their opponents an honorable departure, especially after the courage they had shown.

The following five pyres were more emotional. Many Eclupse could be heard crying as the bodies of Habyss and Okmyss were added to the Mauler bodies. An unknown feeling burned itself across Terrabyss' soul as he saw Wilca and Vozim let out cries of sorrow, joined by Vomi, Zarsyn, Heb, and Jennis. Terrabyss struggled with the intensity of the emotion as he watched Wilca tear herself from Vozim and throw herself into the flames that consumed both her and Okmyss. Vozim held Heb and Jennis tightly as the two pups almost ran after their mother, devastated by her actions. Terrabyss' response was driven by the new emotion, all he could hear was Numa's question, "What will you do when we are no longer just surviving?"

Terrabyss stepped out from those gathered and wrapped his arms around the pups. "Your fathers were braver than any of us standing here." He didn't know if his words would help, but it felt like something he should say, especially since he had been the one who had called for their executions and delivered the sentence. It had been the tactical decision, but Terrabyss had never thought he would need to face the consequences of a logical decision. In the dying embers of the pyre, the Silverbacks fell asleep, exhausted. The suspense of the battle, the injuries sustained, the thrill of the celebration, and the weight of the losses put the whole camp into a very deep sleep as Bakcur, Devyss, Delthyn, and Zelyss all hiccupped and eventually all dozed off.

Epilogue

"Wolf-shit!" I swore as my fist punched through the rubble. It was late and the commune was quiet as I clawed my way out from under the destroyed shack. I stared at the huge wooden beam that had dropped down from above, it had missed me by an inch. I am thankful for that; I hadn't been conscious and would have never known that I had been smashed until I was staring down from the stars above. I breathed a painful chuckle as I looked up at the stars gazing down at me. The moon was starting to drag to the western horizon, and I wasn't sure how long I had been unconscious. Perhaps my Mahzar is up there, perhaps it had been him who altered the course of the falling beam. *Now all I need is Headhunter, and I will know I was spared by him,* I mused as I slowly got to my mutilated paws. My injuries from the battle were still painful, and I struggled to get up.

Looking around for a way out, I noticed that three wooden bars had been half-fitted into the eastern embankment. The western embankment had its three bars comfortably blocking the exit. Smart, I had to admit, *we should have thought of that. Mother Bear, curse them!* Campos Ursyss is to the west, but it would be far easier to sneak out to the east, given the state of the blockade. I looked in surprise to the middle of Kyron. *Wasn't there a keep there?* All that remained now were embers, still glowing faintly, and small clouds of smoke climbing up to the stars from the ashes. Foolish, I thought when I saw the charred foundation of the building. To the south, another faint tendril of fire flickered and then vanished as the stars illuminated other puffs of smoke rising from the charred remains of a massive, single pyre. Behind me, on the western side of Kyron, another five smoke trails rose into the heavens; there were no fresh embers around these five and I figured the fire had been extremely intense to burn so quickly.

I slowly began to move to the eastern entrance, resisting the urge to set some of the many pitch tents alight or to raid Forver's yurt for cushions as I crept past. I didn't see or hear any Silverbacks inside the temporary structures. *It would be easy to just duck in and take some,* but I kept moving forward. Without Headhunter, I didn't feel very confident about getting in a fight. I noticed that the sentries posted at both exits were either leaning against the embankment with their heads resting against their chests, or simply lying sprawled out on the grass. *It will take weeks for Bardell or any other Honcho to respond to Kyron's defeat, but still, this is just sloppy!*

I moved cautiously, not wanting to disturb any of the sleeping invaders that I assumed would just materialize if they heard me try to make an escape. I had to clamp my mouth shut with my hands before I swore out loud, my paw kicked into what felt like wooden planks that had been piled up together. I looked down, half-tempted to pick up one of the pieces of wood and throw it in my frustration. My rage quickly changed to grief and a tear slowly ran down my face as I saw her. *I am so sorry, girl,* I thought as I bent down, picking up my love gently. Her haft had been snapped near the throat and her blade had a few nicks from being swung against the magic vines. I softly held her to my chest, hearing her half-conscious groan.

"*Shhhh,*" I cooed to her, giving Headhunter a nip of my arm. The blood would help revive her. "There you go, girl. Let's get ourselves out of here so I can fix you up," I whispered as I picked my way to the eastern entrance. "Of course I came back for you," I said in a low voice, nuzzling her. "Just rest." I sniffled as I neared the two sentries. The exit was blocked by only two wooden beams here. I wasn't sure if the guards had become lazy and hadn't finished building the blockade, or if the bottom beam had simply fallen. I easily stepped over one guard, who was lying on his stomach. The Mauler twitched and my hand squeezed Headhunter for a moment. If it hadn't been for her whimper of pain, I would have plunged her into that Mauler's ribs. No doubt about it. Even with my head ringing. I wasn't scared, I just knew that if Headhunter wasn't willing to kill the Mauler on the ground, then the one dozing with her back to the embankment wasn't going to be to Headhunter's liking either. I decided to let them be, ducking under the middle wooden beam, after carefully stepping over the bottom one where it was touching the ground. I held the middle beam as I went under, just to ensure that it didn't rotate or fall out on top of me. Given the state of the bottom beam, I wasn't going to take any chances.

I stepped away from the eastern entrance and tip-toed back into the trees. I waited for a moment, hiding and listening to see if anyone gave chase. "We are on our way home," I whispered down to my waist, where

Headhunter hung quietly. "Don't worry, girl, we will make them pay, I promise."

Once I was sure that I was a safe distance from Kyron, I stopped bothering to move quietly and cautiously. Now I wanted to move fast, I wanted to get back to Campos Ursyss as quickly as possible. I had important news for the Honcho, after all, and if I found any survivors on the way back, I would be sure they understood that I was supposed to tell Bardell. I stumbled over a root and landed face-first into the ground.

"Mother Bear, curse those pups," I swore under my breath as I rolled to my back and sat up. I want my toes back, and when I lead the charge to retake Kyron, I will let Headhunter torture all of those whelps and force Groll to bring them back to life so I can do it again and again.

It was close to dawn when I saw a faint light off in the distance. It came from a dying fire, not one that someone was trying to hide or put out. I was starving and exhausted, but I wanted to put as much distance between myself and Kyron as possible. I took another handful of snow that had taken shelter from the heat and rain under a spruce's low branches. I could taste the dirt, but I was so thirsty I didn't care, and didn't mind spitting out the small pebbles as the powder melted. It was the only thing I had to sustain me until I found some food. Headhunter had fallen asleep long ago as I carried us away from the Maulers and immediate danger. I paused for a moment, hesitant at whose fire I was about to walk in on.

Perhaps the Silverbacks had sent parties out to establish perimeter camps to find stragglers from the battle? Perhaps it is another survivor? Perhaps it was just some traveling Ozar, Rodentia, or other Taur that may assist me. I thumbed Headhunter for a moment to rouse her. *Who am I kidding? They are going to assist me; they don't have a choice in the matter.* I stepped out into the fire's dim light, holding Headhunter tightly in my right hand. I felt the twigs snap under my weight before I heard them, but I didn't have the dexterity to pull my paw back before the trap announced my presence. "Wolf-shit," I breathed.

"Are you Ozar?" I asked in a hushed tone as I peered around the camp. "If you're a Silverback, you best run before my allies see your fire and join me in slaughtering you." I figured the lie would either get the visitor running or force them to reveal themselves. I saw an Ozar sit up on the other side of the clearing, peering at me past a log he was hidden behind.

"Mother Bear," he breathed, relaxing and standing up.

"Mahzar?" I managed to stammer in response as I looked at Forver. "You're alive?"

"You don't look so good either," Forver responded crossly, motioning to the missing digits on my paws. "Of course, I am alive." He gave me a curious look. "Also, where were you during the Maulers' assault?"

"You wouldn't believe me if I told you," I finally answered after looking down at my paws and then back to Forver.

"I thought everyone else died," Forver admitted, slowly lowering his shield and stepping over the log.

"They all did die," I responded, gazing half at Forver and half at the axe he still held. "No one else survived the slaughter."

"Well, besides us." Forver laughed nervously, lifting his shield slightly up in front of him as he noticed Headhunter and the way I was looking at it. "This is good," Forver said, sitting with his back to the log and tossing a nearby branch and pinecone onto the embers to bring the fire back to life. "Now we know how strong the Maulers are and we have dealt them a serious blow." I was still upset as this imposter kept talking, trying to ignore his friendly words. "Come, sit," Forver commanded but when no response came, his tone became angrier. "I said sit down, Zolk. This isn't the end for us. We will return and we will crush those barbarians!" Forver announced passionately and fervently. I slowly shook my head no and took a step toward Forver. "Zolk, I gave you a command. I still have money saved away back home; with you as the only other survivor, it is all yours."

I stopped for a moment, this imposter's frantic tone only solidified my assumptions. Forver breathed a sigh of relief for a second, still clutching his shield tightly and guarding himself. I laughed as I looked down at the frightened Norrus. "Forver the Ferocious, now Forver the Frightened!" I sneered. I stopped laughing, giving Forver my full attention. "I don't serve you," was my casual response, "I serve Forver and only the true Forver. You can pay me what you want, but you are not my Mahzar."

"Zolk, I don't know what you are talking about. I am Forver. I am right here. I lived. Is your vision damaged? Do you not recognize me? Stars forbid, were you blinded?" The questions poured out and before I could respond, Forver added, "Groll will gladly fix you, there isn't any need to worry."

"Don't be stupid," I sneered, stepping closer to Forver again. "Of course, I can see you, who you really are."

"Zolk, stop this right now!" Forver commanded, but I just ignored him again. "I am your Mahzar and I order you to stop this immediately. Unbelievable," he breathed nervously as he pushed himself to his paws, I was still coming toward him. "You have lost your mind, haven't you?" Forver shouted but took a step back, stumbling a bit when the log caught his heel. I was within arm's length, all I needed to do was strike and cut this imposter down. "Zolk, stop, you piece of wolf-shit! Stop this right now!" Forver glared at me, making me hesitate as I saw a glimpse of the real Forver shining through in his anger. I still knew what I needed to do.

"Thank you," I responded, sincerely. Forver stood there, his mouth half-open with his claws half-raised to wave humiliatingly at me. "Truly, I do appreciate this last gift. I had not expected you to allow me to see my Mahzar in these last moments."

Forver moved to punch me with the boss of his shield, but he was too slow for me. My left arm shot up, catching the inner edge of the shield and holding it in a firm grip. "You should have never taken my Mahzar from me!" I roared in rage, swinging my right arm around behind it and letting Headhunter live up to her name. The blow damaged her more, but she told me it was worth it to eliminate this fraud. "I will tell the Honcho how we were tricked by your ghost and how your phantom led us on this disgraceful campaign. I will not encourage him to tarnish your name though, stars know the real you needs to be remembered for the good you did." I gave Headhunter a bloody kiss, proud of her. "I had no idea you could decapitate ghosts." I laughed as I kicked the body aside, sitting down in front of the fire to get warm. "I will tell Bardell that the Maulers are back."

Epilogue

Aasha: (Mauler) Alpha of her litter and sister of Brutyss and Foyss. She has black fur with bright golden eyes. She has many scars but the one that defines her the most is the scar that runs down the center of her skull between her ears and eyes. She is short in stature but very muscular.

Adoption: Ceremony that takes place when a pup's pack has died and there are no family members to take care of the pup. When a pup is adopted by another pack, they lose their former pack name and take the pack name of the adopted family.

Alpha: Leader of a tribe of Silverbacks.

alpha: Strongest member of a litter of Silverbacks. Determined by which pup opens their eyes first, until the pups can challenge one another, when one will assert their dominance over their siblings. It is also a term used among the Watchers and Hunters for the leader of their five-male packs.

Alpha Father: Silverback god.

Alpha Hunter: Typically the position of Alpha's mate, oversees the planning and execution of the hunts for the tribe.

Altz: (Eclupse) Brother of Luna. He had gray fur and dull blue-colored eyes.

Ammer: (Mauler) Son of Haxzus and alpha of his siblings, Rellik and Druce. Being groomed to take his father's place as Alpha of the Maulers.

Arn: (Norrus) Patron of the Baore family and Penma's mate. Veteran of Urrah's forces during the Daunkirk conflict. Keeps his facial hair in military braided style, and has black fur which is light brown around the muzzle.

He has dark brown eyes and stands roughly 7'4" with a stocky build.

Arvin: (Eclupse) Pup of Volg and Hild. Looks like his mother with dark gray fur that is speckled white and bright blue eyes. Shorter than his brother Solgar and very lean.

Azbin: (Mahuer) Older guard of Kyron and often employed as a scout. Previously employed at a commune that wasn't on the frontier, but lost his position to Bardell's cousin. He has brown eyes with honey-colored fur, standing 7'9" and muscular. His axe is a garrison weapon, named Biter.

Bakcur: (Mauler) An alpha of a Watcher group.

Balt: (Mauler) Watcher and brother of Narz. One of few Maulers that used actual weapons. He has black-colored fur and gold eyes with a few scars that criss-cross his arms. He is of average height with a lean and agile build.

Banshee Tundra: Tundra at the northernmost point of the continent, bordered by the Berg Maker in the north and the Ice Kraggs to the south.

Barchus: Pack name of the runt that was added to the hunting pack of Terrabyss' litter.

Bardell: (Mahuer) Current leader of Campos Ursyss.

Bear-Shit: Common Silverback curse.

Beast-Back: Typically have fur, scales, or feathers that cover their whole body, with few humanoid features.

Beast-Speech: Common language between all Taurs, but with different accents and dialects.

Belly-Greeter: A coward.

Berbra: (Norrus) Mate of Orald and mother of Gandrie.

Berg Maker: Northern ocean.

Bia: (Mauler) Mother of Tarphyss, Numa, Skoff, and Terrabyss.

Boulder: Well-sized stone that is kept near the Shaman's den and used to measure weights.

Branch Pens: Cages that hang down from the sequoia branches in the southeast of Kyron, outside the commune.

Bravis: (Norrus) Served in Forver's militia alongside Urguss. Has dark brown fur and light brown eyes, is 7'6" and is heavy but still muscular.

Brutyss: (Mauler) Very adaptable and quick thinking, and the sibling to Asha and Foyss. He has remarkable endurance and is very agile by Mauler standards. He has black fur with orange eyes and has no distinguishing scars. He is considered short, although taller than his sister and brother but much leaner than Aasha.

Burrum: (Hax) Half breed of both Norrus and Hax, he was raised in the Banshee Tundra and had a violent temper in his youth. He has dirty white fur with black fur that highlights his lips, eyes, and ears. He has the dark yellow eyes of a Hax as well as their height and weight. Stands over 8' tall and weighs roughly 400 lbs.

Byell: (Eclupse) A member of the lumber pen in Kyron and learned basic smithing from the Herder, Travic.

Calmus: (Mauler) Sickly looking Mauler who is part of the same Watcher pack as Terrabyss, serves as the alpha's lackey. He has black fur with bronze-colored eyes. Stands only a few inches taller than Terrabyss, making him short. He has a compact torso with gangly limbs, which add to his frail appearance.

Compani: Gathering place where both market and government business are conducted in a Rodentia Refuge.

Campo: (Singular: Campos) Ozar settlements that run along the east and northern parts of the Green Wall. Become smaller and less advanced the further north one travels, and are considered simple in comparison to the Daunkirk settlements along the coast.

Campos Ursyss: The last Ozar Campos in the north and considered the end of civilization before the human settlement of Izwin located in the Banshee Tundra. It has two permanent buildings: Middle Market and the Tavern.

Caphri: The Daunkirk capital along the west coast of the Green Wall. A pier city built out into the ocean.

Carloe: (Norrus) The druid currently employed in Kyron. He is young and impatient to test his skill, and from a family of druids. He has black fur that seems to have moss and fungi growing in it.

Charbah: (Norrus) Carloe's father and a druid who was a friend of Groll's.

Circler: A common toy that is essentially a wooden spinning top.

Clipping: A skill that the Daunkirk Madha learned how to perform and taught to the Ozar druids. Used to block a mage's ability to understand sigils, and to block a druid's ability to tap into ley lines.

Council of Elders: The council that helps guide the Alpha's decisions within the Mauler tribe.

Corm: A tribe from the Mino clan who are herders of mammoth out in the Banshee Tundra. Also described as Yak-Taur.

Cuskus: (Norrus) Patron of the Doen family and a possible recruit for Urrah. Recently widowed and has since become reclusive.

Cycyss: (Mauler) Sister to Zelyss and a member of Unkyss' pack for the Hunt. Has an extremely good sense of smell, even among Maulers. She has black fur with a white collar and polished brass eyes. She has no distinguishing scars, and is of average height with a lean build.

Cynwyn: The river that runs east to west across the Green Wall.

Dardyl: (Mauler) Only child and part of the Barque pack; technically the alpha, but she never claims the title. She has black fur and, like Numa who she respects, she uses beeswax to make her head and neck fur stand on end. She has orange eyes and a few scars, and she is average in height but very muscular.

Delthyn: (Mauler) Scout that Numa places in charge while she goes hunting for Hanora.

Dessel: (Eclupse) Mother of Sernna, Essur, and Indel, who passed away from an illness that spared the pups.

Devyss: (Mauler) Retired hunter that worked with Terrabyss in the Raid.

Dhon: (Mahuer) The first and, so far, only female colonel, posted in Kyron. She has dark brown fur that she keeps trimmed along her arms and legs. She has light brown eyes and stands 7'6" and weighs just over 300 lb. Her two-handed axe is known as Carver.

Dio: (Eclupse) Part of an outlaw group that wouldn't join the communes. Discovers the Maulers, and is Luna's father. He has smokey gray fur with white mittens and pale blue eyes. He stands at 6'5" and has a very lean build.

Doren: (Norrus) Female cub of Arn and Penma.

Druce: (Mauler) Runt of the Ballio pack and enjoyed a pampered life.

Druids: The magic users of the Ozar tribes, as well as other Taur clans.

Ebonhuw: Arkem city built by the tribe known as Spilkot in the Charred Cliffs, located somewhere in the Ember Sands. It is supposedly a beautiful and rich city, paved with gold in the day that magically transforms into silver at night.

Erbun: (Mahuer) Mate of Ferda and father of Yoll, patron of the Slen bloodline. Becomes a den dad after being injured in a Vargg revolt in the commune of Dolga. The injury was so severe that his arm was amputated, so he now spends his time with their son and farming honey. He is light blond with dark brown eyes and weighs just over 400 lb., standing at 7'11".

Essall: (Mauler) A senior Scout who is superstitious. She didn't want to be like her brothers and decided not to have a pack of her own, joining the Scouts at the same time as Jabyn. Has feelings for both Jabyn and Skoff, and is a bit abrasive. She has light black fur with gray highlights around her muzzle, eyes, and peppering her torso. She has dull orange eyes and is of average height and weight.

Essur: (Eclupse) Sibling to Sernna and Indel. His mother and father passed away when he was young, due to an illness.

Evems: Tribe of Arkems that live in the northern parts of the Green Wall and in other parts. They are warlike and worshippers of Ploter, the god of disease and poison. They were cast out of Ebonhuw for their violent and unsanitary practices.

Ferda: (Norrus) Youngest of Forver's commanders and known as Ferda the Fearless. She has light brown fur that turns almost black in the winter. She has dark brown eyes, stands 7'2" and weighs 360 lb., is very muscular. She named her axe after her father, Havil.

Fillany: Squirrel-Taurs, Beast-Back with thick, fluffy tails that like to live in trees.

Fintorn: (Eclupse) Pup who lost his father during a lumber accident, hasn't spoken since he lost his mother Trel.

Forver: (Norrus) A very rich Ozar from a very prestigious line known as the Yukon. He had dark brown fur but over the years the fur around his eyes and down his neck has begun to streak with gray. He has dark brown eyes and is considered short for a Norrus, at 6'8" and weighs about 300 lb. His axe is named Ol'Grim.

Foyss: (Mauler) Sibling of Brutyss and Aasha. Runt of his litter and enjoys a pampered life, like Druce. He has smokey black fur that covers his head and tail, but the rest of his body is solid black. He has yellow eyes, but they are very faded, making him appear sickly. He has no scars, is short and slightly pudgy.

Frax: (Mahuer) Veteran of Kyron. Often part of the patrols, like Azbin, and spent much of his earnings having an axe custom-made for him, which he named Hew.

Friggi: Gathering place of the Hax tribe. Their only communal area, housing their ravens for communication and a small market.

Gandrie: (Norrus) Daughter of Orald and Berbra.

Gentra: (Mauler) Runt of the Mallmee pack and sibling to Oryss and Suskyss. She has light black fur with yellow eyes and a few scars. She keeps the fur along her head braided. She is short and lean, which isn't uncommon for most runts.

Groll: (Norrus) The druid of Campos Ursyss. He is very old and is nicknamed Magic Stealer. He has brown fur but the blond highlights on his chest and neck have become gray. His eyes were once a piercing amber but have now become milky. He now stands just 7', having lost half a foot in his old age and is thin.

Groth: (Mauler) Retired Watcher and chosen to work with Terrabyss during the Raid.

Guards: A position created by Grimmis and continued by succeeding Alphas. Reserved for female Maulers.

Gunthil: (Mahuer) Rookie at Kyron and worked as a scout alongside Azbin and Frax. His axe is named Chopper.

Habyss: (Eclupse) Mate of Vozim and the father of Vomi and Zarsyn.

Halfling: Related to Dwarves, but live above ground.

Hamba: (Norrus) A veteran and mate to Urvek.

Hanora: (Mauler) Mate of Haxzus and the alpha Hunter. The mother of Ammer, Rellik, and Druce. She has light black fur that has gone mostly gray, and deep amber eyes.

Harpyn: A Taur that has a humanoid torso, including the arms and hands. Usually, the flesh is still tougher than human skin but not covered by fur, scales, or feathers.

Harris: Hare-Taurs that live mostly underground.

Haxzus: (Mauler) Alpha of the Mauler tribe, son of Grimmis, and patron of the Ballio bloodline. He has black fur with bright gold eyes and numerous scars that crisscross his body, with a very distinct scar that runs from his left ear to the bicep of his left arm. He is slightly taller than most Maulers and is of average weight.

Heb: (Eclupse) His parents gave him and his sister, Jennis, very Ozar-sounding names in hope that the Ozars would be kinder to them.

He-Lah: Prison plane of existence.

Hild: (Eclupse) Volg's mate and mother of Solgar and Arvin. She has lighter gray fur around her paws and hands. The fur slowly darkens until it creates a black stripe down her back. She has bright blue eyes, stands 6'6", and is very gaunt like the rest of the Eclupse in Kyron.

Hoarding: A common game played among the Ozars. Each player starts with five polished stones. Players take turns stacking a stone atop a single tower. The player that places a stone when the tower collapses is out of the game.

Hollow: The dug-out roots of a sequoia that Skoff calls home.

Honcho: The title given to the leader of a Campo.

Howler Grove: The former domain of the Silverbacks. It looks somewhat like a wolf howling, and is outlined by the Ryndell and Cynwyn rivers.

Hown: (Mauler) Kiltra's mate and Dardyl's father.

Hunch: All Silverbacks have a slight hunch to their backs, mainly because of their large shoulder muscles which are used when they run on all fours. Among the Maulers, the hunch is considered prized and is seen as a sign of virility and connected to ambition.

Hunt: Silverback tradition to allow pups to ascend to adulthood. If they successfully complete a kill, they will become adults, or must try again the following year.

Hunnora: (Hax) Burrum and Siya's daughter.

Ice Kraggs: Snowy mountain range that separates the Banshee Tundra from the Green Wall in the north.

Igwulf: (Eclupse) A prisoner of the Branch Pens.

Indel: (Eclupse) Brother of Essur and Sernna.

Ilkyss: (Mauler) Retired Scout.

Inlan: (Norrus) Forver's son and brother to Shael and Jakob. He is very fussy and likes wearing clothes. He often trims his fur to make the clothes more comfortable. He has charcoal-black fur and hazel eyes. He stands exactly 7' tall and is leaner than most Ozars, weighing barely 300lb.

Invasion Council: The war council that is established separately to the council of elders. It consists of Dio, Luna, Terrabyss, Numa, Maxyss, and Suskyss. Eventually, Rymmall is added.

Jabyn: (Mauler) Seasoned Scout and very close with Essall. Bonded with Numa when her father passed away the same winter as Bia. She is the last of her pack. She has jet black fur with bronze eyes and has six significant jagged scars that run down her back when she was attacked by a saber cat. Like Essall, she is of average height and is lean in stature.

Jakob: (Norrus) Forver's son and Shael and Inlan's sibling. He has dark brown fur with light brown paws. His eyes are almost black, and he is the tallest of his siblings even with his injury, standing at 7'6" with a lean and muscular build.

Jennis: (Eclupse) Sister of Heb. Parents gave them Ozar names in hopes that the Ozars in Kyron would be kinder to the pups.

Kaal: (Norrus) Father of Burrum and Forver's elder brother.

Kanabo: The weapon that Terrabyss uses. Shorter than traditional kanabos, it is only about the length of his arm. It is made of sequoia and has inch-long iron spikes attached to metal bands that circle the weapon.

Kellij: (Mauler) The alpha of his litter, part of the Returin bloodline and the leader of the hunting pack that Rellik was a member of. He has black fur with light brown fur around his eyes. He has yellow eyes and numerous small scars crisscross his body. He is of average height and muscular.

Kevkel: (Norrus) Urrah's mate who passed away.

Kiltra: (Mauler) Hown's mate and mother of Dardyl.

Kitren: (Norrus) Carloe's sister and Groll's lover.

Klain: (Mauler) An only pup and self-proclaimed alpha. Has trouble following orders and a rotten personality. Member of Unkyss pack in the Hunt. He has black fur, but it lacks luster and has yellow-green eyes, almost sickly. He is short, with an actual humpback, and thin.

Klarah: (Norrus) Forever's mate and the mother of Inlan, Shael, and

Jakob. She was the first Norrus to have triplets in the history of the tribe.

Kodah: (Norrus) Forver and Kaal's father.

Koff: (Eclupse) Father of Sernna, Essur, and Indel.

Krell: (Mahuer) Cousin of Bardell, and received Azbin's position at a garrison.

Kyron: The commune that is home to some of the Eclupse in the northeast, near the Ice Kraggs.

Lone Wolf: A title given to a Silverback when they are exiled. It is also used to refer to a single survivor of a pack that has not pledged to any Alpha.

Loog Turra: The largest continent on the planet of Sarm.

Lounging: A Silverback custom that is reinstated by Ozars. Essentially, a siesta.

Luma: (Eclupse) Dio's mate and the mother of Luna and Altz. She had white fur like Luna and bright blue eyes.

Luna: (Eclupse) Daughter of Dio and Luma. She is left-handed and has snowy white fur with dark blue eyes. She has no scars and stands just over 6' tall with a lean build.

Madha: The title given to the arcane practitioners of the Daunkirks.

Mahuer: A common Beast-Speech term for 'Great'. It is used among the Silverbacks to refer to the first in a litter to take a mate and start a family. Among the Ozars, it refers to the dominant Bear-Taur tribe.

Mahzar: A term of endearment and a title which means Great Ozar.

Maxyss: (Mauler) Member of both the Elder and Invasion Council. Beta Hunter under Hanora and elevated to Prime Hunter. He has graying black

535

fur with yellow eyes that have milky streaks from an injury during his first Hunt and he is tall and lean among Mauler standards.

Modyn: (Eclupse) Father of Rolg and adopted Sernna, Essur, and Indel.

Molken: (Mauler) Member of the hunting pack that Brutyss led during the Hunt.

Moozer: Mouse-Taurs that often live in servitude to Ozars as they are too small to protect themselves.

Mother Bear: Ozar god.

My Skull: A popular game played at all Mauler events. It consists of as many players as want to play, but needs at least two. The players start in the middle of a circular area and attempt to get a skull across the circle's boundary, although it is contested if it can be any boundary or the furthest from the player's position when they get the skull. When a player is tackled, they must release the skull and form a huddle around it. The skull can also be stripped out of one player's hands by another, at which point no huddle is formed. After a point is scored, the skull is reset to the middle of the circle and the game begins anew. There can either be point totals or the game can be played until everyone is too exhausted to play. Recently, new rules have been added such as being able to kick the skull over the boundary for a single point and running over the line is now worth two points.

Nallus: (Norrus) A widowed cousin of Forver and who raised Shael, Inlan, and Jakob.

Narz: (Mauler) Balt's brother and one of the Watchers that was a member of Oryss' pack. He has black fur and yellow eyes, with a few scars that run along his arms, and is of average build and height.

Nayla: A runt that dies during a stampede in Terrabyss' Hunt.

Needle Arms: A plant construct used by druids. They are humanoid in stature and have thorn-like fingers as well as hard, bark-like skin.

Nill: (Norrus) Ullym's mate who is practically deaf and Groll's mother.

Nio: (Eclupse) Part of the lumber group in Kyron, and Fintorn's father.

Nomi: (Mauler) Guard, chosen by Terrabyss to support the right flank during the Raid.

Nordyss: (Eclupse) Mate of Nordyss and the father of Ordy and Fourdy. A very popular Eclupse name.

Nordyss (Nordy): (Eclupse) Mate of Nordyss and the mother of Ordy and Fourdy.

Nordyss (Ordy): (Eclupse) Sibling to Fourdy and the son of Nordyss and Nordy.

Nordyss (Fourdy): (Eclupse) Sister to Ordy and daughter of Nordyss and Nordy.

Numa: (Mauler) Scout Mother and alpha of the Ravis pack. She has black fur, and uses blood-dyed beeswax in her collar to make it stand on end, to make her appear larger than she is. It also makes her look like she is always fresh out of a fight. She has orange eyes and many scars, although her most notable one runs down her left side. She is short but very muscular.

Obarn: (Norrus) Forver's grandfather and the first Yukon to craft the famous Yukon mead.

Odan: (Eclupse) Father of Ryss and patron of the Kreal pack.

Oflyn: (Mauler) Skrimshander for Skoff and an elder. Known for making very detailed and exaggerated fertility statues.

Okmyss: (Eclupse) Father of Heb and Jennis, and Wilca's mate.

Oulyss: (Mauler) Litter alpha and member of Unkyss' pack for the Hunt. He has black fur with yellow eyes, has several scars, and is tall and muscular. Missing his left ear from a Gorgel attack.

Orald: (Norrus) Named after his father and patron of the Wozon bloodline. Gandrie's father and mate of Berbra. He has dark brown fur with black fur running along his arms and legs. He has bright amber eyes and is average height but very muscular.

Oryss: (Mauler) From the Mallmee pack, and alpha of the Watcher pack that Balt, Narz, Calmus, and Terrabyss belonged to. Has onyx-colored fur with amber eyes and scars along his biceps and chest. Muscular and of average height.

Oscord: (Mahuer) Shael's mate and a distant cousin of Bardell. Positioned in a southern garrison.

Paw and Ear Method: An Eclupse tradition that was implemented when the Ozars conquered the Eclupse. A way of determining if a juvenile is ready to become an adult.

Palgus: A derogatory Taur term that means lackey.

Pellet: A vulgar Taur swear that means herbivore excrement.

Penma: (Norrus) Arn's mate and retired from the military, having been part of Urrah's troop. She has light brown fur and dark brown eyes, stands at 6'10", and is a bit chubby.

Phier: (Mauler) Member of Brutyss' pack during the Hunt.

Philyp: (Norrus) Fishmonger of Ursyss.

Phylyss: (Mauler) Dardyl's grandmother.

Reker: (Mahuer) The Head Herder of Kyron who was replaced by Travic.

Rellik: (Mauler) Haxzus' only daughter and very neglected by both of her parents. She has charcoal gray fur and one bright gold eye with a dull amber eye. Few scars and of average height but a bit lean for a Mauler.

Rodentia: Clan name for all Rodent-Taurs.

Rolph: (Norrus) First cub of Berbra and Orald, who passed away of a fever.

Rolg: (Eclupse) The only son of Modyn and the adopted sibling of Sernna, Essur, and Indel.

Rymmall: (Mauler) Previous Scout Mother before Numa and one of the members of the invasion council.

Ryndell: The river that starts at the Ice Kraggs in the north and then cuts to the south, intersecting with the Cynwyn and continuing into the Warm Wood.

Ryss: (Eclupse) Son of Odan.

Sarm: Planet in this Universe.

Scouts: Female Mauler military division that keeps communication with the outer and inner grove. Also used for monitoring the outer grove for enemies and keep intelligence on other Taur tribes within and around the grove.

Selee: Seal-Taur.

Sernna: (Eclupse) Pup and sibling to Essur, Indel, and Rolg.

Siya: (Hax) Burrum's mate and the mother of Hunnora.

Shael: (Norrus) Daughter of Forver and sister to Inlan and Jakob. She likes to use oil to slick back the fur on her head, neck, and shoulders. She has dark brown fur, with light brown highlights around her face and neck. She has brown eyes, stands at 7'1" and is of average weight.

Shaman: The magic users of the Silverbacks and the Maulers, who was usually also the Alpha.

Skoff: (Mauler) Current shaman of the Maulers and trained by Grimmis. Numa and Terrabyss' sibling, and extremely flamboyant. He loves wearing colorful ponchos and usually carries a gnarled wood staff that has an assortment of bones and teeth tethered to it. He has jet black fur with yellow eyes, and has few scars. The largest runs horizontal to his sternum and across the pectoral. He is short and thin, not very muscular.

Snard: (Mauler) Retired Watcher.

Solgar: (Eclupse) Son of Hild and Volg, and Arvin's brother. He has white fur with sprinkles of gray on his back and stomach. He has dark blue eyes, and is slightly taller than Arvin and a bit more muscular, above average compared to other pups in the commune.

Spilkot: Tribe in the Arkem clan that live in the Ember Sands. They have a very advanced and secretive society.

Suskyss: (Mauler) Part of the invasion council, but chose to have a litter and live in the outer grove. She has black fur and yellow eyes, no scars, and is average height and lean, but very strong.

Surrah: (Hax) Burrum's mother and Kaal's mate.

Tamess: A Norrus family that Ferda recruits.

Tarphyss: (Mauler) The alpha of Terrabyss' litter.

Terrabyss: (Mauler) Runt of his pack, which includes Tarphyss, Numa, and Skoff. Has burgundy fur that usually looks black. His eyes are a mixture of red and yellow, which makes them appear bloodshot or rusted. He has numerous scars, but none that he boasts about. He is shorter than any adult Mauler but is also the strongest.

Thessaul: An Eclupse commune to the southeast of Kyron.

Travic: (Mahuer) The current Herder in Kyron and essentially the liaison between the Eclupse and the garrison in Kyron. Second in command only below Dhon. He has light brown fur that becomes blond toward his head and darker toward his paws. He has light brown eyes with green streaks, and stands 7'6", weighing 380 lb. Has not bothered to name his axe.

Trel: (Eclupse) Fintorn's mother.

Triumph Festival: Ozar celebration of their victories over the Silverbacks and Daunkirks.

Ullym: (Norrus) Groll's father and Nill's mate.

Ulvoue: (Mauler) A young Mauler that Numa likes to spend time with.

Unkyss: (Mauler) Last surviving member of the Sabor pack. He is extremely tall and becomes good friends with Terrabyss. Has an extremely deep voice, and has black fur with yellow eyes and several scars. Along with his giant size, he is extremely muscular.

Urguss: (Norrus) Part of the Kolgur bloodline and lives on the frontier of Ursyss. Was part of Forver's militia that tried to hunt down Dio and the other outlaws. He has light brown fur and light brown eyes, standing just over 7' tall and heavy, having lost some of his physique in his retirement.

Urrah: (Norrus) Second oldest of Forver's commanders. The first female to have any significant military rank. She has black fur and honey-colored eyes and stands at 7'5" tall and is muscular, although has become stocky in retirement. She has named her axe Lopper.

Urvek: (Norrus) Hamba's mate.

Velkurt: (Eclupse) Prisoner of Kyron.

Vockyss: (Mauler) Scout that assisted Terrabyss during the Raid.

Volg: (Eclupse) Hild's mate and father to Solgar and Arvin. He has light gray fur, but is mangy and flea-ridden. Has dark blue, sapphire-like eyes. Standing 6'5", he is very gaunt, showing how malnourished he is.

Vomi: (Eclupse) Sister to Zarsyn. Habyss and Vozim's daughter.

Vozim: (Eclupse) Mother of Vomi and Zarsyn and Habyss' mate.

Watchers: Five-male teams that guard the canyon pass between the Green Wall and the Grove.

What Not To Do's: A list of appropriate behavior and activities for the winter months in Campos Ursyss.
- To preserve food stores, no gatherings (official meetings) were to be held
- To preserve rest, no mingling (visits between friends) was to happen outside of one's yurt
- To preserve serenity, social interactions (no communal gatherings) were to be short and inside one's yurt
- To preserve resources, no hunts were to take place
- To preserve security, no war campaigns were to happen

Whesscire: Halfling settlement in the foothills of the Division Mountains, near the Endless Plains on the western side.

Wilca: (Eclupse) Okmyss' mate and mother to Heb and Jennis.

Wolf-Shit: Common Ozar curse.

Wolg: (Mauler) Part of Brutyss' pack for the Hunt.

Worg: (Mauler) Part of Rellik's hunting pack and part of an outer grove pack. He has black fur and has dark brown eyes with flecks of green. Has a few scars and is of average height and weight.

Woydra: (Eclupse) Rolg's mother and mate to Modyn who adopts Sernna, Essur, and Indel.

Yellow Rest: Former lookout point for the Ozars.

Xurxel: (Eclupse) Prisoner of Kyron.

Yoll: (Norrus/Mahuer) Ferda and Erbun's cub.

Zarsyn: (Eclupse) Sister of Vomi and daughter to Vozim and Habyss.

Zelyss: (Mauler) Member of Brutyss' hunting pack and Cycyss' brother and litter alpha.

Zolk: (Norrus) Oldest commander in Forver's group. His fur is black, with light gray sprinkled throughout his coat. He has bright amber eyes, stands at 7'5" and is extremely muscular for his age. His axe is named Headhunter and seems to have a mind of its own.

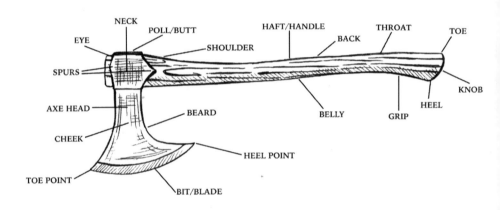

NECK

POLL/BUTT

EYE

SHOULDER

HAFT/HANDLE

BACK

THROAT

TOE

SPURS

AXE HEAD

BEARD

BELLY

GRIP

HEEL

KNOB

CHEEK

HEEL POINT

TOE POINT

BIT/BLADE